THE FLYING AFRICAN

Areg Azatyan

Translated from the Armenian by Nazareth Seferian

Frayed Edge Press
Philadelphia, PA

First English-Language Edition
Published by Frayed Edge Press, 2024

Originally published as T'ṛch'ogh Afrikats'in by Tigran Mets (Yerevan, Armenia, 2013).

Cover illustration by Areg Azatyan.
Interior map illustrations by Areg Azatyan.

Library of Congress Control Number: 2023940378

Publishers Cataloging-in-Publication

Names: Azatyan, Areg, 1986- . T'ṛch'ogh Afrikats'in.| Seferian, Nazareth, translator.
Title: The flying African / Areg Azatyan, translated from the Armenian by Nazareth Seferian.
Other titles: T'ṛch'ogh Afrikats'in. English.
Description: First English language edition. | Philadelphia, PA : Frayed Edge Press, 2024.
Identifiers: LCCN 2023940378 | ISBN 9781642510522 (pbk.) | ISBN 9781642510539
   (ebook)
Subjects: LCSH: Voyages and travels – Fiction. | Journalists – Fiction. | Travelers. |
   Africa – Fiction. | BISAC: FICTION / Magical Realism. | FICTION / Psychological. |
   FICTION / World Literature / Europe (General).
Classification: LCC PK8831.E8 A93 2023 | DDC 891.992 A--dc22
LC record available at https://lccn.loc.gov/2023940378

TABLE OF CONTENTS

Dedicated to all African children

NOTES

Areg Azatyan has written a new book, titled *The Flying African*. Its protagonist travels through the countries of Africa, meeting strangers and encountering all kinds of people. The novel does not have a single storyline, but it is the protagonist that serves as the connection between its different stories, which can be perused separately, each with their own plot, serving mostly as fables with their unexpected resolutions.

The author's objective is not to narrate a real story through this journey, but rather use it as a means for phantasmagoric and allegoric illusions. That is how one should read this book. One should not seek what does not exist within this piece—what should not exist, in this case. Every book should be read according to the rules set by the author. Any dissatisfaction should be strictly within those rules. Otherwise, even some of worldwide masterpieces can end up being considered "unreadable."

I suggest that you get used to this thought from the very beginning, and only then start this book. Reading this book with a very rigid approach is not advisable.

Dear reader, take the trouble of forgetting "normal" books, so that you can truly enjoy reading this novel, especially since the stylistic principles used by the author are very popular in contemporary world literature and had remained unknown to those of us on this side of the "Iron Curtain" for many years.

Perch Zeitountsian
Writer, playwright

The geopolitical context discussed in this book is based on the circumstances prevailing at the time of its writing. However, it is important to acknowledge that geopolitical conditions are dynamic and subject to change. Readers should be aware that developments may have occurred since the book's original publication.

Some historical or geographic facts may also have been slightly altered for reasons of artistic license.

Areg Azatyan
Author

PREFACE

I'm sitting here thinking about what is going to happen. Have I made the right decision? It's possible I could end up disillusioned halfway through my journey, break down, and just hit the road back home. I still don't know why I'm going or what I'll see there. I assume, though, that everything is not going to be as happy and cozy as I might like to imagine. I think of Africa as colorful and strange, magical and indescribable, but I really have no idea what it is like. I am not an "African" yet and I don't know if I can ever become one. In any case, I do want to see that huge continent, shaped like a bird's wing. I want to see it and talk to the people who live there, listen to them and fall in love. I want to see how they live and spend their days, and to write about their reality. Fifty-three countries. This is actually too large a number to allow me see everything I want to, since I can only stay for one day in each country and don't want to disrupt this schedule. I have to return in fifty-three days. The book I intend to write must be a novel, possibly consisting of fifty-three chapters (or days), each one narrating what happened to me at that location. The book should not have a political context; it will be fiction, and it will describe reality through my eyes. I already have the protagonist, whose name I will not mention. Let him be Somebody. He should not meddle in other people's lives or seek information, because I don't want my protagonist to seem like a news reporter. Let him just go to Africa and experience it, like a little parrot that is released once in a while from its cage to fly around and then return.

I am also afraid that I may not come back, but I don't know why; people are unpredictable and it is difficult to say how my destiny will unfold. This destiny is in my own hands though, since I'm the one who has decided to go there, not anyone else. I hope that I will see indescribable things in those fifty-three days, things that I can't even imagine, and that, in the end, I will return home where I've been missed. I haven't yet decided whether to write my book during the journey, or after my return. In any case, my protagonist—Somebody—and I are ready.

"You are going to Damascus, aren't you?" says an Arab at my side, who's been reading a newspaper. I forgot to mention that I am at the airport, and the plane will soon be taking off.

"Yes."

"I have a relative there. We haven't seen each other for a few years."

"I'm going to Africa."

"Africa?"

"Yes."

"But, you said Damascus?"

"Yes, my journey starts a bit further from my destination; I can't travel to Africa directly. From Damascus I will take a flight to Amman."

"Your trip is that long?" he asks.

"Yes."

"There are many countries in Africa. Which ones are you visiting, specifically?"

"I don't know. All of them, one by one."

"What? All of them?"

"Yes, from east to west, from north to south."

"Why?"

"I'm writing a book on Africa."

"So…?"

"So, I must see it."

"Couldn't you just write about it without seeing it?"

"No."

"I know what it is like there. Do you want me to tell you?"

"Yes—what's it like?"

"People are dying of starvation, they are sick, and no one gives a damn. That is your Africa."

"That's *your* Africa."

"Isn't that how it really is?"

"I don't know."

"I'm sure that it is. Africa is a dangerous place. Why should you bother yourself with writing about Africa? Write about Europe."

"Thanks for the advice."

"I'm serious, going there is dangerous. Everyone is sick, the water is undrinkable, the air is polluted, there are people with malaria, cholera, and AIDS all around. It's not too late—give up on the idea of going there. The TV says bad things about Africa all day long."

"The TV shows bombs exploding in the Middle East all the time, so why go to Damascus?" I counter.

"But it's not like that there. The Middle East is a huge piece of land, and Syria is just one state in it."

"Africa is huge, too."

"But Damascus is my home, I have to go."

"I see." I really wish that I, too, could say that where I was going was my home.

"Here's my family, I'm going to go join them."

"OK."

"Have a good flight," he says, laughing. "Although, of course, we will be flying together."

The Arab approaches his wife and kisses her, two children at her side. They are happy and joyful. They excitedly grab the Arab's waist, as if they haven't seen him for years, although it was just five minutes ago that his wife went to a shop with the children and said that she would be back soon. But the important thing is that they are happy.

I want my journey to be full of "Africans" although I know that I won't have time to see all of them, to interact with them all. Although many of them won't be mentioned in my book, they must be sure that my protagonist and I have respect for them all—all the tribes, nations, and ethnic groups, all the speakers of different languages and followers of different religions. It will be impossible to see everything during any journey; nobody can really do that. But I hope that I will at least be able to write my book, to give my impressions. One thing is causing me concern, however: in what language will I talk to them? I'm an Armenian and I speak only Armenian, and some English and Russian. There are so many different languages and dialects in Africa and, naturally, I don't know any of them. It would be good if most people understood English. In my book I will perhaps have to make some corrections, edit the words of some characters without, of course, changing their meaning. I cannot rule out errors and omissions, but I think that the most important things in a work of fiction are ideas and meaning. However, it must naturally be based on a believable foundation. I apologize in advance to all Africans for my protagonist's errors, although I am quite sure that they will be very few in number.

"Going to Damascus?" says a voice behind me.

"Yes."

A man takes a seat beside me. His skin is dark, but I can't really guess his nationality.

"Do you live there?"

"No. I'm going to Amman from there. Then to Africa."

"Africa!" he exclaims.

"Yes."

"It's a wonderful place."

"Yes."

"I've been there. It was long ago, but I remember Africa well. I was a young man and went there to work as a pilot."

"Is it beautiful?" I ask.

"Magnificent. True, I saw it mostly from above, but you can see everything from up there. It's like the whole gigantic continent is lying before your eyes."

"Did you stay there long?"

"For a few years. I'm curious—why are you going there?"

"I'm going to write a book."

"About Africa?"

"Yes."

"Excellent." Tears well up in his eyes and he wipes them away. "Wonderful," he continues. "When will you finish writing it?"

"I don't know."

"Write it, do it by all means. That was the most beautiful period of my life, a time of love and my youth. It was unforgettable. Unfortunately, you can't bring those days back. Have a good trip." He stands up and his legs are trembling as he reaches for his luggage. Then he is out of sight.

"Attention, the flight to Damascus is now boarding. Thank you," crackles the loudspeaker.

It's time to leave. We will soon hear the aircraft engines starting, and my journey will begin.

DAY 1. EGYPT
THE CAVES

I bypassed Al-Arish and Port Said and reached the Suez Canal, from where my journey through Africa was to begin. Without knowing where I was going, I threw myself into the water at once; I didn't even know what water it was—irrigation, probably—heading 100-120 kilometers to the south from the Suez to Ismailia.

Pyramids—the number one thing associated with Egypt. I was very interested in seeing them, but Egypt is a large country, and I unfortunately could not travel to another city on the same day. Throughout my journey, I skipped the capitals of quite a few countries, and my journey actually benefitted from this. I traveled to the city of Suez through the Suez Canal on a motorboat, paying 820 Egyptian pounds to cover a stretch of about twenty kilometers of water. The captain got his point across that this was a service used by tourists only. I failed to explain that I was a writer who had come to write a book; I wasn't a tourist at all. To be honest, it is very difficult to explain something in English to an Egyptian who does not speak any English at all, and this person, to my surprise, was one who spoke no language other than Arabic. He would blurt out some English words from time to time, like a shopkeeper who tries everything to sell his merchandise, ready even to strip from top to bottom and run after you.

Suez did not exactly provide an African atmosphere. True, it was my first stop, so it was too soon yet to jump to conclusions, but I had nevertheless expected something different. The weather was the same throughout the day. The sky stretched over me like the skin of a giant animal that had stubbornly stopped and did not want to move. In the distance, there were some rays left behind by the sun, as if it had grown frustrated at shining down on the same seashore all the time.

In any case, this city located in a gap in the Araga Mountain range (which the locals call Jebel), greeted me with one large and two tower-like structures—at least that was what I thought I could see from the motorboat. There was an enormous mosque towards the southern shore of the beach that had a gray dome and two enormous towers. In the distance, towards the east, there were two industrial cranes, probably being used for some construction work, looking from a distance like two giraffes living underwater. When I got off the boat, I immediately noticed a four-storied white ship with big numbers that said "160." The ship had some flags, like a cruise ship, but it also had a large cargo bay. Arabs with white headdresses were gathered on its deck. There was a five-story yellow building on the other side that looked as if it was made of paper, and all of its windows were of different colors—this was the only thing that reminded me of the Africa I imagined.

There was a three-star hotel, the Summer Palace, on Port Tawfiq Street, where I spent a few hours. It was a good hotel, specially designed to reflect the Egyptian concept of luxury. However, as soon as I entered my room, a story unraveled that provided my most memorable time in Egypt…

There were some Russians in the neighboring room, archeologists, who had come to Egypt to do fieldwork. They were planning to go to the Suez Canal to look for caves. They believed that no archeological explorations had taken place near the canal since November 1869, and they were convinced that they would discover caves. Since I was a foreigner, a non-Egyptian, the Russians confided all this to me. But their idea would have sounded ridiculous to the residents of Suez had they learned of the Russians' intentions. They showed me a journal that had the word "CAVES" written across it in large letters, but this was unconvincing. I thought to myself that perhaps there was one cave, but no "caves" in the plural for sure. Why would there be caves along the canal, and such a narrow one at that?

Two of the Russians were named Anton, and one was called Andrey. It was as if they had been waiting for me; there seemed to be nobody else for them to talk to. They firmly believed they would make a discovery and said that their government had promised each of them a reward of fifty thousand dollars. They asked me to write about it. It was all very strange. I asked them in my broken Russian, "Couldn't you have brought a journalist with you?"

"No, no, it has to remain a secret; why attract more attention than necessary?" said one of the Antons.

"Also, we didn't have the money for it," said the other Anton.

This seemed rather strange to me—their government had promised these large rewards, but they said that there was no money available.

"I'm not a reporter," I said. "I'm an author. I haven't come here to provide news coverage."

"Never mind, you won't be in the way in any case. Come with us," said Andrey, who resembled a large, unripe radish.

It was a very juvenile conversation, as if a bunch of kids were planning to go out to play football, but perhaps the reason it seemed that way to me was my poor Russian. New doubts had crept into me—if everything needed to be secret, then what need was there for any media coverage? These Russians were behaving strangely. I even had a fleeting suspicion that they could be spies dispatched to follow me.

But I set my doubts aside and decided to go with them, not because they asked me to, but rather because I was a writer. I was interested in seeing archeological fieldwork and finding out whether any caves existed.

Not wasting another minute, we set out for the Suez Canal immediately—on the same motorboat that had brought me there. The Russians brought all their necessary equipment and instruments, a load of about a hundred kilograms. Two things particularly interested me along the way: a picture on the captain's shirt, which I had not noticed when I saw him the first time (or perhaps he had changed), and the question of who would pay the 820 Egyptian pounds fee. I gave a sigh of relief when I saw one of the Antons, he also of the radish tribe, pay 1000 Egyptian pounds to the Arab as they started unloading their cargo from the ship.

"Gibraltar," I shouted.

"What?" the Russians asked.

"The Fortress of Gibraltar," I said. "That's what is on the Arab's shirt—see?"

"So what?" Andrey groaned. The last bag that he had carried was probably very heavy.

"I was trying to remember what it was, and I finally got it, that's all," I said.

We proceeded along the shore.

"Why did you pay 1000 pounds?" I asked. "I'd have only paid 820."

"So that he would help us unload the cargo," Anton said.

We hadn't walked for even ten minutes when we noticed a huge black Israeli tank in the distance, half buried in white sand.

"That has not moved in a very long time," said Andrey, who was smoking and speaking at the same time.

I had no idea what the tank was doing there, but it was definitely Israeli. You could tell by its tracks that it had not moved for years. We made our way around the tank and continued walking in the same direction for at least twenty minutes. There was nothing very interesting going on—on the one hand, the Russians were rapidly and incomprehensibly blabbing away, and on the other hand, echoes kept coming to the shore from a fuel-carrying tanker. The sun shone down directly overhead, and I was finding it difficult to walk upright.

"There are the ships. Unfold the map and count," said Anton.

"Approximately two kilometers to the south and half a kilometer to the west," said Andrey, squinting his archeologically-trained eyes.

It seemed to me that Andrey had a particularly professional look, as if he was trying to solve all problems with those eyes. The archeologists opened their bags, and took out a lot of things that were unfamiliar to me—belts, rulers, electrical computation devices, a spade; in other words, a bunch of unnecessary things. They dug a hole in the sand, put the empty bags into it, and then put sand on top. Andrey said, "Remember this spot, in the direction of this wooden stick."

And we were off again. I was walking mechanically, following the Russians. They talked incessantly, cracking stupid jokes and talking about the canal. They said that the construction of the canal had lasted twelve years, employing about one and a half million Egyptians. They spoke about a certain Ferdinand de Lesseps, who had probably been one of the construction developers. They said that part of the canal had been sold to Great Britain for 400,000 pounds sterling. Maybe I misheard or misunderstood, but the Russians seemed to be talking about all this in a way that suggested they had seen it with their own eyes. At one point, when I trailed them by about twenty paces, I took a look at this trio and felt as if there were three shadows walking in front of me, swinging in unison to the voice of the waves.

"What is it, are you tired?" shouted Andrey.

"He's out of breath." said one of the Antons.

"No, no, everything's fine. I was just thinking," I said.

"It's not much further; carry on for two or three more minutes and you can rest once we get there," said Andrey, who was the most enthusiastic.

I caught up with them. It took five minutes, not two, for us to reach our destination.

"Where are your caves?" I asked. "There's only water here and the shore." I was sure that their search had been futile.

They began talking again and then separated, each going in a different direction and leaving me to guard their gear until they got back. An hour passed and they hadn't returned. I called their names one by one: Anton, Anton, Andrey. But there was no one. My suspicions surfaced again and I was afraid that they were plotting something against me. I regretted having agreed to come with them. I waited another few minutes, then ran out of patience and decided to go look for them.

There were some small boats painted in bright colors at a distance of about a hundred meters. I ran in that direction and felt the fine sand filling my socks, which forced me to continue barefoot. When I got a little closer, I saw that the boats were empty.

"Andrey, where are you?" I screamed. "Where did you go, I've wasted my whole day with you, where are you?"

I never got a reply. I remained alone, by the Suez Canal, where I had begun my journey. I decided to go inland and return to the hotel, although I didn't know how I'd get there. Along the way, I noticed an elderly man dressed in grey with a white headdress, his back turned to me. I approached him. He was an Egyptian, his name was Said, and he spoke English.

"Have you seen any Russians around here?" I asked as I greeted him. Said looked at me with a wise gaze, but did not reply. I repeated my question, assuming that he had not understood.

"I know what you said, I understood," Said replied. "What Russians?"

"Archeologists, they came to look for caves," I said.

"Come here and have a look," he said crushing some red clay in his hand. Strange as it was, on the other side of Said there was the entrance to a small underground cave with a crack in the middle. I had not noticed it before. There were dried reeds and fragments of clay at its bottom.

"What cave is this?" I asked, thinking that the Russians might have been right.

"Yes, this is a cave," Said told me with an ambiguous smile. "It is a very old cave. People lived here thousands of years ago, when temperatures were not too high. See, there are traces of clay."

"What about the rushes?"

"The rushes are mine. I sleep here; the rushes are soft and sleeping on them is comfortable."

"You say you haven't seen the Russians?"

"I have. They were taken by the sea."

"What sea?"

"The Red Sea."

"Where did it take them?" I asked.

"I don't know, they were taken," Said replied with a grin. "The Suez Canal was opened on November 17, 1869. On that day, Russian archeologists had come, and while they worked, the waves of the sea came and swept them away. We can hear the echoes of their voices to this day. It is said that they come from the caves…"

DAY 2. LIBYA
THE GREEN TRAIN

Libya, the fourth largest country of Africa (and the only *Jamahiriya*[1]) was the second place I visited. The first thing that caught my eye here was the image on one of their coins of a horseman, fully wrapped in a headscarf and holding in his hand a cross-like staff (that was not a cross). This golden coin—one of five Libyan dinars—I spent within a few minutes of my arrival by purchasing a carbonated beverage that smelled of boiled iron.

Frankly speaking, Libya was also very different from the Africa I had imagined. I saw no colorful dresses here, just children roaming about on their own in the streets, and buildings made of clay. I knew that one could see these things many countries. It seemed to me that Libya was like a dry potato peel that had been flatted and rolled out, with ants gathered on only one small part while the rest of it lay deserted. In Libya, the population density is three to four people per square kilometer. The huge Libyan Desert occupies almost half the country. The cities are in the grasslands and are very hot, like many Central Asian countries. My expectations of Africa had not yet been met. But I was sure that sooner or later I would see the Africa that I anticipated, even though I

---

1. An Arabic word literally meaning "people's state." The word was coined by Muammar Gaddafi in 1977 to describe his political philosophy, which combined elements of Arab nationalism, anti-imperialism, Islamic socialism, left-wing populism, African nationalism, Pan-Arabism, and certain principles of direct democracy. Gaddafi ruled Libya under the principles of Jamahiriya from 1977 to 2011.

suspected it would not give me much happiness. I was somewhat apprehensive that seeing underdeveloped countries would be a difficult experience for me.

Benghazi was where I landed. I suddenly found myself in front of a large seven-story white building that looked like a hotel. I thought that it would be an excellent place to pass the day, but when I tried to enter, two thick-headed guards stopped me and said something in Arabic. They did not know English. I tried gesturing to explain that I needed a hotel, but they escorted me out with incomprehensible words. I felt like they were shouting swear words at me, because those blockheads were probably incapable of saying anything else.

I left the building and noticed the distant trees trembling on the glowing sand, as if they were on fire, with a small two-car train moving between them. The train was painted entirely in green, which immediately reminded me of the Libyan national flag. It seemed like this might be a wonderful opportunity to travel through Libyan cities by train, so I ran towards it. The doors were open. Some people were in a hurry to get on, while the conductor stood close by near the tracks. A small kiosk stood at a short distance, where they were selling hot food.

"Do you speak English?" I asked the conductor.

"Yes, go ahead," he said.

"Where does this train go?"

"Where is it you want to go?"

"I don't know, anywhere. I want to see Libya."

"Then why are you getting on this train? There is no better place than this city."

"You mean Benghazi?" I asked.

"Sure! Don't you know what a wonderful city this is? In 374 B.C., it was named Berenice, in honor of a king's beautiful daughter. Then in 1450, a man named Ghazi—I think his full name was Sedi Ghazi—came to the city and conducted acts of charity, so after his death the city was renamed Bani Ghazi, and later Benghazi."

"But, where does this train go?" I asked.

"Wherever you want. Isn't this city's history of interest to you?"

"Do you have any pictures? It would be better if you could show me pictures."

"I don't have any photos of Benghazi; I'd need to look for them. We'll get into the train car soon and I'll show you all of Libya," said the conductor.

I was overjoyed. That was exactly what I wanted.

"Do you know about the other cities, too?" I asked.

"No, I was born here and this is what we learned at school every day. So, later the Turks conquered…"

"School?"

"No, they didn't conquer school…they conquered Benghazi, before 1911, then the Italians made it a colony until 1942."

"Were you in the war?"

"Of course."

This was quite surprising. He looked to be sixty at most, so he would have been only one or two years old at the time of the war.

"How old are you?"

"Sixty," answered the conductor and, wiping his lips, he invited me in. "Let's move, come in."

"You have a good memory," I remarked.

"Yes, very," he said, smiling. His smile resembled a hippopotamus that had just come out of the river after a good meal. "More than a thousand rockets have exploded in Benghazi; this city has suffered a lot," he went on. "I remember it well, we celebrated with fireworks on December 24, 1951, when Libya finally got its independence. Before that, the British had ruled for several years."

We got on board and at this point I was more interested in the interior of the car and the people there, than in the stories the conductor was telling.

"At that time, the city was second only to Tripoli in Libya."

"Sorry, what's your name?" I interrupted.

"You can call me Muhammed."

"Is Muhammed your name, then?"

"No, but it's easier for you. Everyone here is Muhammed."

"Muhammed, where does this train go? Do you have a specific route?"

"Yes, we do: Zella, Sabha, Germa, Ubari, and then directly to Ghadames."

"I haven't heard of any of them."

"That's all right. You will see them soon and learn about them. We have a very beautiful country."

"What is that building in the city center?"

"Which one, the white one with seven floors?"

"Yes."

"It's the Palace of Culture."

"I had thought that it was a hotel."

"No," laughed Muhammed. "It is of our most important buildings."

"They didn't let me in."

"That's because they guessed immediately that you're not a Muslim; entrance is allowed only to Muslims. Come, let's sit in this car; it has an air conditioner, it is cool here."

We sat down at a table, and Muhammed treated me to water that tasted of boiled iron. I noticed a white vehicle through the window, travelling in parallel with our train.

"What is that car?" I asked.

"A white Mercedes," Muhammed said.

"I know. I mean, where did it come from?"

"Perhaps it's a tourist. Yesterday, there was talk about someone who has come to Africa and wants to write about it. Maybe that's him."

"Are you sure?"

"That's what I heard, but I don't know for sure. Maybe that's not him."

"I'm a writer, too, and I've come for the same reason."

"Oh, that's good," Muhammed said indifferently.

The white Mercedes was speeding in the same direction as our train and I could see that there were two people inside, but I couldn't see their faces. The vehicle also carried something on top, probably a tent.

"Are we in for a long journey?" I asked.

"Not very. We will go around a few small cities on the way: Al Faqan and Idrin. Fifteen hours at the most."

I knew that Libya was very big and the trip could not possibly be so short, especially given that the train was not a fast one. We had a journey ahead of us that covered more than two thousand kilometers. I started to examine the interior of the green train. On the door connecting the two cars, a poster was pasted there bearing the words *Les Têtes Brûlées* and a picture of two guitar players in colorful clothing.

"What is this poster about?"

"It's a band from Cameroon, wonderful performers."

"Are they good?"

"Outstanding. They play and sing."

Then my eye fell upon the wire mesh covering the window, which turned out to be for protection against mosquitoes. The smell of burning wood was everywhere. The passengers were few in number—twenty or twenty-five people. They were all men in white headdresses, sitting silently as if trying to sleep.

We travelled on a monotonous journey for five or six hours with the Mercedes alongside, before reaching Zella.

"This is Zella," Muhammed said.

Zella was in no way different from what we'd previously seen on our journey, except for a small puddle full of rainwater, which looked like boiling milk.

"But where's the city?" I asked.

"We're by-passing it, to save time. We will enter Sabha through the Haruj Desert."

Muhammed spoke with enthusiasm, while I kept thinking about the car and the story of the writer who had come to write about Africa.

We had a little lunch, and Muhammed went off to sleep. It was evening. Everyone had fallen asleep and the sun, too, was tired. I kept watching the vehicle out of the corner of my eye…

"Get up," roared Muhammed, "You'll miss out on a lot if you don't see this."

I had fallen asleep. I jumped up.

"We are approaching Sabha; the city is in the distance. We shall soon see Zwilah, where there is a wonderful mosque lying in ruins."

It was indeed a magnificent mosque consisting of five cupolas; one was fully demolished, and now resembled a caravanserai. The stones looked like leopard skin.

"Is that all?" I asked. "But you said that I would see the country."

"Our country's beauty consists of this. You cannot imagine it, but here each grain of sand has its own warmth; you can't feel all that in one day."

Muhammed was probably right. Yes, I really was an inexperienced novice.

"We shall soon reach Germa. Go to sleep, everyone's sleeping. We'll be there in one or two hours."

Muhammed left again. The Mercedes continued on as before, never falling behind. I slept…

"This is Germa. Have a look," said Muhammed, coming into the car and waking everyone up.

"Are we already there?" I asked.

"It's been three hours. You've been sleeping."

"Are we going to circumvent the city again?"

"Yes, it's quicker that way."

"What's the point of this journey? There's nothing interesting!"

"What about the mosque? We will soon see a few more sights. We'll enter the city when we get to Ubari, where I will have to buy a few things. And I can recommend a good hotel in Ghadames, the Jhadpalm; it is a wonderful place that is perfect for you."

"Alright. So, Muhammed, where did you hear that story?" I asked.

"Which one?"

"About that tourist who has come to write."

"It was in the papers. I am not sure whether or not that's him."

"Could we stop and talk to him?"

"Can't you see how fast they're going? No, we'll lose time."

"Have you kept that newspaper?"

"No, why would you need it? He won't write like you; you'll do a better job at writing."

"How do you know?"

"Whoever sits in my train, writes better," joked Muhammed.

I liked what he said. In the end, it did not matter who was sitting in the white Mercedes. I gradually grew more excited. I started to notice the beautiful sights and views along the way.

"What is that rock?" I asked.

"I don't know, but it is one of the most remarkable places here."

"It looks like Noah's Ark, as if it has the Ararat below it."

"Yes, you guessed right. Qararat."

"What's Qararat?"

"It's the name of this place."

"We have a mountain back home that we call Ararat," I said.

"No, this is Qararat. A very mysterious place."

"Yes, it really is."

"There is another interesting place here; we will reach it soon."

The train lumbered on, the cars sometimes trembling. The Arabs at the back remained quiet for long stretches, with rare grins, a few conversations, and some tea drinking. The Mercedes continued to drive parallel to us on the bumpy road.

"Look," said Muhammed enthusiastically. "This place is called the labyrinth."

There were small stone walls with date palms growing out of them; it was a very impressive place. I had not seen such a place anywhere. This was perhaps the first thing that resembled the Africa I had imagined.

"People used to live here, then their houses ended up in ruins and their roofs collapsed, and only the walls remain. Now, it is a tourist spot."

"It's very beautiful."

"In twenty minutes, we'll reach Ubari. We'll go into the city, where I have to buy sheep wool. Then, we'll finally go to Ghadames and you'll sleep comfortably at the hotel."

I could hear the clicking of the tracks, and then I suddenly noticed that the Mercedes wasn't there.

"The Mercedes is gone."

"It's further off, over there," Muhammed grunted. "It got stuck in the sand, they're trying to shovel out the sand from under the wheel."

"Yes, you're right. I can see one person—it's the driver, wearing a green headdress. The writer isn't there."

"He's on the other side, I can see his legs. He's cleaning the wheel."

The Mercedes fell further behind. We entered Ubari, where there were a few single-story houses, as well as stores and rows of trucks filled with sheep. In every corner of the city, one could see Arab men wearing white headdresses sitting in the sand in groups of four or five. Muhammed bought wool from a dark-skinned boy, and we started off towards our final station, Ghadames. On the way, I saw a caravan of camels for the first time. There were five camels: three of them carried riders and the other two bore loads. They moved very slowly. We passed the camels so quickly that I failed to notice whether they had one hump or two.

"How many humps do they have?" I asked.

"One, I think," said Muhammed. "Take a look at the beautiful rocks in the sand."

The rocks were indeed beautiful. They were round and resembled watermelons, as if thousands of watermelons were growing in the desert. But I was no longer interested.

We had been in the train now for over twenty hours, and I was very tired. I could barely manage to keep my eyes open. It was very hot, and the rails stretched ahead infinitely, towards the sun...

"Wake up, you have fallen asleep. We have reached Ghadames, get up, we will be at the Jhadpalm in a moment. Then we shall have a good rest, and you will experience our culture, our carpets. It is a good place. Get up."

I jumped up, and we were in Ghadames. There was a three-story hotel up ahead built in the Arabian style, with narrow walls bearing colored tiles, and decorated with carpets. One window was closed, its panes adorned with fir trees and geometric patterns. Two people were in the courtyard drinking tea.

"Where am I?" I asked the man in the green headdress sitting next to me. "Where's Muhammed?"

"We are in Ghadames. Who's Muhammed? You struck your head against the wheel; don't you feel better yet? You slept all night, didn't that help?"

"Who are you?"

"I'm the driver."

"What car are we in?"

"It's a white Mercedes."

"Where have I been all this time?"

"With me. You got in the car in Benghazi."

"I've been in the car all this time?"

"Yes," said the driver in the green headdress, wiping his sand-covered forehead.

"Did we see Zella, Sabha, Germa, Ubari, did we pass the mosque, then Qararat, the labyrinth, the sheep in Ubari, and that caravan of camels?"

"Yes."

"Where was I all that time?"

"In the car."

"What about Muhammed?"

"Who's Muhammed?"

"The conductor in the train car. He has a mustache, and a big head. He had a frustrated look on his face."

"What train car?"

"One of the green ones. He was the conductor of the green train."

The driver looked at the setting sun, where the air glowed red and the trees swayed, as if on fire.

"What train? There have been no trains in Libya since 1965. All the stations are abandoned. Come, come, let's go into the Jhadpalm, it's a beautiful hotel," said the driver in the green headdress as he got out of the car and closed the door tightly behind him.

DAY 3. TUNISIA
THE EXILES FROM ANDALUSIA

"Do you speak English?" I asked the shopkeeper in a small store selling leather goods on Taieb Mhiri Avenue.

"Yes, what can I do for you?" asked the shopkeeper.

"Is this bag made of leather?"

"Yes, of course. Everything here is made of leather, of different qualities and with different prices. What do you need?"

"An everyday messenger bag, not a very expensive one."

"This one—forty-five dinars; take it for forty. It's crocodile skin."

The vendor said "crocodile skin" in a way that sounded like it was he himself who had hunted down that crocodile, skinned it, processed the leather, and produced the bag.

"How much is that in dollars?"

"Around thirty-two or thirty-three. Is that too much?"

"No, that's OK, I'll take it. And is the quality good? Will it wear out quickly?"

"No, no, bags like this have been produced for a thousand years. They are always of the highest quality. Not to worry!"

It was the first time that I had bought an important item in Africa, and I was very happy. I'd liked the bag the moment I'd entered the store. It was a little expensive, but it was crocodile skin and looked beautiful. It had three sections, and loops to hold pens and pencils. I decided to keep all my notes and information about Africa in it.

I was in Tunisia, in Sfax—a small city where the population consisted mainly of local people. This city on the Mediterranean is the second largest by population (about 1.5 million) in Tunisia. Everything in Sfax was comparatively inexpensive, and it was considered a tourist area. There were artisans' stalls all around, and narrow streets, but the city also had some newer districts. The islands of Kerkennah were located opposite the city, but I didn't manage to make it there. I was greatly assisted by a small map that I found inside my new bag, with the city depicted on it in great detail. The map was probably a gift, since it was wrapped and attached to the inside of the bag.

By African standards, this comparatively small country (163,610 square kilometers) was very beautiful and left a great impression on me. I already knew not talk to every stranger, or poke my nose into everything. I held my bag tight and walked along Bourguiba Avenue, where the hotel where I was supposed to spend the night was located. It was a three-star, middle-class hotel, well decorated, but in an old and imposing style. It was called Tamaris, and a few bicycles were parked in front of it.

I was walking along and thinking. I actually felt isolated from the outside world for a moment, as if it made no difference where I was; all that mattered were me and my new expensive bag, which for some reason seemed heavier than I thought it would be. I slid my fingers along its front, feeling the softness of the leather surface. It was as if I was holding a small crocodile. The bag had such a hold on me that I did not notice any of the sights, buildings, streets, or squares that were everywhere in Sfax.

However, my revery was doomed to soon end, as it is my habit to be careless. I popped into a store for a couple of minutes to buy some juice, and suddenly realized there was an emptiness under my elbow. Where had I left my bag? I had ended up having less than an hour to admire it.

I took a narrow cobblestone street towards a sleepy quarter where one or two vendors were selling fruit.

"Excuse me, have you seen a thief go by here, carrying a crocodile skin bag?" I asked one of the vendors.

The vendor just grunted; he probably didn't understand English.

"Yes, what do you need?" replied the other vendor, his eyes betraying his honesty. He wouldn't cheat me, I thought.

"Have you seen a thief go by? I entered a store and when I came out, my bag was gone."

"I haven't seen him, but it must be the work of the potter Ali Nafti's son. He has a great penchant for bags."

"Who's that? Where does he live?"

"Go straight, then left; he lives on Farhat Hached Street. Anyone there can point you towards the house of the potter Ali."

"I see. Thank you."

I ran towards the house of Ali. I don't know why, but I believed that vendor. He was a local, he probably knew everyone well. At last, I found the house, but I didn't know how to get in. And all I had was a suspicion; I couldn't be sure that his son was a thief. I decided to wait a little while until someone appeared at the house. Soon, a woman in a headscarf looked out of the window, saw me, and withdrew in fear. I shouted to her. A minute later, a mustached man with a face like an ax opened the door.

"Who's there?"

"Excuse me, is this the potter Ali's house?"

"Yes."

"Are you Ali?"

"No. I'm his brother."

"Is he at home, then?"

"Ali died last winter."

"I'm sorry. What about his son?"

"His son is alive, but we gave him over to state care."

"I've been told that the son collects leather bags, is that true?"

"No."

"In that case, perhaps he steals such bags?"

"What are you trying to say?" The brother of the deceased potter gave me a stern look.

"Is your nephew a thief?"

"It's been three months since Jomas went away. Tell that vendor that he should not blame him for every theft committed."

Ali's brother shut the door.

Perhaps the vendor was unaware of all this. I don't know why, but I believed this man as well. The bag thief must have fled in fear. How was I supposed to find him?

There was an open-air café named La Perla in that area, where they sold mint tea for one and a half dinars. I entered the café and ordered tea. I was depressed. I remembered the bag and thought I would never find it again. I didn't want to buy another one.

"Don't worry, bags like this have been produced for a thousand years," the shopkeeper had said. Maybe it was a thousand years old and that is why it was stolen, I thought.

"Would you like some lemon?" asked the waiter.

"What? No, thank you. Excuse me, could I speak with you for a moment?"

"Sure."

"Are there thieves in your city?"

"Aren't there thieves everywhere?"

"Many of them?"

"I wouldn't say so."

"They stole my bag. It was a good bag; I'd just bought it today. I want to find the thief."

"Ah, I see. It must be the doing of Buazizi. Did you lose it in a store?"

"Yes, how did you know?"

"It is easy to grab them in such places. No doubt, it was Buazizi."

"Who's Buazizi?"

"A cyclist, he wears a black cycling outfit. A terrible person."

"Is he poor? Is he homeless?"

"Where would a poor man get a bicycle? He is a former cyclist who failed at the sport. Now he deals in petty theft."

"Why don't they arrest him?"

"If they caught him, they would," said the waiter. He wiped the lemon in his hand and put it in his pocket. He looked honest, but I guess that all Tunisians seem to be sincere. Perhaps he was telling the truth.

"Are you sure that he is the thief?"

"Who else could it be? He is the only thief I know."

I paid the bill and ran back to Bourguiba Avenue, where I had seen a few cyclists. Where could I find this Buzizi or Buazizi? The waiter's English was so bad that I couldn't get the thief's name right.

I got to the street, but the bicycles were gone. There was only one motorcycle, and its owner soon appeared.

"Excuse me, are you a bicyclist?" I asked.

"No, I'm delivering fish. I'm a fisherman."

"But do you own a bicycle?"

"Yes. Why?"

"By any chance, is your name Buazi or Buzizi?"

"Buazizi?"

"Yes."

"Yes, how did you know that my name is Buazizi? Have we met?"

"Do you like leather bags?"

"What does that have to do with anything?"

I didn't know what to say; his face didn't seem suspicious, especially since he didn't seem to understand what I was getting at. And he wasn't on a bicycle.

"Someone stole my bag, and I'm looking for the thief. Sorry to have troubled you; a waiter said the thief was Buazizi."

"Me?"

"Maybe he meant someone else; he said he was a cyclist."

"No, I don't know who it could be. But you can't find the thief here. Can't you see how narrow the streets are? It's like a labyrinth."

"Yes."

"There are some kids here, they're petty thieves. It must have been them."

"Alright, thanks."

Everyone here spoke with such certainty. One blamed the other, but everyone was innocent, and I couldn't make any sense of it. Searching for the bag had helped me see a bit of Sfax. Yes, I was upset, but I could not fail to notice the luxurious fountains, clay houses, and white arches. It was indeed like a labyrinth. There were houses with low roofs in the old city, and narrow streets with colored tiles. I was confused, but the bag kept guiding me forward.

I had to make a choice. I could suspect anyone—they were all both cunning and kind, with gentle innocent eyes, and talented in deception.

It was already evening and I had to go to the hotel, but my thoughts about the bag kept me uneasy. I decided to stay in Sfax until I found it. I heard someone speaking French, but it wasn't coming from a tourist. French is widely spoken in Tunisia, because it was a colony of France until 1956. There were children running about and screaming. Where these ten- or twelve-year-old children had managed to learn French, I didn't know, but all at once I recalled the fisherman's words.

"Do you speak English?" I asked, thinking that if they knew French, they would also know some English.

"What do you need?" asked the eldest.

I looked carefully at his hands and saw that they were empty. I had nothing on which to base any suspicions.

"Have you seen a good quality leather bag?"

"We have."

"Where? Who had it?"

"In the store."

"No, I know that. I mean, in the hands of a thief."

"But how should we know whether or not he is a thief?"

"You're right. Go home, it's bedtime."

It was a stupid conversation and I felt disgusted with myself. What could these kids have to do with any of this? One shouldn't believe everything others say. It was already late, it was getting dark, and I was tired and hungry from looking for the bag all day. I decided to not give a damn about anything, and just go to the hotel and sleep. I planned to head to Algeria the following day.

I got to the hotel and the doorman opened the door. I glanced at him, and thought he looked distraught. He won't know anything, I thought.

"What is it?" he asked.

"Nothing, I didn't say anything. Has anyone left something for me?"

"No."

"It's late, good night, I'm going to bed," I said.

"Good night. Was someone supposed to drop something off?"

"A bag, a black bag, made of crocodile skin, worth forty dinars."

"They were to give it to me?"

"No, I was just asking. It was lost."

"Did you look for it?"

"Of course; I asked everybody. Somebody stole it."

"Was there anything important in it?"

"A map. The bag was the important thing."

"Was it a good bag?"

"Luxurious, soft as a tangerine. I bought it from the leather store on Taieb Mhiri Avenue."

"That's a good store." The doorman looked as though he was remembering something from his childhood. His eyes sparkled.

"The shopkeeper said that they had produced them for a thousand years."

"That's the truth."

"Have you seen that bag?" I asked.

"Yes."

"Maybe you know who the thief is; you seem like a clever man."

"What can I say?" The doorman looked me in the eye. "Are you sure you really bought a bag like that?"

"Of course I did. This morning."

"Perhaps you are confusing it with something else?"

"How could I do that? I paid forty dinars for it, and the shopkeeper said it was worth about thirty-two or thirty-three dollars."

"Maybe you bought it in another city, or another country?"

"How could I have done that? I bought it today. I'm not crazy enough to forget something like that. Why did you ask that?"

The doorman looked as if he had said the same thing many times. He had really managed to confuse me. I thought for a moment that maybe I hadn't bought the bag there, so then I tried to remember where I had bought it. Perhaps it had been in another city or another country. But no, I had bought it that morning. Everything seemed mixed up.

"Why did you ask that?" I asked again.

"Because such bags have not been made here for more than twenty years. I was the only leather artisan in that store, and there are no crocodiles left now." The doorman once again seemed to be reminiscing.

I could not understand any of it. But his words made sense and he, too, did not seem to be deceiving me.

I knew it was pointless, but I had to ask. "But who stole my bag?"

He looked at me hopelessly. "The exiles from Andalusia[2] must have stolen it…"

"Who are they, and where can I find them?"

"Everyone in Tunisia is an exile from Andalusia." The doorman turned off the outside lights. "Let's go to bed; there will not be any more visitors."

---

2. In 1159–1230, the Almohads were united with the Maghreb countries and Muslim Andalusia. In 1230, the Hafsids exiled them and started a new dynasty in Tunisia.

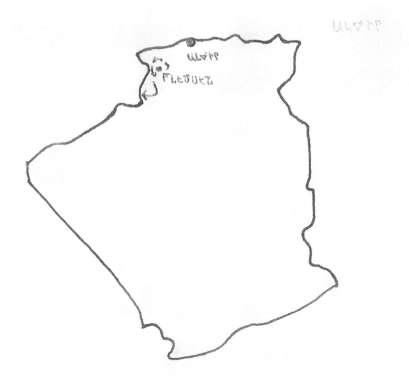

DAY 4. ALGERIA
MEANT FOR FLIGHTS

I tried for a long time to see what was depicted on the tail of the helicopter, but my line of sight was blocked by the rotor blades. Eventually, we landed at Zenata Airport in Tlemcen. I immediately raised the shade, which I had shut earlier, and looked out the window—it was a small airport, mainly used for domestic flights. There were a few small planes, but most of the place housed helicopters meant for twenty-five to forty passengers. The red letters on all the helicopters said "Air Algérie," and on their sides was the image of a swallow or a paper plane—this was the Algerian national carrier. The helicopter rotor finally stopped spinning. The captain announced in Arabic and in French that we had landed; that was the moment I realized that I was going to have language problems.

I was in Algeria, in Tlemcen, a small city with a population of about 130,000. It was a beautiful city that had taken shape in the Islamic and French architectural traditions.

I got down from the helicopter. Posters and announcements in Arabic were everywhere around me; once in a while, I would come across a few in French. I managed to get my bearings somewhat. I knew I needed an interpreter, and this made things more complicated. I roamed around for about twenty minutes, found nothing, and left the airport. Algeria has a lot of tourism, but it seemed like that wasn't the case in Tlemcen and so they had no need for translators there. I decided that I would take a taxi, go to a hotel, settle in, take a walk in the city, then go back to the hotel, have dinner, and go to bed. I had to go to Morocco the following day.

I knew by then that the closer I got to "the bottom of the sea" of the African continent, the more I would encounter nations and languages unknown to me. I was still at the "surface of the sea" and was already having language issues. I would definitely need an interpreter later, but for now I would just go around the city, trying my hand at French.

The taxi driver seemed to understand me, although he had muttered something in Arabic at first, then realized that I didn't speak the language. I handed him the hotel address on a piece of paper. For twenty minutes, I enjoyed seeing the city as we drove. I managed to catch sight of some beautiful buildings, such as the Sidi Bou Medina tomb and mosque, and a fine blue guesthouse-like building (which was the Lalla Setti House, I was later told). We approached a magnificent mosque with three cupolas: the middle section was large and decorated with colored pebbles, while the right and left cupolas looked like candy. There was a huge balcony below, and the roof was separated from the mosque by a series of blue archways and a long wall. The driver said: "Mootich Villa."

"Yes," I nodded, pretending to understand. It was probably the local name.

When we approached another mosque, he said, "La Grande."

"Yes, yes."

He had become a good tour guide for me. With his help I learned a few other names, like Mansourah and the Minaret Mosque. Then the driver suddenly started talking in English in a loud voice.

"The city resembles Fes in Morocco."

"Yes."

In the end, he asked for 1,500 Algerian dinars, around twenty dollars. He had probably included the cost of his tour program in broken English in that sum.

I hadn't even managed to step outside the taxi when the dust from a construction site settled on my teeth and my eyes started to burn. At that very moment, all my plans concerning Tlemcen changed.

"Is this Khadim Ali Boulevard?" I asked the driver, who was already gunning the engine.

"Yes, yes," he muttered and off he went.

But where was the hotel? There was only a newly constructed building in front of me, which was completed on the outside, while work continued inside. Workers were everywhere, wearing heavy coats that bore the letters "PKZ" on the back.

The hotel name, Flamingo Les Zianides, was nowhere to be seen, but I decided to go in.

It was a building that seemed from the outside to have seven or eight floors. Inside, the walls were unimpressive—they were large and had openings for windows but no glass, and the elevator was not working. Everything was white and there were artificial trees in containers on every floor. All the workers were busy. I wanted to approach one and ask questions, but they moved so rapidly that I couldn't venture to speak to one. I went up to the roof. On the roof, there was a small separate house-like structure, and I had to walk up a narrow metal staircase to get to it. The door to the structure was open. Before entering, I looked around from the roof—the view was amazing. I could hear yelling in Arabic from inside the structure. I went in. A man was laying on a folding iron bed. I told him that I did not speak Arabic, only English. He looked at me carefully. His hair trembled as if he was standing in the wind.

"Are you a tourist?" he asked.

"No, I'm a writer; I've come here to write a book about Africa. I'm visiting each country."

"There are many hoodlums in the street at this hour, you should go home."

It was four p.m. The sun shone brightly.

"Is this Khadim Ali Boulevard?"

"Yes."

"Then where is the hotel?"

"We haven't finished it yet. It will be ready in three months. There are a few things left to do."

"What? But I am supposed to spend the night here."

"Here?"

"Yes."

"That's impossible. We haven't completed the construction yet. How can you stay here?" He straightened his hair.

"I was told to go to the Flamingo Les Zianides Hotel on Khadim Ali Boulevard in Tlemcen," I said.

"Who told you that?"

"The travel agency that booked my stay."

"Well, they were right about the location, but you came too soon. We still have three months to go."

"But they told me everything was ready, that my room would have a telephone, TV, air conditioning, furniture, and there would be a swimming pool, all for thirty dollars a day."

"Sounds great. But we haven't finished yet. The ground floor will also have a parking garage, and a lobby area with a bar, cafe, and restaurant."

The man spoke very calmly, as if nothing strange was going on. I had not come to Africa as a tourist, but neither was I a journalist wanting to pry into everything. All I needed was a place to spend the night and the opportunity to see Africa. Then I noticed two huge pipes at the man's side.

"What are these pipes for?"

"It's the ventilation system."

"My room was supposed to be on the fourth floor."

"Was it a single?"

"Yes."

"I know the one, it's good. We've finished everything there, except the windows, but it hasn't been cleaned."

"It's a good room?"

"Yes, very good."

"Does it have air conditioning?"

"Yes."

"Good. It's too bad that you haven't finished it. What's your name?"

"Ali."

He did indeed look like an Ali. Suddenly I noticed a leather bag on the window sill.

"What's this bag?" I asked.

"This one? Ah, yes, I bought it in Tunisia."

"In Tunisia? When?"

"About twenty years ago."

"Did you buy it in the leather goods store on Taieb Mhiri Avenue?"

"Yes, how did you know?"

"I bought one, too. But mine was stolen."

"What were you doing in Tunisia?"

"The same as here."

"Looking for a hotel?"

"No, looking for my bag. Actually, I was acquainting myself with the city."

"I see. Did you say you were a writer?"

"Yes."

Ali pulled out a book from under his bed. To my surprise, it was in Russian. The title was *A General Introduction to Helicopters*.

"Do you speak Russian?" I asked.

"Yes."

We began to speak in Russian from that point on.

"Where did you learn it?" I asked.

"My mother is Russian. I've never been to Russia, but I've heard a lot about it."

"Oh. I never imagined that I would meet a Russian speaker in Algeria."

"I'm a pilot."

"A pilot? What are you doing here, then?"

"I used to be a pilot."

"I see."

"I worked for the Algerian airlines; I used to fly helicopters."

"Is that why you're reading this book?"

"Yes."

"But why do you work here?"

"I love the roof. It's meant for flights. I can lie here for hours and dream about my helicopter. It will go up, rotate, gather momentum, and then soar and fly away. Did you know that Leonardo da Vinci had drawn up a prototype of the helicopter as far back as 1490? Then the brothers Louis and Jacques Breguet raised the first ever helicopter into the air by a few centimeters on August 24, 1907. In the same year, another Frenchman, Paul Cornu, managed to stay in the air for about twenty seconds. Later, Petróczy, Kármán, and Asboth produced the first operational model—the PKZ."

"The PKZ?"

"Yes."

"That's what it says on the builders' uniforms—PKZ."

"Yes," said Ali with a happy smile. "That is my work crew. I gave them that name."

Ali seemed to detour away from his daydreaming about helicopters. I thought that perhaps he had never really been a pilot.

"And what is your current area of specialization?" I asked.

"Air traffic controller. I am a watchman here. But after a while, it stopped working for various reasons."

"What stopped working?"

"The PKZ. After the First World War, a large number of helicopters were produced. In the 1950s, Sikorsky created the first ever civilian passenger helicopter, the S-55. Then Hiller created the XROE-1 Rotorcycle."

I wanted to interrupt him. He was like an encyclopedia, spewing facts.

"The first helicopter with a gas-propelled engine was the Kaman K-225. The Vietnam War raged from 1960 to 1970, and new helicopters were developed—the 209 Cobra and the QH-50, designed for night flights."

He spoke with enthusiasm, but I was not very interested in the history of helicopters. I wanted to find a hotel but, by talking to Ali, that was proving very difficult to do.

"You seem to really love helicopters," I observed.

"Infinitely. Life is for flying."

"Are you a Berber?"

"Yes."

It was very strange—first the hotel, then the leather bag, and now the fact that he was a Berber. Was I being fooled again? Had I once again fallen into some bizarre and mystical African scenario? Was it possible that the hotel address could be wrong?

We were quiet for a moment. Ali's hair seemed to move as if from a wind caused by a helicopter's rotor blades.

It was now dark, but the workers' voices could still be heard.

"Would you like to eat?" Ali asked.

"No."

"Chorba."

"What?"

"A meat soup. Like they serve on the helicopters."

"Thank you. It's getting late. I should go, I feel tired."

"Wait." Ali got to his feet. "Where are you going to go?"

"Can I go down to my room?"

"No, I don't have the key. Besides, that room is not clean."

"In that case I'll go and find another place. This morning, when I got off the helicopter, I had a feeling that Tlemcen[3] would not provide me with a quiet day," I said.

"What did you say?"

"Nothing. Good night, I have to go to Morocco tomorrow."

I went down the iron staircase, and Ali suddenly shouted down at me: "Perhaps you came to Algeria on the helicopter of my dreams, which is why you came so early. My helicopter is very quick."

He pulled out another folding metal bed from behind the door, saying "Come, we shall fly to Morocco together tomorrow."

---

3. Similar to a Berber word meaning "meant for flights" (*Tilmisani*).

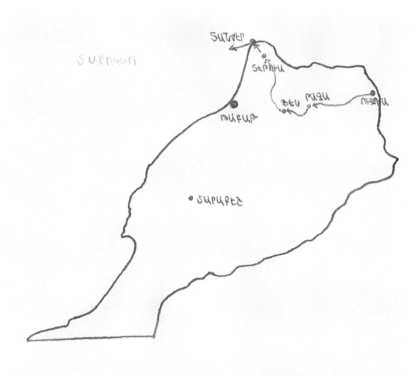

DAY 5. MOROCCO
THE STRAIT OF GIBRALTAR

Avoiding Oujda, Taza, Fes, and Tetouan, we landed in Ali's helicopter in Tangier, the closest port to Europe and the meeting point of numerous trade routes.

The helicopter touched down about fifty kilometers from the coastline, on a grass-covered patch of land that could by no means be called an airport. I was at once embraced by the cold air blowing in from the sea, and decided to continue my journey alone from that point.

I was in the Kingdom of Morocco, a country whose map in geography books I had always associated with a rose. It didn't really look like a rose, but the upper part reminded me of an unopened bud of petals, and I was now at the northernmost bit of that nascent flower. I don't know why, but Morocco immediately felt different from the countries I'd already visited. Everything was different here. I was no longer surprised by anything, and all of Africa's "peculiarities" had started to become completely normal.

Morocco was where I made some important decisions. Tangier was a developed seaport and there were many Europeans.

I walked alone in the suburbs of Tangier.

In the distance, I could see a tall white building (nearly all the buildings there were white). Clouds had gathered in the sky. To the other side, there was a large salt lake that had developed some six million years ago and had split the land between the Mediterranean and the Atlantic Ocean. That was the Strait of Gibraltar, the closest point separating Africa and Europe.

Looking out into the distance, I thought about Africa. My journey did not seem to be going badly, but something kept bothering me. I wanted to see things that were more real, more impressive. I thought about going back home (the first and only time I did so). I would never be this close to Europe again—I could cross the Strait, reach Spain, and from there get back to Armenia through Europe. But was that what I wanted? Was I so weak that I could not withstand the "peculiarities" of Africa? At that moment, I had a serious decision before me, and that decision made at the Moroccan port of Tangier was the most consequential and important step that I had taken. I decided I had to stay here, and that was that. I dove into Africa with new energy.

"What are you doing here?" asked a sailor in French, popping up as if from nowhere.

"I speak English, I don't know French," I said.

"What are you doing here?" he repeated his question, in English.

"Traveling."

"Are you a tourist?"

"No."

"Who are you then?"

"A writer."

"Have you come to write a book about Tangier?"

"No… I mean, yes, but not Tangier—about Morocco, and Africa." I was already bored of saying the same thing to everybody who happened along.

"But why did you come to Tangier?"

"Ali's helicopter landed here. Ali is my Algerian friend."

"Why didn't you go to another city?"

"I don't know."

"I've got a boat, I could give you a guided tour for 180 dirhams," he said, suddenly speaking less formally.

"I have no dirhams. How much is that in dollars?"

"About twenty dollars."

"That's a lot."

"All right then, 150 dirhams."

"No, thanks."

"All right then, 120."

"I can't, that's too much. I'd rather walk around in the city."

"All right. I'll take you into the city in my boat, and I will tell you about Morocco on the way, all for 100 dirhams.

"I won't pay more than ten dollars."

"It's a deal."

We boarded a red boat with white decorations and sailed towards the city.

"My name is Mustafa."

"A pleasure."

"Is this your first time in Morocco?" asked Mustafa.

"Yes."

"You should have seen the Hassan II Mosque first, then Fes, Marrakesh, and then Casablanca and Rabat."

"Why?"

"Tangier is nothing special as a city. There is nothing interesting to see here."

"Is the Hassan II Mosque beautiful?"

"Divine. It was built recently, in 1993. It is the second largest mosque in size in the whole Muslim world, after Mecca. They used sixty-five tons of marble and five hundred lampshades from Venice. It cost two million dollars."

Mustafa's words were overtaking his thoughts. He spoke clearly and it was obvious that he had repeated those words at least a thousand times.

"We will get to the city soon. You will see some interesting things on the square there."

"Like what?"

"Men who charm snakes, shoe shiners, dental kiosks where they extract teeth with no pain relief. You will also see olive gardens. I can take you to Fes, the capital of the former Empire of Mauritania."

"No, thank you," I said, thinking he would probably demand several thousand dirhams for that service. "Do we still have far to go?"

"No, just a few minutes."

In those few minutes, he filled my brain with encyclopedic information and stories, about how the Arabs and the Berbers seized the Iberian Peninsula in 711-720 and created the Caliphate of Cordoba in 765. Later, Morocco became a separate state, and in 985 the coastal segment of Morocco was once again merged with Cordoba. Then, Morocco was seized by the nomadic tribes of the Southern Sahara. Following that, the Spaniards and the Portuguese took over. In 1912, Morocco was divided between France and Spain, while Tangier was declared an international zone. On October 29, 1956, after about nine months of independence, it joined Morocco.

Mustafa proclaimed all this information. No doubt, it was useful to have knowledge of Morocco's history, but not from a random guide who seemed to be an outright fraud.

We finally reached the city. I paid him twelve dollars instead of ten, and we parted ways.

The city looked completely different from inside, and I looked forward to seeing those most interesting things that lay in wait for me there. I was walking along one of the narrow streets of Tangier (although narrow streets were not common there) and felt cold. There was no wind, but it was chilly.

I quickened my steps and went in the direction Mustafa had indicated, where I would see snake charmers, roadside dentists, and shoe shiners. But I found that he had been a swindler and there was nothing there. That square was completely empty. There were only one or two passers-by, and someone was selling ice cream in the distance. I approached him. The ice cream looked delicious. The prices were listed on the refrigerator, next to pictures of each kind of ice cream. I picked the cheapest one—3.95 dirhams, about twenty-five cents.

"What kind of ice cream is that?" I asked the vendor.

He was Spanish, and said something in Spanish. Then he said in English, "Milk."

A very clever answer. What other kinds of ice cream could there be? In turn, I asked in English, "What's in it?"

"Sugar and a few other things. Are you buying it or what? It's melting."

"Yes. Do you know where the dentists and other vendors are?"

"Do you have tooth problems?"

"No, but I was told that there are interesting performances on the square with snakes, that there are shoe shiners and roadside dentists."

"Was it Mustafa who told you that?"

"Yes."

"He's tricked you. All of those things are in the city of Marrakesh. Don't believe that man, he cheats everybody."

"Why?"

"He's simply a liar. If he says it's winter, that means it's summer."

"And is Marrakesh far away?"

"About eight hundred kilometers."

"I see. Thanks."

"If you see Mustafa, tell him his father is looking for him. And don't believe anything he says."

I didn't understand any of this. Was this vendor Mustafa's father, or wasn't he? This could have been the case, since he too was a trickster. When I removed the ice cream wrapping, it was so cold that one could see crystals of ice on it. It was tasty, but after eating some of it, my throat began to ache. I threw away half of it.

After a little while, I ended up in front of a building that was the Continental Hotel, with a large staircase that went up a wall on the left. The middle part of the hotel consisted of four floors, while the sides each had three floors. There were huge palm trees all around. But I had no reason go in; I did not want a room. I had decided to walk around until the evening, and then go on to the next country—through the Western Sahara to Mauritania. But before doing that I wanted to stay a little longer in Tangier to find something interesting that I could compare with what I had seen in the other countries I had visited.

"Roses, roses, winter roses," yelled a flower vendor standing near the hotel entrance. His voice echoed. "Come here," he shouted to me in a mixture of English, Spanish, and French.

"What is it?" I asked as I walked up to him.

"Wouldn't you like some roses? These are winter roses."

"Winter?"

"Yes."

"Do roses grow in the winter?"

"Yes, of course they do. These roses grow only in the winter."

"Can I take a sniff?"

"Go ahead."

The smell was indescribable; it was like a mixture of every single fruit and flower. This was the first time I had ever seen a winter rose. I was reminded of how the map of Morocco used to make me think of a rose bud.

"Would you like to buy one?"

"Just one. How much do I owe you?"

"As much as you like."

"One dollar."

"Good."

"Where did you pick these?"

"Near the Caves of Hercules."

"Where is that?"

"Nearby, just two kilometers to the north."

I turned northwards, my throat still aching. A shiver went through my body. My palms were sweating and my skin was red, and I felt the rapid flow of blood through my veins. My head was heavy; my eyelids were swollen. It was cold. Temperatures in Tangier are usually high, reaching thirty degrees Celsius and higher, while in the winter it does not goes below eighteen degrees. But it was summer now. I was falling ill. I hadn't brought any warm clothes with me. Since it's always warm in Africa, I hadn't thought that I would need a jacket or coat.

"It's winter, it's snowing," yelled someone, who turned out to be Mustafa.

"Mustafa, your father is looking for you," I said.

"I have no father," he said, and he ran off like a madman.

It was indeed snowing; my body cramped. People were walking around in short sleeves and did not seem to notice the snowflakes falling quickly onto the white streets and roofs. They were indifferent, except for Mustafa, who had not been lying for perhaps the very first time…

I hid myself in the Caves of Hercules, looking at winter roses emerging through the snow. The snow kept falling, and I was losing my sense of balance.

The last time there was snow in Tangier was very long ago, at a time when Africa had not yet broken off from Europe and the Strait of Gibraltar had not yet come into existence…

DAY 6. MAURITANIA
THE CAMELS

"Stop, or I'll kill you, you can't escape! I've got you, you won't get away. Stop, stop, you beast! I'll smash your head with this rock. Come here, you little… I'll cut off your humps. I'll thrust my knife into your throat. Where did it go?"

I was in a desert and could see, in the distance, some bales of hay in a big abandoned clay trough. I didn't know where I was, but I knew that if I didn't milk the camel standing in front of me and get some milk down my throat, I would breathe my last in a few hours. I had no idea where the camel had come from. I didn't even know what I was doing there. I was feeling dizzy and my throat was dry, but there was no water anywhere. My only hope was this old camel that was somehow pulling itself away from me and escaping. "Don't go, please!" I yelled, almost losing my wits. I felt drained, and saw black spots before my eyes. At that moment, the camel began to run. I tried to catch it, but in vain. I hurled my knife (I had no idea where that had come from) at the beast. It stuck in its back, and the camel staggered and dropped onto the sand as if struck down by a bullet.

A few minutes later, I also collapsed. Both of us seemed to give up the ghost at the same moment.

I woke up. I was being carried away on a stretcher. My right hand was dangling and constantly rubbing against the hot grains of desert sand. My body swayed. Four Black men were carrying me. My body was covered by pieces of colored cloth that had a particular smell, one that indicated they had probably been used to cover animals for years. I had a fever; I remembered Tangier and its unforgettable weather, but I couldn't think. My only desire was to sleep, and for as long as possible.

I was in Mauritania, one of the most Muslim countries in the world. I did not know how I had gotten there. In general, I remembered nothing after the Caves of Hercules. Someone had probably carried me and brought me to Mauritania, although nobody knew my route besides myself. So it was either a coincidence, or someone had known my plans and brought me here. But who? It was quite obvious that, by coming to Mauritania from Morocco, we had passed through the city of Semara in the Western Sahara. Unfortunately, I had probably been asleep at the time and had not been able to see anything.

But now I was in Mauritania for sure, because the edge of the stretcher had writing in French—Republique Islamique de Mauritanie—and also in Arabic, which was incomprehensible to me. I examined the clothes worn by the people around me; near the collar of their shirts was a horizontal crescent embracing a star, with trees on both sides. It was the Mauritanian coat-of-arms.

I quickly sat up, the stretcher creaked, and they all turned to look at me.

It's a pity that the written word cannot reproduce a melody. These were roughly the words sung by one of them: "Go-go, dim ro di, akoo-va, va zi, go, go, va akoo va zi, go-go…"

His language seemed to suggest that he was from a minority ethnic group, since the state language of the Mauritanians is a form of Arabic, Hassaniya. I couldn't say which ethnic group this might be, but his song seemed to be one of an upset man. He was sad and seemed to be singing a requiem for someone. The heat had given his hair a strange color—it had grown red and slipped out from under his yellow headdress. I also saw his eyes, which looked as if they were expecting something. This stranger had eyes filled with hope; he was probably the group leader.

"Where are you taking me?" I asked. "I can walk, put the stretcher down."

They were silent and raised the stretcher even higher. Beside the four stretcher-bearers and the one who was singing, there were two other people there—a woman and a child. In the distance, there was a caravan of camels indifferently moving forward toward us; they were probably the camels belonging to the man who was singing.

"Where are you taking me?" I asked again. "I feel better, let me down." I clutched at the stretcher.

But they were quiet and didn't even look at me. They walked calmly. The way they walked did not differ at all from the gait of the camels. One of those carrying me had no headdress, his white curly hair expanded and contracted like a spring. He kept chewing something and this reminded me that I was hungry.

"Let me go, I'm hungry, I'm thirsty, give me water. Who are you? Why don't you talk? Are you afraid of me?"

No reply. They paid no attention to what I was saying. I threw the colored cloth off of me and tried to jump off the stretcher. At that moment, the woman and child yelled out, and the leader stopped singing and yelled, too.

I cannot describe what happened next. I can only say that he had a very loud voice, and most of the words he used had a "g" sound in them. He gave an order, and then continued singing. The men carrying me immediately raised the stretcher higher, holding it above their heads. I did not have enough time to jump, but my shoes fell off.

"My shoes, pick up my shoes. Give me back my shoes. I can't walk barefoot like you!" In reality, they were all wearing slippers.

There was no reply once again. Suddenly, an important thought crossed my mind. I was speaking in English, after all. How could those people understand me? If I wanted to get my meaning across to them, I had to know a language such as Pulaar, Soninke, or Wolof, which were recognized as state languages in Mauritania, to the best of my knowledge. For a moment, I wanted to jump up and flee, but I didn't know where to go. This way, at least I wasn't using any energy as I floated along on the "second floor" as it were. After about twenty minutes or perhaps a little longer, the man who was singing came up to me. He spoke some unfamiliar, coarse words and gave me a small glass of water to drink. From that moment on, I started speaking in Armenian to them. Either way, they didn't understand. I also sang in Armenian…

It was a long journey. I started thinking about Africa. It was as if this time I had ended up in the "real" Africa, and my life was in the hands of a singer, or a camel herder. What if they killed me? How could I visit the remaining countries? Many questions began to agonize me. It was the first time that I felt real danger and I realized that I could face many other difficulties besides language issues. I had still seen nothing in Mauritania, such as cities or sights, but all of this was much more interesting. There were no clouds in the sky here, and if I did not look at the desert or feel the terrible heat, I would think that I was in some northern country where there are no clouds but where the sky, as a whole, looks like a stretch of vapor.

"Go-go-dim-boo, ak va-boo, go za, boo boo-go dim-boo, va-va-zi bo…"

The sounds of the group leader's song could be heard once again, after a few minutes of silence, interrupting my thoughts.

At that moment, I noticed that we were approaching a city. There were buildings in the distance, and a yellow minibus was driving up to us.

"This is a city, a city! We made it, let me get down, I can walk the rest of the way myself."

The four Black men were moving symmetrically towards the yellow vehicle. The singer, along with the woman and child, walked ahead of them. A short distance away, the caravan of camels continued walking. The vehicle was coming directly towards us, raising a cloud of dust as it scattered grains of sand to its left and right.

The leader issued a command, and my carriers finally let me down. My legs were trembling. When I touched the sand, it was as if small pieces of glass pierced my skin, but I tried to ignore it.

"Thank you, can I finally go now? My best wishes to you, you seem to be good people." I walked a few meters, but my ears were flooded by the deep voice of the singer. The men brought me back, sat me down and tied my hands with strong rope. I tried to resist, but believe me, the four of them were stronger than elephants.

"What do you want from me? If you want money, just say so. Is there a tradition here of torturing people this way? Or are you just trying to make fun of me?"

The vehicle stopped in front of the caravan, about fifty meters away from us. I noticed that there was some Latin script on the vehicle. Three men dressed in blue emerged from inside and approached us. Each of them carried a case. When I could see their faces, I immediately felt better; they looked like Europeans, so I assumed they would speak English. The singer, the woman, and the child approached and greeted them, then boarded the yellow minibus. They laid me back on the stretcher and we went to the vehicle, too, which turned out to have French words written on it, something to do with medicine. The newcomers were French.

I was untied once we were inside the vehicle and I spoke to the Frenchmen immediately.

"This is Mauritania, isn't it?" I asked.

"Yes."

"Where are we?"

"Near the city of Atar in the Adrar Region. Why?"

"Why? I've been tortured for the past four hours, these people aren't letting me go, and I've lost my shoes. You're French, aren't you?"

"Yes."

"Please help me. What business do you have with these strange people?"

"We're doctors, and our team also includes a journalist. We arrived at the small airport in Atar on a charter flight, then came here. This is Jean, Louis de Gasse, and my name is Michel. Louis is a journalist, and we two are doctors. We have come here to treat these people and also to report on any interesting cases. We were invited by them to come on this occasion, but we visit Africa frequently anyway. Our organization is called 'Helping Africa Together.' Where are you from?"

"I'm Armenian, a writer; I'd gone to Tangier in Morocco and fell ill there. I don't remember what happened next."

"What illness was it?" asked Jean.

"The flu."

The three of them exchanged glances and smiled, then Michel said, "I see." He looked me in the eye. "They found you."

"These people?"

"Yes, they found you and brought you here."

"How do you know?"

"I told you, didn't I, that they had invited us to come here? They asked us to help."

"And what interesting case are you going to report?"

"Revenge," cut in Louis. "That is what is interesting to us, anyway. But their leader, Zazi, is in mourning."

"Who are they?"

"They're Wolofs. Have you heard of them?"

"Yes, I have. But what do I have to do with them? Do they want to help me or not?"

"No, they want to take revenge on you."

At that moment, my thoughts were all mixed up, as if I were in a complex dream where everything was going wrong—but I couldn't open my eyes to free myself.

"Why?" I asked.

"They think you are a Pulaar."

"A what?"

"Someone from the Pulaar tribe."

"But, I'm Armenian. Explain to them that I'm Armenian, I have nothing to do with the Pulaars."

"They won't understand," said Michel in a harsh tone.

"Do the Wolofs consider the Pulaars their enemies?"

"No, it was just that Zazi had a Pulaar friend who betrayed him, so now he naturally wants to take revenge."

"But I'm not that friend."

"We know, we know, but that doesn't matter."

"What are they going to do with me?"

"They'll kill you."

"Why? I've done nothing!"

"You're asking too many questions. When we arrive, you'll get it," said Michel, whom I started to hate at that moment.

"At least tell me how much longer it will take until we arrive."

"The desert is 320 kilometers in the direction of the capital, Nouakchott. But we're going to the north, to Nouadhibou. We've covered about ninety percent of the distance."

It was very strange: they were doctors who had come to treat the sick, and also to cover my murder? Where was the justice in this? I was to be killed for nothing, while they would provide medical treatment to the killers.

At that moment, I noticed that in addition to the people I had seen before, there was one more person in the vehicle, the driver. I also noticed that the camel caravan was no longer in sight, and I was surprised that it had been left without a herder.

We drove on for another twenty minutes and I began to have a fever again. Was Africa really like this? Would I have to struggle for my life at every step?

"Help me escape, I beg of you," I said.

"We can't do that, they'll kill us, too."

"They're committing a crime, and you're ready to turn a blind eye!"

"This is their national tradition; it is not subject to punishment."

Brilliant. There was nothing left for me to say. Everything was happening so quickly that I couldn't grasp it all. I started to recall things again, and remembered the countries I had visited. Then I decided that I would find the right moment and escape, although I had no idea how to do it or where I would go. My throat was becoming dry, my thirst was suffocating me.

The vehicle stopped at a deserted spot and the back door opened, letting out Zazi and his family. The French took out the cases that I had seen them carrying when they had first gotten out of the vehicle.

"Get out," said Michel. "Understand that we don't wish you harm. We will defend you, but they are in charge in their land and what we say doesn't matter. We must submit. We have been exiled already from our homeland for our irresponsible behavior. Please get out."

I tried to run away, but I was too tired and I stumbled. I was once again tied up with a rope and taken to a sand structure that looked like a tomb.

"Go-go-va zi-boo, va-va-vee, goo-go-go va-boo…"

Zazi was singing again, this time on his knees. His wife and child looked at me with hate. Zazi jumped up and came up to me.

"At least tell me now what it is I have done."

"You will find out soon," said Jean.

They pushed me into a strange place with a green field in front, and bales of hay inside.

"He was betrayed by his Pulaar friend, who gave you the silver knife that Zazi had gifted him."

"What knife? I don't understand any of this!"

"You used this knife to kill the oldest camel in his caravan."

"I have killed no one."

At that moment, Zazi drew his knife and struck my body.

"You were here, not at the Caves of Hercules. And you killed that poor camel because of your thirst."

"Me?"

"Yes, that is why Zazi hates you, and has decided to take revenge on you by bringing you here, where he has buried the camel."

My eyes gradually closed. I only said, "But how did Zazi know all that… wasn't it all a dream?"

"The camels told him, the caravan of camels has seen you in a dream," Louis said as he started clicking away with his camera.

೮೦ ೦೮

When I woke up, a Mauritanian woman in black clothes was giving me some milk.

"Drink it, it is camel's milk, it is good for you. You will soon get well. You've been delirious all this time. Drink this, it's milk from the oldest camel in the caravan…"

DAY 7. CABO VERDE
THE SUN OF FOGO

The tiny country of Cabo Verde was the seventh one I visited in Africa. In all, it consists of four thousand square kilometers, spread out over ten volcanic islands. This was the first time that I felt happy. In fact, it was the first time I felt happy just looking at the sky; I had a sense of satisfaction. Perhaps the camel milk had really cured me—my feet no longer trembled, my fever was gone, and I had energy. I cannot say how I ended up in Cabo Verde, but a few hours after my arrival there, I got my bearings and planned my stay. I had told the Mauritanian woman about my travel plans, and it was quite possible that she had arranged my trip.

The Atlantic Ocean was coming towards me and I was walking towards it, forgetting that I can't swim. The water looked so fresh as it splashed against the mountains; the foam sunk beneath the moss, as if seeking refuge there; and then it came over onto the sand, melting into it like snow. Water a meter deep wouldn't drown me, I thought as I took off my clothes and ran towards the ocean. We made friends at once. The Atlantic Ocean embraced me and carried me downwind. It smelled of strawberries. It was very pleasant to have tiny droplets of water roll over my body as if they had long been waiting for me.

The water was warm, as was the air temperature, but my playful movements cooled the droplets which teased my body even more as they touched it. For over an hour, I enjoyed splashing in the Atlantic Ocean around the city of Mindelo, on the island of São Vicente. I felt a little cold but, ignoring what was best for me as usual, I put on my clothes while still wet and walked to the shoreline.

I looked in the distance as the last drops of water sprang from my hair. I wiped the dry sand from my feet, put on my socks, and saw a young man in the distance, his back to me, with a green bucket next to him. I approached him. Just then, as the sun turned and went behind a mountain, the young man moved his head, revealing the fish he was holding.

"Are you from here?" I asked.

A closer look showed that his skin was dark, but not Black. He looked at me and nodded his head.

"Do you speak English?"

He said nothing, but his face showed that there was a lot he knew, so I decided to spend the day with him. However, it was not clear whether or not he agreed to this.

"The air here is great; it feels good to take deep breaths. You have a wonderful country."

He was looking at me and smiling, then he began to remove the scales from the fish he had been holding. There was a metal dish in front of him with a strange black-and-white salt-like substance that he kept rubbing on the fish. I watched his unhurried actions. It took about twenty minutes before he washed the freshly scaled fish and put them back in the green bucket. He glanced at me and then left.

"Wait, where are you going? What about me?"

He turned around, took another look at me, and kept on walking. I followed him. It was as if Cabo Verde has inspired me very much, so much so that I was running around like a five-year-old child.

"Listen, I'm hungry. You'll treat me to some of that fish, won't you?"

The poor fisherman stayed modestly quiet and never said a word. Anyone else in his shoes would have given up a long time ago.

"Hey, Chao," I said, giving him a name that I just made up for him. "Let's eat the fish together. I'll pay you if you like, but give me some fish."

He had already grown so sick of me that he didn't even turn around.

"I've been to many countries; I can tell you all about it. Come on, let's eat together. Please?"

While I was pleading with him, we walked through a whole neighborhood. He did not pay attention to me even once. Of course, I could have gone and bought myself something to eat, but what I really wanted was to walk with him. I felt like there was a lot he knew, and I expected to hear interesting things from him.

I forgot for a moment that I was in Africa. It felt as if I were in a European country; everything seemed so clear and colorful. The city was clean, and there were no unnecessary buildings; it reminded me of Croatia or Slovenia. Cabo Verde was probably the happiest country in Africa, at least among the ones that I had visited.

Chao entered the market. Interestingly, the only other country where I had seen a market like this was Armenia. It was very similar, with the only difference being that the space was well lit, and each vendor had his own scales. There was a decorative pattern on the floor and there was an abundance of items for sale. Most importantly, sales kept rapidly occurring, and it seemed to me as if every item had the same price. Chao finished his business in five minutes, and we headed back towards the ocean.

"Chao. Will you finally talk to me?"

He looked at me again. Once again, he nodded. And then we boarded a boat.

It was strange. Chao wasn't talking to me, but he also did not object to my company. It felt like he did not notice my presence. Chao was very serious. His arms seemed twice as long as normal, but Chao was not a dwarf; in fact, he was a very tall man. He did not smile. That even scared me for a moment. It seemed like just another game. I pushed my hands down into my pants to feel my underwear, to check to see if they were wet, just to be sure that I had indeed taken a swim. They were wet, so everything was real.

"Chao. How come the water on your coast tastes like strawberries? You don't know? Neither do I." Chao probably knew, but did not understand the question. He would probably have answered if he did. He would have said that there were strawberry bushes at the bottom, or that the wind brought the smell from the mountains, or he would say that it was none of my business. But unfortunately, Chao did not wish to speak to me. Nevertheless, I stuck to him like a flea that did not want to come off.

"Chao. What kind of fish is that? It looks like a whitefish, like the ones that we have in Lake Sevan, but you wouldn't know them. Is this fish delicious? Or does it taste of strawberries?" Chao would probably say "I don't know," or "yes," or that it was a zanka, a species that could only be found in the straits between the Mindelo and Tarrafal islands, or he would ask what business it was of mine. He started the boat motor and we sped towards the south.

Chao was silent. He did not look at me; he seemed fully focused on his boat.

"Chao, are you Portuguese? What is the nationality of the local people? You look like a Latin American; you have dark skin and dark hair. You've been under the sun so long that you look like a raisin."

He would probably have said Portuguese, or Cabo Verdean, or Manjak, or perhaps even none of your business. In any case, whatever he would have said, it would not have surprised or offended me. I liked Chao a lot, and I did not intend to leave him.

He was holding his bucket with both hands, while the small steering wheel of the boat was left uncontrolled. It felt like we were being driven by the wind.

"Chao, where are we going? Are you finally going to say something, or not? I know that you're sick of me, and I know you don't speak English, but how is it possible to be so indifferent? What would it cost you to exchange a few words in Portuguese with me? Come on, answer me, where are we going?"

Once again, he did not reply. I felt as if Chao's thoughts were very far away. It was not that he was ignoring me, he was simply looking at a mountain that was moving along with us. If Chao had wished to answer me, he probably would have said we're going towards the sun, or we're going to have lunch, or perhaps he would have said mind your own business.

We sped along, two hundred kilometers to the south. The boat moved so quickly that I felt as if our journey had taken less than two hours.

At last, Chao looked at me. His gaze resembled drops of water that had momentarily separated from the ocean and were enjoying their freedom. Chao's skin was coarse, his neck was rough, his knees were reddened, and his bones could be seen in some places.

"Chao, what is your profession? Are you a fisherman? You look more like a laborer or a shepherd. No, I think you have no specific profession," I said.

Chao smiled. He glanced at me several times and continued to smile. I didn't know why he was looking at me that way, but it was clear that some reason had come up.

I had finally grown tired of him. All my efforts had been spent in vain. I waited for us to reach the shore, so that I could get off the boat and leave. I wanted to walk around Cabo Verde a little more, to see something interesting, and then head to Senegal.

We heard the screeching of seagulls; Chao switched off the boat engine and we could see the shore and the people on it. Just then, the sun came out from behind the mountain and lit up the shore. Chao momentarily shut his eyes, then picked up his bucket, brought the boat to a stop, and jumped out.

We had arrived, but I didn't know where we were. However, it was clear that Chao had come home; there were some people who had come to welcome him, and they hugged. Chao pointed to me then, and one of his friends approached me.

"Hello," he said in English.

"Good, at least someone speaks English. Where are we?"

"In Fogo. Who are you? Boa told me that you kept asking questions throughout the journey here. What do you want here?"

"Nothing. I just wanted to go around with Chao."

"Who's Chao?"

"Your friend. He's a very nice guy, but he didn't give me any fish. And he kept laughing all the time at the end of the journey."

"His name is Boa. What makes you think it's Chao?"

"I asked him, but he said nothing. He didn't want to talk, so I decided to name him Chao."

"He's deaf and dumb. How could he talk?"

At that moment, I felt as if the whole Atlantic Ocean had been poured over me.

"Deaf and dumb?"

"Yes. He hasn't spoken since the day he was born. The only thing he does is fishing. We often send him to Mindelo, because the fish there are very nice. He catches five or six fish and brings them home. He cannot do anything else. But there is really nothing for him to do anyway, we do everything for ourselves."

"Who are you?"

"I'm his brother, and these are his other brothers," he said, indicating the others. "Boa is the youngest."

"He looks very intelligent."

"I know, that's what everyone says. But he suffers a lot."

I did not feel like saying anything more; I wanted to nail myself to the sand on the beach. I wanted to leave Fogo and Cabo Verde as quickly as possible. Chao's gaze had turned to stone in my mind, even as his smiling eyes were looking at me again.

"Come, Boa is asking you to eat some of this fish," said his brother, putting his hand on my shoulder.

"But how did he end up like this? What was the cause of his deafness?"

"The Fogo sun."

"What?"

"Do you see that mountain?"

"Yes."

"This city is named Fogo, after that mountain. Every time the sun approaches our city, the Fogo Mountain embraces it and takes it away from us. On the day when Boa was born, Fogo had seized the sun and did not let it go, and it never enlightened Boa. The poor thing grew sad and went deaf. To this day, he hates the sun. Now come on, Boa is waiting for us. Let's go…"

We went up to them; everyone was laughing, and apparently my underwear was completely wet.

"Did you say that the sea tastes like strawberries?" asked one of Chao's brothers.

"Yes, how did you know?" I asked, surprised.

"Boa told me."

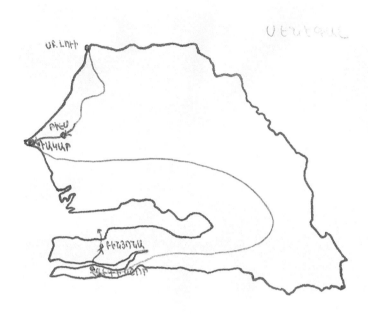

DAY 8. SENEGAL
THE ROAD TO DAKAR

The gradually increasing sound of sand grains scraping metal could be heard, and the ship arrived at its destination. I had come from Cabo Verde to Senegal. What caught my eye at once was the Great Mosque of Touba, looking like a Gothic tower in the distance, and the fishermen standing on the beach. It was the most terrible type of fishing I had seen in my life. I had never witnessed a scene like that—about a thousand fishermen, twenty centimeters apart from one another, stood in several rows, and the fish they had landed were floundering before each of them. The fish crawled out of the baskets but, just before they reached the water, they were struck on the head and their eyes popped right out. All that was made even more horrible by the noise and the stench of the fish. It was like a market with only vendors.

I walked through them and within minutes I felt sick of both the fish and the fishermen. There were so many fish on the shore that they had to be moved in boats.

I was in Saint-Louis. It was a pretty city, but I did not stay long because I had made up my mind to go to Dakar. On the way to Dakar, I passed the city of Thiès, or rather, I circumvented it. I had become more confident as I visited more countries, and the more my confidence grew, the greater was my desire to communicate with everyone and to see strange and unique things; I had finally grown adventurous. Nothing scared me anymore; I even started actively seeking out unusual or arcane stories, places, and people.

All of a sudden, I felt as if Africa was familiar to me. It did not matter what I would see in which specific country. All that mattered was that I take note of what I saw. I was even content to experience just one city, one place, and sometimes even just one person.

English was not spoken in Senegal, but that issue did not worry me, either. I knew that I would need an interpreter in some countries, but I was quite sure that Senegal was not one of them. Besides, things like that had to be arranged in advance.

Senegal was the first country where I met the type of people that I had imagined. They were from Basari[4] territory and they had a fascinating way of life, with their amazing handmade huts and cattle sheds. The Basari had very long legs, and their feet looked like stretched-out duck paddles. I was going to Dakar on foot and if one of the locals had heard this idea, he would simply have laughed and said "Go." I took along two 1.5-liter bottles of water that I bought from the Oasis Hotel in Saint-Louis.

I walked slowly in order to avoid drinking water unnecessarily. Of course, I could have avoided walking that road, or I could have taken a car, but it seemed much more interesting on foot.

The first bottle of water ran out, and at that moment I noticed the traces of horse hooves in the sand, as well as a straight line that looked like the tracks of a wheel. It was clear that there were other people around besides me and, based on the depth of the tracks (which were fresh and had not yet been filled in by the winds), I could assume that they were no more than one or two kilometers ahead of me. With only that thought on my mind, I quickly drank the remaining water and hastily ran in the direction of the tracks.

I had guessed correctly—I reached them after one or two kilometers. There were four people, all sitting in a small cart with one wheel that was bigger than the other. One of them was completely covered in red clothing, while the rest were dressed in white. The horse was out front, resembling a kangaroo (at least in its jaws), with the gaze of a down-and-out hobo. It looked like it had made a few attempts at suicide. It moved forward slowly, like a whimpering newborn, dragging behind it the bent cart which had a number of sacks arranged in the back.

They noticed me and stopped the cart. One of them said, "*Ey, e, e.*"

That voice evoked the memory of a strange echo, but there can be no echo in a desert.

"*Mangi fi,*" the voice continued.

"What? Do you speak English?" I was forced to ask this question once again, with a stupid smile.

"*Mangi fi, Salam Aleikum,*" said the man.

"*Aleikum Salam,*" I replied. I knew that much, at least.

---

4. A tribe living in Senegal as well as its neighboring countries.

"*Nanga def.*"

"I don't understand," I said, gesturing with my arms and legs.

"*Nanga def, naka ligeie bi.*"

At that moment, I wanted one of two things: either for an interpreter to descend from the skies or for me to miraculously end up far away from those people, although they appeared to be very interesting characters.

Strange as it sounds, once again things seemed to end up the way I wanted them to. Someone appeared as if from nowhere and said that he could interpret. He was on a motorcycle and wore a metal helmet with the shield fully covering his face, so nothing was visible. He was dressed in professional motorcycling gear. He asked me to avoid asking any unnecessary questions.

"What can I do for you? You don't understand the language of the Wolof, do you?" he asked.

"The Wolof?"

"Yes," said the motorcyclist.

"It sounds familiar. I think Zazi was a Wolof," I said under my breath.

"What?"

"Nothing, I was just remembering Mauritania. Did you say they're speaking Wolof?"

"Yes."

Meanwhile, the Wolofs sitting in the cart were following our conversation very attentively, trying to understand us.

"What's your name?" I asked.

"Thierry Sabine."[5]

"Are you French?"

"Yes."

"What are you doing here?"

"I said no unnecessary questions, didn't I? I don't quite know what I'm doing. All I know is that I'm lost."

"Can't the Wolofs help you?"

"I don't know, I'll discuss that with them later." Then, addressing the Wolofs, he said, "*Salam Aleikum.*"

"*Aleikum Salam,*" said the one in red.

"Are they Arabs?" I asked.

"No," said Thierry, who was not very good at speaking their language. "I told you they were Wolofs."

"So why do they say *Salam Aleikum*?"

---

5. Thierry Sabine was the founder of the Paris–Dakar competition. In 1976, he got lost in the Liberian desert when he was participating in the Abijan–Nice race, and then he returned to his home country and decided to establish a new competition. Thierry Sabine died in 1986 in a helicopter crash.

"Why shouldn't they? They're Muslims."

"Yes," I said ambiguously, as I had been aware of this previously.

"*Ana vaa ker ga*," continued Thiery.

"*Jere jef, jere jef*," answered the one in red clothing.

"What did you say?"

"I asked how their family was doing."

"But what were they saying to me?"

"Nothing serious. They just said hello and asked how you were, how things were going."

"But I don't know them. Are you acquainted with them?"

"Everyone knows everyone in the desert," said Thierry. "I have to go now. Are you coming with me?"

"No, I decided to go on foot intentionally. I want to talk to them. If you leave, how are we going to talk?"

"I'll tell them that you don't understand Wolof. They speak French well, so I'll ask them to try and speak English. They're merchants and often communicate with foreigners; no doubt they will know some English."

"I've asked them already; they don't know any."

"You haven't asked well enough." Thierry approached them, whispered something, and then returned. "They know some English and will try to talk with you. It's true, they speak badly, but you will surely understand some of it. *Be beben jung*." The motorcycle engine kicked in and sand grains jumped right and left, some hitting my face.

"Wait, what did you say to them?"

"I said, 'See you next time.'"

Thierry vanished in an instant; he had seemed very suspicious. He had asked nothing. A normal man would have been surprised to see me in the desert, but he didn't even hint at it. It was also strange that he told me not to ask any questions—his appearance had been so sudden that anyone would have wanted to ask questions.

I approached the Wolofs, hoping to start a conversation.

"You say you speak English?"

They were confused. They started to blabber something in French. This was followed by Wolof, after which, following a long wait, they produced some words in English.

"May I join you?" I asked, taking a few steps towards the cart.

"No, no, no," they cried in unison. "That's impossible, we can't do that."

"I'm a writer. Do you understand? A writer."

"No, no, the right side is also occupied, no."

"A *writer*, I said, a writer."

They had confused the word "writer" with the "right" side. I took out the notepad from my breast pocket and gestured to help them understand.

"We understand now; still, you cannot come."

"Why?"

"You are not from our group."

"What group?"

"Our team," the Wolof in red said. "Have you ever heard of the Paris–Dakar car race?"

"Yes, the starting line is now in Lisbon. That competition is probably the best-known event related to Senegal. But what do you have to do with it?" I asked.

"We're going to Dakar. We're competing in this event. We're now on the last leg to Dakar."

That was the one thing I had least expected to hear. If they had said that they were ghosts, or that the wind had brought them there, I would have believed it. But who on earth participates in the Paris–Dakar Rally using a horse and cart? Surely, they meant something else?

"This is the year 2006, isn't it?" I asked, to see whether I had somehow deviated from the reality I knew.

"Yes, yes," they said in unison.

"Are you ghosts?"

"No."

"Are you dead?"

"No, why?"

"That rally doesn't take place this month. It's September now, but the race happens from December 31 to January 10, if I'm not mistaken."

"That's right."

"So what competition are you taking part in? And besides, who competes in a motor rally in a cart?"

The Wolofs were silent. The wind shook the sand in the distance, and dust approached like a cloud of vapor.

The Wolofs scratched their heads and straightened their headdresses, while the groaning horse chewed needlessly, moving its empty mouth.

"A wind is coming," they said. "Come with us."

"No, a short while ago you said you were a team. And now you want to take me along." They told me to hurry up, but I objected.

"What's in the sacks?" I asked.

"Salt."

"That much?"

"Yes."

"Where are you taking it?"

"Dindéfelo country, Basari country, the place that Sidi[6] liked."

---

6. Baye Sibi (not Sidi) was a ten-year-old Malian girl who was run over during the 1988 Paris–Dakar rally.

"Who's Sidi?"

"A girl. We're going to her grave."

"Is she dead?"

"Yes. She was ten years old."

"Your daughter?"

"Yes," all three replied.

"My condolences."

"No need for that. Eighteen years have gone by. In 1988, Sidi got into an accident. At that time Senegambia[7] had not yet collapsed."

Suddenly I noticed that the Wolofs had started speaking English very well.

"But you said you were going to Dakar?"

"Yes, first we will complete the rally circuit, win it, and then go to Dindéfelo."

"How did Sidi die?"

"A Frenchman ran her over with his car."

"What was the car doing here?"

"He was participating in Paris–Dakar. Sidi had gone to bring water from the well and saw a beautiful sunset in the distance. She put her bucket down on the sand and leaned against the spring. At that moment, the racecar appeared and ran her over."

The story they told was a brutal one. I had at least three questions to ask, but I restrained myself.

"Are you coming or not?" they asked again.

"No, you go ahead and win your competition."

"Take care."

Everything was clear now. As for their competition, either the father had lost his mind or it was a national tradition of some kind. I could see no other explanation. I immediately thought of the motorcyclist who had shown up, interpreted for me, and then vanished.

The wind grew stronger. The desert reminded me of camel humps, which slid closer and closer together as they approached. I sat down on the sand, bowed my head and covered my eyes. I sang the same parts of a song seventeen times in my mind until the storm ended. When I opened my eyes, all traces of the Wolofs' cart and the horse hooves had vanished, blown away by the wind. Meanwhile, a motorcyclist was approaching in the distance. When he came closer, I assumed from his attire that it was Thierry.

"Have the Wolofs left?" he asked.

"Yes, but who are you? They told me a very strange story about a racecar."

"I know, I know. Do you think it was me who ran the girl over? I know that story. Don't believe them."

---

7. From 1982 to1989, Senegal and Gambia were parts of a united state called Senegambia.

Thierry removed his helmet. His hair was blond and curly, his eyes dark blue, and he had a yellow beard. His eyes looked honest.

Thierry looked at the sunset, then he looked at me, then again at the sunset, and said, "I'm lost, I had nothing to do with that incident." He turned off the engine and continued speaking. "In the winter of 1988, Baye Sibi had gone to the well for water. Seeing a beautiful sunset, like the one before us now, she put down her bucket on the sand and leaned against the well. A short while later, an SUV racecar, which was taking part in the Paris–Dakar rally, approached her at high speed. At that moment Sibi had turned around and seen it, but could not manage to get out of the way. Sibi fell to the ground, but just before falling, it seemed to her that it was a horse and a cart ridden by four Wolofs, one in red clothing, the others in white. The poor girl had never seen an off-road vehicle before…"[8]

---

8. Dedicated to the memories of Baye Sibi and Thierry Sabine.

DAY 9. THE GAMBIA
WHERE ARE YOU, ANTONIO?

I needed rest. Nothing comes easily: all the discoveries that I had been making were taking their toll on me. In all this time, there had not been a single time, in any country, when I had encountered simple reality. Of course, Chao could be regarded as "real," but the game of Africa had continued around me and maybe I was the guilty one in all this. In any case, I continued my journey and kept enthusiastically moving along. My next stop was the Gambia, a country that I had always considered unusual. It is peculiar in that it is bordered by only one country, Senegal, on the north, south, and east, while the Atlantic Ocean lies to its west. I couldn't name another state with a similar geographic setting, at least not in Africa.

It was no coincidence that Senegal and the Gambia had been a united country for about ten years. There are many similarities between the two countries—their architecture is very much alike, as are their climates, their ethnic groups and tribes, and their cities. The only significant difference—quite conveniently for me—was that the official language of the Gambia was English. I'm sure that an insider could list thousands of other differences, but none of them were visible to me.

Trying to forget the sad story of Baye Sidi with its unexpected ending, I crossed Senegal's border and entered the Gambia. I entered from the southern part of Senegal, where the cities of Ziguinchor and Bignona are located, and decided I would leave the Gambia by ocean to go Guinea-Bissau; my travel itinerary was meant to avoid visiting the same country twice.

A border guard noticed that I was a foreigner and asked, "What is the purpose of your visit?"

"I want to see the country," I said. "I'm looking for interesting things."

The border guard asked me to follow him.

We went to a small hut-like structure that seemed out of place with its surroundings. There was a big wooden box inside. He asked me to step inside the hut and opened the box—there were little crocodiles inside! I counted twenty or twenty-five before I started to mix them all up. They were the size of shoes, dark green to black in color, moving slowly like crabs.

"Here is something interesting," said the border guard. "Everyone says they're lovely, aren't they? What do you say?"

"Yes, very."

"You can buy them."

"What would I do with them? Crocodiles are predators; they'll grow up and eat me up."

"You will release them into the river."

"I want to avoid unnecessary expenses. In any case, one day you are going to have to release them yourself."

"No, we do business with a zoo, they'll buy all of them. You can save at least one, if you like."

"Is that what you would like?"

"What I'd like doesn't matter. I am responsible for every one of them. If I'm found to be missing one, I'll have to pay for it. I'll give you a good deal; save the poor thing."

I felt obliged to buy one, although I had never in my life needed a crocodile. The words of the border guard had been convincing.

"How much do I owe you?"

"1400 dalasi."

"And in dollars?"

"About fifty dollars. OK, thirty. Isn't it worth it? You're saving a life."

"Yes, the life of a crocodile who will grow up and devour everybody. Or maybe he won't make it to adulthood, but just end up as prey for something else in the river."

The little crocodile was looking at me and moving his mouth. It was like a raw cucumber. I put my finger in its mouth. It wanted to bite it off, but it did not have any teeth and its jaw muscles had not yet firmed up. I paid for it. The border guard let me pass without checking my documents. He just opened the so-called border and wished me well; the crocodile was wrapped in a white cloth in a small basket.

Having bought the crocodile, this gave me an excuse to see the Gambia River. The best thing would probably be to go to Banjul, the capital of the Gambia. That was where the river starts, or rather, where it ends as it flows into the ocean.

With my basket in hand, I slowly made my way to the nearest bus stop. The border guard had told me how to get to the river; I had to take a bus from there to Serekunda, and then on to Banjul.

I thought about the many sick people who sacrificed everything they had to seek a cure and live, but who died all the same. They don't know what to do, and every step they take brings them to clinics, medications, and international relief organizations that work day and night to save them. And here I was, holding my basket carefully with both hands and heading towards the Gambia River to save the life of a little green animal. He was moving about inside, letting me know that he was angry.

The bus doors closed and its engine stuttered, sounding like an elephant's heavy breathing. A Gambian with jaundiced eyes asked me, "What is that?"

"A basket," I said. I was scared for a moment, although there were also a few women on the bus in addition to this man.

"I can see that it is a basket, but what's in it?"

"The border guard gave it to me." I took out the quivering crocodile and saw that it had soiled the white cloth.

"He gave it to you?"

"Well, he sold it to me."

"For how much?"

"Thirty dollars."

"He's cheated you; they sell them in the shops for ten or fifteen dollars," interjected a woman who had been sitting nearby all this time with her eyes closed, playing dead. "If you're not a tourist, you can find even cheaper ones. That Antonio is a liar."

"They're no good," came the voice of another woman sitting opposite the man with the jaundiced eyes. She kept shaking something in a big package in her hand. "You shouldn't have bought it. I've tried them several times, but they're no good. They're right about Antonio, too."

"It's true," said the woman playing dead. "I've also tried it a few times."

"Really? I'm trying it for the first time. The border guard said I was doing a good deed. Is his name Antonio?"

"Yes. What good deed?"

"Well, saving them."

Suddenly there was a fit of laughter in the bus. Even the driver, who had a moustache that did not suit him at all, dragged deeply at his cigarette and produced a mixture of laughter and coughing.

"What's so funny?" I asked.

"You should have bought fish; their meat is more delicious."

Everything became clear to me at that instant. I looked at the surprised crocodile. I was irritated and my desire to save the poor creature grew stronger. As if it wasn't bad enough that they were taken to a zoo—now it turned out they were eaten, too.

I reached my destination in a few hours. The people on the bus looked half asleep, which I guess meant that they had slept half the way.

I was in Serekunda. I got into a taxi there and left for Banjul, or rather to some place where one could throw a crocodile into the river.

"Why bother? It will be hunted down all the same," said the driver who seemed to be a good man, if one ignored his suspicious grey cap smelling of melted paraffin.

"I don't know; this is what I want to do," I said.

"Do you like fish?"

"Yes, why?"

"You eat fish, right?"

"Yes."

"Well, here they love to eat crocodiles. You can't approach 1,455,842 people one by one and convince them to give up eating crocodiles." At that moment I understood that he was very dangerous, given that he knew so precisely how many people lived in his country. That meant he would know many other things, too.

"Yahya Davda," he said.

"What?"

"That's my name. You can call me Yaya, that's easier to pronounce. We still have a lot of time to spend together."

At that moment, a woman appeared in front of the taxi and almost slipped, dropping the bags that she was holding, while Yaya stepped on the gas and accelerated.

"You ran her over," I shouted.

"It's nothing, don't worry."

"How can I not worry?"

"It's nothing," Yaya mumbled as he slowed down his green Peugeot. He'd said his car was a 1966 Bentley, but I knew it was a Peugeot because only French cars have a surprised look.

"Is there a post office here?"

"Yes."

"And a telephone?"

"Sure. Who do you want to call?"

"Home."

"Where's that?"

"Armenia."

"What's that?"

"A country."

"Ah, I thought it was the name of an office."

"No. Can I call from this place?"

"I don't know, you can try when we get there."

I kept track and we were at the post office in seven minutes. I lost twelve dollars trying in vain to get a connection. I wrote a letter and asked them to send it as soon as they could. I handed the letter to the post office worker, and two minutes later we hit the road to Banjul again.

"They love you, don't they?"

"Who?"

"Your parents," said Yaya.

"Yes," I said, taking a look at the crocodile. "They love me very, very much."

"How come they let you go so far away? You're still a child."

"Because they really love me. I'm writing a book."

"Good. You'll write about me, too." Yaya smoothed his hair with his hand, as if he was preparing for a camera. "What are you going to do when we get there?"

"I don't know."

"You don't know?" he asked, surprised.

"Yes."

"Why are you going there?"

"To throw this crocodile into the river."

"And?"

"And what?"

"That's it?"

"Yes."

"And here I thought you were a serious writer."

I didn't understand what Yaya meant. I remained silent for the rest of the journey, thinking only that I wanted to get there as quickly as possible. I wanted to throw the crocodile into the river and then leave for Guinea-Bissau.

"Did you know that the Gambians were the first Black people to adopt Islam?" Yaya asked to break the silence. "I think it was in 1066."

"No."

"Then we were part of the Mali Empire, and then we were ruled by the Portuguese. The Polish, the Lithuanians, the British—we're been ruled by them all. Antonio is the one to blame for all of that."

"Why?"

"He sold the Gambia River to the British, who then closed all its banks."

"But isn't Antonio a border guard?"

"A border guard? Antonio was a scoundrel, a crazy servant. He was a slave-trader, he sold slaves. But his soul was that of a slave, too. He was a villain. He was the reason they exported three million slaves from our country in three years. Never mention his name again."

"But you were the one who brought him up."

"Yes, that's true."

"What about the border guard?"

"What border guard?"

"Someone on the bus said his name was Antonio."

"I don't know, you must have gotten something wrong."

Perhaps I had gotten something wrong, as always. But Yaya could quite easily be ignorant of his own history since he couldn't even tell a Peugeot from a Bentley.

"Couldn't there be another man named Antonio?" I asked.

"In the Gambia? Impossible. There could be a Jameh, or a Javara, but not an Antonio."

"Maybe he had a Portuguese father?"

"No, impossible. He had four hundred years to change his name. If it were an English name, I wouldn't be surprised; we were a colony of Great Britain up to 1965, but Portuguese…no."

Yaya's green Peugeot was clattering through Banjul's long streets and it was clear that we were going to arrive soon. I looked at the green animal again and this time it was sad and curled up, as if having guessed where we were going.

"There it is, go about your business, save a meaningless and temporary life," were Yaya's last words to me. "Then go tell others about your heroic deed." He closed the rusty, re-painted door and then left.

I had arrived. But at that moment, the only thing I could think of was the river with all its banks closed. It was impossible to reach the edge. The crocodile looked at me, as if trying to persuade me, then he came out of the basket and jumped onto the grass. I suddenly recalled that crocodiles were amphibians, so I hadn't needed to make this long journey at all.

Only one question bothered me. Where was Antonio? It didn't matter which Antonio. I had something to say to both of them…

DAY 10. GUINEA-BISSAU
CRAZY MIKE

A small iron sphere, painted dark blue and bearing the image of the moon and a few stars, slowly rolled off the table and fell to the floor. It was then I understood that there was something inside the sphere that produced beautiful music, like ringing church bells, when it moved.

I put the sphere close to my ear and slowly shook it, trying to slow down and speed up the sounds it produced. But it always remained the same.

Soon the one thing that had made me happy began to bore me, and I put it back in the same place from where it rolled down. The ball moved off again, rolled about and returned to its former place—the center of the table opposite the window sill of room 318 on the third floor of Hotel Hotti Bissau, Avenida 14 de Novembero Street, in the city of Bissau, Guinea-Bissau. At that very moment, I heard another sound that also reminded me of music, this time coming from my left—the hotel corridor.

The music gradually turned into noise and the sound of fighting. Guinea-Bissau remained a mystery to me. I can say I have seen the country, but at the same time, it's true that I never left the hotel when I was there, and I spent all my time in that four-story building. I had initially planned to go out into the city to walk, go around to various places and take pictures, although I didn't have a really professional camera and was forced to use amateur devices like my phone or a digital camera, sometimes asking others to take a picture of me. I also planned to start writing my book. I thought I could write about Egypt, Libya, Algeria, Tunisia, and the other countries that I had visited so far. I wanted to write only about what I had seen and what I had experienced.

However, I wrote nothing that day, and would probably not write anything for another few days. At that moment, the thing disturbing me was the loud noise coming from the neighboring room or the corridor, which had blended with the sounds of the city and the turned off but constantly leaking tap in the bathroom.

"If things go on this way, I won't manage to get out into the city, although the important thing is that I am here in Guinea-Bissau. I'll start feeling sleepy soon, it will grow dark, the street lamps won't work because they look really pathetic, and I'll go to bed," I thought. I had picked up the iron sphere in my hand again, when the room was suddenly invaded by Joao Gomez Louis de Vieira, an employee of the hotel who had very politely shown me to my room that morning and offered me a complimentary cup of tea. He threw open the door and immediately started shouting. I was overcome by the excitement and felt heat rising inside me as I put the sphere back down on the table.

"Do you speak English?" shouted Gomez in a pleading voice with a Portuguese accent. "There are no English speakers in the hotel, help me, help!"

"I speak English, but not very well. What's going on?"

"Hurry, come with me."

"But what's going on?" It seemed as if Gomez had just escaped death, and was talking in incomprehensible, breathless words, scratching his foam-like white hair at the same time.

"Come, I don't know English well, I can't speak, come, come," he said as he pulled me out of the room. There was no one in the passage, not even the voices that had been disturbing me before.

"What happened? Relax, take a breath, tell me everything calmly." I, too, was starting to feel scared.

"Didn't you hear that crazy noise?"

"Which one?" I asked, although I already understood that Gomez meant the same noises that had disturbed me as well.

"A little while ago it was singing loudly, then the noise grew louder; I didn't know what to do." Gomez started to tremble, tears flowing from his eyes.

"Come with me," I said, as if taking charge of the situation. I brought Gomez back into my room and gave him some water which was probably not meant for drinking; in any case, it was worse than the tea he had given me earlier. Then I looked directly at him and, picking up the iron sphere, continued, "Now calmly tell me what happened, and what I can do to help." I kept thinking to myself, "It's safe here."

"English. If you speak English, that's good."

"I already told you that I speak some English, but what's really going on?" I was forced to repeat my question for a fifth time, because Gomez had gone from being a Black man to being a white man. "What happened?" I shouted.

"A bull has entered the hotel. It's running around everywhere; you must help me get it out. None of the other hotel employees are here right now, it's only me. Help, you speak English, don't you?" This seemed quite strange to me, because leaving just one employee on duty at a four-star hotel seemed unlikely.

"Is the bull British?" I asked.

"No, it's a local bull, with red skin and a white forehead."

"So why do you need an English speaker? Get a gun and shoot it, or call the police."

"It's not just the bull, there's someone on it."

"Who?"

"An Englishman. He arrived yesterday and said he was staying one day, that he would leave today. When I entered his room, he wasn't there. I came out thinking that he might already be downstairs, or that he had left, although he still had some time before he had to check out. Then, just when I was leaving the room, I heard a strange sound from the bathroom. I opened the door and a big, giant bull with sharp horns stared back at me. How he came to be there I don't know, but I slammed the door shut and ran. I came back down and called the police. They said they would come, but in two hours, and that this was nothing dangerous. When I went back up to the second floor, from the other end of the corridor I saw the Englishman riding the bull and coming towards me, kicking pictures off the walls. Then I came up here. That's it."

I didn't know what to say. It's not every day that a bull appears in a hotel, particularly one being ridden by an Englishman. Based on some of the other incidents and strange things that had happened so far on this trip, I asked Gomez, "Were you a colony of England in the past?" I thought that if he said yes, everything would be clear.

"No. Portugal. If we'd been a colony of England, we would speak English."

"We must call the police again."

"I have! I forgot to tell you. Before coming here, I went downstairs and called a second time."

"And?"

"They didn't believe me. When I insisted, they said again that they would come in two hours. But we can't wait two hours, that thing will turn this place inside-out in two hours, to say nothing of scaring the other guests here. That's why I came here, because I thought you would speak English. Honestly though, I was afraid to go anywhere else. This room was nearby."

"But you speak excellent English," I said. "Even your accent has disappeared, and you're using complex sentences."

"Am I?"

"You are."

Gomez cheered up, and grew in confidence. His fear had probably caused him to forget that he spoke English.

"Never mind, let's go together," he said.

Gomez took a fire extinguisher that was hanging on the wall, and I put the iron sphere back in its place; it produced a high-pitched ring this time. We went downstairs to the second floor, and everything in fact was a big mess; all of my suspicions vanished. Gomez went to the left and took another fire extinguisher off the wall, handing it to me.

"But what am I going to do with this? There's no fire."

"Hold onto it, you can blow foam at it."

We walked to the end of the corridor. I felt like I was on a rescue mission, although I was shaking a bit. The roar of a bull could be heard, followed by a squeaky voice. The Englishman appeared at Gomez's side, riding the bull. He rushed toward us at great speed. Gomez pressed down on the fire extinguisher handle and held himself against the wall. The bull eyed me angrily and stopped. While Gomez continued blowing foam from the extinguisher, the bull attacked him. The Englishman had yellow hair and a beard, was short in stature and very ugly. I ran towards Gomez but it was too late; the bull had thrust its horns several times into Gomez' abdomen and his blood was draining from his body. The fire extinguisher had dropped from his hands, the white foam still coming out of it. The Englishman took a look at me. I tried to run but it took him just two seconds to cover a distance of some thirty meters, and he ended up standing in front of me. My jaw started trembling and I couldn't help but think that this was going to be the end of me, although all of this was so unreal that I also thought for a moment that it could all be a dream.

"Who are you?" asked the Englishman.

"I'm here…here for one day. I'm leaving tomorrow," I said confusedly.

"Do you also dislike my horse?"

"Horse?"

"Yes. Or do you also think that it is a Guinean bull or buffalo? That was what he said."

"Yes, no, I don't know… I don't know what to say."

"See what nice eyes it has, its tail, its forehead. I'm Mike."

"Yes," I said, walking backwards a little. Gomez's drained corpse lay further away, his blood soaking into the carpeting.

"Mike Richardson," he pronounced gloriously, as if he was going to draw his sword with his right hand and ride into the Battle of Troy.

Time was passing very quickly. I had not yet come to my senses when I saw the moon through the corridor window. I can't remember what that madman was blabbering about, but after a few minutes, when I had calmed down, I was again back in my room. I was sitting in a chair with Mike in front of me, and the bull had vanished. Mike was waving his hand in front of my face, trying to bring me back to my senses. I jumped up at once and grabbed the linen off the bed, tossing it at him.

"What's wrong with you? You were speaking calmly a short while ago; have you lost it?" he asked.

"Why did you kill Gomez? The police will be here soon and they will arrest you."

"Who, me? The police have already come and they took him out on a stretcher a little while ago." He pulled back the curtain so that I could see. "They shot the bull with a tranquilizer dart; they will calm him down later and perhaps take him to the zoo."

"What about you?" I asked, wanting to get away from there.

"I had nothing to do with it; the bull is to blame."

"You were saying that it was a horse."

"At that time, yes. But when it killed Gomez, it was a bull. Didn't you see its horns?"

"It had horns before, too."

"No, you probably imagined that, just like everything else."

"What do you mean, everything else?"

"Yes. Didn't you know that this little ball has a hypnotic effect on people?"

He picked up the iron ball, jingled it, and left. Outside, Gomez really was on a stretcher and they took him away in an ambulance, then they took the bull away in a truck, and then a police car took away a yellow-haired man who looked like Mike.

I felt dazed and understood nothing. I looked at the table and the sphere was no longer there. I was alone in the same spot—at the table opposite the window sill in room 318 on the third floor of Hotel Hotti Bissau, Avenida 14 de Novembero Street, in the city of Bissau, Guinea-Bissau. I was looking out of the window, and could hear the sirens and see the flashing lights of speeding ambulances and police cars. The moon and a few stars were visible, and I could hear a strange sound that resembled the ringing of church bells.

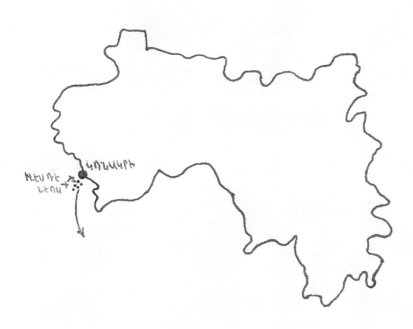

DAY 11. GUINEA
THE COUNTRY OF BLACKS

Not far from Conakry is a place called Iles de Los. This was the only more or less acceptable place that had guesthouses and hotels. I was feeling like I had lost my initial sense of
purpose. I had become an ordinary tourist, who had decided to visit all the countries of
Africa. In actual fact, that was not what I had wanted; what I wanted was to see Africa
and write about it. Perhaps I had not yet digested it all, and there were still many things
which I needed to reflect on.

Nevertheless, I continued my travels, although perhaps with some reservations. I
hoped that all these doubts were just temporary.

I was in Guinea. It was a country which I had previously known nothing about, except
for what I had read online on a couple of websites—they presented it as an underdeveloped country with many problems. But Guinea was the country that created the first
need for radical changes in my future book.

When I approached a market stand in the suburb of Ile de Cassa, the vendor stared
at me wide-eyed. Perhaps he understood that I was a foreigner, and he maintained his
composure while he made a gesture for me to wait. He called for a young man, who
emerged from a two-story house behind the stand and approached me. I wasn't going to
buy anything; I was just strolling around that small street which looked like a market, with

giant umbrellas and a variety of stalls everywhere. As the youth approached, I managed to take a look at my surroundings—the vendors all sold fruits and different kinds of produce on small tables, except for one. That vendor was a middle-aged woman with a blue headscarf decorated with multicolor flowers. She was wearing a bright green apron, also decorated with flowers, and beneath it could be seen a whitish dress, or rather a cloth that had been haphazardly wrapped around her body. She sat there and looked at me with pleading eyes. Then I noticed a round, black lump behind her. That lump turned out to be a child wrapped in an apron; it kept moving its hands and trying to take something out of a blue plastic barrel to put in its mouth. The vendor said a few words and then pulled a small table on wooden wheels forward; she quickly removed a cloth from the table, as if performing a magic trick. On the table there were wooden tubes of differing thickness. The woman said a few words again, then turned around, opened the lid of the plastic barrel, took out something resembling a cucumber and put it into her mouth; then she looked at the child and hit it on its head. I didn't understand why she did that. She then kicked the pieces of a box that had fallen to the ground, and greeted the youth.

"Hello," said the young man. That word rang in my head. I had thought that I would have to talk to the Guineans using hand gestures. This youngish man was about thirty and looked like a matchstick. His body was thin, with a narrow chest and legs, but his head stuck out and he was half bald. He wore denim shorts and a blue shirt, and he held a bottle in his hand with a label that read "Skol." He didn't look like a drunkard, but his "Hello" reached me mixed with the smell of beer.

"Hello," I said.

"What would you like? My mother said that we have a foreign customer."

"What ethnic group do you belong to?" I asked, trying to change the topic. "Have you lived in England? You speak good English."

"I'm a Susu."

"Susu?" It was the first time I had heard that term. "What do the Susu have to do with England?"

"Nothing. I lived and studied in Freetown."

"Where's that? In Sierra Leone?"

"Yes."

"They speak English there?"

"Yes, but besides that I also graduated from a language institute with a degree in translation. Which of these would you like?" asked the young man.

At that moment, a thousand questions arose in me. "Is this woman your mother?"

"Yes, I'm her eldest son, and this one," he said, pointing to the little one wrapped up in the apron, "is the youngest."

"How old are you?"

"Twenty-two," he said.

"And your mother?"

"Forty. Don't you want to buy anything?"

"I don't know what this is. Why would I need wooden sticks?"

The young man said something to his mother. They laughed and the little one tied up in the apron also laughed, but they hit it on its head again, after which the young man said, "These thin wooden sticks are pieces of bread."

"Bread?"

"Yes, this is French bread; my mother wraps them in cloth so that they don't lose their taste." He drank some Skol again and, wiping the foam off his lips, continued, "We have 100-gram pieces and 300-gram ones. Which would you like?"

The three of them looked at me in such a way that I felt like I had to buy one so that I could continue to ask questions.

"I don't know, does it taste good?"

"Just a moment," said the young man as he took some of that unfamiliar food from the plastic barrel, and then pinched off a morsel of bread and handed them to me.

"No, I don't want it."

"Have some."

"What is it?"

"Sea radish," he said—at least that was what I understood from his English.

I ate some. It was sour and salty, tasting of crabs and pickled cucumbers. I could not really taste the bread at all.

"Did you like it? Do you want more?" he asked.

"No."

"How many do you want to buy?"

"One."

He cut the bread with a knife, wrapped it in thin wrapping paper and handed it to me. I paid for the bread, but not knowing what to do with it, put it back down on the little table.

"I'll take it with me later," I said. "I'd like to chat with you a bit."

"About what?"

"Your country."

"We've got no country. Our country is Africa."

"What about Guinea?"

"There are many Susus here, but we are everywhere. I don't know what to call my homeland. I didn't know in Freetown, either."

"Were you born there?"

"Yes, my father died there, and then my family moved here. Then, I went back there to study."

"Couldn't you study here?"

"I could, but I wanted to go there."

At that moment, I stopped looking at him as a salesman. He was an educated and well-mannered man.

"What's your name?"

"Sékou Touré."

"It sounds like a French name."

"Yes. Would you like some beer?" he asked, offering me the half-empty Skol bottle.

"No, thanks. Your English is good, why don't you go to Europe or another developed country?"

"Who would let us leave this country of Blacks?[9] We are cut off from the rest of the world. Who needs us?"

"But have you tried to go?"

"Yes, to Morocco," he said. His eyes brightened; perhaps he did not know that Morocco was not Europe.

"Morocco isn't Europe," I said.

"I know. But what's the difference? They are all the same. They ask you who you are, they hear you say Susu, and then they ask if that is something to eat. I say it is a nation, a big nation. Then they ask, where do you live, which village? I say, in all of Africa. They ask, do you have a country? I say yes, Guinea. They say, you are a Guinean. But there is no such thing." Sékou took another gulp of his beer and continued in the same dissatisfied manner: "Of what use is their Europe to me? Should I go there to be mocked? They ask, do you have family, I say, yes, they ask how many members are in it, I say fourteen—my mother, five brothers, three sisters, my wife, three sons, and myself. They laugh. There's not enough room, they say."

I kept wanting to ask who this "they" was. But I asked nothing, except for a glass of water.

"Come on, we live close by."

Sékou said something to his mother, hit the little one on its head again, and we went to their home.

"Why do you keep hitting that child on the head all the time?"

"He eats too much. He comes to the market just to eat the sea radish in the barrel."

Sékou's home was not really that different from the chaos in the market place, except for the walls and ceiling. The first person I saw was his wife, who looked quite old despite her young age. She carried in her arms one of their children whose body was nearly naked, exposing a poorly cut umbilical cord like a long grape vine. The mother was rocking the child, but the child was scared, perhaps by my sudden appearance there. Then, from another room that I had not noticed earlier, a boy and a girl emerged.

"You said you had three boys," I said.

---

9. "Guinea" means "the country of the Blacks" in Berber.

"Yes."

"This one is a girl."

"I know. She's my sister. My other son died last winter; he was sick."

For about two minutes there was silence, then Sékou said, "Take a seat. It's not like this where you live, is it?"

"What do you mean?"

"Well, I mean that everything is clean and tidy, the streets are tiled, there are beautiful, decorative trees, and luxury vehicles. Luxury vehicles are very rare in my country."

"We have problems, too."

"You live well; you had no difficulty coming to Guinea. It's not that simple."

"I know."

"What do you know? You know nothing."

Sékou spoke angrily, but I didn't blame him. His protest was not directed at me, and even if it were, I wouldn't have been offended. He was sincere, and it was his sincerity that gave me the most pleasure.

"Why did you come here?" he asked.

"I'm a writer," I said, staring to recite again the text that I had committed to memory. "I'm writing a book and going around all of Africa."

"There, you see?"

"What?"

"You are from a developed country, so you can afford to do that. Your country will defend your rights."

"Yes, but..."

"But which Susu writer can go do the same in Europe? No one. We don't even have any writers."

"I'm from Armenia."

"I've heard of it."

"How have you come to hear about it?" I asked. I was surprised, feeling that we, too, were a nation without our own country.

"At university: You used to be in the USSR, and now you're independent."

It felt good to hear that. I stomped my feet on the ground and thanked him on a spontaneous impulse. But I didn't want to talk about that.

"What would you like to have?" he asked.

"Water," I said again.

Sékou asked his wife to bring some water. His wife brought a bottle and opened it demonstratively in front of me.

"Take a look and see for yourself," said Sékou.

"See what?"

"That it's clean water."

When we spoke now, it felt like we had overcome the previous formality of our conversation although, unlike Armenian and some other languages, English doesn't have formal and informal ways to say "you."

"Do you like music?" asked Sékou.

"Yes."

"I like jazz. I want to start a group. Unfortunately, there aren't any good musicians around, you know?"

"Here?" I asked.

"Anywhere."

"One has to ask around."

"Will you ask around?"

"I'll try. Jazz only?"

"Preferably so."

Four more children entered the house, three boys and one girl, all seven to fourteen years old; the girl was carrying a bucket on her head, holding it with both hands, and wearing a dress that had yellow and black stripes, like a bee. The three boys gave me frightened looks, and one of them (I couldn't really tell them apart) gave something to Sékou, wrapped in blotting paper.

"Take this; it's the bread."

I had forgotten that I had bought bread.

"Thank you. Do they know English?"

"No, only I do. I have tried everything to teach them, all in vain; they don't want to. Instead, they speak good French," Sékou said, wiping his face. "What are you writing about?"

"I don't know. Anything."

"Do you write well?"

"Yes," I said, feeling completely at ease. Sékou's eyes seemed focused on something far away.

I understood that he was a man of great depth; his eyes revealed that he had big dreams and that he would try to achieve them by all means. I didn't ask him about it, but rather hinted indirectly.

"What would make you happy?"

"Me? I don't know," he said. His eyes shone as his wife, child, sister, and brothers watched him with awe. "I guess I could become President. This is a good idea, but not for this country; rather, for the country of my dreams."

"Do you like politics?"

"Yes, my father was a politician; they killed him. But my objectives are quite different. If I got the opportunity, I would build a completely different country for everyone. Then, our writers could go to Europe and spread our traditions and ideas."

He was really sincere. I knew he had probably received a good education.

"What about you?" he asked.

"What?" I'd been lost in thought for moment. "Could you repeat what you said?"

"What would make you happy?"

"Finishing my book and going back to my homeland."

"Very good," he said. All of Sékou's relatives were listening to our conversation attentively, although they understood nothing. "You will finish it, of course you will. It's late now, we have to close the market stand; my mother is alone there."

"What about the child?"

"The glutton? He's OK."

I took the bread, thanked the hostess, wished them all well, and left. Outside, I remembered that Sékou must be a Muslim; he had not asked me to take off my shoes, but he himself was barefoot. Opposite Sékou's house there was a scarecrow, guitar in hand, painted in different colors.

"What is that?" I asked.

"The mascot of our new jazz group," he said.

I was very pleased to have met Sékou[10] and his large family. He was very inspiring, and I now understood one simple thing: one should never complain. That encounter provided new energy for the rest of my travels.

I wished Sékou well, and he shook hands with me warmly, then said, "Remember my request about the jazz group…"

"Yes," I said, walking past their market stand, where his mother smiled at me. Finally, I gave some bread wrapped in paper to the child, who had eaten the last sea radish just a little while ago.

---

10. Sékou Touré was the first President of Guinea. After gaining independence from France in 1958, he ruled until his death (March 26, 1984). He was born in January 1922 in Guinea (although nobody knows the exact date) in Faranah, and was a Mandinka by ethnicity. His father was well-known political figure, Samory Touré. Sékou, as President, was very popular in his country. He introduced multiple important reforms. During his Presidency, Guinea established diplomatic relations with a number of countries. Jazz and many other musical styles were promoted under his patronage.

DAY 12. SIERRA LEONE
SLEEPWALKERS IN THE LIONS' MOUNTAINS

A GDP of $500, or perhaps a little more. A ranking of 173-175, or even less, in the United Nations Annual Report: "One of the poorest countries in the world;" "Average Life Expectancy—48.57 years."

The information I had on Sierra Leone did not make for very impressive reading. I had been warned beforehand to be ready for anything. At first, it seemed like I was in the most backward of countries, but then gradually everything changed.

The quickest and most affordable way to get to Sierra Leone was from Conakry to Freetown. In a few hours, the small bus reached the capital of Sierra Leone. I had no trouble with my documents at all. Once again, I was considered very respectable; I was treated with courtesy and high regard. I was probably immediately noticeable due to my skin color, my clothes—which were nothing luxurious—and most importantly the fact that I spoke English. It took me another hour to get from the station to Kimbima Hotel, and that cost 25,000 in leones, the local currency. The five-star luxury hotel with a façade resembling a wooden ship was the first thing that impressed me.

Honestly speaking, I had never expected to see a hotel of that kind there. If it had been in a developed European country, it probably would not have been considered to have five-star status. However, in Freetown, it was of a higher class than expected. After taking a couple of photographs, as always, I decided to walk around the city. I had seen a panorama of the city from the small balcony at the hotel. It reminded me of Yerevan, the capital of my home country, and if not for the Atlantic Ocean, it would have been very difficult to distinguish between them. Everything was like Yerevan, from the architectural styles to the width of the streets. There was, however, one difference—low buildings were abundant, and one of the first ones to stand out was a three-story building not too far away. It was painted completely in bright blue, giving the impression that it was nighttime there with only the moon providing any light. Naturally, that building was the place that I visited first. When I was in the street, the clouds embraced each other in such a way that it seemed as if they were afraid of the sky. They were like children who can't swim, trying to grab hold of something to avoid being carried away by the tide. Unfortunately, the wind was blowing quite hard and a few seconds later, the clouds parted. At that moment I reached the blue building, but it seemed to have nothing of interest any more except cracked windows and voices coming from inside. I entered.

In the very first room inside, I heard sounds of metal buckets, water, and moaning. It seemed very much like a shower room. The first thing I encountered when I entered was a Black female athlete with a naked torso, blocking my path. There were two other athletes at her side, and another who was pouring water over the head of yet another athlete, using an iron bucket. The walls were fully covered with cracked white tiles that clearly showed some dirty black spots. Hanging from the wall were three frames, all empty. There were mosaic figures on the floor, predominantly in black. In the corner, there were some sports shoes. I seemed to be at a sports facility.

"What do you want?" asked the man with the bucket, who had long braided hair with the tail tucked into his shirt collar.

"I just happened to come here. It looked beautiful outside, so I decided to enter."

Surprisingly, the man did not ask me who I was, or what specifically it was I wanted.

"Good for you. This is our club; please wait in the corridor outside and I will be with you soon."

Before stepping out, I took another look at the people there. They were all standing indifferently, and while the female athlete covered her breasts with one arm, it was clear that she wasn't really embarrassed. There was a poster on the door that I could not understand. It had the flag of the United Kingdom on it.

The corridor smelled of rubber and sweat. The same poster was everywhere, along with a few faded photographs.

"Hello, sorry to keep you waiting; I was washing the heads of my students. I'm their coach," said the stranger.

"A pleasure," I said, extending my hand.

"Give me a minute to dry my hand. Joseph O'Reilly;[11] it's a pleasure. Let's go to my office, everything is a mess here. Sorry."

"That's all right, don't worry about it."

"Do you like our current state?"

"What state?" I asked. I had no idea what he was talking about.

"The state of the Federation of Athletics and Weightlifting." He asked me this as if I had been a member of the federation for at least five years.

"I can't say that it's good."

"It's terrible."

"Yes."

"I have been fighting with the higher-ups for over five years, but in vain. Nobody cares about our situation."

"It's a shame."

"It's not a shame, it's a clear injustice."

From the very first minutes, it became clear that Joseph loved to talk. I, too, have a love for talking. But I was already thinking of leaving the place, especially since the stale air was suffocating me and making my eyes water. When we climbed the stairs and headed for his office, he proposed a little walk around the sport facility before going in. This proposal made me happy.

The first place Joseph took me was a small building at the shore where a few local people had gathered.

"This is our only high jump athlete," he said.

"But there are a few of them."

"No, the rest of them are fishermen. They've come to help Quinty."

"His name is Quinty?"

"Yes, the fishermen have brought their rope to help us."

"What's the rope for?"

"You'll see."

Two men on the right and one on the left stretched the rope out at a height of about one and a half meters while Quinty, who was well over a meter and a half tall, ran from a distance to gather speed and jumped over the rope.

"Good, very good," said Joseph, clapping his hands. "Keep it up!"

---

11. Joseph O'Reilly was the Head Coach of Sierra Leone's Olympic athletics team. The names of all the athletes are also real.

"He's a good boy," he continued, looking at me. "He's seventeen years old, from Kailahun. His family escaped to Bo. A promising sportsman."

We moved on.

"This is Lumley Beach."

We approached a few sportsmen who were exercising on the sand.

"Our runners for the 400-meter event."

"Is the sea air beneficial?"

"That's not why they are here."

"No?"

The runners gathered speed and they were all in the water within a few seconds, where they continued their drills.

"This is how they strengthen their muscles. We have no equipment; as I told you, the situation is bad."

When the shore was cleared, a boat came into view in the distance that resembled a raft five meters in length. "DEMOCRACY" was written on it in white letters on green.

"Yes, the situation is bad," I said.

"Very bad."

"What were those posters on the walls at the club?" I asked.

"The white ones, with the flag of the United Kingdom?"

"Yes."

"We knew you were coming, so we put those up as a surprise for you."

Joseph's words made no sense. He seemed to have mistaken me for someone else—but I had introduced myself.

"Were you expecting me?"

"Yes."

"But do you know who I am?"

"Of course I do. You're a writer." That was correct, but the posters with the British flag still made no sense.

"Let's go on," Joseph said quickly, as if nothing unusual had happened. "Come here, this one is our weightlifter."

"He trains here?" I asked. We were at a place that looked like an abandoned cellar. On its right side it had two broad cracks, each about a meter wide; they were letting in the light.

"Yes. This is his home, and here is his wife."

A woman sat on a stone in one corner, with an infant in her arms and a dog at her side.

"He lives here?"

"Yes, the poor guy is twenty years old and has a family already. He's a good sportsman, but has no facilities for training. His parents were killed. He was a little child when the RUF killed his parents, and many others…"

"What's the RUF?"

"The Revolutionary United Front."

"What is it?"

"Don't ask. It was led by Foday Sankoh."

"What did they do?"

"They did whatever they wanted. Haven't you heard about them?"

"No."

"Those were difficult years."

Joseph did not want to talk about it, nor was I particularly inspired by the subject, although it was clear that it had been a political movement with cruel policies.

"Look at those muscles on Sesay."

"Yes, he's a very good athlete," I said.

Sesay held a weight bar with both hands; on either side of it there were unpolished stones.

"Don't you have weights?" I asked.

"We do, but very few of them."

"If he's the only weightlifter, why don't you give him the weights?"

"When I said he was our weightlifter, I did not mean that there were no others. He is the leading one."

"All the more so."

"You're right, but many athletes train at the club and I cannot deprive novices of that pleasure. There, you can see Frank Turay in the distance. I had written about him in my letter, he's a very good athlete." Joseph pointed toward a tree under which there was another athlete. But I was more interested in the letter he mentioned.

"What letter?" I asked.

"The letter in which I asked you to bring the sports equipment, in his name. He had told me to mention it in the letter. He is our senior runner, a participant in the 1996 Olympic Games in Atlanta. The poor guy lives in the house of his brother, who was killed by the RUF. His brother had been a policeman."

"I don't understand."

"What is it that you don't understand?"

"I don't understand any of it. When I entered your club in the morning, I just wanted to look around."

"So, the letter hasn't reached you?"

"No."

"That's very bad. I had written important things in there."

Everything was getting even more confusing. "I am a writer, but I don't understand the rest of it. What letter?"

"Aren't you from the United Kingdom?"[12]

"No."

"But you're a writer?" Joseph was open-mouthed.

"Yes."

"All right then, you can write about our mountains of lions,"[13] he said, and then he was suddenly quiet.

"By all means."

"Don't forget to write about our athletes, please."

"I won't forget. You were probably waiting for another man, is that right?"

"Yes," Joseph said with disappointment, realizing that he had taken me for someone else all this time. He apologized and asked that we return to the club. I noticed how his mood had dropped; his head was hanging, and he was silent for a few minutes.

"Nevertheless, this was of interest to me," I said.

"Yes," he said, raising his head. The ends of his braids sprang out from behind his shirt collar. "Interesting, but nothing more."

"You were expecting help, weren't you?"

"Yes, but never mind. They might come, but who is interested in the lives of these sleepwalkers? We are only of interest to ourselves."

It was evening, and we were slowly approaching the club. Joseph had crossed his hands, like the clouds that I had seen in the morning, and mumbled a local song between deep breaths.

"I'm sorry I took so much of your time. I really didn't want to cause any confusion. I'm very sorry for the misunderstanding."

"That's all right, no problem," he answered, somewhat sulkily. "Don't forget to write about the sleepwalkers."

"What sleepwalkers?"

"Those who light a fire on the beach at night under the moonlight, and even play football, running about with their eyes closed. Do you know what they use for a ball?"

"What?"

"The moon."

Joseph was talking about the athletes.

"Don't forget to write about the Mountains of the Lions."

"I won't forget. I apologize again. I have only one question before I leave."

"Please go ahead."

---

12. In May 2000, Sierra Leone was visited by photographer Seamus Murphy and writer Alex Duval, who attended a few athletic training sessions and took pictures and wrote about it.

13. Sierra Leone means "The Mountains of the Lions" in Portuguese. That name dates from about 1460, when the Portuguese ruled the country.

"Why are these athletes training so hard?"

"What do you mean, why?" His voice grew louder. "For the Olympics."

"The 2008 Games in Beijing?"

"No."

"Then which ones?"

"The 2000 Games in Sydney."

It was nighttime, I walked the streets of Freetown. I saw the moon and heard the shouts of the sleepwalkers…

DAY 13. LIBERIA
LIBERIAN MASKS

This time, I really didn't know anything. It was only my English that gave me a bit of hope. I don't know why, but I was in a bad mood. Something did not seem right. And this was despite the fact that I had gotten into the swing of things and my trip was going well. I felt dizzy and sleepy, as I had almost not slept at all in the airport. I had been forced to stand around for nine hours as I breathed in the smell of Sierra Leonean patties, which had spread so thickly throughout the terminal that it had formed a thin film on my clothes. Added to that, I had not gotten used to the heat. It was summer, so heat was a natural thing—but I would have much preferred a temperature of ten degrees Celsius in those conditions. When they announced my flight, I was so happy that I left my small piece of hand luggage on the bench and rushed to the plane. There hadn't been much in the bag—a few books, papers, phone numbers…

When I shouted out that I had forgotten a bag in the terminal, everyone looked at me and laughed. I asked the flight attendant to help and to stop the plane from taking off, as we hadn't gone on to the runway yet, but nobody took me seriously. Once again, I was the focus of everyone's attention, except that this time nobody shied away from me—I was seen as a newcomer who knew nothing.

"I really did forget my bag. It had important papers and books in it, and some information that I really need," I said to the half-asleep Liberian sitting next to me. He was the only one who listened quietly; he had no teeth and seemed very tired. He nodded, muttered something I couldn't understand, and fell asleep.

"Are you sure you've forgotten it?" laughed some passengers sitting close by, who looked like a family. Their colorful clothes and large headgear forced me to compare them to a bunch of carrots and beetroot.

"Yes, I forgot it. It was in my hand, and then they announced the flight. I left it on one of the benches and got on board."

"Careful you don't forget the rest of your things," said the person sitting behind me, who was most probably a laborer at a construction site. His nails were cracked, his fingers were thick and he very much resembled someone from Tajikistan.

But what's done is done, you can't change the past. The plane was in the sky and I was exhausted. I fell asleep. When I woke up, we were in Monrovia. Ten or twenty minutes later, I was out of the plane. The passport officer took me for an American and questioned me at length.

"What is the purpose of your visit?"

"I'm writing a book. I'm very interested in your country."

"How long do you plan to stay?"

"One day."

"And then what?"

"Then I go to Cote d'Ivoire."

"Why?"

"That country interests me too."

"Why one day? Have you ever worked in America?"

"No."

"How about at any international organizations?"

"No. Why do you ask?"

"Doesn't matter. Have you been here before?"

"No."

"How about any other African country?"

"Yes, I've already been to twelve countries; I'm going to each one in turn."

"Have you been to the US?"

"No. Why do you ask?"

"Don't ask me any questions. I'm the one who asks questions around here. Any other English-speaking country?"

"No." His questions were pointless and I would have replied more rudely had he not been instrumental to my gaining access to Liberia. Actually, even if he had not allowed me to enter—if he had rejected my visa—I was already in Liberia, and that would be enough for me to write about.

"What is the book about?"

"Africa."

"In whose interests is your work?"

"I don't understand the question. I'm not working for anyone."

"Are you writing fairy tales?"

"No."

He looked into my eyes and shook his head with suspicion as the sound of the stamp confirming my entry into Liberia could be heard.

"For your own safety and because the hotel is still being rebuilt, we ask you not to open the balcony door. The hotel management apologizes for this inconvenience"—this note posted on the glass of my balcony door did not make for inspiring reading. I did not know how I could dry the clothes I had washed. As always, I ignored these mundane issues and walked out of this modest hotel where I had reserved a room. I headed for one of the city's central streets, the name of which I cannot recall.

Liberia was the first country where none of the names I encountered stuck with me. I simply forgot them. I had either grown tired of remembering so many names, or something else was wrong in my head.

I crossed a small bridge and happened upon a dirty but very colorful scarecrow, about three meters tall, stuck in the center of a field. The scarecrow reminded me of the yard at Sékou Touré's house.

"It's for sale," someone said, popping out from underneath a bush and giving me a dirty look. He appeared so suddenly that he startled me, and I ran back a few meters.

"Where are you going? The scarecrow isn't going to eat you."

"You startled me," I said.

"There's nothing startling about me."

"Yes, you're right," I said, thinking that he looked like a tortoise without its shell.

"Well? Do you want it?"

"What would I want that scarecrow for?"

"You'll stick it in your yard at home, and it will never rain."

"But rain is a good thing. Why wouldn't I want it to rain?"

"You'll understand when you see it rain."

"No, thanks," I said, as I watched him take the skin off his face, revealing another face beneath it.

"It's a mask, don't be scared. It's one of our traditional masks. Would you like to try it?"

"No." He seemed like a very strange man to me. He had appeared very suddenly and was now trying his hand as a salesman in an attempt to get some money from me.

"All right then, give me some money at least."

"What would you do with it?"

"Get something to eat."

"Don't you have any money?"

"Being poor is common around here. The impact of the civil wars can still be seen in our society. Many people are hungry."

"You should work, then."

"Work where? There is no work. I sell masks like this one."

"That's not good."

"It's very bad. And this is the capital city. Think about what it's like in Yekepa, Harper, and Gbarnga."

"Was the war a long time ago?"

"No. From 1989 to 1996, then from 1999 to 2003. Those were very tense years."

"Why were they fighting?"

"I don't know. I'm an illiterate man. I don't know what they were fighting for, nor do I know what they achieved. They slaughtered each other, then left."

"They didn't have a purpose?"

"Who knows? Perhaps they did. When someone asks me, I say that they were fighting against the rain."

"What rain?"

"Rain. The usual rain. You know, that falls from the sky."

"Were they firing at the sky? Why did people die, then?"

"Whoever you ask around here, you'll hear a different story. Everyone has their own reasons to go to war. For one person, his neighbor might be bothering him. The other one might need money. A third one might want territory. I need for it to stop raining so that my few hectares of land can yield a harvest."

"But doesn't the rain help you do that?"

"The rain here doesn't spare anything; it wipes everything out. It's the rainy season now, so it rains every single day."

"Are you a local?"

"Never ask anyone that question."

"Why not?"

"There are no locals or foreigners here. Some have lived a bit longer on this land, some a bit less. That's the only difference."

"Where are we now?"

"In Monrovia."

"I know that. I mean the street, the address."

"I don't know. Who knows the street names around here? People care about other things."

The man spoke with such hopelessness, that I too began to fear the rain, despite myself. Liberia, in reality, was a bit different from his description of it. There were rich people there, as well as the poor.

"Do you want water? It costs a dollar."

"No, thanks. What's your name?"

"I'll make it easy for you. Call me Kru."

"Is that a nickname?"

"No, it's the name of my tribe."

"What does it mean?"

"It means Kru."

"But what *is* that?"

"I don't know. If it were up to me, I'd say it means 'those who fear the rain.'"

"Why? Is everyone afraid?"

"Yes. Do you want a mask? I'll give you one for twenty-five dollars. It's handmade."

"No, thank you."

"This mask is a particularly good one. If you put it on, everyone will take you for a local. They won't cheat you; they'll treat you well. It's worth it."

"No, I don't want it. It's time for me to go now, Kuru."

"Don't make a mistake like that again. People take great offense here if you pronounce their name wrong, or forget it. It's Kru, not Kuru."

"Forgive me, Kru. It's time for me to go. I want to walk around town a bit. Talk to people."

"There's nothing to talk about around here. Everyone will say the same thing. They'll either ask for money, or they'll sell you rain-harvested water for two dollars—more expensive—or they'll sell you masks."

"Aren't there people in any other trades here?"

"No. Everyone wants God to provide them with a peaceful sky."

"Which God?" I asked, expecting him to say, "The Rain God."

"The Rain God."

"Really? That's what I thought you'd say. Are you pagans?"

"What does that mean?"

"Do you have several gods? Is there a god for each thing?"

"I don't know. Each person has his own god around here. My god, for example, is a giant cob of corn that spins in the sky and warms the soil. Every day, I ask it to drink up the rain and send large suns to the ground in its place.

"That's beautiful."

"Do you have a god?"

"I'm a Christian."

"Oh, you mean the one that was crucified?"

"Yes."

"And you don't ask him to drink up the rainwater?"

"No."

"Why not? Don't you have rain?"

"We do. But each of us has a different attitude towards it."

"I get it," he said, moving his head. "Someone wants rain, someone wants water, someone else might want large balls of sun, another—clean air. Right?"

"I should go. It's been very interesting, but I have to get going."

"This one's a very good mask. At least take this one. I'll give it to you for twenty dollars."

"I don't want it."

Kru seemed like a good man, but he talked so much that my ears had turned red. He kept talking incessantly about the rain, and that was very tiring. The mask was very pretty, but I didn't have anywhere to keep it, even if I had bought it. If I ended up buying one thing in each country I visited, I would have to travel with several pieces of luggage. For that reason, I had decided at the very beginning that I would buy only things that were of the greatest necessity.

"What do you want, then?" Kru asked.

"I don't want anything."

"How about the bag that you lost at the airport in Freetown?"

"What?" He had caught me by surprise.

"That bag—the one with papers and books in it."

"How do you know about that?"

"Do you remember someone sitting behind you on the plane? The one who told you to be careful not to lose everything else?"

"Yes, I remember him; he had hands like those of a laborer. I thought that he resembled someone from Tajikistan."

"Did he?"

"Yes. How do you know all this?"

"I was that man."

"What?"

"Yes." Kru showed me a bag that had dozens of masks in it. "This was the mask," he said, putting one on. "Remember?"

My jaw dropped. I didn't know what to say. I had seen a lot of things in Africa, but I would never have believed that a person could transform himself like that.

"How did you end up here?" I asked.

"By plane. I was with you, wasn't I?"

"Yes, that's right. Are you following me?"

"No."

"Then how come we ended up meeting again?"

"I live here. In that house over there. You found *me*."

"Yes, perhaps. But I don't see a house there."

"What? Of course there's a house there. Behind the trees, take a good look."

"I don't see one."

"It's probably the rain that's making it difficult for you to see."

"There isn't any rain."

"Not here there isn't. But where I live, a hailstorm is pouring down from the sky."

"It's getting late. I have a train to catch; I have to get to Cote d'Ivoire."

"Why?"

"I just have to; I can't tell you why." I decided not to tell him about the book.

"You're a writer, aren't you?"

"How do you know?"

"Don't you remember? Back on the plane, you told the person sitting next to you that you're a writer touring Africa."

"Yes. Was that you, too?"

"No."

"Then how do you know?"

"I was sitting behind you, wasn't I?"

"Yes, that's right. Yes, I'm a writer."

"It's going to rain soon. At least take one mask with you, so you don't get wet."

"What about my clothes? I'd better buy an umbrella. However, I don't think it's going to rain. You've talked about it so much, but we haven't had a drop so far."

"It'll rain, it'll rain. Don't worry about it. But you'll have a tough time finding an umbrella around here; you'd better buy a mask."

"If it's a rainy country, there will definitely be umbrellas for sale."

"There aren't any. Everyone uses masks to drive the rain away."

"That's okay, I'll figure something out. I have to go now, it's late. We've been talking for three hours. I'm going to be late."

It had already become a habit of sorts—in each country, I'd ended up talking to only one person. I had seemingly run out of adventures as well as things to do. I wasn't doing much when it came to touring within the country. That was why I had decided I'd do a lot of roaming around in Cote d'Ivoire.

"Well? Don't you want one?" he asked.

"No, stop trying to persuade me."

"All right, I'll tell you what."

"What?"

"Do you like this mask?"

"Yes."

"It's yours."

"Really?"

"Yes. You're very stubborn; I failed to persuade you to buy it, so I'll give it to you as a present."

"Really?"

"Yes, of course."

"Thank you very much."

Kru gave me his mask, but not the one that resembled someone from Tajikistan. He gave me another one, once again taking the mask off his own face.

"Huh? How many masks are you wearing?"

"Many. My whole face consists of masks."

Kru's face changed completely—and his new face seemed very familiar.

"I've seen that face."

"Yes, I know. Remember now?" He closed his eyes.

"Of course I do. You look like the man who was sitting next to me on the plane."

"Yes."

"Was that you?"

"Yes."

"But how? Didn't you just say you were the guy who resembled a Tajik?"

"I lied. I simply had a mask of that guy."

"I'm confused," I said, my mind becoming a blur. I picked up the mask and brought it closer to my face.

"Not so fast."

"Why not?"

"You'll try it on later."

"Do you have another mask on beneath this one?"

"Yes."

"Whose face is it? It's the man who I associated with a beetroot on the plane, isn't it?"

"No."

"Who is it, then?"

"Yours." Kru took off his mask and revealed my face. It looked so much like me that I ran away in fear; I didn't even say goodbye. Where had he managed to get a mask of my face? His masks of African faces had not surprised me, although it was strange that they had been the faces of the other people on the plane. But when I'd seen the mask of my own face, I had almost fainted. When I was far away, I decided to put the mask[14] on my face, but before doing this, I discovered that Kru had managed to swipe twenty dollars off me...

---

14. These masks are traditional. In ancient times, they were used to gain protection from the rain by scaring the sky so that it would not send down rain. Now, the masks are just souvenirs sold to tourists. They say that the masks have magical effects on all foreigners.

It grew misty. I somehow managed to cross the muddy road. Hailstones struck me on the head and the giant corn cob in the sky spun and sent small balls of sun below. A house was visible in the distance which was the only place where it was not raining. There was a scarecrow there and someone sat in the dry bushes with a bag next to him.

I somehow managed to cross the small path. The rain had grown so heavy that I could not keep my head up…

And the man who had been sitting in the distance was now plowing the dry soil…

DAY 14. COTE D'IVOIRE
THE GATE

"It says in your passport that you can stay in Liberia for another day."

"I know," I replied.

"Come back in one day, then."

"It says I *can* stay, but that doesn't mean that I *have* to."

"What does it mean, then?"

"I can't stay another day and, anyway, no country has a law that requires you to stay."

"This isn't a law."

"What it is, then?"

"You have to stay for a minimum of two days for your arrival to be registered."

"What then?"

"Then you have the right to leave the country."

"Can't I register my arrival now and get the right to leave the country?"

"At which hotel did you spend the night?"

"I don't remember."

"You don't remember the address either?"

"No. I've been to so many places and I'm starting to mix them all up in my head. I have to write everything down somewhere. I forgot the bag I used to have at the airport in Sierra Leone."

"Do you have an address of any kind, perhaps a business card?"

"Yes, I do. Here you go."

"No, this isn't from our country. Neither is this one."

"But my passport is proof that I've entered your country. It's stamped."

"No, that doesn't matter. You need a certificate of registration in order to get the exit visa. You can't recall the name of the hotel, nor any address. You can't even tell me the name of a street. You know nothing. I don't understand why you've come. Are you an American?"

"No. Here, this is an Armenian passport. I'm a writer. The UN has granted me the right to travel throughout Africa without needing a visa, so that I can write about it."

"But how could you have forgotten everything?"

"There is one thing I remember."

"What?"

"A storm, hailstones; I barely managed to cross the path. A giant cob of corn in the sky, swallowing the rain and throwing down small balls of sun."

"Is this your idea of a joke?"

"No."

"I'm the one who makes the decisions here. This is the Liberian border, you're still in our territory. I'm the one who decides whether or not you can get on that train."

"I had the same problem when I arrived here."

"Impossible. You don't need a certificate of registration in order to enter the country."

"No, it wasn't that. The customs officer asked me many questions."

"He was right to do so."

"Fine. What are we going to do now?"

"What *can* we do? Go and stay somewhere tonight. Register yourself there and note down the address in your notebook. Then come back here tomorrow and there won't be any problems."

"I can't do that."

"Why not?"

"I can't stay for more than a day in each country."

"What is that supposed to mean?"

"That's the whole point of my book."

"How is that my problem?"

"Help me."

"I'm just doing my job."

"And I'm just doing mine. I can't just sit here."

"I really want to help, but it's impossible. If you could recall an address, you could contact them and confirm your registration there. Then you could go on to Cote d'Ivoire with no further problems."

"Is there no other way?"

"Absolutely not."

"So I can't go to a different country today?"

"So what if you can't? What's wrong with the country we have? Go back into town and relax."

"The country is fine, but you must understand that I'm sticking to certain rules. If I break them, everything loses its meaning."

"I don't know what to say. I've done what I can. There's nothing else I can do."

"I've been to so many countries. None of them caused me these problems."

"You're probably right about that. But things have changed since the war."

"Yes, now I remember something. You mentioned the war, and now I remember someone I spoke to. His name was Kuru. No… Kru."

"Kru?"

"Yes."

"What's that?"

"He said that I could call him that. He had a house, a few hectares of land, he made masks…"

"Kru, you say? Everyone makes masks here."

"Yes," I replied, "It was easier for me to remember the name of his tribe."

"Ah yes, Kru. He didn't give you another name?"

"No."

"More than eight percent of the population here is from the Kru tribe, and we have a population of around three and a half million. How do you expect us to find your Kru?"

"I don't know. He also asked me where my hotel was, but I couldn't remember."

"Perhaps you have issues with your memory?"

"No. It's just that I've been travelling a lot, so I've been unable to remember everything."

"Well, hurry up. Make up your mind about what you're going to do; I can't spend all this time talking to you."

"What's your name?"

"Didier."

"Is that a French name?"

"Yes."

"But aren't British and local names more common in Liberia?"

"Yes, they are. I'm from Cote d'Ivoire."

"Is everyone working here from Cote d'Ivoire?"

"Not everyone. I'm a Liberian citizen."

"I see. Well, I really want to see your country and write about it. It's very important—do you understand?"

"I understand."

"I'm not just another tourist."

"What are you going to write? Couldn't you just look the country up online? Why bother to come all the way here?"

"No, I couldn't just look it up. I have to see everything with my own eyes."

"What are you writing about? There are many beautiful places here. We have an opera, good stadiums, fancy cars. Abidjan used to be a flourishing city once, but its situation grew worse because of political instability. You could stay at the Ivoire Hotel; it's a lovely place in the style of the 1960s, everything has been preserved as it was, to this day. You could go to the zoo, too, it's a great place. Go to the beach at Bassam, it's the best. We always have good journalists visiting."

"I'm not a journalist."

"I understand that."

"The train will be leaving in five minutes. There's nothing stopping you. All you have to do is stamp my passport, and we're done."

"Do you see the border? On the other side of the tracks?"

"Yes."

"That's another country. It has nothing in common with this one."

"So what?"

"When the train crosses our border, there is another procedure to inspect passengers on the other side."

"And?"

"And you will need to get off in five hundred meters. You won't even spend two minutes in the train before that."

"But if you stamp my passport, I won't have a problem there."

"You will. They will ask for another document on the train."

"Do they demand that all foreigners have that document?"

"Yes. It is a mandatory requirement."

"The train is moving."

"There's nothing I can do. I really want to help, but there's nothing I can do."

The train set off. There were all kinds of women in colorful headscarves, children and men already inside, sitting around small tables, or perhaps in their cabins or lying on the hard wood. I did not manage to get on the train that started at the border between Liberia and Cote d'Ivoire and travelled through the cities of the latter. I had failed to execute the plan I had set to travel around the country on that train. This was the first time I had come across an obstacle like this. Even the fact that I was a writer and mentioning the United Nations hadn;t had an effect. Perhaps the laws were too strict, or something else had gone wrong for me.

"It's gone," I said to Didier.

"Yes."

"When's the next one?"

"Tomorrow morning. You'll be able to get on it with no problems. I'll register you today and you won't have a problem tomorrow."

"Couldn't you have registered me ten minutes ago?"

"No. The date would show. I have today's date on my stamp; I don't have yesterday's."

"I have nowhere to go. I was supposed to be in Cote d'Ivoire today. I've been here for more than twenty-four hours."

"Do you know where you were supposed to go there?"

"It doesn't matter."

"You don't have a place to go? A hotel? A friend? An acquaintance?"

"No. In some countries, you need to book in advance. In others, you don't. I think I had booked in advance for Liberia, actually. But it's too late now."

"You're saying it doesn't matter where you stay?"

"No, it doesn't. As long as I know that I'm in Cote d'Ivoire. I really did want to see that country, though."

"I have an idea."

"What is it?"

Didier left his small booth for a few minutes. As he did so, I caught sight of an American magazine on his table, which had the word "Gate" on the cover in green letters. I also saw a couple of buttons—one green, the other red—that had lights flashing beneath them. While he had been sitting there, Didier's large hands had covered them.

He returned to the hall holding a chair. He held the chair in one hand and scratched the back of his head with the other. He pressed the green button and the small barrier in front of me opened.

"Come through. It's night time now; it's only me and the guards at the station, nobody else."

We dragged the chair forward and ended up near the railway tracks. Didier walked up to the border with Cote d'Ivoire and stopped.

"Here, you can sit on this chair and look towards the east. We've already crossed the border."[15]

---

15. Liberia does not have a railway border with Cote d'Ivoire. The train goes from Buchanan to Yekepa in Liberia. In Cote d'Ivoire, it goes from Abidjan to Bouaké, to Ferkessédougou and then to Ouagadougou (the capital of Burkina Faso).

He left. I looked to the east for a few minutes. I couldn't see anything. I fell asleep without realizing it. It was morning when I awoke, and pigeons from Cote d'Ivoire were dancing around me.

"You can go now," I heard Didier's raspy voice behind me, as if he were speaking through a microphone.

"Go where?" I asked.

"Cote d'Ivoire."

"I don't want to," I said, "I've been there already. Now, I need to go to Mali."

DAY 15. MALI
MALEVICH

The brown spire that stood out from behind the small trees, the walls below it and the large mossy stones ten or fifteen meters to the east were the first things I saw reflected in the puddle. It was my first time seeing a mosque as beautiful and unique as this one. It reminded me of a sandcastle. When I was small, I would spend hours sitting in a sandbox, using wet sand to make all sorts of buildings like that mosque.

I walked around the mosque. It looked the same from the other side. There wasn't a puddle on that side, but everything else was identical. One of the spires ended in a triangular pinnacle with wooden sticks protruding out of it, like scaffolding on an incomplete structure, although it was clear that in this case it was the architectural style. It seemed like a small child had built this mosque out of sand.

I was in Mopti, one of Mali's most beautiful cities. But it was not in Mopti that I experienced several interesting and unusual incidents.

I crossed a territory that was as big as the whole of Armenia, possible larger, before I got to Timbuktu,[16] a city I had heard of before I arrived there.

---

16. Timbuktu-Tumbutu-Tombouctou (fr.) means "difficult to reach" in one of the local languages.

Timbuktu is located about fifteen kilometers north of the Niger River. When I asked the taxi driver to take me to the hotel, he explained in French that he did not know where it was located. I had begun to understand a little French, but did not know enough to ask questions.

"Few people speak French here, even though it's the official language. People here speak Bambara."

"What?"

"Bam-ba-ra," he said, breaking it down into syllables. "You're in the wrong place. Nobody will understand you here." He said a few more words after that, but I didn't understand a thing.

"Nobody knows French here? Are you sure?"

"Yes. Don't you have an interpreter or a guide?"

"No, I'm on my own. But I guess I have to find someone."

I was speaking English, and he was speaking a broken French that was similar to English. I somehow just barely managed to understand him.

"Ah yes, I know. I'll take you to the textile factory. There's someone there who knows everything. Our man Malevich. He'll help you."

"Who?"

"Malevich."

I hadn't expected a driver in Timbuktu to know the name Malevich. It had probably been a misunderstanding.

"Which Malevich?"

"Kazimir."

"The painter?"

"Yes."

"But he died a long time ago."

"Yes, I know. On May 15, 1935."

"So which Malevich are you going to take me to see?"

"Get in the car; you'll see when we get there."

Fifteen minutes later, we were at the studio of the so-called Malevich.

"I've got to go, I've got things to do," the driver said. I paid him and got out of the car, and approached the small one-story building.

Before that, I had seen a magnificent mosque that was very similar to the one in Mopti, but it was much smaller and seemed to have only one spire. In contrast to the mosque in Mopti, this one really was made of sand, and had pieces of wood sticking out at different levels. They had probably been put there to give the structure more stability and make it more secure. It looked like someone had filled a large bucket with mud, then turned it over upside down and stuck it in the ground, before lifting the bucket to form the structure. Two women walked past the mosque with wicker baskets on their heads, probably containing rice. The baskets were multicolored and, from a distance, it looked like two giant lanterns were walking along the street.

"Where did you come from? I heard a car…" said a man who had just stepped out of the one-story building. His head was shaved and he wore a bright yellow shirt.

"Finally! Someone who speaks English. I'm so glad I found you. Is there a hotel around here?"

"Yes."

"The driver said there wasn't."

"He probably didn't understand what you said."

"I assume you're Malevich."

"Yes. Did the driver bring you to me?"

"Yes. He said you're the only one who speaks English."

"No, there are others here who speak English, too. He probably didn't understand you."

"Probably. Can you help me?"

"What do you need?"

"If there's a hotel, give me the address. I'd also like to talk with you for a bit."

"Go to Buktu, it's in the town center, near Azala. Or to Relais, in Azala, the western part of town. I don't know the specific address; you'll have to ask around, someone is bound to know it. Those are the only two hotels in this city."

"What is this place?"

"It's our textile factory."

"Is it yours?"

"No," Malevich laughed. "I work here."

"What do the women do?"

"The women gather wheat."

"Are you the only employee?"

"Yes. There used to be a few more, but they died. I'm the only one left. Come in and sit with me for a while, before you go to the hotel."

"Could I stay here?"

"With me? I don't know. If the owner were to find out…"

"What if I pay?"

"All right, come in. How many days?"

"One night."

"No problem; you don't even have to pay. I thought you were staying longer."

"No. What is this mosque made of?"

"Clay—it's made of the clay from the river. Almost everything here is made of clay."

"It's pretty."

"Where did you come from?"

"Mopti."

"Do you live there?"

"No. I flew from Bamako to Mopti by plane, and then came here from there."

"Is there a flight from Mopti to Timbuktu?" Malevich asked.

"Yes, there is. Three times a week, I think."

"Did you come on a Yak?"

"No, a Let L-410."

"That's Czech. They're a bit old now."

"Yes, it was a noisy plane."

"So, you're from Bamako?"

"No, I'm from Armenia. I'd arrived in Bamako from Cote d'Ivoire."

"The border with Cote d'Ivoire is closed; how did you manage to cross it?"

"I managed somehow."

"That road closed after the 2002 uprising. It had been one of the most well-used roads. How could you come on that road? There are soldiers with guns keeping watch at the border."

"I know. But they saw that I wasn't a local and that I had a permit from the UN, plus I gave them a little money, and they let me go. The road was very bad. They said they'd repaired it in 2004, but it was even difficult to walk on it."

"I see. Where's Armenia?" Malevich took out a couple of spools of thread from a drawer and sat on a stool, which looked like it was made of paper. "Let me get back to my sewing, but please keep talking; I'm all ears."

"Armenia? It's near the Middle East geographically, or the southwestern part of Asia. The South Caucasus. Have you heard of it?"

"Is it a city in the Soviet Union?"

"It's a state now," I said. It seemed like Malevich was lagging behind when it came to current events; everything he knew seemed to be from several years ago. "The Soviet Union collapsed in 1990."

"Ah, I see. I was wondering why they weren't making Yaks any more. And what were you doing in Cote d'Ivoire?"

"Nothing. I slept for a few hours, then I came here."

"Are you serious?"

"Yes."

Our conversation was very one-dimensional, and the main reason for that was probably that Malevich seemed to be speaking mechanically; he was concentrating fully on his work. He was focusing more on his thread than on what I was saying. He slowly wet the end of the thick thread with his mouth and passed it through the huge eye of a needle and pulled the thread through. His head hung low throughout this process. Besides one half-finished item, there was no other cloth in his workshop.

Malevich did not even have any machinery. He had placed a self-made tool of some kind on his knees and used it to make his calculations. The tool was made of thin branches and threads. It looked like a crib.

"When will you finish this work?" I felt like we were growing closer as I asked this question. Once again, my sense of familiarity with people and my readiness to speak openly seemed heightened. "I want to go to the mosque."

"I've got a lot of work to do. You should go on your own, although it's closed and they won't let you in."

"Is there anything else to see in this city? I came here intentionally, because I thought it would be the most interesting place."

"You're right about that."

"Then say something. You've been quiet for two hours. Recommend somewhere good."

"Ours is a city of geniuses."

Suddenly, a question rang out in my mind, one that I had surprisingly not asked so far. And it was that question which changed the whole course of our conversation.

"Why do they call you Malevich? I understand that it's a nickname, but why Malevich?"

"Finally! I was waiting for this question to come up." He put his work aside. "Let's go outside. I have to bring Edel home from school, and we can continue our conversation on the way."

"Who's Edel?"

"My son. My only child," he said, seeming to have forgotten his work.

"But people here usually have…"

"Yes, but I wasn't lucky and only had one child, and my wife left us early. I'm a bit different from the rest."

"You didn't tell me why you're called Malevich."

"Yes. My real name isn't Malevich."

"Of course."

"But I resemble him very much and, in reality, I'm angry at him."

"How do you resemble him?" I asked. In any case, he didn't look anything like Malevich on the surface.

"His father worked in a sugar factory, so did mine. His father had fourteen children, so did mine. Kazimir was the oldest, so am I. Only nine of them survived to adulthood, and the same happened in our family."

"So what?"

"Nothing. But I, too, have painted the *Black Square*."

"The cube?"

"Yes. I didn't know any better and thought that I had made a great discovery. Then it turned out that Kazimir had produced that painting in 1915. But what did he know about applying oil paint to canvas? They say he was a cubist, a futurist, a representative of the avant-garde movement. But he was just a painter; he didn't really understand what he was doing when he painted the *Black Square*. That painting went around the world as an innovation, a discovery. But I'm sure he didn't have a concept behind it at the time, perhaps a subtext at best. But my piece was completely different. I wasn't painting to innovate; I was producing the history of my country. One look at that painting and all your questions would be answered."

Malevich seemed deeply offended and did not want to speak about this anymore. I was slightly surprised by the extent of his knowledge.

"Do you still paint now?"

"No. After the *Black Square*, I found out that some of my other paintings were also the same as his. I had also painted the *Black Circle*, and I swear I hadn't seen his work before that. But when I saw that it was exactly the same… Then the *Black Cross on Red*. What did Malevich know about us that led him to paint that piece?"

"But that wasn't about you."

"But that is our history, that is my life. When I spoke about it, nobody believed me. But the worst thing is that the reason for that was that nobody knew of Malevich. They said I was a genius. I said that Malevich had produced all those paintings long before me. So, they gave me that name. Ah, here's Edel."

A little boy approached us, embraced and kissed his father, gave him his bag, and looked at me in surprise.

"He's a guest of ours, you can say hello. He knows Malevich," Malevich said.

"Hello," I said to Edel in French.

"My son has just started to learn French; all the classes in elementary school are in Songa. But I'm teaching him."

"Where are the paintings?"

"Underground. There are no paintings. There is nothing here. When you said that you'd heard there were interesting things here, you were probably mistaken. The most interesting thing here is that everything is being built from scratch, like our house. We are forced to rebuild our little houses every year. And every year, we leave our property and our memories in the old house."

"Why is that?"

"There are landslides. Clay collapses. Why else?"

"So frequently?"

"Yes. Our city changes every year; we have a new map every year."

"This mosque, too?"

"The Sankoré Mosque has been being built for several centuries now."

"Why don't you use stone to build it?"

"Why did Malevich paint that piece before I did?"

I didn't understand his question. Understanding Malevich was difficult in general. He spoke in a very serious and confident manner, and that seriousness put me off a little.

We walked around the small town for about an hour. We were mostly quiet during this time—he said very little and I had run out of questions. We walked from north to south, then from east to west. And I discovered something interesting during that time. The city was like a square, and we kept going through its central area, which was shaped like a circle, with a cruciform pair of streets in the middle.

"I have to leave, it's time for me to go," I said.

"Yes, go. I hope you'll take good memories of this place with you."

"Yes, of course. Especially of your paintings."

DAY 16. BURKINA FASO
THE *HOGON*

The Mossi, Fulbe, Bobo, Lobi, Senufo, Grunshi, and many other ethnic groups that live in Burkina Faso, which was called Upper Volta until August 4, 1984, all went unnoticed by me. I was only thinking about the Dogon people at the time. Although most of them lived in the Bandiagara Escarpment, in Mali, I managed to find one of their villages here.

Perhaps I was not being fair. I was in Burkina Faso, one of the friendliest and most peaceful African countries, and I had put everything aside to focus my efforts on a people that had a population of perhaps a few hundred thousand, only five percent of whom lived in Burkina Faso.

This time things worked out the opposite way—I was searching for the Dogon but, instead, they found me.

This was already Day 16 of my travels and I had all but forgotten that I was an Armenian. I had become an "African"—even the color of my skin had changed. Gradually, I had begun to understand that I was in the place where I had always dreamed of being, something which had at first seemed impossible to realize.

Naturally, I had really wanted to meet the Dogon in Bandiagara, but because my book was based on the principle of spending no more than a single day in the same country, Burkina Faso ended up being the most suitable opportunity to do so.

Having found an interpreter who could translate directly from English to the Dogon language, everything began at the moment when he escorted me past a series of their small clay cottages to a two-story house about which I knew nothing.

An elderly man sat in the *toguna*,[17] which was made of clay and painted with various kinds of colorful patterns and symbols. The old man was probably past eighty, but had the facial expressions of a child and he gave the impression of always wanting to play children's games. He had tied a cloth around his head with thick black-and-white cords, and various kinds of stones, decorative pieces, pebbles, metallic items, and shells—all sorts of things, basically—hung from his beard. He was dressed almost fully in black; only his collar was red.

The old man looked down on us from an open balcony and the interpreter requested that he come down. He did so and greeted us, then invited us to his house, which was a short distance away from the *toguna* and resembled a large salt shaker. In general, the houses of the Dogon look like salt shakers or small chests of drawers, reminding me of houses drawn by children—they are simple structures with one large door, two windows, a smooth or domed roof, and a small yard of about five or six square meters.

The interpreter's name was Eboe Atul Diarra and his own ethnic origin was a mystery; before we arrived at the village, he kept requesting that I avoid asking any questions about his past. With the exception of the simple questions that people ask each other in everyday conversations, one could say that I had fulfilled his request. And this despite the fact that I was very interested in the little necklace that kept rustling on his neck as he moved.

The old man's house was different from the ones around it and the main reason for the difference were the four masks that hung from its walls, each of which resembled something.

When we entered his house, it seemed to me that he had been waiting for us for a long time. But in reality, I'd had no idea of where exactly Eboe had been leading me. He had probably told the old man in advance that we would be coming. The old man took the masks from the walls and brought them to me. We sat near a window, or rather, near a rectangular crack in the wall. The light from the sun lit up a section of the wall and a flower pot that held a lemon tree bearing dark green lemons. Throughout that time, one question kept tormenting me as it ran through my mind: do lemons grow in Burkina Faso?

"Look, these are the masks I was telling you about," Eboe said.

"You didn't tell me anything about any masks," I said.

"Of course I have. Think harder. You must have forgotten."

"No, you haven't said anything like that; I'm certain. I would have remembered."

---

17. A toguna is a two-story hut built only for men. It is where they make important decisions and also relax. The roof of a toguna consists of eight layers of millet stalks. It is a low building where one cannot stand upright, which is done intentionally to avoid violence when discussions get heated.

"I haven't told you about the Sigui?"

"No, but I've heard about it."

"How so?" Eboe found a thin twig on the ground and put it in his mouth. "Who told you about it?"

"I read about it in a book."

"Ah, I get it now. I thought for a moment that you really knew about the Sigui."

I thought that I did know a thing or two about the most mysterious of ceremonies celebrated by those odd people, but it turned out later that I really knew nothing at all.

During our brief conversation, the old man had remained standing in the middle of the room, confused, using a small piece of cloth to wipe the dust off the masks which had probably been hanging there for years.

"How should be we begin?" Eboe asked.

"Begin what?"

"Our conversation."

"With the old man?"

"Yes."

"Who is he?" I asked.

"Let's do it this way. I won't add anything on my part; I'll just directly translate what the two of you are saying. Do you agree to that?"

"Yes."

"I won't interfere in the conversation and I won't give my own analysis of anything that is said. Fine?"

"Fine."

"This service costs fifty dollars an hour. It's not a lot, but it's not very cheap either. Nobody else can help you at the moment except for me."

"Done," I said, looking at my watch which now had a slight crack on the crystal.

"Who are you?" I asked.

"Me? I'm nobody," said the old man. He looked at Eboe, understood that he had translated everything with accuracy, and continued, "I'm awaiting my death now."

"Why?"

"Who needs a lame deer in a field full of tigers?"

"Who are the tigers?"

"The tigers are all the deer who no longer wished to remain deer, so they became tigers."

"And who are the deer?"

"The deer," he said, looking out the window where a few deer were grazing, "are there."

I was surprised by the old man's reply. His child-like facial expression seemed playful. I could not tell what was real or unreal in what he was saying.

"I really want to hear your story about the Sigui," I said.

"What story? I don't have a story, just one or two childhood memories, that's all."

"Well, at least those, then."

"Why bother with someone else's pain?"

"It's interesting," I said. I feared that I might offend the old man as I said these words, but instead he started laughing.

"It's like a huge snail that the sea has carried away, while his shell remains in someone's hands. He wants to remove the snail from the shell, not knowing that he would have to jump into the sea to do that."

"What are you talking about?" I asked.

"Myself."

"I have heard that the Dogon have superhuman powers, and they are often thought to be aliens."

"Who considers us to be aliens?"

"That's what I've read."

"In Griaule's books?"[18]

"No. Who's Griaule?"

"A Frenchman. I haven't spoken to him, but I know that he's written books about the Dogon."

We were quiet for about a minute. He looked at Eboe, Eboe scratched the back of his head, and a roll of skin became visible where his necklace was clasped. Then he looked at me. I waited.

The old man, who had not yet introduced himself and seemed very mysterious, put one of the masks into my hands, making me think of Kru's masks. However, this one was made of wood. It was rough and reminded me of the clay houses.

"It's the mask of a rabbit," the old man said, and he put it on his face. He proceeded to tell me the story of the rabbit.

The Story of the Rabbit

"We were in Bandiagara. I was six years old. It was one of the happiest years of my life. There were seven children in my family, all of them boys. I was the middle one; I had three elder brothers and three younger ones. I remember, it was during one of our regular rehearsals. We were preparing for the Sigui, but I did not yet know anything about that ceremony; it was a game to me, a child's game, which often ended in an incomprehensible manner. We had to wait for more than twenty years for the ceremony, because it was due to take place in 1967, while this was still 1940 or 1939. We were all waiting impatiently, especially me. Every night, when I looked at the sky, I felt that as the festival

---

18. Marcel Griaule was a French anthropologist who visited Sangha (Mali) in 1931 and was overwhelmed by the Dogon, and their masks and cosmic performances. He was so awestruck by the Dogon that he set himself the objective of revealing them to the world. As a result, he wrote the book *The God of Water*, in which he provided an interpretation of the legend of the Dogon. Marcel Griaule died in 1956.

approached, so too the stars would come closer to me. I was a child then and did not see anything wrong with that happening. I thought that the Sigui was the meaning of life, that people were born to prepare for the ceremony. Perhaps my great love for the Sigui came from the fact that my mother was an actress while my father made masks. This mask is associated with the warmest and most emotional of my childhood memories. Once, it was a rainy night and I ran to our hut. I could hear my brothers shouting from a distance. Our hut was a small one, and they were incapable of being quiet as they ran around. I guess that was why they suddenly pushed the wicker door open and rushed outside. They were playing. I don't know what had gotten them so excited, but I was not in a good mood that evening. That would happen to me often back then. When I stepped inside, the hot aroma of rice immediately struck my nose. My mother called me to dinner and asked me to fetch my brothers as well. She was a wonderful cook when it came to rice, but buying rice was no easy task for us; we were not rich. For that reason, whenever we had rice for dinner, it was like a special occasion; I even felt like the Sigui was about to begin. I remember that moment well. I turned around to go get my brothers, but I noticed this mask—the rabbit mask—on a small rock which served as our table. It had different kinds of decorations on it before, but none of that remains now. Naturally, I loved to eat rice, but I couldn't resist the temptation; so far, I had only seen masks during rehearsals, and it was forbidden for me to wear them at home, as my father kept them in his workshop. So, I forgot my mother's request and rushed to put on the rabbit mask. I thought that I would see the universe through it, everybody would be dancing, there would be music; instead, I saw nothing. I think my father had not yet made the holes for the eyes. I walked a few meters and then turned, and as I prepared to take off the mask, I heard a loud noise. I snatched the mask off—all of the rice had spilled on to the floor; I had overturned the plate full of rice. I was the unhappiest person in the world at that moment. Everyone was back at home and they stared at me with open mouths. My mother gathered the dirtied rice and threw it away. I was quiet. I put the mask down on the rock and ran outside. My mother ran after me and told me not to cry, that everything was all right, and that she would ask the sun to send a few plates of rice. I grew happy again, and when I entered the house a few minutes later, I saw that everyone was having dinner, and that a plate had been set for me. 'A miracle has taken place,' I thought. 'Mother has been able to talk to the sun and ask for more rice.' When we finished dinner, I stepped outside again. It wasn't raining any more. I looked up at the sky, and the moon was out. Perhaps that was the reason I doubted my mother's words; had the sun still been in the sky, I would not have doubted anything. All at once, the tears began to fall from my eyes like hailstones when I saw my mother going to the neighbor's hut, the plates all stacked on top of each other. It had been a lie; they had tricked me and I was the one to blame. I had never cried so much in my life.

"The next morning, my life changed dramatically when I woke up and saw that the rabbit mask had been placed on the rock again. I wasn't going to touch it, but my father walked up and put it on my face with his own hands. I opened my eyes and saw the universe, people dancing, colorful costumes; it was all real. When I told him that I had seen the universe, he laughed and said that he had made holes in the mask so that I could see everything.

"I swear, I really did see the universe that morning. Nobody believed me, of course. To be honest, when I would put on that mask afterwards, I kept trying to see it all again, but it happened only once and it would never happen again."

"Was the universe beautiful?" I asked.

"Yes. At the time, it was the most beautiful thing I had ever seen."

"How many times in your life have you been a part of the Sigui?"

"Once."

"That's all?"

"The Sigui is held once every sixty-five years and it lasts for six to seven years. It takes place in a different village every year. It starts and ends at Youga Dogorou. During the ceremony, the men wear masks and their faces are unrecognizable; they talk in a secret language that the women don't know. They live in hiding for three months and nobody should see them during that period. The men participating in the ceremony are called *Olubaru*. The villagers are afraid of them and prefer to stay indoors at night."

"Please tell me more about the ceremony."

"Very well, but first I will tell you another story."

The old man removed the rabbit mask and put it aside, then put another one on his face—the antelope mask. Then he told the story of the antelope.

The Story of the Antelope

"This reminds me of one of the most unfortunate moments in my life. I have had many masks, but these four are related to the important stages in my life: the most memorable, powerful, happiest, and saddest moments.

"I was eighteen years old, and I hadn't yet lost hope of participating in the Sigui ceremony. But I was being told that one or two of my elder brothers would participate and I would be a spectator. Yogo and Yago (my brothers' childhood nicknames) were very excited. They too were preparing for the festival, although it had always seemed to me like I was the one in the family who loved the Sigui the most. We have had many festivals— Amma, Binou, Mono—but the Sigui continues to remain the most important event in my life. I felt that, once it was over, I would die and only then would my soul be happy. Many people thought I was sick, because not all of the Dogon love that festival so much.

"I remember that it was windy. The creak of a cracking tree could be heard and a tree trunk fell in our yard. It was almost four meters long—dry wood, an excellent fuel.

But I didn't rush to think of it as firewood, because I thought that it was a sign that had been sent to me. My brothers were happy that the tree had finally fallen and were getting ready to chop it up. I asked them not to rush because a tree symbolizes many things and some of them are not good signs, especially when a tree has fallen. My brothers did not listen and said that the wood could be used to make pretty masks, and it would be a great opportunity to surprise our father. This appealed to me too; naturally, it would've been better to leave the tree as it was, but the idea of making masks excited me very much. They chopped up the tree into several parts, took the branches and rough sections into the house for firewood, and saved a few smooth pieces to make masks. I ended up with the knot—the worst piece for a mask, especially given that I wasn't very skilled in the process. Yogo and Yago cut up their wood in a few minutes, attached pieces together and soon ended up with rectangular items resembling masks, but I felt that I could make the most beautiful mask of all and impress everyone during the rehearsals.

"I wanted to make the antelope mask: the most beautiful of them all, and also the most difficult to make. I shaved the wood for more than two hours, but what I ended up with was a rectangular, ugly mask. I put every ounce of strength I had into scraping that wood into shape, and moved so fast that I could smell the burning wood. My fingers had gone red, blood was boiling inside me such that it seemed like a prick of my finger would produce a gushing fountain. I decided to go into the forest; I remember my mother asking me where I was going and I said that I wouldn't be late, that I had a pretty secret that I wanted to share with her first of all. She grew happy and I noticed her dreamy eyes for the first time; she had never looked at me so happily before then, as if she were proud of me. We were very close, she loved me most of all. When I left the house, she said that I should ask God for an antelope. I didn't understand what she meant at the time, to be honest; I thought that her mention of an antelope had randomly coincided with the mask that I was making. I was going to the forest to hunt an antelope; I needed its horns and skin to make the mask more beautiful.

"I returned after I had succeeded in hunting an antelope and had prepared a beautiful mask. I had painted the front of the mask and attached the horns. I had stuck some of the skin onto it and sewn on various decorative items. I was very happy at that moment. I kept thinking of the Sigui; they wouldn't be able to ignore me anymore with a mask like that. But my happiness did not last long. I entered our home with the mask on my face. First, I heard my brother scream, and then the sad news reached me. My mother had died. I didn't remove that mask for more than a day, so that no one could see my tears. I only found out later that my mother had secretly seen my mask. That, of course, was the saddest day of my life, but then I began to look at it another way. My mother had been proud of me, and the most important thing was that I was close to achieving my dream."

"The Sigui?"

"Yes. I was finally given the opportunity to participate."

"But it was still another ten years away, wasn't it?"

"Yes, it was, but that was very little time for me; it passed by like a second."

"So you finally took part?"

"Yes," he said as he took off the mask, "but not with this one." He put the antelope mask aside and picked up another one, a brown bear. Then he told the story of the brown bear.

The Story of the Brown Bear

"The Sigui began in 1967. I couldn't see the festivities that year; as I said, it starts in Youga Dogorou. But the following summer, my life's dream began to be fulfilled. I had become an *Olubaru*. Perhaps it was nothing special for some other people, just another form of entertainment, after which they would get back to their everyday lives. But I had been living with one purpose only since the day I was born—to see that festival and then die in peace. I know it sounds foolish, but there was nothing I could do about it. My father and mother had planted these thoughts about the Sigui inside me from the day I was born. That summer, the festivities arrived at our village of Koundou. I remember how the guardians of the masks, the *Awa*, were doing a traditional dance. I had the brown bear mask on my face and I was running. A few thousand people had gathered, most of them from neighboring villages. Our main group, which was performing the Sigui ceremony, had gathered around a tree with a large trunk.

"Hundreds of women and girls had put on hats on their heads with intricate designs. They formed a circle and danced. Dust had risen up to cloud the sky but, despite that, there was nobody who was sad or in a bad mood. We were performing one of the seven episodes of the Sigui. It was the scene of the creation of the world. The Sigui is in fact a festival dedicated to the *pō-tolo* (Sirius),[19] and everything begins with the *pō-tolo*. Our whole history is based on this. I was happy to participate in this episode about the creation of the *pō-tolo*. I remember it well—I had been asked to wear the brown bear mask because we didn't have a fox mask and, according to the legend, I should have been playing a fox.

"First there was the *Amma*, which was in a huge rotating egg, in the center of which a small grain of wheat had formed. When the wheat grew, it burst open the egg and the universe was formed. *Amma* used the remaining fragments of the egg to make the first living creatures, four pairs of twins. They looked like amphibians: half human, half animal, with soft limbs, red eyes, and snake-like tongues. One of those animals, *Ogo*, occupied a part of the ground and created the earth. *Amma* was angry and sent forth a drought, and she transformed *Ogo* into a fox. Later, *Amma* decided to rebuild the universe

---

19. Sirius is invisible to the naked eye and was only discovered in 1862. Astronomers believe that in the first century B.C., Sirius was in a binary star system before its two component stars smashed into each other. The Dogon probably witnessed that event and are passing down this information through the Sigui, which was being performed for the thirty-fourth time.

and sacrificed *Nommo*, the fox's brother. A lot of blood was spilled into the universe, as a result of which the first star appeared, the giant *pō-tolo*.'

"This was the main story of the first scene and I enthusiastically played the role of the fox, even though I had a bear mask on my face. Behind that mask, however, was my joyful face as I proudly ran and hid myself from *Amma*.

"That was the happiest day of my life. At that moment, I could think only of death. But fate had another surprise in store for me. As often happens, the game turned into reality."

"What do you mean?" I asked.

"Everything seems to be so easy, but in reality nobody does anything for you just like that."

"Do you consider yourself to be unfortunate?"

"I can't describe how I feel, to be honest. At that moment, I felt like my life could come to an end at any time. But in reality, I would live for another forty years. Perhaps that would have caused joy to many others, but not to me. My game was over."

"Did you stay in the village?"

"Yes. The Sigui ended in 1973 and the enthusiasm died down. And the thought that I would have to wait another sixty-five years, until 2032, caused me only sorrow."

"But life goes on, right?"

"Life did not go on. It had turned into a clock that had stopped, the kind you keep only because it looks good."

"What is bothering you so much?"

"My meaningless life. I suddenly realized that the Sigui and my life had run in parallel, they were similar to each other. My life was also like a defeated fox, which roams in caves because it is homeless."

The old man removed the brown bear mask and I noticed that his eyes were red, and there was white powder on his eyelashes, probably from inside the mask. He put the brown bear mask aside and, with trembling hands, picked up the last one, a mask with snails. Then he told the story of the snails.

The Story of the Snails

"I lived alone in Bandiagara till 1998. Everyone knew me and respected me; they would come to me with all kinds of questions. I was the only old man who didn't have a family. It was strange but none of my seven brothers had a family of their own, and they all left Bandiagara early. Like an unfortunate donkey, I dragged myself here and there with a walking stick in my hand. I remember that day very well—it was April thirtieth, a sunny day when the smell of cactus had filled my room. Cactuses don't really smell, but if you cut a small opening in them, an aroma begins to spread immediately. I had gone out for a walk; I'd never seen a sky like the one I saw that day—the sun was on one side, the stars on the other. I remembered my mother's words. She had said that she would take all the stars in the sky and give them to me for play. When she'd said that, I had truly believed my mother, and she hadn't lied.

"As I stood awestruck by the sky, my house burned down. I saw for the first time how clay can burn. I had no strength to run. I pushed my stick forward and barely made it home, and the only thing that I managed to save was this mask. Everything else I had burned down. I don't really know what had caused the fire. Many people blamed the Bambara, the Tuaregs, or other tribes, but I knew that this was a punishment sent down by the *pō-tolo*. This was its curse. The great fire of 1998 was not that great; many people didn't even hear about it. I was forced to leave the village. I searched for shelter for a year before I came here. I crossed the border and entered Burkina Faso like a shivering deer.

"I remember, when they saw me here with a snail mask, everyone thought I was a knight who had lost his horse. They gave me shelter in the *toguna*, then built this hut. I kept my face covered for more than a year so that they wouldn't see how old I was. I told them that this was a tradition we had in Bandiagara, and that nobody should see me until the next Sigui.

"My secret didn't last long. When the Dogon here saw me, they couldn't believe that I was the man with whom they had been living all this time. That's all I have to say. You've come at the right time."

"Why?"

"I don't know."

The old man took off the last mask, the one with snails. He gazed outside at the sky with a cold stare. Then he said, "That was the story about the Sigui."

Eboe put his hand on my shoulder and suggested that we leave. I refused, but he pushed me out.

"Wait, I didn't even ask who he was, what his name was."

"He is the *Hogon*; come, we must go," Eboe said.

"*Hogon*? Is that his name?"

"It's not a name."

"What is it?"

"It's a Dogon word, or rather, a title."

"What does it mean?"

"It's the Dogon's spiritual leader."

I didn't understand why Eboe was pushing me out with such urgency from the *Hogon*'s hut. But then I saw a few Dogons with sickles in their hands enter the old man's hut, only to emerge a few minutes later and break the sickle handles, leaving them by the wall.[20]

---

20. There is a Dogon tradition to break sickles in two when somebody dies, to symbolize the fact that that person will no longer be able to reap any harvest.

DAY 17. GHANA
THE GOLD COAST

I had heard a lot about Ghana. And, just like in all the other countries, I expected to see anything here except for the ordinary.

The round, gigantic sun that appeared the very minute the plane landed in Ghana was the first thing that surprised me. This was truly a unique sun; it was golden and seemed to be rotating as it approached me. I had never seen the sun this big. And I had never seen anyone selling umbrellas right in the middle of a road, people pasting crocodile skin in the hollows of trees, or locals living in hat-shaped huts. Perhaps these are not common in Ghana, either, but these were the very things my eyes spotted, including a woman with yellowing hair who came out into the street and yelled, "Essien, Essien, come home quick."

Essien was not young and obviously had health issues of some sort. One of the locals had even told me a parable that he had thought up and dedicated to Essien. He said that, one day, the sun came out into the sky and saw that there were hundreds of suns there. That made it sad, so it started to cry, and its tears dropped down to the ground and set fire to a huge village. All its inhabitants died in the flames, except for one, who had looked in awe at the rays of the sun that morning, before it had started to cry.

"Essien, Essien, come home, before the crocodiles attack," the woman shouted. "Come quickly; you can go back later."

I was in Bolgatanga, the largest city in the north of Ghana. It was very pretty, especially its suburbs. There wasn't a crocodile in sight, except for a tree hollow that had a patch of crocodile skin stuck on it.

One of Essien's eyes was considerably smaller than the other and, besides that, his eyes were of different colors—one was yellow, the other brown. Essien limped, and it was clear that his right leg did not belong to him. His appearance fascinated me the most, although I realized that the more I looked at him, the more "faults" I could find. But the fact that his facial features were the most unusual I had ever seen forced me to follow him.

Although the official language in Ghana is English, I hadn't expected Essien—a resident of Bolgatanga, or more specifically, of a little hut near the Tonga hills—to speak the language.

"Excuse me, could I speak to you for a moment? I'd like to ask you something."

"Ask what?" Essien looked at me with disdain.

"Are you from here?"

"No."

"I thought so."

"I'm from those parts," he said, indicating the east. "That is where I come from."

"Perhaps from Japan or Malaysia?"

"Japan, Malaysia?" the woman interrupted. "Essien is a native Mole—Dagbon. He thinks he's from those parts. But look at his face. Malaysian? He has the face of a monkey."

The woman was very rude to Essien, while he listened with his head hung. Essien's loose leg made the whole scene even more melancholic, as it emitted creaks similar to a rusty bicycle.

"Come in, then, don't stand there like a fool. Is this the first man you've ever seen? He's just a regular guy. Hurry in, or the crocodiles will be here in two minutes."

Essien grabbed his head and, screaming tragically, rushed into the hat-shaped hut. He had forgotten his umbrellas, which remained out there in the middle of the street.

I was forced to knock on the wicker door for around five minutes, until the woman opened it and gave me a loathsome look.

"What do you want? Can't you see that he's sick? Leave my brother alone."

"I've brought the umbrellas, that's all. I thought someone might steal them."

"We don't have any thieves around here. You could've bought them, instead of bringing them here. That would've been better."

"But do you get rain around here?"

"Of course," the woman said mockingly. "We get everything around here."

"Excuse me, but you were very rude to your brother."

"That's none of your business. I've cared for him all my life—I've fed him, cleaned up after him, found work for him, I've done everything. I have the right to be rude."

"He's a human being, not an object. He might feel hurt."

"The mentally ill don't have hurt feelings. How is any of this your business? Go away." The woman spoke good English and the words poured out fluently as she complained about Essien.

"How old is Essien?"

"How do you know his name?"

"You were calling him earlier."

"He's fifty-seven."

That reply shocked me. Essien did not look a day over twenty; he didn't even have any facial hair.

"What is his illness?"

"What it is to you? Haven't you said enough? Go away, I've got a lot to do."

"Why are you trying to scare him by saying that crocodiles are coming?"

"Because he doesn't listen. At least that way, he's frightened into it."

"But that might make him even more mentally ill."

"That's my business. He's not your brother. Go away."

The woman slammed the door shut, although I still had a few more questions. At that moment, I was ready to give anything for him to be healthy, although I had nothing for him except for my questions—questions that kept coming spontaneously and demanding to be answered. I knew that I was a very unwelcome guest for Essien and his sister, but my stubbornness meant that I managed to spend several more hours with them.

I didn't know what I wanted from them, either, but I felt that the more I "submerged" myself into Africa, the more I was concerned with relationships with people, and with feelings and emotions.

"What do you want from them? Go away, don't stick your nose into other people's business," an old man said, suddenly tapping me on the back. He had a pointy mustache, a sharp nose, and dark skin. But he didn't look like an "African" at all. "I'm serious. Go about your business. Don't bother Kaune; she helps out her brother a lot. What do you know about them, anyway?"

"Who are you? I hadn't noticed you here."

"I'm Luis de Gomes Oliveira, born in Ecuador, but a Creole by ethnicity."

"What are you doing here?"

"I've escaped to here."

"From where, Ecuador?"

"Well, I actually wanted to escape to Spain. But the border guards spotted our boat and we were all deported, so I arrived in Morocco, and came to Ghana from there."

It was surprising to see an Ecuadorian with such a past in Ghana, especially one who seemed so happy with life there, as if Ghana was his homeland.

"Well, I wasn't sticking my nose in… it's just that his sister…"

"Kaune?"

"Yes, Kaune was very rude; that kind of talk could drive anyone insane."

"But what is it to you? You suddenly show up and want to intrude into their lives and change something? Who do you think you are?"

"I'm a writer and local life is one of my interests. If I can leave things a little better after I'm gone, I'm willing to make any effort to do so."

"Yes, but in this case Essien is sick, and changing his life is impossible. You think his sister isn't suffering? Oh, how she's suffering! She cries so much at night that all of us in the village are woken by her sobbing."

"How come you speak English?"

"I learned it, since I was traveling to Spain."

"But they speak…"

"I know, it doesn't matter. Fate has brought me here. My life is very similar to Essien's; we are alike in many ways."

"In what ways?"

"I have overcome a number of difficulties as well."

"What difficulties has Essien overcome?"

"I don't know."

"But you just said that you were alike. How can you not know?"

"Yes, I don't know. I see that similarity in his eyes. Only his sister knows everything about him, and Kufot knows a little as well."

"Who's Kufot?"

"A benefactor who makes umbrellas for the poor."

"He told me a parable."

"I know, he tells that parable to everyone."

"What is Essien's illness?"

"You can't see it?"

"No."

"He isn't sick." Luis de Gomes Oliveira looked into my eyes, smirked, and said, "Go away, this place isn't for you. You can't understand the mentally ill people here."

Those words hurt me, but it seemed that the locals were not happy to see me.

"Open the door, I have to talk to Essien," I said, and started knocking again.

"There's nobody home," Essien shouted from inside, probably having been frightened into doing so by his sister.

"Who's speaking from inside?"

"A snowball."

"Essien, how do you know about snow? Have you ever seen snow?"

"Yes."

"Where?"

"In a dream."

"Was it pretty?"

"Yes. The snow was yellow and fell on my head like teardrops. It was hot."

"Have you seen cold, white snow?"

"There's no such thing." A loud noise could be heard from inside, and Essien jumped out of the arched window and ran towards the Tengzug, which was about seventeen kilometers from the city. I'd only learned about it, naturally, once I had asked the taxi driver to follow Essien.

"Why bother? He's going to die in a few days," the driver said.

"Why?"

"Don't you have any cases of mental illness in your country?"

"We do."

"Go cure *them*, then."

"I'm not a doctor. But the things that Essien says have left an impression on me. He isn't mentally ill; he has a wonderful imagination. There's something strange within him, that other cases of illness don't have."

"They're all the same. One hundred cedis. Or rather, ten dollars."

Finally, I saw Essien by himself, without anybody else around him. At that moment, I asked myself why I wanted to speak with him so much. Did I have my own personal interests at heart, or was it something else? Perhaps the first thought in my mind was seeing him as a literary character.

"Essien, I've followed you here so that we can talk."

"Go ahead."

"I'm very interested in your past. Everybody thinks you're sick, but I'm convinced that they're wrong."

Essien entered a hut that looked like a place of worship. It was a house made of sand, but it seemed like a giant stump whose roots had emerged from the soil.

"This is the house of the blind man," Essien said as he caressed its walls.

"Essien, don't you want to talk?"

"I'm sick; everyone is right. What do you believe? I'm really sick and you shouldn't bother yourself with me; I've got no time."

"What happened to your leg?"

Essien looked at me. His look seemed to be one of wisdom.

"A crocodile ate it."

"Is that why your sister keeps frightening you?"

"Perhaps. But the crocodile wasn't alone. There were six of them. I walked through crocodiles in order to get here."

"But what had happened?"

"A fire; the village was burning, and only I survived. I ran and tried to save everyone, my father shouted for help; I was six years old, I ran through the fire, through the crocodiles, and ended up on this coast. Everybody died, but I found out later that Kaune had survived, too, but I was insane already, insane," Essien shouted and slammed his hand on the wall. "I'd gone crazy; nobody believed me when I said a crocodile had eaten my foot. They said that it was a family illness, but I knew the truth. They thought that nothing existed on the other coast, but they were wrong. Besides the slaves and the sick people, there were happy people there, too. But when I was six, after I ran through the crocodiles and ended up here, I was miserable. My family remained on that coast; they all burned, they are all ashes."

Essien spoke very clearly, but it was hard to keep up with his thoughts. I tried to imagine his sorrow, but it wasn't easy.

"You don't know what it means to be crazy. I'm not crazy, I'm an unfortunate child. My father told me to run, he told me to escape, but I couldn't leave him. Who needs a life where you have everything, but not a family? And they are the ones to blame."

"Who?"

"Those who don't know how to experience awe, those who look at the sky and see dozens of suns instead of just one, those who drove me away from that coast."

I couldn't understand what he meant and there was probably no need to. The only thing I understood was that I needed to go; it was already evening, and my journey had to continue. Before I left, I asked him one final question.

"Essien, where are you from, what is the name of that coast?"

"The Gold Coast."[21]

---

21. On March 6, 1957, Ghana gained independence through the efforts of Kwame Nkrumah. It used to be a British colony and was called Gold Coast.

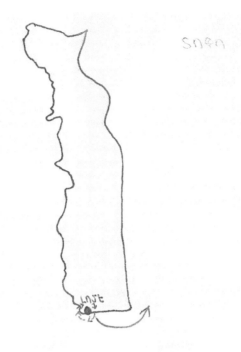

DAY 18. TOGO
THERE ARE NO WINDMILLS IN TOGO

I was very tired. The worst part was that I was forced to close my eyes sometimes and pretend that everything was perfect, because I had no desire to see anything that could cause me pain, feelings of compassion, or simply displeasure. This wasn't the first time I was in a situation of this kind, and I had already seen such cruel scenes in Mauritania, Liberia, and Sierra Leone. I didn't want to discuss or analyze sick people like objects; they too have their aims in life which they want to achieve. So I was forced to close my eyes when I saw people suffering from AIDS, malaria, or mental disorders.

I was in Togo, a country that had come to be known in recent months through the unprecedented success achieved by its soccer team. Conversations about that continued everywhere. The only strange thing was that some people here seemed to believe that Togo had become world champions.

I was in Lomé, the capital of Togo, which had an overall population of no more than 400,000 people, or 700,000 counting the suburbs.

I understood right away that I needed to be careful because, in the space of just three minutes, I lost the hat I had bought in Morocco—it had grey and white stripes, was 100% wool, and had been made in Tunisia. Somebody had probably swiped it.

I was walking through one of the parks in Lomé, where there were several trees with large trunks, and a small stall. I suddenly noticed a Black man who was leaning against a tree and reading a book. What surprised me most was that the book was in English. I realized at that moment that he could be my guide.

I watched from a distance for about five minutes, until he grew tired of reading and closed the book.

"May I join you?" I asked.

"Where?"

"I mean, is it okay if I lean against this tree, too?"

"Go ahead."

"That's an English book."

"Yes, I know."

"How are you reading it?"

I forgot to mention that this man was around my age, with glasses that resembled a pince-nez with a dusty right side. Some of his hair was a pronounced white, as if it had been dyed. In general, he looked like an astonished porcupine.

"With these glasses," he said.

"No, I mean English."

"I know it," he said, and took out a notebook from his pocket. "I know English very well."

"Where did you learn it?"

Perhaps my question offended him.

"In Lomé. What's so surprising about that?"

"No, no, nothing. I thought you were a foreigner," I said, trying to make up for what I had said.

"Like a Dutchman or a Canadian, right?"

"No."

"They're made of rubber, like raw uncooked meat. I'm an Ewe. Have you heard of us?"

"Not really, to be honest. You're probably a student, right?"

"No. A Professor."

It seemed to me for a moment that he was older than I had thought.

"How old are you?"

"Nineteen."

"A professor?"

"Yes. What's so strange about that?"

"You teach English, I assume?"

"No."

"Then what?"

"Sports journalism."

"In English?"

"No. What's English got to do with it?"

"You speak it well."

"So what? I'm even better at cycling."

"Cycling is a sport. Is that a part of your profession?"

"I'm a journalist."

"I'm writing a book about Africa," I said.

"Mosie, Mosie Moe is my name."

I started to laugh.

"What's so funny?"

"Oh nothing. '*Mozi*' is an Armenian word, that's all," I said, thinking that he looked like a *mozi*—a young calf—too. "That's why I was laughing."

"What does it mean?"

"Umm... a harvester," I said. It was the first thing that came to my mind.

"That's good, it's got a nice ring to it. Mosie the Harvester. What else would a *mozi* do, besides harvesting?"

"Eat grass... no, no, I mean eat bread."

"Well, we all eat. What I mean is, what would a *mozi* do for a living?"

I found it difficult to describe what a *mozi* would do if it were human.

"What everyone else does... what else would it do?"

"So you're a journalist, too."

"No, I'm a writer. It's not the same thing."

"How come? A *mozi* can be a journalist, right?"

"I guess so," I said, barely containing my laughter.

"What are you writing?"

"I haven't started yet. I'm still visiting different countries. At first, I wanted to start writing during my journey. But I've changed my mind now. I guess I'll just take notes and then do the writing later."

"So you're a journalist?"

"No. Do only journalists take notes?"

"No. But you look like a reporter."

We talked for a while about many interesting and uninteresting things. Mosie gave me a brief summary of his country's history and told me a few engaging things, but none of that was of any interest to me until someone showed up who looked like the literary character of my dreams.

He was short, had green hair, earrings, and large, thick shoes, each of which must have weighed at least three kilograms. His cheeks were puffed out like balloons that had been blown up for a long time and had now suddenly started to leak. The gap between his front teeth was so big that another one could have fit there comfortably. And the distance between his eyes was at least five centimeters. He was wearing a yellow outfit, looking like a Buddhist monk, but it was probably a national costume of some sort.

Mosie started speaking to him in his language, and then switched to English.

"My name is Java," said the newcomer. Java was broader than he was tall.

"Java is a soccer player," Mosie said.

"A coach, I assume?" I asked.

"No, no, a real soccer player. I'm a bit fat, but I play well. I also have a lot of knowledge about the game," Java said.

"Okay, you two keep chatting; I've got to go. I'll see you later," Mosie said, putting his papers in his bag. Pointing at me, he told Java, "He's a journalist."

"A writer," I said.

"What difference does it make?" Mosie said, and left.

"That's good. Journalists and soccer players have a lot in common."

"Please, call me a writer."

"But what's wrong with being a journalist?"

"Nothing. But would you like it if I called you a basketball player?"

"I'd love to be able to jump that high."

"But you can't, can you?"

"No."

"So, you're not a basketball player."

"I know I'm not."

"And I know that I'm a writer."

"I get it. What interesting facts would you like me to tell you?"

"Anything you wish."

"Have you heard? Our team is the world champion."

"Which team?"

"Our soccer team."

"When did they become champions?"

"This year, 2006."

"In Germany?"

"Yes."

"Do you mean street soccer?"

"Street soccer? No. Real soccer. World soccer."

"Italy is the champion."

"Our team beat Italy through penalties."

"Italy-France, Olympiastadion, the match started at eleven pm Yerevan time, the game ended 1:1 at full time, and Italy was declared champion after a round of penalties. Trezeguet missed a penalty for France," I recited.

"Yes, yes, I know. He's a stupid player; he's no good."

"That was the final. What's Togo got to do with it?"

"You're confusing things, but that's okay, I won't hold it against you. We're the champions."

"Is that what everyone here thinks?"

"No. Some of my friends don't believe me, like you."

"So, you see?"

"They think that Ghana is the champion."

"I'm sure you'd really want it to be that way, but the world champion is Italy."

"Should I believe what I saw with my own eyes, or what you're saying?"

"What have you seen?"

"Our team lifting the Cup."

"Where?"

"In a sports magazine somewhere."

"Maybe it was a different kind of magazine."

"No, that's impossible."

Java began to smoke, and his eyes seemed sad. We were quiet. We leaned against the tree, Java on the right, me on the left. The rustling of the leaves gave me goose bumps. He gazed into the distance and slowly released some smoke from his mouth.

His dreams were obvious to me. That soccer player, who easily weighed one hundred and fifty kilograms, had a dream and believed in that dream. My words had made him sad, and he no longer wished to speak with me. He shook his head.

"I have to go," he said.

"Where? Don't you want to be my guide?"

"You already know everything; what kind of guidance could you need?"

Java left. He had probably taken offense.

I left the park; there were a few old French cars parked in the street. The sun seemed pale, as if I was looking at it through Mosie's dirty glasses. A conversation between some people could be heard in the distance, one or two streets away. I didn't want to approach them. I walked slowly through one of the central streets of Lomé, I'm not sure which one, and thought that everyone looked the same to me. They all had sad eyes and sorrowful looks on their faces; their smiles were similar and, most importantly, they could all dream.

I suddenly recalled that nobody had swiped my hat, I'd hung it on a branch of one of the trees. I returned to the park. Something had changed there, like a storm was sweeping through it. It was difficult to see anything in the dust and dirt, and there seemed to be no explanation for the way this wind was blowing.

After a long search, I finally found my hat. It was dusty and faded. After leaving the park again, I saw Mosie for a second time; he was wiping his glasses.

"Where are you going?" Mosie asked, taking out a copy of Alphonse Daudet's *Letters from My Windmill.*

"Home. I mean, eastwards, to Benin."

"Porto Novo?"

"I don't know, we'll see. That's a good book."

"Yes, I know."

"Are there are windmills in Togo?"

"No," said Mosie. He looked at the red windmill depicted on the cover of the book and replied sadly, "There are no windmills in Togo. Oh, I almost forgot. I've written an article about you."

"Really? What article?"

"About our conversation. And I've called it *Mosie and the Harvester.*"

"That's nice."

Mosie left. I didn't ask him any more about the article. I could tell from the look on his face that it had been a very important article.

I was sure that Mosie would have liked to see beautiful windmills. That would have made him a little happier. Java would have been happy, too, if the Togo soccer team had won the World Cup.

When I left the park, I caught sight of a poster stuck to one of its gates, which said, "AIDS Patients Treatment Center No. 1."

I crossed the street and continued my journey…

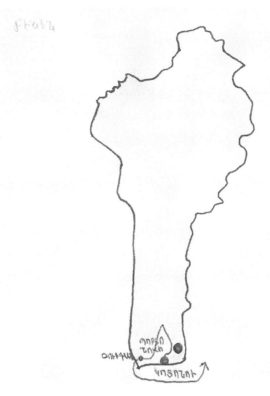

DAY 19. BENIN
THE FEATHERED DRUM

Mosie's and Java's words were still fresh in my memory; after meeting them, it wasn't easy to adjust to the completely different natural setting and atmosphere in Benin.

From the very first minutes, the giant sun in Benin looked down and, as if taking a deep breath, doubled in size. Many people who have been to Benin might say that the sun is small there, and some might even say that they haven't seen the sun there at all.

I read this in a magazine once: "The grass sighed and burst through the soil, rising higher, and the hungry cow rushed to it and swallowed it instantly. This is why there is no longer a sun in Benin, nor any grass…"

But I saw both fields and a large, very large sun, which seemed to have run a long distance and was panting, puffing up to double in size with each pant.

I travelled east from Cotonou to Ouidah, but it would be more correct to say that I didn't know where I was going. I was like a wild animal, moving with my head hung low, to any place where I could find shelter. Northern Africa had been completely different from this. You could spend the night at any hotel there and walk into shops in the city, use public transportation, and eat food. It was ten times more difficult to do that here;

there was no hotel where I could have made a reservation in advance. I had to be careful at every step not to ingest a dangerous bacterium and catch something.

I once again faced a serious problem—nobody understood me. No one spoke English. Even at the stand where I decided to buy a beer and had asked the vendor to give me the bottle with the red label that said "La Beninoise," all he did was look at my hands, then turn around and go into the back room while picking his nose. I never managed to buy that beer. When I got to Ouidah, the sun was no longer as large as it was before, and the natural landscape had changed. It had rained, the soil was wet, and muddy bubbles would sometimes appear in the rainwater puddles. The Gulf of Guinea was just ten kilometers from there, possibly even less.

I could hear thumping, like a drum. It came from far away, barely audible. The sound of the drum was clearly distinguishable from the surrounding noise. It was constantly in the same rhythm and listening to it for a few minutes gave me a headache, as if someone was deliberately trying to get on everybody's nerves. But focusing on the rustling of the leaves on the giant poplars, or the sound of a car on one of the few streets in the city, would cause the drum beat to move to the background immediately.

When I wanted to go to the beach, I noticed a small "African"—perhaps four or five years old—standing in front of one of the huts nearby. He had wrapped himself like a little koala around the trunk of a tree that was at least twenty times larger than him, and he had stuck one of his hands into its hollow while his cheek was pressed against the tree and the wind mildly blew against his brown hair. The little one's belly stuck out in front of him and shone in the sun's rays; his belly button protruded. He was barefoot and had put one foot on top of the other, scratching the left one with his right, dripping wet sand from one onto the other. He only wore a piece of faded green or blue underwear, which looked like a skirt. His eyes bulged out, as did his nose, lips, and chin. The child remained immobile while he looked at me for five minutes. Only his abdominal muscles contracted, betraying his apprehension.

I realized that he was scared of me; perhaps I looked very foreign to him. I walked slowly towards the tree. He remained rigid; only his chin began to tremble. When there was less than five meters between the two of us, I saw that the child really was not scared at all; he simply looked very sad. I wanted to know whether the child was a boy or a girl. I'd taken him for a boy at first glance, but he also seemed to be very delicate.

"What's your name? Are you a boy, or a girl?" I asked, softening my voice. He was surprised, let go of the tree, and ran into the hut so fast that his underwear fell off. He was a boy, that "little African," whose sad and defenseless expression could have been the symbol for the whole continent.

Because I had to wait till nighttime to return to the airport in Cotonou, I decided to go out into the streets and walk around. I saw a car at the end of the street had that slowed down as it approached me, and then stopped. I thought it had stopped on purpose. There were at least twenty or twenty-five wicker baskets on top of the car, as well as several humongous knitted sacks. The load on the car was bigger than the vehicle itself, which was a red Fiat, probably from the 1980s. I could see inside from the rear window: five or six spotted lambs sat there and immediately began to bleat when they saw me. Three locals got out of the car. I said hello to them and they responded in kind. I opened the rear door to take a look inside and the lambs hopped out suddenly, each one running away in a different direction. The locals, who were either Fons or Yorubas, grabbed their heads and ran after them. I don't know why they had stopped the car when they saw me, but it was obviously dangerous for me to remain standing there. I left the street and ran along the muddy curb. A short while later I ended up in a pretty place that looked like a small lake; it was surrounded by trees on all sides and in the middle, in the water, stood a circular fence made of thin wooden branches and thatch. It was as if someone had drawn a border in the lake. Within the fence, thousands of fish raised their heads above the water and reveled in the mild whispering of the wind. I was probably close to the sea since I could see a gigantic structure that I knew well in the distance. It was Benin's monument to its slaves, faded red in color and consisting of a large archway with two rectangular passages next to it. There were bronze images on its façade and slaves were depicted to its left and right, lined up like soldiers. The sea was right behind it.

The sound of the drum pierced my ears once again, this time sounding sharper and rougher; the rhythm hadn't changed, but the sound seemed to be coming from somewhere closer to me. It seemed to originate below the water, but the sound of the drum also seemed to come both from my left and my right, from in front of me and behind me, and it even seemed to come from above.

It felt like there were drummers hidden all around me, playing simultaneously. But, in reality, there was only one drummer and he was not too far away—just a few meters to the south, towards the Gulf of Guinea, where the monument to the slaves stood. I found the drummer easily and there was someone else standing next to him. When I saw them, I felt like time had spun back a few hundred years and they were still slaves of the Kingdom of Benin,[22] who would work day and night. However, no matter how strong my feeling was, they really were far from being yet another illusion, and they knew well who they were and the time period in which they existed.

The drummer was a boy of ten or eleven with bright eyes and curly hair; his forehead was shining and his twisted locs slowly writhed like worms with the rhythm of his movement. His arms were thin, as was his torso, while his belly was red (perhaps he had been carrying the drum on it for a while). The drum was now between his legs as he bent over

---

22. Tribes that formed a part of the Kingdom of Benin lived on the coast of Dahomey. In the 15th century, the Portuguese colonized these territories. For several centuries, this was considered one of the centers of the slave trade.

it and struck his drumsticks against the drumhead with the same rhythm. His cheeks were puffed out, like the sun I had seen in Cotonou and he panted, forced to open his mouth for each breath, while water kept flowing from his nostrils.

The person next to him was close to thirty. He stood calmly and watched the drummer.

When I took out my camera to take a picture of them, the one who was standing by quickly approached me and blocked my view.

"What are you doing? You can't do that."

"Did you just speak in English?" I asked, because grasping his English was almost more difficult for me than understanding something in his mother tongue would be.

"What do you think I did? Do you think that only white people are educated? Do you think we're cavemen, running naked in the fields with sticks in our hands?"

"No, I was taken by surprise. Nobody here seems to speak English; it's been very tough for me to talk to locals. You are the first person here who I've met who speaks English, so I was surprised."

"Nothing to be surprised about. Put that away. You can't take pictures. This is a secret and you'll be in danger if they know."

"If who knows? What secret?"

"This is a spiritual ceremony, and I need to complete it."

"Who is he?"

"The accused."

"What do you mean?"

"He is the accused, and I am the witness."

"Accused of what? I don't understand. Who are you?"

"You can call me what you like. I don't have the right to introduce myself."

"Who's he?"

"I already told you: the accused."

"What is he accused of doing?"

"That's also a secret."

"Why is he constantly beating that drum?"

"That is his punishment."

"What punishment? I don't understand."

"He has to beat that drum until he dies. He has been sentenced to death. And I must wait until that happens. You've asked too many questions. Go away and don't bother us."

"How long do you have to wait?"

"I've been waiting for three days already. I guess there will be three more, and that'll be it."

"But why? What kind of death sentence is that—to play the drum until you die?"

"This isn't just any drum. It's a feathered drum."

"What's the difference?"

"The whole city can hear the sound of this drum, and when the residents hear this sound, they take lambs and offer a sacrifice."

"Why?"

"As a sign of gratitude. They are grateful to God for the elimination of one of their enemies. When the drumbeat stops, then the accused no longer exists. His soul soars into the sky and is cleansed, the sun takes a deep breath and starts to run."

"And what if none of that happens?"

"What?"

"What if the car stops and the lambs escape; what if the drummer stops beating the drum but nobody dies? What then?"

"No, that cannot happen. That isn't how it works in Ouidah. If the drumbeat has stopped, then the drummer is dead."

"And who knows about this?"

"I do."

"Who else?"

"I'm here to bear witness to this event."

"Have you been doing this job for long?"

"No, this is my first time. When the drumbeat stops, I'll go home."

"Do you know this little boy?"

"Yes."

"Who brought him here?"

"I can't answer questions like that."

I felt like he was hiding something. But I didn't insist further on finding out who had organized this unique punishment. The face of the drummer suggested that he could not have committed a serious crime, however. He seemed too small and too honest.

"He must be hungry," I said.

"I know."

"Maybe I'll buy him something."

"I don't think you get it. If he eats, he'll never die."

"Listen, Jacques, can I ask you a favor?"

"Who's Jacques?"

"You said I could call you what I liked."

"Yes, but why Jacques?"

"That was the first name that occurred to me."

"Okay, but I'm not French, all right?"

"Yes, I know, Jacques. Why is he being punished? His parents must be looking for him now."

"He has no parents, just a younger brother—four or five years old—who wraps himself around a tree all day and waits for his brother. Their house is at the other end of the beach, and their grandmother looks after them. Their parents are dead."

"Did they die by drumbeat, too?"

"No, malaria."

"What's his name?"

"His brother's?"

"No, his. The one playing the drum."

"I don't know."

"Can he understand us?"

"No."

"What ethnicity is he?"

"I don't know that, either. What is the favor you wanted to ask? Say it and leave. I'm not supposed to talk this much and it is getting late; it'll be dark soon."

"Jacques, what if we escape?"

"Where? Are you crazy?"

"Why? Tell him that the law has changed, that he's free. And let's get out of here."

"Where would we go? That's impossible. He must be punished."

"But nobody will know. I swear, I won't tell anyone."

"No, stop being so stubborn."

"What is this unforgivable crime he has committed that cannot be forgotten?"

The little one's lips trembled; tears flowed, and blood dripped from his hands. It fell drop by drop onto the feathered drum, which did not have a single feather on it.

"What has he done, you ask? Do you want me to tell you? Which side did you come from?"

"From the right side, where the street is."

"So, you've seen the lake?"

"Yes, that pretty lake over there?" I asked.

"Yes."

"With the fence made of wood and thatch?"

"Yes, that's it."

"What about it?"

"What about what? That's the very thing he did."

"What did he do?"

"He set up a border[23] on the lake, and now many of the fish have gathered there and are slowly dying. That is why he is being made to beat this drum."

---

23. The locals prepare traps like this to catch fish.

"But I saw the fish. They were happy. They had gathered in a particular spot and were looking at the sun in awe. And the border only exists near the surface. I'm sure that the bottom is open."

"Are you positive?"

"Yes."

Jacques seemed to believe me. I wasn't lying to him, and I did want to help the little drummer. But it was late and I couldn't wait any longer. I had to get to Cotonou. I said goodbye, after asking him again to release the boy, and I walked out to the street. I came across a motorcycle about five minutes later. There were many such motorcycles around there; they worked as taxis and they called themselves something that translates to "take me quickly." The driver spoke good French and knew a couple of words in English; I asked him to take me to the airport.

We hadn't left Ouidah yet when I saw the red Fiat on the road, on its way back, with the lambs quietly sitting in the back and watching the street.

"So the locals found them and didn't offer a sacrifice," I muttered to myself.

"What?" the driver asked; his metal helmet was so big that it almost covered his whole head.

"I said that the drumbeat seems to have stopped. I can't hear the drum anymore."

"What? I can't understand what you're saying."

"Jacques must have listened to me..."

"I can't hear you. What? I don't understand."

"That little guy has probably found his brother now and has given him a big hug. They're probably happy now."

"I can't hear you," the driver said, stopping the motorcycle. "What are you saying?"

"Nothing. I just said that the drumbeat has stopped. We can keep going now."

The driver laughed, used five fingers to scratch his face, then started the engine again.

"Ah, I was wondering what you meant. Yes, the festival[24] ended a long time ago; it's late now, so the drumbeat has stopped..."

---

24. Ouidah is known as a city of magic and voodoo, and the people there have a unique set of religious beliefs. There are often festivals celebrating these in Ouidah.

DAY 20. NIGERIA
THE MINERS OF LAGOS

"I know that there have never been any miners in Lagos. They're not real; they're characters made up in a story. What would a miner do? There aren't even any mines here. I know that there aren't any; one-hundred percent, it's a lie…"

"I've seen miners, but I don't remember where. I think it was in Sokoto or thereabouts. But they were foreigners, not locals for sure. There was a white cross on their hats, probably the logo of an international organization… I don't know… Ah yes, I remember that they were white, they were from New Zealand, but I don't know what they were doing here."

"Why all the commotion? There are no miners in any of our neighboring countries, so how could there be any here?"

"I don't agree with that. That's like saying that zebus exist only in Madagascar and cannot be found in any of its neighboring countries. I don't agree."

"Our domestic economy is not well developed; that is why there aren't any miners. We have a population growth of 2.5% every year, but our economy only suffers as a result."

"What do you expect? We've got a population of 130 million. We're the biggest nation in the world!"

"Says who? The Chinese are the biggest nation, then come the Indians…"

"We're number three then."

"What about the US, Indonesia, Russia, Brazil? We'd barely make it to number ten."

"That's no small number, either. Where are the doctors?"

"Step aside, you're all crowding too much here. Stop arguing and step aside to open up some space; the doctors will be here soon."

"This is a huge city, but there are no doctors."

"Lagos is a big city. What did you expect? The doctor is only going to show up by the time the patient's dead. Who asked you to go into mining anyway?"

"That's what I'm saying, too. If you were in another occupation, you wouldn't have ended up like this."

"Nothing to do: that's the problem. Who would've thought it—miners in Lagos!"

The siren of an ambulance could be heard, and then the vehicle itself appeared on the scene a couple of minutes later. The people who had gathered spread out and the paramedics secured the two men to stretchers and loaded them into the ambulance.

It was a hot day. I was in Lagos, Nigeria. This was the first place where I had seen so much activity. There were a lot of people, there was plenty of construction going on in the streets, and public transport bustled about. The noise was constant; it blew in from all directions like the wind.

"Where are you taking these people?" I asked one of the paramedics. He didn't hear me because his attention was focused on the victims, who did not look particularly different from the other Nigerians present.

"How did these miners end up in Lagos?" the doctor muttered to himself, as he took off their metal hardhats.

"You didn't answer my question—where are you taking them?"

"To the hospital," another doctor said loudly. He looked like a piece of cotton dipped into a jar of ink.

"Are they dead?" I asked.

"They've been dead a long time."

"What happened?"

"Higher, higher—good, that's enough."

The doctors paid no more attention to my questions. They were surprised, and the cause for their astonishment was not that they were transporting two corpses, but that the dead men were miners.

"You're the one who was here, and you're asking *us*?" the other doctor replied belatedly.

When the ambulance left, I noticed that there were also police cars in the area.

When I approached one of the police officers, he put on a pair of black sunglasses and asked, "Are you a reporter?"

"No. I arrived from Abuja a short while ago. As soon as I arrived here, I saw hundreds of people gathered and I couldn't understand why. They said that the victims were miners."

"There are no miners here."

"But what happened?"

"You're asking me? You were here before me. Instead of knowing the answers, you're asking me. How am I supposed to know? Those people are dead; what can we do to change that? What was supposed to happen, happened. This misfortune has occurred; that's all."

The policeman's words honestly did not strike me as a suitable reaction for someone in his profession. He sounded just like any of the other people who had gathered and—except for the incident itself—had something to say about everything.

"Does it often happen that…"

"That we find miners?"

"No, that people die in the street."

"Not really," he said. He took off his glasses and brought his head forward, revealing two protruding teeth, bent to such an extent that they looked like two pieces of wood that had swollen from humidity. "Come to the station," he said.

I must have seemed suspicious. Perhaps I had asked too many questions. In any case, I ended up at the police station with a policeman standing in front of me with the facial expression of a hippopotamus. There was a mirror behind me and the rooms next to me were separated by glass dividers, such that I could see inside them. It wasn't a very intimidating setting and I was treated with respect by them. This is how I ended up having to provide a statement to the police within the first few hours of my arrival in Nigeria.

"Start from the beginning. Who are you, and where are you from?"

"I'm from Armenia," I said, and I was forced once again to go through my whole biography in detail.

"Now tell us what you saw."

"At eight thirty in the morning, I arrived from Abuja to Lagos, and I set off for the hotel on Maitama Sule Street. I went to my room and left my things there, then I went out for a walk."

"Then what happened?"

"Then I walked into one of the bars on that street and I ordered a drink."

"Do you like drinking?"

"No, but at that moment I felt like trying one of the local drinks. The bartender offered me something that had a strange name, something like *kunun*, but I said no. I was afraid of a bad reaction to it, so I ordered a beer in the end."

"*Kunun* is a good drink. How much did you drink?"

"One bottle. Half a liter."

"Then what?"

"I decided to talk to some of the local people."

"Weren't you afraid of being misunderstood?"

"No, is that a crime? I just wanted to get some information about Nigeria."

"What information?"

"Things that one can't find in books, magazines, or on websites."

"Gossip?"

"No, on the contrary, I don't care about local gossip, especially because I know that any native of any land can complain about their country. What I'm more interested in is your history, and any interesting things that are characteristic of Nigerians only."

"Then what happened?"

"Then, I left the bar and went to Tafawa Balewa Square. The bartender had told me that there are always lots of people there, and it would be a good place to have interesting conversations with some of them."

"Were you drunk?"

"No, I was in a good mood; I felt energized and wanted to talk to people. But I definitely wasn't drunk, I was in full control of myself."

"And then?"

"When I got closer to the square, I heard a noise, something like the sound of a helicopter engine, but it also reminded me of a steam engine locomotive. I looked up and saw a gigantic blimp."

"What?"

"Yes, I saw a large blimp—white with grey stripes, and some letters on it that I couldn't read. It vanished after a few seconds."

"Blimps don't exist anymore; what nonsense is this? Well, there aren't any here, anyway."

"I saw it, I'm telling you what I saw. I'm not lying. The blimp looked like a gigantic rocket."

"And then?" The policeman wiped his sweaty forehead, brought his hands closer to his nose, and sighed heavily. "What happened in the end?"

"When the blimp vanished, I thought for a moment that I had indeed been seeing things, but then I saw the smoke it had emitted and I was convinced that it hadn't been an illusion."

"What kind of a balloon was it? Perhaps it was something else?"

"No. It was a large, passenger-carrying blimp, not one of those hot-air balloons with a basket. This thing was huge, it could probably hold fifty people."

"But blimps don't emit smoke, from what I understand."

"I don't know about that, really; all I'm saying is what happened. Perhaps it wasn't smoke, maybe it was something else. But there was something in the air."

"Then what happened?" the policeman asked with a sigh.

"When I tried to run away, a woman stood in my way."

"Why did you want to run away?"

"I was surprised by this at the time, too; I ran to clear my head. When I saw the woman, my knees weakened and I started to tremble. Then my whole body started to convulse."

"Why?"

"The woman looked very scary, like a wicked witch from some children's story. She had a stick in her hand. She asked me to hold the stick for a few minutes. It was a very strange request; she could have leaned the stick against a wall somewhere, or put it on the ground."

"Perhaps it was valuable?"

"Hardly likely, the woman didn't look like she was rich. She entered a shop, or rather, a closed space of some kind, that looked like a small cellar. Sounds of animals could be heard from inside."

"What animals?"

"I don't I know, I can't say. A goat or a sheep or a cow... I don't know."

"Why didn't you go in?"

"Why would I have gone in? The woman asked me to hold on to her stick for a few minutes. She came out quickly and had an iron cup in her hand. She said that she'd milked it for me, and I said thank you, but I didn't take the cup. Then she said something that is still ringing in my head."

"What did she say?"

"She said that it was bull's milk, and that there was no better milk in the world."

"Bull's milk?"

"Yes, bull's milk! I thought I had misunderstood, but she insisted that her bull gives milk."

"She lied."

"No, she didn't. I thought so, too, at first. But when I went into the cellar, I was convinced that that bull could indeed be milked."

"What? A bull? How would one milk a bull?" he stuttered.

"Yes, I'm telling you what I saw with my own eyes. They were milking the bull, and the bull was bellowing so loudly that cracks appeared in the walls."

"Impossible! First a blimp, then a milk-giving bull... you're talking ridiculous nonsense. I've been a policeman for thirty years; I have a lot of experience, but I've never heard such things in my life. You've only been here for an hour and already you've turned Lagos upside down."

"What have *I* done?"

"Can anyone bear witness to your account?"

"I don't know. That woman perhaps, but she left after I didn't take the milk; she mumbled to herself and left."

"But the bull is still there, right?"

"I guess it's still there."

"Fine, we'll check that out later. Continue."

"The sun was burning down and I had covered my head with a kerchief. There was noise everywhere. I haven't seen such a populous city in Africa yet. I finally got to the place that the bartender had recommended."

"Tawafa Balewa Square," the policeman said.

"Yes. And I saw that there were indeed lots of people there. Dozens or hundreds of people had gathered."

"What had happened? That many people never gather there. Yes, the bartender's right, a lot of people can be seen there, but never that many. You're exaggerating. You haven't done anything wrong, but you're saying impossible things."

"Should I go on?"

"Yes."

"I could hear the various things people were saying, from a distance."

"What were they saying?"

"I don't know, different things. They were all surprised and everyone was saying something, but I only heard whispers and fragmented bits of speech. I stood a slight distance away from the crowd and had the impression that something was happening at the center of the spot where they had gathered. And, indeed, based on what they were saying, something *had* happened."

"But you didn't mention *what* they'd been saying."

"They were saying that Nigeria is a huge country with a large population. They mentioned zebus or some such thing."

"It's a kind of animal."

"They were making various comparisons. They were discussing the country's economy and said some other things."

"Why had they gathered there?"

"When I came closer, I saw in the center two Black men who had fallen. They lay still, but it seemed to me that they were still alive. Everybody was watching, as if it were a street performance. But nobody tried to help them; everyone was waiting for the ambulance. I wanted to do something, but I didn't know what. The two people who lay on the ground weren't moving, and they had metal helmets on their heads."

"What else?"

"Nothing. That's all. A crowd, two corpses, and me."

"Why wasn't anybody helping them?"

"I don't know. I shouted, 'This is a huge city, but there are no doctors,' and someone replied at that moment, 'Lagos is a big city. What did you expect? The doctor is only going to show up by the time the patient's dead.' And then he added to himself, 'Who asked you to go into mining anyway?'"

"To go into what?"

"Mining. The crowd said several times that the victims were miners. Everyone seemed surprised at that idea, even the paramedics. When they were loading the corpses into the ambulance, they were talking in amazement about how these miners could have ended up there. It was as if they had fallen from the sky."

"There are no miners in Lagos. Even if there were, how did they know that the dead men were miners?"

"I don't know; I honestly don't. I was surprised, too."

"Then what happened?"

"Then, when they took the corpses away, the crowd broke up, and I saw one of your fellow officers; I walked up to him and he brought me here. All I wanted was to know why those people had been so surprised and how they had come to the conclusion that the deceased had been miners."

"Why not? You were the one who told us about the blimp, the milk-giving bull and the old woman, and now about the miners. All of this is nonsense. It's impossible. I've been an inspector for forty years; I've seen many things in my time, many improbable things, but you've said so much in one hour that I'm at a loss. Go, go on, get out of here... You can leave, the questioning is over. Goodbye."

The inspector called his assistant and the latter showed me to the door. I left the police station. I felt relieved in a way, as if a heavy burden had been lifted off me. I didn't understand what was going on, what they had wanted from me, why they had brought me to the station, or what I'd done.

My head ached. I wanted to quickly get back to my hotel, Bogobiri. I wanted to pack my things, take a final stroll outside, and head for Niger. The street was full of people. After standing around for a few minutes, an *okada*[25] came up. The driver first spoke in a language I didn't understand, then he switched to English.

"Where are you going?"

"Maitama Sule 9, Bogobiri Hotel."

"All right. Put on this helmet," he said, giving me a metal helmet and starting the motorcycle's engine.

We were going quickly towards the hotel and the wind blew in my face. I held the driver's body tightly. His metal helmet was right in front of me, moving slowly in the wind. It seemed very familiar to me, but I couldn't remember where I'd seen it before...

---

25. An *okada* is a mode of transport in Nigeria, a motorcycle-taxi meant for short distances. *Okadas* are driven carelessly and at great speed. There are often many road accidents involving okadas because the drivers are under the influence of alcohol. That is why taking an okada is considered very risky, even if the driver has a metal helmet.

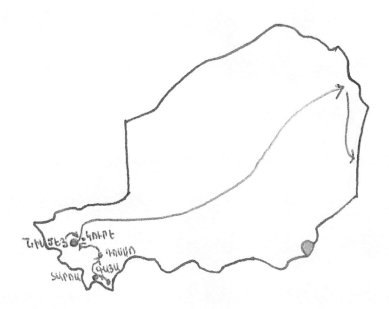

DAY 21. NIGER
TEARS OF THE GIRAFFE

I circumvented Gaya, Tahoua, and Dosso as I made my way to Niamey, the capital of Niger. It was hot inside the car, as it was outside, and there was nothing left to drink. It's true that there was a slight breeze thanks to the half-open window, but it didn't have a cooling effect; it burned like fire, scorching my arms.

"Do we still have a long way to go before we get there?" I asked the driver, whom I'd met in Nigeria. He would use his small car, a six-seater, to take tourists from Nigeria to Niger. When I'd first heard the driver's name, I thought he had a speech disorder; and indeed, a name like Akonkgnawu is very hard to pronounce. And that wasn't the end of it. He presented his full name as Benedictus Akonkgnawu Ikpeba. There was nobody in the car except me, but I had to pay for five passengers. Otherwise, I would have had to wait for hours until the right number of passengers had turned up.

"This is Niger, there is little time here."

"I don't understand."

"I mean that anything can happen here; you have to be ready for the worst."

"Like what, for example?"

"I don't want to scare you, but sometimes these ten hours, on the Nigeria to Niger route, can take three times as long."

"But we're getting closer to Niamey, aren't we? We should be there soon."

"Yes, we should be there in another two or three hours, but who knows…I can't say," Benedictus said indifferently.

"That's okay, I'm in no hurry. In any case, there's no way I'm going to see the whole of Niger. Whenever we get there is fine, as long as we get there."

"Yes, of course. It's only one in a thousand cases that there are attacks on the way, or that we come across wild animals, or something like that. Things are calmer now, anyway. It used to be more dangerous, especially at the northern border."

"On the Algerian side?"

"Yes. But incidents can happen anywhere."

I didn't want to believe what he was saying. I was interested in knowing what could possibly go wrong in this boundlessly barren terrain. The sun also seemed fatigued, and everything around me was very quiet and monotonous. Even the sand flowing from the curb which, coming into contact with Benedictus' wheels, rolled away with such indifference that it made you lose the desire to think about anything.

"Are you tired?" he asked.

"Yes, it's hot. I wasn't expecting this."

"You haven't seen hot yet. If we take the right road, we'll get to the city quickly. If we don't, we're going to be thirsty for a long time to come."

"I don't understand," I said. It was as if the two of us were speaking different forms of English. "Don't you know the way?"

"I do, but there's a small section here which is dangerous in this season, so we have to go around it. And I've never been on that road."

"You've never taken tourists in this season?"

"I have, but the danger is much greater this year."

"Why?"

"The giraffes. There are so many of them, that…"

"They're herbivores; what danger could they pose?" I interrupted.

"You can't imagine what I mean. This isn't one of those nature shows that you see on TV. The giraffes here are very dangerous. You're right, they're herbivores, but they're huge animals, and if fifteen giraffes block the road at once, there's no way to get through them."

It was obvious that Benedictus was mostly concerned about his worn-out car. I had been unable to figure out its make or model, despite the Bentley logo that adorned the windshield. Benedictus drove the car slowly, trying to cross each pothole and section of rough road with the utmost care.

"Are you worried about your car?" I asked, though I knew the answer.

"Yes. You can picture it, right? Giraffes are huge creatures. Even if they end up in front of the car by chance, we're done for."

"What kind of car is this?"

"A Bentley."

It was impossible. His car couldn't be a Bentley, especially because, despite the logo, none of it looked like a car of that make—the side windows would not go up all the way, and there was no air conditioner or any of the sophisticated systems that cars have nowadays. I was sure that he'd found a sticker with the logo somewhere, and he'd just stuck it on the car.

"It looks more like an old car that has been around for a long time, with no new models being manufactured anymore," I said.

"Yeah, it's old, but it's a Bentley. That's why I don't want to end up having to face any giraffes. You get it, right?"

He had said the same thing for the third or fourth time already. What was there to get? I didn't know, but I was forced to agree with his statements.

According to Benedictus, we had gone around a large section of road. He sang on several occasions, stopped the car, cooled the engine, and bought food from a roadside stand along the way, until we reached a strange place where he said, "I don't understand. We're going around in circles. We're lost."

I felt frightened at that moment. I believed him, and I thought that we wouldn't be able to find our way on that convoluted road anymore.

"What are you trying to say?" I asked.

"I don't know where we are; nothing looks familiar to me here. We've taken a wrong turn somewhere. Wait a bit; I need to think."

Benedictus knew well that if he delayed things any more, he would be forced to return the money I had paid him. He was ready to do anything at that moment to avoid hearing me say those dreadful words.

"What are we going to do?"

"Don't be afraid; we'll do everything necessary."

To be honest, the situation wouldn't have scared me if I had been certain that we were in a safe place. I wasn't in a position where I had to remember the names of places, know any addresses, or ask any names…I was sitting comfortably in Benedictus' desperate old "Bentley" and waiting for giraffes to appear. The only question that bothered me was: how safe was the area in which we'd ended up?

"Does it rain here?" I asked.

"I don't know, everything happens here; don't you worry, we'll figure something out," he said again.

Benedictus had stepped out of the car and was using his foot to clean off a bit of mud that had stuck to a tire.

"Does it snow here, too?"

"I don't know about that. But we'll do everything necessary; don't worry."

He referred to himself in the plural, obviously trying to encourage himself in this way. It was as if he knew that there was nothing he could do, but the expression "we'll do everything" inspired confidence in him.

Benedictus had not yet suspected that he had become my protagonist. He was still worried about the money I had given him, but he didn't know that I couldn't care less about the money at that point. I was gradually turning him into a literary character. Within a space of ten minutes, I had taken note of his facial features—he had brown eyes, in which his Bentley's tires seemed to keep spinning. His eyelashes were sharp and his eyelids were quite broad. His hair was slightly braided, as if braided by the wind; his nose was broad and flat, and he bore a slight resemblance to Java, whom I had met in Togo. Benedictus also had a blue earring in his right ear. I didn't know the name of the stone in it, but that earring added a certain charm to his face. His neck was thick, with broad veins that would tense and rise each time he swallowed. He had on a green coat, although it was not cold; it was probably an item that was just as dear to him as his car.

Benedictus had probably never smoked, but he took a puff from a cigarette in my presence and nearly choked. I couldn't understand what he was scared of the most—that I would take the money back, or that giraffes would attack his Bentley. Those two situations were probably causing him equal distress.

"Come back inside the car," I said. "Let's sit and think together."

"No, thanks. I like thinking on my own. There isn't much to think about; I want to wait until it gets dark so that we can continue our trip."

"Why? It's easier to get lost in the dark."

"We won't get lost. I already know the way we should go. We just need to wait till it gets dark, so that it's safe, so that the giraffes don't attack."

Benedictus must have been around thirty, and I couldn't say that he lacked life experience, but he looked out into the desert with such naïveté, that I, too, felt for a moment like a herd of giraffes would soon attack and devour the two of us.

The air was thick and there was no wind; my only hope was the half-open car window, stuck in its current position such that I couldn't lower it any further. I could have gotten out of the car, of course, but that wouldn't have changed anything. I was like a piece of fruit that had been overdried, left out in the sun for so long that it had stuck to the surface beneath it and if you plucked it up, a piece of it would unavoidably be left behind.

"What kind of a name is Benedictus?"

"I don't know; I'm no scientist. We've got names that nobody's ever heard of anywhere in the world, even back in the times of the Renaissance."

"I've heard your name, but I just don't remember where. What do you know about the Renaissance?"

"Nothing, I've just heard about it. I like art, and from what I know there were some good painters, sculptors, and thinkers during that time."

"Which artist's works do you like?" I asked, realizing how artificial the query sounded, like I was a teacher questioning him.

"I don't know, nobody specific; I don't remember. But I've heard that there were some big names. If they had cars back then, I can only imagine how grand the designs would be."

Both of us looked at his car at that moment—I looked from the inside, he from the outside.

"I've always loved drawing," Benedictus continued. "I used to draw quite well back in the day. It's too bad I didn't end up becoming an artist."

"You Nigerian?" I asked more informally.

"No. I mean, I live in Nigeria, in Abuja, and I have a family there. But I'm from Niger by birth; I'm a Jerma."

"So you probably know Niger well."

"I didn't live here long; I was six years old when my parents moved us to Abuja. Niger is so big that even if you lived here for a hundred years, you wouldn't know it well. But, as a driver, I know the roads well," he said, coughing.

Our glances fell upon each other once again at that moment.

"You've never smoked before?"

"I have. But you can't smoke the same way in this heat; the smoke grabs you by the throat—you can't swallow it, nor can you exhale it. You can't do anything in this heat."

"I caught cold on a hot day once. I remember I felt so bad that I had to be carried on a stretcher."

"Where?"

"From Morocco to Mauritania."

"But it's hot there; how had you managed to catch cold?"

"I don't know; it was winter."

I was just rambling. My body felt weak and I couldn't feel anything, not even the seat on which I was sitting.

Suddenly, I began to hate Benedictus. I don't know why, perhaps the only explanation was that he had put me in an extremely uninteresting situation. My hatred for him continued to increase, and the sun's rays burned the windshield so hard that I could see Benedictus reflected in it. I was forced to bear the presence of two Benedictuses. That made me even angrier. He smoked in the real world but, in the reflection, I couldn't see his hands. That was good in the sense that the smoke from the cigarette held by one of them did not bother me. I don't know why we had gone quiet; we had both probably realized that we had run out of things to say. I wanted to get up and flee, but there was the risk that I would get lost even further and would end up unable to leave Niger for days.

A bug of some sort kept buzzing around, also seemingly disappointed. I didn't know where it was, I just kept hearing it buzz, but at that moment I felt a strong desire to talk to the bug.

Besides the sun, the bug, two strange trees in the distance, and us, there was nothing else in that place.

"I guess we should get moving," Benedictus said after a long silence.

I saw him disappear from inside the windshield and then sit behind the wheel. It wasn't dark, but I supposed that he, too, had realized that it was impossible to keep staying in that place. We left.

I left my hate in the windshield, where Benedictus' doppelganger remained, who was honestly more attractive than the one sitting at the wheel. We sped along at about a hundred kilometers per hour. The road wasn't bad and there were few turns, and the twittering of long-beaked birds that I didn't recognize had a calming effect on me.

I was so tired that it seemed like I hadn't slept for twenty-one days. I fell asleep.

∞⌘

I was in Kouré, a small city about fifty kilometers to the southeast of Niamey. They say that there are many giraffes there, especially in the fall. It was summer now, but I managed to see a few of them. They were very far away, unfortunately, so I didn't get to see them close up. Kouré was the small city where we had gotten lost, where Benedictus had stopped for hours and frightened me. I didn't know that Niger was so beautiful, especially its suburbs and small towns. They say that Niger is one of the most backward countries in the world, and the Nigeriens—the Hausa, Jerma, Sonrai, Fula, Tuareg, and the other ethnic groups—are the most backward and illiterate. I don't believe it.

I never got to Niamey. I didn't see the two-star Rivoli hotel on Luebke Avenue, I didn't get to Agadez, which has a grand mosque resembling the one I saw in Timbuktu. I never got to see the mosque in Niamey either, the one which has one tall minaret and three domes—one large, the other two small, with a prayer room beneath each of them.

The giraffe slowly licked my face and…I woke up.

∞⌘

"What happened?" Benedictus asked.

It was nighttime. The lights were on in one or two places along the street.

"Huh?" I said, jumping. "Nothing. It was a dream. I was talking in my sleep."

"What are you saying?"

"Where are we? Have I been sleeping long?"

"Who's been sleeping? You?"

"Yes. Have I been sleeping long?"

"You haven't slept. We were looking at the giraffes together. There weren't many of them, just a few in the distance, but we did see them."

"Stop the car, I want to walk."

We stopped. I walked a bit. Then we drove on.

"So, you say you fell asleep?" Benedictus asked.

"Yes."

"So, who was I talking to for the past two or three hours?"

"Have I been sleeping that long?"

"You haven't been sleeping, I tell you. We watched the giraffes in Kouré, then we arrived in Niamey, saw the mosque, and you kept describing them."

"Where are we now?"

"Niamey."

"Where are we going?"

"I don't know. I've been asking you for an hour, but you keep saying that the giraffe is licking your face. I don't understand; perhaps you've suffered from sunstroke."

"I never saw Niamey."

"Says who?"

"I didn't see it. I only remember the giraffes."

"We're doing the rounds of Niamey for the third time. What else did you want to see? I've done my job; I have to get back to Abuja now. Where should I drop you off?"

Benedictus spoke with confidence. I wanted to believe him, but I suspected that he had seen my dream—or rather, the other Benedictus had seen it, the one who had remained in the windshield back in Kouré. There was another problem. The dream I'd had was like a thought—poor in imagery and action.

There was nothing left for me to do but to say goodbye to him.

I moved on to Chad, never having seen Niamey.

৪৩

"Niger is a state that consists of large villages and small towns. There is a place here where one always gets lost. You think you see something, but it is actually a dream; if you're not alone, the person who is with you sees the same dream as you.

"It is a dream of giraffes who miss you and shed tears from time to time. I had never seen their tears before; each was like a small dream…

"We forget that we are often surrounded, and among those who surround us there are also our doppelgangers, who appear in the rays of the sun, in anything that shines…"
— Dhodom Agoshe, *Tears of the Giraffe*

DAY 22. CHAD
THE DEAD HEART OF AFRICA[26]

The main cause of my problems is probably the fact that I give life much more importance than necessary. Had I not been that way, that is to say, had I entered Chad, roamed around and left, my trip probably would have made much more sense.

Everything started from the moment when a tree was uprooted and fell across my path. The tree had calculated its trajectory such that it fell right in front of my feet; I was actually quite lucky. The collapse of that tree was so silent and stealthy that I wouldn't have noticed it, if not for the particles of dust that settled on my body. The sun rocked itself in the sky once more, but had no thoughts about setting. The heat pursued me.

It had probably once been a fruit-bearing tree, then perhaps it had dried and rotted. My eyes sought out its swaying shadow, which was slowly moving back and forth in the sand heated by the sun. It wasn't a large tree, maybe about six meters high. They say that a fallen tree is a bad sign, and I even recalled the words of the *Hogon*, who had mentioned one in his narrations.

I don't know, perhaps all of this was symbolic of something, but at that moment I decided to not pay any attention to it and continue my journey. I was in Chad and I was

---

26. Because of its dry, desert-like climate and its distance from the sea, Chad is often called the "dead heart of Africa."

moving towards N'Djamena, the capital. Actually, I had just crossed the border and although I kept trying not to pay too much attention to anything, I was failing. Just looking at the horizon was enough for me to understand how far I had to walk; I couldn't see anything in the distance, and dust particles kept flowing over me like waves in the sea. There was nothing, not even a large rock, a building, a cactus, or an animal, nothing except for the fallen tree, which I had circumvented. Nothing else could be seen in the distance and it was impossible to determine the direction in which I was supposed to walk.

According to the map I had, I was not too far from the city of Massakory. All I needed to do was choose the right direction to go in. It was Day 22 of my stay in Africa. I had changed, my thinking wasn't the same as before; I had experienced many things first hand. I had lived a whole separate life over these days, a lifetime of twenty years. Perhaps this was nothing unusual for an "African"—though probably not all of them—but I myself couldn't stand it. There had been too many tragedies. I tried to close my eyes to them, to give no importance to them. I tried to speak of only good things, pretty things, because bad things can be found anywhere.

I had become an alien, mostly to myself. It was as if I had split in two—my right side had separated from my left—and although they had not become enemies, my left side—which thought independently—kept getting more emotional despite myself; perhaps the reason was that my heart had remained on my left side. I considered myself to be on my right side, so I ignored my left, but I wanted to gradually free myself entirely from my body and become a ghost. Seeing all of the chaos of this "African game-playing" had left me dizzy.

And it was no coincidence that I saw an old woman in the vicinity of Massakory who thought that I was lame. She approached me and held my left hand, and we walked slowly for about ten minutes. Then she looked into my eyes for a long time; she wanted to take out her heart at that moment and hand it to me, but I couldn't take it—it would have been too precious a gift for me. It wasn't easy for me to walk with one eye, one arm and one leg; I suddenly realized that I had lost my left half when the tree had fallen.

I was in Massakory, a small town a hundred and sixty kilometers to the north of N'Djamena, and the capital of the Hadjer-Lamis region, located near Lake Chad. I had initially planned to go to the capital, but ended up staying longer in Massakory than I thought I would. This city was well known as the source of most cholera epidemics, especially in the rainy season.

By some strange coincidence, I met a woman in Massakory who resembled that other woman, but was younger. How she had ended up there, I don't know, but she was following me. I found it difficult to figure out why, at that point, but the woman's expression was very sad. She was like a newborn foal; her whole body was covered in black cloth with only her face revealed. I had no idea what her ethnicity might be. She linked her arm through mine and pushed people aside as we walked. I was afraid for a minute and even wanted to run away, but then I remembered that I had "lost" half my body. We walked in silence for around twenty minutes. I didn't like the scenery around me and wanted to break free from her, but she held me so tightly to her hip that I was helpless.

We walked on a sand path and there was nothing around us except for one or two houses with thatched roofs, some camels, a scorching sun, and the sky. We walked very slowly, and the whole thing seemed quite artificial to me, like a scene from a badly staged play. On the other hand, it was very interesting; I was walking like a lost man, a strange Black person was beside me and we were quiet—it was true that I had asked one or two questions in English, but there had been no response; it was as if she were mute. Her hands shivered at one point, and she embraced me and began to cry, her tears quickly flowing down the black cloth and drenching the yellow sand. Then she let me go and fell down on her knees before me, and bowed. Despite myself, I felt the need to encourage her, so I fell down on my knees as well, and embraced her. I had never hugged an African before. I felt her thin bones at once. I wanted to lift her up, but she kept crying. Then she began to rub sand on my legs. For close to two minutes, she poured sand on my feet. I think this was supposed to mean something.[27] Then she rubbed some sand on my pants. At one point, I thought she was insane.

Her hands trembled, her body did so, too, and I was also forced to hear her song. I didn't know what she was singing, but she sang like crazy, and I noticed that every single part of her trembled. The melody reminded me of the sound of water when a large rock is thrown into it.

Now I was the one pushing her forward, dragging her along; her legs had gotten entangled, and she could only use her hands to indicate where we had to go. I couldn't have left her there, although it was probably not an unfamiliar place for her. It was different from the other places I had been to; I had never seen a place so dry and yellow. It was as if the desert was the hump of a gigantic camel.

"Where should I take you, where do you live?"

"Ah, ah."

"Why were you following me in this desert?" I asked. It wasn't really a large desert; people could cross it on foot, if they had enough food and water and knew the right way to go.

"Ah, ah."

"What are you saying? I don't understand. Whatever you say, I'm not going to be able to understand it. There's probably nobody else here except for us. Who are you, what is your ethnicity?"

"Ah."

---

27. The locals (I never did manage to find out what their ethnicity was) try to seduce people in this way. In other words, it is a symbolic gesture that seems to suggest that the person whose legs are being enveloped in yellow sand will live the rest of his life covered with gold. The more they do this, the greater their desire.

The woman was actually moaning, but I kept thinking that "ah" meant something. It was only when I grew tired of dragging her along that I understood that it had been an expression of exhaustion on her part as well.

It started to rain. This was unexpected, but I had been wanting it to happen for so long. It was a hot rain, the drops were large and round, as if cherries were falling from the sky. The rain grew heavier and the yellow sand turned gray instantly; the small stones—remnants of inexplicable origin—began to shimmer. The sky had emptied. The woman began to scream again and her tears mixed with the rainwater. The black cloth she wore clung to her, revealing her lean body.

I felt her fear grow with the coming of the rain. Now, she was the one pushing me. It was only then that I understood that she was in a hurry to get somewhere, and she wanted me to come with her.

The two of us were running—she would overtake me, and then I would pass ahead of her. She looked like a young person from a distance but, in reality, she was about thirty or thirty-five years old. We were both barefoot. She probably knew why she was running, but I didn't, and that made me happier. I had not run so energetically before, nor had I experienced Africa in this way yet. The rain was probably to blame for this; its drops were striking me with such force that they seemed to double my speed.

We had probably run a couple of miles when I saw the city in the distance. At that moment, I thought we had arrived at N'Djamena but, of course, it was still Massakory—the residential part of the town, with small buildings.

The city welcomed me with a beautiful sunset. The yellow sun descended in a red sky hanging over black sand, and there were one or two clouds above, hiding in semi-darkness. Then I saw a hole with a person inside, sitting in a clay pot. When I greeted him, he looked at me and threw a stone. This man should have a book written about him as the main hero, but I had no time; the woman was waiting for me. When we entered the city, the first thing I noticed was that I was the center of everyone's attention. They were all looking at me, but this was natural since I stood out as a white person. The woman was pushing me, urging me forward. We ran through the uneven roads of the city and along its muddy sidewalks, and I didn't see a single tree. It was dark, though, so perhaps there had been some trees.

The rain kept getting heavier and had been coming down for about twenty minutes nonstop. Along the way, I saw someone pushing a carriage filled with hand-made clay boats. The boats looked like worn-out slippers. I didn't see any cars; it was as if the city was sleeping, or full of sleepwalkers or ghosts. Looking at people's hands, the only feeling I had was one of compassion.

It was as if everyone was sick, and I even thought I saw some corpses on stretchers.

The woman screamed again, as if trying to get my attention. We walked through the narrow streets of Massakory to a hut. She took me inside. It was humid and wet everywhere. Water leaked through the roof and onto the sand on the floor. There were several metal plates inside which I immediately noticed because of their large size. The hut had two more rooms and there was a narrow corridor between them, with a curtain hanging at the end of it. I wanted to see what the other two rooms held. But the woman grabbed my hand, washed it in a large bowl that held rainwater, and then held my hands against her chest. At that moment, I once again felt that it was very difficult to understand these Africans. The woman became emotional again and fell to her knees, then in this position dragged me into the other room that I had wanted so badly to see. I found it difficult to speak, as if shrimps had gathered in my throat and were forcibly holding my tongue and my lips shut from the inside.

What I saw in the room stupefied me to the extent that tears flowed from my eyes instantly and I held my head in my hands as I walked out. The woman ran out after me and tried to bring me back in, but I did not dare reenter that room. She fell to her knees again and poured more sand from the ground onto my feet, but I breathlessly fled as far away as possible from her, from her hut, and from Massakory in general. I ran as quickly as I could; I wanted to escape that nightmare which pursued me like a ghost. Strangely enough, I had imagined Massakory to be completely different, and perhaps I needed to come here another time to see it in another way, to not meet that woman, to not circumvent the tree,[28] and to not enter that woman's hut.[29] I would have probably seen a happier town if that had been the case.

---

28. I only found out about the tree later. In reality, the tree itself had not been in Chad, but in northeastern Niger. I had probably thought at the time that I was already in Chad, but I had really been in Niger. It was the Tree of Ténéré, which had once been located in the region that bore the same name and was considered the loneliest tree in the world, with no other trees for more than 400 km. Strangely enough, it turned out that a Libyan truck driver had driven past the tree in a drunken state in 1973 and knocked it to the ground. There is a story that whoever passes by the spot where the lonely tree once stood would see its ghost. And someone would die in the city at the same time.
The tree was moved to Niamey, to the Niger National Museum.

29. The hut was a regular one, there was nothing special about its shape. But inside the room, there had been the woman's child. His body had turned yellow and was covered all over with bruises. His ribs stuck out like small bridges rolling over before reaching the pit that was his abdomen. His head was swollen (or it may have seemed that way to me because he was so thin) and dozens of flies had gathered around his eyes. He could barely move his legs. Next to the child was the old woman I had seen in the vicinity of Massakory. She held compresses in her hand. She kept putting the compresses to the child's forehead, and the latter kept coughing.
Perhaps the woman had taken me for someone else, thinking that I could heal her child.

DAY 23. CAMEROON
LES TÊTES BRÛLÉES

I had initially planned to continue my journey to Sudan but this proved impossible, as all of the borders between Chad and Sudan were closed; so I left for Cameroon to the southwest. I went first to Yaoundé, and then to Douala.

Douala was quite a pretty city and did not resemble most other African towns. It isn't the capital of Cameroon, but I was sure that its beauty was not inferior. Douala got its name from the local people, most of them being from the Douala tribe.

I didn't plan on spending the night there; I was supposed to leave the city as soon as darkness fell. I quickly walked out in the streets of Douala and tried to see as much as I could, but none of it stuck with me. The people of Douala looked at me with strange smiles and I felt like one of them might approach me and ask, "What are you doing here? Are you looking for something?" That made me uncomfortable, of course.

Douala is a big city, the largest in Cameroon. It is also a port and you can see the sea for at least one or two kilometers into the distance. I was in the center of Douala and a three- or four-story bright yellow building stood in front of me, shining like the sun in the distance. The windows of the building were blue. I was unsure of whether or not it was a residential building, but it looked nice. I stood near a shop on the opposite side of the intersection where that building was located and I followed the light from the sun as it gradually swept over the building. Within ten minutes, the sun had set and the city was now being illuminated by that yellow building.

The semi-dark city immediately quieted. The sidewalks emptied, many of the shops closed, and the number of cars decreased. I watched the city as it gradually slipped into slumber; it was as if Douala was yawning. In that perfect silence, a song emerged, coming from the next street. The lyrics were in English and I thought that it must be a homeless person who had gotten drunk and was singing at the top of their voice, but the melody was actually quite pleasant. I ran towards this "singing street." At the corner of the street, beneath a gray building, a man had curled up. He had long hair and when he saw me, he raised his voice.

"People are so greedy, they aren't satisfied even after death. They keep wanting and wanting more. They emerge from beneath the soil and kill each other all over again to their heart's content, after which they go back underground. Hey, dead people, you're all very greedy…"

When I came closer, he went silent, then took a few sips from the bottle he held in his hand, which probably had beer in it, and then he looked at me. He coughed, came closer, and held the bottle out.

"What is it?" I asked.

"Mützig. Good beer," he said in English. "It's Guinean, or German actually, but made in Guinea. Take it and drink."

"No, thanks. I meant the song. What is the song you were singing?"

"It's just a regular song, but a very good one. *Les Têtes Brûlées*."

"What's that?"

"You've never heard of them?"

"No."

"Strange. You've *never* heard of them?"

"No, I'm telling you."

"That's very strange."

He turned away, poured the Mützig down his throat, and then came closer with a cough.

"Do you have a cigarette?"

"No, I don't smoke. Smoking is bad for you."

"Don't preach to me, now. Smoking is better for you than Mützig," he said as he swung the bottle into the air. A few seconds later, the sound of shattering glass could be heard. "So you say you don't know *Les Têtes Brûlées*?"

"No."

"That's strange."

He got down on his knees, looked up to the moon and sang, almost screaming, in a raspy voice, "Here I am, almost dead, greedy people. You, who sleep in your graves like worms, get up and devour each other, show everyone how people like you swarm everywhere, I'm not afraid of you…"

His song slowly turned into a scream; he had lost control over himself, his vocal cords were strained, and he barely moved. Although he was drunk and this long-haired, yellow-eyed Black man looked disgusting and repulsive, I had to confess that he was saying very interesting things. He didn't look like a regular homeless person who would think like a leech about where to cling to next in order to get drunk. Perhaps, back home, I wouldn't have come any closer to him. But here, in Douala, he looked like he was in harmony with the semi-dark streets and the vehicles that passed through every once in a while. Besides feeling compassion, I wanted to understand him, and I felt sure that the lyrics of his song were not just any old words put together.

"Do you want me to take you home?" I asked.

"I don't have a home. Do you want to visit me? Be my guest?"

"I don't understand. If you don't have a home, how can you host me?"

"Can you clap?"

"Why?"

"Clap and I'll tell you. Louder, louder, yes, that's good, now keep clapping with the same rhythm. 'Hey you, greedy people, who are in the sky, you've been rotting there for so long you've begun to stink, see how they clap for me, someone still needs me, see how loudly they clap, do you hear? Someone is still interested in me…'"

He began to cough again and collapsed to the ground. I approach to help him up, but he resisted.

"You keep clapping, I like that better. I'll get myself up."

I continued to clap, seeing that he really enjoyed it and had even become emotional.

"Yes, this is my home. You wanted to come over? The louder you clap, the sooner you'll enter my house. That's it, lose yourself; too bad we've run out of Mützig. Clap, yes, yes. 'Hey you, miserable people, those who've fallen asleep long ago. You, who are rolling about heavily underground. Come out and see the performance I am giving.' Will you buy me a Mützig?"

"From where? It's already past ten o'clock."

"There's a little stand at the corner of the next street. Tell Mark to give you two bottles; tell him that Jean-Marie sent you. Tell him to put it on my tab, I'll pay for it later. Go and come back quickly. I'm waiting."

I left. I didn't have to go, of course. But Jean-Marie was a very interesting person and he spoke very well. When I approached the stand, which had a large advertisement for Coca-Cola on its front window, I thought for a second that I had come to the wrong place, but the curly-haired vendor had already greeted me and asked, "What would you like?"

"Are you Mark?"

"Yes. I speak good English and I know French, too. What do you need?"

"Two bottles of beer."

"Which one?"

"Mützig."

"500 francs."

"Do you know Jean-Marie?"

"That crazy guy?"

"Yes, that vagabond."

"Yeah, I know him. Did he send you?"

"Yes."

"Did he ask for this to be put on his tab?"

"Yes."

"I'm not giving you the beer," he said rudely. "That madman doesn't have a tab. Are you a crazy friend of his?"

"No, no, I mean, I'm his friend, but I'm not crazy. I'll pay for the beers, don't worry about it."

"That drifter has become a huge problem for all of us. Every day, we sit and wait for him to die, so that we're rid of him. Every night, he loses control and drags himself through the streets, singing foolish songs."

"And you want him to die for that?"

"No, but he isn't a good guy, besides all that. He's an idiot. Or rather, he's a bit immature. We didn't know him before. Some people say that he was forty years old the moment he was born. He isn't a local; he's from Cameroon and he speaks good English."

"Thank you, good night," I said. I picked up the beer and left the stand quickly.

"Good night. If you see him, ask him when the departed spirits are going to come pick him up."

I left for the next street. Jean-Marie was lying on the ground and I thought that he wasn't breathing. When I squeezed his shoulder, he jumped up.

"You're here? I'd fallen asleep. You know what I saw in my dream?"

"What?"

"Me and you. We were in London. Sorry, I forgot to introduce myself. Jean-Marie Ahanda. Did you bring it?"

"Yes, here you go."

"Did you get it from Mark?"

"Yes."

"Was he alone?"

"Yes."

"Did you tell him to put it on my tab?"

"Yes."

"Mark is a good man. He has a good heart. We've been friends for a hundred years. He really respects me. Drink up. Why are you looking at me like that? Drink up, this is good beer. Don't you drink?'

"No, I don't want any. I'm going to travel tonight."

"Where are you going?"

"Malabo."

"By ship?"

"Yes."

Jean-Marie looked towards the sea with a dreamy stare.

"Have you ever been on a ship?" he asked.

"Yes, but a small one. A boat, really."

"No, a ship is something else. Travelling by ship is a completely different experience."

"Have you been on one?"

"I've travelled the whole world by ship."

"To be honest, I could tell that you know a lot about the world. What was your profession? I mean, what do you do?"

"I'm a louse. A louse born in someone's hair. I don't want to talk; I want to sing. When I sing, I feel lighter, I become happy. Do you know what distinguishes the fool from the smart man?"

"What?"

"The fool knows he's a fool, whether or not he drinks, but the only time a smart man will confess this is when he drinks. So they're both idiots in the end. But I'm no idiot; I'm a philosopher."

"And I'm a writer; I'm writing about Africa. You know what? I love Africa and, this might sound a bit self-assuming, Africa has become home to me; I don't even want to leave anymore."

"What's the point of writing? Who needs that, who's going to remember you, who needs you? In the end, you're going to be swinging bottles of Mützig like me," he said, swinging the bottle he was holding into the air again. "Give me the other bottle, too. I know what I'm saying—life is a cruel thing. Do what you want, but in the end, you're going to end up living for what Mark sells in his stand."

It was obvious that Jean-Marie was very unhappy with his life. He was complaining and I didn't know why, but I assume he had his reasons. He took a pair of socks from his pocket, pink with white stripes, and put them on. He began to sing, "People are so greedy, they aren't satisfied even after death. They keep wanting and wanting more. They emerge from beneath the soil and kill each other all over again to their heart's content, after which they go back underground. Hey, dead people, you're all very greedy, even after dying you give me no peace, but you watch me from above and mock me."

"*Les Têtes Brûlées*, you say?"

"*Les Têtes Brûlées*, yes. Never heard of them?"

"No."

"Well, I've heard a lot of them. They're my favorite band. They're Cameroonian. Their name means 'the burning heads' or 'the hotheads.'"

"Is this their song?"

"Yes. It's a good song, right?"

"Yeah, it's not bad. It's a good song."

"You see? And you say you want to write a book. There isn't much to do here in Cameroon. There's a volcano in the north, near Rhumsiki. Everyone says it's extinct, but I'm certain that it's active. The seafood is good, too—prawns and oysters. Ah yes, and there's good football. Crazy stuff. But there's nothing else. That's what I think, anyway. Do you have a cigarette?"

"I told you I don't smoke. You shouldn't smoke either."

"I don't care—you think I don't know that it's harmful? You think I don't know that nobody cares about me? Nobody likes me. You think I don't know that Mark is the worst of the scoundrels, the worst among the vendors? I'm sure he told you in the end that they're asking themselves when I'm going to die, so that everyone is rid of me. I know all of that. What, do you think I'm crazy, that I'm incapable of doing anything? It's a lie. It's just the way life is—one day you're at the bottom, the next day you're at the top. One day you're dead, the next day you're alive. It's all like that. Why are you staring at me like that? Go on, get lost, I'm not saying anything. You say it's not a bad song? Do you know that this song is genius? What do you care, anyway? You slip your body left and right like a worm, and you write your words. You don't stop to think about me for one second, you don't think about how Jean-Marie howls out here every night. You know what the worst thing is?" Jean-Marie pressed his hand against my shoulder in a slightly threatening manner. "The worst thing is that people are losing the desire to be happy. They ask themselves what they want and they realize that, like a hungry worm, they simply *want*—it doesn't matter what it is, as long as they eat-eat-eat. Everyone is a worm, a worm! 'Do you hear me, you worms up there, I'm talking to you. You're sleeping in our beds and keep wanting to eat more. You have no peace...'"

Jean-Marie repeated this at least ten times. I realized that he was growing more and more irritated. Mark was right. When he lost control of himself, he was completely out of hand. I wanted to leave as our conversation was growing more absurd by the minute and, to be honest, I was slightly afraid.

"What are you looking at? You don't know them, do you? You don't know anything."

"What don't I know?" I asked.

"*Les Têtes Brûlées.*"

"No."

"It's a good thing you don't know them. Nobody will know me when I die, either. What's it to you? You're enjoying life in London, while I…"

☜☞

It was nighttime, around eleven o'clock, and I was already on my way to the harbor. I popped into Mark's stand on the way; for some reason I wanted a Mützig.

"Is he dead?" Mark asked.

"Yes," I said.

"What did you do?"

"Nothing, I left him there. I didn't want to stay with him for long."

"Did you tell him about me?"

"What was I supposed to say?"

"That I was waiting impatiently for the spirits to come pick him up."

"Yes."

"What did he say?"

"He said that he likes you very much, that you've been friends for a hundred years and that he greatly respects you."

"Whatever; Jean-Marie was a fool," Mark said after a moment's silence.

I walked slowly towards the harbour, my body trembling; I wanted to sleep. I suddenly remembered the poster that I'd seen in one of the train cars in Libya, behind the door connecting two cars. I remember Muhammed the conductor, whom I had asked about the group on the poster, and how he had said, "*Les Têtes Brûlées.*"[30]

---

30. *Les Têtes Brûlées* is one of the most well-known bands in Cameroon and in Africa in general. They represent the genre of so-called "soft" pop or bikutsi dance. They gained fame in the 1980s for their style of music. *Les Têtes Brûlées* is French for "the burning heads" or "the hot heads." They soon gained fame throughout the world, from Europe to the USA and Japan. They would dress in bright colors like clowns, with striped socks, painted faces, and long hair. In 1988, the guitar player in the band, Zanzibar, committed suicide and this threatened to cause *Les Têtes Brûlées* to break up, but the group managed to survive for a few more years and release more records. At that time, an important role was played by the founder of the band, Jean-Marie Ahanda. The character in this story is imaginary and does not bear any resemblance to the real Jean-Marie Ahanda.

DAY 24. EQUATORIAL GUINEA
FERNANDO PO

"But do we really have a port? We don't have much of anything; how did you come up with the preposterous notion of having arrived here by boat, and from Cameroon? You've probably gotten something wrong. Perhaps your English isn't very good?" said the uniformed official, who had gotten off the ship with me.

"My things were stolen. I'm sure they're on the ship; I have to get back on that ship at all costs," I said.

"I'll explain this all to you again. We don't have a port, and there are no ships. The last ship in Malabo was probably Fernando Po's. So, you're a little late."

"What do you mean you don't have a port? I'm not crazy. The two of us arrived from Douala together. You offered me some juice on the ship and told me that you were involved in politics in Equatorial Guinea and that the country owed you a lot."

"I'm a very serious person; do you take me for a fool?"

"No, but I've lost my bag and you don't want to help me find it."

"There's no way I can help you. You can go into the sea and search for it there; maybe it's somewhere in the remains of a sunken ship."

This was the absurd start to my stay in Equatorial Guinea.

I was in Malabo, the capital. I'd lost my bag again and, for some reason I couldn't explain, I felt like this stranger could help me. We stood in the port on a small bridge, with a gigantic white ship a few meters to our side with large letters saying in Spanish: "Freedom to Equatorial Guinea."

It was a grand ship: four floors on the top level with gold-plated pillars and iron leaves painted green. The ship's deck was full of people. There was a small café there installed with huge umbrellas.

"Are you blind?" I asked. "My things are on that ship. I don't speak Spanish or Portuguese; please help me get back on the ship."

"There is no ship here; enough of your having fun. I've got to go; I don't have time to listen to your stupid chatter."

This interaction surprised me, but I had gotten used to such things even though I had at first thought that it was a language issue.

The stranger, who had introduced himself on the ship as Francisco Nguema, looked like a swindler—he had a broad forehead, wide open eyes, short cropped hair, and thick lips with a slightly thinner and longer upper lip. His eyelids were broad and his face was large with pointy ears. The muscles of his jaw were visible, and parallel creases descended from both sides of his nose. His nostrils were wide and pronounced. In brief, he looked like a bad guy and it seemed like no coincidence that he was trying to pass himself off as blind.

80 C3

I continued on my journey. At first glance, Equatorial Guinea reminded me of a fairy tale that had everything and nothing at all.

This small state, which is mostly populated by the Fang and Bubi peoples, seemed gloomy and it was no coincidence that, when I found a shepherd who spoke to me in his language (I don't know what language that was) and told me an interesting story, it may have been a miracle, but I understood what he said.

He wasn't like the shepherds I was used to seeing back home; his clothing and the way he carried himself were very different. In reality, calling him a shepherd was not correct, because he only had two sheep, a buffalo (at least, it looked like a buffalo), and a dog. What he was doing in the northern part of Bioko Island, in one of the suburbs of Malabo, I can't say. "Raffael—with two f's"—the shepherd asked me to call him that. But that name didn't seem to suit him well.

"Look, in the distance, on the other side of the bogs, almost at the edge of that hill, some people have gathered and are coming towards us. They're sinking, and one of them has died," Raffael said.

"I can't see it, where? There's only the sea and the sky, there aren't any people there."

"You won't see it; only I can see it."

"What do you see?"

"A funeral procession is approaching in the distance. Someone has died, one of the villagers."

"So what?"

"They're coming to me. They have to see me before they bury him, then…"

"Why?"

"Do you see these sheep?"

"Yes."

"I have to give one of them to those people. If the sheep follows them, the dead will come back to life. If it runs away, then they can bury him."

"Where will the sheep go?"

"As far as the cemetery. When the coffin is lowered into the ground, the sheep will bleat twelve times and that is when the relatives of the deceased will decide whether to bury him or take him home."

"Then what happens?"

"If the sheep bleats, then they take the coffin home and wait for seven days, after which the person comes back to life."

"Why seven days?"

"That's how much time it takes."

"What if the sheep doesn't bleat?"

"Then they fill in the hole with dirt and go back home."

"And the sheep?"

"The sheep? It comes back to me. These two always come back, they're faithful."

"Can you make them bleat each time?"

"No, I have no control over that. It depends on the relatives of the deceased. If they really want it, the sheep will bleat."

"Why wouldn't they want it?"

"I don't know; I can't say. There are many reasons."

"Is that a tradition?"

"Is what a tradition?"

"This story about your sheep."

"No. I made it up. Interesting, isn't it?"

We were near a puddle; Raffael sat on a rock and his animals stood behind him. It was a cloudy day and the clouds had fused with the water in the distance and a fog had formed. Perhaps that fog was why I hadn't been able to see the funeral procession, which was indeed coming closer. There was probably a cemetery nearby. When they arrived, two of the people approached Raffael, spoke with him in Spanish, then paid him some money and tied a rope to one of the sheep before leading it away.

"You see? They bought Francisco."

"Francisco?"

"Yes," Raffael said with a laugh, putting the money in his pocket. "They took him to make a sacrifice."

"Is that the sheep's name?"

"Yes, Francisco Macías Nguema. Is it a familiar name?"

"Very much so. I met him at the port today."

"What?" Raffael asked, standing up. "What did you say?"

"Yes. We arrived together from Douala today by ship. He offered me some juice and after we left the ship, I asked him to help me get back on board, because he'd seemed like quite a dignified person. But he didn't help me, and I never found my lost bag."

"What did he look like?"

"He was Black with a large forehead, wide nostrils, and big cheeks; he looked like a swindler."

"That's impossible."

"I'm serious, he looked like a bad guy."

"That's impossible; you must be mistaken."

"What would I be mistaking?"

"Francisco Macías Nguema was our President, and he received the death penalty on September 29, 1979. I hated him so much that I named the sheep after him, although it would have been a much better name for my dog."

"But then who was the person I saw?"

"I don't know, it must be a mistake. Or perhaps you're not describing him correctly; maybe you don't see very well. Or he gave you the wrong name."

"No, everything was right; I'm sure it was him."

"I don't know what to say, in that case."

Raffael was thinking. For about a minute, he stuck the stick he was holding into the ground with a steady rhythm.

"He was a dictator," Raffael continued. "In 1968, when Equatorial Guinea became independent, Francisco was our first President. He was a violent dictator who was disdainful of the intelligentsia, and he gave himself many different titles, including "President for Life." He had a large number of Bubis killed and even prohibited fishing, which was the only livelihood that many locals had. He wasn't a good man. Then, his nephew toppled his regime. He was accused of attempting genocide and was sentenced to death. So you could not have seen him. It must have been a dream."

Raffael left. After he'd gone, it started to rain and, at that moment, I thought that perhaps he hadn't been real either. I began to run. I'd pulled my shirt over my head, so I could barely see ahead of me. My whole body was drenched. The rain was hot and pleasant, especially when the water ran down my spine. All I could think about at the time was whether or not it was really raining in Equatorial Guinea.

⁍⁎

The huge field had been transformed into a large puddle, like a bog. In the distance, about twenty meters away, an animal was running around. I couldn't see it well—it was either a zebra or a cow. The animal stopped and looked at me or, rather, I felt like it was looking at me. Then, something happened that I'd only heard about in fairy tales—someone emerged from within the animal and walked up to me. I was afraid. The person coming closer was unshaven, with short hair and European features, and was wearing gray pants, a yellow checked shirt, and suspenders. His hair was the color of rust and his eyes were green. He put some kind of a green wooden stick in his mouth, and he was moving it around with his tongue. He said something in Spanish, then realized that I didn't understand him and switched to English.

"Where are you from?" he asked.

"Who are you?" I asked in turn.

"I'm Spanish. Why are you looking at me with such fear, as if you've seen a talking animal?"

"Isn't that what I've seen?"

"What do you mean?"

"That zebra—you came out of it and walked over here."

The Spaniard laughed. "That zebra is my tractor."

When I wiped off the fog from my glasses—I hadn't noticed it accumulating—I realized that it had been a tractor in the distance.

"I hadn't wiped off my glasses. It was raining, and they had fogged up. I didn't realize what it was," I said.

"Yes, that was a lot of rain. One drop of it could fill my palm. Did you get wet?"

"That's okay; it's hot. I won't catch cold."

"I'm not saying you'll catch cold, but it's not a good thing to get caught in the rain."

"Why?"

"There's a tradition here. The locals made it up. Come with me and I'll tell you what it is."

We walked to the tractor and got in it, then he started the engine. It was strange, like the tractor had been built a thousand years ago. It was wooden inside, and the so-called engine was a large rock which used its weight to roll the wheels.

"I made this," he said. "The soil here is wonderful, and it's a shame not to have a tractor. The locals don't know about this. If they find out, they'll immediately ask me to make ones for them, too."

"You haven't told me about the rain."

"Ah, yes, I forgot about that, you're right. See that hill?"

"Yes."

"The villagers, slaves and laborers, cultivate the land there. Those lands belong to the Spanish."

"To you?"

"No, not to me, to the Spanish. Well, to me, too, but really to our government."

"But I thought the Europeans no longer had any land in Africa."

"No, you're wrong. That land is ours. Most of the revenue is ours, too. The locals satisfy themselves with food and shelter, but sometimes they don't even get that."

"Who are the locals?"

"I don't know," he said. He took the wooden stick out of his mouth and began to spin it with his fingers. "They're Black people. I don't understand them at all."

"So what? What does the rain have to do with any of this?"

"Those Black people hate us, but they don't show it. They're afraid. They know that they have no way out, and deep down they want us to die. They're waiting for us to give them their independence." The Spaniard stopped the tractor. "I'll be right back," he said, and he got out. I could see that his bottom was completely wet. He returned shortly.

"Here, put this on. I know what I'm talking about; things won't end up well otherwise."

"I don't understand."

"I'll explain everything in a minute. When it rains, those wretches think that it's crying. They believe in the power of rain; it must be part of their local religion. They curse the drops that fall and, whoever the rain touches, that person dies. I don't know how they do it, but that curse works. Their leader is a man named Raffael."

"About a half hour ago, before the rain started, I saw them take a dead person to be buried. It had probably rained before that," I said.

"Perhaps."

"But I don't believe in such things."

"Whether or not you believe it, the locals do. They are witches, and they can make the sun set late or keep the moon from appearing in the sky."

"Then why can't they free themselves from you?"

"That's the one thing they cannot do."

I didn't tell him that I had met Raffael, because I wasn't certain that it had been real. I wiped myself with the towel he had given me and changed my shirt. I could have stayed a bit longer and talked to the Spaniard, whose name I never found out, but for some reason I was in a hurry and I felt like the whole of Equatorial Guinea, and Bioko Island in particular, had dragged me into some kind of a game.

When I bid the Spaniard farewell, he said with scorn, "Wherever you go, they will come with you. They won't take their eyes off you. And if you think you've rid yourself of them, then you're mistaken; dead or alive, they will always pursue you."

Perhaps the Spaniard had thought that I was also a colonizer like himself. Why would the locals curse or punish me? This Spaniard seemed like an arrogant man to me. He was scared, and he was trying to cover over his fear with fake confidence.

I continued on my way. I was very interested in the opinions of the locals, especially the ones who were his subjects.

I wasn't lucky this time and couldn't find anyone who could speak a language that I understood. When I entered the town, it was as if it had come alive; I don't know what had changed. Perhaps nothing had changed at all. Perhaps the rain had stopped and it was just the noise of the town that had created this impression.

I stood behind a beat-up truck and watched quietly as five or six Black men and a white woman loaded sacks of potatoes onto the truck with great difficulty.

It turned out that the woman was a photographer and journalist who had arrived from Braga in Portugal. I waited for them to finish their work, and then I asked her to ask the men where they were from. She happily agreed to be my interpreter for a few minutes. When she questioned the men, they replied that they were locals, the residents of a suburb of Malabo. They had come to the market to sell their products, but they hadn't found any buyers and now they had to return.

I asked Estefania (that was the woman's name) to ask them about the Spanish and the tradition about the rain that I had heard about in the tractor. They grew angry and shouted at both me and my interpreter. After they said a few things, they got in their truck and drove away.

"What did they say?" I asked.

"They thought that you and I are both crazy. They hurled a few insults at us."

"That's it?"

"Yeah. And they said that there haven't been any slaves here for a long time, that this wasn't Fernando Pó's time anymore."[31]

---

31. Fernando Pó was a Portuguese explorer. In 1472, he left in his ship to go to India, but ended up on Bioko Island instead. Having "discovered" it, he named it *Formosa* ("beautiful" in Portuguese). The island was later renamed Fernando Pó (and called that until 1972). In 1474, the islands of Fernando Pó and Annobón were colonized by the Portuguese. Later, Maria I (the Queen of Portugal) and Charles III (the King of Spain) agreed to an exchange, and these territories became part of the Spanish Empire. Later, from 1827 to 1843, these territories engaged in slave trade. In 1900, Río Muni (the mainland) and the remaining islands were once again colonized and renamed Spanish Guinea. On October 12, 1968, Equatorial Guinea was granted independence. The slave trade was then stopped and the influence of the Europeans gradually waned.

It was nighttime. I was alone, and it was time to leave "magical" Equatorial Guinea. Perhaps I had seen things incorrectly, or been left with the wrong impression. I don't know. In any case, the "fairy tale" seemed to come to an end, and when I left the café where I had treated Estefania to a cup of coffee, I noticed the huge white ship again. It wasn't as crowded this time, and it seemed to have been standing there for several centuries…

DAY 25. SÃO TOMÉ AND PRÍNCIPE
THE FLYING AFRICAN

São Tomé ended up being a continuation of the "fairy tale" that had started in Equatorial Guinea.

At the beach on the Gulf of Guinea, the foamy waves were being absorbed into the yellow sand and the weather was hot, but clouds had gathered in the sky. Many pigeons, standing in pairs, were swaying together as the thick, green forest could be seen in the distance on one side, and the city appeared on the other.

There was silence; only the voices of a few São Toméans could be heard, as they returned to the coast in their fishing boats.

I was walking through the small capital, which featured a beautiful natural landscape and looked like a picture drawn by a child. Nature still dominated here. People were happy, although the history of São Tomé and Príncipe had been anything but joyful.

When I crossed one of São Tomé's main streets, I thought it looked more like a path in a dense forest; the only difference was that it was paved. Three Black men appeared in front of me on wooden bicycles. They sped by so quickly that it seemed like they were going a hundred or a hundred-and-twenty kilometers an hour. But of course, a wooden bicycle—and this was the first time I had even seen one—could not generate such speeds.

They rode over to the side of the street and stopped. I thought that they had stopped for me, so I walked over to them without hurrying. Just when I was a few steps away, they gathered speed again and left, laughing as they did so.

I finally got to my hotel, which I found with great difficulty. It was called Miramar, and the first thing I noticed there was the flag of Germany, with the São Tomé flag next to it, and a third flag that was completely blue. It was like the flag of the European Union, but there were no stars to be seen.

It was a pretty hotel, almost more like a resort than a hotel. I decided to go into the town and roam about. When I left the hotel, the cyclists once again cut in front of me.

I was on the beach, lying on the sand. There were birds above me, their screeches piercing my ears. The sound of the waves could be heard, slapping against my feet with the same rhythm. The water was cold, but it didn't bother me. Suddenly, I felt a sharp sting in one foot and I jumped up.

"It's cold, don't lie around like that. The wind will get you."

This voice came from a swarthy, black-haired man who was around thirty years old.

"What?" I asked. I noticed that it seemed like my own skin color had changed, starting a long time ago. "Are you a tourist?"

"Yes. I said it's cold." He used the stick in his hand to once again deliver a soft blow to my foot.

"I don't feel cold."

"I know what I'm saying. I've been here for a month. I put my feet in the water two times, like you, and then…"

For a second, I thought he was going to say that the locals had cursed the water. But thankfully, the story was much simpler this time.

"…and then I fell sick," he said.

"Who are you?"

"I'm an Indian. My name is San. I'm from India and I saved my money to come here; I'd always dreamed of seeing this country. But I'm not particularly impressed."

"Why not?"

"My money was stolen. Now I don't know what to do."

"Who stole it?"

"I don't know. I originally intended to stay for twenty days. I've already been here a week longer than I'd planned."

"Are you sure it was stolen?"

"Yes, it seemed well planned out. I'd left to go to Principe for a couple of days before my departure. The plane ticket cost 125 euros, but I wanted to see that part of the country, too. Then, when I returned, I came back to the city and my pocket was empty."

"Perhaps you lost it."

"No, it was stolen. The people here steal everything from us tourists. They don't like us." He sat down on the sand.

The Indian told me about himself and I did the same. We "felt cold" together out there for about an hour, and then he said, "Well, the sun's going to set soon. Where are you going?"

"Avenida Marginal 12."

"The hotel? I've been there. I stayed there for twenty days," he said. "I don't have money for a hotel now, but you know that already. I've made a friend, so I'm staying at his place. He's Portuguese, but he has a Black child. Interesting, isn't it? We manage to communicate somehow. Do you want to come? We'll talk a bit."

"I'll come another time."

I didn't want to believe that the locals could be thieves, as they all had innocent looks and sorrowful eyes. We parted ways, San heading towards the east, while I went towards the west.

I was still on the beach. Suddenly, I heard a guitar. Someone was playing and singing in the distance. I found the guitar player; he was a huge man, more than a hundred kilograms, and he was disabled—his right leg was missing. He sat in a chair and moved his gold-plated guitar up and down as he sang in a loud voice. When he saw me, he grew even more animated.

I waited for the song to end. The melody was beautiful, but it was clear that he couldn't play very well. It was dark and when I approached him, I saw that he was white. When he finished his playing, a small Black boy approached and held out a metallic bowl in front of me.

"Don't be afraid, pal; put some money in," the guitar player said with a laugh. "Don't you have any dobra?"

"I don't have any small change," I answered.

"That's okay, you can put in a large note; you heard a lot of the music," he said as he laughed again. When he laughed, his cheeks moved and hung down toward his neck.

"Come on, come on, don't be stingy, we're pinning our hopes on you," he said.

The little boy put his hand to his heart at that moment and said, "You're breaking my heart."

It was very funny hearing him say that. Embarrassed, I put a 20,000 dobra note, worth about a dollar and a half, into the bowl.

The guitar player laughed again and asked me to come closer.

"He's my son; he did a good job, right? I taught him that—when someone doesn't give money, he comes closer and asks them again in a heartbreaking voice, and everybody melts."

"He's your son?"

"Yes, I understand what you mean. My wife was Black. I've been here a long time, around forty years, from back in the time when we weren't independent. I was a fisherman, and then I met Dodoy's mother and we got married. I couldn't go back to Portugal after that. It's nice here. It's a wonderful place." He began to cry. His cheeks were so puffy that his tears couldn't roll downwards. He straightened up, and called the boy over and put his hand on his head. Then he kissed the boy's head and embraced him. Dodoy started to cry, too. The two of them cried for about a minute.

"Your name is Dodo?" I asked the boy, trying to lift his mood.

"He doesn't understand English," the man said emotionally. "And it's not Dodo, it's Dodoy."

"What does that mean?"

"Nothing, I made it up," he said with a smile. "Once, when he was small and his mother was still alive, he saw a parrot on the beach and shouted 'Do-do-doy.' We decided after that to name him Dodoy. The names here are similar to the ones we have in Portugal, but I wanted his name to be unique."

"Is this how you make money?"

"No, I have fishing boats; I rent them out. The local fishermen are good people, they respect me. Everyone here is good. There was a time when I used to go out fishing but now, after my illness…it's difficult."

The Portuguese man started to play again and it turned out to be a better effort this time. He looked so much in harmony against the dark sky, shimmering waves, and palm trees that I didn't want to interrupt him. I felt sleepy and I needed to get back to the hotel, but I wanted to stay for a bit longer.

Dodoy came up to me again with his bowl.

"I have nothing to give this time," I said with a laugh. I really had nothing. Then the Portuguese man laughed. So did Dodoy.

"There are many birds here. The sky is like a zoo for birds. When an animal dies on the beach, eagles instantly appear and attack the corpse. There are so many of them that sometimes, when you look at the clouds, you'd think they are birds in flight."

"Yes," I said tiredly. "There really are a lot of them."

"Do you like fish?"

"Yes."

"Let's go eat, my treat. It's delicious."

"No, thanks, I'm not hungry. Also, I'm getting sleepy."

"I'll tell you a story; it'll wake you up in an instant."

"Go ahead."

"Have you been to the eastern side?"

"Yes, that's where I came from."

The Portuguese man settled in his chair and told Dodoy to put the guitar in its case.

"There's a very interesting tradition there. A São Toméan had once decided to fly over the ocean and go to Europe. This was a long time ago—some five centuries past, in an era when the sugar industry was well developed. He had gone hungry that day and told everyone that, once he arrived in Europe, he would make São Tomé rich. He would send back money, and build the place up. It wasn't even a country then, it was far from being a country; the slave trade had just begun to take hold."

"Did he make it there?"

"Nobody believed him and, after a few days, everyone realized that it had been a big lie. But now I think that he did actually make it to Europe. Time is an amazing thing. All it takes is for you to look at the same thing a second earlier or later, and everything changes. Right, Dodoy?"

Dodoy nodded, although I thought he looked tired and wasn't really listening to what his father was saying. He was counting the stars in the sky.

"When the São Toméan flew," the Portuguese man continued, "he asked all his friends to close off the beach, so that the wind wouldn't stop him. Naturally, they couldn't close off the whole beach, they only managed to do this for one part. He said that if he didn't get to his destination, the sharks would devour him."

"Then what happened?"

"They say that he really flew and disappeared in the sky. The pessimists made up a version of the story in which he fell into the water and ended up as a meal for the sharks. But in those days, another story was also told about the flying São Toméan. The local slaves said that his soul had split into three parts: one had drowned in the ocean, another had fallen victim to the eagles in the sky, and the third had reached his destination and died there. Since that time, people are afraid to go out into the street at night, because they say that his three spirits ride on wooden bicycles at the speed of lightning. They're a very strange people. I think it's just a story. In any case, seeing the state of the country now, perhaps that flying African is only now about to reach Europe. Dodoy?"

Dodoy had fallen asleep. He had wrapped himself around a leg of the chair and stuck his feet in the sand.

"It's late; let's get going," the Portuguese man said.

"Yes, it's very late."

"Dodoy, get up, come on, we're leaving. That poor Indian guy, San, must have grown tired of waiting for us. Get up, put out the fire, bring my walking stick, and let's go."

The curly-haired boy finally woke up, put out the bonfire, which I hadn't noticed earlier, and we left. They walked towards the east, while I went west towards my hotel.

Before we parted ways, the Portuguese man asked, "Do you believe in dreams?"

"I believe in mine."

"Good for you; so do I."

I was walking along the tree-lined street once again. I was scared; there were no cars and the moonlight was the only thing that kept me company. I began to run, but this time I didn't come across the three Black men who were speeding along like lightning on their wooden bicycles.

When I got to the hotel, I noticed that the third flag was in fact that of the European Union. The twelve stars on the blue background were now visible. I entered. Inside the hotel, it felt like I was in Europe. But the atmosphere didn't feel familiar to me. The Portuguese man's company had been much more interesting…

I was hungry. When I entered the hotel restaurant, a man approached. He was a German in a white coat and pants, black shoes, and a tie. He apologized for bothering me and asked if he could sit down, and I said yes. He asked the waiter to come over.

"Are you a tourist?" he asked.

"Yes."

"Is this a good hotel?"

"Yes."

"You've settled in all right?"

"Yes."

"Would it bother you if I smoked?"

"No."

He took a large cigar out of his pocket.

"Would you like to try it?" he asked.

"No, thanks, I don't smoke."

"It's good. It's from Cuba. What would you like?"

"Thank you, but I'll order for myself."

"It's no problem at all. Please tell me what you'd like to have."

"I don't know. Why don't you order for me?"

He asked the waiter to bring some fish, cooked in the local style with spices, and then he ran his fingers over his waxed hair.

"The local fish is delicious. Do you like fish?"

"Yes," I said. I felt sleepy and I wasn't particularly enthused by this person's presence. "Who are you?"

"Sorry, I didn't introduce myself. Oliver Hemmler."

"Are you a tourist, too?"

"Almost."

"Are you on vacation?"

"No, I'm one of the owners of this hotel. I like sitting and talking with people in the evenings. Ten years ago, in 1996-97, we built this hotel with the Americans. Now it's the most beautiful spot on the island. It's great to visit here—there's a wonderful pool, a bar, and we have 10,000 square meters of garden area. The rooms are wonderful. You can stay here and not have to go anywhere. Did you like this hotel?"

"Yes."

"The local residents come and look through the gates at it in the distance," he said, putting the cigar in the ashtray. "It's good; I feel at home here."

"Have you been here a long time?"

"What do you mean?"

"Have you been living here for a while?"

"I come here once or twice a year for ten to fifteen days."

"Do you know the locals?"

"No. Just the ones who work here at the hotel."

"Have they told you one of the local legends?" I asked.

"Which one?"

"The one about the São Toméan who decided to fly over the sea to Europe."

"And?"

"And how he said he would send wealth to São Tomé once he had gotten to Europe, and he would build this place up."

"No, I haven't heard that one. It sounds like a foolish children's fairy tale. Those kinds of things happen only in science fiction movies," he said, laughing with self-satisfaction. He paid for the meal. Then he invited me out into the garden. I was tired and, to be honest, did not wish to talk with him anymore, so I said goodbye and went up to my room. I kept thinking about the flying African and I didn't want to tell Oliver Hemmler that the São Toméan had made it to Europe; he wouldn't have believed me anyway…

The next day, as I was preparing to leave heavenly São Tomé and Principe, I walked down the stairs at the hotel and suddenly felt a sharp sting in my foot. I bent down and saw a wallet that had a considerable sum of money in it, including some Indian rupee notes and a map of India.

I realized that, before going to the airport, I had to find the house of the Portuguese man…

DAY 26. GABON
THE ROBBERS OF THE LAMBARÉNÉ GOD

The flight to Libreville (the name translates to "free city"), the capital of Gabon, took one hour and forty-five minutes.

This was a country with at least forty ethnic groups, one of the biggest (if not the biggest) and best-protected natural parks, a unique natural landscape, and dozens of languages and language groups. It was home to the Fang, Bandjabi and Nzebi, the Myene, and the Bakota, as well as the Balumbu, Eshira, Bapounou, Okande and many others; the Bantu are considered to be the ancestors of almost all the "Gabonese." It was a country that was considered to be one of the more or less developed states in Africa.

It was cloudy. The clouds had grown red in places and the sun could not be seen. It was about eleven kilometers from the airport to the city. That was how far we had to travel, according to the taxi driver. And add another few kilometers to get to the hotel, which was on the beachfront side of the city.

When I came out of the airport, a crowd of taxi drivers swarmed around me. This is a common sight, even in developed countries, especially following the arrival of flights with many foreign passengers. It was a great way to make money. Several drivers immediately lunged at me near the entrance, which perhaps did not happen as often in Gabon, but they were so aggressive that I ran away from them. I was lucky that there were several other foreigners at the arrivals terminal of the Leon M'Ba International Airport, which was named after their first President. When I stepped into the street, I was beginning to panic and, seeing a car with a taxi sign on it, I went right up to it and opened the door, causing the driver to fall out of the car—he had been asleep inside, his body leaning on the door. He woke up and began to shout in a language I did not know and to swear (or so it seemed), so I turned around and ran away quickly.

Perhaps this incident was my fault because I hadn't taken notice of him, but I hadn't expected him to be asleep and leaning against the door. I didn't get a good look at his face but I did notice the large knife that he had in his pocket.

Another car was a few steps away from that one, and the driver was definitely awake. I approached the car and said hello, and I was about to get into the car when he got out, asked me to wait, and ran in the direction of the airport. A short while later he returned, accompanied by two other drivers whom I had come across at the arrivals terminal. I thought for a moment that he had asked them here to translate. But it turned out that he had called them because it wasn't his turn to take a customer—it was theirs. Although it was with difficulty, I eventually thought I understood; the two drivers seemed happy and led me away.

But, unfortunately, it turned out that I had not understood correctly and I only discovered this once we were already on the road. It turned out that I had to bear the company of two other drivers besides the one at the wheel. According to them, they only had one car between them and they kept switching places as the driver so that each of them had a turn at earning money.

"Eleven kilometers to the city and add another few kilometers to get to the hotel," the driver said; the man currently at the wheel was the only one of them who spoke English.

"How far to the hotel?" I asked.

"What's the address again, please? I'll calculate it."

"B.P. 74, the Atlantic Hotel."

"Around five kilometers," he said very seriously, after what seemed to have been several very complicated calculations.

I don't know whether or not he was fooling with me, but then I've always had my reservations when it comes to dealing with taxi drivers. It was my bad luck, too—the car was at least thirty years old, the seats were uncomfortable, it smelled bad, and the engine made a lot of noise. In addition to that, the two men in the back seat had fallen asleep, leaning on each other, and were snoring.

"Is this a very old car?" I asked. I was trying to make myself feel better, especially after noticing that there were many newer cars being driven as taxis in the city.

"Not that old. Are you comfortable?"

"It's not bad."

"If you want, I can stop and you can switch seats. D'hol can come sit in front with me."

"No, thanks, it's fine, it's fine, don't worry about it," I said. There was nothing I desired less at that moment that ending up "in the embrace" of that other driver.

I was quiet; there was nothing more to say. I was interested in the culture, population, national parks, architecture, and people of Gabon. Perhaps I was being a bit arrogant at that moment, but I didn't think that these topics would be of any interest to the driver of that green Peugeot.

I heard a shout behind me and I jumped in my seat. D'hol and the other driver were laughing.

"What happened?" I asked.

"Nothing," the driver said. "Llama had a dream and was telling us about it, and we were laughing. Llama always has stupid dreams."

Llama did indeed look like a little llama.

"His name is Llama?"

"No," he laughed, "But what animal does he look like to you?"

"A llama?"

"Yes. That's why we call him Llama. Do you want to hear about the dream? You'll like it."

"Go ahead," I said.

"Llama says he saw a gigantic plane that blew up in the sky, and its pieces turned to gold and fell to the ground. He says he ran to grab that gold and as soon as he took it in his hand, he woke up to find that he was holding D'hol's nose. They'd fallen asleep so soundly that they'd ended up in each other's face!" He laughed again.

I laughed, too, and turned toward him. "Do we still have a long way to go?"

"A little further before we enter the city. Things will slow down as soon as we get into town—but don't worry, we'll get there soon."

"Why do they keep sleeping? Are they that tired?"

"No. But there's nothing else to do."

"But how do they manage to sleep if they're not tired?"

"People here are always tired. Even if they sleep at night, they can sleep again the next day. We're a tired nation."

"Who do you mean, 'we'?"

"We—what does it matter? All the Bantu. Let me put it that way so that I don't offend anybody: we're all one nation."

"But…"

"Yes, if you look at it that way, each of us is from a different ethnic group. So what? We're brothers. That's what I think."

"What about the others?"

"What others?"

"What are their relations with each other?"

"How would I know? Which country doesn't have its enemies? Good people live here."

Malu, the driver with whom I was talking throughout the ride, lit a cigarette.

"Would you like a smoke?"

"No, I don't smoke."

"It's complicated… It's growing more and more difficult in this country."

"Are you unhappy?"

"Who's happy?" he sighed.

There probably isn't a taxi driver in the world who's happy, but Malu did not seem like a "typical" taxi driver. He gained more and more of my sympathy and something about him led me to believe what he was saying.

"Are you a professional?"

"Yes, I'm a professional driver."

"You misunderstood my question. I meant your educational background."

"Mathematics."

"What?" I laughed. "What's your real profession then?"

"I'm a mathematician. This is my Renault, I bought it from D'hol ten years ago, and D'hol bought it from Llama ten years before that. We're friends. I'm thirty-two years old, they're forty. You can't make money with mathematics. My parents were educated people; I got married after they died and pinned my hopes on this Renault. Now, I support my family with the money I make each day," he said, tossing his cigarette away.

It wasn't a Renault in reality; it was a Peugeot. Malu's mood fell slightly and he began to look ponderous. He held on to the wheel more firmly and accelerated. Another laugh could be heard from the back at that moment; this time, it was D'hol who'd had a dream.

When I asked Malu to translate this dream, he said that it had been the same dream and that it was no longer funny, but D'hol and Llama laughed so much that they shook the car.

I was quiet again. It seemed to me that we should be arriving soon. I was thinking about Africa and these "Africans." Naturally, I'd had these thoughts before, but now I also began to have a sense of familiarity. It was like I was their kin and, to be honest, I liked that feeling.

A short while later, the sound of the car engine grew worse and then it died. Malu steered the car to the curb and braked. The three of them got out. That was when I noticed that Malu limped on his left foot.

"What happened?" I asked.

"What do you think? It's dead. It's dead again."

Malu's eyes filled with tears, though it looked more like they were just watering. He raised the hood and stuck his head under it. D'hol and Llama crouched under there as well. My view was blocked.

Two minutes later, it seemed like they were arguing, and they were shouting loudly. A crackling sound came from the car (the engine was probably cooling) which prompted me to get out.

"What's going on, are you arguing?"

"Go sit down."

"Is something wrong?"

"We'll figure something out; go sit down," Malu said irritably.

I sat down. Llama tried to close the hood, then D'hol tried to do so, after which Malu slammed it shut. They got in the car. Malu lifted his hand to his forehead and smacked his lips like a fish. D'hol and Llama were very serious, too.

There was a grand building in the distance—several stories high, it resembled a structure from the Renaissance. It had beautiful arches, pillars, and large windows. The building had five or six stories, but their dimensions could have actually accommodated eight to ten floors. It was yellowish and there were no other buildings like it in the area; in fact, there was nothing else around it. I wanted to ask them what it was, but they were so tense that I was afraid to do so.

It was hot and the sun was still not visible, but the gray clouds were slowly dissipating. There was a hot wind. It was quiet in the street; only one or two cars rarely went by. A long way away, there was a forest, or perhaps it was a part of a cloud which had descended and closed off our view.

After a long silence, Malu said, "Would you wait for a bit? Llama and I will go to a shop and be right back." He named a part for the car that they needed to buy.

"How long?" I asked.

"You stay with D'hol. We'll be back soon; half an hour maximum," he said and they left.

He didn't even wait for my reply. D'hol seated himself behind the wheel. He smiled. He offered me chewing gum. He took out a bottle full of water from the glove compartment, but it had grown so hot that it had steamed up on the inside and bubbles had formed. He drank from it. He opened the door and rinsed his oily hands. He leaned the seat back, and lay down and closed his eyes. Half an hour went by. Then one hour. Llama and Malu had not returned.

D'hol took the bottle again and this time washed his face. He looked at me.

"Gabon," he said with a smile.

"Yes, Gabon," I replied. D'hol didn't know any English at all, nor did he speak French.

"D'hol," he said, pointing at himself with a finger, then he took out a booklet from the glove compartment that had pictures in it. "Malu, Llama."

"Yes," I said, smiling back.

D'hol was uneasy. We had already been waiting for about an hour and twenty minutes. The sun had been gradually heating up the car, and it became impossible to keep sitting inside. I got out.

Malu and Llama finally returned. They quickly began to change some parts on the car. Malu woke D'hol up, sat at the wheel and asked the three of us to push the car. While pushing, I saw an empty taxi in the distance, one that looked much more comfortable and newer. For a moment, I wanted to make a break for it, to get away from there, but I stayed. We pushed the car for about a hundred meters, until Malu shouted for us to get in.

We were back on the road.

"When will we get there?" I asked.

"In twenty minutes at the latest. If the car doesn't break down again. What was D'hol doing all that time?" Malu asked.

"He fell asleep twice."

"Yeah? He didn't laugh?"

"He smiled."

"D'hol's always laughing, when he isn't sleeping. He's like a child. He's forty years old, but he hasn't achieved anything in life; he just keeps dreaming. And he doesn't even know how to dream."

"Everyone dreams for themselves. Everyone always believes in something," I said.

"There's nothing worth believing. Here, or anywhere else in the world, there's no good thing out there. There is no God. God died two years ago, in May. He burned and died… I've thought about that for a long time. One shouldn't believe in anything, it's foolish; the only faith here is in money and this old Renault."

I had meant something different, but I didn't want to interrupt Malu; he was speaking very passionately, and also with great sorrow. He seemed sincere, as if he were seeking someone new to whom he could open up.

"Life is frozen here, like inside a freezer. For a long time, I've been feeling like a fish that has been caught and frozen, one that nobody even wants to eat. There are a couple of gas refineries here, but that's not enough. Who cares?"

"You mean oil production?"

"What difference does it make? Here, or elsewhere, it's all the same. Do you think you live in a good country? We all have the same problems."

"Are things bad here?" I asked.

"Where are they good? Is there a place where things are good?"

"In what sense? I know many places where I feel happy."

"It's one thing to feel that, but it's something else to be in the same surroundings and situation all the time. Don't believe the people here, they're swindlers; they might give you fake smiles, treat you well, compliment you, but all that is for profit. If they see no good for themselves in you, they'll ignore you and won't take you seriously. People are like that all over the world."

I felt like no matter what we spoke about, Malu would keep changing the subject and want to speak badly of people and the world. He was getting more and more agitated and making the car go faster. It was as if he hated everyone. He had a negative attitude towards everything.

"When you said that God had died, what did you mean?"

"I was right. He died exactly two years and four months ago. It was spring, the end of May, and God burned and died. I was on the balcony, drinking coffee, when I suddenly saw that the dining room was full of smoke. I went inside and ran to the kitchen, bringing a bucket of water to put out the fire, because the room was burning. Then I heard a voice, and ran to the first floor and the whole living room was in flames. The crackling of the flames was like a bunch of worms attacking. I had nowhere to escape. I wanted to put out the fire, but I could no longer do that; the upper floor had turned to ashes, and the bedrooms were melting like butter before my very eyes. I wanted to get upstairs at any cost, but I had hurt my leg; my left knee had gotten burned and was swollen. I shouted, but there was no reply. I somehow managed to drag myself out."

Malu's eyes welled up. His hands began to tremble. He stopped the car. His chin was trembling, too. He wiped his face with his hands, which had at least ten birthmarks. The ends of his fingers were trembling too.

"'My house is burning, it's burning,' I kept shouting. 'Come, help us, save us, it's burning.' There was nobody around. Everybody had disappeared into thin air. In twenty minutes, it had been razed to the ground. The firefighters came one hour too late. They lay me down on a stretcher and tried to convince me that I had been rescued from the smoldering wreck."

"Was there anybody else at home?"

The tears flowed quickly from the spaces between his reddened eyes as he used two fingers to grab the bridge of his nose and apply pressure. He smashed his hand against the glove compartment once, then again, and it opened, dropping out several empty plastic bottles.

"Justine, my wife, was home. In her room. But I didn't see her. I couldn't hold her one last time. I didn't even hear her make a single sound."

"They didn't find her?"

"No, they don't know what happened. I had no idea either and I don't even want to know. None of that interested me. I wanted to kill everyone, especially God. When I was discharged from the hospital, I met him. It wasn't far, just a stop or two by bus. Then I started to follow him; I was waiting for him to go somewhere that wasn't crowded. I struck him on the back and then stabbed him three times with my knife. He didn't put up any resistance. He didn't move. He didn't even say anything. Only I did. I said, 'If you saved my children, why didn't you save Justine as well?' He didn't make a sound. I wanted to leave him like that and run, but nobody else could see him except for me. I left him but came back in the Renault, wrapped him up and put him in the trunk. He's still there."

After he said this, I couldn't bear it any more. I opened my door and ran out. Even D'hol and Llama were startled. The rusty taxi didn't move. It just stood there at the curb, under the shade of a palm tree.

I ran for about a kilometer, far enough away that I would not be able to see them anymore. I no longer knew where I was. I entered a shop. I was thirsty and my body was trembling. In my mind, I still saw scenes from Malu's story. The shopkeeper recommended a local beer, which was called Regab, sold in the unusual size of 660 ml. After drinking it, I felt sleepy.

"You all right?" the shopkeeper asked in broken English. His hair was so long that I couldn't help but stare at it when he spoke.

"Where am I?"

"Gabon, Gabon."

"I know. What part of it?"

"This is Libreville, Gabon."

"Am I already within the city limits, or not?" I was shouting, as if talking from the half-open window of a truck.

"Yes, Libreville, yes, right."

The shopkeeper didn't understand my question correctly but, in any case, I knew that I was in Libreville, and I assumed that I could get another cab that would take me to the hotel, although I no longer felt like going there. Only one thing surprised me: why had Malu grown so angry and told me this story? Perhaps I had been talking too much, and that forced him to open up and say what he did.

It had already been three hours since I had gotten off the plane, and I did not know where I was going. I was drinking the beer and, looking out into the distance, I could see two or three elephants, and the elephants seemed to be moving slowly in sync with me. I stopped moving. I suddenly asked myself why there would be elephants in Libreville. Naturally, Gabon did have elephants and very diverse wildlife in general, but I wasn't expecting to see them in the city.

I sat on the curb. It was hot, and the clouds had grown white. I was waiting for a taxi to come by. Some cars did pass me, but they weren't taxis, and the locals slowed down as they approached me, not because they wanted to stop, but simply to get a good look at me. The beer had not been strong, but my head began to spin. I had lost hope that anyone would stop their car for me. I was afraid for a moment that I wouldn't get to my destination. I even thought about going back and finding Malu, although he would probably not still be there.

I went back into the shop and asked for some water. They didn't have any, so I drank some juice. This time, the person running the shop was not the same person with the long hair.

"Need anything else?" the vendor asked, speaking better English than the other shopkeeper.

"No. There was somebody else here a moment ago instead of you."

"Who?" He laughed. "How could someone replace me? There's nobody here except for me."

"I bought a beer here some thirty or forty minutes ago."

"No, I'm seeing you for the first time."

"Same here, but there was someone else here instead of you, with long hair."

"No. Perhaps you went into another shop, although there are no other shops here; the next one is two kilometers away."

"I know I was in this shop. I'm definitely not wrong about that."

"I don't know. I don't understand any of this," the shopkeeper said.

I knew I wasn't confused about the shop; it had definitely been this one. I didn't understand what was going on, but I did know that I had a headache.

"Where are we?" I asked.

"Near Lambaréné."

"The other shopkeeper said it was Libreville."

"What other shopkeeper? Did you fall from the sky? There is no other shopkeeper here."

"Which city did you say this was?"

"Lambaréné, Lambaréné."

"Is Libreville close by?"

He laughed.

"It's about three hundred, four hundred kilometers away. We're in the south."

It was impossible for Malu to have driven that distance in two hours. Something did not make sense. He said it was eleven kilometers from the airport to the city, plus a bit more to the hotel. He couldn't have flown across so many kilometers. Yes, he had been driving fast, but he couldn't have traveled three hundred kilometers!

"Do you have elephants here?"

"Yes."

"I saw two of them. How can I get to Libreville? Is it very far away?"

"Five or six hours. Do you want me to arrange a car? I can, but it'll be expensive."

"Do I have any other options?"

"You could wait a few hours for the bus to come, but I don't know exactly when it'll get here. It's comparatively cheaper."

"Call me a taxi—just make sure the driver can speak English and the car is comfortable."

I was afraid for a second that he would call Malu, but felt relief when I saw that the car that came was a different one, and relatively more comfortable. The driver was a man past sixty with a wrinkled face. He was thin and kept drinking water.

It was dusk and the large sun was on the horizon, and the elephants were walking in front of it. They were moving towards the west with the same speed as the sun. I felt sleepy and wanted to reach Libreville, and the hotel, where I could sleep and then leave.

"Have you been here long?" asked the driver, whose name was Benjamin.

"I don't know. I thought I hadn't, but it turns out that I had."

"Yes, time flies by here. One hour is like a day; everything is densely packed."

"Perhaps. Are you a local?"

"I'm a Balumb, from Gambia."

Benjamin drove his car quickly. We were quiet. I was tired. It was dark. The car's headlamps lit the semi-darkened streets. I nodded off and when I woke up, we were only a few kilometers from our destination.

"Life is fascinating," Benjamin said. "A strange thing happened today. I had a near brush with death. I fell out of my car and hit my head on the ground."

We entered the city and I finally saw Libreville, by night. It was a wonderful city and, although many of the streets were dark, I still managed to see a few things.

"What happened?" I asked. I was sleepy and didn't really feel like talking.

"I had a lot of trouble. Luckily, Sebastian, the shopkeeper, called and ordered my services; otherwise, I would have spent the whole day thinking about it."

Benjamin stopped the car in front of my hotel. Then he got out of the car, wiped the windshield free of the dust that had gathered unnoticed, changing the color of the vehicle. It was cold. Colorful lights shone in the distance, very low; it was probably from the cafés and bars nearby. There were many stars in the sky. I paid the driver.

"Do you believe in the stars?" Benjamin asked.

"What?" I gazed blankly.

"You look at the sky—there are thousands of stars up there. And I ask you: do you believe in them?"

"Everyone always believes in something," I said, realizing that I had said the same thing to Malu.

"It's a lie, don't believe in them. I have a friend in one of those stars, he's probably a hundred years old by now. But he can't figure out a way to come and see me; I miss him. He, too, looks up into the sky and thinks like you do. But there's nothing to think about, we live in different realities. Anyway, it's late; I've got to go. There's a good flight coming in at the airport today, with many foreigners arriving, and I don't want to be late. I have to be there at one."

"Do you work there?"

"Yes."

Benjamin turned to get back in the car, but I suddenly stopped him.

"Do you know Malu, D'hol, and Llama?" I asked.

"Those crazy people? Yes, they go to Schweitzer's[32] hospital every day, but nothing ever works out for them there. They don't treat psychiatric patients. Those are the idiots who keep robbing gods."

"What do you mean?"

"Do you think I know? He says to me every day, 'Do you want to see the trunk of my car? God is there.' But I ignore all that now."

"What about the fire?"

"What fire?"

"The one that happened two years ago, in May."

"I don't know anything about that. I have to go, otherwise I won't make it to the airport on time, and the other drivers will grab my customers."

"Where is that hospital?"

"At that same spot where I picked you up. In Lambaréné."

Benjamin turned around and got in his car. At that moment, I spotted the huge knife in his pocket. It was the same one I had seen that morning…

"Which star is your friend on?"

"You wouldn't know it, it's really far away. Only I know it."

Benjamin left. His friend probably lived in Europe. I went up the stairs to the hotel. There were fountains in the distance. The wind blew so hard that drops of frozen water flew at my face.

---

32. The city of Lambaréné is famous through the renown of Albert Schweitzer (1875-1965)—physician, theologian, philosopher, physicist, and musician. After graduating from the University of Strasbourg, where he studied philosophy and theology, he moved to Paris and continued pursuing philosophy and music (he played the organ and was also a music critic). Despite having a promising future, he decided to change everything and move from Europe to Africa. In 1913, he and his wife (Helene Bresslau) left for Gabon, specifically to Lambaréné, where he began to provide medical services and founded a church.

He returned to Europe from time to time in order to raise funds for his hospital. In 1952, he was awarded the Nobel Peace Prize. The hospital has now been converted into a museum and bears Albert Schweitzer's name. A new hospital was built next to it and is considered one of the best equipped hospitals in the whole of Africa.

But why did he go to Africa? Nobody can answer that question, including the man, Schweitzer, himself,

"Society cannot treat man like a means, it cannot see humans as executive bodies. It will inevitably find itself in a position that demands compensation towards the general good, at the expense of the love of separate individuals."—A. Schweitzer

DAY 27. CONGO
THE VILLAGE OF DRAGONS

Everything began quite strangely. The interpreter accompanying me asked me to get on a local bus and head to one of the nearby villages. I already knew him; he worked with a local agency whose services I had used several times.

The yellow bus surprisingly arrived on time. Its doors opened with a sound reminiscent of a tiger's growl, and Nap—Napoleon De Sica, my interpreter—and I got on. The smell of coffee wafted from inside. There were two or three other passengers. We sat at the very back, on the only seat that could fit two people.

Nap, who didn't like to talk about himself—I didn't even know his ethnic origin—said, "Don't look left or right like you're new to all of this; people here aren't used to just anyone—especially a white person like you—sitting in their village bus."

"You forced me into this; it's not my fault. This bus is so strange that I can't help but show my surprise."

We waited for around three minutes until the driver pressed the button that shut the doors, and then started the engine. He had a cap on, but from a distance it looked to me like he was bald. There were a few small, bad-quality posters in the bus cabin from various political campaigns.

"Is there going to be an election?"

"No, those are old. The locals probably didn't even go to vote. They're unaware of everything. The village we're going to now is cut off from the rest of the world. Its inhabitants are not connected in any way to the people in the rest of Congo's cities, especially Brazzaville."

I had earlier asked my interpreter to take me to a place that would be different from everywhere else, a place that would be completely new to me.

When the bus started moving, a few people suddenly appeared from nowhere, jumped inside and took their seats.

"Who are those people?"

"Passengers running late. People here always wait for the vehicle to start moving before getting in. The villagers don't like the way the inside of the bus smells. They prefer to wait outside for as long as they can."

"How long do we have to travel?"

"If everything goes smoothly, half an hour."

"What do you mean by 'goes smoothly'?"

"We have to go up a mountain in this miserable bus. Sometimes, its engine can't muster up the power, and then we're forced to walk halfway. Anything can happen."

"Is the road very bad?"

"No, but it's all uphill."

There were a few white sacks piled on top of each other in the bus, with wet coffee inside. There were two young people sitting in front of us who would often look back at us and whisper to each other. I was sure that they were talking about me, although Nap didn't want to talk about that. In front, near the driver, there was a woman with a red headscarf. She was very fat; I had never seen such a fat woman before. Her breasts were bigger than the heads of the young men sitting in front of me. Her cheeks sagged and moved up and down with the vehicle's movements. She also looked at me often and seemed very dissatisfied with something. She wore a long, colorful dress, the hem of which touched the muddy floor. In front of that woman, there was someone else whose face I couldn't see at all. Only the long walking stick in that person's hand was visible, which served as a leaning pole and helped maintain balance when the bus turned. That passenger would look back sometimes, but I would never be looking in that direction at the same time.

There was a curly-haired child to our right, around four years old, with a woman who was probably his mother. The child kept eating something; his feet couldn't touch the ground and he kept swinging his legs, causing his dirty shoes to rub against his mother's skirt. Watery snot flowed from the boy's nostrils and slowly slipped down to his lips. He even used his tongue to clean it off once or twice, but nothing changed. When the child turned towards me, his mother would strike him on the shoulder in what seemed like a warning to not look at me.

There were two other people next to them who had been the last ones to board the bus. One of them was elderly, about seventy years old, with white, curly hair. The other was younger. I didn't know why but they were standing and holding on to each other, even though there were two free seats right there.

"Why are they standing?" I asked Nap.

"I don't know; they're most probably scared."

"Of what?"

"You."

"Why?"

"Do you want me to ask?" he joked. "I told you, didn't I? It's strange for people here to see someone like you. You're probably the first white person the people here have seen. There's no sightseeing in their village, nothing that would bring tourists over. Nor are these villagers wealthy enough to leave their birthplace and travel. They have no televisions, no telephones…perhaps their only wealth is this bus, but even this doesn't belong to the village—it's a city bus. During the revolution, the villagers somehow managed to hold on to it and not return it." He was talking about the assassination of their president in 1977 and the political events that followed it.

"How do you know that?"

"My friend told me."

"Is he from the village?"

"Yes. When we get to our destination, we'll go see him."

The bus slowly went up the hill. Those two standing passengers kept looking at me and did not sit down. I couldn't see outside the window because the glass was dirty and it had cracks in some places. It was very muddy and some dirt entered through the cracks and blackened them, spreading throughout the glass like a cobweb. In the silence, the banging of the door could be heard; it was constant and monotonous and often went unnoticed. The back door, which hadn't closed completely, was also moving back and forth. This allowed a wind to constantly enter the bus and blow directly into my right ear. Nap was sitting to my left, near the window.

There were at least a hundred flies inside the bus, if not more. They were quiet, but did not want at any cost to be plucked off of the heads of the young people in front of us.

The person sitting in the very front, whose face I couldn't see, held a bag in his hand that was half open, and two horns could be seen in it. There was probably an animal inside, although it didn't make a sound.

"Is everyone going to get off in the same place?"

"I don't know; I don't know them. All I know is that there are no other villages on this route. But who knows? They might get off elsewhere, but only once we're on level ground again."

"That person in front keeps looking back at us, but I get the feeling that he's hiding his face so that I can't see it."

"Who, the one with the walking stick in his hand?"

"Yes. And the bag. With the horns in it."

"Those aren't horns. They're wet branches."

"Wet?"

"Yeah."

"Why would he need wet branches?" I asked, although I was sure that Nap had it wrong and that those were in fact animal horns.

"Nature is very bountiful here. The people make herbal medicine from wet branches, mainly for themselves. But it's only somewhat effective, of course. People here don't live long. Everyone has a disease."

"What kind of disease?"

"Different kinds, all fatal."

I myself had taken precautions against various diseases in advance. Otherwise, I wouldn't have been allowed entry into many of the African countries. One needs special vaccinations before being permitted to enter some nations.

"We've been traveling for about twenty minutes already, right?"

"Almost."

Nap didn't like talking very much, especially when asked to offer an opinion or comment on something. Perhaps he wasn't used to expressing his own ideas to other people, because his work involved mostly translating other people's thoughts. I was trying to get a conversation going with him, to exchange some opinions, but he was cold, like a thick baobab, saying just a few words or sentences and then shutting up.

The child sitting to the right of us vomited and fell to the floor. His mother, who had been sleeping, jumped up. The child was coughing. It was a serious cough. He drew his knees up to his belly and was crying. His mother was trying to help, but the child was sobbing and hitting his hands on the floor. The young men in front of us got up as well. I wanted to help, too, but Nap made a gesture warning me to stay put. The child's mother shouted at the driver to stop the bus.

"Why isn't he stopping?" I asked.

"Where would he stop?"

"Here."

"If he stops, we'll be stuck here."

"Why?"

"Because the engine won't start again. I'm sure of it. Everyone here knows that."

"But that child is suffocating."

"So what?"

"We must help him."

"Help him with what? Whether he dies inside the bus or outside it—what difference does it make? Even if we stop, it won't change anything."

"I'll stop the bus."

"No. Stay in your seat; this is not your business. Everyone is staring at you as it is. There's no need."

"Is the child ill?"

"Of course." He said this very matter-of-factly, as if I had asked him the time. I seemed to be the only person besides the mother who was concerned. Perhaps it was because I wasn't used to such scenes, but I was also recalling the child I had seen in Chad.

A short while later, I bore witness to a much more horrific scene. The mother reached out her hand to the half-open door that kept banging against the side of the bus, and she opened it. She grabbed her child and pushed him out the bus, and then followed suit. The bus was still moving. I jumped up from my seat to see what happened, but I couldn't see a thing. The fat woman looked upwards and made strange gestures with both her hands, and then turned to me with a look of hate and contempt.

"What does she want from me?"

"Who?"

"That woman."

"Nothing. She was talking to God. It's a local custom, probably praying for the child's soul. She's looking at you because she thinks you're to blame."

"What have I done?"

"What do you think you've done? You haven't done anything. Just being here is enough. Don't be surprised. Many people will take you for Death, or the opposite. The people here live with stories and parables. One person's life is nothing; it's like a leaf falling off a tree. Everyone understands that they will leave this world sooner or later and they weave legends around this."

"Is there a school in the village?"

"There was one. But they don't have it any more. There was a time when there were schools, although they were far away and many people didn't attend them." He was referring to the time between 1981 and 1992, when the Republic of Congo was an ally of the USSR and had various bilateral agreements.

"Those schools were better suited to other villages that were closer to them," he continued. "It was like a stable and there were one or two teachers who had come from the city. There is no need for that anymore. This is a place that has been cut off from the world. The people here have their land, their own lifestyle…"

I was wondering one thing: if the passengers were all from the same village, why didn't they seem to know each other? When I asked Nap that question, he said that they didn't get along very well with each other.

"How many people live in the village?"

"The last time I was there was a year ago. There were around a thousand then. Now their numbers have gone down, to maybe seven or eight hundred. Many of them have died."

"What's the village called?"

"It has different names. Each of the locals has their own version. So, I can't really answer your question."

"What's it called on the map?"

"What map? Do you understand what you're asking? Who could find that one village in all of the country's 342 thousand square kilometers? No map has the names of all the villages. I've never seen one that does."

"Did the child die?"

"Naturally."

"Is that why nobody helped?"

"Of course."

"What about the mother?"

"I don't know," Nap said calmly as he wiped his pinkish lips. "The road will level off soon, we're near the end of the slope. There's not much further to go. You wait here, I'll be right back."

Nap went up to the driver, took some money from his pocket, paid him, and came back.

It was humid and slightly cold—a gloomy day. There were trees above us, a forest, one could even say "forests" in the plural. When we got off the yellow bus, we walked towards the east, and Nap took me to meet his friend.

"Are you still thinking about the child?" he asked on the way.

"Yeah."

"Don't think so much. I know you're not used to this. But this is how it is here. One replaces the other. One dies, another is born. Several new children will definitely be born today to replace that curly-haired little one."

"But why did nobody react? It was as if one of the coffee sacks had simply fallen to the ground."

"I told you already—this is how it is here. This would be strange even for a resident of Brazzaville or someone from another city."

"Is it like this in all the villages?"

"I don't know, but it's definitely this way here. The people here don't live out full lives. Their lives are very brief."

"What ethnic group do they belong to?"

Nap was quiet and didn't want to answer my question. Perhaps he was from the same tribe. In any case, I didn't repeat my question. We were walking along a narrow path that was paved with stones and curved, like an archway in the Vatican. The stones in the ground glittered, and we could see the reflections of our faces in them. The land to our right and left was deserted—uncultivated land, glades, forests.

"How are we going to get back?" I asked.

"The same way."

"Will the bus be running?"

"If it doesn't break down, yes. It's going to come back down to the bus station in the evening—I checked on this with the driver. He said he lives in the city, Loubomo, and that he needed to fill the bus up with gas to make the trip back in the evening."

"What if he doesn't come back?"

"Then we'll walk."

We walked for about ten minutes on the uneven path before we got to Nap's friend's house. He lived in a half-ruined hut, and there were no other structures in sight.

"What's his name?"

"Lala Loule."

"Does he live in this village?"

"Yes. He's a fisherman. He used to work with tourists in the past, but then he came here and has been living alone ever since."

"Why? Doesn't he work anymore?"

"Loule fell ill. They fired him. But he knows the country very well. He was very good at his job. I hope he's still alive."

When we went inside, Loule was not in his hut.

"Sit down," Nap said, pulling up a chair.

Inside the room, which was barely five meters square, there were two chairs, two sacks that probably held vegetables, one small metal bed, and a table. The room was brightly lit from windows on all sides except for the side with the main door. But only one of the windows had glass in it. The floor consisted of packed soil with cardboard placed on top. There was a small fishing net in one corner, along with a rod and a few other items. The hut was probably self-made and very old.

When Lala Loule came in, he didn't recognize Nap. They spoke a couple of words in their language and then embraced. I greeted him, too.

Lala sat on the bed. He raised his legs, covered in yellow socks up to the knees like a soccer player, and shook off the mud that covered them. He was around thirty-five years old, thin, with a wrinkled and worn face. If Nap hadn't already mentioned it, I would have guessed myself that he was ill. He wore a thick, long-sleeved hoodie. He looked sad and lonely.

Nap and Lala Loule spoke in their language for a few minutes, then switched to English. Lala knew English, but he didn't speak it well. He spoke better French and pronounced most of his English words with a French accent.

"Nap said that you've come to see something special," said Lala Loule.

"Yes," I replied.

"In that case, let's step outside." Loule smiled for the first and only time.

We all went outside. We walked for about a hundred meters. The weather was amazing. Loule had brought his fishing rod and was spinning it as we walked. We reached a wonderful spot. The valley was below us and, for about forty meters, there was dense forest. A small stream flowed through it. There were glades and meadows in some places with thousands of flowers, pink like Nap's lips and yellow like Lala's socks. There was wind blowing below us, but it didn't reach up to our height. The distance between the two gorges was around a hundred meters.

"It's a beautiful place; I haven't seen it before," Nap said.

"Do you see the stream?" Lala asked.

"Yes," I said.

"That's where I go fishing," he said, and he coughed. It was a grave cough.

"How do you get down there?"

"It's very difficult, and it takes several hours. Sometimes I stay there and spend the night, then climb back up in the morning."

I wanted to talk to Lala with respect, simply because that seemed to be the right thing to do. In general, I feel like people who live short lives spend their years with much more intensity, making thirty years quite a mature age. Perhaps that was the reason why each day could pass by so slowly for them, but at the same time, very intensely.

"I didn't know that Congo had such high altitudes."

"No, we're only about 500 meters above sea level. This village is on a mountain. All right, let's go, the day passes by pretty quickly here. I have to go down."

"Going fishing?" I asked.

"Sort of."

In the distance, on the mountain, there was a structure that was barely visible. It was made of yellow stones.

"What building is that?" I asked.

"It's a church," Lala said.

"The village church?"

"No, the mountain church. I don't know who it belongs to, or whether there's anyone there anymore. I don't know. All I know is that it's very old and..."

"But why was it built? Isn't there a road leading to it?"

"I don't know. The locals say it's a monastery."

"Monastery?"

"Yes."

"That high up?"

"It's so that you're closer to God. I don't know if that's true or if someone made it up. I think there's nobody in that church, just some spirits. Life is like that," he said, before quickly changing the subject. "People live and live, and then suddenly get the news that they must leave. And everybody leaves without exception. Literate or illiterate, thin or fat, hungry or full, poor or rich. A rich person here is someone who has several animals and a place to sleep. This is a village of sick people. I, too, got a letter yesterday."

I didn't understand what he meant for a moment, and then Nap corrected him.

"I had a dream," Lala Loule continued. "I was fishing in a swamp in my dream. The fish were splashing on the water's surface. I could catch any that I wanted. But when I cast my line into the swamp and pulled it out, I saw that the fish were dead and rotting. I changed to a different place. Now I was fishing in an old truck. The truck was surrounded by fencing and the floor was a long strip of cardboard with water in it, but murky. There were hundreds of fish inside, buzzing around like bees. It was surprising that the water stayed within the fencing. When I got a bite after a long wait, I pulled it out and saw a fish that looked like a spider. It was so disgusting and strange that I couldn't tell its head from its tail. I went back to my previous spot. I cast the line into the swamp again and when I again got a bite very quickly, I pulled out the line with joy. I had caught two fish at once, they were moving, but they had no heads. Then I woke up."

I imagined Lala Loule's dream so vividly that I got goosebumps; my feet went numb, and for a moment I couldn't walk. Nap was stunned, too. He was translating for me and making a few corrections along the way, but the dream that Lala narrated was mostly understandable.

After being quiet for a while, when Lala had gone a few steps ahead of us, I asked him, "What is the name of this village?"

He gestured with his hand and said that we were bothering him. When Nap repeated my question, he turned, saying, "You can call it what you like; people give it whatever name they want. For me, this is the Village of Dragons. A place where everything is destroyed."

He picked up his pace. I noticed that he was limping.

"Come on," Nap said.

"Where?"

"Let's go back. Let's leave him alone. He has things to do…"

We left and went back to the hut. Nap went in, picked up one of the sacks and put it over his shoulder, and then asked me to carry the other one. He closed the rotting, crooked door behind us and we set off.

"This will rot here; we'll take it with us and give it away. Lala doesn't need this anymore."

The sacks were heavy. I barely managed to keep holding on. There were peanuts inside, or something that resembled them. We walked slowly but took big steps back down the same path that we had taken to get there. It was much more difficult this time around. We were quiet. Along the way, after we had walked quite a bit, Nap saw a child. He walked up to the child and spoke to him. Then he gave him his sack.

"Shouldn't we give him mine, too?" I asked. I was barely managing to carry it.

"We'll give it to the next one. We'll meet someone else."

"What did that boy say?"

"Nothing. He just said that the bus isn't going to come."

It was dark, almost nighttime. All I could hear was the tapping of our feet and the rustling of the peanuts under my ear. We would stop every once in a while and catch our breath. There was nobody else for me to give my sack to. We walked along the dark road. Nap didn't feel like talking, and neither did I. I kept thinking about Lala Loule, his stories, and everything I'd seen. The wind came up from behind us and pushed us along. We still had a long way to go…

DAY 28. DEMOCRATIC REPUBLIC OF THE CONGO (DRC) THE RIVER THAT SWALLOWS ALL RIVERS

The Democratic Republic of the Congo (DRC), or Congo-Kinshasa, is the largest state in the central and southern parts of Africa, and third largest in size in the whole of Africa. It did not welcome us with much joy.

Nap continued to accompany me. We arrived by boat from Brazzaville, the capital of Congo, to the DRC. We paid about twenty US dollars each to a guide who would take us there smoothly and in comfort. But, as we found out later, comfort is a very relative thing. We barely managed to make it to our destination in an overloaded boat.

When we finally got off the boat and crossed the border, I noticed a half-ruined single-story building in the distance. It had a sign on its façade saying, "Volcano Hotel." There were a few pillars in the front and single door. It looked like the hotel had not been functioning for a long time. Its roof was blackened and I thought that it looked like soot deposited from a fire.

"It says 'hotel,'" I said. "Looks like an interesting place."

"It would be better to go into town; there are many things there that would interest you. The local boys do graffiti. Let's go; it's dangerous here."

"Why?"

"There are many reasons, it's just better that we go. This place is not clean, the air is dirty, and if any of the locals sees you, a whole gang would attack you."

"Why?"

Nap gave me a long stare, as if I was supposed to already understand this on my own.

"Things aren't so simple here," he said. "In a country with more than 240 languages and 700 dialects, can you imagine how difficult it is to live? It's good that French is around, otherwise this place would be the Tower of Babel. There are 250 ethnic groups and as many languages, and overpopulation to add to all of this. The population has gone up by twenty million people in the last ten years." By 2007, they had a population of 65.7 million.

"There are that many languages in use here?" I asked.

"No, only French and four others—Congo, Lingala, Tshiluba, and Swahili—have the status of official languages. But everything is complicated here; nothing is straightforward. Except for the capital and possibly a few other cities, nobody even knows what is going on in the rest of the country."

We were walking along the muddy curb. It was cold and the sky was gloomy. The soil was fragile and soft. Our shoes were completely covered in mud.

We were walking against the wind, and the cold air seared my face. I was still lost in my thoughts and worries. I was unable to forget the sick child whom I had seen on the village bus, as well as Lala Loule.

"Nap, why did we go to the Village of Dragons?"

"You're sorry we went?"

"No, but I was expecting something different."

"Let's go in here," Nap said, quickly changing the subject. Moving ahead, he entered a small café or bar, which didn't look like a very pleasant spot, to be honest.

I felt an emptiness for the first time during my travels; it was a horrible feeling that didn't allow me any peace of mind. I felt like getting drunk and forgetting everything. The last several countries had neither amazed me nor caused any joy; they only brought sorrow. I began to consider myself an "unfortunate African"—an "African" because I had grown so comfortable here, and "unfortunate" because any "African" would be unable to go through all that with indifference.

In reality, this had all started a few days earlier, but none of the countries were really to blame in this case. It was an issue between me and reality. I wasn't sad because I was in any particular country, but because all of this had wrapped itself like a snake around my throat and was not letting me go. A thought had suddenly begun to haunt me: why had I started this journey? What was the point of seeing all this suffering, and suffering myself? The things surrounding me had become unpleasant. I had had similar thoughts in Morocco, and in Tangiers. But the question was now tormenting me in a different way. I had no intention of returning home, but at the same time I had lost my original enthusiasm. Perhaps the reason for this was the absence of the mystic, fairytale-like Africa; I hadn't seen that side of the continent for several days in a row.

In any case, the question of what I was seeking—and what I would like to seek—in Africa would not let go of me.

"Bring us some *momambe*," Nap said to the waitress, who was a pretty woman close to thirty, with short hair. Then he turned to me, saying "*Momambe* is a tasty dish. It's local. Do you want something to drink?"

"No, thanks." I really did want a drink, but not there. That bar seemed unsanitary, and I didn't really even feel like eating there. There was a small stage behind me, or rather a platform, where two musicians were making a real effort to play and sing a pop song. There were many people smoking in the place, and the smoke had gathered and occupied the ceiling area like fog. The place was dimly lit by red bulbs and was reminiscent of a photo laboratory. It was a good thing that the music wasn't loud.

I felt like it must be nighttime, although it was still daylight outside.

"This is a good bar. Young people usually come here, but there's no rowdiness. The management is strict," Nap said.

The waitress brought the food a few minutes later. It was delicious. Then Nap left. He didn't tell me where he was going, but I assumed he was headed to the outhouse.

I don't know how it happened, but then everything changed. The waitress came up and said that the bar urgently needed to close, and that I had to leave. She asked everyone to leave. Chaos ensued.

"Where's Nap? Where did he go?" I asked, taken aback.

"What? Speak louder," the waitress shouted. "I can't hear you." There really was no need to shout, but I tensed my vocal cords and asked again, as loudly as possible.

"Who's Nap?" the waitress responded.

"We ordered this food a short while ago. The man who was sitting next to me… don't you remember?"

"No, no, I don't remember anything. Get out, leave. It's dangerous here."

The chaos kept growing and the other customers were leaving without finishing their meals. They were shouting and pushing each other around in order to leave as quickly as possible. It was very strange; I found myself unable to understand what had happened in the space of just a few minutes. The waitress didn't wait. She pulled the tablecloth off the table, and the food that was on it spilled onto me and the floor.

"Get out, it's dangerous here," she shouted again, so loudly that the pictures hanging on the wall fell to the floor.

I was no longer interested in knowing where Nap was at that moment. The stone walls rumbled, and the large chandelier hanging from the ceiling, which only had a few bulbs in it, swayed. Everyone was shouting. The musicians had stopped playing a long time ago and had disappeared. The whole building began to shudder—apparently, the pictures had not really fallen off the wall because of how loudly the waitress had shouted. A short while later, a long, sustained sound like the engine of a tractor rang out; the right wall collapsed and a large tank entered the place. When I got to the door on the other side of the place and was getting ready to escape, I saw the gigantic tank parked in the middle of the room.

I was out in the street. It looked like a battlefield. People were running around, in a panic. Shooting could be heard constantly. There were tanks in the distance. Some people were in military fatigues and held bullhorns in their hands that they shouted into. Suddenly, someone with a familiar face came up to me, though I couldn't remember where I had seen him.

"Are you looking for Nap?" he asked.

"Yes, do you know him?"

"Of course. Do you see all this? This is all because of him."

"What do you mean?"

"It's a long story. I'm in a hurry now, so I can't hang around. I'll explain later; I'll tell you everything later." And he quickened his pace.

"Wait. Who are you? What is it you have to tell me? I don't understand a thing."

"I'll tell you later. We'll meet again at this same spot. But I have to go now; they're waiting for me. You get out of here; it's dangerous to stay."

"What's going on? Who are you? Why is everyone running away? Who's shooting? This is like a battlefield; I don't understand any of it."

"Yes, we're in a war; what else do you think this could be? Don't you see the tanks going back and forth? They've occupied the city; it's a state of emergency. I can't talk any more, I have to go. But I know you, I recognize you."

"Where do you know me from? I don't get it. Wait, I'm coming with you."

"No, you can't come. Try to find Nap. If you find him, he'll explain everything."

The stranger left. Then I noticed that there were other white people in the street besides myself. Soldiers were chasing them and putting handcuffs on them, after which they were being forced into trucks. It was like a prison where each inmate was tormented separately and taken inside. One of the soldiers noticed me, too, and ran towards me. He wasn't carrying a gun, and his gear was heavy. I managed to outrun him.

Some people had lit a fire in the middle of the road and were dancing around it, singing in one of the local languages, Lingala, as they embraced each other. The shooting continued in the distance and a crowd of thousands of people was heading in my direction. Everyone was shouting; there wasn't a single person in the whole city whose mouth was shut. Absolutely everyone was saying something. And I had no idea at all about what Nap had to do with this.

One of the buildings collapsed and huge pieces of it blocked off the road. A few ambulances which seemed to have a red cross on them (which is how I saw it; I couldn't see well at that distance), sped by me with their sirens blazing. There were wounded people, possibly even dead ones, laying in the streets. The smoke rising from the city was so thick that even the sun couldn't be seen. I also sensed that there were helicopters in the sky. The chaos continued and worsened as time went by. Some of the people picked up stones, others used agricultural tools or guns to strike at shops, stands, buildings, and cars that had writing in foreign languages. There was nobody I could ask for information about what was going on.

It was evening already, and a relative silence took hold of the streets. The bar where I had been earlier in the day no longer existed and a huge crack had appeared in that street following the explosion of a grenade.

I had a headache and wanted to sleep, but it was too dangerous. The sky was gloomy, but in some places, the rays of the sun hit my face through the spaces between the clouds and the smoke. The smoke swirled above and even in that state it was the calmest thing about the city at that moment. I leaned on the wall of a semi-collapsed building and began to think. All of this was better suited to be called "City of Dragons," the name of Lala Loule's village. He probably didn't know that, not too far from his hut, stream, and village, there was a place with a completely different rhythm of life. It was like dragons were roaming the streets of the town with open mouths and were breathing fire on whatever they came across.

"Who are you?" a fat woman asked me in French. She resembled the woman that I previously had seen on the village bus.

"What?" I asked. I was scared, although the woman had questioned me very politely.

"Are you a customer? Can't you see? There's nobody here, everyone has left; I can't offer you anything. It's a bad situation."

Nap had taught me a bit of French and I managed to understand the woman, albeit with great difficulty.

She was the owner of a brothel and I later discovered that I had been leaning on the wall of the building that Nap and I had seen earlier that day, the one bearing the words "Volcano Hotel." I guess Nap hadn't known that it was a brothel.

The woman closed the door and left. I wanted to stop her and ask her questions, but I didn't feel like speaking French anymore.

I didn't know what time it was, but the sun didn't want to set. I was certain that the sun had been in the same position for at least three hours. At first, it seemed like this was because of the geographical position of the country, but it was not. Something was wrong, but I couldn't understand what it was.

I then entered a store which, to my surprise, was still open and had not been damaged. The shopkeeper looked at me with fear and I felt like he was getting ready to attack. But I was wrong—he simply was very angry.

I asked him for water and something to eat. He didn't say a word; perhaps he hadn't understood what I had said. Then he gave me a soft drink and went over to a child sitting at a table near the dark corner of the wall. The child was around four years old and held a piece of bread in his hand, which he was slowly chewing. His feet did not reach the ground but he kept swinging his legs and his dirty feet kept rubbing against the shopkeeper's clothes. Two people stood in the corner of the shop and looked at me with amazement: one was old, about seventy, with white, curly hair, and the other was younger. I don't know why, but they held on to each other and did not let go, even though there were two empty chairs in another corner of the place, which was better lit. I drank the soda and, just as I was getting ready to leave, the child started to cough. I ran out. It was as if my eyes were replaying the scene from the village bus.

It was probably nighttime, but that was hard to tell because the sun had been hanging in the same spot for four hours now. There was some noise in the distance, but the city had regained its serenity. There were no tanks, nor was there any artillery or shooting. But there were still many people in the streets, and doctors were moving the wounded onto stretchers and carrying them to ambulances. From one side of the street a crowd of people was approaching, shouting as they walked. Some fireworks went off. I melted into the crowd as well.

Everyone was shouting, "Colonialists, get out of Africa, go back to your countries."

I joined in the shouting automatically and walked with them for about two kilometers. We marched through some of the central streets, and then the protest broke up. The slogan they were chanting was disturbing, but I didn't pay any attention to it. I wanted to find a place to spend the night. Suddenly, I saw a tank in the distance, and Nap was on it, holding a bullhorn in one hand. He was in military uniform and was shouting something that I couldn't hear. At that moment, someone drove up from behind me in a European car. It approached him, stopping in front of the tank. Two people got out of the car and attacked Nap, firing guns at him and then fleeing. It was like a story, perhaps like the story I had wanted to experience, but that had been evading me for the past few days.

Suddenly, the sun began to move and the city again calmed down to some extent. I ran towards Nap, but they had covered his body and taken him away in an ambulance. It was dark, but Nap's body could be seen through the ambulance window, bouncing on the stretcher. He was just lying there, and the doctors weren't providing any sort of assistance. A large crowd quickly gathered at the spot of the murder. They were talking and looked stunned. I didn't know what language they were using, but they kept repeating the same name. I felt like it would rain soon; the clouds rumbled and there was lightning, but not a drop came down. Suddenly, I saw the same stranger in the crowd. I went up to him and squeezed his shoulder.

"You came to me this morning and wanted to tell me something. You said we would meet again."

He seemed like he wanted to leave for a second, but then he nodded and dropped the bag in his hand to the ground and looked at me. He had a stick in his other hand.

He leaned on the stick.

"I recognize you; you're Nap's friend. But Nap wasn't really an interpreter."

"What was he?"

"I can't say for sure. It is dangerous to talk about things like that in the presence of foreigners such as yourself. You're all cowards; all of this is fun to you, but one day you, too, will understand why we're fighting like this. This is no random occurrence; we're not just useless slaves, we're human beings just like you, except that you're white. But what's the difference? If it's nighttime and the sun is not in the sky, do you think that's a bad thing? You can only imagine life with the sun. Imagine that you're the sun and we're the moon. Do you know what would happen?"

"What?"

"You'd see the sun the whole day. Even when it grows dark, you'd still see the sun. It would be in the sky in the morning and at night; it wouldn't go anywhere. Is that what you want? Nature will reestablish balance one day, in any case. And you, and people like you, will finally understand that our struggle was not senseless. Nap was no ordinary guy; his death was not a random act. To me, he was a hero. But not one of the heroes that you imagine, who only know how to kill and win."

He was speaking with passion. I don't know who he'd taken me for, but I didn't want to interrupt him. It seemed normal for him to address me, not as an individual, but as the representative of all white people.

"There was war here today, but there will be peace tomorrow. Yes, my friend Lala Loule will not see all this, because he'd been ill for quite some time and now he's dead. But we'll see it."

"Lala Loule? You know him?"

"We'll see," he continued his thought, "that the next generation will live in a country that's free. And nobody will remember this incident."

"Where do you know me from? Have we met?" I asked.

"Yes."

"Where? I don't remember you. Who are you?"

"It doesn't matter. I've got to go, but I'll say one thing. If you want everything to go smoothly, for people to live and enjoy life, for nighttime to be nighttime and for daytime to be daytime, then leave Africa; we have no need for you."

Then the stranger left. He picked up his bag from the ground and walked through the empty street, which was much calmer than it had been in the morning. It was nighttime and quiet. I kept trying to remember when I had seen him. He walked along the dark street and in the silence the tapping of his walking stick could be heard, striking the ground with the same rhythm, along with another familiar sound that came from his bag. That sound resembled bleating, and a pair of horns was visible, sticking up out of the bag…

I walked along the street, the wind lashing against my face and searing it. I didn't want to think about anything. I was tired. I took a small postcard from my pocket which Nap had given me that morning on the boat. There was a small picture on the postcard—blue, green, and light blue; there were thin people in the picture who were chained together. The corner of the postcard had the caption, "Slaves Yoked Together," and in one corner there was text that said "31x48 cm, Mode Munti, 1973, Zaire."[33]

Music could be heard coming from one corner of the street. It was the bar-café where I had been earlier in the day. I was hungry. I walked inside so that I could finish the *momambe* I had left half eaten…

---

33. The Democratic Republic of the Congo was called Zaire (officially, the Republic of Zaire) from October 27, 1971 to May 17, 1997. In the 1960s, a struggle led by activists who were against the colonialists, which was accompanied by civil unrest, internal political tensions, and disaccord, laid the foundation for the creation of the Republic of Zaire. The word "Zaire" originated in Portuguese and is a mispronunciation. The actual word comes from *nzere* or *nzadi* in the Congo language, which means "the river that swallows all rivers."
The names of all characters in this story have been changed intentionally.

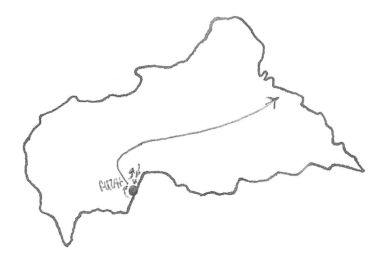

DAY 29. CENTRAL AFRICAN REPUBLIC (CAR)
THE TOWER

"In order for you to understand me, we must be on the same level. But you can't be on the same level as me—you'd have to have seen everything I've seen throughout my life, feel everything I've felt, and that is not fair...

"You can't take someone else's place. You're you. If someone takes out your eyes and puts my—ordinary—eyes in their place, or if they replace your heart with my worn-out heart, you still wouldn't understand. Life is like that—we are born and die; each one of us unique. The rainbow seen by each of us has different colors. I could talk for hours, if it doesn't bother you, of course, but then what would you do with what I have to say? I don't want you to look at me and my family as helpless, poor, and miserable people; we aren't like that. Perhaps you're laughing to yourself; you probably think that I'm making excuses, or trying to pretend to be an honorable person. No, I'm being sincere; I, too, have something to lose, perhaps something more precious than you. But that's not important—what's important to me is you. Yes, you. Don't be surprised—just as you have discovered me, I have discovered you, too. I'm not a useful tool for you, nor am I something you've just found along your way; on the contrary, I have found you. Your presence is proof that my dreams were correct. Tired? I can shut up if you like.

"I forgot, there's one more thing I wanted to say, it's stuck like a thorn in my throat and, if I don't say it now, I'll never get an opportunity like this again. Is the tower still there? Once, when I was a small kid, they took me to Paris. I don't remember the name of the tower, but it's the only thing I remember from that trip. Probably because of its size. I remember, when I saw it, I immediately had the desire to build something like it back home. Do you know how long I've waited? My friends say that I'm supposedly a wise man. They come and tell me their problems, they ask for advice; they think I know the answers to everything. But, tell me, what's so smart about me? Which wise man would send his wife to prostitute herself in order to make money? Which smart man would give away his children and agree to an exchange, handing over healthy ones in exchange for sick, disabled, and malnourished ones? You're silent. I understand. You don't want to accept it or understand. I'd probably do the same if I were you, I wouldn't accept it. I'd want so much to be able to argue with myself. I often want to commit suicide, but that's foolishness, who would I play *momba* with then? Do you know what *momba* is? I made it up. It's the only game that you can play by yourself. You choose several stones that have different colors and you throw them up into the air, but you have to throw them in such a way that they all disappear into the air together. After that, you have to wait for a while, until one of the stones falls back down. You have to pay attention—the whole point of the game is in the first stone that falls down. That stone is considered the winner. I have several thousand victorious stones. And that's not all. When you pick up that stone, you look at it carefully, and it tells you what is about to happen, like a soothsayer, and whatever you think about first at that moment, that will come true. I don't need a lot in life; I'm not a greedy man. You wouldn't understand what I want, no, you wouldn't understand it, and I don't blame you. I know that you're not to blame. Do you know what the three most interesting things in life are? I don't know. I thought I knew, but I only know two and can't figure out the third for the life of me. But I know that there are three of them. The first two are simple: *momba* and my tower… Man is always striving for something, he always wants something new, more resources, more money, but in the end, he wants the same thing. Man does not know what he wants. I'm tired. I've talked so much, that's why I can't think of the third most interesting thing. It's going to rain soon. I have to go feed my pigs. You didn't answer my question: is the tower still there, or have they torn it down?"

I can't remember the name of the village, but it was close to the capital. I had arrived there in half an hour on foot. I stopped in front of a pig farmer's house, lost. It was evening already and I had to return to Bangi, but I had lost my way. The air was humid and there was a slight breeze. Clouds had gathered in the sky.

The pig farmer was a man past forty, with yellowed eyes, dry, thick hair, and a raspy voice. When I asked him where the road was, he began to talk about completely unrelated things.

"Which tower? The Eiffel Tower?" I asked.

"Yes, that's the one. I'd forgotten the name. Is it still there?"

"I don't know. I suppose it is."

"You sound doubtful; they've probably torn it down. They must've torn in down." He got up and walked slowly along the stony path to his pigs. "Why would they keep it? They must've torn it down. Wait, I'll be right back. Stay there."

I could hear the snorting of pigs; the pigsty was around twenty meters uphill, but the noise coming from there seemed to be right in my ear. The pig farmer, holding a muddy bucket, went inside.

"It's loud, isn't it?" he said with a moan.

"What is?"

"My pigs and their groans."

"Yes."

"Do you know why?" he overturned a bucket that held rotten food onto the ground, "The wind is blowing and the sound can be heard even a kilometer away. If you stand against the wind, you can hear different sounds coming from long distances away. They say that you can even hear the sounds of people's souls. I haven't heard any, but I believe it. When I die, my soul will come to feed the pigs, so that they don't go hungry. There's a small bell on my tower, I'll ask for them to ring the bell seven times that day; seven is my favorite number." He moaned again and came up to me breathlessly. He looked at me carefully as if he had never seen a man before, then he brought his hand to my shoulder, squeezed it powerfully, and coughed in my face. "I'm a writer, too. Surprised? But I'm not limited like you; I write about the whole world. That's why I was saying that it's not you who found me; I've found you."

"How can I get to Bangi?"

"Why go to Bangi? Stay here. You'll help me, you'll tend to my pigs. My children can't help me; they're bedridden. Stay, stay," he said, then walked back toward the pigsty. "Come, I'll show you how."

"How do I get to Bangi?" I asked again. "It's getting dark, I want to get there while there's still some light. I know it's close by, just point me in the right direction—up that way, or down there? I have to be in Sudan tomorrow."

"Why go to Sudan? The situation there isn't good. Stay with me. I won't be around forever. You'll look after my pigs. Come, I'll show you how. Come, come. The rain is late," he muttered to himself.

I went up to the pigsty. There were about ten pigs there, all of them lying in the mud with no desire to move.

"They're nice, right?"

"Which way to Bangi?"

"Go down and go straight along the right side. You'll get there in half an hour," he said in an angry tone. "You didn't like my pigs. I knew you wouldn't understand me."

"I have to go. Down, you said?"

"Yes, yes, down, then straight, don't leave the path." He followed me for a bit and then said with some worry, "There are cannibals in the village; be careful."

"Cannibals?"

"Be careful, will you? Ah, yes, one more thing," he said in a calmer tone. "Learn how to play *momba*."

The pig farmer's words caused me to worry a little, although he gave the impression of being a bit absent-minded. He left his thoughts unfinished, and one thought was not connected with the next. The road was uneven, but I could see small, one-story buildings in the distance and I thought that must be Bangi.

I walked for a while, around twenty minutes. The road seemed to go on forever.

But the pig farmer had seemed like an honest and wise man, indeed. I didn't know what it was I was supposed to understand, but he had kept mentioning it. I really liked the story he had told about the wind, although I didn't hear a sound during my walk. I also had no idea why he was so interested in the Eiffel Tower; he spoke about it with such emotion. I would have happily stayed with him and worked for days, or years. But not this time. Perhaps on another occasion, after completing my journey.

I'd collected a few colorful stones along the way, so that I could play *momba*. All I could think about at that moment was getting to the city. Then the weather changed suddenly. The air grew heavier. At first, it was strange and unpleasant, like it had a chemical smell. Then, it changed gradually. It was the smell of petrol. It wasn't unpleasant, but it was very concentrated and it prickled my nostrils like alcohol. I could breathe comfortably, but I felt a buzz, and my feet seemed to grow heavier. A short while later, I noticed a small stone house in the distance which I thought was an outhouse. I came closer. I went in. When I lowered my pants, someone spoke very loudly, and the voice echoed, "What are you doing?"

"Can't you see what I'm doing?" I replied; it seemed to me that it was the pig farmer's voice, carried to me on the wind.

"Get out of here!" Someone laid a hand on my shoulder and pulled me outside.

The smell of petrol inside had been very strong and unnatural. It was as if they had mixed something into it. Three young men stood in front of me. They looked at me in surprise. Then the one who had dragged me out slowly came up to me and unfastened the buckles on my jacket. I thought that these must be the cannibals that the pig farmer had warned me about. I wanted to run away, but the other two stood by, ready. He unfastened all the buckles, took the coat off of me, and put it on.

I wanted to understand why he was doing this, although at the same time I was ready and waiting for an opportunity to make a run for it.

"That's all," he said.

"That's all?" the other two behind him asked.

"Who are you?" I asked.

"Who are you? Didn't you see that big sign?" he responded.

Behind us, on the top of the house, there was a small sign, or rather a board marked in red paint, that said in French: Petrol. This was probably a gas station. I hadn't seen the sign and had mistaken it for an outhouse.

"Give me back my jacket," I said, holding out my hand to take it back.

"It's hot here, you won't feel cold," said the man who had put it on and, taking a few steps backwards, he joined the other two who had gone to the opposite side of the road.

"Are you selling gas?" I shouted after them, resigning myself to the fact that I would not get my jacket back.

"Yes, but we don't have any now. No gas, just oil. The villagers don't need oil anymore, because the village now has electricity," said the young man wearing my jacket. His reply sounded like a thank you for the fact that I wasn't still demanding my jacket back.

"Where's Bangi?" I asked. We were talking to each other at a distance of around twenty meters.

"Where it's always been."

"I know that it's where it's always been. It couldn't have run away. But where is that place? I've been looking for it for a while, and it's going to get dark soon."

"Don't be so sure. There are times when the wind blows hard and the city flies away and is lost forever. You have to be careful or you'll never find it."

"Flies away where?"

"I can't say. It gets lost… it disappears into thin air."

"Where should I look?"

"No need to look. The rain will come and the city will come back with it."[34]

"What rain?"

"Regular rain. But I have no idea when it's going to rain. There are clouds in the sky and the wind is blowing. But it doesn't seem likely that it will rain now."

He spoke with such conviction that I couldn't help but believe him. When they left, I noticed that they all exchanged glances and laughed, as if they'd found an idiot whose leg they could pull.

---

34. This is a local belief that the elderly still hold, but that many others don't even know about. In the past, when the wind blew away the villagers' houses, they believed that the rain would bring them back. When it rained, they believed that God was sending gifts to them from above and they stood there for hours, getting wet, expecting their houses to return and the village to be put back in its place.

It was getting darker and no rain had come. I no longer wanted to walk, convinced that I was in Bangi already but that the city had flown away. Why the pig farmer had mentioned nothing of this to me I didn't know, but he had been waiting for the rain, too, so he had probably known about the disappearance of Bangi.

Suddenly, the silence was broken and I heard the noise of a crowd approaching from afar. The group had white people in it, as well as cameramen recording the proceedings. Perhaps they were reporters. A large crowd of locals accompanied them. Everyone was happy and proud, as if returning from war after vanquishing the enemy. I joined them.

"Where are you going?" I asked one of the cameramen.

"The village has been supplied with electricity. We're going to shoot a story."

"It didn't have electricity?"

"No, it never did. Or rather, I don't know, perhaps they did, but not for the past ten or twenty years. Now, people are starting to return to the village. Many people are coming back home. The electricity here is several times cheaper than in other places."

"Why?"

"Various reasons," he said. He wanted to list the reasons, but did not seem convinced about them. "It's low-voltage electricity," he said, as if justifying it to himself.

"Is the village close by?"

"They said it was close, but we've been walking for more than half an hour and we still haven't reached it."

"Are you a reporter?"

"Yes, from Euronews."

"Are you French?"

"No, Polish."

The reporter's name was Bojan. He was in the Central African Republic (CAR) for the first time and, like me, he was a bit confused. He wanted to keep talking, but I could tell that he didn't know what to say. He was tall, thin, and bald. He had on prescription glasses and an item hung on his back that kept making a hissing sound.

"It's a radio," Bojan said, realizing that the hissing sound had caught my attention. "But I can't connect from here. They gave it to me so that I can keep in touch with people in the city, but for some reason, I've lost the connection."

"It's the city that's lost," I said.

"Yes, that's right," he smiled. "It's not that well developed." He smiled again.

"The wind has blown it away," I said.

I did not agree with Bojan. Bangi was indeed not a well-developed city, but his comments had another subtext. I had found the city attractive. I don't know what it was, but there was something magical in that small city in the vicinity of the Ubangi River.

"It has to rain," I said.

"Why?"

"So that you get the connection back."

"No, I don't want that. I'd rather not get the connection. If it rains, I won't be able to shoot my story."

"You won't be able to use your camera?"

"No," he said with concern. "I can use the camera, but there won't be any electricity if it rains. I've been told that the electric supply is cut when it rains. The cables can't work when they're wet. And we're going there to report on how happy the villagers are, now that they finally have electricity. If they don't have a connection at the time, the report is pointless." Bojan narrowed his eyes and looked towards the distance, then said to himself in a low voice, "When it rains, they switch off the power up there, so that there isn't a fire."

"Who switches it off?"

"Up there. I don't know his name, but I was told that the main power station is over there."

"So why don't you shoot your story there?"

"Because strangely enough, the very day we arrived, we were told that the person who had built that power station to supply the village with electricity had died."

"Today?"

"Yes. Some of the villagers left to go see him a short while ago, otherwise this crowd would be double the size."

Bojan kept squinting, as if looking for someone.

"What's wrong?" I asked.

"Nothing, except I can't find our correspondent."

"What? Look again, he couldn't have just vanished."

"I don't know," he said, his voice once again loaded with concern.

"Where could he be? Could he have already made it to the village?"

"Hardly possible. I'm afraid the cannibals may have gotten him."

He said this with such seriousness that it reminded me of the pig farmer. Bojan stretched his long neck forward for a moment and started walking more quickly. Then he came back and said, "No, the other reporters haven't seen him, either."

I didn't know what to say; I was sure that without rain there was no way I would make it back to Bangi. We walked along the semi-demolished, rocky path lined with yellowed grass and shrubs, many of which were covered with worms. The wind was blowing, but nobody's voice could be heard in the distance, just the excited sounds of the children who were slightly ahead of us and singing with their arms raised. They were naked except for a small wrap below their waists, which was translucent.

"Can't you do the story without him?" I asked Bojan, although it seemed like an impolite thing to say.

"I can, but how? I can't get a connection."

"It has to rain," I said again. "When it rains, Bangi will come back, and the connection will be restored."

Bojan was stunned and brought his face closer to mine in order to get a good look into my eyes. Then he demonstratively turned away, trying not to pay me any attention, and went in the opposite direction. Perhaps what I had said sounded absurd. I went after him and said rudely, "Where are you going? The village is that way!"

"I have to go back. I just remembered where my correspondent could be. We had met there previously."

"Where?"

"Near the gas station. He met three young men there…"

I didn't go with Bojan. On the contrary, I headed back with greater confidence towards the village, the name of which I didn't know, the location of which I had no idea about—I knew nothing, except for the fact that it now had electricity, and that everyone was going to witness that event.

I felt good for a moment, realizing that every foreigner here was just as foreign to the locals as I was.

The road seemed endless; we had walked for nearly an hour, the sun had set and the sky had darkened, thousands of stars had appeared but they did not shine brightly because the sky was not yet completely dark and this dulled their light.

I kept thinking about Africa. I was still a bit groggy and couldn't quite understand everything I had seen. Everything seemed so intense here that it was difficult to understand it all at once. Every day, another strange thing occurred, as if in pursuit of me. And, while these things had surprised me or seemed unpleasant at first, I could no longer imagine my trip without them. I felt like a spaceman, whose one day in space was equivalent to several days on the Earth. I was also a spaceman in the sense that I had "flown" over half of Africa without feeling the weight of my own body.

It seemed like none of this would have happened if I hadn't come. I'm sure this wasn't the case, but it felt like something that seemed big in one place could be small somewhere else. And it was no coincidence that the locals had been so excited because of the electricity, which is a very common thing for other people.

My nose felt wet. It was the first drop that caused dismay among the gathered crowd. It started to rain. It was soft and mild, but it was raining.

Some of the villagers were sad, but it was mainly the foreigners in the group who were the most disappointed. They had walked for almost an hour to see the illuminated village.

When we got to our destination, it was already nighttime. The mild rain gave me certainty and I had no doubts that Bangi had returned. Out of curiosity, I entered the village in order to see the electric station. The village was lost in darkness, and nothing could be seen clearly—there were small houses, narrow streets…

Only in the distance, lit up by the moon, there was a tower. It wasn't very big, but it looked very grand, and it resembled the Eiffel Tower. I came closer and stood beneath it. I looked at it for a few minutes and suddenly noticed the small bell hanging from it. This tower was the power station that so many people had gathered to see.

Nothing could be heard except for the sounds of nocturnal birds. I had long left the village. I was finally returning to Bangi. It was windy again. I suddenly remembered the colorful stones in my pocket. I took them and threw them upwards. When the first stone returned, I picked it up and waited for something to happen. I remembered the pig farmer's words and put the "victorious" stone in my pocket. Then I heard the sound of the bell ringing. One, two… six, seven. Seven rings.

I remembered the story the pig farmer had told me about the wind, that it could carry a sound for kilometers.

The ringing was coming from his tower…

When I entered Bangi, the rain had already stopped. In the distance, very far away, a small village could be seen, shining like a star and giving off light.

The pig farmer had probably made up that whole story on purpose, so that I could see the tower he had built…

DAY 30. SUDAN[35]
THE CIRCUS OF DARFUR

Nothing was clear. I wanted to understand where the two policemen were taking me. Their rubber batons would rub against their uniforms as they walked, causing a rustling sound. It seemed to me that they were conversing with each other in whispers, but in reality they weren't even opening their mouths. We were going through a narrow corridor that was dimly lit and looked like a basement. It was humid and cold. There was no wind, but the light coming from the torches hanging on the walls was moving. Each step we took caused an echo, and I heard each one three times. We were walking slowly; the policemen were in no hurry. The corridor seemed endless.

One of the policemen was Black, with large eyes. He had a miserable, sad look on his face; you couldn't tell by looking at him that he was a policeman. He could have been a violinist or a writer. His police uniform, which looked black, although I couldn't really tell in the darkness, seemed "tougher" than he did.

I felt like he would soon take a violin out from under his coat and start to play. If he indeed did have a musical instrument under his shirt, he wouldn't be able to find a way

---

35. South Sudan (Republic of South Sudan) gained independence from Sudan (Republic of Sudan) on July 9, 2011, making it the newest independent country on the African continent.

to remove it—his clothes were a tight fit. His pants also looked gloomy and dissatisfied, making even his gait seem discontented, while his shoes looked like those of a murderer, although I was sure that they housed the feet of an honest man. This Black policeman also had large cheeks. He was young, but his clothes did not allow him to look young.

The other policeman had dark skin, too, but he wasn't Black. His facial features looked more like those of an Arab. He seemed like a good man, too. His eyes were small, his lips thin, his nose a bit pointy; he had combed his hair back and had a thin mustache that grew haphazardly and looked like fuzz. His police uniform, which looked green, although I couldn't really tell in the darkness, was also "tough." He didn't look like a violinist, but he could have been hiding another musical instrument in his breast pocket. His shirt buttons strained against his body tightly and he could barely move. The two maintained a distance of about one meter from me. The gap between us never changed, even when I quickened my pace.

I could have escaped. But the whole problem was that there was nowhere to run. There were long corridors both in front of me and behind me, and while small windows appeared from time to time to the sides, nothing could be seen through them.

The corridor was like a tunnel dug during the Second World War. The floor had shiny tiles, but that shine had probably developed as a result of a lot of walking being done on them. For a moment, I even thought that I was in the palace of a prince of some kind and that it was the 17th century. But my imagination came to a complete halt when the Arab-looking one took a small device out of his pocket that I thought was a mobile phone at first glance; he pressed some buttons, took a set of earphones from his pocket and put them in his ears, and then happily waved me on to keep me moving. At that moment, I realized that my assumptions had not been wrong. He liked music, too, just as the darker man did, in whose case I had no doubts whatsoever.

I noticed how much joy the Arab (as I called him from that point on) felt when he switched on the music.

"What are you listening to?" I asked. He didn't say anything. He just looked at me and continued to listen.

The Black man, whose name I never managed to pronounce (I called him Ja Ya for short) looked at the Arab and said something in their language, which was Arabic. Then the Arab replied, but I didn't understand anything; the only word familiar to me was Bach's name.

We finally left the corridor. The Arab and Ja Ya approached me and asked that I hold out my hands so they could handcuff me. For the first time, I thought that I was being taken for a criminal. But I couldn't remember what I had done; in fact, there was nothing to remember—I had done nothing.

"Why?" I asked.

"Security," Ja Ya said and, without asking my opinion, he handcuffed me. It was the first time in my life that I felt those heavy pieces of rough iron on my hands.

Ja Ya knew English, because he had worked as a doctor on an international medical staff.

"Where are we going?" I asked.

"Not much left," the Arab replied; unlike Ja Ya, he only spoke Arabic and a few English words—"hello," "not much left," "goodbye," and one more word that he kept using when he pretended to speak English: the word "if."

"But where are we going? It's been more than twenty minutes that we've been walking. You were quiet at first, then you started talking. I don't understand any of this—where are you taking me?"

"A prison cell. You'll wait for your trial. You will be tried and then you will be set free. Then you'll go home."

"What have I done? I was just standing around when the police car drove up and I was attacked. I hadn't done anything…"

"Don't tell us about it. When they interrogate you, that's when you can talk. We're regular police. We do whatever we're ordered."

"What are your orders?"

"They don't concern you."

We stepped outside into a deserted area that only had a few trees. It was hot. The grass had grown yellow. The sun burned like a flame. I tried shielding my eyes with my hands, but the handcuffs didn't let me. I remembered Nigeria—I had been interrogated there, too, but I had only been a witness there; here, I was the accused. And if I were to go to trial, I could forget about being a writer. My trip would come to an end. I wouldn't be able to return home for a long time. Sudanese prisons are only slightly different when compared to hell.

"Where will they take me?" I asked.

"A concentration camp."

"Then what?"

"What do you mean—then what?"

"Will I end up staying there?"

"Isn't that bad enough?"

"But why? I haven't done anything."

"You have. If you hadn't done anything, you wouldn't be with us now and we'd be happily listening to our music."

"Am I going to be staying long?"

"I don't know." Ja Ya was trying to act cold and distant, but he wasn't really that way.

"I have to get to Khartoum" I said, which is the capital.

"Why?"

"I want to see it."

"See what?"

"Khartoum."

"Nothing special to see there."

"I have to get there. I was supposed to go there first. But then they told me that there's a road in from the border."

"So what?"

"They said I could get to Khartoum by train."

"What train?"

"A local train. Isn't there one?"

"Here?" He asked a question to the Arab, who had been listening to music this whole time. Then he continued, "There is a train, but it takes several days to get to Khartoum. And it also takes several days to get to the train. Sudan is the biggest country in Africa."

I knew that, of course. I was actually supposed to go to Sudan from Chad, but because of some discord between the two states and the dangerous situation on their closed border, I had been forced to postpone my trip to Sudan. The same issues had also existed on the border with Egypt, as well as with the DRC. So, it turned out that this biggest state in Africa (of more than 2,505,813 million square kilometers) was isolated and there was no way into it, except from the east. I had decided to enter Sudan directly from its border with the CAR, travel to Khartoum by train, and continue my journey from there. But I hadn't taken Sudan's sheer size into consideration. Right at the border, after I had walked just a short way and had reached the highway, some police cars had shown up and they arrested me. They then took me to a city whose name I cannot remember and handed me over to the Arab and Ja Ya, who had emerged at that time from a tent.

When I first saw Ja Ya, a stethoscope hung from his neck and, in all probability, he had been treating someone in that tent. The tent was round with a pyramidal top and looked like a miniature circus tent. I could hear the sounds of children in the distance, as well as crying and shouting.

If I weren't in Africa, I would have thought that there was some kind of a theatrical performance going on inside the tent.

I don't remember how we ended up in the long corridor; I just remember being handed over to the Arab and Ja Ya, who had been asked to take me to the police station. At that time, Ja Ya had called over the Arab, who had been lying in the sun, squinting his eyes, barely managing to look up to the sky.

"What are you doing in Sudan?" Ja Ya asked.

"I've come to see it."

"See what?"

"The country."

"Which country?"

"Sudan."

"There is no Sudan now. You should have come from the east side. There is no Sudan here."

"What is there, then?"

"Not much left," the Arab interrupted.

"What is there?" I asked again.

"Nothing, there is nothing here. There used to be people, but now there are none. Everyone now…"

"Are you Sudanese?"

"Yes."

"What about the Arab?"

"Who's the Arab?"

"He is."

"He's Sudanese, too."

"Why have you arrested me?" I asked this in a softer voice, as if forcing them to respond.

"Tell the truth—why are you here?"

"I'm telling the truth."

"You are accused of illegally crossing the border. In addition to that, they want to know why you've crossed the border and come to this side. All of this could even lead to your death. They probably would have already have killed you if you were Black. You're lucky that you look like an Arab."

"I'm not an Arab."

"I know, but you're not Black, either."

Ja Ya stopped for a minute, as if wanting to say something important, then he straightened the clothes he was wearing and continued to walk. I noticed once again that his police uniform hugged his body tightly and did not allow him to move freely. The buttons of his shirt were fastened so tightly that it seemed like he would suffocate if he spoke any more.

"I'm a writer. I'm very interested in Africa, which is why I'm here. I'm really a writer." I came closer to Ja Ya.

"So what? If you're a writer, does that mean you can break the law?"

"No. I didn't know that I was breaking the law. When I crossed the border, I didn't even know that I was already in Sudan. I only understood this once I saw the police. Even my passport didn't help; it just complicated the situation further. They probably took me for an inspector or something. My questions and explanations didn't help at all. They looked like Arabs. They were probably Arabs. Then they brought me to you. I thought for a minute that they were letting me go, but when I saw you, I knew it wasn't going to be that easy."

"Why?"

"I don't know. There were lots of people in the distance. If I weren't in Sudan, I'd think I was at a movie studio or something. And I could hear shouting and shooting from the other side. I thought that people were being killed. I didn't want to see anything. I tried to escape at one point, but one of the Arabs gave me an evil look and that threatening gaze really scared me. Then I saw you. You came out of the tent. It was like a small circus: it was red on top, and green below. It was a small tent, but I got the feeling that there were many people inside."

"A circus?"

"Yes."

Ja Ya gave me an ambiguous look. His eyes welled up. He suddenly moved his head to the side. After being silent for a moment, he said, "There are many such circuses here; didn't you see them?"

"I did. There was a smaller one in the distance, and several other tents. But there was shouting everywhere."

"You sound like a writer," Ja Ya said.

"Yes. I've told you that I am."

"Lucky you."

We were walking slowly. The heat was unbearable. The Arab had fallen behind slightly, still listening to music. Ja Ya was tired. He offered me some water, which tasted like plastic.

"When I saw you," he said, "I understood at once that you were not a local. I thought that you had been brought here for another purpose, but when they took you out of the car, I understood that things were not going to end well for you. Usually, they solve such problems in a different way. I don't know why, but you've been lucky so far."

"In what way?"

"In many ways. First, they didn't kill you; second, you're with us; finally, that you've seen so many circuses. When I was small, I would dream of becoming a clown. I would do magic tricks in my village, making people happy. They liked me a lot, they called me the 'happiest person in the village.' There were special days when dozens of people would come to watch my performances. We had a small stage, and I would dance there and make faces, making people laugh. I would dream about the circus. We never had anything like that in our parts. I believed that, one day, a large number of people would gather and would enjoy my performances. But my childhood dreams were dashed to the ground. There was no longer a stage, no villagers, no village. They needed a doctor then, not a clown that makes people happy. Nobody wanted to be happy. There was no time for that. People were suffering, leaving their homes, their villages. They were fleeing in the thousands to neighboring countries, and some went to the eastern cities—Khartoum, Port Sudan, Omdurman. People no longer wanted to dream; everyone's faces had changed, nobody was smiling. They only thought about seeking asylum. I couldn't live with dreams. People were dying, there was a famine, sick people were everywhere…

They took me to Europe; I was lucky like you—I was saved instead of being killed. I became a doctor in Europe and, along with other foreigners, we were sent to several African countries. I picked Sudan, because it was my homeland; I couldn't have chosen anywhere else. Nothing had changed here, it was the same situation: fires and corpses everywhere." Ja Ya stopped again, blocking the sun from his face with his hand. "Look, do you see that hill?"

"Which one?"

"There should be a hill there."

"No, I can't see anything."

He called to the Arab and asked him, too. He couldn't see a hill, either.

"It's over there. Block the sun with your hand, and you'll see it."

"I've blocked it, but I can't see anything."

"Our village was on that hill. Sometimes I think there are people there. They wave to me. But I suppose there really is nothing."

"The village doesn't exist?"

"No. The hill probably doesn't, either. Otherwise, you would have seen it."

"And then?"

"What?" Ja Ya asked, as if from far away. He was staring blankly.

"What happened then?"

"Then? Nothing happened then. I was also forced to become a policeman, in order to keep my own body safe. But I've never killed anyone. I put on this uniform only to feel safe, although I'm not that safe in reality."

"Do you like playing the violin?"

"No."

"I think you do like it."

"No, I don't. I don't know how to play," Ja Ya kept looking into the distance, wishing he could see something.

"Are you looking for the village?"

"Yes, but it's not there."

"You would see better from up close."

"We'll leave it for another time. We have to get to the police department now."

"Not much left," the Arab said, joining us.

I was between the two of them. The Arab had taken out his earphones. He had a twig in his mouth and he was moving it around with his tongue. Ja Ya continued to look at the deserted fields around us, hoping that he would find his village there.

I was tired. I had been walking for more than an hour. There was only the sun in the distance and one or two dried trees. There wasn't even a road.

"Do we still have far to go?" I asked.

"Not much left," the Arab replied, and he sat down on the ground. I thought for a second that he was praying.

"Are you in a hurry?" Ja Ya asked.

"Yes."

"What's the point? You can't change anything."

"There isn't even a road here. Where are we going?"

"The police station. We'll get there soon."

"Remove the handcuffs."

"Why?"

"I can't bear it any more. The cuffs hurt."

"You'll run away."

"I won't. Where would I run to?"

Ja Ya called the Arab, and took the keys—I hadn't noticed when he'd handed them over to him—and unfastened the cuffs.

"Thank you."

Ja Ya smiled. Then he gave the keys back to the Arab, who said something.

"What did the Arab say?"

"He said that the sun will set soon."

"Doesn't he speak English?"

"Just a few words. He doesn't know anything besides that." He called the Arab. "Do you have something to say to him?"

"No, it's just that he's been quite."

"He was listening to music."

"Is he a policeman, too?"

"No. He's a childhood friend. He used to own animals in the village once. But that business shut down."

"Is he an Arab?"

"No."

"What is he?"

"I don't know. Do you want me to ask him?"

Ja Ya spoke to the Arab.

"He says he's an Arab," he said.

"From here?"

They spoke again.

"Yes."

"Why is he quiet?"

"He isn't quiet. He speaks to himself."

Indeed, the Arab wasn't quiet. When I looked carefully at his lips, I saw that they were constantly moving.

"Will I be interrogated?"

"Yes," Ja Ya said absent-mindedly.

"What should I say to them?"

"Whatever you want."

"Will they let me go?"

"Of course not."

"Will I be tried?"

"Yes."

"How long will it take?"

"Around a year. Prisons are hell in Sudan."

"Then?"

"Then what?"

"What should I do?"

"When?" Ja Ya asked absent-mindedly. He was acting coldly again and had lost the sincerity he had shown a short while ago. We were getting closer to a city, which actually seemed like a small town. I could sense that there were people close by.

"Now," I said.

"What do you want to do?"

"I want to escape."

"From us?"

"Yes."

"Where would you escape to?"

"I don't know. I don't want to go to prison."

"You shouldn't have crossed the border."

"I didn't know I was breaking the law."

"Would you have broken it if you'd known?"

"No."

"How would you have gotten here?"

"I don't know. There was nobody at the border. There wasn't even a border. How was I supposed to know that I was already in Sudan?"

Ja Ya laughed. He asked softly, "Are you really a writer?"

I didn't reply. Ja Ya spoke to the Arab again for about two minutes. Then he said, "Do you see that tree?"

"Yes."

"Go there. Wait until we are so far away that you can't see us on the horizon. Then you go to the east. A military helicopter will be landing there soon. They're peacekeepers. They're from Khartoum. Go with them. Forget about us, don't tell anyone about us. Tell them you're lost, tell them you've just landed from the moon, say whatever you want, but don't mention our names."

"All right," I said, realizing that I didn't even know their names. "So, you're letting me go?"

Ja Ya was quiet. The Arab was quiet, too. They both looked at me and smiled.

"Goodbye," the Arab said. "If…"

He wanted to continue, but he didn't know how to speak. Ja Ya didn't say anything; he just slapped my shoulder with his hand and they left. I didn't know what to do. I was surprised that they had let me go. I stood under the tree and waited for about half an hour until their bodies, quivering in the sun, vanished. They were walking slowly, side by side—the Black Ja Ya and the Arab Arab.

Then a military helicopter landed, looking more like a jet. A few people in military gear came up to me and asked in English, "What are you doing here? This is a danger zone."

"I'm lost," I replied.

"Come with us to Khartoum; you'll give your explanations there."

I sat on a trembling iron seat and watched the deserted spaces from above. I kept looking, wanting to find Ja Ya's village, but there was nothing. When the colorful tents appeared, the ones that reminded me of a circus, a few people in the helicopter said, "Darfur."[36]

I looked at the tents and it seemed to me that I could hear laughter…

---

36. In the western part of the Sudan, in the region of Darfur, military operations began once again in 2003. The main conflict in the region was between the Arab and the Black populations. The (Arab) Janjaweed militia had destroyed and razed several villages and towns over the course of a few years. Various calculations suggest that up to four hundred thousand innocent locals were subjected to genocide. Around 2.5 million people were left homeless, seeking asylum in neighboring cities. The genocide in Darfur is continuing to this day, and the number of innocent victims just keeps mounting…

DAY 31. ETHIOPIA
THE BOY WITH THE BALLOON

This wonderful country, which is considered one of the oldest states in the world, was the second country, after Armenia, to accept Christianity. It is the second in size by population in the whole of Africa, and it greeted me with a huge sun shining brightly and two schoolchildren who accompanied me throughout the capital city, Addis Ababa, for more than an hour.

I don't know why or how, but Ethiopia was different from the previous countries I'd visited. I wouldn't say that the difference was obvious, but something about it made me feel different.

The two schoolchildren, who weren't really schoolchildren but were simply carrying schoolbags, happened by me at the airport. They answered my questions with pleasure.

From the very beginning, I suspected that they wanted something. One of them took on the role of interpreter and began to translate for the other. They were probably fifteen to eighteen years old.

"Ethiopia is the oldest state in the world," Haile, one of the youths, said.

"I know," I said, although I really didn't know much information about the country.

"Mankind originated from here."

"I know."

"We're the oldest nation," said Mahmoud, the other young man.

I wasn't sure if Haile and Mahmoud would be able to answer my questions, but they did want to present their country and culture to me. They even went with me to the National Museum of History, the market, and many other places.

Only at the end, when we were saying goodbye, did I find out that they were orphans. We were at the train station and I was waiting for a train.

"We don't have any parents; they died of hunger," Mahmoud said.

"My parents are from Dire Dawa, near Mount Gara Muleta. They died a long time ago, in the eighties. I was one or two years old. I don't remember them. Mahmoud and I are from the same orphanage. An English family adopted us. We've been living in Great Britain for fifteen years now. But Mahmoud never managed to learn English."

"I know English," Mahmoud said.

"We've come here to tell tourists about our country. Back in those days, twenty or twenty-five years ago, there was a famine. There was a famine before that, too. More than a million people died and several million suffered, including our parents. We're fundraising to help the children who've suffered, the ones who are homeless or living in orphanages."

"We need money," Mahmoud said.

"What will you do with it?" I asked.

"We're collecting it now, then we'll figure out what to do with it. We have to help them."

"How much have you collected?"

"We haven't collected anything yet; we've just started. You're the first person we've approached."

I couldn't refuse them. But I wasn't sure that they were entirely honest. They had small eyes with lids that would blink quickly. They would smile sometimes, but with a very childish smile. Because they had accompanied me for so long and had not complained even once, it would have been unkind of me to refuse their request.

"Thank you, take this picture," Haile said, taking out of his bag a small piece of cardboard which he held out to me. "This is a picture of one of the children."

"What children?" I asked.

"The hungry and suffering."

"The orphaned and abandoned."

"The homeless and miserable."

"One of the children who needs our help." Haile and Mahmoud spoke in turn.

I took the picture and said goodbye. A small Black boy was in the picture, standing in a field and holding a blue balloon in one hand. The balloon seemed to want to soar upwards and take the boy with it. He had curly hair and large, sad eyes. The picture was very colorful; it had been made using water colors, and seemed to have been freshly painted a few minutes ago.

When I got to the cashier's window, which looked like a small chapel, a man touched me on my shoulder from behind. I turned around immediately. He was an old man, at least sixty years old. He had a white wavy beard and a protruding jaw, and wore a transparent green shirt and a checkered jacket that did not suit him at all. He also wore a cowboy hat.

"Where are you from?" he asked, bringing his head closer.

"Armenia."

"Are you a tourist?"

"Yes, I want to buy a ticket," I said; I was in a hurry.

"How much did you give?"

"Give?"

"To the boys collecting money."

"Why?"

"They owe me money."

"You?"

"Yes."

"How do they know you?"

"I'm a conductor and a porter; I guide people"

The old man didn't look like a porter, and the jacket he was wearing looked like it had seen better days; he looked more like he could have been an actor or an opera singer.

"Who are you guiding?" I asked.

"I could guide you."

"I have to buy a ticket."

"Where are you going?"

"Anywhere."

"There's only one route here. No other way."

"That's okay, I don't care. As long as I get on that train."

"Are you running away from someone?" he asked in a low voice.

"No," I said. I turned back to buy a ticket, but the old man touched me on the shoulder again.

"I'll guide you for free."

"Thanks, but I don't need a guide."

"Follow me."

And, despite everything, I did follow him.

"Where were you from, did you say?" he asked again. I noticed that he limped, and seemed to breathe with difficulty.

"Armenia."

"Ah," he said ambiguously.

I didn't know whether he had heard of my country or whether he was completely unaware of it. I felt like he didn't know anything about us.

"Come this way. The train will leave in twenty minutes. We'll wait till everyone goes on board, then we'll slip in."

"Do you have a pass?"

"I do, but you…"

"I could have bought a ticket."

"No, no, there's no need. Relax," he said very casually, "it's going to be fine. We'll get in just fine. Do you want gum?" He took some gum out of his pocket that looked like it had already been chewed, even if it hadn't, and he bit off half.

"No, thanks."

"There's not much left. Everybody will get in, then we'll walk up. Where did you say you were going?"

"I don't know."

"How can you not know? Why are you here, if you don't know?"

"I've come without knowing."

"Do you regret it?"

"No, on the contrary. I'm very happy."

"What are you so happy about?" he asked with dissatisfaction.

"I'm happy to be here."

"Why am I not happy then? I've been here fifty-six years."

The old man looked at me. The look he gave me was a bit disdainful.

"What's it to you? You're going to leave; that's why you're happy. If I were to leave, perhaps I would feel the same way. You can't be happy in the same place, even if you're in the most developed country. It'll bore you someday. We want something new. It's like a glass full of water that is being held under a faucet—they want to fill it with water, but it's already full. What's the point of that glass? It is no longer useful. Either the glass full of water must be emptied, so that it can be filled again, or the glass needs to change."

"Or, you can shut off the faucet."

"Yes," he said, smiling. "Let's go, it's time."

A short while later, we were standing in front of the closing doors of the train, and the old man was trying to stuff himself in. Dozens of villagers had gotten on board with their things at the last minute and there was no place to sit. I regretted listening to the old man. Finally, we managed to pack ourselves in.

The train car was hot and the air was unpleasant. Everyone was sweating, but they couldn't even wipe the sweat off; everyone was packed in so tight that there was no way to move. Luckily, nobody asked to check my ticket.

"Will they get off along the way?" I asked.

"Yes, yes, don't worry," the old man said, trying to calm me down.

"Is the next stop far?"

"We just got on; you have to wait a bit."

I was looking carefully at people's faces. Most of them had a sad look.

I was surprised that nobody seemed to be paying me any particular attention.

"Where did you say you were going?" the old man asked me for the third time.

"I don't know. I don't have any particular place to go. I have to go to the end, then come back."

"What's the point?"

"That's why I've come."

"To sit on a train? There are other interesting things here, too."

"I know. I was hoping to see something from the train window, but I can't even see the window, unfortunately."

"Ethiopia is a magnificent country."

"I know."

"You can't see the country from the train."

A few people got off at the next stop and the train grew less crowded.

We finally found a place to sit. The old man did not want to sit at first, then came forward demonstratively and sat down.

"I don't want anyone to think that I'm doing my job badly," he said.

"What is your job?"

"Going back and forth, like you want to do."

"And?"

"I keep watch so that people don't argue, so that there is no disorder. I help old people. I carry light loads. There's always something to do."

"Are you paid well?"

"I don't know," he said, looking at me suspiciously.

The train was uglier on the inside than the outside, but the scenery outside the window was so nice that I forgot about that. The window was half open, and the cool wind blew over my hair, bringing with it the smells of animals and trees. It was a very bright day. A few kilometers later, the train suddenly stopped; it seemed like someone had used the emergency brake. Many of the passengers moved to the windows to see what had happened.

"Has there been an accident? Have we hit something?" I asked.

"Yes," the old man said, yawning.

"Really?"

"Yes, I said. Happens all the time. Do you want gum?" He plucked the other piece of gum out of his pocket and put it in his mouth.

"Has the train derailed?"

"No," he laughed. "Relax, this happens almost every day. It's nothing dangerous."

"Why are the passengers surprised?"

"They like surprise. This is an opportunity."

"Are we going to be waiting long?"

"Isn't it all the same to you?"

"In principle it doesn't matter, but I wanted to get to the end."

"Don't worry, we'll move soon. In a few minutes."

The car began to shake, the window pane trembled and the handkerchief hanging above my head—I don't know why it was there—swayed in the air. I stuck my head out the window and saw that a herd of elephants was passing by. They were moving calmly, in no rush.

"So many elephants!"

"It's not always elephants. It could be zebras on another day, or rhinoceroses, giraffes, deer—it's not just the elephants that make the train stop in these parts. Good thing it didn't run any of them over."

"Has that happened?"

"Yes. Several times. Doesn't it happen everywhere? It's only natural. When it's only one or two animals, you might not notice them from far away. When they're in a herd, it's different."

We waited for another twenty minutes, and then the train began to move. I thought that the incidents with the animals must happen very rarely, and that the old man was simply exaggerating a bit.

"My name is Abebe Noratu."

"That sounds nice."

"You never told me how much money you gave those collectors," Abebe said in a more serious and business-like voice. His name, like his clothes, did not fit with his demeanor at all.

"Those young kids?"

"Yes, the ones you met near the ticket window."

"They arrived there with me. They'd been accompanying me since the airport."

"I get it. So, you don't want to tell me?"

"What's to tell? They gave me this picture."

"Let me take a look. Did they give it to you or sell it?"

"No, they just gave it to me."

"I saw you giving them money. They owe me, that's why I'm asking."

"I don't remember how much I gave them, but it wasn't much."

"Why did you give it to them?"

"They said they were collecting money for homeless children. They told me that they were orphans and that an English family had adopted them a few years ago. They had come back to Ethiopia to help the poor children living in orphanages. They said they were fundraising."

"And?"

"And I gave them money."

"Did they tell you anything about me?"

"No. Were they supposed to?"

"No." Abebe was quiet. He turned his head away. He had an angry look and gazed into the distance at the rooftops of houses that were visible from the window, and his jaw muscles clenched. Then he turned back to me with the same look.

"They've lied to you."

"What do you mean?" I asked.

"They're not from an orphanage. And they don't want to help the homeless."

"They said that their parents had died during the famine."

"That's the only thing that was the truth. Many people died during the famine."

"They said they were from the same orphanage."

"From that point on, it's all a lie."

"But I met them at the airport and they spoke English well, or at least one of them did, the other not so much. His name was Haile."

"Yes, Haile speaks well, but Mahmoud knows English, too; he just pretends not to."

"You know them?"

"They're my grandchildren. They tricked me and asked for money, and I loaned it to them. It's been several days now, but they haven't returned it."

"You loan your grandchildren money?"

"Yes. I'm not rich, so I can't just give it to them. They have more money than I do."

There was anger in the old man's words, but it wasn't hate. I could believe that Mahmoud and Haile were family to him. I didn't want to ask him any unnecessary questions, so I simply asked, "Do you live together?"

"We don't have a house. I sleep at the station. That is my home. I have a room there. They sleep wherever they can manage."

"They're homeless?"

"No."

We both stared blankly for a second. Abebe Noratu seemed to feel that we were thinking the same thing at that moment and he said, "Yes."

"I thought so. And this picture?"

"I don't know. They don't tell me anything. Perhaps they painted it. I'm not good with pictures. My only dream is to see Jesus. That's why I ride trains."

"See whom?"

"Jesus."

"Which Jesus?"

"The one who was crucified."

"Why do you want to see him?"

"I've got business with him."

"What business?"

"Nothing. It's not important."

Abebe said nothing more. He was quiet and, then, trying to change the subject, he said, "I'll step outside for a while, but I'll be back soon. I don't want them to see me sitting."

I thought I wouldn't see him again. I still had many questions to ask. When the car rocked and the train moved again, I realized that he had secretly gotten off. Staying on the train was no longer interesting.

I got off of the train, too. I didn't know where I was, which city or village it was. There were fields and semi-ruined houses everywhere. I walked. I was quite far from Addis Ababa. I walked for an hour along the track, its wooden trestles rotting in places and the surface rough. I felt like a train engineer might mistake me for a zebra or deer at some point and run me over. But there was no train. There was nothing—just the bright sun and the deserted fields. I walked for another couple of hours. I was tired. Then I noticed a train approaching from the other direction. I crossed over to that side of the tracks and ran towards the train, signaling for it to stop. The engineer noticed me and braked. He stopped about a kilometer away. I ran.

When I got to the train, the conductor asked, "What are you doing in these parts?"

"I'm lost. I got off the train, but it was the wrong station."

"Do you have a ticket?"

"No."

"How did you get on the train if you didn't have one?"

"Yes, I do—well, I did have one, but I lost it."

"We can't take you if you don't have a ticket."

"I'll pay."

"No. I can't do that," he said, straightening his uniform.

"Abebe Noratu is my guide."

"Who?"

"Abebe Noratu, that train's conductor."

"Which train?"

"The one heading west a short while ago."

"Yes, there was a train. But who's Abebe?"

"The conductor—with a cowboy hat, a white beard, a protruding jaw... an old man. He lives at the station."

"No, we don't have a conductor like that, you're mistaken. He might be living at the station, but he doesn't work for us."

"He limps."

"No, we don't have anyone like that. We never have."

"He has two grandchildren; they're orphans."

"How do you know so much about him?"

"He told me."

"What grandchildren?"

"Haile and Mahmoud."

"Ah, I know them. But they have nothing to do with that man you mentioned."

"What? He's their grandfather. He even said that they owe him money."

The conductor laughed. He was a young man in his thirties. He had short hair, a blue uniform, a large mouth, and a happy smile.

"Haile and Mahmoud are our friends; they've come from Great Britain. They come every year, so I know them well. They were both from the same orphanage. They're involved in charity work now. They help homeless and orphaned children living in poverty. They're good boys; they're going to come again this year."

"They're already here."

"Even better. They'll use our train service for sure, then."

"But they…"

"I'm sorry but this train has to move. I can't keep it here any longer. Everybody's waiting. We should have been in Akaki already. We lie to people and tell them that elephants have blocked the tracks or some other animals have slowed us down but, in reality, we waste a lot of time because of tourists like you."

"I saw the elephants when I was on the other train. The train stopped then."

"There are no elephants here. This is a holy place."

"Can't there be elephants in a holy place?"

"There can, but there aren't any here that could be roaming around freely in a herd."

"So how do you lie to the passengers, then? Don't they know that there are no elephants?"

"They do."

"So?"

"They don't believe us. They know we're lying."

"But I've seen the elephants."

"I'm sorry, but we have no more time. We have to move. Give me a ticket, or that's that."

"Can't I just pay?"

"No, we can't do that."

"Where are we now?"

"Near Adama."[37]

---

37. The city of Adama is in the central part of Ethiopia, around sixty-five miles to the southeast of Addis Ababa. It is also called Nazret (Nazareth). Some locals believe that this is where Jesus was born, and they search for him to this day.

"Is the capital far away?"

"Quite far."

When the conductor gave the order for the train to move, I showed him the picture that Haile had given me. He recognized it immediately. I told him that I had donated to their cause. That made him happy. He finally let me come on board.

I sat beside the trembling window, and the same handkerchief hung above my head. I didn't want to think about anything. The silence and the rocking of the train wheels had sunk me into a state of pleasant harmony.

The huge sun lit up the train cars in front of mine, and the light reflecting off of them hurt my eyes. I looked at the picture that Haile and Mahmoud had given to me; the Black child was smiling, but he no longer wished to fly upwards. He seemed to have punctured the balloon with his finger. I had probably ended up helping someone.

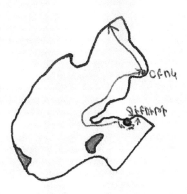

DAY 32. DJIBOUTI
THE PUREBLOODED ITALIAN

The train went all the way to the end. It got to Dire Dawa, where the parents of Mahmoud and Haile had lived, then arrived in Aysha, from which it went on to enter Djibouti. I saw a boy at the border who smiled and took balloons of different colors from his pockets. It seemed like a coincidence at first, but this boy was trying to sell the balloons, not soar away with them. I bought some and crossed the border.

I was in Djibouti, the capital of the Republic of Djibouti. I was walking in the street, seeing people about whom I knew nothing, and I felt like a foreigner. Perhaps I was tired, but for the first time during my trip, I felt like breaking the rules I had set. In fact, the next country that I was supposed to have visited was Eritrea, but the border between Ethiopia and Eritrea was closed, so I had actually ended up crossing into Djibouti.

It was evening. The curved lines of the train tracks were visible from the gaps in the low trees, yellowed in the rays of the sun and lighting up their surroundings like lanterns.

I walked through the semi-dark streets of Djibouti. I had nowhere to spend the night, because I hadn't planned on being there. It was getting dark and I was unable to find a hotel. The locals, mainly Issas and Afars, did not speak English. Neither did the taxi drivers. One part of the street was crowded, where people were selling things. It looked like a wholesale market. There were a few small trucks and porters with carts, vendors who spoke to each other in very loud voices, and several boxes in one corner with plastic bottles arranged in them, one on top of the other—probably drinking water.

I walked up to some vendors to ask where I could spend the night, but nobody responded to me. Like any vendor, they pushed their products towards me in the hope that I would buy something. I noticed at that moment that someone had approached the boxes with water and was carefully removing several bottles from them. It was dark in that area and the only light was coming from a car that stood a small distance away. But the man near the boxes continued to remove the bottles even after the car had driven away.

At least twenty vendors, most of them speaking Arabic, had rushed towards me and were showing their wares. It was mainly food and clothing. I wanted to run away; I was scared, but then I got lucky. One of them noticed the person stealing the bottles, and all of them ran towards him.

I left the market. A short while later, I heard shots fired, followed by shouting and different kinds of metallic sounds. I thought that they had killed the person who was stealing the bottles. That thought scared me even more than the sounds. I wasn't looking where I was going. All I needed to do was to keep moving, I thought. I had to move and move until nobody could see me. But there wasn't a single corner without people.

Without seeing where I was going, I entered a dark street where there was no light at all; the brightest thing on that street was probably my blue jacket.

After walking a few meters, my foot suddenly caught on something and I fell down. I thought I had slipped. I got up and dusted off my clothes, and something suddenly pulled at me from behind. My fingers froze in fear and I began to tremble. Several things were going through my mind at the same time.

The first thing I thought was that it was a dog who was pulling at my shirt with its mouth and, based on the force with which it was pulling, it had to be a large dog. Second, it could be a gang, and one of them had a tight grip on my shirt. The third thing I thought was that I hadn't known where I was going in the dark and that I had ended up in some trash cans. And finally, I thought that it was one of the vendors, who had run after me, caught up with me, and wanted to show me something else he had to sell.

But there was no canine barking, no human voice or shouting, no smell of trash, and no footsteps to be heard. The street was quiet.

I turned around. At first, I didn't see anything. Then, my eyes got used to the darkness.

It turned out that I had accidentally stepped on someone's leg, and he hadn't even noticed. He was still comfortably asleep, one leg to his right, the other to his left, his head facing downwards and his hands under his belly.

I kicked him softly in the leg, but he didn't move; for a moment, I thought it was a dead body and I remembered the man stealing the bottles. But I could hear him breathing in the darkness. I brought my head closer, and I could smell alcohol on his exhaled breath. One could have assumed that he was an alcoholic. I looked at his face for a few seconds—it looked like it was made only of bones; his lips were thin, and he had a small piece of cloth over his body that served as a cover. I wanted to adjust the cloth to better cover his body when he suddenly opened his eyes wide as a bat and said, "Boo!"

The drunk laughed. He had probably just pretended to be asleep. He said something, then realized that I didn't understand him. He stood up and said something else. Then he lay down again and went to sleep.

From that moment on, I really regretted my unplanned stop in Djibouti. I was sure that if I had come later, as planned, I wouldn't have come across any drunks, I would have had a place to spend the night, and I wouldn't be forced to run in dark streets at night.

Eventually, I managed to find a spot that was more or less well lit. It was a small square where there were cars, people on the sidewalk, and shops that were still open. The sidewalks were paved, and not in bad shape; I even noticed trash cans in several spots. The women covered themselves in a one-piece cloth, with only their faces showing. They even looked like streetlights to me from far away. They moved like waves on the sea. I walked behind them and I felt like somebody would hit me on the head with a heavy object at any moment.

Without realizing where I was going, I had ended up back at the market through some amazing coincidence. "Djibouti is a small city," I thought. "No matter where I go, I end up in the same place." There was something else that bothered me besides its small size. I couldn't see well. But my eyes certainly weren't to blame. Whatever I looked at seemed foggy and gloomy.

"Careful!" someone shouted. I only saw him from behind. He had hit me with his bicycle. He was moving very fast and rode his bike in the middle of the street as well as on the sidewalk, among the people. It was a man in a yellow jacket and yellow pants, who disappeared as suddenly as he had appeared.

The vendors had noticed me. I tried not to pay any attention, and walked along the sidewalk with my head hung low, when suddenly someone grabbed my shirt and pulled me back. I was so certain that it was one of the vendors that I was getting ready to turn and run, but when I turned, I saw that it was a woman wrapped in a black cloth, although I couldn't really make out the color well. She was one of the women who looked like lanterns, with large pretty eyes, heavy lips, and dark skin. She looked like an Arab. She was short and thin. She apologized in their language and left. A minute later, a man approached her, grabbed her by the arm and led her forward, pushing her along. The woman had probably confused me for her husband, because her husband was curly-haired like me and wore similar clothes. The woman was shouting, and her voice could be heard from the other street as well.

I was tired. I couldn't keep my eyes open. The sky was full of everything but the sun. The sky was just as confused as I was, nothing was in its place. When I got to a street with a beautiful mosque, I saw a small shop with a sign that said "Souvenirs." The shop looked very different on the outside from the rest. It had metallic shutters and large windows, and there were many colorful items inside. I spotted the shop just when it was about to close. A man was locking the door and lowering a metal shutter. I ran towards it. A beautiful scene revealed itself to me—a small mosque with its minarets, looking like they were made of ice, white and shimmering. There were curved windows on the lower section, with decorations and small, colorful ceramic tiles. I came closer to the shop.

"Good evening," I said.

"Hello," the man said with suspicion; I later found out he was the shop owner.

"Are you closing?"

"Yes."

"This early?"

"Early? I close two hours later than most shops. My shop is probably the last to close in the city."

"I'm so glad I've found you."

"Do you need to buy something?"

I realized that if I said no, he probably would not help me find a place to stay.

"Yes."

"What? But be quick."

"I don't know. A souvenir."

"For whom? A woman? A man? A child? What's the occasion?"

"A child. I need something interesting," I said, beginning to make things up.

"Come inside. Everything here is interesting. I've got things that you won't be able to find anywhere else. Come inside."

I went in. He didn't raise the shutters but had left them half-closed. He shut the door and looked at me with authority.

"Do you need a souvenir?" he asked. "Or something else?"

"What else do you have?"

"Clothes, for example. Upstairs."

"No, not clothes. I'll choose something from here."

The shopkeeper was uneasy. He wanted to understand what I needed and what the value of my purchase would be. If I didn't pick something in the next few minutes, I would definitely arouse suspicion. I tried to distract him. I felt that I would be able to find a place to stay more easily if I kept talking to him. But I definitely had to buy something.

"There are no price tags on them," I said.

"Tell me what you want, and I'll tell you the price."

"How much is this necklace?"

"120 dollars," he said, coming closer. The way he spoke made it clear that the price was variable and subject to bargaining. "This is a great piece of work. It's pure silver. I've brought it from France. I've got some unique items." He placed the necklace, which depicted the heads of various animals, in my palm.

"What do you have that's local?"

"The local stuff isn't good," he said with contempt. It was clear that it was more an issue of the local stuff being cheap, rather than not being good. The shopkeeper didn't like that.

"That's okay. Can you show me some of it?"

"There are some things, but they're not for children. I'll show you if you like. Does it have to be a necklace?"

"No, it doesn't have to be."

He took out a box from inside a table drawer. He put it on the table. I could barely hold on. My eyelids kept closing shut. I was ready at that point to buy all his souvenirs, if only he would arrange a place for me to stay the night. But I didn't dare ask him about this yet.

"Girl, or boy?"

"Who?"

"Your child."

"Oh… boy."

"How old is he?"

"Five."

"Why have you come to me then? Buy him a toy. A car or some other gift. I have no gifts for a five-year-old," he said with disappointment.

"I've bought a present, but I need a souvenir."

"What is the present you've bought?" the shopkeeper asked slightly impolitely, in an irritated voice, pushing his belly outwards as he came towards me.

I suddenly remembered the balloons that I had bought from the boy. I wasn't obliged to show the shopkeeper what I'd bought, of course, but his threatening gaze scared me. He looked at me with dismay and envy, but I wasn't sure why.

"These balloons," I said, taking them out of my pocket.

"Let me see."

He took them and examined them for a long time. He held them up to the light. He picked at them with his fingers. And then he gave them back to me with a laugh. What there was to laugh about, and why he needed to examine them for that long, I didn't know, but his mood was bolstered suddenly and he roared with mirth as he said, "There are holes in them."

"Holes in what?"

"The balloons. Like someone has used his finger to make a hole in them. You've been tricked." And he laughed again.

For a moment, I did feel tricked. But I couldn't understand the reason for his enthusiasm. Perhaps the boy selling the balloons had indeed tricked me. But this had made the shopkeeper much happier than I would have expected.

"That's all right, I'll find other balloons."

"I can gift you some, as many as you want. Consider them a present from my shop. If you buy this necklace," he said, holding out the French necklace, "I'll give you a box of balloons."

In reality, neither the balloons nor the necklace interested me. But I bought it. I wanted him to be happy.

"Well, good night. You've made a good deal; your son will be happy."

"Are you closing?"

"Yes. Do you need anything else?" he asked with enthusiasm.

I felt at that moment that he was ready for anything. I could understand his excitement—just when he was closing the store, he had managed to sell one of his most expensive necklaces, and now he might be able to sell something else as well.

"I have a question," I said.

"Go ahead."

"I wasn't supposed to be here today; I was supposed to come tomorrow. I was supposed to be in Eritrea today, according to my plan. But I miscalculated and had not known that the border between Ethiopia and Eritrea was closed. I haven't been able to plan anything for my stay here, since this was unexpected. Could you please show me somewhere where I could spend the night?"

"What?" The shopkeeper was left open-mouthed. He had a nice set of teeth—white and shiny. At that moment, I noticed for the first time that he wasn't African. He had black, curly hair. He looked like a clown, with a round nose that pointed upwards, long lashes, and large black eyes.

"I said I'm looking for a place to sleep. I've been walking around town for several hours now, but I haven't been able to find a place. And I've had quite a few scares."

"Who scared you?"

"Different people, but it doesn't matter."

"Don't be scared. I know the people here well. I can bring my gun if necessary."

"There's no need for that."

"I've got three guns. They're upstairs. They're for sale, by the way—do you want one?"

"No."

"I'll be right back, wait here."

"I asked for…"

The shopkeeper thrust his heavy body forward and went up to the second floor of the shop, which wasn't much different from the first. He didn't even hear what I had to say. He soon came back downstairs with a long-barreled rifle. At that point, he looked like a cartoon character to me.

"Let's go. Let's see who's scared my guest."

"There's no need. Don't concern yourself about it; I'm perfectly fine now. It would be better if, instead of all this, you would just tell me where I could spend the night."

"I've already killed one person today, so I can kill someone else, too—anything to rid the city of these sick people."

I noticed that the shopkeeper had a foreign accent, but not that of an "African."

"Where are you from?"

"I'm a pure-blooded Italian."

"But your skin is dark."

"It's not Black. It's grown darker here. People's brains also grow dark here, so the skin is no big deal. Where are these criminals?" He was acting quite crazy. The Italian had stepped out into the middle of the street near the mosque and shouted out. Many people ran away as soon as they saw him. It seemed like they recognized him.

"Don't worry, everything's fine," I said, trying to calm him down.

"What's fine? Do you know what you're saying? What do you understand of all this? What do you know? All you need is a place to spend the night. I need so much more. You can't live in freedom for a day among these disgusting people. They just exist during the day, or they end up drunk in a corner, or dying of hunger. They're like lice. If my shop were not on this street, this whole place would be a dump. Everything's ugly. There's nothing beautiful." The Italian pointed the rifle to the sky and fired a few rounds. I was completely unable to calm him down. "I've killed one person today, so I can kill someone else, too," he continued.

"Why did you get so angry? All I said was that I was scared, but there's no need to go crazy over that."

"You don't understand. An honest Italian like me who's never committed fraud of any kind, never tricked anyone, always helped people—I can't take it anymore! As soon as I see something bad, I want to eliminate it."

"Everything's fine. There's no need to get angry. Take the gun inside."

"I was selling things this evening—not here, but in the market. I have a stand in the market as well, besides this shop. It's not too far from here."

"I know, I know."

"Unexpectedly, a thin, ugly Black man stole my bottles."

"What bottles?"

"I had put plastic bottles in boxes in a corner of the market. I saw him steal several bottles, and then he got lucky. A tourist came to the market and we all got excited and flocked around him; that idiot picked up several more bottles in the meantime. But I have good eyes, I spotted him at once. Not too far away, the light from a car hit him directly. He saw that I'd noticed him and he ran away at once. I told everyone, and we all forgot the tourist and ran after him.

"Then what happened?"

"We killed him. But he got away."

"I don't understand. Did you kill him, or did he get away?"

"We killed someone. But the bottle stealer got on the bicycle of the person we had killed and sped off."

"What was in the bottles?"

"Vodka."

"What could he do with so much vodka?"

"They're all drunks, they're all good for nothing."

"Who did you kill?"

"I don't know. We never found out."

"An innocent person?"

"There are no innocent people here. The only innocent one is you," he said with scorn.

I had never seen anyone change so much in just twenty minutes. He had looked like a normal vendor who owned a shop. But then he had inexplicably erupted.

"It's things like this that destroy all hope you have for the future. You feel like committing suicide," he said.

"Why didn't you call the police?"

"Why should I? What policeman would organize an investigation for a street robbery like that? People don't do their jobs well here."

The Italian fired into the air several more times, and then he suddenly calmed down. He lowered the gun. He took several deep breaths and said, "What were you asking me?"

"What was I asking you?"

"You were asking me something," he said very calmly.

"When?"

"Ah, yes, I remember. You were looking for a place to spend the night. If you want, I can take you to my house. You'll sleep at my place. You'll rest up. Today was a tough day. I'll show you around Djibouti tomorrow; I'll take you to the market. My house is close by; it's just a few hundred meters away.

The shopkeeper re-entered the shop and put the gun down on the table on the first floor, next to a box—I never found out what was in it—then he quickly left and locked the door, lowered the shutter, and came back to me.

"Should we go?"

"Where?"

"Weren't you looking for a place to stay? There are no hotels nearby. You can spend the night at my house," he repeated.

It was late at night. The sky was gloomy, but it looked like the sun would rise at any moment, and a new day would begin. The street was noisy. I refused to go to the Italian's house. I no longer felt sleepy, to be honest. I preferred to walk in Djibouti at night. I saw several grand mosques and buildings; all of them seemed to be made from ice and had a unique glow.

After walking for several hours, I heard a loud noise in the distance. There were sounds of police sirens, and I slowly walked in their direction. The police had blocked off a corner of the street. There was an ambulance there as well. I couldn't see anything, and they weren't letting me get any closer. From a distance, I just saw them put somebody on a stretcher and cover his whole body with a piece of cloth.

I slept on the street, just like that other homeless drunk. I left Djibouti without having understood much about it from my stay there; it probably had taken offense at my mistaken arrival.

I went into another souvenir shop at the end of the street, where I was told that the French necklace I had bought was a local piece and would cost a maximum of 800 Djibouti Francs, or about four and a half US dollars.

DAY 33. ERITREA
TWILIGHT

They say that everything stops moving at night, that things stop where they are and only continue their movements in the morning.

They also say that weddings take place at night, and that people wait for the sun to set.

I don't know who says all this or where, but the car I was in, heading to Asmara, stopped on the way and we were forced to get out. Beyene, who was accompanying me, and I were going to the capital city of Asmara—Beyene had to visit his sick brother and attend his wedding ceremony.

It was dark. It was nighttime, not just evening time, and nothing could be seen in the distance. It was a rainy day. The soil was wet. This beautiful country, which I'd always likened to an elephant's trunk on the map, greeted us with a twilight scene. On this side of the twilight, there were three women wearing similar clothing and a camel herder next to them with long, thick hair. They came toward us like an illusion, but we never saw them up close. Beyene said that they were going to a wedding ceremony and that those three women were the camel herder's wives; their clothes—which I could not see well—were their festive dresses. Beyene said that they were Rashaida. But the Rashaida lived only in the north of the country and they never married into other ethnic groups. Unless I was mistaken, the Afars made up most of the population where we were located, and they constituted eighty percent of the overall population when combined with the Tigre people.

"How would any Rashaida have ended up here?" I asked.

"I don't know," Beyene replied.

"Do they marry other people?"

"Probably not."

"What business could they have here?"

"It's an illusion," said Beyene, whose full name was Beraki Beyene Weldemichael.

He was from Jordan, or rather, that was where he lived. He was a doctor. He worked at an American hospital which, he said, had been founded by the Jordanians. Beyene was in his early thirties. We had met near the city of Obock, and then gone together to the border village of Moulhoule, from which we had taken a taxi to Kulul. We weren't that far from the capital, but there was no transportation to get us there.

Beyene was dark-skinned; he looked like he was covered in chocolate. Except for his eyes, his whole face was of the same color. The expression on this face did not differ much from the looks on the faces of "Africans" that I had seen before—sad and melancholic, as with the others.

"What were you doing in Djibouti?" I asked him. We stood motionless and watched a foggy bridge that was visible in the distance.

"My other brother lives there. We were split up during the war. We separated: Bahra went there, I went to Amman, and Gerbu remained in Asmara. I had gone to see my brother."

"Did you see him?"

"No."

"Why not?"

"He's dead."

"I'm sorry to hear that."

"We hadn't seen each other in a long time. We'd become strangers. The last time I'd seen him was ten years ago. But I was going to Djibouti now to tell him that he wasn't alone, that he has family."

Beyene was feeling bad. When I looked at him, I noticed tears in his eyes that were the same color as his skin.

"I didn't have the money to visit him earlier. My family is huge. Bahra was my elder brother."

"Had he died a long time ago?"

"I don't know. They told me that he lived on the streets and that he didn't have money to support himself. The landlord of the place where he used to live had thrown him out; they said he was sick."

"And then?"

"Then what?"

"What did you do?"

"Nothing. I left and came here. I'm very sad. The hardest thing for me is not losing my own brother, but being unable to tell him what I had wanted to say."

"Had many people escaped back then?"

"I don't know," he said moodily. "Our fight for independence took almost thirty years."

"Is that why the border's closed?"

Beyene did not reply. He didn't want to talk about it. Perhaps he had lost other family members as well in the war. We were leaning against a rock that looked like an unfinished statue.

"Do you see that bridge?" Beyene asked.

"Yes."

"Good. It's good that you see it."

"What's good about it?"

"That's an illusion, too."

"In what sense?"

"We can see it here. But, in reality, it's in Asmara."

"But some camels went over it."

"That's an illusion, too. The twilight is keeping us from seeing reality."

Beyene was discouraged. I understood how he felt.

"Is your other brother older than you too?"

"No, he's younger," he said, smiling. "He's the youngest in the family. I haven't seen him for ten years, either. I don't know how he's doing. I got a telegram saying that he was getting married. I'm going to see him now."

"Doesn't he have a phone?"

"He does."

"Don't you have one?"

"I do."

"So why haven't you spoken to him yet?"

"I don't know. I'm scared. I'm afraid he won't recognize me. That he won't want to speak with me. I don't know how he remembers me. I was fourteen years old back then. When I left, he was already disabled and had lost his smile. He has a large mouth; when he was a child, he would open it from ear to ear."

"What happened to your brother?"

"One of his legs was amputated following a grenade explosion. He can't walk, he's trapped in his wheelchair; the poor guy was just beginning to start his life. He had dreams. He was a dancer. He danced well."

"Was that because of the war?"

"There was no war yet, but there was tension. We lived in a place not too far from Kulul, near the border. Then, he moved with my parents to Asmara. We split up. I haven't heard his voice since that day. Gerbu was a good boy; I always remember him as a little guy."

Beyene spoke about his brother in the past tense. I thought for a minute that he might have ended up sharing the same fate as his elder brother, but I avoided expressing this thought.

"You think he might be dead, too?" Beyene said.

I was taken aback.

"Yes," I said, after holding back a little. "How did you know?"

"I thought the same. I'm afraid of that. I think anything could have happened. I didn't get the telegram from him; I don't know who sent it. It said that my brother was getting married and that I was being invited to be with him. So, I decided to visit both of my brothers at the same time."

"Did you get the telegram a long time ago?"

"Around a month ago."

"Perhaps he's already married?"

"Even better. If he's married, then he's happy and he isn't suffering."

We crossed the bridge. It was cold. There were trees in the distance. There was a fog on the other side of the trees and the wind was damp. It was even visible. I had never seen the wind before. A short while later our view was blocked by smoke, and the smell of something burning reached us; then something exploded in the distance. It was like a small sun that had somehow burst through the clouds, but was then dragged back down. The air grew thicker. My eyes started to water.

"Don't be afraid," Beyene said.

"What was that?"

"It sounded like a grenade."

"Does that happen often?" I asked.

Beyene stared at me for a long time.

"The last time I was here was ten or eleven years ago. Our house was around here somewhere."

"Maybe someone wanted to attack us," I said.

"Hardly likely."

"Why?"

"I think that was an illusion, too. Did you see the grenade?"

"No, I saw the explosion."

"So did I," Beyene said, and he took some food out of his metal case.

We were walking on a damp, narrow path. There was nothing close by. We were about a hundred and fifty kilometers from the city.

"Will we get there today, or won't we?" I asked.

"We won't get there on foot. We have to find a car. We'll get there in two or three hours in a car."

"Where would there be a car?"

"I don't know. There's nobody to ask. I've told you so much about myself, but you have never said where you're going."

"I'm going to see Asmara, and Eritrea in general."

"See what?"

"Everything. I'm writing a book about it."

"What's the book about?"

"Africa. People. I don't know; that's a difficult question."

"Why Africa? You could have picked Asia, or America. Was it out of a sense of pity?"

"No. It's simply what I wanted to do."

"What is it you expect to find here?"

At that moment, I thought we were both the same. We were both seeking something, we both had certain expectations, but we were both uncertain that we would find what we were looking so hard for. But I was different in one way—I didn't even know what exactly it was that I was seeking.

"You didn't respond."

"What am I supposed to say?"

"Why did you come to Africa? Does that question bother you?"

"It bothers me. I don't want to think about it. I like Africa; that much is enough."

"Are you going to write about me?"

"I don't know."

"If you were to write about me, would I be a good guy or a bad guy?"

"A good guy."

"Will you write about my family, too?"

"Yes."

"Don't write all of it. There are some things I told you that I don't want everyone to know."

"I won't write all of it."

We continued walking, and looking for a car so that we could get to our destination sooner. It was probably still daytime. I could hear the sound of thunder, but the rain had not yet come. Beyene looked at the sky absent-mindedly—his eyes looked one way, but his thoughts were somewhere else.

"What are you thinking about?" I asked.

"Nothing. Looking for a car."

"Were you thinking about your brother?"

"No, I remembered that I'd been in these parts when I was a child. There's a place here where there used to be a rainbow every day. I don't know how. We would all come every day to see the rainbow. I always loved looking at rainbows. I haven't seen a rainbow since then, you know? Whenever I've seen one, it always seemed like one color was missing; I think it was yellow. Have you ever seen a rainbow?"

"Yes, but not in Africa, I think."

"There're no rainbows here anymore. The rainbows here are the gloomy sky and the twilight."

"How do you know? You haven't been here in a long time."

"I feel it. People are becoming sadder and sadder. They've stopped looking at the sky to see rainbows."

"Weren't they sad before?"

"They've always been sad. But when I was a child, there were a lot of things I wouldn't think about. But now, even the kids think of those things. Many people try to help, but that help is a result of pity. Sometimes rich people adopt the children; they come from various capitals. They adopt one or two, sometimes even a larger number of kids, and they take them back with them. They tell the whole world about it, as if they've saved all the sick and orphaned children. But that is just advertising. It's for their reputation. They pick the child like they're buying something in a shop—they want the child to be relatively pretty and healthy, and they adopt them. They can't imagine any of it in reality. They come and make a donation, but all of it stems from their own interests. They want to have a better reputation so that they can sell more autographs. I find all of that to actually be quite funny. Most of the children are sick; you can't treat them with presents and autographs. And you can't prevent the healthy ones from falling sick."

Beyene was very convincing in his speech and even named a few names, which he asked me not to repeat.

We heard the sound of an engine. It was a small truck. We rushed to stop it. Beyene spoke to the driver in Arabic, and we got on board, or rather we climbed into the back and sat on some wooden boxes. The truck was very small, old and muddy. There were different things in the bed of the truck—sacks, boxes, pieces of wood, rope. It was moving very slowly, but Beyene said we would get to the city in three hours. We managed to hold on somehow to a couple of protruding parts in the back, as we bounced up and down as the truck progressed. The road was very bad.

"Wasn't there a seat next to the driver?" I asked.

"There was only a place for one."

"Couldn't the two of us have managed to fit?"

"Perhaps, but barely."

"Why didn't he let us sit inside? Did I make him uncomfortable? You go ahead and sit next to him."

"No, both of us made him uncomfortable. He said that we were strangers. It's a good thing that he let us sit here at least," Beyene shouted; the engine was so loud that we could barely hear each other.

"Where's he going?"

"Probably Asmara."

"You didn't ask?"

"No, but I think there's no other place to go on this road."

"Did he ask for money?"

"No, he said there's no need for money. I offered some, but he refused. Fuel is very expensive here. I said we would buy some gas, but he refused that, too. He's a good man."

I couldn't remember the driver's face. I could only see him through a small glass window. The window had fogged up and not much could be seen.

We were tired. We both fell asleep. I had probably not slept much. When I woke up, we were still on the road. Beyene was still asleep. I saw a rainbow in the distance. It seemed to occupy the whole of the sky. I wanted to wake Beyene up, but then I thought he would call it another illusion and he wouldn't believe it. When I looked carefully, I got the feeling that the color yellow was missing from the rainbow.

My back hurt, I wanted to get up and walk. I shouted to the driver a couple of times for him to stop, but he didn't. I tried to sleep again, but I couldn't. When Beyene woke up, he shouted at the driver, too, but the man kept driving the vehicle without hearing our voices, oblivious to everything.

"I saw a rainbow in my dream. I was telling you about it, remember?" Beyene said.

"Yes."

"The color yellow was missing again."

He looked at me with a gleeful face, then opened his metallic case which held various medical instruments, and took out some food.

"Where might we be now?" I asked.

"I don't know."

"How much longer before we get there?"

"How long did we sleep?"

"I don't know."

"Look at your watch," he said uncomfortably.

"It's past six."

"When did we fall asleep?"

"I don't know. I don't think we slept much."

"Me, either. We'll probably get there soon."

"Have you told him to drop us off at Asmara?" I asked.

"No."

"Why not?"

"I forgot. The driver told us to get in. He quickly agreed to take us, and I forgot about the rest. I assumed he understood where we were going."

We shouted again, but the driver was lost in thought. I didn't think he was ignoring us on purpose. The noisy engine and the muddy road were to blame. We decided to calm down and wait a little longer. But suddenly, it started to rain. It was a hot rain with large drops. That didn't stop the driver either; on the contrary, he picked up speed. He was probably afraid of being stuck halfway. The soil had grown soft and was sticking to the wheels like melted chocolate. We picked up some of the sacks to cover ourselves with. When I shook one of the sacks, a few things fell out of it. I heard a crashing sound, but I ignored it; I assumed they were unimportant items. But a short while later, I saw a pair of eyes looking at us from a corner of the truck bed. I shouted to Beyene.

"You probably imagined it," Beyene said.

"Look, something's moving there."

Beyene managed to get on his feet somehow, muttering with irritation, and walked over to the side of the truck. Then he came back, trembling.

"They're hyenas," he said.

"What?"

"Hyenas. There are many of them here."

"Real ones?"

"Yes, but they're pups, so don't worry; they don't have any teeth."

"They won't attack us?"

"No. How would they attack us? They were scared when I approached them."

Beyene trembled as he spoke. He was scared, too. There were two or three hyenas. They were very small and only their eyes were visible, shining like diamonds. When the rain stopped, dawn began to break.

"What are they doing here?" I asked.

"Maybe he's a zoologist," Beyene replied, indicating the driver with his head.

"Why didn't he warn us?"

"I don't know."

The hyenas began to behave aggressively. They came closer to us. Beyene found a long stick and held it near the driver's window, then struck it several times.

"Look, there's a church in the distance, and a tower next to it," I said.

"Asmara," he said with an awestruck voice, and he began to hit the window with even stronger blows.

There were two beautiful towers in the distance—one looked like Big Ben in England, and the other was an Islamic mosque. There was another building in front of them with two domes that had two circular signs, which I could not see well. Behind those buildings, the whole city could be seen, and it was an architectural wonder—grand, colorful buildings, churches and mosques followed one after another.

"Do you see that tower on the left side?" Beyene said.

"Yes."

"It's the Roman Catholic Cathedral. Beautiful, isn't it?"

"Very."

"Look to your right. See the other tower, with the green dome?"

"Yes."

"Al Khulafa Al Rashiudin mosque. Wonderful, right?"

"Yes, it's magnificent."

"Look ahead, that building with the two domes."

"Yes."

"The Enda Mariam Orthodox Church. See how many churches and mosques there are?"

"Yes."

"There are lots of buildings here that resemble Italian architecture. Both the old and the new architecture of the city has been recognized by UNESCO as a cultural heritage site. This used to be an Italian colony. The Italian Empire. Heard of it?"

"No."

"It was made a British protectorate after the war. In 1950, it was part of the Ethiopian Federation. But that doesn't matter now. What matters now is that it is independent. Do you see what a bright and shining city it is?" Beyene said. He was happy.

"Enough with hitting the window with that stick," the driver called out. Apparently, he spoke some English.

"What?" Beyene said.

"You'll break the glass!"

"We want to get off; would you please stop the truck?" I said.

"I've stopped already, can't you see?"

Beyene switched to Arabic and asked a few questions. Then we got off the truck and said goodbye to the driver. While speaking to Beyene, he said the word "Dekemhare" several times in an angry voice. Beyene's mood worsened immediately after talking to the driver.

"Did you ask him who he was?" I asked.

"We'd guessed right, he's a biologist."

"Why are you sad?"

"He said we're in Dekemhare."

"Meaning?"

"Meaning that we've gone past Asmara. He said that I hadn't told him, which is why he hadn't stopped."

"I don't understand. Why did we get off? Did we go around the capital?"

"Yes," he said, feeling guilty.

"What about the tower, the mosque, the churches—we saw all that, didn't we?"

Beyene gave me a crooked look and walked on. While we were sleeping, we had driven past Asmara.

"Are we very far away?" I asked, catching up with him.

"No, the driver said that we hadn't reach Dekemhare yet, we're about fifteen kilometers away from the capital, maybe a bit more."

We walked. Beyene was once again lost in thought. It was twilight and we couldn't see well ahead of us. It was late evening. The sun could be seen but its light wasn't even enough for the clouds.

"They say that everything stops moving at night, that things stop where they are and only continue their movements in the morning. The truck was an illusion also," he said after thinking for a long time. "It wouldn't move if it had been real. The driver wouldn't have picked us up, and the hyenas would be back in the jungle."

"So how did we get here?"

"I don't know."

"You mean that we imagined all of this?" I asked.

"Yes."

"What about Dekemhare?"

"What?"

"Aren't we in that city now?"

"I don't know, I don't know. I'm even beginning to think that my brother's wedding isn't real. The twilight isn't letting us see anything; the horizon is beyond our sight."

A light approached us. I thought that it was the hyenas, but this light was much brighter. It was someone on a bicycle, wearing a yellow shirt and yellow pants. His face seemed familiar to me.

"Do you see that man in the yellow clothes?" Beyene asked. "Do you see him?"

"Yes. Should we stop him?"

"No, no, let him go," he said angrily. "Did you get a good look at him?"

"Yes," I said again.

"That's my brother."

"What?" I said, shocked. "Doesn't your brother have a disability?"

"Not that one."

"You have another brother?"

"The one living in Djibouti, the one who died. He always liked bicycles."

We went our separate ways after that. Beraki Beyene Weldmichael went to his brother's wedding ceremony, and I went by car to Asmara, and then by the Red Sea to Mogadishu.

My time in Eritrea was up, although I never did figure out how much of it I had actually travelled through.

The car arrived in Asmara and the driver had some trouble waking me up.

"We're here, get out," he said.

"Where are we?" I asked.

"Asmara."

"We got here so soon from Dekemhare?"

"What Dekemhare? Get out, I have to go back to the airport, I don't have time," the driver said, and opened the door.

"What about Beyene?"

"Who's Beyene? Get out!" And he muttered under his breath, "These tourists are all crazy, they lose their minds as soon as they get off the plane."

It was a sunny day. I was in Asmara and it was morning, I was heading for Massawa, so that I could get to the Red Sea. I saw a bridge in the distance with a young man dancing on it by himself. He had opened his large mouth from ear to ear, and was laughing...

DAY 34. SOMALIA
THE AFRICAN HORN

Almost all tourism websites say that Somalia is not a country for tourists and that it is very dangerous to go there. I read in some places that the probability is very small for a foreigner to stay alive there, that it's difficult to avoid falling victim to local gangs and bandits. Traveling by air is dangerous, because the shelling of the Somalian airport by Ethiopian forces often leads to delayed flights or emergency landings. Traveling by land is also dangerous, either because there are no real roads, or because they're closed or impassable.

But I wasn't planning to travel to Somalia by air or land. I was planning to go by way of the Red Sea from Massawa, passing through the Bab al-Mandab Strait, reaching the Gulf of Aden, and then getting to Mogadishu, the capital, from there.

This was all born in my imagination, and in reality, that trip at first glance looked both dangerous and also pointless. But I only understood all this once I was on the Red Sea and had met a strange sailor named Abdi Aziz Mukhtar. The Sailor (he asked me to call him that) had come out onto the sea in his boat—which looked more like a tub—in order to hunt pirates. I never found out his nationality nor the ethnic group to which he belonged. The only things I learned were interesting facts about Somalia. The sailor

Abdi Aziz knew almost no English, but he had found a very unique way to communicate. He had a very sharp instrument for wood carving. He made all sorts of images on small thin pieces of wood using this instrument.

I had met him when I arrived at the beach. The Red Sea was magnificent indeed. The water was hot; a strange warmth embraced it from below. Two leopards were depicted on his boat.[38]

"Do you see those hills?" the sailor Abdi Aziz asked, motioning to the east with a strange instrument in his hand.

"Yes," I said.

"The Dahlak islands. Pirates used to live there once."

"What about now?"

"Now it's the Rashaida. Had I lived a few centuries ago, I would have destroyed them all," Abdi Aziz said, as he etched into the wood.

The picture he produced had several cannons and pirates. He had drawn himself on the right side and the pirates on the left, with the sea between them.

"There are no pirates now," I said.

"Yes, there are. I have destroyed a few, and even if we don't see any here, they're definitely there in Somaliland."

"Do you have to go there?"

"Yes." He etched the map of Somalia onto the wood.

"I have to go there, too," I said, talking about Somalia.

"Let's go together," he said. Then he drew the two of us into the wood, with both of us standing in the boat with guns and firing towards the pirates' boats.

"No, I haven't come to kill people."

"If you don't kill them, they'll kill you." He drew me in the wood as a dead man with two armed pirates next to me, their mouths open. The pirates he drew did not resemble the images of pirates with which I was familiar. They looked more like gang members— they wore military fatigues, had modern guns, their heads were wrapped in cloth like Muslims, and they had cigarettes in their mouths.

Abdi Aziz depicted his heroes very well. He wasn't really sculpting them; it was more like drawing. I had to wait about ten minutes each time, until he finished drawing the next scene.

"This isn't a pirate, it's a bandit," I said.

He wrote today's date on the piece of wood and drew the same pirate next to it.

"These are the pirates of today," he said.

---

38. Somalia's coat-of-arms consists of two leopards standing face to face, with a gold crown between them and a five-pointed star on a blue background in the crown. Abdi Aziz Mukhtar's boat had an image that was more or less like this.

I had been sitting in his small boat; it rocked, but did not move. We had been talking for more than an hour already. Some birds were in the sky that were unfamiliar to me. Some of them looked like seagulls, but their beaks were long and sharp, like a heron's.

"How can I get to Somalia?" I asked.

"Like this," he said, and began to draw. As he was drawing, I looked carefully at his face, which was different from those of the other locals. His eyes were cloudy, as if covered by a film, while his hair was long and partly covered his face. Abdi Aziz showed me the picture—he had drawn a dusty road with several vehicles coming from the distance. There were six of them, six trucks, but the picture didn't show what they were carrying.

"What is this? You mean I should go by truck?" I asked.

"No," he said, showing me the previous picture, in which the pirates had killed me.

"I don't understand."

"The trucks have pirates in them. They don't spare the life of anyone or anything who crosses their path. They'll kill you," he said.

"What does that have to do with Somalia?"

He took the picture with the trucks and wrote in large letters above it: "Somalia."

"I can't go."

"Well," he said, then continued to draw.

The picture showed the map of Djibouti and a plane.

"I should go to Djibouti?"

"Yes, and you can take a plane to Somalia. But in the air…" he drew again.

This time it was a crashing plane.

"The plane will crash?" I asked.

"It could."

"How do you know? You're sitting here, how do you know what's going on there?"

"I know many things."

"Like what?"

"Like the fact that there are no butterflies here. They are what the pirates hate the most."

"Why?"

"They're afraid of them."

"Of butterflies?"

"Yes. They're afraid of death. Butterflies are poisonous, but we don't have any here, unfortunately."

I had never heard of a poisonous species of butterfly. Perhaps Abdi Aziz had been mistaken or, then again, maybe they did exist.

I could have stayed with him for a few more hours, but I was in a hurry. I had to get to Somalia before nightfall. Before saying goodbye, I asked him, "What is that in your hand?" indicating the strange device he was holding.

"It's a telescope. When I look into the distance with this, the pirates don't appear in the picture. Everything is beautiful."

The Sailor began to draw again. This time, he drew a beach, people, birds, trees, and animals.

"Everything is joyful here, there are no pirates, they've vanished into thin air."

"Can I look through it?"

"Here you go."

I couldn't see anything. There was only darkness.

"I can't see anything."

"Not everyone can see with that device."

I said goodbye to Abdi Aziz Mukhtar and continued my journey. He gifted me one of the pictures—the one in which the six trucks were driving on the sand, raising a cloud of dust.

It was evening. I was walking along without knowing where I was. I assumed that I would be in Somalia soon. The wind whipped at my back, making it easier for me to walk. I was like a paper boat, going left and right with the wind, not having a route and not knowing where I'm going.

I had travelled quite a bit already. When I tried to remember where I'd been—which cities and villages—my memory would confuse things, mixing them up. I felt like I was gradually becoming an "African." The only things that upset me were the sad and cruel events that I had witnessed in the last few countries I had visited. I understood well that the more I focused my attention on all that, the worse I would feel. I tried to see and to notice as little as possible, to not pay attention. Africa was growing sadder. It was sad at the very beginning, too, but now it seemed like a sad child who had lost his toys and would never find them.

I didn't want to see Africa this way. I had already visited more than thirty countries and I had seen so much, but I felt like there was still something I had not witnessed. There was something else that would cause joy to the whole of Africa. I was walking along, lost in thought, when something struck me on the shoulder. I thought it was the wind but, shortly afterwards, I felt a sharper sting, and I turned around in fear; a bird resembling a heron stood behind me. It seemed a lot bigger and scarier close up than it had in the sky. I don't know why it had come there but I was sure that it was looking for fish. It brought its beak forward several times and tried to strike but I evaded it, then it stuck its bill into the sand and began to dig into it like a woodpecker.

It dug a small hole, almost half the size of its beak, and then it opened its mouth—and several fish poured out of it. They were small fish. The heron—I didn't really know what kind of a bird it was—covered the hole and flew away.

I continued walking. I felt like the bird continued to fly behind me and that it would strike me with its beak at any moment. This thought made me go at an even slower pace.

I had walked quite a bit, but Somalia was still nowhere to be seen. The sun was slowly beginning to set.

Something struck me on the back once again. This had happened once in Djibouti, and at that time it had been a homeless drunkard; on this occasion, I didn't even have the wildest guess as to what could be happening. Perhaps the only thought I had was that this was either the heron or bandits. While I needed to run to save myself from the former, even the quickest sprint would not spare me in case of the latter. I looked around; a camel stood behind me, striking at my back with its hoof. Sitting on the camel was a Black man, whose face was even stranger than the fact that the camel was pawing me. The Black man had a thick beard that resembled a woolen hat, and he wore dark glasses, a white shirt, a black tie, and black pants with the crotch torn. He had a gun in his hand. The man was bald, or he had had his head shaved and shined. He got off the camel and took some heavy steps toward to me.

"Welcome to Fully Independent and Free Somalia," he said, syllable by syllable, as if reciting something. Then he loaded his gun. At that moment, I thought for the second time that my book would remain unfinished. My legs, arms, and body all slipped away. Only I remained standing there. This is probably what death feels like, I thought.

The Black man lowered his gun, threw the strap over his shoulder, and took off his glasses. He dried his moist hands on his tie and looked at me with a smile. I relaxed a little. But I had had such a clear picture of death that, at that moment, I was even ready for suicide.

"You're not going to kill me?" I asked, barely hoping that he would answer.

"No," he said with a gleeful expression.

"Do you speak English?"

"Yes, of course."

"Why aren't you killing me?"

"Why should I kill you? Was I supposed to kill you?"

"I thought you would."

"No, I don't kill people."

"What's the gun for?"

"Defense."

"From whom?"

"Would you believe me if I said from pirates? From bandits, naturally."

"Who are you? You gave me quite a scare," I said.

"I'm a border guard."

"I've never seen a border guard with a camel and a necktie."

"And you never will again. I'm the only one. There's no other border guard like this in the world."

"Where's the border?"

"You crossed it a short while ago."

"Where was the border marked?"

"Nowhere."

"But then how did I cross it?"

"Just like that. You walked, and then you'd crossed it."

"But there was no border. No sign, no poster, no barricade. There wasn't even a fence. It was just an empty road."

"Yes, that's right. If you really want to see it, here's the poster." He took a piece of paper from his breast pocket that was about half a meter square. He unfolded it and held it above his head. The paper said, "Welcome to Fully Independent and Free Somalia."

"Well?" I asked.

"This is the announcement of the border."

"Which border is this?"

"The land border."

"Isn't there another border guard here?"

"No, there never has been. I'm the only border guard."

"Where did you come from?"

"Behind you."

"But this is the first time I'm seeing you."

"I have a hiding place; it's for my own protection. When I saw you, I realized that there was no need for me to protect myself from you. So, I came out."

"Where am I now?"

"Fully Independent and Free Somalia."

"Am I far from town?"

"Which town?"

"Any town. I need to get to a city."

"Why?"

"First of all, I'm thirsty, so I want to buy some water. Also, I don't want to leave without having seen anything."

"But you've seen the most important thing that nobody else has seen. You've seen Fully Independent and Free Somalia."

The unknown border guard, whose appearance had seemed very suspicious and strange, spoke as if we were in a country that did not really exist, as if a new country had just been created between Djibouti and Somalia called "Fully Independent and Free Somalia."

"There's almost nothing here, just roads and deserted spaces. This isn't how I'd pictured Somalia," I said.

"And how had you pictured it?" he asked with a slightly rude tone. "A country rich in multicolor flowers, abundant meadows, beautiful buildings and streets? Or ruined and gloomy, with demolished and rickety buildings, burnt fields, streets full of sick and dying people? This is the real Somalia—where there is nothing, but it is peaceful and there is nothing to be scared of. These are deserted spaces now, but it will be very grand later."

"If it's peaceful, why do you need a gun? You said earlier that you're defending yourself from bandits, but now you're saying it's peaceful."

"Yes, it's peaceful. This is for unpredictable circumstances. No bandits come here, but protecting oneself just in case is not a bad idea."

"You didn't answer my question—how can I get to a town?"

"If you mean Berbera, I have to say that you've already passed it. If it's Hargeisa you want, then you have to go southwest. If it's Mogadishu, you should keep going east, and then south; perhaps you'll get there in a few months if, of course, you manage to stay alive. Come with me to my hiding place; it's cool there."

"Is Mogadishu that far away?"

"Of course. But what do you need there that you can't find here?"

"I don't know."

"In that case, come with me."

The border guard sat on his camel and beckoned with his hand. To be honest, I couldn't persuade myself that he was being truthful; it was like the story with the Sailor starting all over again. That camel rider, with his black tie and white shirt, looked more like an illusion than a real border guard. But I had no alternative. In this empty space, it was better to talk to an illusion, especially since he understood me.

"Where is your hiding place?" I asked.

"A few kilometers that way. Not too far. We'll get there soon."

"How come you speak English?"

"Everyone in this country does."

"But, as far as I know, Somalia's official languages are Somali and Arabic."

"Yes, Somalia's," he said with emphasis.

"What is your nationality?"

"Somalian."

"So, you know Somali and Arabic, too?"

"I do. But in this country, we speak English with foreigners."

"Is it really unsafe in the city?" I asked.

"I don't know a safe place on this planet."

"Why didn't you ask me for any documents?"

"Why would I need to?"

"If you're a border guard, then…"

"If you'd entered from another border, you wouldn't have been allowed in. They would have examined you a thousand times, they would have checked a thousand different documents. But everything is a lot easier with me. It's time to think freely."

The camel walked slowly; it also looked skeptically at its owner. The border guard, who had not introduced himself on purpose, afraid that I would betray him, asked me to stay alone with the camel for a few minutes so that he could go and bring his hiding place to order. In his opinion, it would be bad to host a guest without preparing in advance.

I waited for around ten minutes. The hiding place looked familiar to me. I had seen huts like that in Chad, but it only resembled them on the outside. Inside, it was a deep pit and had a ladder. It was a spot isolated from the rest of the world, a place cut off from civilization.

"Don't be surprised; you're probably used to all kinds of luxury," the border guard said.

"I'm not surprised, I'm already used to this," I said.

"Things like this stay stuck in your memory." He went into the pit and continued from there. "Happiness passes quickly, but sad moments stay on." He came back up with a plastic bottle in his hand and two glasses. "Drink this. It's boiled, it was left under the sun."

"Is it safe?"

"I always drink it. It's an old method. Because we don't have electricity, we keep it under the sun and it stays there for a few days. The harmful bacteria settle at the bottom of the bottle, and the upper part is safe to drink."

I drank. I should have opted to stay thirsty for another day. The water had a chemical taste.

"I have nothing else to offer you."

"There's no need for anything," I said.

The border guard took the bottle and descended into the pit again. I thought it was quite strange that he never asked who I was, where I was going, or why I'd come. His own life seemed to interest him more.

"Are there herons around here?" I asked.

"Yes, shy herons. But not in these parts."

"I saw one today. It dug a hole in the ground, poured several fish into it, and then covered up the hole."

"Ah, I know it. It was a pelican. We have two kinds here: the ones with a pink tail, and the ones with a white one. You've seen one with a white tail."

"A pelican?"

"Yes. Don't be surprised, they eat fish."

"But pelicans eat live fish, right?"

"Yes."

"But the one I saw buried the fish in the soil."

"It's only natural," he said. He came out of the pit and sat down next to me. "It's a common white pelican, native to Somalia. See that pit?"

"Yes."

"Do you know what's in there?"

"What?"

"My things. Everything I have is over there, in that pit. My stores."

"And?"

"In Somalia, the animals think that way, too. Everything could change suddenly. The animals here have deviated from the natural course of evolution."

The border guard's words seemed somewhat senseless to me and exaggerated, but I had no reason not to believe him, since I had seen it with my own eyes.

"If the trees could, they'd grow underground," he said.

"Why?"

"It's safe that way."

"Do you have butterflies here?" I asked.

"That I don't know."

"A sailor told me that there aren't any wild butterflies here. He said that the bandits are scared of them."

"He probably meant the mosquitoes. There are mosquitoes, but I haven't seen any butterflies. What is that picture?"

"The sailor made it. He said that Somalia was a dangerous country, that there are bandits everywhere, and he drew this picture. These are six trucks." I had intentionally avoided using the word "pirates."

The border guard looked at the picture for a long time and then he asked, "Has he drawn the sky at the bottom?"

"So what?"

"The person who drew this was probably blind."

Suddenly, I recalled Abdi Aziz's cloudy eyes and the telescope.

The border guard was a good host, but many of my questions remained unanswered. I had to leave. It would be night soon, and I had to find a city. According to the border guard, he knew all the short, safe roads. He wanted to accompany me to Hargeisa, but asked that I spend the night at his place and set off only in the morning, because it was extremely dangerous at night.

I slept on his narrow, moist bed. We set off in the morning. We headed northwest; the border guard had procured an all-terrain vehicle from somewhere. He didn't say anything on the way. He was as quite as his camel. I didn't speak, either.

My visit to Somalia had been, in all probability, the most difficult and complicated one. Although I had planned my route to a certain extent, I never managed to go anywhere in Somalia; it was like a dead end that was very difficult to enter and just as difficult to exit.

When we got to our destination—although it was still not clear how I was supposed to "slip into" Hargeisa—the border guard said, "In reality, the horn is to blame for all this."[39]

"What horn?"

"A deer horn," he said, laughing.

The only thing I was thinking about at that moment was leaving Somalia.

I said goodbye to him. It was hot, the sun was by itself in the sky. It seemed for a moment that it, too, had found a hiding place, but it was a good thing that this was not so. On the road, there was a rusty sign that said "Somaliland."[40]

There was a rocky road in the distance; its other end was invisible. Suddenly, I noticed smoke. It was a cloud of dust rising from beneath a set of wheels. A short while later, I saw a truck, followed by another, and then another; six trucks rolled into my field of vision and then drove past me. There were armed men in the trucks who looked like the pirates that Abdi Aziz Mukhtari had drawn.

The bandits sat in the back of the trucks packed tightly, their heads covered with cloth, holding tightly on to their guns as they swayed with the motion of the vehicles. One of them noticed me, smiled, and waved…

---

39. The African Horn is a geographical term. It includes the eastern part of Ethiopia, Eritrea, Djibouti, and Somalia, which is on its edge. The horn is also considered a sharp object that is linked to failure and misfortune.

40. Somaliland is a self-proclaimed state that is located in the northwestern part of Somalia (in the African Horn). On 18 May 1991, the residents of this region declared themselves independent. However, no international organization or state has recognized its independence. The territory of Somaliland constitutes around 134 thousand square kilometers, and its population is around 3.5 million people (2005). Somaliland is populated by Somalilanders. Besides Somaliland, there are also some other self-proclaimed territories in Somalia like Puntland and Galmudug. All of them have tense relations with Somalia. Internal political strife and clashes continue in the country to this day. After independence (on June 26 from England, and on July 1 from Italy, both in 1960), led by President Siad Barre, violence continued to occur in Somalia. Since 1991, Somalia does not have a functioning government. The internationally-recognized government only has control over a part of the southern region, including the city of Baidoa. Somalia is now considered a highly unstable and dangerous state.

DAY 35. KENYA
THE RED SUITCASE

"You know what I like the most in the world?" said the rich Arab who was sitting next to me on the plane.

"What?" I asked.

"Shaving. And you know what I like the least?"

"No."

"When I'm unshaven." He straightened his long beard and looked out the window. "We're about to land."

This was the Dubai to Nairobi flight. For the first time during my journey I had been forced to leave Africa, because the best option for me to get to Kenya from Hargeisa was to go by way of Dubai. Our plane was now landing at the Nairobi airport, which was the largest in the region.

The Arab, who had not been quiet for a minute throughout the flight, asked me to take down his suitcase from the overhead bin. I somehow managed to go around his massive stomach and was about to open the bin when he pushed me.

"Sorry," he said, "it was an accident. I've been sitting so long I can no longer feel my body."

"Which one's your suitcase?" I asked.

"They're all mine."

"There's only one here."

"Bring that one down."

The suitcase was very heavy. I was surprised that he had managed to get it on board.

"That's not mine," the Arab said rudely.

"But you told me to give you the suitcase in this overhead bin, and that's what I did."

"Someone must have stolen it!" he shouted.

The flight attendant approached us at that moment and asked us to remain seated until the plane came to complete stop.

"They've stolen it. I've been robbed. Robbed!" The Arab kept shouting this to everyone in the cabin. The plane was mostly full of locals with the exception of a few white people who were on the other side of the curtain, in business class.

"What suitcase was it?" I asked.

"It was red."

"Maybe it's in another bin."

"No, it was in the one right above me."

"Hold on, it couldn't have gone anywhere. We'll find it."

"Whose suitcase is that?" he said, pointing to the black bag I had lowered from the bin.

"I don't know," I said.

"Isn't it yours?"

"I don't have a suitcase."

"Well, whose is it then?" he said loudly.

Nobody replied.

"Whoever stole my suitcase, this one is theirs," he said.

"But the thief couldn't have left the plane since we've been flying," I said.

"The thief is in this cabin. I've barely just arrived and I've already been robbed. Nobody leave; I'm going to check each and every one of you."

While the Arab opened all the bins and directed all kinds of abuse at the passengers, the plane came to a stop at the airport bearing the name of Jomo Kenyatta, the first President of Kenya. I saw a British Airways plane from my window and heard the raspy voice of the pilot who ended a long-winded speech with the words "*Karibu Nairobi.*" I later learned that this translates to "Welcome to Nairobi."

I left the plane and saw a passenger bus waiting for us on the tarmac. The Arab was the last one to get off the plane, and he was pulling a brown suitcase along as he walked. When he got on the bus, I asked, "Did you find it?"

"No."

"Whose suitcase is this?"

"I don't know, I found it. I searched everyone, but my red suitcase was not there."

"Doesn't this bag belong to someone?"

"No, I waited till the end and nobody took it, so I assumed that it was mine."

"But yours was red."

"So what? This one's brown."

"What about its contents?"

The Arab's eyes doubled in size at that question. He seemed to have forgotten about that. He opened the suitcase; it was full of Kenya Airways blankets and pamphlets. There were also napkins, plastic cups, and a few t-shirts with the airline's logo. The Arab began to panic, and everyone started to stare at him. His face went red and he immediately shut the suitcase. He wanted to get off the bus, but one of the staff members stopped him.

"What did the suitcase have in it?" I asked.

"Didn't you see?" he asked in surprise.

"Not this one. Yours."

He pushed the suitcase beneath the legs of another passenger, distancing himself from it. He then took a few steps back and said in a whisper, "Fossils of prehistoric creatures."

"What?"

"Fossils."

"Where did you get them?"

"I'm an archeologist."

I had never met an archeologist before. But the Arab looked suspicious and I had been tricked into thinking that he was a rich man. He had never mentioned his line of work during the flight. Before me stood a large-bellied archeologist, looking like a newly-baked, soft and warm loaf of bread, wiping his forehead with a paper napkin taken from the Kenya Airways suitcase.

"Don't tell anyone," he said after a moment's silence.

"I won't. What specifically was in your suitcase?"

"Fossils from a very rare dinosaur that lived around two hundred million years ago, in the Mesozoic Era."

"Which dinosaur was it?"

"I had taken it to get answers to that very question. But I've ended up being unable to. We have to continue our research."

"What body parts did you have?"

"I don't know that, either. I didn't find it myself. The archeological group from the University of Utah discovered it. I simply registered the find."

"Registered what?"

"That it had been discovered. Then we have to bring it here and allocate a special spot to it in the museum."

"What are you going to do now?"

"I don't know. I'll run away. I don't know," the Arab said in confusion; he kept walking backwards till he reached the back of the bus.

When we arrived at the terminal, he didn't want to get off. After we spent some time persuading him, he finally got out. We walked to the customs area and then left the airport.

The Arab, whose name was Muhammad Al Moi, was panicking. He was only just beginning to realize what he had lost. He didn't know where to go or what to do; I did not envy the situation in which he had ended up.

It was morning. It was a hot day. The sky had darkened slightly but was generally cloudless. We were walking through the streets of Nairobi. The city seemed very cheery and colorful to me. People were friendly, warm and hospitable.

Kenya is considered the most developed country in the region, with a huge port in the city of Mombasa, two international airports, and a population of around thirty-seven million that consists of more than thirty ethnic groups. These are predominantly the Kikuyu, Luhya, Luo, Kalenjin, Kamba, Kisii, and Meru.

Kenya got its name from Mount Kenya, which is one of the highest mountains in the whole of Africa at 5,199 meters. This country is also unique in its indescribably abundant flora and fauna.

Muhammad and I headed for a hotel on Moktar Daddah Street so that we could get some rest. Muhammad would have had other plans, of course, if he hadn't lost his suitcase. Because he was in a very bad mood, I was trying my best to make him feel better. But, in all honesty, it looked like I wasn't succeeding.

We were sitting on the only bed in the room; he was as sullen as a four-year-old child as he looked at the lamp hanging on the wall.

"What are you going to do?" I asked him again.

"I don't know," he said, his head hanging.

"Were you planning on staying here long?"

"One month."

"What about now?"

"I don't know. If they find out—twenty years."

"What if they don't find out?"

"That's hard to imagine. You can't hide something like this."

"What if you ran away?"

"Where?"

"To the Emirates."

"What would I do there?"

"Live."

"I'm a citizen of Kenya and my home is here. What would I do there?"

"Your compatriots there will forgive you."

"I'm a Kikuyu."

"You're not an Arab?"

"No," he said, laughing for the first time.

"I thought you were an Arab."

"I'm not an Arab. But you can call me one if you like; there have been Arabs in my bloodline."

"Isn't Muhammad Al Moi an Arab name?"

"I was christened Muhammad Al because I look like an Arab. But Moi is my real name—Daudi Moi."

"But we arrived together from Dubai."

"Yes. I was in London before that. We were running our tests there."

"Perhaps you lost it in London."

"No, I thought so too for a moment, but I remember well getting on board the Nairobi flight with my red suitcase."

"So, you live here?"

"Yes."

And here I was, thinking that I was "hosting" him, but it turned out to be the contrary. This fact disappointed me a little, because I thought that we would take a walk together and see interesting things as tourists, but Daudi Moi was not enthusiastic about any of that. He kept thinking about his suitcase. Had I been in his place, I too would not have known what to do. Perhaps I would have taken it even harder.

"How much would that fossil be worth?" I asked.

"I don't know; it was priceless. If someone finds it, they'll get really rich."

"Isn't it a national treasure?"

"No. I mean, it should've been one; we had received state funding. But because the origins of the fossil have not yet been fully established, it's still a private discovery. If someone finds it, they're not obliged to give it to the authorities. They can even sell it. Meanwhile, I'll have lost my job and reputation, not to mention gaining a criminal record."

"Let's go for a walk."

"You go, I'm staying," he said and, opening the door of the mini-bar, he took out a beer.

"Couldn't you have flown directly from London to Nairobi? Why did you go through Dubai?" I asked.

"No, there were no flights."

"I've seen a plane from there; how could there have not been a flight?'

"There wasn't," he said, chugging at the bottle.

The bottle had a label that said "Tusker Lager." It was a local beer.

"When our flight landed, I saw a British Airways plane next to ours."

"No, you must be mistaken. Perhaps it had similar markings, but it couldn't have been a British plane."

Perhaps this was true, though I remembered having seen it quite well.

"I'm going to leave and take a walk. You coming?" I said.

"They'll spot me and arrest me."

"Nobody knows about it, relax." I was pretending to calm him down, but I too was uneasy.

"Why did they discover those fossils? Wouldn't it have been better if they'd been left underground? I would have lived in peace," he said, wiping the beer foam off his beard.

"Are we very far from the city center?" I asked.

"Or how wonderful it would be if dinosaurs still existed today. Their bones wouldn't be worth anything then, and I wouldn't be in this situation," he continued.

"Are we far from the city center?" I repeated.

"No. If somebody finds the fossils, he won't know what they are. Maybe he'll throw them in the trash without realizing that he's found a real treasure. How could I ruin the work of so many people? Why did it have to happen to my suitcase; couldn't yours have gotten lost?"

"I don't have a suitcase," I said once again.

"They'll kill me, and the museum will ban me."

"Let's take a walk. It's a nice day."

I finally managed to persuade Daudi Moi to come out with me. Although he had no desire to talk, he continued his monologue by muttering under his breath.

"If a huge brachiosaurus stood here instead of this building, people would lose their minds. But if we lived in the Mesozoic Era, it might be the brachiosaurus that would panic at the sight of humans. It would have been good if people could have seen them; perhaps then the director wouldn't be sad when he finds out I've lost the fossils. We always like to discover things; we keep sticking our noses in various places."

Daudi was so carried away by his thoughts that he was nearly run over by a car. I was trying to change the subject, but he kept thinking about the lost suitcase. Even in the city center, on Tom Mboya Street, at a restaurant called Jikone, he asked the waiter for a Diplodocus. After thinking for a while, the waiter said that they had run out, not knowing that a Diplodocus was a kind of dinosaur that had lived around 150 million years ago. There was a poster on one of the restaurant walls featuring a meal made of zebra meat. The waiter said that it had been quite some time since a ban had been placed on killed zebras and giraffes.

"What are you going to do?" I asked Daudi again.

"I'll commit suicide. My life no longer has any meaning. What would I live for?"

He was serious.

"Do you see that waiter?" he said.

"Yes."

"He's going to come now and say that I'm under arrest. Let's get out of here before he comes."

He pulled me by the hand and forced me to leave without paying. When we stepped outside, a truck that was yellow like a school bus passed in front of us. The truck stopped. A thin man stepped out and opened the back of the truck.

"Let's get out of here; quick, they've come to get me," the Arab shouted, dragging me along.

When I turned around, I saw that the thin man was unloading bottles from the truck. We were running on Parliament Street, and there were two or three tall buildings in the distance. The Arab, for some reason, had got it into his head that the whole country knew his story, and I was forced to follow him. We sat on a bench in one of the parks.

"See, see what a huge shadow that is," Daudi said.

"Where?"

"It's moving. Look at the skyscrapers over there."

"I don't see it."

"Over there—it's like a huge tail. A huge shadow… it's the shadow of an Allosaurus. Can't you see it?"

There was indeed a shadow. I didn't know what was casting the shadow, but it did look like a moving tail.

"Maybe it's the wind," I said.

"The wind? What wind? You think I don't know what I'm saying? It's an Allosaurus. They've come to get me."

"Calm down."

"Look, there's the shadow of a brachiosaurus on the other side. But where is the creature? All I see are the shadows."

I would have thought that the Arab had lost his mind had I not seen the shadows myself. Unfortunately, they did indeed look like dinosaurs—moving, large—although I was not sure that the Arab was right that I would not have noticed any of this if not for the lost suitcase.

Daudi got up and started running again. I thought I would never see him again. I was transfixed by the shadows; indeed, I was frightened, but because they were not yet real, they looked very beautiful. I was waiting impatiently for the creatures to appear, but they never did.

It was evening, and I returned to the hotel after a long walk through the streets of Nairobi, which were slightly dirty, but very pretty. As I was preparing to open the door to the room, I heard sounds from within. I thought for a moment that one of the dinosaurs the Arab mentioned had found its way inside the room. When I opened the door, I saw the Arab curled up on the bed. I didn't ask him how he had gotten inside. I walked up and sat down next to him. He was serious. He was straightening his beard.

"Did you see them?" he asked.

"See what?"

"The dinosaurs."

"No. They never appeared."

"What were they doing?"

"Nothing. Just moving around."

"Did anybody ask about me?"

"No."

"I knew it. I'll leave now; don't worry," the Arab said, changing the subject abruptly.

"You can stay; you're not bothering me. I'm leaving tomorrow. I'll leave you the room."

"There are many rooms here; I don't need this one. I've got a question I want to ask."

"Go ahead."

"Do I look like a miserable man? Be honest."

"No."

"A lie! Why am I so sad then?"

"I don't know. Perhaps you like being sad?"

"Yes, I like it. It's surprising, but true. Many people won't understand this. I truly like being sad."

He hadn't been sad on the plane at all; he had constantly been laughing.

"People want to be sad sometimes. It gives me pleasure. I've had many occasions to be happy, but I haven't used any of them. There are some things in life that you can't bring back. Remembering those things gives me pleasure."

The Arab began to speak with great seriousness. His face froze. It was as if his blood stopped flowing. He wiped his eyes, although there were no tears, then he continued monotonously.

"I wanted to change so many things. But it's impossible. Time can't go backwards. When I lost my family, my life changed, and I decided to quit everything and focus on archeology. I wrote books, began to lecture, all of that to help me forget the past. I threw myself into research like a fool. And then I realized one day that it wasn't my life I was living, it was the life of the dinosaurs. I am in their reality. But it was too late; I couldn't bring anything back. On the other hand, I felt like there was no need to. By dedicating myself to archeology, I managed to heal. The Albertosaurus and Protoceratops became members of my family. I was no longer of this world; I had concentrated all my focus on different kinds of academic research and discoveries. I haven't even shaved once in the past two years. I was in mourning."

"What happened?" I asked.

"When?"

"What happened to your family?"

"I don't know. If it had happened now, I would have thought that the dinosaurs had gotten them. They died. They were sick. I don't want to talk about it; don't ask any questions. I've got a headache," he said, and he took another beer from the mini bar. "And now the suitcase. I can't take it anymore. I've tried several times, but I don't have the strength for that, either."

"The strength for what?"

"Suicide. Can I come also?"

"Where?"

"With you."

I had told him about my journey: all the countries I had visited, the people and interesting incidents I had seen; I thought I had found a companion. We spent the night in the same room. When I woke up the next morning, the Arab wasn't there. I waited for three hours, but he didn't return. He hadn't written a note, or left a message for me at reception. The time came for me to check out. I walked down the narrows stairs, handed in my key, and stepped out into the street.

It was a hot day. There was no sun, but I was told that this is normal. On sunny days, the sun can't be seen in Nairobi. It was dispersed light. I was walking the streets since I still had time before I had to be at the airport. Suddenly I heard voices blaring on a loudspeaker. The sound came from several streets away. I went there immediately. There was a small stage and large speakers had been set up; dozens of people had gathered. Everyone looked at the skyscrapers in the distance, which featured the shadows of various animals—giraffes, zebras, elephants, camels. With the help of mirrors placed at various angles, the shadows seemed to move like real animals. It was a nice show.

The time had come to leave Nairobi and Kenya, which had left a wonderful impression with its beautiful tall buildings and bright sky. When I got to the airport, I saw the British Airways plane again. I specifically checked this time, and I was told that it had indeed flown in from London. And when the airport employee saw that I was very interested in that flight, she said, "Have you lost a red suitcase?"

"No," I answered.

"There's one left from the previous flight. Someone forgot to pick it up before getting off the plane. The tag wasn't on it, so we were forced to open it. But we couldn't find an address inside, there was just some shaving equipment.

The Arab—Muhammad Al Moi or Daudi Moi—had disappeared. Perhaps the dinosaurs had gotten him, or perhaps he had gone to shave.

DAY 36. UGANDA
THE GREY CROWNED CRANE

Sometimes, a city is not well known. The only thing I knew about the Ugandan capital before arriving there was the Kampala International Airport, which is actually located in Entebbe. The boda-boda[41] driver told me that the road was very good and that I would get to the capital in about forty minutes. He also said that if I took his boda-boda, it would take twice as long and be half the price. He said he would talk to me about Uganda on the way.

After we left Entebbe, he forgot about his promise and, when I asked him why he wasn't telling me anything about Uganda, he said there was nothing to say.

When we'd covered more than half the distance, the driver stopped and, without telling me where he was going, asked me to wait. He asked for half of the fare money, saying that we had already covered half the distance, so I gave him 250 shillings (around twenty-five cents).

I waited for ten minutes, then twenty, then thirty, but he didn't return. His boda-boda grew "tired" too and a gust knocked it over. I waited a little longer, but the driver still

---

41. Boda-boda are bicycle taxis that are common in East Africa, particularly in Uganda. The name comes from a distortion of the word "border" and originates in the words commonly shouted by the drivers: "Border, border."

didn't turn up. A passer-by told me that if I walked, I would reach the city in one or two hours. I liked that idea. I left the boda-boda on the curb after covering it with a cloth that I found in a small compartment, and I hid it in some bushes that had grown all the way up to the edge of the road. I thought I was doing the driver a favor so that nobody would steal his boda-boda.

Uganda, like Kenya, has wonderful flora and fauna. It also has beautiful streets and buildings that are not inferior to some of the most developed cities in the world. This was also a multi-ethnic country.

After walking for a long time, I grew tired and decided to rest a bit. But there was no place to take a break. There were only some trees and a couple of small shops set up right next to the street, which I felt posed a danger to traffic. I walked up to one of the shops because I was hungry. When I opened the door, I heard a ringing sound. There were some bells hanging behind the door. There was a strange kind of smell inside. I didn't spot anything to eat; the only things there were some wrapped items with pictures of birds on them. A few moments later, the person running the shop appeared, emerging like a ghost from beneath a table.

"What do you need?" he asked, smiling.

"What does this shop sell? I'm looking for something to eat," I said.

He laughed. Then he slapped himself twice in the face, trying to grow serious, and said, "Take some and eat it, you'll start chirping later."

"What do you mean?"

"Before coming in, did you check to see what this store is?"

"No. I thought there would be food here."

"You thought right, but it's not for you."

"Who's it for, then?"

"Mountain gorillas," he said, laughing.

"Are you serious?"

"No. Can't you see? It's bird feed. This is a bird shop."

"But where are the birds?"

"No, not in that sense. I meant this is a shop for birds. We sell feed, cages, books, and many other things. Do you have a bird?"

"No."

"I can't help you with anything, then." He laughed again and this time struck himself on the chest.

"Is there a shop with food anywhere close by?"

"I don't know. If you keep going straight, you'll find something in Kampala. But that's far away. You should buy something here."

"But it's bird feed."

"We have grains here. People can eat that, too. It's harmless. We've simply ground them, so that parrots can swallow them. I'll bring you some. It's really tasty. I eat it, too, sometimes."

I realized at that moment that the salesman looked like a parrot himself—perhaps he'd had too much grain? He brought back a plastic package. There was no writing on it. It seemed to contain crushed bread.

"250 shillings," he said. "You should take a boda-boda, you'll get there faster that way."

"I'm going to Kampala."

"Yes, that's obvious. If you're on this road, you're going to Kampala."

"Why?"

"Where else would you go? Do you want me to call you a driver?"

"No, thanks, I'm fine. Walking is fine; it's more interesting."

"One of them was here a short while ago. He bought some bird feed and left."

The sky seemed to be painted in watercolors. Small clouds swum along like waves. I was walking along the street and wondering whether or not to eat the grain. When I opened the package, the smell that came out was so bad, I wondered how the birds could eat it. I couldn't see any trash cans anywhere, so I held on to it.

There was a forest to my right. I didn't know how deep it was, but it seemed like there were only trees on that side. The trees swayed slowly in the wind, making an unusual sound. It was as if I were on the beach. Suddenly, I noticed a pair of eyes watching me from afar. I thought for a second that it was a boar, but I didn't think that one would come up so close to the road. When I got nearer, it looked like a deer. I couldn't see it well. It sat on a rock and slowly moved its back. When I got even closer, it turned out to be a five- or six-year-old child. He kept staring at me. He was splashing his feet in a muddy stream and they were covered in moss, and he rubbed his body against a rock. He seemed to be covered in moss, too. When he saw me come closer, he curled up and stared with wide eyes like a cat. I felt like he would hit me with a stone if I took another step forward.

"Don't be scared. Were you swimming?" I asked in a low voice. He dropped the stone he was holding, rubbed his protruding belly and emerged from the stream. He was naked. He used a leaf to cover himself and stared at me again with the same look.

"What's your name? Do you live here?" I recalled the little boy who had wrapped his arms around the tree and stared at me with those same eyes. That one had lived in Benin, while this one was a Ugandan, but they looked alike. There was a purity in the way they looked at me, and their eyes were miserable but sincere. The boy clambered on the rock and raised his arms in the air, as if calling someone for help. When I started to walk away, he once again slipped into the stream and picked up a stone. He rubbed his legs together, splashed some water on his face, then smiled and shouted, "Hello," as he waved goodbye with his hands.

"Hello," I shouted and walked away.

I thought that he must live alone. Looking at him, you wouldn't have thought that he was a child; he was just small in size.

"What do you want?" I suddenly heard someone shout.

"What?" I was taken aback and then suddenly noticed that the street was full of chairs and beds. I suppose I had been lost in thought and had not realized where I was going.

"What do you want?" a man standing a slight distance away from me repeated.

"I don't want anything," I said.

"Why are you so surprised? We've got some great chairs, starting at 10,000 shillings."

"I don't need a chair," I said.

"A bed? Great quality."

"No, thanks. I don't need furniture."

"What do you need?"

"How can I get to Kampala?"

"Go straight, then straight, then straight again. One hour, at the very least."

"That much?"

"Yes. You can take a boda-boda. Do you want me to call you one?"

"No, no need. Walking is better."

"Are you sure you don't need any furniture?"

"No. Is there only furniture for sale on this street?"

"Yes. For about a kilometer. We make furniture here, and we sell it," he said, indicating some huts behind him, which were single-story workshops. "That is our area of work."

"Do you have any buyers?"

"Why would we do this work if we didn't have any buyers?"

"There's so much furniture here that I can't imagine anyone buying it all."

"Many people buy it. There's nowhere else to buy furniture in these parts. People even come from other cities: Masaka, Jinja, and even from Kampala sometimes."

The whole street was covered with furniture. The vendors had lined it up against the curb. There were beds and chairs made of wood of various colors, and the chairs went all the way up to the horizon. There was even a place where some chairs were stacked on top of each other, and it seemed like they would collapse at any moment.

"What are you doing here?" the vendor asked after a long silence. He was wearing his hat in a way that created the impression that he was relaxing at the beach. He had a thin mustache and a long jaw. His eyes were blue. Perhaps I was mistaken, but I had never seen an African with blue eyes, bright blue ones at that.

"I'm walking," I said.

"Our country is beautiful, isn't it?"

"Yes, very."

"Are you going to the city?"

"Yes."

"Come, let's have breakfast together."

"No, thanks. I have to go."

"Come in," he said, indicating the green door of one of the workshops. "I'll tell Rajat to bring us some *luwombo*. Rajat, Rajat," he shouted. "He'll be here soon. Come on in."

I walked in. The hut contained different kinds of machinery of varying sizes. There was a pile of sawdust in one corner and pieces of glass in another, covered in cobwebs. It was stuffy. The vendor opened a window.

"The air in the room will clear up in a moment; the place was closed for a few hours," he said.

"You work here?"

"Yes, we close the windows before starting to work."

"Why?"

"Not everyone does it that way. It's a tradition. They say that it keeps bad thoughts from coming in through the window. People sleep on what we're making, after all."

"Do you only use wood?"

"Yes. Almost everyone here uses only wood. We don't like soft furniture," he said with a laugh.

"Why not?"

"We've got hard backs," he laughed again. "Rajat? Rajat! Where is that Rajat? Somebody call him."

"Where's the wood from?"

"From the trees. It's natural wood, it's not a synthetic blend. We throw this sawdust away; we don't use it in the furniture."

"Why?"

"Well, it sounds funny, but we believe that the wood cries when we cut it, and those tears fall to the ground and pile up. How can we make furniture using tears?"

"Is that also a tradition?"

"No, it's something that my brother and I think; our father taught us. We're continuing his line of work. I can show you how we make furniture; do you want to see?"

"No, thanks, there's no need to do that. What are these pieces of glass for?"

"To shape the wood. That's how we give it the shape we need."

"But there are cobwebs on it."

"Our father was the last person to shape the wood."

A young man came in who was about thirty years of age. His features suggested that he was the brother. He also had a red cap, a narrow mustache, and a sharp jaw; only his eyes were different.

"This is Jean, my brother," the vendor said.

Jean came closer, stared at me for a long time, then sat down next to us.

"What happened to Rajat?"

"I've told them to call him; he'll be here soon," Jean said.

"Do they let you cut the trees?" I asked.

"Yes," the vendor replied, "but not all kinds of trees. Mainly the ones that are dried up and are rotting. They let us cut the healthy ones too, sometimes, if they're growing too close to each other. The whole of Uganda is covered in trees and forests. It's our livelihood. I know that it's like a sin to cut trees, a grave sin. That's why I go to church every day. But what can I do? This is the only way we can make a living. Are we harming anyone?"

"We don't steal trees, we don't burn the wood, we don't spoil the fruit—we make furniture," his brother said.

They were good people, honest and simple. You could tell that they liked their profession and worked with pleasure. When I was getting ready to leave the hut, they wanted to give me a small stool as a present, but I refused.

"Wait a little longer. Rajat will be here soon and he'll bring some *luwombo*."

"No, it's late, I've got to go. I still have to get to Kampala, and then get back to the airport. I'm leaving Uganda tonight."

"At night?"

"Yes. Is it dangerous?"

"No, it's not dangerous here. You can take a boda-boda to the airport," Jean said.

Suddenly, someone opened the door and said, panting, "Rajat is swimming. Do you want me to call him or let him swim?"

"Let him swim; our guest is leaving," the vendor said. "Rajat is my son. He wallows in mud the whole day. Now he's swimming."

I said goodbye to the vendor in the red cap and his brother, and then continued walking. The sun had hidden itself behind the beds. I had already walked for half an hour and I felt like I would be in Kampala soon. Suddenly, a bird flew over my head. I remember the pelican I had seen in Somalia, but this one looked completely different. I didn't get a good look at it; I just saw its golden crown. It seemed like the bird had lost its head, as if it were in mourning. It looked like a crane. I didn't pay it any more attention and continued to walk. At that moment, I noticed that there were several people standing between the trees. They were hunters who had hidden themselves in the foliage and were looking at the sky.

"What's going on? Why are you walking in this direction?" one of the hunters shouted. Then he raised his gun.

"Nothing's happened, I'm lost," I said.

"Come closer, don't be scared."

"Are you hunters?"

"Yes," all three of them replied. I came closer. I sat down in the bushes.

"Who are you hiding from?" I asked.

"Nobody. This is the nature of our work."

"What are you hunting?"

"Everything. There's everything around here."

"Big game?"

"No, birds mainly. The forest is close to the city; you won't find any big game here, they're too scared. But we go to them instead of them coming here," the hunter said, and everyone laughed. "Wait, you'll see in a little while what we're hunting today."

"What?"

"They'll be here soon; they'll bring it with them."

"Who'll be here soon?"

"Our other group. They've killed a boar."

"Is that permitted?"

"If I say we've hunted one, then it must be permitted. They'll bring it a little later, and we'll eat it together. This is the first time I'm seeing you. Are you a local?"

I thought for a second that my skin color had changed. I'd never been asked that question.

"No, I'm not a local. Are you from Entebbe?"

"Yes, this is where I live."

"What do you do with the meat?"

Everybody laughed. One of them—a fat man past forty—came closer, put a hand on my shoulder and said, "What's your line of work?"

"I'm a writer," I said.

"What do you do with the things that you think up?"

"I write them."

"And we're hunters. This is how we live. Frogs eat mosquitoes, cows eat grass, hunters eat boars. We're just as human, and we know quite a few things."

I wasn't sure why he spoke that way. Perhaps he thought that I looked down on him because he was a hunter, but that hadn't been my intention. On the contrary, they seemed like kind and jolly men.

"Is Kampala far from here?" I asked.

"The road is over there, you should have kept going straight, you shouldn't have come into the forest. Go back to the road, there will be some boda-bodas there. Take one of them and you'll be in the city in half an hour. But don't leave yet. They'll bring the boar soon. We'll eat together, and then you can go."

"Thanks, but it's late. I have to go."

"If you hear gunfire, don't be scared. It's just us. We haven't shot any birds today."

"Got it," I said, smiling.

I left the forest. As they had said, I heard gunfire within the next twenty minutes.

It was getting darker. I kept walking but didn't seem to get anywhere. I began to think that I should have taken a boda-boda, but I didn't see one anywhere. I was forced to keep walking. I was hungry and remembered the grain I had bought in the bird store. I took it out of my pocket but couldn't bring myself to eat it. There were still no trash cans nearby so I had to put it back in my pocket. Then I saw someone nearby. He was standing on the curb and looking at the cars going by.

"Excuse me," I said. "Are there any boda-bodas around here?"

"In the village," he replied.

"What village?"

"In the forest."

"I was in the forest a short while ago. There weren't any roads there."

"Walk that way and you'll see a house in the distance. Ask for Moses; he has a boda-boda. If he's at home, he'll help you. Where are you going?"

"Kampala."

"Yes, he'll help you. Keep going straight. There's a shortcut through the trees."

I didn't know what that man had been doing standing there, but it seemed like he had been standing there just for me, in order to give me directions. I walked along the narrow path. There really was a hut in the distance, but when I walked up to it and knocked on the door, nobody answered. It was a hut made of wood. There was a small scarecrow above the door, swaying in the wind. I shouted a few times, but nobody responded. When I turned to go back, I suddenly heard crying and shouting coming from the forest. They were human voices. I ran in that direction. There were two men and a woman. The woman had wrapped herself around one of the men and was rubbing her eyes. The other man had taken a wet branch in his hand and was sharpening his knife.

"I'm looking for Moses, do you know him?" I asked.

The woman bawled in an even louder voice and hugged the man more tightly.

"Moses is dead," the other man said, and threw away the branch.

"When?" I asked; I was taken aback.

"A short while ago. Why? Did you know him?"

"No."

"Then why are you asking?"

"I needed a boda-boda," I said, feeling awkward.

"I see. Well, it's too late now. You should have come earlier. It's much too late."

"What happened?" I asked, although I guess I shouldn't have asked that.

"Moses had a beautiful grey crane. He loved it very much. It was time to feed it. He had come home to feed it and then he had to go out again. I'm his brother. He came to me and told me that he couldn't find the crane. We began to look for it. It turned out that the crane had heard gunfire and had escaped its coop. We found it. It was perched on top of a tall tree. Moses decided to climb the tree."

"He fell out of the tree?" I asked.

"No. He's great at climbing trees. He wouldn't have fallen. He asked me to go back home and bring some rope, so that he could tie the crane's legs. When I came back, I saw him lying on the ground, poor Moses. And the crane was gone. But he hadn't fallen."

"What happened? Did hunters shoot him?"

"No. The tree was cut down. They cut the trees and use the wood for furniture."

A child arrived then; he had brought a boda-boda with him. The child panted for a few minutes, then said, "I barely managed to find it. Someone had hidden Moses' boda-boda in the bushes and covered it with a cloth."

I left. It was evening already, and it did not seem likely that I would get to Kampala. I had to return to the airport soon.

I left the pack of grain in the grass. Perhaps Moses' crane[42] would like it. I walked out onto the road.

---

42. These cranes are called grey crowned cranes. They are considered the national bird of Uganda and are depicted on the national flag. I was told in Entebbe that it is considered a bad omen when one of them escapes…

ɲ ɲ ʀ ʞ ɴ ʞ ʌ ʞ

DAY 37. RWANDA
IMMACULÉ

It was nighttime. I couldn't find a single cab at the airport. I was forced to walk until I happened by a vendor. I saw him in a dark corner of the street; he was selling something I didn't recognize. The vendor approached me and said in a very raspy voice, "Are you looking for a cab?"

"Yes," I said.

"There aren't any. It's nighttime. If you don't have anyone to pick you up, it's dangerous to be out on the street at this time. You should find a place to spend the night, then find a cab in the morning to take you to the city."

"Am I far?"

"I don't know. Where do you want to go?"

"To the city center."

"Of Kigali?"

"Yes."

"You should wait and go in the morning."

"But this place looks deserted. Is there a hotel around here?"

"No hotel, but I know a place nearby where you can spend the night."

"A house with a room for rent?"

"Something like that. See that tower?"

"Yes."

"There's a two-story house next to it. The owner will put you up for a night's rent."

"It's not dangerous?"

"No. He often provides tourists with accommodation. That's how he makes money. See that tower?" he asked again, indicating in the distance a tower around ten meters in height which, for some reason, was leaning.

"Yes."

"He lives there. Walk up to his place, knock on the door, and tell him that you just got off a plane and have nowhere to go. He's a good man, he'll be happy to help. His name is Immaculé."

"What does he do?"

"I don't know. He hasn't been working for the past few months. He used to stand in that tower and watch people from there. The tower is in the airport's vicinity, so he always has business. His house is excellently located."

"Won't he be asleep now?"

"No. He goes to sleep very late at night; don't worry. God be with you."

"Thank you. Sorry, one more question. What's that you're selling?"

"Zinger. It's a kind of food made from animal bones. But I'm not a vendor. I'm a mason. I tear down and build walls. I've got to go now."

The stranger left. I didn't even get a chance to ask him his name. He disappeared suddenly.

I walked towards the tower. It seemed close, but I had to walk for at least five minutes. There were thousands of stars in the sky; I'd never seen so many stars. The stars twinkled like butterflies flapping their wings. It was hot, but I noticed a strange thing—small droplets of water were falling from the sky. It was foggy in the distance, and the droplets had created a mist. It seemed like the weather would clear soon, but I never managed to see the other side of the tower.

The house that the mason had mentioned did indeed seem quite lavish and comfortable. I walked up the metal stairs; none of the lights inside the house were on. I could hear the sounds of owls and dripping from a tap somewhere. I knocked on the door. Nobody answered. I knocked again. My knuckles hurt. The door was made of iron and it was uneven. I shouted, calling out the man's name. Nobody answered. I sat down on the cold steps. Soon afterwards, a voice from inside said, "Who is it?"

"It's me," I said, but nobody reacted. I continued, "I've been told that you offer rooms for rent. Have I come to the right place? I need to stay for one night. I'll pay."

"The door's open, come in."

"It's closed," I said.

"Turn the handle upwards," the voice said.

"I can't, it's frozen."

"Is it cold outside?"

"Yes. I mean, no. I don't know why, but your door's frozen," I replied. His question seemed slightly strange to me.

"Is the sky pretty?" he asked.

"Yes."

"Are the stars out?"

"Yes, many of them."

"What color are they?"

"I don't know. Different colors."

"Are they shining?"

"Yes. They're fluttering like butterflies."

"I know. I love them. The sky here is amazing. Is the tower leaning?"

"Yes."

"Which side is it leaning towards?"

"I don't know. East, I suppose."

"Can you straighten it?"

"How? Don't you want to open the door?"

"The door's open, you need to push hard. But wait. I need to ask you to do something. Please go to the tower and climb to the top. Perhaps you'll be able to straighten it."

"Why do you want me to do that?"

"I haven't seen it in a long time; I miss it."

I walked to the tower. To be honest, I considered not returning for a moment, but then I returned, for some reason that even I couldn't understand.

"Did you walk up to it?" the voice asked.

"Yes."

"And?"

"And what?"

"Did it straighten?"

"No."

"Did you go up the tower?"

"Yes."

"Was the sky just as clear there?"

"Yes. It was clearer; the stars seemed to be right in front of me."

"Seriously?"

"Yes. Will you open the door, or should I leave?"

"Wait, don't go. Let me ask you one more thing. Can you hear the dripping of the tap?"

"Yes."

"Is the tractor in the distance in the same condition?"

"I don't know what condition it was in before today. I think I should go."

"Wait, don't go. I need to ask you one more favor."

"Yes?"

"Tell me something happy."

"What?"

"I don't know. A happy story. Don't you know any?"

"I don't remember any."

"I'll wait."

"Why don't you open the door, and I'll tell you the story when I'm inside."

"You won't tell the story when you're inside. Please, tell me the story now."

"I was walking on the beach one day, and a small boy walked up to me and started singing. Then he put his hand on his chest and said that I was breaking his heart. He was joking. He wanted money. He and his father were standing on the beach and singing. His name was Dodoy."

"Then what happened?"

"That's it."

"What was so happy about that?"

"I don't know. I can't recall any happy stories."

"Do you want me to tell you one?"

"Go ahead."

"Once, when I was a schoolboy, my classmates came to my house, because I wanted to introduce them to my parents. When my father saw them, he laughed. He said that those weren't my friends, they were my brothers. It is only now that I understand what he meant."

"What?"

"I won't tell you."

"That wasn't a happy story."

"It was a happy story for me."

"Will you open the door?"

"Yes, yes."

The sound of a lock could be heard. It clanked several times from inside and then the handle slowly turned, and the voice from inside said, "I thought it was open, but it turns out I'd closed it. Come in." The door opened.

"Are you Immaculé?" I said to the man, who walked backwards to the only chair in the room and sat down, without turning around.

"Yes," he said.

"I was told that you rent out rooms, is that right?"

"Not anymore."

"Couldn't you have told me that sooner?"

I was getting ready to leave, when Immaculé said, "Wait, don't go. I'll think of something."

"I only need a place to stay for one night. I'll leave early in the morning."

"I understand. Sit down. I'll think of something," he repeated.

"Where should I sit?" I asked.

"Wherever you like."

"But there's no place to sit."

"You're right."

Immaculé got up. That was the first time our eyes met. I'd never seen anyone with a face like that before. I was unable to tell how old he was. He could have been both thirty and eighty. He looked young but, at the same time, there were hundreds of wrinkles on his face. When I spoke, I felt like I wasn't looking at a man but at a ghost who had died a long time ago. He seemed to be asleep. His eyes were open, but they stared into nothingness. He wasn't blind, nor was he ill. The room where I stood made me uncomfortable; it reminded me of a prison cell, although there were no iron bars and it was very clean. Immaculé was thin, his back was hunched, and when he walked up to me really close, I felt like he had several eyes. His face looked like a rough and uneven African road.

I was scared and wanted to leave. But the thought that it was dangerous out in the street forced me to come to terms.

"Sit down; the chair is yours now," said Immaculé.

I walked up to the chair. When I sat down, the chair turned over. He cackled like a witch and said, "You should've been careful. I forget to tell you that it was broken."

"That's OK."

"Are you hurt?"

"No."

"Wait, I'll bring another one from upstairs…"

"That's OK. I'll stand."

"…for myself."

He left. I felt even more uncomfortable then. I started thinking that spending the night out in the street perhaps would be more pleasant.

"Come here," Immaculé's voice rang out.

"Where are you?"

"Up the stairs."

"Where?"

"Come out of the room."

I left the room. The corridor was like a royal palace—it was huge, decorated with pillars and expensive paintings. The stairs were quite broad, with large flowerpots at the ends. There was a red carpet on the floor and gold-plated chandeliers hung from the ceiling. It seemed to me that I had ended up in a completely different place.

"Up the stairs," he shouted again.

"I can't find you; where are you?" my voice echoed.

"Keep climbing. I'm on the roof."

"How many floors are there to your house?"

"Twenty," he laughed. "Three."

"But you can only see two floors from the outside."

"I made up the third one."

"You were going to bring a chair down, weren't you?"

"Come up here. It's nice up here."

The broad staircase seemed infinite. When I got to the roof, I could hear a piano.

"Keep coming, keep coming, you're in the right place," Immaculé said when he saw me. He was sitting at a piano, randomly striking its keys.

"What was it you wanted?" he asked.

"What do you mean?"

"Why have you come here?"

"To spend the night."

"Don't be so surprised. I'm a bit weird, aren't I?"

"Yes, to tell you the truth."

"I know. It's fine. Each of us is from a different world, to a certain extent."

I didn't know what he meant, but I would have said myself that he was completely from a different world, and not just to a certain extent.

"Do you know how to play?" he asked.

"No."

"Neither do I. But I love it."

"You said you'd give me a room. Where is it?"

"I've given you one. Take your pick."

"You're not going to tell me where to spend the night?"

"What difference does it make to you? Spend the night wherever you wish."

"All right. How much do I need to pay?"

"Pay whom?"

"You."

"Why would you need to pay?"

"I don't need to. I'm assuming *you* need me to."

"I don't need you to, either. Can't you see? I'm very rich or, rather, I have a lot of money."

The sky could be seen from his roof. The stars were gigantic. We could see them through the large square windows that reminded me of a greenhouse.

I left and found a room that was furnished with many valuable items. I locked the door and lay down to go to sleep. But I couldn't fall asleep. I was both scared and uncomfortable. I heard a crashing sound a little later, as if something had fallen from above. I got up immediately and went out into the corridor. The pieces of the broken piano lay below. I ran up to the roof. Immaculé was sitting in a rocking chair and looking up into the sky. He seemed very indifferent and didn't even notice me when I stood right next to him.

"What was that crashing sound?" I asked.

"You didn't see?"

"Was it the piano?"

"Yes. Why ask if you already know?"

"Did it fall?"

"No."

"How did it end up on the stairs in the corridor?"

"I threw it there."

As soon as he'd said that, I decided to leave.

"My weirdness shouldn't make you uncomfortable," he said.

"It's already made me uncomfortable. I should go."

"Don't be afraid of me."

"I'm not afraid."

"I understand. But I wasn't always like this."

"I wouldn't have come if I'd known."

"Wait. One minute," he said, running downstairs. "Let's talk."

"Talk about what? I haven't come here to talk."

"Wait, I'll explain. If you'd been in my place, you would already have ceased to exist a long time ago."

Those words brought me to my senses somewhat. I suddenly realized that the man I was facing wasn't insane, he was just very sad. We went back into the room where I had first entered. He brought out two chairs and sat down in front of me. He looked like he was getting ready for a confession.

"I'm afraid of heights, which is why I haven't jumped off the roof," Immaculé said. "I made up the third floor so that I could jump off from an even greater height, but I'm scared all the same. Funny, isn't it? Have you ever met a man who wanted to commit suicide, but was afraid that it would be painful?"

Immaculé spoke in a frightened voice. He often panted, took a deep breath, and sighed.

"Do you see this house? This lavish estate? These things, the furniture, paintings, chandeliers—all this is mine. I have several kilograms of gold. I can give you all of it."

I wouldn't have imagined that a Rwandan could be so rich.

"I have everything," he said, and then suddenly changed the topic. "Do you believe in God?"

"What do you mean?" I asked. I had been asked this question before.

"Do you believe, or don't you? I don't believe in God. Or, rather, I'm disappointed. There was a time when we would talk to each other, almost every day. I'd talk to the sun, to the sky, the stars… But now, even the stars have turned away from me. They no longer smile at me. They are silent. They stare at me, their eyes wide open, as if mocking me. When my wife and children were taken away, I thought they would ask for a ransom. I waited for a few days, but nobody called, nobody demanded anything. Then it turned out that a maniac had gotten them. And what he wanted was not money at all. I had no news of them for several days. I'd looked everywhere for them, I'd told everyone what had happened, but nobody helped me. A week later, I was told that the maniac had killed them. When I was summoned by the police to identify their bodies, it seemed to me that a gigantic sheep—the size of a building—was pursuing me. I began to be chased by horrors. I haven't left the house in almost three months. I don't want to see anybody. I don't want to come into contact with anyone. You're lucky you're a foreigner; you can't understand me well."

"Who was it?" I asked in a low voice.

"I don't know. I don't want to think about it. He destroyed my life, he ruined it, just like the piano that crashed a short while ago. From that day on, I felt like God would punish him, that He would kill or torture him, but He did nothing. In fact, it's like He forgave him—He rewarded him with wealth. Tell me, is that fair?"

"No."

I automatically recalled Malu and the story of his family. Malu was also "on bad terms with God." He, too, had gone through a horrible experience. His house had burned down and he had lost his family.

"Don't be quiet. I want you to speak," he said.

"What should I say?"

"I've decided to kill him."

"Who?"

"The maniac. Massacring people like that is the least one could do."

"How much time has gone by since the incident?"

"I told you—around three months. I probably haven't slept a day in all that time. It was strange to hear someone knocking on my door and asking for accommodation."

He stood up, covering his face with his hands and twisting it. Then he asked me to wait for a few minutes. When he returned to the room, there was a small gun in his hand. He put it in his pocket and said, "Shall we go?"

"Where?"

"To find him."

"The murderer?"

"Yes. If nobody has punished him, why should I forgive him? That won't change anything."

"You want me to come, too?" I asked.

"Yes."

"I don't want to."

"Don't come if you don't want to. I'll go alone."

"Where is he?"

"Close by."

I recalled the vendor then. I thought for a second that he was the murderer. I was even sure of it.

"A vendor told me about your house. He was selling animal bones. I met him near the airport. He said that he was a mason. He told me that you were a good man and that you would put me up for the night. When I wanted to ask who he was and how he knows you, he vanished. I didn't even see his shadow slip away."

"Let's go to the tower; you can see the whole city from there," Immaculé said.

"You didn't say whether you know that man."

"No."

I was sure that he'd say that he knew him, but he didn't. Immaculé had already left the house. I stood on the outside stairs and looked at the abandoned tractor. I'd never seen a smiling tractor before. Immaculé walked over to the tower. I noticed a poster near the entrance, which was half stuck to the window and fluttered in the wind. There was a photograph on it of a few men, including Immaculé. Below it, in large Roman letters, there were two words—"*Interahamwe*"[43] and "*Impuzamugambi*."[44] After standing around for a few minutes, I left his house and decided to return to the airport. At that moment, I heard a gunshot. The whole sky roared, as if the stars had banged together. Perhaps he had found the maniac and killed him, I thought, or maybe he had just fired into the sky.

I saw the same vendor at the airport. It was late at night, and he looked like a shadow once again.

---

43. Meaning "those who fight and die together."

44. Meaning "those with the same goal."

"Have you seen the time?" I asked. "Do you know how late it is? Who would buy bones from you at this hour?"

"Nobody," he said in an extremely calm voice.

"Why are you standing here?"

"I have nowhere else to stand. Can't I stand here? Are you forbidding it again?" he said angrily.

I couldn't understand what he was trying to say.

"You forbid everything. You've even taken away my right to sell these old bones."

"But who would buy them?"

"Are you trying to say that they're useless?"

"No, that's not what I meant. It's really late, that's all."

"Why did you get Immaculé so upset?" he asked in a tone that was both rude and distressed.

"Me?"

"Yes. Did you have an argument?"

"No. He's a bit weird."

"But why did you upset him?"

"I didn't do anything. He went to kill the maniac."

"What maniac?"

"I don't know."

The expression on the vendor's face changed completely.

"He went in the direction of the tower," I said.

"I saw."

"Did you hear the gunshot?"

"Yes. Poor Immaculé, poor Immaculé," he said syllable-by-syllable. "He never managed to come to terms with it."

"With what?"

"His wealth, his lonely life. He was very rich. But he was miserable. I don't know why he was miserable," the vendor said.

"Why are you speaking about him in the past?" I asked.

"Immaculé jumped off the tower."

"But he was afraid of heights!"

"He shot himself first, then fell off the tower."

I left the vendor, left the airport. I set off for the city on foot. The road was dark. I arrived in Kigali at dawn and walked around the "little capital," which seemed upset, before leaving Rwanda.

When I was returning to the airport, I saw the tower and suddenly heard the tap dripping, and then I saw the small droplets falling from the sky.

The tower continued to lean. Nothing could be seen in the distance. I remembered Immaculé and his story, and I felt that, by committing suicide, he had killed the maniac...[45]

---

45. The Genocide that occurred in 1994 was the darkest chapter in the Rwandan civil war. More than five hundred thousand Tutsis and several thousand Hutus were killed. Based on varying sources, the total number of victims has been estimated at one million. Extremist militia called Interahamwe and Impuzamugambi were the organizers, and many of their leaders are still at large today. There is a bounty of five million US dollars on them.

It is difficult to visit Rwanda today and not notice the traces of that horrible crime...

This story is dedicated to the memory of the innocent victims.

DAY 38. BURUNDI LABYRINTH

After walking for a long time, I realized that I wanted to be happy. I wasn't tired, nor was I disappointed. Like someone who hadn't slept well, I simply couldn't open my eyes wide and see. It felt like my eyelashes had penetrated into my pupils and blocked my field of vision. Several thoughts and analyses would go through my head before I would come to the realization that what I was seeing was perfectly normal.

It had become a habit: whatever country I visited, I found a topic, a protagonist, or a character of some sort and I would spend my day with them. That would help me take certain predictable steps. I had not planned any such thing this time around. The only thing that I kept thinking about was a happy story—I wanted to see smiling children, with round apple cheeks and mouths that opened wide up to their ears. I wanted to see happy people who would not have sorrow or misery in their eyes, people who would not dream hopelessly but who would believe with conviction. I wanted to see people healthy in their old age, who were not lying in the shadow of a tent, and whose bodies were free from thousands of flies.

"Stop plucking off those branches." Someone tapped my shoulder and coughed. I turned around.

"Who are you?" I asked.

"Who're *you*? I should've asked first."

"I was lost in thought; I felt cut off from the world. I'd forgotten where I am," I said.

"*Do* you know where you are?"

"In the capital of Burundi, Bujumbura."

"That's not what I meant."

"What did you mean?"

"You were plucking branches off the trees in my garden a moment ago, and you would probably have continued to do so if I hadn't stopped you."

"I'm sorry. I was lost in thought. I hadn't noticed. To be honest, I didn't know that this was anyone's property."

"This is my garden, my forest, and every branch is valuable to me."

"I'm sorry. How can I compensate you for this loss?"

"No need. Next time you're lost in thought, leave my branches alone. I haven't grown them for someone to pluck them off in a few seconds."

"Got it," I said and I got up from the yellow bench, which was at least one hundred years old by my calculations. The stranger, who had been speaking in an angry tone of voice, was a fat man in his forties with curly hair. He was as broad as the trunks of his trees and well built; his stomach reminded me of a barrel. When he had first seen me, he had stared at me for a while, for around two minutes, watching how I automatically plucked the branches off the trees.

"Wait," he called after me.

"What is it?"

"Where are you going?"

"I'm leaving your garden."

"You're leaving?"

"Yes."

"Did I upset you?"

"No. Why would I get upset? It was my fault," I said.

"I didn't mean to be rude. I just don't like seeing people being disrespectful of trees."

"I understand. I wouldn't have done it if I'd been more aware of my actions."

"A couple of kids went into my stream yesterday and they were throwing stones. All the ducks that I had flew away. By the time I got there, the fish had all fled, too."

"Where did the fish flee to?"

"How would I know? They were gone. There were hundreds of fish there once, but now you won't find even a single one. And my ducks flew away. The strange thing is that they were domesticated ducks, but they flew away. Domesticated ducks don't fly."

"Who were the kids?"

"I don't know, they were from the other street; they live around here. But they don't understand anything. They don't get that this forest is going to belong to them in the future. They just keep fooling around. I'd occupy myself with something more serious if I were them." He changed the subject and said, "Well, come in, I'll offer you something."

"Offer me what?"

"What would you like?"

"I don't want anything. I was just asking."

"Do you want a good barbecued duck, or fish?"

That was the moment I said goodbye to the gardener and continued on my way. I tried not to think too much, afraid that I would once again end up plucking off someone's branches.

The weather was wonderful; the sun had been hiding for several days now. But it was bright. I don't know how the sun managed to light things up, but the low buildings in the city were shining.

I felt happy for a moment. It was like I had been freed of all my unpleasant memories. The cold air entered my lungs, and I continued my journey in a completely different mood.

I had walked quite a bit, but the day was only just starting. I had the impression that people were still asleep; the streets were empty, the working day had not yet begun. I noticed two young men in the distance, wearing army uniforms. They held each other's hand and walked slowly along a small sidewalk that was on an incline, a slight distance away. I decided to approach them, especially since there was nobody else around. When they saw me, they seemed upset at first and spoke in their own language, which was probably Kirundi, after which they switched to French. They realized that I didn't understand a thing, and they started to laugh. They had on wristbands with small military jets on them, probably meaning that they were pilots. One of them took a camera from his pocket and asked if they could take pictures of me—first with one, then with the other. They took the pictures and then again held hands and continued walking up the incline. There was a small shop at the corner of that street that had open doors which had some unfamiliar writing on it. The only word I recognized was "Café." The entranceway was painted black, and the walls featured colorful caricatures. I walked in. A blonde woman walked up to me and smiled, her mouth opening in such a way that its ends reached up to her ears. She probably understood that I wasn't a local, so she called another employee. When the other person arrived, I thought she was her twin sister. She was blonde, too, and had the same smile.

"What would you like to have?" she asked, wiping a table with a piece of cloth.

"Is this a café?" I asked.

"Yes, of course it is."

"I managed to understand that with great difficulty."

"I know, but that's not our fault. There are two naughty kids on the other street. As soon as we fix up the café, they spray paint our walls the following day. They painted caricatures on our walls two days ago. And they painted the entranceway black."

"I noticed."

"No matter how much we ask them not to do this, we can't prevent it from happening. They're naughty. They don't understand that what they're doing is wrong."

"Are they that naughty?"

"Yes, very. We've tried punishing them several times. We completely shaved the head of one of the kids, even his eyebrows. But they continue doing these bad things, like little monkeys. Anyway, forget about them. What can I bring you?"

"Water."

"What else? Nothing to eat?"

"No."

The woman left. During that time, someone else appeared in the other corner of the place and began to sweep up pieces of glass that lay next to the wall. I hadn't noticed them before.

"This was their doing. They used a sling," the stranger said.

"The kids?" I asked.

"Yes."

The woman returned and brought a bottle. She opened the bottle cap in my presence and poured the water into a glass.

"And they broke our window yesterday," she said. "Would you like anything else?"

"No. Thank you."

A little later, I noticed that the waitresses were standing near the entrance and arguing with a tourist who was most probably European. I waited for the argument to end, and then I called one of the women over and asked about the incident.

"Who was that?" I asked.

"The local priest," the woman replied.

"Who?"

"The priest. Don't be surprised. In the villages, tourists come from time to time to give 'spiritual nourishment' to the locals. It's a temporary job. He'd come to collect taxes."

"What taxes?"

"Well, it's more of a contribution to the church that he was seeking. We call it a tax. He wanted us to make a donation. But how could we? We don't even have the money to replace this glass."

I left the small café and continued walking up the incline. I was either in a suburb of Bujumbura, or in one of the villages close to the city. People began to gradually appear on the streets. I even managed to see one or two old French cars, one of them a taxi, the driver of which braked abruptly when he saw me. There were two men inside. One of them stuck his head out of the cab and asked in French who I was and where I was from, and I replied. Then he asked where I was going. I found it difficult to respond, because I don't speak French very well, and also because I really didn't know where I was going.

The man had big cheeks, round and protruding. There was a large scar on part of his face, and it looked fresh. The person sitting next to him, the driver, was slightly older, around forty years old. He was silent and barely even looked in my direction. I even thought that he was falling asleep.

They eventually managed to convince me to get into their car. They switched on some music several times and laughed, exchanging some words with each other. But I barely understood any of it. The music was local.

When the car turned off the uphill street, the driver asked, "Do you speak English?"

"Yes," I replied with surprise.

"I know a little, but I understand well."

"That's good. Where are we going?" I asked.

"You tell me."

"I don't know."

"Neither do I."

"The city seems to be asleep. Where are the people? I've been walking around since morning, but I've barely seen anyone."

"Yes, yes," he said, smiling but not understanding anything.

"There are very few cars, either."

"Yes."

"What point is there in working as a cab driver, if there's nobody around?"

"Yes, yes," he said a short while later. "Most of the population is in the villages. They raise animals. There's nothing for people to do in the city."

The man sitting in front of me suddenly shouted. I didn't understand what he had said, but it had sounded like he was swearing.

"What did he say?" I asked the driver.

"He got angry," he replied, laughing.

"At whom?"

"Two kids. He noticed them a moment ago, and got angry."

"Why?"

"For several days they've taken rides in the car, but have then refused to pay."

"Where do they live?" I asked. I suddenly had the urge to see them.

"I don't know."

"I want to see them," I said.

"Why bother? They ran away. They saw us and ran away."

"I didn't see them."

"You were talking to me."

"Stop the car."

I saw the priest from the car window. He was talking to himself and walking angrily on the uphill road. The strange thing was that I seemed to be going around in circles in the same place all the time. It was like being in a movie that had a limited number of actors. I'd seen another street going uphill like that one, but it had been a different street.

"Excuse me," I shouted. "Can I talk to you for a minute?"

I got out of the car. I said goodbye to the driver and the person sitting next to him.

"What is it?" the priest asked. He was surprised to see me.

"Are you going to church?"

"Yes."

"Is it close by?"

"No."

"Can I come with you?"

"Who are you?"

"I saw you at the café," I said.

"And?"

"Where are you from?"

"France."

"Are you French?"

"Yes, no," he said.

"The waitress said you were collecting taxes."

"She lied. What taxes?"

"For the church. She said it was a donation."

"No, she lied. I'd come to collect money, but it wasn't for the church. They owe me money."

"Is that why you'd been arguing?"

"Yes. They were saying that they didn't have any money. They said that the kids had broken their window and they didn't even have any money to replace it. And I said that they had stolen my clothes and dozens of candles, but I wasn't complaining. They were going to leave sooner or later, after all. They should take care of their own problems."

"Who are those kids? Everyone's been talking about them."

"Who are they? They're just a couple of stupid, illiterate kids."

"I want to see them."

"What's there to see? Instead of going sightseeing, you want to see a couple of kids." But the kids did truly interest me more.

"I'm sorry, I have to change plans and go in another direction," he said.

"You're not going to church?"

"No, there's one more thing I have to do. I'd forgotten about it."

"Could you please tell me where the church is?"

"So you've changed your mind? You want to see the church now?"

"I've been walking around since morning; it's like being in a labyrinth. I have no idea where I'm going. And there's nobody on the streets. I've barely seen anyone at all."

"Keep going straight on this road, about one kilometer. You'll see a large rock, then take a left from there. That's where the church is. It's very beautiful. But go quickly. Don't be late for mass."

I forgot to ask the priest how mass could start without him. I walked with enthusiasm, as if I finally knew where I was going, and headed for the church. I walked for a kilometer, but didn't come across a rock. There were some small shops on the road that featured advertisements from several well-known companies. I entered one of the shops to ask for directions to the church.

"What do you need?" a young man who was a tailor asked.

I was surprised that everyone spoke English—at least everyone I met.

"Excuse me, I'm in Burundi, right?"

"Yes," he said with surprise.

"In Bujumbura?"

"Yes."

"What street is this?"

"Du Stade Avenue. Why?"

"Is there a church here?"

"Yes, there is."

"Where is it? The priest said that I should go up the street and turn left."

"The French one?"

"Yes."

"He's crazy. He isn't a clergyman; don't believe him. Go downhill. There's a garden there, several kilometers to the north. That's where the real priest is. He has a large garden. He'll tell you everything you need to know. By the way, your pants are a bit too long; they're dragging on the ground when you walk. Take them off, I'll shorten them for you."

"Here you go," I said, taking off my pants. "Shorten them; I'll wait."

The tailor grew excited. His mood lifted.

"Does everyone here speak English?" I asked.

"No. Only a few people do. I know English because I studied languages at one point. But not everyone here speaks it. Why would we need it? Our life is so monotonous, there's nothing to do. Life has almost come to a standstill. I'd gone to the village this morning, because one of the farmers I know has a cow that had given birth, so I'd gone to see the calf. When I got there, hundreds of people had gathered and were dancing. I didn't know what the occasion was. When I came closer, it turned out that the cow had given birth to two calves instead of one. The farmer was beside himself with joy. He'd arranged a feast and more than a hundred people had been invited. We celebrated. We had a great time. Then we found out later that a tragedy had occurred; I heard about it after I had left the village. It turned out that one of the calves had gone savage and attacked the other one. It had killed him. Then it killed the cow and escaped. I'd never heard that a cow could act so wildly, especially a newborn. Many of the villagers didn't believe it, either. Everyone decided that the spirit of a wolf had entered the calf; that it was cursed. The poor farmer will be bankrupt. He'll be forced to sell his truck now."

"Did they find the calf?" I asked.

"No. They say it committed suicide. It committed its evil deeds and vanished into thin air. I'm done—here, put this on."

The tailor's face suggested that he liked to make things up on the spot and tell exaggerated stories.

"So the church is downhill?" I asked.

"Yes. Go straight down, then take a left at the café."

I walked back down the same street, past the same houses, and saw nobody.

"Hey," someone shouted. I turned around; it was the soldiers I had seen in the morning. "Where were you? We were looking for you," they said.

One of them took a picture from his pocket and held it out to me. I took it—it was a picture we had taken together. I said thank you. We parted ways. I don't know where they had been looking for me, but I was surprised that they had taken the effort to print the picture and give me a copy.

I never found the church. I searched for it for more than an hour, but it was in vain. I decided to return to the spot where I had come from. And then I suddenly realized that I didn't remember where I had come from. The only thing I remembered was sitting on a yellow bench in a garden, pondering and plucking off branches. I didn't remember anything before that. It really was like I was in a labyrinth.

ဆာ၄

"Do you want to go to Bujumbura?" the truck driver asked. I had stopped him along the way, after leaving the airport.

"Yes," I said.

"Where are you going to stay? Do you have a place?"

"No, I'm not going to stay for long, just a few hours. I'm leaving in the evening."

"Do you want me to give you a tour in my truck?"

It was morning. Late night, even.

"Well, do you want a tour?"

"No, thanks. Please take me to the city center; I'll figure something out from there."

"Okay. If you don't want to give me any money, you can just say so," the driver said, supposedly joking.

"No, it's just that I want to walk."

"Okay, okay."

"Do you live close to the city?" I asked.

"Yes, two hours away. Do you want to go to the village? I'm celebrating today. My cow is giving birth to a calf. It's a happy day. We have to celebrate; I've invited everyone over."

"Thank you. I'd love to come, but I can't."

"What's there to do in the city? Why are you going there? A couple of state buildings and several streets. And emptiness. And the streets are dangerous, too."

"Why?"

"There are two kids in town, floating around like ghosts and causing trouble. Nobody's been able to catch them. It's like they can't be touched. Nobody knows where they live or who their parents are. Many people say that they're ghosts that possess children and make them do bad things. And they pick the kids who aren't innocent—although nobody is completely innocent anyway. Good thing they can't possess animals, or else…" he laughed. "Here we are, this is the city. I've got to go now."

"Thank you," I said, "Whose house is this?"

"It's the gardener's. Sit down on this yellow bench, he'll come and show you around. He's also a priest; you'll probably have a good time with him."

DAY 39. TANZANIA
CHACHAGÉ'S RETURN

The miserable cart-driver somehow managed to get me to my destination, and then he started to sing. He looked like the root of a rotting tree which essentially should not have existed. The cart-driver stopped his bulls and embraced me tightly. He wept and continued to sing.

I had heard such a song only once before, in Mauritania, when I was being taken away on a stretcher. But the cart-driver sang a different song. He sang sweetly; he was smiling. He hugged me again at the end.

"What song is that?" I asked.

"It's a good song," he said, and he rubbed my shoulders with his hands, pulling my body towards him and hugging me tightly.

The cart-driver was an old man, burned under the sun. He barely had any teeth. There were one or two teeth in his mouth that seemed to be made of wood—yellow and twisted. He was wearing a piece of cloth, which he also used to cover his head.

He was looking at me.

"Where are we?" I asked.

"In outer space," he said.

"What song were you singing?"

"I was making one up. About you."

"What were you making up?"

"That you are lost, three demons are chasing you, you're running away, they're chasing you and emitting fire, they're flying. You no longer know where to escape, and you approach me. I see you and embrace you tightly. And then, you run once again."

"Then what happens?"

"That's it; then it's the chorus."

"Why did you decide to sing about me?"

"Who else should I sing about? There's nobody else here."

"Where are we?"

"I already told you," he said. The cart-driver got off the cart and began to caress his animals. Then he took a long stick from behind the cart and started to rap them on their thick hides.

"You scratch them," he said, "and they like it. They like it when I give them my attention."

The cart-driver was rubbing the bulls very slowly. There were one or two huts in the distance, some animals moving about, and acres of mud. It had probably rained. The old man went about his work in a monotonous and indifferent way, as if I was not there. He would probably have kept on caressing the bulls for hours had I not interrupted him.

"Is there a lot left?" I asked.

"For what?"

"For you to finish."

"I don't plan on finishing; it'd be better for you to say what you want."

"I asked you a question a moment ago."

"What?"

"You don't remember?"

"No."

"You said that there was an airport on the other side of the border. You also said you'd take me there. You said you were headed in that direction. But now we're standing in this deserted place, where there is mud everywhere, and we're not moving. Can't you tell me where we are? I have to get to Dar es Salaam."

"You're a strange man," he said, climbing back on the cart. He lay down on the sacks in the rear, which probably contained grass. "Don't you have anything else to do? Nothing to occupy yourself with? Why do you always repeat the same question? My bulls are hungry, and there is no grass here; we have to get to a place where they can graze a bit, and then we'll continue our journey."

"What's that in your sack? Isn't it grass?"

"No," he said, as opened one, "it's cloth."

"Where is there grass?"

"Do you see those huts? In that direction."

"How do you know?"

"One of them is mine. Lie down, rest. We'll go soon."

"I'm not tired."

"Lie down, lie down. We still have a long way to go."

"Are we very far from the airport?"

"Yes. Didn't you know?"

"I did know."

"Why did you decide to cross the border on foot? Wouldn't it have been quicker by plane?" he asked, yawning.

"It would."

"So why didn't you go that way?"

"This is more interesting."

"Strange." He rolled over to one side. "You're complaining, and yet this is more interesting—very strange."

"How long do we have to wait?"

"I don't know; until the animals are rested."

"How will we know that they're rested?"

"They'll tell us. The animals here can talk."

"You mean you understand their language?"

"No, the animals here are happy. Nobody bothers them. The lion has a full stomach, as does the rabbit. The zebra drinks water from the stream without fear, and the crocodile is asleep. All the animals are happy. There are no predators or domestic animals here—they are all together, side by side."

"What do they eat, if they have a full stomach?"

"I don't know. Sick animals, I guess."

"When will the bulls tell us that they are rested?"

"Lie down, lie down, you can settle down comfortably on these sacks."

I was forced to lie down. There was so much mud around us that I didn't want to walk around. The cart-driver curled up and fell asleep in a few minutes. I was a bit angry at him. A few moments later, I fell asleep, too.

ഉ⊙ങ

His bulls had walked through the mud and reached the hut. The cart-driver was asleep. It started to rain shortly afterwards. The pouring rain turned everything to mud in no time. The mud covered the bulls' hooves, as well as the lower section of the cart. It was like we were in a swamp. The bulls tried to move forward, but were finding themselves unable to do so. I called out to the cart-driver once or twice, but he didn't wake up. I nudged him, but in vain. It was like he had turned into stone.

"Maybe he's dead," the bull on the right said under his breath.

"Why do you think so?" asked the bull on the left.

"He isn't breathing."

"He's in deep sleep."

"I know him well. He's dead. This other man must have killed him."

"What did he do? I didn't see anything."

"You had your back to him."

"So did you."

"But I saw it. He was shouting at him. He must have died of fright."

"What are we going to do?"

"I don't know."

"Can he hear us?"

"I don't know."

"If he can't hear us, then everything is fine. We'll pretend that we haven't noticed."

"What if he can hear us?"

"Hardly possible. He can't hear us."

"How do you know?"

"He won't be able to understand our language."

"What *is* our language? Do you know our language?"

"No."

"You see? We must be careful. In any case, we have to try to get out of this mud. Then we can think about the rest."

"I've already made a decision."

"What have you decided?"

"We have to kill him."

"How?"

"I don't know. We'll wait till he gets off the cart, then we'll attack him. We'll stick our horns into his stomach."

"That's cruel."

"Well, why did he kill our master?"

"Perhaps it wasn't him."

"But you said a few moments ago that you saw him shouting at him."

"Yes, but perhaps the old man was ill."

"He was healthy. I've never heard him complain of his health. And he was singing this morning."

"Do you know why he embraced him?"

"No."

"I think it was longing. He misses his sons."

"He hasn't seen them in a long time, has he?"

"No."

"I wonder if they're alive."

"Probably. They shouldn't have left, in my opinion."

"You're right. They shouldn't have left the old man alone. His life lost its meaning."

"How old is the old man?"

"I don't know; I don't remember. He'd had many animals before us. He had a large farm once."

"Did he like his animals very much?"

"Yes. He didn't slaughter any of them. Only for ceremonies, and sometimes he'd drink blood."[46]

"The old man died a natural death."

"I think so, too."

I was waiting for them to finish their dialogue. But they would have continued to speak forever if I hadn't interrupted them.

"Excuse me," I said, "Where is the airport around here? Your master was supposed to take me to the airport. You don't know? Why aren't you speaking? You were speaking a moment ago."

The bulls were quiet. I felt like I was gradually losing my mind. This was the first time I'd had a lifeless person lying next to me, and in a place so deserted.

I nudged the man a few more times, but he lay there inanimately. He had died. The bulls did not move when I told them to. I was afraid to get off the cart at first, but then I gathered up the courage and did so.

I had goosebumps. Water had attacked and invaded my clothing on all sides. I was in mud from the knees down, I couldn't feel my feet, and it was like I was walking in wet clay. I kept feeling like somebody was pulling me down from below.

The huts looked like small salt and pepper shakers; I'd seen ones like them before. When the rain stopped, the day transformed at once. The mud on my pants dried and turned yellow. When I looked back, I saw that the bulls were very far away. I'd walked about a hundred meters and had reached the huts. There really was a lot of grass there. I was beginning to panic. I began to hurry for some reason, I felt like I was running late and had to be somewhere. I couldn't keep pace with my thoughts. Suddenly, I saw an

---

46. Most of the Maasai live in northern Tanzania. Before going to hunt, the men often mix cow's milk with blood and drink it. They believe it gives them strength and courage. The Maasai speak Maa, Dinka, Nuer, and other languages, and some of them understand English. Many of them live in a fantasy world to this day…

old man approaching in the distance; walking ahead of him was a child who was seven or eight years old and had curly hair. There was a long stick in the child's hands, and the old man was holding on to one end. The child walked slowly and guided the old man, who listened to the child and held tight onto the stick, walking towards me. When they came closer, I heard them speaking in a language I didn't understand, probably Swahili, which disappointed me. But, surprisingly, as soon as the old man noticed me, he shouted, "Come closer."

"It's so good to see you," I said.

"S'hafi, stop. Can't you see that there's someone standing in front of us? Say hello," the old man said to the boy.

"Hello," S'hafi said.

"Hello, do you live here?" I asked.

"Yes."

"Who does this hut belong to?" I asked.

"Chachagé… He'd gone to see his sons, but he must have returned by now."

"His name is Chachagé?" I asked.

"Yes, do you know him?"

"Is he an old man?"

"Yes."

"Thin? A few teeth in his mouth?"

"Yes, thin. The teeth in his mouth aren't real. They're made of wood."

"I was with him a little while ago."

"Really?" He smiled, "S'hafi, say hello to this man again; he is a friend." S'hafi came up to me this time and embraced me. I embraced him back.

"Is he your grandson?" I asked.

"Yes. He is my most precious possession. But where is Chachagé?"

"He died a short while ago. I didn't know what to do. I left his body in the cart. I came here to find someone. We met at the border with Burundi. He said he would guide me, and I agreed."

"Where is he?" the old asked sadly.

"There," I pointed, "with the bulls."

"Cows."

"Do cows have horns?"

The old man pushed the stick and the child moved forward.

"Let's go see," he said.

"What is this stick for?"

"S'hafi is my guide. I don't see well. Little ones should take care of the elderly. He will ask his children to do the same someday."

"Do we have to go back across this road now?"

"Yes. I cannot bring back the body on my own. You must help."

"Can't the cows bring it?"

"Come, come."

We walked through the mud. Only half of S'hafi could be seen, the other half was submerged in mud.

"Did Chachagé have children?" I asked.

"Yes."

"They left him?"

"Yes. How do you know? Did he tell you?"

"No. The cows did."

"Ah yes," he smirked. "That's right, his cows know everything. The only thing I don't understand is how they know so much. Had you gone to help him?"

"No. I was in Burundi. I came from there."

"You live there?"

"No," I said, beginning to slowly suspect that I no longer looked like myself. "I asked him how I could get to Dar es Salaam, and he said that there was an airport in these parts. I didn't want to go back to Bujumbura, so I came with him."

"You did well. He probably felt lonely and realized that he was going to pass on. He didn't want to be alone. S'hafi, stop. Our friend is tired."

"I'm not tired, we can continue."

"S'hafi, continue. Why are you going to Dar es Salaam? It's so far away. What do you have there? Are the people there more advanced? Do they know more than we do?" he asked sarcastically. "Yes, life is advanced there, everyone is rich, the sun rises twice a day. But that doesn't mean anything."

"I don't think people are rich there," I said.

"Even worse. So those people walk here and there in the mud like we do."

This was the first time I'd met someone who was so ignorant of the capital of his country. But Tanzania was such a big country—945.1 thousand square kilometers—that it was possible to be ignorant.

"Don't be so surprised. I'm not that ignorant. It's just that we don't need to know very much," the old man said.

"Why?"

"What would we do with so much knowledge? Who would we talk to about it? There's nobody here. Chachagé had probably spoken to his cows so much that they had learned everything. Even how to speak!"

"Where are we now?"

"Near Lake Tanganyika, in Kigoma."

"Is it a big city?"

The old man laughed.

"S'hafi, stop. Hold the stick. Help me up."

We had finally reached the cart. I was afraid to go any closer. I stood near the cows, who had hung their heads and laughed like bashful children.

"Come closer," the old man said to S'hafi.

He climbed up into the cart, too. They tried to revive Chachagé for a few minutes, but it was in vain. They climbed down.

"He's dead. You were right."

"What should we do?" I asked.

"What can we do? Get in the cart."

"Then what?"

Chachagé's body was heavy. We placed him on our shoulders and somehow managed to walk.

"The body of the deceased is heavy," the old man said.

"Yes."

"Do you know why?"

"No."

"All the spirits enter his body and organize a feast. They light a fire around the trees and start to dance."

"Why?"

"They celebrate his return."

"Where is he returning to?" I was barely managing to speak.

"He's returning to them."

"To whom?"

"To those who live well," he said with a smirk. "What do we do in this life? Everything changes once we're gone, anyway. It doesn't matter how many people remember him. He won't remember us. It doesn't matter how many people cry at his grave—nothing will change for him. Even if his sons return."

"Where should we take him?" I asked.

"I don't know. We're walking, for now. S'hafi, do we still have far to go?"

"No," S'hafi responded, his eyes closed, with one of them opening from time to time to look into the distance. He would also glance at me sometimes and pull at the stick in fear.

"Let's get to his hut, then we'll call the villagers."

"Why?"

"To bury him. You think we should leave him like this?"

"No. I mean, don't you want to call his sons?"

"Who knows where his sons are? They've probably been taken away as well."

"By whom?"

"The spirits." He turned to S'hafi. "Don't listen to any of this."

"Couldn't the bulls have moved him?"

"Cows."

"Well, couldn't they have? I can't go any farther; I need to rest."

"Don't put him down on the ground. He'll get muddy," he said.

"Where should I put him?"

"It's not much farther. S'hafi, aren't we there yet?"

"We're almost there," S'hafi said.

"Why is it so muddy here? Why doesn't anyone cultivate the land?"

"We cultivate the land, but it always rains here, almost every day and at every hour. There's no need to cultivate land in these conditions."

"Isn't there a better road to the village?"

"There is. But what can we do if this is where Chachagé chose to pass on?"

"I can't go on," I said.

"Not much farther; hang in there. You'll get a good rest afterwards. He probably has many spirits inside him, which is why he's so heavy. He was an old man. He'd come to know many people, one way or another. All their spirits have probably come to him."

"Couldn't they have organized their feast elsewhere?"

"No," he said with conviction, "they only celebrate in the bodies of the deceased. That is how it is."

"I can't go on any more," I said.

"S'hafi, is it much farther?"

"No," S'hafi said.

Chachagé's body slid off my shoulders and ended up in the mud. I failed to catch him. I had run out of strength.

"What have you done?" the old man asked angrily.

"I couldn't go on; he was too heavy," I said.

"They'll all flee now. There were just a few meters left; couldn't you have kept going?"

"Who'll flee? Why are you getting angry? Let me rest a bit and I'll continue."

"It's too late."

"Too late for what?"

"You scared the spirits that had gathered. Chachagé will never find peace. He was miserable as it was."

"What could I do? I couldn't go on. I can't feel my feet."

"They couldn't celebrate his return in peace."

It seemed like the old man was more concerned with the spirits than the deceased. When he got angry, I thought he would berate me for getting Chachagé's body dirty, but it was only the spirits' feast that seemed to concern him.

"What should I do now?" I asked.

"What can you do? Nothing. Leave the body here and go away."

"We're going to just leave it like this?"

"No, I'll call the villagers, and they'll come. They know the right way to see Chachagé off."

We walked for a bit more and got to the village. A large group of villagers had gathered near the path and they gave us strange looks as they stared at me and at Chachagé's muddied corpse. Some of them had on body paint; they were probably from different tribes. The villagers eyed me with suspicion. S'hafi, who had been walking ahead of me so far, suddenly vanished. I didn't see the old man, either. When I emerged from the mud, it was like I had ended up in a completely new world; the villagers surrounded me and made strange noises. I felt like I had gone back to prehistoric times. I suddenly came to my senses and realized that it would be better for me to quickly leave this village. The only thing that surprised me was the fire that burned in the space among the trees and the people gathered around it, dancing…

∞∞

The bulls were in their place, Chachagé lay next to me. My eyes hurt, as did my head. I don't know how long I had slept. When I tried to wake him up, I saw that he was lying there lifelessly. I shouted once or twice, but it was in vain. Chachagé had truly died.

There were two huts in the distance, and a boy sat in front of one of them. There was a thin, long stick in his hand. He would throw the stick into the air and then catch it. I came down from the cart. I ran in that direction. The soil was wet and had turned into mud here and there. I approached the boy.

"Is your name S'hafi?" I asked.

"Yes," he said with surprise. It seemed like he didn't speak English well.

"Do you know Chachagé?"

"Yes. But he isn't home. He's gone to see his sons," he said. "They'd left him; he's gone to find them."

"Where do they live?"

"In Burundi."

"See that cart?" I asked.

"Yes."

"He's over there. I was there a few moments ago. He's dead. Can you call someone?"

"Grandpa," S'hafi shouted.

"Wait. Let me leave, then you call him. All right?"

The boy nodded. The only thing going through my mind at that point was to quickly flee.

"Where's the airport here?" I asked.

"There is no airport here."

"Chachagé said that there was one. He brought me here. I have to go to Dar es Salaam."

"There is no airport here."

"Impossible. Are you telling the truth?"

"Yes. Wait, I just remembered. He probably meant the military airport. His sons are military men. He must have been talking about the military airport. But that's on the other side, closer to Burundi. His twin sons are pilots there."

"Got it, thank you," I said and ran, just as the boy shouted after me, "One of the legs of your pants is shorter than the other," and he started to laugh…

When I put my hand to my breast pocket, I remembered the photograph given to me by the two young men I had met in one of the narrow streets of Burundi.

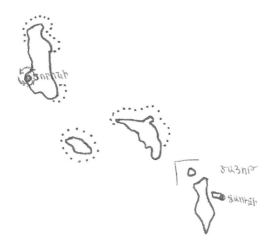

DAY 40. THE COMOROS
THE UNDERGROUND CITY

I'd never seen a mail cart like that one before. As far as I knew, horse-drawn carts had not been used for mail delivery since the 18th century.

The hooves of the horses, splashing in the water, made a strange sound as they cut across my path.

"How can I get to Mayotte?" the stranger asked as he got down off the cart.

"I just arrived here a little while ago and don't know anything, to be honest. I don't even know where I am," I said.

"You're in Moroni," he replied.

"Is this a mail cart?"

"Yes."

"I haven't seen carts like this for more than two hundred years."

"How old are you?" he laughed. "This cart was built before Christ."

"Wouldn't it be more convenient to use a car to deliver the mail?" I asked.

"No. A car is weak. I can cut across the Indian Ocean on this cart, but you can't even drive across a muddy road in a car nowadays."

"You mean over the water?"

"Yes. My horses are very strong. They run so fast that the cart doesn't sink."

"Were the horses born back before Christ, too?"

"No, they're even older," he said, laughing again. "I bought this cart from some slaves, or rather, from my forefathers. It's been handed down from generation to generation. They used to transport grain in it at one time, then newspapers and vegetables, and before that—slaves. This cart has seen so much. Now I'm making use of its services. I take letters from Moroni to Foumbouni and Bambao. But my employer made some changes today and my route has been modified; I have to go to Mayotte today. Dzaoudzi. But I don't know how to get there. I've never been there; I'm afraid that the horses will get confused and sink, that they won't be able to swim. Worse yet, I've been told that I have to get there today. There's a letter that has to make it today. It must be important; that's what I've been told, anyway."

"You haven't checked?"

"We have no right to read the contents of the letters. All we need to do is get them to their destinations. It's none of our business what they say."

I thought it was quite strange that he had asked me where Mayotte was, and that he didn't know its location.

"Fine, it looks like you can't help me," he said.

"Yes. I'd have loved to help, but I guess the locals would know better. This is their country, after all," I said.

"Yes," he laughed again. "Of course, this is their country."

The horses neighed, their hooves struck the ground and the mail cart and the mailman disappeared. I shouted after him, but he didn't hear me. I wanted to ask him if he'd ever opened a single letter that belonged to someone else.

I was in Moroni, the capital of the Comoros. The boat trip from Zanzibar, in Tanzania, to Moroni had cost about 100 euros, even though I had bargained with them to reduce the price. The trip had been long and boring. But when I got to the capital of that small archipelago, everything changed. I'd never been in a place like that before. I could already feel that certain "games" were afoot.

At Moroni, I was greeted by a small pretty mosque and old rusty boats along its shores. The boats seemed to be made of wood—grey, rotting wood, with many cavities in them. I'd never seen such boats before. The mosque was really beautiful. It had two stories, arches and pillars, and a decorated roof. On the rear side, which wasn't clearly visible from the coast, there were towers of four stories, the domes of which stuck upwards like little hats. The mosque was so white that it seemed to be made of ice; I'd seen one like it in Djibouti. But this one was large and grand. The coast was not very clean—besides colorful grains of sand and stones, there were many pieces of trash on the beach. The water was black. It wasn't murky, but you couldn't see through it despite the fact that the sunlight was falling directly on it. I never got to see the bottom.

I walked around several rickety buildings and came to a busy street, which was probably one of the main streets of the city. There were many people in it, as well as cars, and a lot of commerce was taking place on the sidewalk. Most of the vendors were selling cheap clothes—made in China and India—and also some food.

I didn't know Comorian or Arabic, so I was forced to try my hand at French. I threw in some English, but the locals didn't understand any of it.

I don't know whether or not it was a coincidence, but two cars crashed into each other right there before my eyes, and both drivers were injured. An ambulance arrived after a slight delay. People crowded around the scene. I'd last seen a crowd of that size in Abuja, when the people had gathered around and said that they had never seen miners before. This time, I couldn't understand what any of the people were saying. The only thing that was clear, even without understanding the language, was that the paramedics and the police spent a long time negotiating, as a result of which the conditions of the injured continued to grow worse. One of them was a bald man with a long beard, about forty years old, who had covered his head in a green cloth and wore a brown cape. His eyes were open but they stared into nothingness. The other was a young man, in his early twenties, thin, with a long jaw and a mustache. His eyes were open, too, and, like the bald man, stared away. The bodies of the victims swayed on the stretchers. It seemed to me that they weren't breathing. I'd already grown used to seeing lifeless bodies, and I could easily make out who was still alive and who was dead. I left the scene and continued to walk on to the next street, where most of the vendors sold food. I saw a stall that had the word "Food" on it in English. I walked up to it. The vendor wasn't there but there were bananas lying all over the place, dark green in color. I'd never seen bananas like that before. A piece of paper, handwritten in black, said "250 KMF," meaning Comorian Francs, which was around fifty cents. I left money on a stool there and picked up one of the bunches. To be honest, it was how they looked that had attracted me. I wasn't particularly hungry, but I really wanted to taste them. The bunch was heavy and uncomfortable to hold. The bananas tasted very different from what I was used to; they hurt my throat and I felt short of breath, like I was eating a raw potato. A little later, after I'd already eaten three bananas, someone shouted and came running after me.

His face looked familiar; I felt like I'd seen him somewhere before. He said in English, "Why did you steal my bananas?"

"I didn't steal them," I said, putting the bananas on the ground. "I paid. There was a stool there, and I put fifty euro cents on it."

"That's too little. You bought three bananas and stole seventeen."

"I didn't steal anything. Three is enough for me, to be honest. The note said 250 francs. So I calculated using the exchange rate and left the money there. I couldn't find the vendor. And I didn't even know that the person selling them would be able to speak English. If I'd known that, I would definitely have waited."

"The vendor didn't speak English." He stroked his long beard, scratched his head and covered it with a green cloth. "The vendor doesn't care what language he speaks." He was talking about himself, and continued, "The vendor doesn't exist anymore; he's dead."

I hadn't heard such a frank confession ever before.

"How did it happen?" I asked, surprised.

"Yes. I no longer care what language I speak. Did you see the accident, two streets away?"

"Yes."

"You don't remember me?"

"No." I still couldn't understand what he was getting at.

"I was driving the yellow Citroen. I died a little while ago. I still don't feel very well. This is a slightly strange situation, but an interesting one."

"You're dead?"

"Yes. Didn't you see them arguing? I took my last breath while that was going on. Or rather, in the ambulance, on the way to the hospital. My name is Ahmed."

"You're dead?" I asked again.

Ahmed looked at me with a beautiful smile and pressed his teeth together. He had round eyes and a broad forehead. He directed a joyous gaze at me and seemed proud to have died.

"Yes. I was in a hurry to get to the market, so that I could serve people like you. My bananas are placed at various points in the market, and they can't be sold without me. My car has been giving me problems for the past couple of days. I didn't manage to brake in time, which is why the cars collided. I don't know how that other vehicle appeared in front of me. I didn't manage to steer the car away in time. You saw what happened as a result. But I feel all right, that is, if you give me the remaining 1250 francs."

"Can other people see you?" I asked.

"Don't change the topic. You owe me money."

"Is this your ghost I'm seeing?"

"No. I'm not a ghost. I told you: my name is Ahmed. I just died a little while ago, that's all. You were my first customer today, so I've come after you. Otherwise, I wouldn't have come."

"Can the others see you?" I asked again.

"What difference does it make?"

"It'd be interesting to know."

"I don't know. But I like this life. It's like I'm drunk. It's like I'm flying. If I'd known that death was such a wonderful thing, I would've thrown myself off a tall building a long time ago. Do you want us to go somewhere like that? You can try it out, too."

"Try what out?"

"Jumping off."

"No, thanks, I've still got a lot to do. I'll try it out another time."

"Do you see those clothes?" He showed me some clothes hanging in front of a house, which had probably been wet and were swinging slowly in the wind. They were so colorful that it was like there was a small rainbow in front of the house. "That's my house. Interesting, isn't it? My house is so close to the market, but I drive there in my car. Do you know why?"

"No."

"Because I deliver several bunches of bananas there every day. As you can see, each of them is quite heavy, and they're not comfortable to hold."

"They also don't taste good," I said.

"I don't care. You've eaten them, so pay up. I had a good reason for not being at my stall. If I hadn't died, I would've been there, and I would've asked for the money right then. But it makes no difference. What matters is that you pay."

"I'll return the seventeen remaining bananas to you."

"No, you've taken them already. Give me the money."

"What are you going to do with the money? You're dead, after all."

"So what? Even better. Instead of having some compassion, you're rejecting me? It's just 1250 francs. Give me the money and I'll be on my way, and so will you."

"I'd give you the money, but I can't understand why it's so important to you. You can't do anything with this money, but you still want it. It sounds like all you want is to cause someone else some inconvenience."

"I'm a good man, with God as my witness," he said, coming down on his knees. "I've never stolen, never tricked anyone. I've always been an honest salesman, and I've weighed even the smallest of items fairly. Why would I cause any problems over some bananas? You don't believe that I'm an honest man? The underground cities are my witness."

"What cities?"

"The ones underground."

I hadn't yet come to terms with the fact that the person standing in front of me was a dead man who was moving around animatedly. We were standing in one of the busier parts of the street and I was constantly getting the feeling that everyone was staring at us. In all probability, they couldn't see Ahmed, which is why I was trying to suppress my own movements, so that people wouldn't think that I had lost my mind. I could have paid him 1250 francs and said goodbye, but that would mean ending a very interesting conversation, of a kind I had never come close to having before, especially now that he had said something even more fascinating.

"You mentioned some cities," I said.

"Yes."

"What does that mean?"

"I told you already. I'm an honest vendor. And the whole world knows that. I've never tricked anyone, I've never lied. When someone's asked for five bananas, that's what I've given them." He began to repeat himself: "When they've asked for six, I've given six. I've never given one more or one less. I'm an honest man. If it's twenty bananas, then it's twenty. You've paid for three, now you must pay for the remaining seventeen."

"Did you make up the part about the underground cities?" I asked.

"No."

"They exist?"

"Why wouldn't they? People are too lazy to dig. But once they *do* dig, do you know what they find? Anywhere, any island, just dig a few meters and you'll find anything you could ever imagine."

"How do you know?

"I just know."

"Are you an archeologist?"

"No. I'm a vendor. And vendors know everything."

"So you're saying that there are other cities underground?"

"Of course. But they aren't there now; they used to be there. The same way that I used to be, but I no longer am. The cities used to be there, too, just like that. The Comoros looked very different a few thousand years ago. But there were definitely cities, there were people, and now they are a few meters below us."

"How far below?"

"I don't know. Twenty, thirty meters. If they dig, they'll see that I'm right. But they won't dig. They'll build new buildings instead—a new house, a new street, a new city; all that is going to end up underground at some point, anyway. Cities, like people, end up with their bodies buried underground when they die. The only difference is that they live slightly longer. But don't you think about that too much. Give me the money, and I'll leave."

"Where will you go?"

"I don't know. I'll go home. I'll rest up a bit. Then I'll get my car fixed. I've got to stop by the market, too. Nobody's looking after my bananas there."

"But why would you need anyone to?"

"What do you mean?"

"You're dead, remember? Why get your car fixed? Why go back to the market? You're gone. Have you forgotten?"

"No, I haven't forgotten. But what difference does that make? Don't I have any rights if I'm dead? Have I been deprived of my rights?"

I'd never heard such questions in my life. I thought that I was delusional. I couldn't make out what was real, and what was not. The bald vendor standing in front me, who had just breathed his last a little while ago, was standing and walking around like a healthy man. But the strangest thing was that there seemed to be no difference for him whether he was alive or dead.

"I can invite you to my house, and we can be friends; you could be my guest—but only if you give me the money."

"I will," I said.

"Wonderful. Well, come on. I'm in a hurry. I've got to get the car repaired."

"Why did you mention the old city? Is there something you know about it?"

"Of course. After I died, I ended up being able to speak English. Why wouldn't I also know history? I've become clairvoyant."

"If you hadn't had the accident, and had stayed alive, what would you do?"

"I don't know. I don't want to think about that. God forbid that should have happened," he said and knelt down once again. "I'm an honest man, I've never tricked anyone, I've never lied. God gave me this gift."

"Death?"

"Yes. What's so bad about it? You don't believe me? You can try it. I assure you, there's nothing more wonderful than this."

"Will you be around forever?"

"No, I'll die again," he laughed. "Did you see the people in the crowd? They were looking at me like they envied me. Come, let's go to my house."

"No, thanks. I'll give you your money, but I don't have much time."

"Oh? Alright, as you wish. What matters is the money, right?" he laughed.

"Aren't you planning on leaving?" I asked.

"I'll go home soon; I've got things to do, as I said."

"That's not what I mean. I meant leaving the earth."

"Soon, soon. I'll end up underground, too, and I'll go to the cities that used to exist but no longer do, and I'll walk on the streets that have vanished into thin air. There's no sun there. There's no air, either. Just ghosts like me, walking around like cockroaches. Life is frozen there. Don't worry, I'll leave." Then he changed his tone. "I wonder if they have bananas there?"

"Why? Are you planning on being a vendor there?"

"Yes."

"Are the cities very old?"

"A few thousand years old. There are several layers of them, and the different layers consist of different cities."

"Here's your money."

We said goodbye. I didn't know whether or not I should believe him. He could have been mistaken. He was a vendor, after all, and wasn't expected to know about other cities. When I returned to the market, I didn't see anyone there. His bananas lay there randomly, in various parts of the place. People continued selling on the streets.

Suddenly, I remembered the mailman I had met in the morning. I remembered his cart and his horses, and the thought crossed my mind that he, too, could have been from that city, or perhaps he was going there. He said that he didn't know the way to Mayotte,[47] but if he had been a local, he would definitely have known…

I kept thinking about what could have happened to the other person who had died. When I returned to the scene of the accident, there was nobody there. Life in the city went on as usual. People were walking about, there were cars on the street, but nothing remained that could remind one of the incident that had occurred earlier that day. I received confirmation of the accident from a medical officer who was moving wooden boxes from the trunk of a minibus to the yard of the single-story building opposite us, where there were many exotic trees in gigantic flower pots. It was the office of an international organization, the name of which I ended up never finding out. The medical officer heard me out and said that he was aware of the accident that had happened, and then he added that both drivers had died. Both lives had ended in their cars. The older one—the bald man—has died of a heart attack, while the second one had died of cerebral trauma. The police had taken their vehicles away, but the medical officer did not know where the deceased were located. When I asked him about cities that had ended up underground, he laughed and told me politely that I needed to see a doctor. He also said that the elderly liked to make such jokes, and I had probably misunderstood what someone had been saying.

Time began to slip by quickly. It was the middle of the day already and the sun stood in the center of the sky. I was tired, and the bananas were heavy. I put them on the ground and sat down to rest a bit.

---

47. An insular department that is ruled by France. More than 190,000 people live in Mayotte. Most of them are locals who were born there. The rest are immigrants from the Comoros, Madagascar, and other countries. French is the state language, while the most common ones are Shimaore, Kibushi, Arabic, and others. As a result of a referendum that took place in 1972, the Comorian Islands (now the Comoros) gained independence from France. Only the residents of Mayotte rejected independence and preferred to stay under French rule. Nevertheless, the United Nations recognizes the authority of the Comoros over Mayotte.

It was evening. It was hot. I was walking on the street. I was so engrossed in thinking about Ahmed's story that I wasn't watching where I was going.

"Hey, where're you going? Watch where you're stepping," someone shouted behind me.

I could have sworn that it was the other dead man, whose ghost I was only seeing now. I turned around at once.

There was a vendor behind me, around fifty years old, with round cheeks and thick lips. He was Black, but I could tell from his appearance that he wasn't a local.

"You speak English?" I asked.

"Yes, I'm from Zanzibar; you know the place?"

"Yes, of course."

"It's good that you know it," he said. It seemed like he felt proud. "What are you doing around here?'

"Talking to ghosts," I joked.

"Good. How many ghosts have you managed to find?"

"One so far, but I was almost certain that you were a ghost, too."

We were standing in a corner of the marketplace. I got the impression that the marketplace occupied the whole of Moroni and that, no matter where I went, I'd end up being in the marketplace. The man from Zanzibar was selling clothes. He'd shouted out to me because I had been standing on one of his products.

"What's that in your hand?"

"Bananas," I said.

"I know that they're bananas; I'm not blind," he said, slight rudely. "What do you need so many bananas for?"

"I don't know. I'm just holding on to them. I bought them at Ahmed's stall. But they're not good. I ate a few, but they didn't taste good; they prickled my throat."

"Yes," he laughed. "You're not used to them. They're good bananas, but you have to eat quite a few of them to get used to the taste. Where did you say you bought them?"

"At Ahmed's."

"Which Ahmed?"

"The bald guy, who drives a yellow Citroen. He died this morning."

"I don't know him. But there's no Ahmed among the banana vendors that I know. Did you buy them over there?" He pointed in the correct direction.

"Yes."

"There's no Ahmed there," he said with conviction.

"His name was Ahmed. He died this morning."

"Are you talking about the accident this morning, when two cars collided?"

"Yes."

"What does that have to do with the bananas? Muhammed is the one who sells bananas in that part of the marketplace. From what I know, he has no plans of dying yet."

"Are you trying to say…"

"Yes, you've been tricked."

The large-bellied Zanzibari pushed his body forward, taking broad step after broad step as he walked towards the vendors. A little later, he returned with an old man who was so thin that he looked like he could die at any moment.

"This is Muhammed. This is who you bought the bananas from," the Zanzibari vendor said.

"I haven't seen him before. There was nobody there. I left the money on a stool and took a bunch."

"That's right. That's what Muhammed told me. He saw you, but didn't approach you. He saw you take a bunch and leave the money. He is grateful to you."

"But I only paid for three bananas."

"No, he says you paid for the whole bunch; everything is fine."

"In that case, who's Ahmed?"

"I don't know. But be careful; don't walk alone on the street. Don't talk to strangers."

I left. The vendor shouted after me,

"Don't you need to buy any clothes?"

I never did find out who Ahmed was—the deceased driver of the yellow Citroen, or someone else? In any case, it didn't matter much to me. What mattered was that I had met him.

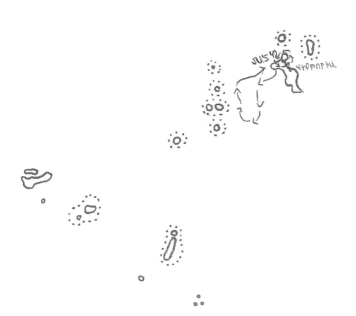

DAY 41. SEYCHELLES
PEOPLE WALKING ON THE OCEAN COAST

I'll never forget what I saw in Seychelles; it was much more than anything my imagination could have produced. Everything was so beautiful that I was forced to think that I wasn't in a new country, that it was all just a dream.

I only spent one day—or, rather, ten hours—on the beach of one of Seychelles' 155 islands, Mahé. During those ten hours, all I managed to do was walk along the beach and look at, or watch, or perhaps see, the Indian Ocean, the joyful sky, the small cliffs that looked like rhinoceroses, the sun, the clouds, and many other things.

Spending the night in Seychelles is comparatively expensive, the costliest among all the other nearby island states. The contrast with the Comoros was obvious—there's no real reason to make any comparisons, of course—but this small state (the smallest in Africa—451 square meters) is probably one of the most developed on the continent.

At first, I thought that there were no people here and, like the suburbs of Bujumbura, they had concealed themselves and did not plan on coming out. But the difference was that only about 81,000 people live in Seychelles, and many of them had become invisible.

When I arrived in the capital, Victoria, the first thing I did was to leave the city, as the ocean immediately attracted me. The sun and the unusual sky attracted me, too. I'd have liked a sunset like this when I was in Fogo, Cabo Verde. You could see a cloud of every color in the sky, a wave of every color in the sea, and a ray of every color on the horizon. I thought to myself that the people and the animals here must be so good that Nature rewarded them with this marvelous sunset.

It was evening, but everything could be seen clearly and it was obvious that the light would last for several more hours. I was walking along the beach, looking for people. I was no longer in the capital, and there were no guest houses or fancy hotels nearby.

I noticed first the gigantic fish, and only later saw the fisherman standing next to it. He was singing, and the blowing wind carried his words to me.

"I'll care for you, bathe you and embrace you, and together we'll sleep in one bed. You'll be my protector, and I'll never be afraid again. We'll spend the whole summer and fall together. I'll let you go in the winter; you'll go and swim in peace. I want nothing else. This is enough; what matters is that I caught you, and you are mine alone. You will make my wishes come true, and I'll never forget you. Perhaps we'll meet again next year."

His song seemed strange to me. It sounded like a regular song at first, one that could have been a folk tune or a modern piece, but I learned later that the fisherman was just making it up.

When I approached him and saw him up close, I understood that it made sense, that a man like him would sing such an unusual song. His yellow velvet pants, which were at least three times his size, had slipped below his waist and looked like a worn-out sack. He'd tightened them using a belt, but they could have fit three people in the lower section either way. He was wearing an old green shirt, and had black winter boots on his feet, the kind of shoes one would usually wear in the snow, while the weather in Seychelles was always warm and it never snowed. On his head, the fisherman wore a large, broad-brimmed straw hat that was patchy in parts. He looked like a drunkard—swollen eyes, broad eyelids, ruddy cheeks, and open mouth; he had a thin mustache, a protruding abdomen, short arms, and he always put one of his feet down at an angle. The fish was around two meters long. It had a sharp, protruding snout and teeth; it was probably a predator, and had no scales. It had an aggressive look on its face, which it directed to the sky. The fish was dead.

I approached the fisherman from behind and ended up startling him. He looked scared for a minute, but then continued singing, "My dear fish, we are no longer alone, the evil spirits have come to get you, to take you away, but I don't know which of us died first. We must escape, or we will be gobbled up. We're helpless, weak, wretched, and dirty. He'll take us to hell, no questions asked and no explanations offered. He or his ghost are evil, but what's important is that if we don't pay any attention, he might leave us alone," he sang, hugging the fish.

"Hello," I said.

"He said hello and is trying to talk to us, he wants to know everything about us, but we'll keep standing here quietly, as if nothing has happened, and we can't see him."

"I heard your song; it's beautiful. What song is it? Are you a fisherman? Your fish is so big that I'm scared to come closer."

"Did you hear that?" he asked the fish. "He's scared of us; we've succeeded in keeping him away."

He continued to sing, "We'll sleep on the beach tonight, under the green leaves; all the winds will blow to us, but we will be warm in bed."

I'd never heard a person speaking to a fish like that before. I considered the fact that he might be slightly deranged but, on the other hand, he was the first person I had met on the beach, and the people there possibly lived in a different world.

"You don't want to speak with me? I'm not a ghost, and I'm not evil. I'm just a regular guy. But I admit that it would be interesting to keep watching how you talk to your fish."

"You see?" he said, looking at the fish. "He's blackmailing us; he realized he was failing and he's now trying to scare us." Then he turned to me abruptly and said in a normal human voice, "So you're not an evil spirit?"

"No," I said.

"How do you know?"

"I'm sure of it. I've never stolen people's souls."

"What about fish?"

"No fish souls, either."

"Sure?"

"Yes."

"Well, that's good," he said, and turning to the fish, he continued his song. "All our wishes will come true today. We'll watch the Indian Ocean and sleep in the warm rays of the sinking sun. The ghosts have stopped pursuing us. We are free." He turned to me, saying, "I've removed the evil within you."

"Thank you. Are you a fisherman?"

"My name is George; I'm a painter. But I love fish very much." He put the fish down and brought it closer. I took a step back. "Don't worry; it's dead. It won't bite. Its eyes are crossed. If a wild fish does not have a focused stare, then it's dead."

"What was that song you were singing? The wind carried some of your words in my direction from the distance. I didn't understand what they meant."

"There's nothing to understand. I found a dead fish on the beach—imagine, one this big! It died recently, so we can eat its meat. Do you understand? Do you realize how many days I'll have a full stomach?"

"What about sleeping together and making all your wishes come true? What was that about?"

"Have you read Pushkin's *Golden Fish*?"

"Yes."

"That's what it's about. Don't I have the right to dream? To imagine that I'd caught a golden fish?"

I was a bit surprised that a painter living in Seychelles knew about Pushkin.

"Do you live here?" I asked.

"For the time being, yes. I studied in Russia once, then in Great Britain. And now I'm living like a bum on these islands cut off from the rest of the world."

"Where do you live?"

"On the beach. This is my home. I have the largest house in the world, seventy million square kilometers! Isn't that great? The whole Indian Ocean! Nobody can throw me out of here, nobody can evict me. I've paid my rent and nobody can bother me. Do you know who the Indian Ocean belongs to?"

"In what sense?" I asked.

"Which country it belongs to?"

"No."

"That's because the seas and oceans don't belong to anyone. Nobody can fight over them. They're mine—at least this one is. I'm telling the truth. I haven't lost my mind. This isn't a nut you're talking to, nor are all the people here strange like me. No, they're very smart, a hundred times smarter than me. I love them. But I am the way you want to see me. You've probably seen the beautiful sunset, the lovely clouds and waves. I painted them."

"Very well painted," I said.

"You don't believe it? I know, it sounds funny. But I'm not delusional, never have been. You don't realize what I'm saying now. But anybody else would feel the same in my place. Tell me, have you ever felt lonely?"

"Yes."

"How long?"

"I don't understand. What do you mean?"

"Have you ever dreamed of being alone?"

"Of course."

"Has your wish come true?"

"Perhaps."

"Now imagine that you dream of being alone, you want to cut yourself off from the rest of the world, from other people, you don't want to hold on to material things, you don't want to move quickly from one place to another. Imagine that you're cutting yourself off from everything and sinking into solitude. Have you imagined it?"

"Yes."

"Tell me now—is that good?"

"Yes."

"Would you want to go on like this?"

"Yes."

"How long?"

"I don't know. Until I got bored of it, I suppose."

"What if you didn't?"

"Even better. I like being alone. But I'm sure I wouldn't want to be cut off from the world for long."

"Now imagine that that world doesn't exist. Imagine that there is more ocean on the other side of the ocean. Imagine that if you keep moving in one direction, you'll cover the circumference of the Earth and end up in the same spot because no other place exists."

"Then what?"

"You'd be sad, right?"

"Yes."

"Your memories, your past life, your experiences—none of it exists anymore. They've vanished into thin air. You might remember it; it would be difficult for you to let go of your experiences. It would be difficult for you to adapt to this new world, no matter how much you wanted to."

"So?"

"That is my current situation. I've travelled the whole world, I've enjoyed life, spent nights in the most luxurious of hotels, and worn the most expensive clothing. I was a world-famous painter. But who am I now? If, a few years ago, you'd plucked this fish out of the sea, even it would recognize me. I'm sad; I'm a sad and despairing fisherman who lives on fish lying dead on the beach. Why are you looking at me like that? You don't believe me?"

"What's your problem?"

"I don't have a problem. That's my problem."

"What do you mean? You just said that you used to be a famous painter. So you miss that life, but you don't have the money to go back?"

"No. You haven't understood anything, just like those stupid Americans; you don't get it. The problem is that I don't miss anything at all. It's like I'm hypnotized. Two years ago, when I came here, my only objective was to take a vacation. I'd come for three weeks. But gradually, the ocean, sky, beach, and mountains seduced me. It was like they intoxicated me. They swallowed me up. I fell in love with all of it and forgot about the world, about other pleasures. So I surrendered myself to this sand. I enjoyed life for about a year. And then I gradually began to get used to the everyday sunrises and sunsets, and they became a habit. At the same time, I'd estranged myself from my previous life, and I was afraid to go back. I didn't have the desire to start all over again. I stayed. Another year went by. I slowly used up my savings, ending up bankrupt and homeless. I enjoyed that lifestyle for a bit, and felt that it was a welcome punishment, but then I looked at the shining sky and changed my mind, understanding that this magical place is truly magnificent. But everything has changed now. I'm in a completely different state now; I'm a different man. No other world exists for me—I look out into the distance and only see myself, because the other side of the horizon again consists of me and these cliffs. This place is an island, and man has no need to be an island here, because it is on a land that is cut off from the rest of the world, and bewitched."

I didn't say anything when he'd finished. To be honest, I was having a hard time understanding him. I don't know why he opened himself up to me like that. Perhaps he had long desired to speak to someone. But, in any case, I didn't want to see him sad.

"Haven't you told anybody about how you're feeling?" I asked.

"No. You're the first one."

"What does the sea hold?" I asked, trying to change the subject.

"The sea holds everything. Don't digress."

"I have to go. The sun will set soon, and I have to get to the airport."

"Take me with you."

"Where?"

"I don't know. Get me on board the plane, then drop me off in the sky somewhere."

"I have to get going."

"Haven't you seen my painting?"

"What painting?"

"My most famous painting."

"No," I said.

"'People Walking on the Ocean Coast.'"

"No, where is it?"

"Right here," he said, and pointed. "About a kilometer to the north."

"On the beach?"

"Yes. My painting is there. Two people are walking on the beach, but they're in a mist; you can't see their faces, you can see their shadows, and they're constantly walking. Do you know when I painted them?"

"When?"

"About a year ago. A couple in love was walking, embracing, kissing, rolling about in the sand. Then the woman went into the water and called out to her husband for help. They never returned. I was far away and couldn't help them. But I decided to paint them, so that people remember them.

"Go straight and you can see their painting, too. Take your time, you won't be late. I'll paint the sunset late today."

"Goodbye," I said.

"Where are you going?" he shouted after me. "Their painting is in the opposite direction."

If I stayed a little longer, I too would have ended up remaining on the island for at least another two years. I could hear George singing as I was leaving; he propped up the fish, hugged it and shouted loudly, "We tricked the evil spirit and he left. We're free now, you and I. We'll run in the sand, kiss, embrace each other, and dance; we'll be the happiest of couples."

I saw fishing boats in the distance but they weren't regular boats, they were meant for tourists. This was how the locals made money, by taking tourists out on fishing trips with them.

When I got closer, the boats had already returned to the shore. I had assumed correctly—besides two local Creoles, the rest of the people were tourists. I said hello and asked one of the locals to put the boat back into the water. They told me I had to wait and that there had to be a minimum of five passengers, otherwise I would have to pay in their place. I paid. I wanted to float, to sink… I wanted the cold wind to blow so hard that the boat would lose balance and overturn.

"Where do you want to go?" the boatman asked.

"Let's just go around and smell some of the sea air."

"Can't you do that on the beach?" he laughed. "You paid a lot of money for some air."

"I don't care where we go, let's just go."

We pushed out the boat and entered the Indian Ocean. I was seeing it from the "inside" for the first time. The boatman was young. He was quite thin, and I wondered where he got the strength that allowed him to maneuver with the oars.

"It's a beautiful day," I said.

"Yesterday was a better day. The weather changes every day here. One day is pleasant, the next is not."

"Does the temperature change, too?"

"No. Not every day. I meant the sky and clouds. It was magnificent yesterday. There were five tourists in my boat and they were awestruck. The further into the ocean we went, the closer the clouds seemed to be, and the sun floated in the sky."

"Yes. The painter hasn't done as good a job today."

"What?"

"Nothing."

We went around this magnificent ocean for about an hour. I felt like a piece of bait that had been thrown into the water to tempt a giant fish. The sun wasn't moving. The day seemed to have come to a standstill.

"Are there any big fish here?" I asked.

"Yes. But not close to the shore. We have to go out very far for the big fish. It's dangerous there."

"But when they die, don't they wash up on the shore?"

"No," he laughed. "Who told you that? There's no such thing. Who could imagine a big fish dying and washing up on the shore? There are no human-sized fish anywhere in these parts, from what I know."

"But you're a fisherman, aren't you?"

"No," he said and laughed again. "I work for a tour agency, I'm a guide. I can row, and I know how far away each island is. I don't know anything about fish. But I'm not ignorant to the extent that I wouldn't know about fish washing up to the shore. A big fish is not a shell, nor is it a crab, digging itself into the sand. This is a tourist area; if such things happened here, they wouldn't have built so many buildings." And he pointed at the hotels in the distance, which I hadn't noticed up to that point.

"I saw one a short while ago," I said.

"Saw what?"

"A huge fish. Human-sized. Dead."

"And?"

"The fisherman told me he'd found it on the beach."

"What?" he laughed again. "Impossible! He's probably tricked you. You know how many hundreds of meters you have to go into the ocean for a fish that size? It's a lie."

"That's what he said. He was very happy to have found it."

"Then the fishermen must have left it there. There was probably something wrong with that fish. They'd left it for the birds. And then he found it and was happy."

"How are such fish caught?"

"I don't know; I'm not a fisherman," he said disdainfully. "I know what that island is, or that other one over there. I know interesting stories, fairy tales, which we use to charm the tourists. They get excited and leave these 'magical' islands in awe."

"Could you tell me one?"

For some reason, I wanted to be fooled; the sensation of being taken in fascinated me. I had already assumed that the guide would tell me a false story, especially since he had already hinted at this.

"They say that a couple used to live here on the beach. They used to have a house, but then they preferred spending their nights on the beach. They loved each other very much. Every evening, they would build a fire with wet twigs and dance around it, then kiss. They were together for days and months; they say it was the most beautiful love in the world. They spoke little, always smiled, and were happy. They lived at the shore for 350 days, got wet in the rain, dried under the sun, ate the fish from the water and the fruits on nearby trees, and never went into town, always hiding from people. They loved each other so much that they were afraid of losing each other. They would always hold hands when they walked, because of this fear. They thought they were in Paradise, in the sky, near the sun. People would even say that they would go around naked. They didn't have any children, but they loved the ocean like their own child; they would always sit on the shore and cast small grains of sand into the water, making wishes. And one day, the 351st day, the woman went into the water for a swim. She swam absent-mindedly for such a long time that when she looked back at the shore, she realized that she had swum a hundred meters away. She turned around and wanted to return, but something pulled her from beneath the surface. A big fish, as you call it. She shouted out to her husband. But he didn't see her. He was asleep. The woman struggled with the fish for ten minutes. But she ran out of energy eventually. The fish pulled her beneath the surface. When her husband woke up and saw that his wife was not next to him, he shouted, lost control, and went into the ocean. But he only saw the reddened water, nothing else. He returned to the shore and lost his mind."

"He didn't die?"

"No, the husband stayed alive. He lost his mind. Nobody's seen him since that day. Nobody's heard anything about him. They say that his wife lives underwater to this day and sometimes surfaces in the form of a fish, in order to see her husband. But I've never seen them. Small clouds gather in the sky in the evenings, but those clouds have been growing larger more recently. They say that the husband has wished for it to be this way, but I don't know why."

"Are you sure the husband didn't die?"

"No. He's alive."

"Was this a true story?"

"That's what they say." He smiled cynically.

"What was the husband's occupation? Do you know?"

"He was a painter. They both were. I forgot to mention that they loved to sit in front of the fire and make beautiful paintings. But people say that they would paint in a unique way, as if they were not painting, but imagining. And the paintings they imagined would appear before them."

"I saw the husband today," I said.

The guide immediately stopped rowing. Then he began to paddle the oars once again. "You saw him?"

"Yes. Didn't you say that this story is supposed to be true? I saw him. I'm sure of it."

"Where?"

"On the beach. One or two hours ago."

He was quiet, but seemed to be laughing inwardly. He looked at his watch and said, "All right, it's time to go back, it's getting late."

"The painter said that the sun would set later than usual today," I said.

We returned to the shore, and the guide said nothing. He was lost in thought. It was as if he had discovered that the lie he had grown used to telling had actually been true. He seemed slightly anxious.

I walked over the white sand, the exact color of which I was unable to say, because it kept changing with the rays of the sun. It was almost nighttime, but part of the sun could still be seen, although the giant clouds covered it and did not let it poke out its head. I was trying to catch a glimpse of its face, but was unable to do so. Gradually, I began to understand George, his misery. It was clear to me why he didn't tell me that the woman was his wife. Or perhaps I hadn't understood him at the time, thinking that he was insane.

When I walked back to the spot where George had been standing, the place was deserted. The ocean waves were uneasily moving back and forth, pushing the grains of sand. The sun had already escaped. Strangely, it hadn't descended in the sky, but instead had risen up and disappeared. Perhaps it stays in the sky at night, but in a place that nobody can see.

When I got into town, I remembered George's painting, "People Walking on the Ocean Coast," but it was too late. I couldn't return. The city was bright; illuminated buildings stood everywhere, as well as smaller structures and squares and parks. Once or twice, I came across huge flower pots; I'd seen flower pots like those before in Rwanda, at Immaculé's house. The airport was close by, although it wasn't really walking distance. I did have some time. I walked the grand streets of Victoria and it felt like I was on a completely different continent, in a completely different world. I kept thinking about George and his wife, their joyous love and misfortune.

That story was still tormenting me when I heard someone shout, "Watch out! Got a death wish, or what?"

"What?" I turned and saw a huge truck in front of me, an unusual sight on the streets of Victoria.

"Don't stand in the road. I almost hit you with my truck," the driver said.

"Sorry."

"You should thank God that my brakes are working well," he smiled, opening the door. "Are you headed this way?"

"Yes, to the airport."

"Get in, it's on my way."

I got in. He gave me a weird look, then smiled again.

"What's up? You seem upset," he said. It was as if we'd known each other for ages.

"I just got back from the shore. I'd gone to look around. I met a painter there. He looked like a crazy person at first glance, but when he started speaking, I realized that he was simply in misery. He held on to a huge fish and was singing. Then I got into a boat and the guide told me a sad story."

"About a painter?" the driver said immediately.

"Yes. You know it?"

"They were a couple who loved each other boundlessly; they lived together. They would be together day and night, and then one day the women went into the ocean and swam far away. The husband had been sleeping and when he woke up, he realized that a huge fish had taken his wife away. The painter went mad that day. And the wife would take on the form of a fish and visit her husband. They embrace, kiss, and sing songs."

"Yes," I said.

The driver was quiet. He took a cigarette from his pocket. He put it in his mouth, took a lighter from the glove compartment, and lit the cigarette. He inhaled. He blew the smoke towards the window. He turned on the radio and then turned it back off in irritation. He looked at the side window, used his hand to wipe off a section that had fogged up, and inhaled on the cigarette again.

He looked at me cynically and said, "They've tricked you. It's all part of a show they make up for tourists. One of them stands on the shore holding a huge fish, and the other one tells everyone this story…"

⋅⋅⋅

As my plane was getting ready to take off, I looked out at the shore. I wasn't too far away and could make out the people there, to some extent. Two of them seemed to be in a mist, holding hands as they slowly walked together…

DAY 42. MAURITIUS
THE DODO

The bright blue ocean and the white shore seemed to be a continuation of what I had seen in Seychelles. But there wasn't a crazy fisherman here or a woman in the form of a fish, nor was there a painting of people walking on the ocean coast. This triangle of countries, the Comoros-Seychelles-Mauritius, felt like it was located in a completely different world. In every corner of that triangle, I saw life from a completely different angle, and each of them was different from the countries that had preceded them.

I was in Port Louis, the capital of Mauritius. It was a small, fancy city, where there were dozens of sights to see from one end of the city to the other.

The Mauritians here were very different people and, at first glance, it looked like there were huge differences among them. In a single spot, I managed to see Christian, Muslim, Buddhist, and Hindu Mauritians, and even one who practiced a local religion. Even back at the airport, I was told that there is no such thing as a Mauritian—there were just locals with different cultures, customs, religions, and languages. Although they had been living together for a long time, they were at peace with each other and in harmony. That surprised me. It was the first time that I was in a place where the locals were so different from each other, yet coexisted so peacefully.

Not too far from the city, I was in a field with hectares of planted beetroots. But when I came closer, I discovered that they were actually pineapples. That was where I met the happy Mauritians. They were on their break and having lunch. When they saw me, they called me over. I didn't manage to figure out what they were eating—they told me what it was called, but I didn't recognize the name. They were all young. They didn't talk much—they smiled more, looking at each other, and it seemed to me for a minute that they were gossiping, but I was wrong; they were simply very direct and sincere in their communication.

"Are you all farmers?" I asked.

"No," the Christian Mauritian said. "I'm a fisherman, a carpenter, I keep livestock, and I'm also a farmer."

"All of us have several occupations," the Muslim continued. "This land and these fields bring us together."

"Each of us has a share in this, and we have no complaints. Whatever God has given us has been sufficient," the Buddhist Mauritian said.

"What matters is peace, and we have that here," the Hindu Mauritian said.

"Yes," the one with the local religion said.

Their words reminded me of poetry events back in school, when we would each say a line in turn. I was unable to talk with all of them at the same time, because they said that only one of them would stay to keep watch on the field after lunch, while the rest would return later. The one that stayed was named Raj, or Raji, or Rachi, and he said that he wanted to take a nap, so he settled down in the bushes. I recalled Chachagé at that moment. For some reason, I felt obliged to poke him, so he wouldn't fall asleep.

"Get up," I said.

"What is it?"

"I want to talk; get up."

He looked at me, as if asking himself why I'd appeared and started to disrupt his routine, and then he leaned on one arm and asked me, half asleep, "Okay. What is it you want?"

"I want you to tell me a story," I said.

"What for?"

"I'm expecting something interesting."

"From me?"

"Yes."

"I'm an uninteresting person. What could I say that would interest you?"

"Nothing. Just say something."

Raj rolled around in the bushes, stretched his arms up and yawned. He looked at the sun.

"Couldn't you find someone else? Am I the only one you've come across among our million and a half citizens?"

"I'd come to the shore. I was looking at the ocean and my eyes fell on a field that seemed to stretch out to infinity. I was surprised that a country this small could have such a large field. So I decided to walk over. It looked like a white sea in the distance. That's how I met your group. The four others left and you remained. I've walked a long distance and I have no desire to go back."

"If you're tired, you can take a nap, too. There's place here for you, too."

"No, I want us to talk. I have no desire to sleep."

"All right," he said. He sat up, straightened his back, stretched his arms up, yawned again, and looked at me.

Raji was about thirty years old. He looked vaguely Asian, had dark skin, and his face had some fuzz on it. His hair was long and black, and braided unevenly, looking like a painting. His eyes were big, with one them constantly shimmering in the light. Raji looked like he was short, although I hadn't seen him standing; his legs seemed short. He was thin and had a long face.

"Go ahead, I'm listening," Raji said.

"I've come from Seychelles, and I saw something interesting there. Something strange also happened in the Comoros. So I'm waiting now, expecting something to happen here as well."

"What's going to happen?"

"I don't know. But I have the feeling that something will. I'm waiting for it."

"Good for you. I'll wait, too. I've been waiting for ten years already."

"For what?" I asked. I thought he would say something romantic.

"The pineapples. A good harvest."

"Why so long?"

"I don't know that, either."

"But the harvest looks like a good one."

"No. It's not real—have you ever seen an illusion?"

"Yes."

"Well, this is like that. This pineapple is there, but it's not good. In reality, it's a small, wrinkled, and dry fruit," he said, picking up a huge, juicy pineapple and cutting it in half with a knife. "See? It's empty inside," he said, as the juices flowed from the fruit, "and the peel is so thick that you have to clear it with an axe." I could barely see the peel, but he continued, "And it tastes like you're eating a tree branch, so tough that you can barely chew it." He gave me a piece and it melted in my mouth; the taste was fantastic, but he said, "And you start to feel nauseated after you eat it, and you want to sleep it off, otherwise you'd have to carry it around in your stomach all day."

"It's very tasty and very pleasant; on the contrary, I no longer feel tired."

"Can't you see that it's not yet ripe?"

"Seriously?" I asked. I was a bit scared. He was being extremely pessimistic.

"Yes! This pineapple should be thrown in the trash, I've wasted my whole life on it. And to no avail. There is no sun for us to have a good harvest." He looked at the bright sun and closed his eyes.

"What about that huge sun? Is that really what you think?"

"Yes," he said, and he shut his eyes, rolling over on his side.

I wanted to leave. At that moment, he started to laugh. He curled up and his laughter grew even stronger. He turned around.

"I was just joking," he said, still laughing. "Our pineapples are amazing. They're unique. Come back. Come back," he shouted after me.

I came back and sat down.

"I'm waiting for my favorite bird," he said.

"I don't understand," I said.

"I've been waiting for it for ten years. But it's not coming. Perhaps it's lost."

"What bird is it?"

"I don't know," he laughed. "I really don't know. I haven't seen it. But I'm waiting for it."

He was quiet. He didn't say anything for a few minutes, then he continued in a stronger voice, "We're five brothers. They're very hard working; they don't muck about. I'm the smallest one. After we have lunch together during the day, they go into town, and I stay here. I either take a nap, or talk about absurd things with people like you."

"They were your brothers?"

"Yes."

"From the same family?"

"Yes."

"You have the same parents?"

"Yes. Why?"

"Well, I thought that all of you were different people, with different ethnicities, religions, and cultures."

"They're different people, but they're my brothers."

"That's not good."

"Why?"

"Well, I've already put one of them down as a Muslim, one as a Christian, the other a Hindu, the fourth one a Buddhist, and you as having a local religion."

Raji laughed. "All right then, if that's what you've put us down as, so be it. Don't change anything; they won't mind. Everyone is different here."

"Are you sure?"

"Yes."

A little later, Raji said, "Where have you put us down that way?"

The sun followed us from above—it was a bright and sunny day, and there were many birds in the sky. Raji was a few meters ahead of me; he walked slowly and swayed, leaving the impression that he was limping. His build seemed crooked.

"Why are you walking that way?" I asked.

"Limping?"

"Yes."

"I hurt my leg in the water."

"Did a fish pull you down?"

"No. It froze."

"In this heat?"

"Not here. In Antarctica."

"What were you doing there?"

"Research."

"Seriously?"

He laughed. "Yes. I'd gone there to bring a polar bear back for the zoo."

"For real?"

"Yes. But I failed. I came back empty-handed. The bears didn't want to come to Port Louis. They were too lazy."

"Are you being serious?"

"Yes. The only lie was that I hurt my foot in the water. It actually happened on land. I had been standing for a long time without moving, and my foot went numb. I tried to move it but it didn't move. A few days later, I found out that I'd hurt it."

"Are there bears in Antarctica?"

"Yes, as big as these pineapples. They're everywhere."

"But what would a farmer do in Antarctica, and one from Mauritius at that?"

"It wasn't my idea; it was the idea of my brothers. They put me up to it. They'd set their minds on going to Antarctica. Who knows why they wanted to? They made the decision in a month, pulled everything together, collected the necessary money, and we were off. I only found out at the end. As always, they told me last. But I'm used to it; I don't mind. People like me are always the last to find out any news."

"Was it an easy trip to make?"

"No. It took us a few days to get there. Throughout the journey, I kept asking them why we were going, what the point was of the trip, but they never managed to give me a straight answer and said in the end that we would bring back a polar bear. Maybe Antarctica has soil that's well suited for pineapples," he laughed.

"There's a shimmer in your eye. Several times already, your pupil has looked like a diamond to me. Why is that?"

"Yes. So, it's that obvious?"

"Very."

"When I was small—five or six years old—I had tied a hammock to a tree and was swinging in it; one of my brothers was in the tree, and another was near our house, not too far away. I asked my brother to throw a coconut down from the tree. At that moment, my other brother called out my name. I looked up to reply to him, forgetting that my brother was about to throw down a coconut. The coconut fell right on my left eye. I couldn't see anything for two days, and on the third day I realized that I had seriously damaged my eye. That's why my eye shines. There's a crystal in it; it's not a real eye."

"You can't see?"

"I look at bad things with this eye," he joked.

"What do your brothers do?"

"I don't know. Who knows? They just talk. Everybody talks here, but it's difficult to know anything for a fact."

"One of them said that he was a fisherman and had livestock. Is that true?"

"It's true, but what kind of a fisherman could he be? He can only dream. That's what they all do: dream. They don't understand anything when it comes to life. They're five to ten years older than me, but they have no families. They live like four-year-olds."

"You were saying a short while ago that you were happy, at peace."

"Yes. We're happy, at peace… but you can't just live and do nothing."

"What do you do?"

"Me? I imagine. Don't compare me to them. I'm sick. I'm not healthy like them. They can do whatever they like. They can enjoy every aspect of life. Me? I can walk a little, sleep, eat, and dream a bit. I can't do anything else. I'm not healthy like they are."

"But what's happened to you? You don't look sick."

Raji was quiet.

"I'll go. Maybe we'll meet again someday," I said.

"Go. I'm tired. I'll take a nap. My brothers will be back soon."

We said goodbye. He went northwards, and I walked towards the south.

I was walking in the pretty streets of Port Louis, where many different areas felt familiar to me. But I didn't stop. I wanted to keep moving, as if sensing that I would find what I was seeking at any moment. As had often happened in the past, someone stopped me. A man appeared suddenly and blocked my path.

"Excuse me," the stranger said, "could you speak with me?"

"Yes," I replied.

He was a man of about forty years, with dark skin that was almost Black. He was slightly fat, with puffed cheeks, short hair, and a protruding belly. He was wearing a uniform.

"I'm the doorman at the Shandrani Resort. Would you be willing to come with me to the hotel, so that we could talk there?"

"Where is it?"

"Not far. We can walk."

"What do you want to talk about?" I asked.

"Let's go; I'll tell you there. Don't worry," he said, and he took out an identification document that had his name and a stamp on it.

"Indir?" I asked. "Your name is Indir?"

"Yes. It's an Indian name; I'm an Indian. Or of Indian descent, actually. Have you been to India? It's a huge country."

"No."

"You should go; they have everything there, and it's cheap."

"All right. Where are we going now?"

"I told you—the Shandrani Resort. I work there," he answered, and indicated the identification document again.

We walked quickly to the hotel, but I didn't know where he was taking me. I didn't know whether or not I should trust him, but I felt like he had something important to say.

"How did you find me? Do you know me?" I asked.

"No. I don't know you. I could tell from your face that you are a foreigner. That's why I came up to you. I need a foreigner."

"Why?"

"Let's keep going; we're almost there. We'll sit down and talk comfortably."

"If you don't tell me, I won't come."

"All right. But if I tell you, will you come?"

"I don't know."

Indir realized that insisting was pointless. He began to calm himself down, using his hands and his feet.

"Okay, I'll explain now. One of the employees at our hotel hasn't come in; he's ill. Can you replace him today? I'll pay you well for it."

"What do I need to do?"

"You have to wear a polar bear costume and move around in a cage, as if you had just been caught and you wanted to escape; as if you're angry and would break out of the cage at any moment, freeing yourself of your shackles. We need a small show. We'll pay a lot."

"If it's a costume of an animal, what difference does it make if the person wearing it is a foreigner or a local?"

"The eyes will be visible."

This was the first time that someone had suggested that my eyes resembled those of a polar bear.

"What is the performance for?"

"We organize small events from time to time to entertain the guests. It's nothing serious, just an exotic show."

"When do you need me?"

"Right away. The whole show lasts two hours. It starts in the evening. You can come now and rehearse."

"Is your sick coworker a foreigner as well?"

"No. But his eyes resemble a bear's."

In reality, this proposal, which had seemed ridiculous at first, intrigued me. Indir and I went to the Shandrani Resort. He kept me waiting in the lobby for around half an hour, then returned with someone else.

"Hello," the stranger said, taking a long rope from his waist. "Get into the cage. We'll try it without the costume for a bit, then you'll put it on."

"What's the rope for?" I asked.

"We're pretending that I'm training you. I won't hurt you."

"Indir didn't say anything about this."

"It's nothing serious; don't worry."

"Who are you?"

"I'm playing the role of the bear tamer."

He was a giant, with a shaved head and a huge jaw. When I entered the cage, I felt very sorry for myself. My body barely managed to fit in there. I'd never played the role of a bear before. At that moment, I regretted having agreed to it. It was like being punished for all my past sins.

We rehearsed for around three hours, then they gave me some food to eat. And then the performance began. When I had the costume on and was walking from side to side in it, my eyes fell upon Raji's four brothers. Suddenly, it became clear to me that it was Raji who was supposed to be in this costume in my place. His eyes were different from everyone else's, weren't they? When the show ended and I left the hotel, some people called out to me. It was Raji's brothers. One of them walked up to me.

"Thank you," he said.

"What for? I did this because the doorman asked me to. I was curious to see what would happen. Had I known it was going to be this difficult and tiring, I wouldn't have done it."

"We're grateful, in any case. You have no idea how much you've helped us."

"What have I done? I've just moved around for two hours."

"Yes, but if you hadn't moved that well, we would have lost our jobs. Raji, too. He probably told you that we'd gone to Antarctica, to bring back a polar bear."

"Yes."

"That was the bear you were playing."

"What do you mean?"

"I mean that you were a big help to us," he said, and he embraced me and left.

I didn't understand what he meant. All these straightforward but complicated stories had confused me. I kept seeking the amazing and magical, but nothing else happened. Why had I ended up playing a polar bear, why I had listened to Raji talking for hours, or why his brothers were so grateful—I understood none of it. Nobody would be able to make sense of this story, I thought. It was just an exotic story that happened to me in Mauritius, on a beautiful and happy island.

When I was preparing to leave the island and go to Madagascar, I unexpectedly heard a short story that was very interesting, although it wasn't related to my story.

Two Mauritians sitting next to me were having a conversation,

"One day, the bird left its cage and abandoned its family. It was the Dodo. The Dodo flew over the whole world and looked at all the poor people."

"Then he helped all the people who limped and whose eyes didn't see—all those who had a disability. He flew upwards, and nobody saw him anymore."

"To this day, many people remember the Dodo, worship it, dream about it, and wait for him to come and help them. Come and help them…"

I remembered Dodoy, the Portuguese boy, who I'd met on the beach at São Tomé; he had been named in honor of this bird. Perhaps he had seen one.

"The Dodo flies every morning, rises high and watches us from there."

"One can understand this; he can no longer comes down, because he no longer exists."[48]

---

48. The dodo is considered to be the symbol of Mauritius. This bird has long been extinct.

DAY 43. MADAGASCAR
THE LITTLE BOY'S DREAM

This country of baobabs, considered by the locals to be a separate continent, greeted me with a very beautiful story. When I left the airport the taxi driver, who was a francophone and could not understand me at all, sped along in his old car to the south of Antananarivo. I knew why he had decided to do that—he had probably decided that I looked like one of the Malagasy that lived there, or he had assumed so after hearing me speak. In any case, we were zooming through Antananarivo's broad and narrow streets, which consisted mainly of low buildings. The driver's name was Muhammed, but he was a Christian. When I asked him whether he knew that his name was Muslim, he said, "Yes, yes, I'm a Muslim," and he kissed the gold cross that hung from his neck. "What's the difference?"

Muhammed's Renault was probably new, but it was designed like an old car especially for this region; it was probably impossible to find another one like it anywhere else.

Besides not knowing where he was taking me, Muhammed also had the desire to pick up a few more passengers. That was probably the reason why he chose a convoluted route and went around in circles to the same spot from time to time.

I was very surprised to find that his yellow Renault could fit eight passengers. That would have seemed impossible to me at first glance. The other seven were villagers and spoke Malagasy, and they would sometimes turn to me and ask my opinion, but I had no idea what they had been talking about. The air grew stifling after a while. The window handle had come off and so rolling down the window was not an option. And I was unable to convey to the driver that I was suffocating.

"Fifty francs," Muhammed said.

"Which francs?" I asked. I had gotten out of the car.

"French francs," he said, with a shimmer in his eye.

"French francs?"

"Yes," he said, smiling happily.

Muhammed refused to take euros and, after a long debate, I paid him in ariaries, the local currency. He didn't seem very happy about that.

I didn't know where I was, just that I was in the southern part of Antananarivo. I walked along the wet, muddy road that reminded me of red clay. My shoes had turned red. There was no rain and it was hot. The wind blew in my direction and small particles of sand mercilessly assaulted me.

The tops of the baobabs could be seen in the distance. If I hadn't known where I was, I would have assumed that ostrich feet had sprouted up from the ground. The baobabs were scary; I was seeing such trees for the first time, and they seemed to pull me over to them. Standing beneath a baobab, the scene seemed much more serene and there was nothing frightening. But when I looked up and saw the ostrich foot swaying in the wind, I got goosebumps.

There was a river nearby. Looking at that river, I got the feeling that I would never be able to leave Madagascar. The river seemed hopeless and forlorn, and I saw a woman in the water at a distance. She was old and there was a small child next to her. There was a small net in the woman's hand; she would put the net in the water, swing it about and raise it slowly. Small fish or shellfish would end up caught in the net. She would give them to the child, who was holding a bucket that was larger than he was, barely managing to move it forward. It was like the river had not yet seen the sunrise, and that it was still early morning there.

I watched them for a long time, after which I continued walking on the red path. There was nobody around, there was nothing. I regretted having gotten out of the car and thought that it would have been better to die of suffocation than to lose my way in a muddy forest, my steps growing heavier under the frightening watch of the giant baobabs. It started to rain a little later and that made my situation even more difficult. I ran for a few hundred meters, until I lost my energy. Then I leaned against a baobab, whose thick foliage was impervious to the rain. I waited a few minutes to catch my breath. At that moment, I noticed that someone was sitting on the river bank, making a boat, but I didn't have a clear view. I was afraid of approaching him for a moment, but the presence of a potentially maniacal stranger seemed preferable to being drenched in solitude.

As I had expected, the stranger did not speak English and barely spoke any French. He was happy to see me. He got up, said hello and embraced me. He asked me to sit down. He was making a small boat, which was probably not meant to be rowed. We talked a little. It turned out that he and his wife lived in a nearby hut that wasn't visible from the road. The stranger, who was past fifty, called out to his wife. The woman came, half-naked, with her breasts exposed. I'd never seen breasts like that before—long and narrow, around thirty centimeters long, flopping downwards like a pair of rabbit's ears. She spoke with her husband briefly. I didn't understand a thing, but I recorded their conversation.

"We have a guest," the husband said.

"Where's he from?" the wife asked.

"He's a writer, from the North. He's hungry."

"Invite him in. He's not dangerous, is he?"

"No."

When I had it translated later, I couldn't understand how the stranger had managed to know these things about me. After being hosted warmly by them, I stayed in the hut for a few hours. When I left them, the husband and wife embraced me tightly and saw me off.

"Where's he going to go?" the wife asked.

"I don't know. He doesn't know either."

"Won't he get lost?"

"Let him go. He'll walk around a little. Where else could he see such things?"

I was walking along the river bed—I wasn't sure if it was a river or a stream. The road was just as muddy as it had been several hours earlier. I had nowhere to go. My only objective was to find someone—anyone who could understand me, anyone who could speak to me without an interpreter.

First, I heard the strange bellowing of some cows, then the sound of hooves, and then seven or eight Malagasies appeared in the shadows of the gigantic baobabs, sitting in carts. Their cows moved faster than the average cattle. This "motorcade" was coming in my direction and I didn't know whether I should hide, or stand in front of it. While I was thinking about my next step, they noticed me and stopped.

There were three carts with six Malagasies, sitting in pairs. In the front cart, there was a half-naked man of about forty years, and there were wooden boxes behind him. Someone else sat on the boxes, but his face was not visible. The second cart had a young man, sitting in the same position, his arms held out, with some sacks and a woman behind him. In the third cart, there was a young man, and a small child, four or five years old, sat behind him. The cattle, which were actually called zebus, are the symbol of Madagascar.

They had an intelligent look about them and their sharp horns were pointy and curved inwards. Zebus look like buffaloes. The Malagasy sitting in front had a much softer voice than I could have imagined.

In a voice that was almost feminine, he asked, "Where are you going?"

"I don't know," I said.

"If you don't know, come here and sit down, we'll take you."

"Where are you going?" I asked.

"We don't know, either. We have a very long way to go."

"How much do I need to pay?" I asked.

They exchanged glances. Only the Malagasy in front seemed to know English.

"Sit," he said.

I sat down in the front cart. It was completely made of wood, tied together in some spots with wires. The cart seemed weak and I was afraid it wouldn't be able to take so much weight.

"Go ahead, talk," the cart driver said.

"Talk about what? I'm lost."

"Talk about something happy."

"I'm not good at telling stories. They never come out well. It'd be better if you told a story."

"I only know sad stories."

"That's okay; I'd be very interested in hearing one."

"How many hours should I go?"

"What do you mean?"

"Do you want a long story, or a short one?"

"It doesn't matter. I'm in no hurry."

"I'll tell you a story that you'll find very interesting. But don't let it get to you. My stories are like tempting, poisonous fruit—they look delicious, but eating them will kill you at once."

"I don't understand."

"I mean to say, don't tell anyone this story. It's a family secret."

"Is this your family?"

"Yes. That's my wife, my son, my other son, the third, and the fourth. This is my family," he said, pointing at the zebus.

"The cows, too?"

"Yes, they're my family, too. Zebus are considered sacred here. If you have many zebus, then you're rich. If you don't have any, there's no point in living."

I remembered Lala Loule's village.

"Don't your family members have names?"

"They do, but why do you need to know them? Their names are too long for me to pronounce."

"So, what do you call them?"

"I don't call them, they come. They know when they need to come and when they need to go. Just one look and we understand each other."

"Are you Malagasies?"

"Yes. Ancient ones."

I didn't know what he meant by "ancient," but the man I was speaking to seemed to have a profound personality. He was literate and educated. The look in his eyes suggested that he was sad, like almost all the other "Africans" I had met.

"Should I start?" he asked. "You wanted a story."

"Yes."

"Do you see that mountain?"

"Yes."

"My story will last until there. It is the shortest story I know. That is the direction in which we are heading; we have to get to the ocean."

"But the ocean is very far away."

"We are going very far."

"How long will it take?"

"What? Getting to the ocean?"

"No, your story."

"A few hours. If you don't interrupt me."

He was talking about the story as if it was a ceremony of some sort. The other members of the family were quiet, half-asleep, or urging the zebus along automatically, although the zebus seemed to know the way quite well. The woman was asleep and her head bobbed back and forth because of the bumps in the road. The smallest boy had curled up like a bear cub, his body covered with a piece of cloth.

We were on the same path and no matter how fast we went, we couldn't seem to circumvent the forest of baobabs.

"See my son?" he asked, pointing at the little one.

"Yes," I said.

"My story is about him. But I have to start with a prologue, before the actual story. My family was very big; I don't remember everyone. My father loved me very much, and he had sacrificed several zebus for me. One day, I had stolen a few zebus from our neighbor—that's a common occurrence now, but I had committed a major sin at the time. So I had to be punished and, despite the fact that I was the smallest in my family, my father punished me. He banished me from the house. Exiled me. He said that although he loved me very much, he couldn't forgive such a crime. I was eleven years old. After working for a few years for different families, I got married. Gradually, I began to grow rich. Now I have more than ten zebus and a large house; I even have a car without a working motor. I achieved all this on my own. I didn't ask anyone for anything; my journey was a slow and difficult one, desperate and dangerous, but I managed to save my family from starvation and provide them with a life of security. Do you understand? I didn't have anybody's help. I compare my life and all my experience with that of our country, which is moving forward slowly, very slowly. And imagine all of that vanishing in an instant. In a few seconds, it turns out that your life, your past, none of it exists, you don't exist. You're like a rat, or you've been crushed like a cockroach. It's not only that nobody cares what you say, it's like you don't have the right to exist as a person. All my life, I've carried my family around on my back like a slave. My father's punishment was fair and it turned me into a man. In contrast, I don't want my child to suffer. He lives in a different world. Life today is completely different. He has another future in store. I have no right to punish him so strictly."

"Has he done anything wrong?"

"He's had a dream."

"What dream?"

"A bad dream. I wanted to tell you his dream. I don't know, perhaps you'll find it interesting. But I assure you that it's more dangerous than stealing a zebu."

"His dreams come true?"

"That's not the problem," he said, lowering his voice. "It's just that I don't have the right to allow any of my children to have such a dream."

"What has he seen?"

"There's a type of cactus in Madagascar that is used to make many dishes. It's also a medicinal herb and it has a liquid core that quenches one's thirst. There are places where the locals survive on this plant and they would die of hunger without it. In his dream, my son was walking through the forest. Then he approached a stream and drank water, only for a huge crocodile to emerge from it and bite his foot. My son felt no pain. He shouted and called for help, but nobody was around. Why had I let him wander off so far? He limped back to a village somehow—and I don't even know which village it was—and he saw that cactus there. He walked up in order to pick one and tie it around his foot when a huge bug flew at him and bit his neck. We don't have huge bugs like that; my son had made that one up. After that, one hand holding his neck and the other around his foot, he managed to make it out onto the road, having almost bled dry. At that moment, he saw a huge helicopter. The helicopter landed in front of him. My son asked them to help, to take him home, but he was told that he didn't have a home, that the sky was the right place for people like him. At that instant, he heard a loud noise. My son said that the noise was so loud that all the baobabs fell over. A little later, the whole island had exploded. Everyone died, including him. Only the white people in the helicopter had managed to stay alive. They lifted up and flew away. When he told me this dream, I was very scared. I wanted to understand how he could have managed to make up such a dream. Why should a five-year-old have such a horrific dream? So now we're going. We're going to the sacrifice. I've decided to sacrifice four zebus for my son."

"But what was the scariest part of all this? Were you surprised that he had a dream like that, or do you want to avoid him asking you any questions?" I asked.

"Both. I don't want to talk to him about bad things. I don't want him to imagine anything bad. His imagination is important to me. It must be infinite like the sea and warm like the sun."

The dream of the cart driver's son had truly shaken me. I was also surprised and wondered why he would have had such a horrible and sad dream.

"The sun is light blue in his dreams," the cart driver continued. "The clouds are green and yellow. He sees zebus flying in the sky. How could anyone who has such beautiful dreams suddenly see something that was so terrible? Do you know what the first thing he said was?"

"What?"

"My son asked me to promise that such a thing would never happen. He asked me to swear that our continent, our Madagascar, would never be blown up by anyone, that the poor would continue to be able to use the cactus, and that everybody would be able to afford it. I promised him. That's why we're going to the ocean. We have a lot to do there."

"What are you going to do? Is that where you will sacrifice the zebus?"

"I don't know yet. Maybe. If that is what the ocean wants. In any case, the first thing we must do is narrate the dream to the ocean, so that the water washes it away. The dream will sink into its waves and that will allow it never to become reality. Maybe we'll throw the zebus into the water. But then they might not die, and the sacrifice will fail. I cannot allow my son to be afraid."

He spoke with great emotion. I didn't feel like asking any questions. Even without this story, it was clear that he'd had a difficult past. He had led a tough life and seen many bad days. He truly believed in the ocean, in his zebus and his son. He believed in many things that some people would simply see and be content about. I felt the power of the ocean in his words. I also felt like talking to the water about all of my problems.

"Does the ocean only wash away bad dreams?" I asked.

"No. It'll help you with any problem; all you need to do is believe. You don't even have to drown a zebu. Just believe."

It was growing dark. I was lost in thought, but I suddenly realized that if I were to stay with them any longer, I might end up being completely lost.

Before our goodbyes, the man said, "I told you this because I know that nobody will believe you. But, in any case, please be quiet about this. There's no need for the whole world to know about my son's dream."

He helped me get to town. He gave me directions and we parted ways.

I was walking along the streets of Antananarivo. It was a bright day even though the sun was preparing to depart. I kept thinking about the child's dream and the Malagasies. They really seemed to be isolated from the rest of the world. And, in contrast to the smaller islands, Madagascar did seem like a whole continent. The locals were all hospitable and warm.

I had to get to the airport. Although I didn't have any more time, I wanted to look around a bit more. After walking for a few more kilometers, however, I realized that I was running late.

"You're running late." The waiter somehow managed to get those words out in the café where I had decided to sit and shield myself from the sun. I hadn't ordered anything and this had probably not been to his liking.

"You're running late," he repeated.

I was forced to get up and leave the café.

I didn't know how to get to the airport. I felt like I was close, but I didn't know where it was located. The airport there had large intervals between flights, so I couldn't see any planes in the sky. At least that way I could have known which direction to go in.

I walked further on a narrow road. There was some sunburned grass on the curb and the road itself was separated by a thin fence. There were a few houses in the distance. I decided to walk up to them and ask for directions.

"There's no airport here," said one of the residents.

"There is an airport here, but it's very far away," said the other.

"The airport here is closed," said the third.

After thinking long and hard, they understood my question and gave me directions to the airport. I managed to get to the airport in a pousse-pousse.[49] The "driver" was a miserable-looking man who, naturally, spoke no English but sang well and, surprisingly, his songs had English lyrics. I sat in his pousse-pousse as we made our way very slowly to the airport. I felt a bit awkward, to be honest, and even embarrassed, but this was his job and if people like me didn't sit in his pousse-pousse, he wouldn't be able to make a living. I looked carefully at his sweaty back, covered in rags from different pieces of cloth. He grunted as we moved forward and I came closer to the airport meter by meter.

---

49. Pousse-pousse comes from the French, meaning "push, push". It's a means of transportation that often acts as a taxi in Madagascar. It consists of a cart with two wheels and uncomfortable seats, and two long handles protruding towards the back which the "driver" holds on to as he pushes the pousse-pousse.

On the way, the "driver" sang a song which he said was African. Where he had heard it and whose song it was—neither he nor I could answer these questions. But the lyrics seemed to be the epilogue of my stay. The pousse-pousse driver sang, "Go away and leave, take all the bad memories with you, yearn for me and leave, you will remember me always… I'm with you, you'll never be alone, but go, leave, take all the memories with you, forget the dreams you have had today, may your heart have only happy thoughts, and may your soul never feel sorrow… don't remember any of this and tell this to no one, but always recall that I was your love… don't tell them the dream that has abandoned my soul…"

I paid him for the pousse-pousse trip as well as for his song. We said goodbye and he left, pushing his pousse-pousse along. I saw the blisters on his hands, his tense muscles, and how much difficulty he was having in pushing the pousse-pousse. And I remembered what the cart driver had said earlier that day—how his life was similar to the story of Madagascar, which was moving forward slowly, very slowly…[50]

---

50. A series of chemical experiments led to the destruction of many hectares of cactuses and other flora in several regions of Madagascar. Several kilometers of land were also destroyed during atomic bomb tests. All of that could not happen without consequences…
On June 26, 1960, France recognized the independence of Madagascar.

DAY 44. MOZAMBIQUE
THE PINK SUNSET

"Close your eyes and see what you can see now. You'll feel like you are in the past, in someone's memory, and you'll think that you're in an alien body. But, in reality, you will be within yourself, not too far from yourself; you will be sitting on top of a huge rock on the road to Nampula, and it will seem to you that you are seeing it from outer space… But there is nothing worse than memory. I suffer when I remember. It will seem to you that it is a regular occurrence; anybody can remember and be saddened, but my story is completely different. I'm an ordinary person when I start to think about beautiful things, and when I understand that they are very far from me, I suffer great disappointment… Don't look at me as if I'm a regular person. I am, it's true, a regular person, but my thoughts are worthy of attention. When I tell people a sad story, they give me a reaction, whether good or bad. They grow sad, or they become happy. But they never feel what I feel. They watch from above, from the top of the huge rock of Nampula. They don't know that my story is the most tragic in the world, the most tragic—if only for the reason that I believe it is. But they don't believe it; they only express compassion, and that's it."

"How can I get to Maputo?" I asked him for the third time already.

"I'm like a cyclist who has lowered his yellow bicycle into the Zambezi and is pedaling. He keeps moving, not looking at his feet, thinking that the water is shallow, thinking that he'll be able to cross the river in his bicycle, not knowing that he will drown. He takes pleasure in that situation, thinking that the deeper he goes, the closer he will get to the end of the river. Poor man! He doesn't even know that rivers have no end, that they are endless, they are incessant. The river will end, the lake will begin, the lake will end somewhere and the sea will begin, the sea will end... The name of the river will change, but it won't stop flowing, it won't dry up. And here he is, his green bicycle in the water, pedaling. The wheels are partly submerged, the pedals are wet and his feet are touching the water. He's barely managing to keep balance and he's shivering as he's moving ahead. The riverbed is rocky; small shells and muddy moss have assaulted his bicycle. I saw somebody like that a few days ago. He was in the water just like I've been narrating, with his blue bicycle, floating. It was sunset. From a distance, the cyclist looked like a monster that had emerged from the water, its huge head lifted out of the water and its body still concealed. He was moving forward slowly, as if afraid, unwilling to cross the water all at once. I called out to him. He did not respond. He didn't even wish to look in my direction. The only thing he was thinking... I don't even know what he was thinking. How should I know? If I were him, I would think of happy things."

The person I was speaking to did not wish to tell me where Maputo was, although I think he might not have understood me. He was speaking Portuguese and I didn't understand him at first, either. But at that moment, I had no option but to understand—I was alone, there was nobody else around, I had somehow crossed the Indian Ocean and ended up in Mozambique. I wanted to get to the capital, but I didn't even know where I was. However, I was even more surprised when the stranger said, "Do you think I don't know what you asked me? I know it very well. It's just that I don't like answering other people's questions."

"You understand me?" I asked.

"If you can understand Portuguese, then why wouldn't I understand you?"

I relaxed a great deal then. I thought that I would no longer have any difficulty talking to him. I hadn't yet managed to say anything else, when he asked, "You've come to Mozambique?"

"Yes."

"How?"

"From Madagascar."

"Was there any water in the ocean?"

"Yes."

"Was it easy to get here?"

"No. I was on the wrong route three times, until I finally found the place."

"Were you alone?"

"No, I'd rented a boat."

The stranger laughed.

"You're lying. I saw how you came, swimming to the shore."

"I swam to the shore because the wind wasn't letting us bring the boat to the beach. I don't know how to swim. But the water in that area was shallow; I was lucky."

"You crossed the whole ocean and the wind didn't stop you, but just as you got to the shore, the wind was an obstacle?" he asked cynically.

"Yes."

"Come up."

The stranger gestured with his hand. He was standing about a meter above me, slightly away from the shore. He looked old. He had a short, white beard, and his hair was also white. I couldn't guess his ethnicity and never found it out, but I could tell that he was a man of strong belief. He acted strangely when he first saw me; he walked up to the water and gestured like a monkey, then he scratched his body and walked up on the sand.

"Maputo is in that direction," he said. "You have a long walk ahead. But why are you going there? Stay here."

"I want to see the city. I'm writing a book about Africa. I'm trying to spend time in every capital."

"What for?"

"I want to see it up close."

"It doesn't matter; it won't work," he said cynically. "You'd have to be one of them to do that. From the inside. Who will let you see it? Eyes like these aren't good enough for that." He brought his fingers up to his eyes. "In order to do that, you have to convince someone to take out his eyes and give them to you." He was quiet for a minute, then said, "I can give you mine. Yes, I don't see very well, but I do see. With my eyes, this sea is pink, as are the sky and the mountains in the distance. See that island? It isn't often that you can see it from here. It's the island of Inhaca. I see that in pink, too. I can give you my eyes, for what they're worth. They're almost always closed, anyway."

"What would I do with my eyes, then?"

"Put them on the shore, far from the water so that the waves don't wash them away. Eyes that have been removed tend to shine like diamonds, and make for a lovely sight at night. When I look at the sand, a million shining eyes light up the shore, like reflections of the stars."

"And what if I can't find my eyes?"

"They'll be shining the brightest. You'll find them. If you can't find them, then you'll remain blind, or you'll keep seeing things through my eyes. I switched my eyes once and then couldn't find them. I walked around without eyes for a long time, but then I found them."

"What are you doing here? I get the impression that you haven't left this place for years."

"That is true. Sometimes I feel like I've been here for more than a hundred years. I can't feel time any more. The cyclist that I told you about really resembled me."

"Where do you live?"

"Not too far away; there's a hut there."

"You said that your story was the most tragic one."

"Yes. That's what I think. It's not a story, it's one of the saddest incidents in my life."

He wouldn't have talked to me if he hadn't known that we would be speaking different languages.

"Will you tell me?" I asked.

"What for? It's not a very good thing to listen to other people's stories. I already told you: it's like looking at someone from above and not understanding a thing."

"I'll try."

"There's nothing to try."

He moved up a little higher, then leaned on the sand and said, "Are you writing about us, or about yourself?"

"Why?"

"To what extent are you interested in our lives? Our problems. Our feelings. How the locals live, who their neighbors and enemies are, what problems they have, what diseases they suffer, why they are poor, why they are hungry and thirsty, why nobody helps them, why the situation here doesn't interest anyone, the fact that Africa is only used to describe the evils that exist in the world. Most of the people here are considered backward, homeless, diseased, poor, uneducated—why don't you write about that? Why doesn't that interest you?" he said, his voice gradually growing louder. "Why do you think that by describing the story of an old man, by seeing the city, you'll be able to understand us correctly? You should have been interested in all the things I just mentioned, and not just in my story." He was quiet for a while longer and then drew a deep breath, after which he continued slowly, "You're writing about yourself."

I was unable to contradict this statement. He was essentially correct. This wasn't the first time I was told something like this. I well understood that the pain of the Africans was very profound, that smiles and sweet talk wouldn't bring them any happiness. This old man ended up as one of the pillars of my trip, someone who forced me to think about this, to come to a conclusion.

After a long silence, he continued speaking. "Do you love Africa?"

"Yes."

"There's one thing I can't understand. If someone loves someone or something, how can he remain calm? After all, fear is a part of love, isn't it? If you love that much, why aren't you afraid?"

"What should I be afraid of?"

"Afraid of losing it, afraid that it won't smile at you. If you look and see that it is no longer looking you in the eyes, isn't that reason enough to be worried?"

"Yes. That has happened, when Africa has not smiled at me."

"And weren't you worried?"

"I was worried."

"Everyone is the same. I don't like the fact that people like you keep coming here and analyzing, writing opinions, ruining our name. What for? For you own reputations, your own success. What's that to us? This is the biggest issue."

His words made his suffering even clearer. I would have really preferred for him not to have said all that, for him to just start telling his story. But on the other hand, the bile that had gathered within him had to burst out sooner or later.

"I'll take your eyes," I said.

"What for?"

"You were insisting on it a short while ago."

"You don't need to do anything for me."

"I'm not just doing this for you. I'm truly interested in seeing the world through your eyes."

The old man got up and walked to the sea. He called me over.

"Look," he said, "Maputo is over there, and Xai-Xai is a bit to the northeast; Beira is further north, Nampula—even further. I was born there. There's a huge rock there, near one of the roads; I can't remember the exact location now. I used to love going there very much, climbing up on that rock and looking at the city. Nothing much could be seen, nothing at all could be seen, just the road and the trees, and the mountains in the distance. But I felt like the whole city could be seen from there, that I could even see the people. When I was a child, I imagined that there was a huge city under the rock, and when I climbed the rock, I would rule over everyone, like the Europeans. Later, I was forbidden from playing that game. My father told me to stay the way I was, to not pretend to be someone else. Before, I was happy, truly happy. I don't know now whether it was because I would stand on the rock, or because I was a child. I don't know. But at the time, I didn't understand anything either, like you. Life was passing me by, and I wasn't seeing it, like I was not a part of life. I met my future wife on top of that rock. But everything changed from that moment. Everything turned upside down. I was young, I couldn't support a family. We had three children; all three were boys. I wasn't ready for that life, I was still dreaming, but real life had attacked me and gave me no peace. I was jealous of everyone who would go to the rock, stand on top of it and look.

"There was no time to even play with my boys. My only game was work. I couldn't understand whether I was working to make a living, or living to labor and suffer. There were almost no slaves left at the time; a new order had supposedly come about. But that didn't mean anything; people were the same. I would torment myself at three different workplaces every day. I wouldn't see my wife or my children, but they were with me, in my heart; they were rarely far from me, even though we didn't see each other for days. My wife was forced to sell her body, and in truth, she had been obligated to do so, against her will, because her surroundings made her do it and she had no other option. That's what they wanted, that's what suited them. When she fell ill, nobody needed her anymore. I wasn't even able to say a final farewell to her. I never found out where they took her. My boys had seen a boat from the seashore and they thought that it had emerged from one of the stories I'd told them. They got into the water and were a few dozen meters away, but the boat was from above and those people—the Europeans—hadn't noticed that they were children, so they had opened fire. All three were wounded, but not killed. When the boat came closer, they saw that my boys were still alive, so they brought them to the shore. My boys fought back, defending themselves, resulting in a few more shots being fired. According to one of the witnesses, they took their bodies by boat to the depths of the sea and dumped them into the water." He was quiet. "You asked what I am doing here. I'm waiting for their bodies. I'm waiting to find favor with the sea and get my sons back. But it doesn't want to do so. It doesn't love me. My family lived very briefly—just seven years. Not even that long, really. I came here after that. I didn't want to stay in Nampala after that. I didn't want to see the huge rock, the happy faces at its peak; they didn't understand the times in which they were living, the lives they were leading. Their dreams would come true there, on the rock, but as soon as they came down from it, that's it, a cruel and empty life would attack. That is why I say that they could never feel what I feel, because they look from above. I understood very important things later, but the most important one is that love is fearsome. I would probably have had a different fate, had I not loved. The colors before my eyes began to fade with each passing day. My vision worsened and I began to see everything in pink. I don't know why it was that specific color, perhaps that was what my God had wanted. He did not wish to give me any other color. I'm standing here now and regretting the day that I was born. I'm being honest, and if you had come down from that rock, too, you would understand me."

"I don't know what to say."

"If you don't know, then don't say anything. I've said all there is to say. There's nothing left," he said, then abruptly changed the subject. "Look, there are three children over there. They're the ages that my boys were, but they're hungry. They're wandering around here and there in their hunger; they have no time to dream. You shouldn't live in a dream world, but every person has the right to dream. And what are they doing?

They're carrying weapons, they're holding guns and learning how to shoot. What for, who are they fighting against?"

The old man stepped backwards. He sat down in his spot. He yawned and went quiet. There were colorful chains on his hands. He looked at me and then condescendingly turned his head and dropped them behind his back, out of my view.

"So you aren't giving them?"

"What?"

"Your eyes. I want to go to the city, and I want to see it through your eyes."

"Are you crazy?"

"Why do you say that?"

"How can I give you my eyes?"

"But you said that you could."

"You took me literally?"

"Yes."

"Can you take out your eyes?"

"I don't know."

"Well, why don't you try it? As soon as you can, I'll give you mine."

"So, you lied?"

"You really are crazy," he said softly. "Where did *this* guy come from?"

"What about the diamonds shining on the beach?"

"What?"

"Was that a lie, too?"

"I haven't lied about anything. You've misunderstood, that's all."

I came to my senses. I immediately changed the subject.

"What are those chains on your hands for?"

"I'm counting the happy days of my life. There are four rings, each is one occasion of joy. I've been happy four times in my life."

"Really?"

"Yes," he laughed. "It's just a regular chain; I found it somewhere."

"I've got to get going."

"Goodbye," he said indifferently. "Did my story help you with anything?"

"Yes. Very much."

"Good."

I said goodbye to him. For a long time, I was unable to think about anything but the story he had told me. My thoughts were confused. I had heard so many stories that I was barely able to keep walking. I felt like I was a box into which too many things had been thrown while it kept being dragged around.

I left the shore and headed for Maputo. I didn't stay long in town, but I roamed through the streets, saw many smiling people (especially children), many beautiful buildings, and the white Catholic church located in the city center. It looked marvelous, as if it were made of waffle sticks. There was a beautiful cross on top and behind that the dome, which was slightly pointy. The church was large and could be seen from various points in the city; its façade featured a large circular window. Despite its gigantic dimensions, I was unable to see its shadow. The sun lit it up from behind and I assumed that its shadow would fall in front of it, but I never found it. This main church in Maputo didn't have a shadow; it did not block the light.

I had dinner there and continued my journey. I had no intention of returning to the shore; I had to go north, towards Lilongwe in Malawi, but for some reason, my heart took me back there. When I returned to the shore, I saw the hungry boys, as the old man had called them, in the distance. I sneaked up behind them so that I could avoid being seen by them; I was afraid that they would open fire. When they grew clearer in my field of vision, I realized that they weren't holding guns, but wooden sticks. They were smiling and training with the sticks. I could tell that they were athletes. The boys didn't notice me and I rushed down the shore; I wanted to see the old man again and tell him my discovery.

It was evening by the time I got there. The shore was empty, there was nobody there. I could only hear the sound of the bubbles in the waves. The gigantic sun was visible in the distance. I lay down on the moist sand for a few minutes. I closed my eyes. When I opened them, I jumped—one of the boys was standing above me.

"Are you looking for the old man?" he asked.

"Y-yes," I stuttered in reply. "How come you speak English?"

"We understand what we need to understand."

"Were you following me?"

"Yes. I've been following you for a few minutes now."

"Why?"

"I noticed that you'd come and you were watching us. My friends saw you, too. We were scared at first. Then we decided to follow you."

"Why were you scared?"

"I don't know. You should always be wary of strangers."

He wasn't that small; he was around fifteen. His body was half naked. He was spinning a stick in one hand.

"What's that for?" I asked.

"We're training."

"The old man had thought that you were firing guns. He thought these were your guns and that you were hungry children."

"We train every day. We need to be in good shape. We don't know how to fire guns."

He was quiet for a moment. He looked at an anthill located a slight distance away, where thousands of ants had built a home that was more than two meters tall. It was like a pyramid. The ants moved about quickly, taking small pieces of food inside. They were closing all the holes in the anthill.

"They're preparing for the rain," he said. "They're building a house that nobody will be able to destroy. They're blocking the entrances so that other ants won't be able to come in, although ants are strong insects and know how to defend themselves."

He was quiet again and put his stick aside. I noticed how tight the muscles in his body were and how they tensed with each movement. The boy asked again, "Are you looking for the old man?"

"Yes. Where is he?"

"He's gone."

"Where?"

He indicated the ocean, using his head. "He went to be with his sons."

"What?"

"Yes, he's gone. But he probably knew that you were going to come. He asked me to give you something."

"What?"

"Wait until nighttime. You'll see. I have to go now."

"But I can't wait," I said. "I'm in a hurry."

The boy left. I waited for more than an hour, but nightfall didn't come. But when the sun had set, my eyes were pierced by shining objects that were lying in the sand. They were shining like diamonds, like the reflections of stars.

I looked into the distance; there was a beautiful sunset in the distance, a pink sunset…

DAY 45. MALAWI
THE MONSTER

When I wanted to think, a herd of thousands of cows attacked me from behind; I was being overcome by that wave and there was no time to stop it. In reality, there was no herd; it was just memories that were perturbing me. My sense of responsibility began to gradually grow stronger, and it began to suffocate me. I had lost myself for a moment.

Africa had turned into something quite usual. That scared me; it meant that I would have to suffer as well, sooner or later. I thought I had followed all the instructions in the medical booklet. I thought I'd followed all the rules. I even suspected that all of it may have started several days earlier.

"Have you had sexual relations with any women?"

"No."

"How old are you?"

"Twenty."

"How long have you been here?"

"Forty-five days."

"In Lilongwe?"

"One day."

"What have you been doing all day?"

"Nothing. I had a headache. I felt cold. I couldn't feel my body. I was lying in my room."

"Have you drunk any water?"

"Yes. No."

"Yes or no?"

"No."

"Have you eaten anything?"

"Yes."

"What?"

"I don't know. It was like a round bread. A sausage. An egg."

"Are you married?"

"No."

"How long were you planning to stay in Malawi?"

"I was planning to leave tonight."

"Today?"

"Yes."

"Why?"

"I don't know."

"Where to?"

"Zambia."

"When you stand up, do you feel dizzy?"

"No."

"Stand up again."

"I don't feel dizzy."

"Do you have any abdominal pain?"

"No."

"Toothache?"

"No."

"Chest pain?"

"No."

"When you flex your muscles, do they hurt?"

"I don't feel any pain."

"Take a deep breath. Deeper. In which part of your body do you feel a shiver?"

"Near my legs."

"Squat. Get up. Have you taking any preventive medication?"

"Yes."

"I don't know what to say. It's not like any particular condition. But you are not well. It would be better for you to spend a few days in bed, and then we'll examine you again."

The doctor's words seemed hopeless and inadequate. I wasn't really as bad off as he thought. But the conversation with the doctor disappointed me. We had met in the hotel lobby, and he was probably the hotel's in-house physician. I began to be filled with doubt. It would be in their interests for me to stay longer, I suspected. But, on the other hand, the doctor seemed like a reliable man. He wasn't alone; there was someone else with him who had been quiet the whole time. He kept watching the people walking around and offered his help to carry their luggage.

But I really wasn't feeling very well; I felt piercing pain unlike anything I had known before. A shivering had numbed my legs, such that I could barely keep my balance when I walked. It was windy outside. Sunny. The window glass was slightly dirty, but the foggy city could be seen through it. The sound of cars could be heard from the half-open windows, as could the sound of the broom being worked by the hunched janitor, who was indifferently cleaning the corners of the lobby. There was nobody else in the room. Strangely enough, no other staff members were there at the time, either. I sat on the worn leather couch located in the upper part of the lobby and I looked at the scattered magazines in the room.

It had been more than an hour since the doctor had left. I continued sitting there in the same place. For some reason, I wasn't even trying to stand up. I had lost faith that the unpleasant tremor would not return when I was on my feet. There was one more thing that constantly worried me. It was the sound of water that I would constantly hear from the room next door, and every time it grew louder, the janitor would say, "It's the sewage system."

And I would ask, "What?"

"I said it's the sewage system."

"How do you know?" I would ask. And he would mutter under his breath and continue to sweep. There wasn't actually anything left to clean. He had long since finished cleaning the room, but it was like he was obliged to stand and sweep that corner of the lobby for eternity, like he had nothing else to do in life.

Another hour went by. I felt like everything had changed. I got up. At that moment, my eyes grew heavier and I once again ended up on the couch. The janitor asked, "You dead?"

"Not yet."

He laughed. I began to hate him. He was probably to blame that I was in this state. Perhaps he had nothing to do with it, but I wanted to kill him.

"Should I call the doctor?" he asked.

"No."

"He'll help."

"I don't want him."

"The builders are running late."

I realized that he wasn't talking to me. He had absolutely no interest in what I was saying.

"What builders?" I asked.

"They have to come and rebuild the third floor. We're starting renovations very soon."

"Inside the hotel?"

"Yes. They're running late."

"But what needs renovation here? Everything's new."

"I don't know. They've told me that we need to renovate the third floor. I'm only doing what I've been told to do."

"There is no third floor here."

"There was one, once. Then it collapsed. They sucked it up. Now the time has come to rebuild it. Who sucked it up and why, I've never asked."

"Have you been working here a long time?"

"Yes."

"Do you do the same thing every day?"

"Yes."

"Aren't you tired of it?"

"No."

At that moment, the strange noises once again came from the neighboring room.

"It's the sewage system," the janitor said and he left the lobby.

A little later, he was out on the street, greeting some people I didn't know. They wore laborers' overalls and carried some metal cases. They went up a few stairs and into the lobby from there, as I heard the sound of a car engine, probably the one that had brought them to the hotel. I found it strange that nobody else had come out to meet these builders except for the janitor.

"Come in," the janitor said in a tired voice. "This is a patient we have, don't mind him; keep going straight ahead."

I felt hurt by that attitude.

"Hello," the first laborer said.

"Hello," the second one said.

"Hello," I replied.

They were much more polite.

"What would you like to drink?" the janitor called out from a distance.

"Coffee," one of the laborers said.

"What about you, patient?"

I did not reply. He was calling me a patient, but in fact he was probably ill with several diseases himself. My hatred for him kept growing. I wanted to kill him but, unfortunately, the laborers were in the lobby. That was a major inconvenience.

"What are you going to do?" I asked them, in order to calm my nerves down.

"Build," said Willy, one of the laborers, the thin one.

"We're going to make our city prettier," said Gospely, the other one, who was also thin.

"But the building is pretty," I said.

"Yes, and the number of guests keeps growing. We need more rooms."

"He's right. A few months from now, there won't be an empty room in this hotel."

"How will the two of you manage to finish it on time?" I asked.

"There's isn't enough money to hire a whole team. A lot of the work has been done already, so there's not much left to do. We've done lots of work like this, we're used to it. We're trusted professionals, we're the best builders in the business."

"We've got to put up a couple of walls, smooth them out, paint them… not much else to do," Willy said, putting his professional terminology to use.

"You know what the good thing is here?" Gospely continued.

"What?" I asked.

"It's calm. I never want to leave."

"He's lying. You wanted to leave," Willy said.

"I didn't want to. I was a bit desperate at one point but now, thank God, there is work."

"Sure, easy for you to say now. But you were desperate and complaining back then."

"I've never complained. And have you forgotten that you wanted to go to South Africa?"

"Yeah, so? They pay well there. Of course I wanted to go. Did I say anything when you wanted to go to Europe?"

"Your coffee." The janitor's unpleasant voice interrupted the conversation—gradually growing into an argument—between the two laborers. He looked at me. "Would you like one, too?"

"No, I don't drink coffee."

"Why? Afraid it'll poison you?"

"No."

"It's good coffee."

"I don't want any," I said. It was as if he was intentionally trying to make me angry. I had such a powerful headache that I could easily lose control of myself.

"The doctor said you should go and lie down—why aren't you doing so? I could tidy up your room, if you like."

"No," I said. I could just imagine him tidying up my room. Just the thought of it kept me from wanting to return to my room at all. "I'm fine here."

"Fine," he said with a sarcastic laugh and he walked away, muttering to himself.

While the laborers enjoyed their coffee, my eyes rested on a vending machine with soda, which I had not noticed earlier, near the wall opposite me. It had a sign saying that it only accepted coins. It was making some sounds and generally seemed to be in working condition. But nothing came out after I hit it a few times. I somehow got back to my place and sat down next to Willy and Gospely. They were not arguing.

"When are you going to start?" I asked.

"Right away; we'll start as soon as we drink our coffee."

"What's in the cases?"

"Different kinds of tools—a saw, hammer, paint, building tools," Willy said.

They were good men and looked honest.

"We could saw off someone's head," Gospely said, laughing, and he stretched his hand out to the case and withdrew a rusty saw; he ran his finger over its teeth.

"Put that back," Willy said.

"Why?"

"It'll scare the janitor."

"He knows that we have tools like this. Why would it scare him?"

My eyes gleamed as soon as I saw the instrument. I no longer felt my body, and my eyes looked red in the mirror hanging on the nearby wall. The time was right to pick up the saw and kill the janitor; I even imagined various scenes to figure out which would torment him most. The bluntness of the saw's teeth made me happy. But everything changed when Gospely tapped me on the shoulder and asked in a calm voice, "What has he done?"

"What?"

"Do you know the story of the cannibal?"

"No," I said, confused.

At that moment, a few foreigners walked in, luggage in hand. They walked up the stairs and entered the lobby. They said hello—with particular warmth when it came to me—and then went up to the second floor.

"You haven't heard it?" Gospely continued.

"No," I said.

"A cannibal used to live in our house. He used to kill each of his relatives in turn. He was accused of doing all sorts of horrible things. But he never tortured anyone. He would quietly kill and eat them."

"Shall we go?" Willy asked.

"You go, I'm telling an important story here."

"We'll be late. We shouldn't delay things."

"Go, I'll be there soon."

Willy smiled. I didn't see where he went. It was just me, Gospely, and the janitor left in the lobby.

"Should I continue? He was a thin man and ugly; naturally, he was scary to look at and nobody wanted to talk to him. But he just a regular mortal like the two of us. Except that he was a cannibal, that's all. His relatives were scared and didn't know when he'd be hungry again, and whose leg, arm, or ear he'd grab at that moment. He wasn't a wild predator, as many people thought. He was just a regular guy—good and honest. When he was alone and full, one could talk to him for hours. But you had to be careful not to stay with him for too long. The cannibal liked women very much. He tried not to eat them. He would have sex with them, talk to them, but he was afraid to eat them. The women were afraid, too, although some were very excited to go to bed with him, uncertain at every moment as to whether or not they would end up being his victim. One day, the cannibal ended up eating my sister this way. When I came home, I saw how he had attacked her. Like a monster."

"Who was the cannibal?" I asked.

"It was me," he laughed. "I don't know. When I came upon that scene, I ran away. I left my family, my home, everyone. I decided to live separately. Live my own life. And I didn't really care who he was, whether or not he existed, whether I had imagined him or not; what mattered to me was that I had found myself. I had left those oppressive surroundings in which I had lived for many years. Do you know why I'm talking about this?"

"Why?"

"Because I saw how tempting the saw was to you."

I had never thought that a Malawian laborer would say things like that to me.

"What's going on outside?" I asked.

"Where?"

"On the other side of this window."

"It's sunny. Hot. Nothing's going on. Stay here. I'm saying this for your sake. Stay here and get better."

"Why did you run away from your family? Did you feel like a stranger to them?"

"No," he said, growing serious. "Yes. A little. Everyone feels like a stranger in a place where he is loved very much."

"Why?"

"He becomes a toy. Which toy feels powerful among people? None of them."

"Willy said that you wanted to go abroad."

"Yes, I wanted to go to a better country. Make some money. He wanted to, too. Many people wanted to. But a lot has changed since then. I'm seeing many fewer cannibals than before. Life is a little better now." He scratched near a hole in his pants. "People are becoming kinder."

The doctor and his assistant entered the lobby and cast a worried glance in my direction. I felt obliged to get back to being sick and weak. The doctor squinted and asked in a delicate voice, "How are you feeling?"

"Bad," I said, because that was what he wanted to hear.

"Very bad?"

"Yes. I'm close to losing consciousness, if I haven't lost it already."

"That's not good. Did you lie down? Rest a bit?"

"No, he hasn't lain down," the janitor butted in.

"Why not?" asked the doctor.

"It's fine here. I see people come in and go out. I look out at the city through the half-open windows. This couch is comfortable."

"He hasn't even had any coffee. He's afraid of being poisoned," the janitor said again.

"Go and get some rest. You won't get any better this way. Go to your room. You need to rest. We don't know what it is you have. It could be very serious."

"I have to go," Gospely butted in. "He's waiting for me."

"Go. What symptoms do you have?" the doctor asked.

"I'm a builder," Gospely said and left.

"Go and lie down," the doctor said, turning back to me. "I'll tell Chaziga to tidy up your room." And he called to the janitor.

"No need. I don't want to."

The janitor looked at me with hate. I felt at that moment that he would kill me, if he had the opportunity. I even suspected that he may have poisoned me.

The lobby was empty once again, except for the elderly Chaziga, who did not move from his spot and had turned his back to me as he gazed out the window. Small bells hung above the main entrance. They were supposed to ring every time someone opened the door, but they were not hung straight, so the door made them move a little, but not enough to ring.

It kept growing darker, and I noticed that the lights were on in the lobby. I noticed the blue coming in from the outside. The city was calling out to me, but I was in no position to overcome my pain and go outside. The monster was stopping me from doing so; it had sat down within me and wanted to torment me. It wanted to come out from inside me.

I dozed off for a bit, although the presence of the janitor frightened me. I hadn't managed to start dreaming when Willy and Gospely tapped me on the shoulder.

I jumped. "What's going on?"

"We're leaving. Bye."

"So soon?"

"It's nighttime. You've slept for a few hours. We didn't want to bother you, but the janitor said that you weren't in deep sleep and that we could say goodbye."

"Aren't you taking your tools with you?"

"No. We're coming back tomorrow. What's the point?"

"We'll be working here for two months."

They left. The hate I felt had grown so much that I was ready to strangle the janitor with my bare hands. But I didn't feel strong enough.

I don't know why I felt this evil, but my illness bothered me so much that I couldn't think of anything other than hanging, killing, or drowning someone, just to escape this unpleasant feeling.

Suddenly, people began to appear in the lobby. I hadn't expected any of them. They seemed unpleasant to me, too. But it was nighttime already, and it was time to leave. I had to get to the airport. Somebody called out to the janitor. It was a strange and monotonous voice. Chaziga leaned the broom against the door, as if nobody else was supposed to enter, and went up to the second floor. It was probably the sound of the sewage system.

I looked at the pictures on the walls of smiling children, who were probably locals. They were looking at me and smiling sincerely. "They were sick once, but now they're well again and they can smile; they are our future, our hope, our love," the message at the bottom of the posters said.

Suddenly, a cry rang out, and the cry turned into shouting, and the shouting turned into howling. It was as if somebody was being skinned alive on the second floor. The sounds kept growing worse. Even my swollen ears could hear them. Then, I heard footsteps. The second floor was slowly descending into chaos; all kinds of horrible sounds rang out above my head. Something terrible must have been going on there, something that had shocked everybody. I wanted to see what was happening, too, but I had no control over my body. My legs were nailed to the couch.

The footsteps headed downstairs. A few more seconds and I would know what had happened on the second floor of that small hotel in the city of Lilongwe. It was one of the hotel employees coming down the stairs, the one who had given me the key to my room the previous night. She was a young woman in a white uniform with a skirt, and black shoes. When she saw me, she tried to gain a bit of control over herself, but failed. Her hair shivered with fright and her muscles had tensed; the cuffs of her shirt were undone, and her chest heaved. She hadn't even managed to catch her breath when I asked, "What's going on?"

"He's dead. Brutally killed."

"Who's dead? Who killed him?"

"Our janitor. There was a strange monster in the room; it attacked and killed him. Everyone's scared. The monster is still there; everyone's terrified. The monster attacked him."

"What monster?"

"I don't know. It doesn't look human. It's a monster."

She went back up to the second floor. The shouting and crying continued. I got up, and my body felt light. My headache was gone. I came down from the lobby, hung my keys on a nail at the reception desk and left the hotel. I could still hear the sound of Chaziga's broom behind me and I was sure that he was back in his spot, indifferently cleaning up one of the corners of the lobby. But I didn't turn back, I didn't want to look behind me. I left…[51]

---

51. Millions of people die of a disease in Africa every year. Some of them end up with mental disorders and grow violent…

DAY 46. ZAMBIA
CLOSE YOUR EYES

It was night, a dark night. I was in a noisy place; I didn't know whether it was a harem or a guesthouse, but I could hear dozens of screams. The sounds came from the neighboring rooms. There was a round, wooden table in front of me, with two bottles of beer and another round item that I couldn't see well from where I was. The light coming towards it had been blocked and the shadow made it difficult to discern what it was. I'd arrived in the morning, or perhaps during the day, but I couldn't recall what I had been doing for the past few hours. It was as if that time had simply disappeared.

I was slowly getting drunk. Strange things continued to pursue me, seduce me, as naked women walked in front of me and I had no idea what was happening. If I had been somewhere else at that moment and seen the same things, I would definitely have thought that I was losing my mind. The women here were pretty. Although nothing much could be seen, their bodies were a bit different from the other African women I had seen. They were attractive to me, and smelled nice.

Suddenly, a shot rang out. I ran outside and came to my senses for a moment, trying to understand what had happened. Outside, many young people had gathered; they had stacked up dozens of rubber tires and set them on fire. Then I came back inside.

"What happened?" I asked.

"Nothing has happened, sit down and be calm," said the naked woman sitting in front of me. "All you need to do is close your eyes."

"Why are they shooting? They'll kill someone!"

"Let them shoot. If they want to shoot, let them do it."

"But why?"

"Relax," she said. She put her hand on my forehead and pressed hard.

I felt cold suddenly and I momentarily recalled the lobby at the hotel in Malawi.

The gunfire continued. I didn't know who their target was. A moment later, several of the windows in the room shattered and pieces of glasses scattered inside. The noise kept growing louder, but the people inside did not seem to be particularly perturbed.

"Does this happen often?" I asked.

"Yes. They're very aggressive today."

"Why?"

"They're young. They're unhappy with something."

"But is this disorder really necessary?"

"If they're doing it, then it must be."

"Is it a political rally?"

"I don't know."

She left, but I felt like she would be returning soon. I closed my eyes then and decided to think of something else. I had an immense desire to have a pet leopard. Why could other people own a horse, or a cat, or a dog, but I couldn't have a leopard? From that moment on, I was sitting on the back of my leopard, and we were racing along. It had a very sleek body, like the women here, but muscular and able to leap several meters in one bound. We were racing across the whole of Zambia, over the Muchinga Mountains, along the Luangwa River, on the narrow and thin streets of Lusaka, and through Kafue National Park. My leopard was running very quickly. I was barely able to hold on to its thick neck.

We stopped for a minute. The leopard looked at me and said thoughtfully, "It's dangerous here; we have to get back quickly."

"Where are we?" I asked the leopard.

"I don't know. But I can sense that it's dangerous. There are hunters nearby. They could open fire at any minute."

"We'll run away. They won't be able to touch us."

"I'm tired. We have to hide."

"Where? There aren't even any trees here."

"In a cave, somewhere. As long as they don't find us."

I grabbed the leopard's warm head and pressed it against myself hard. It tensed its eyelids and shut its eyes. I don't know whether it was water flowing from its eyes or tears, but at that moment, we both felt protected.

It was hot inside the cave. I couldn't see whether it was daylight outside, or night. I could hear the leopard's breathing, which seemed to be very slow and deep. Each breath was like a motorcycle engine being turned off. As I caressed its furry skin, a painting on the cave wall grabbed my attention. It had on it the phrase "One Zambia, One Nation."[52]

"Do you want some water? They're firing again," said the woman who had left a short while earlier.

"No," I replied.

I didn't want to know her name; I liked the fact that we were strangers to each other. There was fear in her eyes, and that fear was strange. At first it had seemed like she had nothing to lose. But I had been wrong.

"What's wrong? You're behaving strangely," she said, as if we'd known each other for a long time.

"Nothing. Nothing's happened. We're hidden," I said.

"Who?"

"My leopard and I. He's afraid they might kill us."

"Who?"

"The hunters."

The woman laughed. "What hunters?"

I was surprised. Instead of asking "What leopard?" she was asking about the hunters.

"The hunters I hate, the ones who are chasing us," I said.

"Tell your leopard not to be afraid. There are no hunters here."

"How do you know?"

"I know," she said, smiling.

The room was quiet for a moment. I could hear the breathing of an overweight man sitting several meters away, the one who hadn't taken the cigarette out of his mouth the entire evening. He was holding on to the bottom of a woman who was as heavy as him, and he was smiling. Even the buzzing of the mosquitoes that had gathered on the ceiling was now audible, and they had their own conversation with each other:

"There's a huge river down there."

"No, there are people down there, having fun."

"No, there's nothing down there."

And they burned.

I drank another glass of beer. The sounds grew more frequent from then on. We were in the basement, and the noise from above blew in my ears like the wind coming

---

52. This motto is featured on Zambia's coat-of-arms.

from one direction, then the other. The ceiling swayed, and the people gathered in the room were happy.

"Where did they find all those cars whose tires they're burning?" I asked.

"Why should you care?"

"I waited for an hour for a car to arrive this morning so that I could get from the airport to the hotel. There weren't any cars around."

"That's probably why—they were all burning."

"But why? What is the protest against?"

"I don't know."

A minute later, a thin man who looked like a caricature passed in front of us, shouting.

"My finger! I've cut my finger! Help, help!" he cried.

"Perhaps the broken glass caused the injury," the woman said.

"But why is he shouting?"

"He's afraid he'll get infected."

She left again. I didn't understand why she went—perhaps a customer had come in who was more attractive, I thought. But the only thing interesting me at that moment was my leopard.

"Get up," I said to it.

"What's going on?" the leopard asked.

"Get up; let's leave the cave."

"Why?"

"I've been told that there aren't any hunters here."

"Who told you that?"

"I don't know her. A woman. In one of the city harems."

"There are no harems in the city."

"I don't know. It's a guesthouse, then. She said that we didn't need to be scared; there are no hunters here."

"I'm not so sure."

"She was sure. She even laughed."

"So what?"

"You want to keep hiding?"

"A little while longer. We can't believe what any old slut would say."

"I believed her."

"That's not enough," the leopard said, and it fell asleep.

The disorder continued above us. Despite my indifference, I still had a desire to find out the cause of all this. When I got up and walked along the narrow staircase, the large chandelier hanging from the ceiling fell to the ground. The small bits of glass that hung from it scattered across the room. That had happened once before; I remembered the incident in the DRC, when I was sitting in a café and the ceiling collapsed. But on that occasion, the walls of the room had crumbled and a tank had driven through them.

Within moments, I was outside, in the street, where a few young men were pushing each other around. They were all smoking and looked angry.

"Were you the ones making all the noise?" I asked. "You've made a mess downstairs. Glass is broken everywhere, and the chandelier collapsed a minute ago."

"What?" They looked at me, laughing.

"I asked if you're the ones causing all this ruckus."

"Yeah, so what if we are?" one of them replied in local slang. He was fifteen at most, and took a gun out of his pocket. "Get lost." Then he began to spew out a string of expletives.

"But why?" I asked.

"What we're doing is none of your business," another one of them jumped in. He had a gun, too.

"You have no right to say anything to us," a third one continued.

"You're bothering the people inside," I said.

"There are no people there. There's just trash. Filth. Garbage that should be thrown away. They're sick people who live a completely foreign life. There isn't a single healthy person among them. They're all from another world."

"But they're not bothering you."

"Yes, they are. If they're alive, then they're bothering us. We hate all those who can be bought off."

"There was a fire here a few minutes ago, and a crowd had gathered. Where's everyone now?" I asked.

"The police took them away."

"Then they'll take you away, too."

The first boy aimed his gun at me. He threatened to kill me and shouted that I should go back inside and not come out again.

"Who are you fighting against? Why are you so angry?" I asked.

One of them made a movement with his gun and a fake sound, pretending to have fired, then the three of them started laughing again.

"Get back down there, before it's too late."

I was back in the guesthouse a few seconds later. I was sitting in front of the round table again, drinking beer. I'd lost count of the number of glasses I had drunk so far.

"It's the seventh," the woman said, smiling. She had long been sitting in front of me, watching me with interest.

"What's the seventh?" I asked.

"It's the seventh glass."

"Really?"

"What happened? Did you talk to anyone?"

"Yes, but they ran away. As soon as they saw me, they got scared and left the street," I said.

"Good. The noise has died down. People won't be scared now."

"But they weren't scared before, either."

"They're used to it."

I suddenly realized that the men in the room were foreigners, as were the ones coming out of the neighboring rooms.

"What kind of people come here?" I asked.

"Different kinds. They're not locals. The local men don't come to this guesthouse."

"Do you disgust them?" I asked.

"No, *you* disgust them."

"Why?"

She looked at a white American, or perhaps he was English, standing some distance away whose protruding belly was so huge that he was unable to button his pants. He was walking like a duck, and his face resembled a huge sausage placed in a freshly baked bun. He walked towards us with slow steps, smiled, somehow shoved himself up a few stairs, and then fell down. He got up again, dusted himself off, and then his pants fell down. He didn't pick them up, but still somehow managed to walk out of the guesthouse.

"I don't know," the woman replied.

"What is that?" I asked, and indicated the dark item on the table.

"It's an apple. Do you want it?"

"Yes."

I took the apple.

"Get up," I said to my leopard, who had been sleeping for more than twenty hours.

"What happened?"

"I've brought you an apple. Get up."

"Is it light out?" it asked.

"I don't know. I was sleeping, too. Let me check. Yes, it is."

"Let it grow dark, then we'll leave."

"Do you want an apple?"

"Yes."

"I want to soar in the sky. I want to hold on to your neck and enjoy life," I said.

"Enjoy it then."

"You're afraid of the hunters."

"I'm afraid of death."

"But there are no hunters here."

"I don't believe it."

It kept insisting on this. I didn't want to have the same conversation over and over again, so I returned to the guesthouse.

"Isn't there anyone else around?" I asked.

"Why do you say that?" the woman said.

"It's silent."

"Those young men were here a moment ago. They attacked a few people and fired their guns. They've been taken to the bathroom."

"Who has?"

"The victims."

"Were they killed?"

"Yes."

I felt ashamed for a minute that I had lied earlier and said that the young men had run away.

"Did they kill many people?"

"Yes. Twenty."

"How many?"

"Twenty."

I was shocked. Then I recovered. My head started to ache.

"Is that where the corpses are?" I asked, and pointed at the bathroom.

"Yes."

"Only men?"

"No."

"What are you going to do?"

"I don't know. The police will arrive soon."

"Then what?"

"They'll take them away."

"Where?"

"I don't know. Wherever."

"What about the guesthouse?"

"What about it?"

"What will happen to it?"

"It'll continue to operate."

"They won't close it down?"

"No. If they wanted to close it down, they would have done so a long time ago."

"Are there many foreigners in Zambia?"

"I don't know. If you ask me—yes. Because I don't see anyone else besides them. But when it comes to reality, I don't know."

"Who are they?"

"Those two?"

"Yes."

"They're police."

"Why aren't they coming here?"

"I don't know."

A few tables away, two Black men sat indifferently, caressing the women around them. They were drunk, too.

I was surprised by everyone's indifference.

When there was no noise, and everything was calm, the people gathered in the room seemed more uneasy. But now, with all the glass broken, the staircase damaged, the huge chandelier shattered, and more than twenty dead bodies piled on top of each other in the bathroom, they were calm, indifferently kissing and not looking in the direction of the bathroom.

I felt like I was in the wrong place. I had come to see the city, to see Lusaka. To talk to people, to see their reality. And no matter how ugly it was, I had been ready to resist all of that.

"Get out." The voice of one of the young men could be heard; he was afraid of his own voice. His voice trembled, and his hands trembled, too, but he held on to his gun, and I was sure that he would fire it. "Get out; I'll kill you all. Get out. I'll kill you. Get out of here, you filth."

He began to fire, and the other two joined him. That was the moment when I was asleep and was eating the apple with my leopard. I saw them cruelly kill one man or woman after another. Shouting could be heard from the neighboring room. People were being killed there, too. The young men were attacking everyone, and nobody was resisting. They were piling up their victims, one on top of the other. The young men had killed more than fifteen people; I tried once again to stop them, but I failed. One of them fired—and they killed me, too. They threw me on top of the others and ran out. They killed twenty people and disappeared.

"Have they killed me, too?" I asked the woman.

"Yes, although, I really don't know. You can see for yourself—the bathroom isn't far away. If you can recognize yourself, that is."

"What about you?"

"I'm alive," she said, and she was quiet. "They want law and order; they're not to blame. You shouldn't blame them. Anybody would have done the same in their place; many of the women gathered here are their relatives. Can you imagine what they feel each time they see someone like you?"

"What would they do if the customers here were only Black men?" I asked.

"I don't know," she said, getting emotional. "I don't know."

It would probably be the same, although perhaps they would have allowed it, I thought. The leopard struck me with its thick paw at that moment.

"What is it?"

"Did they kill you?" it asked.

"I guess so. I never went to the bathroom to see."

"Why would you bother? Either way, you had nothing to do there."

"Yes."

"Should we go?"

"Yes."

It came to me. I sat on its back and we sped off. The leopard ran more quickly than the cars on the streets; people looked at me and smiled, they had never seen a white man who had his own leopard.

I felt strange, like I was at a worship service. I had fallen in love with all the Africans and didn't want to leave them. I wanted to stay by their side. I would have happily changed my skin, even if I had been offered thick, velvety, yellow and black fur instead, if only I could stay here by their side.

It was morning. I was standing in front of a white house. There were small buildings behind me. The street was clean; there were trash cans placed here and there. It was a bus stop, where colorful buses were replacing each other minute after minute. My bus was running late. A schoolboy appeared next to me a few minutes later. He was a young boy of ten or twelve years, with large eyes. He hung his schoolbag from his shoulder and gave me a stony stare.

"Going to school?" I asked.

"Yes," he said.

"Is the bus late?"

"Yes."

"Do you get good grades?"

"Yes."

"What's your favorite subject?"

"Geography."

He hadn't blinked his eyes this whole time.

"Do you know it well?"

"Yes."

The bus arrived. We got on.

"I like it, too. Especially Africa."

"Me, too," he said and smiled. "What's the longest river in Africa?"

"I don't know," I said.

"The Nile," he laughed. "The tallest mountain?"

"I don't know," I said.

"Kilimanjaro," he laughed again. "The biggest lake?"

"Tanganyika?"

"Lake Victoria," he said. His teeth were white and crooked; he had a happy smile.

"What about the biggest island or country, the most populous city?" he asked. He grew excited, his feet barely touching the ground.

"I don't know. You tell me."

"I don't know, either. I'll tell you the next time we meet."

The boy got off the bus. He walked towards a school. I had noticed that the driver had been watching us through his small rearview mirror. When I was getting off the bus, he asked, "How can you love Africa, if you don't know all those things?"

It was a beautiful day. At that moment, I closed my eyes and saw many strange animals flying in the sky that looked like my leopard.

DAY 47. ANGOLA
IT FEELS LIKE THE WAR
NEVER HAPPENED

I had lost myself over the last few days; I had become freer. This was noticed even by the person selling flowers, who had directed an indifferent glance in my direction. I had seen a flower seller like this one in Morocco. When a bicycle rode past us, she opened her eyes wide to stare at it and said a few words in Portuguese. I understood nothing. But I felt like she had noticed how free I felt in Luanda, their capital. In reality, her words had not been directed at me and perhaps she hadn't noticed me at all; I may have imagined it. In any case, I was happy that she had looked at me; I was happy because it felt like she was thinking about me.

Then, the bicycle rode past one more time. The woman spoke again. Then this same thing happened once again.

The bicycle was causing me anxiety because it was rolling past me at random, with no particular objective. Nobody was even riding it. It kept going, then coming back, then going again. This went on for several minutes, as if it were bewitched.

I was standing outside one of the buildings on Rua Paralela, where there were very few people. A shadow covered the whole length of the street, a large area of shade, and low buildings lined the sidewalk. It was a hot day. The past few days had slipped by very quickly; I was lost in dreams. Africa was gradually becoming easier for me to perceive, as if I could feel its whole weight. I wanted to close my eyes and soar, grab someone to bring along with me and escape. After the dream of the small Malagasy, everything had changed—the story of the old man in Mozambique and the builders in Malawi had also changed me completely, and the leopard I had met in Zambia seemed like it had been following me all along.

"You're blocking the road; stand to one side," the flower seller said.

"Am I bothering anyone?"

"Yes."

"I was lost in thought," I said.

"Go think somewhere else."

She was rude to me, but perhaps she was right. I had bothered her. But I hadn't any desire to make her angry.

"May I speak to you?"

"What do you need?"

"Nothing."

"Need flowers?"

"No."

"What do you need, then?"

"I don't need anything. Could I ask you out to a café?"

"Me?"

The flower seller was a woman past sixty. It's true, she didn't necessarily look that old, but the wrinkles in her cheeks were particularly pronounced. She was heavy, had large eyes like her flowers, and wore a colorful dress. Her bulbous lips reminded me of motorcycle tires.

The flower seller had misunderstood me.

"What do you want?" she repeated. She did not speak English well, although she knew enough to sell flowers to tourists. Her flowers were unique and very expensive, so the locals rarely bought any.

"Would you have lunch with me?" I asked.

"Why?"

I was not confessing my love to her, nor did I feel any attraction. "I don't know; it's just a thought that crossed my mind," I said.

"But why?"

"Hasn't an unusual thought ever crossed your mind?"

"Like, what are zebras doing in the city?"

"Yes," I said.

"It happens."

"Will you come?"

"No."

"Why not?"

"What do you want from me?"

"Nothing."

"In that case, go away. You're bothering me."

I really hadn't wanted to bother her. I was feeling a strange audacity that I hadn't experienced before. I felt like I could do whatever I wanted, but it wasn't a feeling of arrogance, simply a belief. Africa had forced me to believe that everything was possible in life, everything.

"Why have zebras come to the city?" I asked the woman, whose attention was now focused on a family—three white people, including a curly-haired child—who were coming towards us. They were still a distance away, so I expected us to be able to exchange a few more words.

"What zebras?" she asked rudely.

"You said a little while ago that zebras were coming to the city."

"I never said anything like that."

"I asked you whether any unusual thoughts ever crossed your mind, and you talked about zebras."

"So what?"

"I'm curious. Why are zebras coming to the city?"

"Who said that they were coming here? It was just a thought that crossed my mind."

"Will you come with me?"

The woman turned her attention to the family, which was—or at least I thought so, for some reason—from France. The child was holding a chocolate ice cream cone. I decided that the boy's name must be Loris, and that he had brought his ice cream with him from Paris. Or rather, he had come from Paris, licking his ice cream along the way. His father was a man around forty years old, tall, thin, wearing spectacles and a jacket, and with a leather bag in one hand that looked like the one I had lost in Tunisia. He was, in all probability, a lawyer, and I was prompted strongly to think this by the sharp fountain pen sticking out of his breast pocket and the thin envelope next to it, which must have contained at least 10,000 euros. His wife was tall, too, even taller than her husband, and had blonde hair and a long jaw. She was wearing a short red jacket and pants, and her shoes had no heels, making her gait ungainly. The woman looked like an important professional, too, but it was difficult to make an assumption immediately regarding the sector in which she worked. They walked up to the flower seller, and I watched carefully as the large woman focused her whole attention on this "French" family, beckoning to them with every single part of her body. Loris finally succumbed, running up to us, grabbing a flower and then running away. Naturally, the polite lawyer came up to pay for the lost flower. At that moment, I didn't know who to watch—the boy or the flower seller.

"Loris!" the boy's mother shouted.

For some reason, this was in English, although it would be fairer to say that one couldn't tell the language in which she spoke, because she had said nothing else other than the boy's name.

Loris had put his ice cream in his pocket and was admiring the flower.

"Loris," the woman shouted again. She continued saying more this time, and the language was foreign to me. I was very disappointed. They had turned out to not be French.

The flower seller managed to sell them several flowers. Besides that, she spoke warmly with the lawyer for about three minutes. When the family left, I walked up to her once again.

"Who were they?" I asked.

"What do you want?" she asked, smiling. She was in a good mood.

"Who was that man?"

"I don't know. But he knew my father," she said as she continued smiling.

She was pondering something. She had recalled her father.

"Is your father deceased?" I asked.

"Yes," she said, looking at me happily. "He was a hero."

"What did that Frenchman have to do with any of this?"

"What Frenchman?"

"The lawyer."

She laughed again.

"He's Portuguese; the woman with him was his wife. They came to Luanda to adopt a child."

"Did they complete the adoption?"

"Yes, the little one who stole my flowers. He was born here, although he's white."

"Loris?"

"Luis. His name was Luis."

"So he's Angolan?"

"Yes," she said, stretching out the word. "Luis has no idea of what is lying in store for him."

"What *is* lying in store for him?"

"A happy life."

"Why?"

"He'll go to a good school there, he'll become a good professional, he'll get a good job. He'll be happy. He won't even remember where he was born."

"Are they going to take him to Portugal?"

"Yes."

"Doesn't he have parents of his own?"

"I don't know. How would I know? You're asking some strange questions. How would I know if Luis has parents?"

"You spoke to his father for such a long time."

"So what? We were talking about other things."

"Like what?"

The woman gave me an angry look. I realized that I had overstepped my bounds and so I quickly changed the subject, saying, "Where is there a café around here?"

"Go straight; there should be one at the end of the street."

"Will you come with me?"

The woman once again looked at me angrily.

"What would you like to order?" the waiter asked.

We were at the café. It was an old-fashioned place, modeled to look like something out of the fifties. A pianist played the piano in one corner, and pictures of people hung in every possible spot on the walls and the ceiling. They looked like politicians, judging by their ties, but perhaps I was wrong, the same way I'd been mistaken about Loris and his "French" family.

"What kind of a hero was your father?" I asked.

"A war hero."

"Which war?"

She thought for a second. "There've been so many wars, even I don't know. Maybe the World War?"

"Did Angola take part?"

"No. My father lived in Brazil. My grandfather was a slave. He moved to Brazil at a young age in a small boat. My father was born there. He went to an aviation engineering school, unless I'm mistaken. Then the war broke out, and he destroyed everyone from his plane in the sky."

The woman's story was so simple that it sounded like a little child was recounting it. I enjoyed hearing her speak.

"How did that man know about your father?"

"He'd heard about him. My father was involved in many battles. He had simply heard of him."

While we were talking, I looked out the window and saw the bicycle slipping past once more, with no rider on it again.

"Were you born in Brazil?"

"No. Here. In Luanda. The war went on and my father moved to Angola. He married my mother and my brother was born, then the other, and so on. They had eight boys, and then I came along. They decided not to have any more children after me."

"Did your father die here?"

"Yes."

The woman ate very slowly; I was watching her carefully. She would look at me bashfully sometimes, as if she thought that I was in love with her.

Half an hour went by. We finished eating. She looked at me and I looked at her. There was nothing left to talk about. I had run out of questions and she didn't know what to say. Finally, I spoke. "Shall we leave?"

"No. I have to go somewhere else. But I have to ask you something."

"Go ahead," I said.

"Why did you want to have lunch with me so much? There are so many pretty girls here. They're a thousand times more pleasant than I am, they can talk about more interesting things and, finally, they'd be happy to talk to you."

"Do I have to answer that?"

"Yes."

"I don't know. I really can't say."

"You like older women," she said confidently and left.

"Perhaps," I responded, although she could no longer hear me.

I felt slightly awkward about what I had done. I was afraid that she had misunderstood me, and I hadn't said anything that could have helped her understand correctly. I'd only asked her questions, as if interrogating her. I left the café, but before going out, I walked up to the pianist, who looked at me and said, with a look that was very serious, immensely serious, "Do you know who Beethoven was?"

"No," I said.

"He was a global great. I worship him."

I gave him a few kwanza, which is the local currency, and stepped out. He said thank you and then shouted, "I'll tell you about Mozart the next time you come. He was a genius, too."

There were many people out on the street. There was very little public transportation; instead, motorcycles and bicycles were everywhere.

One thing bothered me. I regretted that I hadn't asked the name of the flower seller's father. However, it had seemed to me that she had made up the story about her father, and that there really had been no pilot, no hero. I thought that she had probably just wanted things to be that way.

From where I stood, I could see the other half of the city; several construction cranes had risen up, probably building skyscrapers. The cranes were green and I wondered how people had motivated themselves to paint all those large pieces of iron, one by one.

"Hey," someone shouted behind me. I thought it was the pianist from the café, since I hadn't gone very far yet. "Stop."

I turned around. It was the waiter.

"You forgot your change," he said.

"I haven't forgotten it, that's your tip," I said.

"What tip?"

"For your service."

"But I hadn't asked you to pay for service; that's free."

"I know, but that's my way of saying thank you."

The waiter knew very well what a tip was, he simply didn't want to accept this one.

"This is a large sum of money; you could pay for another meal with this," he said.

"That's okay. Take it, in exchange for the warm treatment you gave us."

"My warm treatment is not for sale," he said. It was a matter of honor for him.

"How can I express my gratitude then?" I asked.

"What for?"

"For the fact that you served us with warmth and consideration."

"Say thank you."

"That's it?"

"Yes. Give this money to your mother; she probably needs it more than I do."

"She isn't my mother. She's a flower seller. There's a small stand on the other side of that street; that woman sells flowers there."

"Sorry," the waiter said, blushing. "I thought she was your mother and that your father was a white man, and that you hadn't seen your mother for many years, so you'd decided to come back and finally give her a hug."

"Really?"

"Yes. Sorry about that."

"No need to be sorry. I make mistakes like that, too, sometimes. Did we give the impression of being that close?"

"Yes, I even felt certain that you hadn't seen each other for many years."

"How many?"

"Seven."

"That long?"

"Yes."

The waiter put the money in my pocket and walked away slowly, his steps ridden with guilt.

"Are you an Angolan?" I shouted after him.

"Yes."

"What war took place here?" I asked.

"When?"

"Several decades ago; I can't say which year exactly."

"I don't know; the World War, I guess. Although… I don't know."

"What about after that?"

"I can't say. I'm too young; I don't know."

I walked along Rua Paralela, I hung my head down low and did not want to look up. Something was getting me down, but I couldn't understand what. I had to go back to the hotel, because the time had come to leave colorful Luanda. I saw a beggar in front of the hotel, although he was the first one I'd seen all day. He looked at me and smiled like a cactus.

"Do you need money?" I asked.

He didn't understand me. He had used some rope to hang a piece of cardboard around his neck; it had some Portuguese writing on it. It probably said that he needed money for food. One of his legs had been amputated, and the text probably mentioned this, too. He was old and had a white beard, but he seemed very absent-minded, which is perhaps why I had compared his smile to a cactus. The old man shook the piece of cardboard hanging on his chest several times, trying to get my attention, but I couldn't understand what it said.

"I speak English; do you know any English?" I asked and gave him a few coins.

He nodded his thanks and took out a modern remote control from the bag that lay next to him. I'd seen things like that in toy stores; they were used to drive toy cars. The remote control was somewhat large, and I couldn't understand what it was for. I heard a ringing behind me a little while later, and the bicycle I had come to know so well zoomed by. It stopped, turned around, and rode up to the old man. The old man picked up his bag, reached toward the handlebar, and asked for my help. He somehow managed to get on the bicycle, after which he pressed on the remote control. The bicycle left. I'd never seen a remote-controlled bicycle before. Perhaps he'd made it himself, and his cardboard sign had mentioned it; perhaps he had fought in the war, too, like the flower seller's father.

I saw many people with disabilities in Angola, especially middle-aged men. I thought that the old man may have been an inventor and was collecting money to make some new device. I walked into the hotel and immediately asked the doorman about the old man and his bicycle.

"No. I don't know him," the doorman replied rudely.

"He'd been standing there for hours; he probably stands there every day. He has a white bicycle," I said.

"No, I haven't seen him. You haven't paid for your room yet."

"Yes, I'll pay. I didn't have cash in the morning. I'll pay now."

"That's not the way we do things; this is wrong. If someone occupies a room, they're supposed to pay on time. If they can't, they should be so kind as to leave the hotel."

I had forgotten to pay. It was my mistake. For some reason, I'd decided in the morning to take a walk before coming back to pay. But I'd forgotten that I had to return early from my walk, and I'd only come back in the evening.

"It's five o'clock," the doorman said.

"I know, I'll pay now."

"No need. We've taken your things out of the room. We've given your room to someone else."

"Who?"

"What difference does it make? You weren't here on time. We thought you'd slipped away."

"What about the things I'd left here?"

"It doesn't matter. They could have belonged to someone else. We have certain conditions; everyone is supposed to comply."

"So, you don't want me to pay now?"

"Pay for what? For the fact that a notebook and two pens were lying in one of our rooms for four hours?"

"And a bag."

"No. Don't pay."

"Do you know anything about the old man?" I asked again.

"What old man?"

"The one I told you about a few minutes ago. He has a bicycle with a remote control."

"Ah, yes," he said, as if remembering. "I know him. But I don't remember him having a bicycle. He's probably a drunk. He often begs for money. He'd probably been involved in criminal activities before, and has been in prison for a few years, where he caught some disease and had to have his leg amputated. Now he doesn't have a family. He has nothing. He's probably a drunk."

"Probably?"

"Yes."

"Thank you," I said.

"What for?"

"For not throwing my things away," I said. I left the hotel and was about to make my way to the airport, when the Portuguese, or rather the "French" family appeared in front of me—the man, the woman, and the little child, whose pocket was lined with traces of ice cream. He had removed all the petals from the flowers and wore them in his hair.

"Hello," I said.

"Hello," said the husband.

He was a bit surprised; he had been startled when I began speaking to him.

"Hello," the wife said, smiling.

"How's your son?" I asked.

They looked at each other and replied in unison, smiling. "Good."

"A happy future lies in store for him, doesn't it?" I asked.

"Yes," the man said anxiously; the envelope in his pocket now looked twice as thin as before.

"Why do you ask?" the wife asked, fearfully.

"He'll go to good schools, become a good man, and have a great future," I said.

"Thank you," the husband said. "Thank you for the good wishes. But why are you saying all this?"

"Just because. I hope that your son will come back here someday and remember Luanda."

"Really? Why? Why should he remember it? What is there to remember here?"

"He'll remember it, for sure; he'll remember some things," the wife said. "Especially how he stole the flowers."

"Don't be too hard on him, he's still small. He didn't know what he was doing. He looks like he'll be a great person," I said.

"Thank you, we're very grateful," the husband said.

"I saw you when you were buying flowers from that woman. I was there, near your son, and saw how kindly you spoke to him."

"Really? That's nice," the husband said somewhat absent-mindedly, not understanding why I had mentioned this.

"Shall we go to our room?" the woman interrupted, probably thinking that I was behaving strangely.

"I know that you knew the flower seller's father. She told me. But I forgot to ask which war he had fought in."

"What?" The husband looked at me in surprise.

"Georges, I'm going," the wife said. "Fabien, come here," she called to the boy.

"What war? What woman? What father?" the husband asked.

"The flower seller told me."

"What did she tell you?" he asked rudely.

"Aren't you Portuguese? Haven't you come here to adopt that child?"

"No," he said with surprise, "She must have imagined all that, or perhaps that was how she had wanted things to be. Excuse me, I have to go. Fabien isn't well, and we need a doctor."

Fabien had probably had too much ice cream, or perhaps he'd caught a cold, and that was why he was ill, although I couldn't rule out that the flowers had been poisonous.[53]

---

53. The Civil War in Angola began in 1975 and ended in 2002. It was one of the longest wars in history, lasting for over twenty-seven years. Various sources place the number of casualties at around half a million people, with tens of thousands forced to leave their homes.

As for the cause of the Civil War, different people have imagined different things…

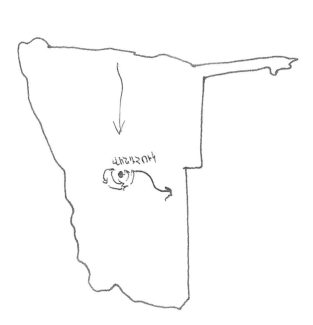

DAY 48. NAMIBIA
THE DIAMONDS

"Windhoek, this is Windhoek," the first man I met said simply and warmly. He seemed just as sincere to me as the mountains behind him. He had a Mexican sombrero on his head that covered his face in shadow. He looked at me and was filled with a desire to speak.

"Are you looking for Windhoek?" he asked.

"I'm not looking for it," I replied.

"This is Windhoek," he said, smiling.

"I know."

"This is Windhoek," he repeated. "I was born here."

"I don't know anything about you," I said.

"But you were looking for me, weren't you? Isn't that so?"

"Yes, of course," I said cynically.

"Do you know me?" he asked. His hands trembled.

"No. I don't know you."

"Not at all?"

"No."

"That's bad, isn't it? It's bad that people don't know each other."

"Yes," I said.

"Are you well off?"

"I don't know."

"Neither do I. It amazes me how people can decide what it means to be well off, and what it means to not be. It's impossible to know. That's what I think."

"Who are you?"

"Excuse me, I didn't introduce myself."

If I'd walked back another meter, I would have ended up in a gorge. I had stepped outside a few moments ago and had happened upon the courtyard of a factory after walking past several intersections. It was an abandoned spot; all the windows were dirty and cracked, there was paint on the walls—graffiti, some of the windows had bars, and something was moving intermittently in one of the upper windows, like a mill. We were standing at the mouth of a gorge and it seemed to me like he was going to throw me down there at any minute. But his eyes looked miserable, as did the bicycle abandoned in the distance, and he had a kind look on his face.

"My name is John Sebastian Hitzfielder. You can call me John. It's a fake name; I don't know what I'm really called. I don't know who my parents are, I don't remember them. When I think about that, I get a headache. It's like thinking about where this hat came from."

"You don't know?"

"I found it."

"Don't you have a home?"

"No. I live here. This huge building is my home."

"What is it?"

"I don't know. I guess it was a factory. You can't tell now. I don't know what this building contains. It's huge. One room is enough for me."

I was sure that the room with the mill was his.

"That's my room over there, do you see it?"

"What's that moving in it?"

"I've put some wet clothes on the fan."

"There's nobody else here?"

"No. This is the most distant place that is close to the city."

"What's that supposed to mean?"

"The closest hiding place."

"In what sense?"

He looked at me with surprise. "Forget about it."

"It took me only a few minutes to get here," I said.

"But why did you come?"

"I don't know. I just wanted to walk, to think. I was looking for a place where I could escape the city noise."

"And you found it," he interrupted, "because many people feel attracted to this place. People want to escape everything, so they come here and speak their minds. Sometimes they're sad, sometimes desperate, sometimes lost in thought, and sometimes they come here and try to throw themselves off from this very spot. This is where people lose themselves."

"Who are you?"

"Me? A street rat who has a bicycle, a room in a huge building, and a few metal cups."

"Are you following me?"

"No."

"You look different now."

"Really?"

"Yes. A few seconds ago, you looked like the kindest man in the world."

"Why? Because I was silent?"

"No."

"Perhaps you'd liked my hat?"

"No. But you looked simple."

"Like I'd come down from heaven?"

"No. But now I feel aggression in your words—as if you're this close to killing everyone."

"Why?"

"You seem cold-hearted, as if nothing's happened."

"But what has happened?"

"I've got to go," I said.

"You're behaving like a girl."

"Why?"

"You don't even want to have a cup of tea with me," he said.

"I'd better go."

"Why? Were you looking for someone else?"

"I don't understand."

"Everyone's always looking for someone. Isn't that so?"

"What do you mean?"

"Forget about it. I like playing mind games with people. I'm pretty good at it, huh?"

John Sebastian Hitzfielder was at least thirty years old. He was white. He had narrow eyes and thick lips. He was unshaved and his face was wet. He had black hair. I had the feeling that something could happen here which would put an end to my travels. I was so close to finishing the journey, all it would take was another meter backwards and I would end up at the bottom.

"I'm a kind man; you noticed correctly. I'm the kindest man in the world. And the kindest man in the world is inviting you over to his place. Will you come?"

"Why?"

"We'll talk."

"I've got to go."

"Why?"

"I don't want to stay."

"Don't be scared," he said. "Writers are always scared, aren't they?"

"You know me?"

"No."

"How did you know I'm a writer?"

"Only someone writing about Africa would come here and then not know what to do. I assumed."

We walked towards the building.

"That used to be a pool. Over there, there used to be a small playground. I've gone swimming there," he said.

John was drunk. I realized this for the first time when the wind blew from his side and then once again when he fell on the stairs, like the American who rolled down the stairs at the guesthouse in Lusaka. We were in his room. He took out a half-liter bottle from this pants pocket and raised it to his lips. I don't know what was in the bottle, but it smelled of alcohol. His room was not very dirty. His face looked familiar, but I couldn't remember where I'd seen him. John lay down on the bed. There was a chair in the room, a fan, and a small set of drawers, but the right corner of the room was a mess of items where one could find anything one imagined.

"Have I seen you before?" I asked.

"No," he shouted and covered his head with a pillow.

"Your face looks familiar."

"Does it? We met in Germany; do you remember the Berlin Wall? We were there…1989, wasn't it? We were drinking beer together and celebrating victory?"

"What are you talking about?"

"You don't remember?"

"No."

"How would you remember? You weren't there," he laughed. "Do you know why you're not leaving? Because I'm interesting. When you came to the factory and looked awestruck at the windows with bars, I saw the fear in your eyes."

"So what?"

"So I understood that everyone feels fear," he said, and rolled over in his bed. "Everyone feels the same thing. The color of your skin doesn't matter, a sad man doesn't care about his ethnic background. He just wants to cry and cry. You hate me, don't you?"

"No. We're strangers."

"But I'm unpleasant. You're thinking 'Who is this idiot, blabbering foolishly when he's drunk?' Why did you come? Answer me."

"Where?"

"Here."

"You know why. You said yourself, didn't you, that I'm a writer?"

"I mean why did you come to me?"

"I didn't come to you."

"Are you sure?"

"Yes."

"I could've sworn that you were looking for someone to talk to. You looked so terrified. When you entered the factory, your face was completely red," he said.

"Yes, but I don't want to talk about that."

"I forgot to offer you something. Wait here," he said, and got up.

"No need."

"When you walked up to me, I realized that your heart was pounding and I said, 'Windhoek, this is Windhoek.' I thought you were lost, that you needed help. Green tea?"

"No, I don't want any tea."

"I wanted to help you. But it wasn't confusion in your eyes; you were scared. I saw fear there, as if someone had been killed in front of your very eyes a few moments earlier. I'm right, aren't I?"

"I don't want to talk about it," I said. "I've got to go."

"Where? Stay. I have a confession to make. What do you think—is there anyone better to confess to than a total stranger? A total stranger is the most sacred of them all. Do you know why?"

"Why?"

"Because he doesn't care about you. And that thought forces me to be more honest. Look at me," he shouted.

"I'm looking."

"What do I look like?"

"A man."

"What kind of man—am I good, or bad?"

"I don't know; that's a very strange question."

"Could I be an angel, helping people, or is it only murder that seems to suit me?"

"I don't know."

"Take your tea."

"I don't drink tea."

"Why, does it disgust you?"

"No."

"You see? I'm unpleasant, I don't look like a good man."

John's speech was full of pathos, as if he was an actor on stage, performing his final monologue before committing suicide.

"Tell me, can a person be forgiven?" he asked.

"I don't know."

"If I were Black, would you respect me, or pity me? Be honest." He struck me on the shoulder with his hand and the teacup nearly flew out of my grip.

"I don't see any difference."

"Why? Are they any good? Tell me. They have to be much better for you not to see a difference. Isn't that so?" He took a small stone from his pocket; it looked like a diamond.

"No."

"Why are you looking at me like a ghost? As if you're looking for something mystical or magical? Do you know that there is nothing more magical than reality? Isn't that the whole point of life—this small piece of rock for which people are willing to kill each other? But it has no value now. Do you know why people make up magical and mystical things?"

"Why?"

"So that they don't lose their minds. Otherwise, reality would seem too horrible. They need a fairy tale. I've killed someone; do you understand? I've killed someone."

"When?"

"What does it matter? Do you care at all about what I'm saying?"

"No."

"I'd never killed anyone before. There were times when I'd shot at someone, or robbed them, but I've never killed anyone, I swear. When I saw you, I thought you'd come to get me, I thought you'd come to take me away. I thought you were my angel, but when you cynically said that you were looking for me, I realized that you were a person just like me. There was no angel."

"Do you regret it?"

"The murder?"

"Yes."

John stood up and turned off the fan; he removed the clothing and put it on. He sat down and started to smoke. I popped my head out of the window. Outside, there were police cars a few streets away. I sat on the bed. He stopped smoking and then turned the fan back on, turning it in the direction of the smoke.

"I regret being born. In reality, had I not been born, nothing would have changed. Tell me: would you, for example, feel any sorrow in knowing that a woman or child in a village somewhere in the villages of the Philippines had not been born?"

"I don't know," I said.

"Of course you wouldn't. Why would that make you sad? As long as you don't know that person, they don't exist in your mind. They're dead, because a person is truly born at the moment when they are known. Nobody knows me. I have nothing." He drank again.

"Have you always lived here?"

"Yes. But I don't remember how long it has been. I've always wanted to be loved. But I've never been loved. Why would I be loved?"

"Don't you know anyone here?"

"I know some, but only those who need me, not the ones I need. I know the criminals, the swindlers, the murderers, the bad people. And if you're a stranger to everyone and you have nothing, then you would make a great criminal."

"What are you drinking?"

"I don't know, I've mixed some things together. I've been promised a house and some money. I've been promised a way out, finally, of this factory. But it's too late. Because I'm weak, I managed to achieve this only after committing a murder. That's the truth. If I were to be born again, I would want to be one of the bad guys."

"Why?"

"I would commit suicide, and the number of bad guys would go down by one."

I realized then that the man I was speaking to was a murderer. I was in the room of a murderer who had taken a gun in his hand and was speaking with great emotion. His voice kept growing softer. The sounds of police sirens grew louder. The fan wasn't working well; the smoke had gone closer to the window but did not want to leave the room. John Sebastian Hitzfielder would commit suicide a few minutes later. He would pick up his yellowed pillow, cover his face with it and scream, asking me to leave him, threatening to kill me as well if I didn't leave the room, and I would go down the stairs with my eyes closed, trying not to see the pillow feathers flying out of his room.

The shot rang out; I was in a beautiful city that had a small number of people, but everyone looked kind. Windhoek did not seem very large; I saw a beautiful church there, a Lutheran structure, that had a statue of a horseman in front of it. It was a gothic church and looked wonderful. I walked along Freedom Avenue, which had many buildings, and spent some time in the city center. I saw the Kudu Statue.

ഇ൦ങ

I was still lost in thought regarding Angola. I had just arrived in Windhoek and everything seemed wonderful. I recalled all the countries I had visited and felt a unique sorrow. At one point, I felt a great desire to not return home at all, especially when I remembered the pig farmer in the DRC. I felt the urge to quit everything and go back there to his place. But not just yet; I still had a few countries to visit and a few more smiling people to see. I had to make it in time to love everyone, and perhaps only after that I could go back to the pig farmer.

I was in Windhoek, the capital of Namibia. Actually, I was a short distance away from it already, because the tourist bus was headed to a suburb of Windhoek, where some diamond mines were located. Everyone in the bus was from England. They had come as tourists and wanted to see the beautiful sights. Namibia was of great interest to them, especially the diamond mines. Many of them had small cameras in their hands, which they held up to their left and to their right, taking pictures of everything, even me.

"My name's Steven," the man sitting in front of me said as he held his camera to my face. "We're going to see some diamonds, aren't we?" He was looking at me through the lens of his camera and moving his hand anxiously, signaling that I should speak.

"Yes," I said, smiling.

"Would you like for all the diamonds in the mines to be yours?"

"No," I said.

"What a strange man," he said to himself, the camera still pointing at my face. "I would like that."

We arrived. I separated from them. The white, freshly washed minibus and the tourists inside it were of no interest to me. There were a few huge trucks in the distance, some tractors, and some people. Next to them, there were a few manually excavated mines, or rather, pits. There were also some houses there, where the diamond miners lived.

I was watching from above and all of this was not really very close. I was forced to traverse the rocky and muddy road on foot. Everything seemed much more spread out below. The mines and living quarters were on one side, while the pits that I had seen were in a completely separate area. I walked up to one of the houses. At first, I had no desire to go in. I was just walking past it. But everything changed when I walked around to the other side of the house, where the entrance was, and I read the announcement on the door: "Dear tourists, if you wish to do so, you're invited to throw a few coins into the box near the door. I would be very grateful to you. Even if you don't help me, but you read this note, I will still be grateful. Respectfully yours, Moby."

There was no box near the door. I walked around the house three or four times, but couldn't find anything. The thing that interested me the most was finding out who Moby was. I knocked on the door.

"Who is it?" someone shouted from inside with a raspy voice. I thought that it sounded like an old man past sixty, with white hair, lying on a bed with his head on his pillow and no desire to come to the door.

"May I come in?" I asked.

"Who is it?"

"I can't find the box."

"Look again."

"I really can't find it."

"How could it not be there?"

"I've looked everywhere."

"All right, hang on," he said, and he came to the door and opened it.

We were in his room.

"So they've stolen it."

"Yes."

"I wonder how much money there was inside."

"I don't know," I said.

"Wasn't there anyone around?"

"No. Some people came with me, but they headed off in the opposite direction."

Moby was barely past thirty. He hadn't been sleeping, nor did he have white hair. He did not speak clearly, or rather, he spoke in a dialect, and it was very difficult to understand him.

"Why have they come here?" he asked.

"They're tourists. They probably came for the diamonds."

"Yes," he smirked. "I'm asking stupid questions. What about you?"

"I don't know. I came to see."

"Me?"

"Everyone."

"That's good." He settled down in his chair. "Would you like something?"

His house was very small, it was like a wagon. There were very few items inside that seemed unfamiliar to me. They were mainly work tools. Looking at Moby, one could assume that he worked in the mines. He lived alone and in poverty in that house. But he always smiled when I asked him a question or made a joke.

"Did I bother you?" I asked.

"No. I was watching television. On the contrary, it's good that there's someone with me; I'm tired of sitting here alone."

I looked at him in surprise.

"What's wrong?" he asked.

"There's no television here."

"I know. But I've made one up. Look out that window. There are foreign miners there. They collect truckloads of diamonds. And I watch them. How's that for a television?"

"Not bad," I laughed.

"I have only one channel, but that's enough; it has several programs. For example, there are shows about how the trucks come out of the mines at night and go back in during the day. Or about how the foreigners argue with each other. I sit on my chair and watch."

"Why do they argue?"

"They don't like each other." he said. He was quiet, then asked, "How much were you planning on giving?"

"A few cents. But the box isn't there."

"So you won't give anything?" he asked anxiously.

"I'll give the coins. But they won't help, will they?"

"Help what?"

"You."

"That's okay, give me the money. I'm not begging or anything, but my salary is too low. It's not enough to live on."

I gave Moby the coins. The room grew darker as a car parked in front of the window. I was surprised that it had managed to drive down that rocky road.

"My television is out of order," Moby said. "Let me go see who that is."

He returned a few seconds later.

"Somebody was asking if I was home," he said.

"Why?"

"I don't know, that's all they said."

"You didn't ask why?"

"No. I guess they were just checking up on me. This has happened before. They don't like it when I leave the house."

"Why?"

"It bothers them. This is private property and I'm supposed to be an employee. But you know how I'm paid?"

"How?"

"By being allowed to live here. You probably saw the small pits. I dug those, with my hands and a spade—these are my tools. Look around you, there are huge mines every-where, diamond mines, millions of carats that are worth billions. I'm sitting in the middle of it all, and I'm going hungry. What do I care that a foreigner makes several thousand from that piece of rock? All I want to do is live. I cast aside sand every day, I dig in the same spot to find a few pieces of diamond, but they grab it away from me. They give me small pieces of gravel and say that they are diamonds. But everyone knows that this is not the truth. I work on a rock for several days, transforming it into a precious stone, and they throw a few cents my way in return, telling me to live and be happy that I'm not killed. They'll cover these pits soon and I won't have a place to work."

"Who are they?"

"People, regular people," he said, then he changed the topic abruptly. "What's life like in the better part of the world? Are there many Namibian diamonds there?"

"I don't know. I guess so. I don't know much about diamonds."

"I have to know a lot about them. What worries me the most is human greed. They've grabbed everything in their own hands and aren't allowing anyone else to have any of it. What fault is it of mine that I was born here? Imagine a cow being born in a field where there are thousands of hectares of grass, but she isn't allowed to eat any of it and is told that none of it is hers."

Moby spoke in a very sad voice. He was afraid and offended; someone had oppressed and scared him. There was a shiver in Moby's facial expression. He did not look away from his television.

"Is there anyone else like you around here?"

"I don't think so. There might be some in the other sections. But there are many people in the same situation, of course. They're not loved at all. Like me, they're digging somewhere, and they're looking for rocks in a sieve day and night. But, in the end, they sell what they find practically for free, otherwise they could be hunted down at any instant."

"Can one piece of rock solve so many problems?"

"Of course. But we don't even see its dust."

"Are the people who work here also in the same situation as you?"

"No. They're contracted foreign workers. They get their pay. We're not in the same situation; we face different conditions. I have a rock," he said enthusiastically. "Let me show you." He got up, opened a metallic box that was hidden behind the wall and took out a small diamond from within it. His hands were trembling, "Look, I found this. I don't know how it had ended up in the soil; it looks like it's been cut. It might be two or three carats. It has a magical value. I take it out every day, polish it, then put it back in the box. Beautiful, isn't it?"

"Yes. Why don't you sell it? Sell it and get out of here."

He looked at me.

"Sell it to whom?" he asked. "I know that it's worth a lot, but I don't need it to provide me with money; it's priceless to me. It's only for me to look at. Even if I'd found a diamond the size of a potato, all they would have said to me would be, 'Be grateful you're being allowed to live.'"

"Why don't you just go?"

"Go where?"

"Somewhere else."

"There are no diamonds anywhere else. What would I do there?"

Moby sat down. I didn't want to ask too many questions, although I felt like he wanted to talk. When I was preparing to leave, the small car once again came and blocked the window. I realized that it was better for me to just go.

"Wait," Moby called after me.

"What?" I asked.

"Tell everyone about me. Let people know that a diamond is not as valuable a thing as they think."

They called Moby again from inside that strange car. They saw his metal box. Moby waved at me and I left.

They would kill him a few minutes later; they would take him to one of the pits dug behind the house and they would shoot him in the head three times. They would take the metal box and cover him up with soil. Meanwhile, I would be running up the hill, my eyes closed, ready to get into any car that happened by and head back to the city. I would stop on the way, catch my breath, then keep going.

The shot rang out. I was no longer in the diamond mine. There were huge windows with bars in front of me. My body was covered in goosebumps. After crossing several intersections, I'd ended up at that strange place where there was a huge building, a swimming pool, and a gorge in the distance. My legs were trembling. I was scared. I'd never been this scared, and I'd never seen anyone who was scared of being alive. A bicycle lay on the ground beneath a wall, and a stranger stood in the distance, walking towards me with slow steps, a large Mexican sombrero on his head. The stranger walked up to me and said, "Windhoek, this is Windhoek."

DAY 49. BOTSWANA
THOSE BURIED BENEATH THE KALAHARI

Everything changed in the Kalahari Desert. I lost myself for a moment. I began to see things as though through a fog in the distance, and the yellow sand beneath my feet was delicate and soft like snow. It was probably no coincidence that this path was like an obstacle or yet another hurdle that I had to overcome. The thought that I was searching for something kept guiding me, but I felt fear on top of that: a feeling that everything could turn upside down in just a minute.

This beautiful country, which is huge in size (almost 581.7 square kilometers) but very small in population (around two and a half million in 2021), greeted me with lizards, women in colorful clothing, and a huge cactus that I saw in the center of Gaborone, the capital. It wasn't real—when I looked at it up close, it turned out to be a display for one of the cafés nearby. That disappointed me; I would have given anything to see a real cactus there.

"It's tasty, you can eat it," I heard a voice say. And as had often happened before, I turned around and started in surprise.

"What?"

"It's tasty, eat it," said the man, who was probably past fifty. His skin was darkened from the sun, but I wasn't sure that he was Black. He had an apron on and a tray in his hands.

"I thought you were talking about the cactus," I said.

"I *am* talking about the cactus," he said. He removed a piece of cloth from the tray. "It's fresh."

"Is it cactus?"

"Yes. It's hot; try it. My treat."

"I've never eaten cactus before."

"I know—it's natural, don't worry about it. Everyone here has had some; this is a special offer. I'm a waiter in this café, and we have an amazing offer today. We're treating everyone to cactus for free!"

"Is it good?"

He smiled that characteristic African smile and took one of the pieces of cactus, which must have been ten-to-fifteen centimeters long, and put it on my lap.

"Where do you get cactuses from?" I asked.

"We grow these cactuses specially; these are not regular cactuses. If you want to see these giants close up, you have to go to the Kalahari Desert; perhaps you can see them there. But I wouldn't recommend it, because you won't see anything there besides dry desert and yellowish-red sand. It would be better for you to step inside our restaurant; we have some delicious dishes."

I was in the Kalahari Desert. From the beginning of my journey, I had dreamed of being in the desert and, although I had spent some time there in Mauritania, Chad, and other countries, the Kalahari was something completely different. There was nothing there, but when I looked, it was as if I was seeing the whole of Botswana's history in front of me. I had read on a website that there was nothing to see there besides grey lions, yellowish-red sand, cactuses, and reptiles. But I saw none of that—although the sand was indeed red in some parts, it looked nothing like the pictures I had seen online. The first incident happened at the very moment when I heard a rooster crowing; the sand rocked and spun in a vortex beneath me, pulling me down like quicksand. I was drowned in sand for the first time in my life. I thought my breathing would stop but a few moments later I had ended up in a dark space, like a cave or perhaps a bomb shelter. How could such a place exist beneath the desert? I remembered the history of the Egyptian caves for a moment, but this was something completely different. This shelter was not visible from above, and inside it there was only darkness. Everything became even weirder when I met a man who had wrapped some cloth around his whole body and looked at me in fear.

"Where are we?" I asked the stranger.

"My house," he said.

"How did I end up here?"

"You stood on slipping sand, it swallowed you up, and you sunk down here to me."

"How come the sand doesn't pour in here?"

"I don't know; it's magic."

"There's no light here, but I can see you. How do you get the air from above to enter here?"

"I don't know."

"How can I get out of here?" I asked.

"Why would you want to?"

"It's dangerous here."

"It's dangerous *there*. There's nothing to fear here."

The stranger had extremely Black skin; he had curled up and looked upwards as he spoke.

"What is up there?" he asked.

"I haven't seen anything yet."

"Are there any living beings?"

"I don't know. I came here to find cactuses. They say that this is where the biggest cactuses can be found."

"You should have gone to Mexico," he laughed. "There's nothing here. This is no place to live."

"Why not?"

"Because there is everything, but nobody knows about it."

"First you said that there is nothing, now you're saying that there is everything."

"Because nobody knows about it. People don't see what there is, they see what they want. Do you know why I'm here?"

"No."

"I'm angry with my cows. They had left to graze and were supposed to return in the evening. It's been several weeks, but they haven't come back yet. First, I thought the gray lions had gotten them, but there were no traces to be seen. I was very upset; I thought they'd cheated on me, that they didn't want to live with me. That's why I'm upset with everyone. I've come here and I don't plan on ever going back up. What matters to me is their happiness, but they never had any sense of appreciation. How can I look them in the eye after all this and smile? They don't deserve my respect."

"How many cows were they?"

"Two."

"Oh. I thought it was a huge herd."

"What difference does it make? If one of them betrays you, you can still find a way to come to terms with that. But all of them? No. The number doesn't make a difference in this case."

"But there is no grass here."

"I know. That's probably why they left."

"Are there any cows in the Kalahari?"

"It was just those two. I don't know now. But it's not the cows that bother me."

"What is it then?"

"The fact that nobody wants to believe what they don't see. Everyone thinks that only what you see can be real. But just like this shelter of mine, there are billions of things in this world that you can't see from above, but when you're inside them you can see the outside."

"When I came here, I heard a rooster crowing."

"You heard that? Wonderful. That rooster is so that I know when I have guests. I thought for a moment that it was my cows."

"Where does that sound come from?"

"From the same place where the biggest cactuses can be seen."

"Which is?"

He looked at me like I was supposed to understand what he was saying. Then he said cynically, "You don't believe your dreams."

"Why?" I asked.

"Before you stands a miserable man who has wrapped himself up in his bedsheets and is telling outrageous stories, while instead you were supposed to be in a beautiful place. Isn't that so?"

"No."

"That look on your face tells me otherwise. But it's not your fault."

"Aren't there any cactuses here?" I asked.

"There is nothing here. You are in a deserted place where there is nothing."

"How can I get out of here?"

"Turn around three times and you'll be up there again."

I turned. He laughed as I did so.

"People always believe the most incredible things only when they are in a difficult situation. Why is that? If I'd told you that you had to swallow several handfuls of sand, you would have done so, wouldn't you? But you didn't believe the stories about the cows."

"How can I get out of here?"

"Spin around again and you'll be up there."

This time he was right. I turned around three times and appeared in the desert again. The sun had occupied half the sky and the cactuses were nowhere to be seen.

That was the end of the first incident, but the second one began immediately afterwards. This time there was no rooster crowing and nobody said anything, but the sand once again started bouncing like a spring and I ended up below it. I was in a small cell again. Once more, there was somebody there.

"Who's there?" he shouted and got up from his bed.

He was wearing a golden garment. He had a large belly and a humped back. There were some pictures in one corner of the cell; they were in the shadows. In the other corner, there were two cows. They had metallic rings on their necks. The cows were standing very close to each other and one of them was licking the sand.

"Sorry to bother you," I said. "It's not my fault; the sand brought me here. I slipped through and ended up here."

"Who are you? I was sleeping, and you came in without warning." The stranger covered his hairy abdomen and smiled as he walked up to me. "Sit on the sand. What would you like?"

"Where am I?"

"In my home."

"You live here?" I asked.

"Yes; is it a bad place? It's cool, quiet, and you can sleep the whole day. Relax. I have a small office here. What matters is that nobody knows about this place."

"Why?"

"They won't ask how I came to have it. I feel safe here. I have everything, while those who have nothing are jealous and think that people like me are criminals, but we're trying to live like they do. We can't live with dreams; this is reality—this cell of sand located under the desert."

"But what about sunlight? Air?"

"I have a special device up there that is like a filter. It catches the air and pushes it downwards, like an air conditioner. Light? Why would I need light? There is electricity here. This is my planet, where you can do whatever you like and nobody will know about it. Good, right?"

"Where are the cows from?"

"What? Oh, the cows? I bought them. I'm very rich, but there's no need for everyone to know that."

"There's someone else here who lives like you do. He also has a shelter beneath the desert."

"Who is it?" he asked, startled. "Tell me, and I'll get my gun. Who has the right to live in my territory?"

He ran to the other room. I wanted to get out of there. I spun around several times, but it didn't work. I did somersaults, but then I realized that I had to find another way to get out of this shelter. Before he returned, I walked up to the cows. They looked like Chachagé's cows, but they didn't speak. They just looked at me sadly; one of them licked the sand indifferently with its huge tongue, while the other moved its tail and opened and closed its empty mouth.

"Where is he? Come, let's go and kill him."

He fired the gun. I instantly appeared above ground. From that moment on, I ceased to hear any gunfire. I tried to walk carefully, because I felt that there must be many spots with slipping sands and hidden shelters in the Kalahari.

It was difficult for me to say who the people I had just met were. I even thought that they were dead souls who had ended up beneath the sand for many centuries and had then started to speak out of boredom. But the gun that the second one held was a modern weapon, as were the metal wires that were used to tie the cows.

Suddenly, the sky darkened and a torrential rainfall began. I hadn't run under the hot rain in a long time. I could no longer distinguish reality from the unreal. The only question that really tormented me was: where were the giant cactuses?

The sand moved back and forth again, and I ended up in a pit. But it was different this time—I couldn't breathe, the sand assaulted my body on all sides, I was itching unbearably, the hot sand touched my feet and froze there like pieces of hail. A little later, I was in a cell again. There was someone there on this occasion as well. He was a young man, and had I not spoken with him, I would have taken him for a local. But like me, he too was lost.

"Have you been here a long time?" I asked.

"Very. A thousand years."

"Really?"

"Of course," he laughed. "Ten or fifteen minutes."

"I thought for a minute that this was your house."

"Of course it's my house," he said with sarcasm. "I was born and brought up in this hole. This is my favorite spot in life. My home. Well said. This isn't a home. This is hell. I've jumped up more than fifty times. But I can't manage to get out of here in any way. It's like being punished."

"What were you doing here?" I asked.

He held out his hand to the grains of sand and ran a finger over them, then he walked up to me. He gave me a cold stare. I noticed his white hair.

"I came to get some cactuses," he laughed. "Don't say you did the same thing."

"Yes, so did I. How did you know?" I asked.

"I don't know. But there are no cactuses here."

"I've walked several kilometers and I've found nothing."

"Where would you find them? They've all been eaten."

"By whom?" I asked.

"The gray lions."

"There are no gray lions anymore."

"They've all been eaten, too. Tell me how to get out of here," he said.

"Spin around three times and you'll end up on top," I said.

"Are you making fun of me?"

"No."

"How do you know?"

"It's magic."

He spun around three times and vanished. I was left alone. I made several attempts as well but couldn't get out. For almost an hour, I was spinning there in that pit and the air grew progressively thinner as I did so, while grains of sand kept pouring down on my head. I was trying to get out, but my situation was growing worse by the minute. Then, my feet went numb and I fell on my back onto the sand. I was shouting, but no sound came out. There was no light, no electricity, no air conditioner, no neighboring room.

Eventually, I managed to get out. I ended up not tasting death as a tractor lowered its scoop into the sand and picked up my body, like a dinosaur closing its mouth on me. I didn't even try to resist. I was above ground a few seconds later. No trace remained of the rain. Instead, three people surrounded me and were looking at me in shock. They had metal helmets on their heads.

I would have continued to stare at them for a long time, trying to understand who they were, but one of them came up to me and opened a metallic bottle. He thought that I must be thirsty, and that I would die if I didn't drink some water at that instant.

"Who are you? Why are you looking at me like that?"

"Water; drink some water now! Don't ask questions!"

"I'm not thirsty. What do you want?"

He had brought the bottle up to my lips and was now pressing hard. I held the rim of the bottle with my teeth, but he was trying to force it in with every ounce of strength he had.

"I'm not thirsty. Leave me alone."

"Drink it, drink it," the people standing behind him shouted.

"I don't want to, let me get up!" I pushed him back with all the strength I could muster with my hand. The bottle dropped and the water turned to vapor in a few seconds. "Who are you? Why are you looking at me like that? Did I do something wrong?'

"Yes."

"What?"

"What business did you have in the pits?"

"I don't know. You should know that better than me. I'm not a local. I don't know what traps the Kalahari holds. The fact that the sand here can slip out from under you and that there are pits every few meters—I didn't know any of this."

"What did you want from here?"

"I was looking for cactuses."

I realized that my response was absurd, to put it mildly. They smiled at each other.

"Did you find any?"

"No."

"Why do you want a cactus?"

"I wanted to see one. I'd heard that Botswana has the world's biggest cactuses. I'd decided to come here and look for them. I'm very interested in your country."

They liked what I was saying. One of them said to the other, "He's a serious guy. Yes, he probably knows what he's doing."

"He even managed to find the pits and enter them."

"Yes, very successfully."

"Yes."

"He's studied the place well; he can talk about everything there, then."

"Yes, the Europeans have found the right person to send."

I couldn't understand any of it.

"He probably pretended not to know who we were in the beginning, to not know the place. He asked some incomprehensible questions."

"Yes, that is the Europeans and their extra precautions; when they're afraid to reveal their intelligence, they pretend to be stupid."

"Yes. Now he wants to regain contact slowly. He's trying to make us talk."

"He wants to convince himself that we're doing our job well."

"Yes," said one, and he turned to me. "Now tell me, what are we supposed to do and how? We're waiting for you to tell us. You've been in all the cells and you'll have a correct assessment of the situation."

"What situation? What do you want? I was just walking around."

"I understand. But now that you've walked around, can you tell us something?"

"Tell you what?"

"We're waiting for your opinion," the other one said, "after which we have to continue our work."

"What opinion? I don't understand any of this."

"That's surprising."

"That's very surprising," the other one intervened. "It's as if you don't understand what we're talking about."

"Yes. I really don't understand what you're hinting at."

"Nobody's told you anything about us?"

"What were they supposed to have said?" I asked.

"About the construction?"

"No."

They looked at each other and then one of them, with a slightly softer voice, said, "We're builders. A European architect was supposed to come here, and he was supposed to draw the blueprints for our new restaurant. We were told that he would come, examine the progress we'd made, and say something. We were expecting him. A huge restaurant is going to be built here. These pits have been dug for cactuses. We've dug them in such a way that they can't be seen from the outside. It's a complicated technology. When you said you were looking for cactuses, we understood that you could be the person we were waiting for."

"But there are no living things here," I said. "There's nothing here, it's just some deserted place. Does it make sense to build a restaurant here?"

"It makes sense. You tell us this—are you the architect, or aren't you?"

"No. Does he have white hair?"

"Yes. Maybe."

"I was with him a little while ago, in a pit. He wanted to get out."

"And?"

"He did get out."

"How?"

"He spun around three times and disappeared."

They looked at me with suspicion and left.

"Wait," I shouted. "You didn't tell me how it makes sense to build a restaurant in such a faraway place. There's no water here, no roads, no natural landscape; who will your customers be?"

One of them turned around indifferently.

"The people living in the pits; the ones who believe in life."

It was evening. I was walking along the streets of Gaborone.

DAY 50. ZIMBABWE
A SMALL STORY FROM A MAN'S LIFE

"Come, come this way, this way. Hang on, Nozipa."

"He needs oxygen. Nozipa, Nozipa."

"Run this way; it's calmer here."

"How do you know?"

"There are no shots being fired."

"But there are wounded. I just saw some people who couldn't stand on their feet. They were barely managing to drag themselves using their arms. They were bleeding. There were more dead people."

"Bring him here, he's suffocating; he'll go into cardiac arrest, he needs air."

"But there are no ambulances here."

"I don't know; do something. He's losing too much blood."

"I know, John. You grab his feet, I'll take his arms—all together now—one, two, lift him up. Good, good. Take him. Mungosh, don't let your hands tremble."

"I can barely hold on, he's really heavy."

"That's okay, there's not much left to do. There's a doctor close by."

"How do you know?"

"There was a small kiosk in a yard here when I was small. When we went there, when we were up to no good, the vendor in the kiosk would always warn us to behave better, otherwise she'd call the doctor to come and give us an injection. That would scare us, and we'd leave."

"How old was he?"

"Who?"

"The doctor."

"I don't know; I never saw him."

"Has anybody seen him?"

"No. Stop, I can't go on; I'm out of breath. Let me rest a bit."

"There's no time. There may be some more wounded; we have to get them to a safe place as well. If we move this slowly, there won't be anyone left alive by evening time."

"Let John and Mungosh keep watch over them, while we go and find the doctor's house."

"I won't go. I'm scared. They might shoot."

"I'm scared, too."

"Mungosh, there's no time to protest; everyone's scared now. Go there and get things ready; we'll find the doctor and we'll come for the other wounded. Leave Nozipa with us."

"Fine."

"Shall we go?"

"Yes."

"Where's the kiosk?"

"What kiosk?"

"The one with the vendor who would frighten you."

"In the yard of that building in front of us."

"But that building isn't there anymore."

"What do you mean, it isn't there?"

"Yeah, it's not there. Lower Nozipa's foot from your shoulder and you'll see that there is no building in front of us."

"Maybe we're going the wrong way."

"No—there are no right or wrong ways here. There's only one direction in which we can go; the other ways are dangerous."

"What should we do?"

"I don't know. We can ask around."

"Whom?"

"Well, someone has to pass by here."

"At this hour? This city is in the middle of a war; who's going to just happen to pass by?"

"I don't know. What can I do? You were the one who decided that there's a doctor in this building; what do you want from me now? I listened to you."

"Don't shout, it's not my fault. I only heard about the doctor when playing as a kid, when we were down in that yard."

"Maybe the kiosk is still there?"

"So what if it is?"

"We'll ask the vendor. She'll remember you."

"Yes, but I was a kid then. She used to scare us like that then, but why would she scare us now?"

"I'm not saying that she'll scare us. I'm saying that we'll ask her whether or not there is a doctor."

"And what if she says no?"

"What if she isn't there at all? You're coming up with stupid ideas. It'd be better to leave Nozipa here and find the kiosk."

"Maybe you can stay, and I can go."

"No, I don't want to stay alone."

"Fine, let's go together. He's almost dead; we have to hurry. Let's run."

"Do you see anything?"

"No, there's too much smoke in the distance."

"Any armed men?"

"Doesn't look like it. If there are any, they'd be our boys."

"Haven't we gone past where the kiosk is supposed to be?"

"I don't know. I haven't seen it yet, anyway."

"Someone's coming. We have to ask him."

"Yes, he's old. He would probably know."

"He's walking so slowly. Let's go in his direction."

"Hello, sir."

"Hello."

"We're looking for a kiosk. It's supposed to be here somewhere."

"I'd come to this yard to play when I was a kid. Do you know where the kiosk is?"

"I don't remember."

"Think hard, the vendor was an old woman; everyone would be surprised that she managed to stay alive. I think her name was Tinashe... yes, Tinashe. You don't remember?"

"No."

"You don't remember a kiosk?"

"No."

"Maybe you'll recall the building opposite the kiosk?"

"If I can't remember the kiosk, how would I remember the building?"

"What are you doing here?"

"I left home and heard gunshots and noise, shouting—are we at war? I wanted to check. What are you doing here?"

"Us? We're looking for that kiosk. Or rather, a house. Or rather, the doctor who lives there."

"It's your lucky day, then. I'm a doctor."

"Really? Why didn't you say so earlier?"

"Did you ask?"

"Please, you have to help us, there are several wounded people; we've left them near the gas station. We need a safe place where the wounded can get medical assistance."

"Yes, but what is this fighting about? What's going on? Tell me something. I'll help, of course, but I need to know what's going on."

"You don't know?"

"No, of course not."

"Come, we'll tell you on the way. We have to run. Otherwise, the number of fatalities will go up."

"Let's run."

୨୦୯୧

I had just arrived in Harare, the capital of Zimbabwe. My memories were still fresh of the Kalahari Desert and the people who lived there. But on the streets of Harare, there were neither any cactus vendors, nor any cafés with cactus-shaped signs. Zimbabwe gave me complete freedom—it was as if I had become a witness to what had happened there, and at the same time it was as if I had seen nothing and left there like a blind man. It all began when I was walking through one of the poorer neighborhoods and a boy struck me in the head with a stone. When I turned to reprimand him, I saw him standing in front of me, apologizing.

"I didn't see you," the small boy said. He bent down low to pick up the stone, then walked away, backwards. "Sorry."

"You speak English?"

"Yes, so does my brother. But I speak it better."

"Why did you pick up that stone?"

"I'm playing. It's a game we've made up—I throw the stone in the air, my brother does the same, and we have to throw them in such a way for them to touch in the air. Whoever manages to do this, wins."

I remembered the pig farmer's game.

"Are you playing with your brother?"

"Yes. But he doesn't know how to play. This is his stone—instead of throwing it upwards, he threw it in your direction," he laughed.

There were gaps alternating with his teeth. Perhaps he was still losing his milk teeth.

"Why didn't he come to pick up his stone?"

"I told you, didn't I? He speaks worse English than I do," he said, laughing again.

The little boy had probably eaten chocolate.

"Would you introduce me to your brother?"

"Why do you want to meet him? People avoid him, even at school."

"Why?"

"He's…" he said, hesitating. "He's different from everyone else. He doesn't like playing this game."

Led by the child, we entered a yard where there were several women and some children. Most of the women were looking at me, mumbling in the Ndebele or Shona languages, while the kid, his belly thrust forward, was walking towards his brother, who was lying on a cot and staring at the sky. The colorful clothes hanging on a clothesline caught my eye.

"Hobo, get up," the little guy shouted. We hadn't yet reached the cot.

"His name is Hobo?" I asked.

"No; Alexander."

"So why are you calling him Hobo?"

"Because he looks like a Hobo."

"Do you know what a hobo is?"

"No, I don't know," he said, shaking his head. "It must mean something."

Hobo must have been ten years old; he was lying on his back and had closed his eyes.

"Get up, there's someone here who wants to meet you."

Hobo jumped up, looked at me and then laid back down in disappointment, as if he had been expecting someone else.

"Get up, this man has something to say to you."

"Let him say it," Hobo said.

"Hello, Hobo," I said.

"Hello."

"Your brother tells me you're an unusual boy."

"He isn't my brother; he's a bad boy."

"Why?"

"He forces me to play stupid games. As soon as I say no, he tells everyone I'm crazy or something, or that I've lost my mind or I know nothing."

"But he hasn't complained about you," I said.

"Impossible. I'm forced to play that stupid game every time, so that he doesn't tell the people at home who's stolen the chocolate."

"I don't understand."

"I apologized to this man on your behalf. You were the one who should've said sorry, and now you're blaming me?" the little child said.

"Weren't you the one who asked me to play with you? Otherwise, you'd tell our family at home that I had stolen the chocolate—even though both of us had eaten that chocolate."

"Well, you shouldn't have stolen it."

"But am I to blame if I wanted something sweet? What was I supposed to do?"

"You shouldn't have eaten any."

"But you ate some too, didn't you? You ate it and you also forced me to play with you. You aren't letting me think about more serious things."

Hobo spoke English quite well.

"What would you think about?"

"Serious things."

"Like what? How many years it'll take for you to be an adult?" the little guy said.

"You've always been stupid."

"This man has come specifically to talk to you, but you're lying there and ignoring him. That's not polite."

"You're seven years old. Who gave you the brains to decide what's polite and what's not? You only know how to throw stones."

"And you only know how to steal chocolate from others' shops."

"Why do you care, anyway? You can go and try to steal some, if you're brave enough. I'm a good person. My God won't punish me for one piece of chocolate."

"He will, and even if your God doesn't, my God will for sure. I'll tell my God to come at night and take you to the moon."

"Let him, that's even better. It's very pretty there."

"How do you know?"

"I've been there."

"See, I've been right all along. You're a weird guy, Hobo. There's no fun in either playing with you or speaking with you."

"You can call yourself Hobo. Keep your stupid names to yourself. I have a name."

"This man has come here to make your acquaintance. He finds you interesting, but you, for some reason, didn't even want to say hello to him."

"Where is that man? He's left already."

"What do you mean, he's left?"

"Yes. Look behind you. Where is he?"

"He's gone?"

"Yes. While you were discussing my theft, he got bored and left."

"But he'll come back to talk to you. Why'd he leave?"

"He left. You leave, too, and let me lie here in peace."

❧☙

"Where's Nozipa? We left him here, didn't we?"

"Yes, near this gas station."

"Has it blown up?"

"No, doctor. How was it supposed to blow up? Our friends returned so that they could bring the other wounded back, and we were looking for you in the meantime. We left Nozipa so we wouldn't have to carry him with us."

"He's gotten up and left."

"He couldn't have. The way you're talking, it's like you're not a doctor at all."

"Why couldn't he have left?'

"Because he'd been shot in the leg and he fell down from a height. He had several fractures for sure."

"He's right. He couldn't have run away."

"I didn't say he ran away. I said he left. Those are different things. He might have hidden himself somewhere out of fear. That can happen when someone finds himself in a very mentally challenging situation. He no longer feels any pain—the pain numbs—and he can do anything, even run, if he really wants to."

"It's interesting, isn't it? First there was no doctor to treat the wounded, now we have a doctor but no wounded."

"It's just our luck."

"What does luck have to do with it?"

"It's good one day, bad the other. It's black one day, white the other. Nothing to be surprised about."

"Nothing black over the past few days, only white."

"Coming back to your wounded friend, I hope he hasn't died. Young people have strong will power; they can overcome any problem at any moment. So, if someone really has the desire to do something, he will definitely succeed."

"We have great desire, but over the past few days, desire hasn't been enough. You have to fight in the name of everything dear to you. We have to fight for our sake, for our family's sakes; we have to fight and win."

"Let's find Nozipa first, then we'll come back to this."

"He's right, doctor. You go there. We'll find Nozipa. They need your help there more than we do. Some people have died, and there are many wounded. You have to get there quickly."

"But I'm a family doctor, what am I supposed to do there?"

"Go, go. For our sake, go and help with something. If we don't resist, no good will come of this."

"All right, I'll go. Don't shout, I understand. I'll go."

"We'll look for Nozipa and bring him there. Tell the boys that you're a doctor. If there are any other doctors, bring them there, too."

"Okay."

"He won't run away?"

"No. If he finds out that there are many victims, he might be very scared. But he's a doctor, isn't he? His job is to help people."

"But we need more people helping us. Just one doctor isn't enough."

"I'm not about to go back to the same place looking for a kiosk, if I can save several people's lives instead."

"All right, you've convinced me. Forget about the doctor, we have to find Nozipa and get back. Otherwise, we've abandoned the battlefield and are roaming about this way and that while our brothers are fighting on."

"There's one thing bothering me."

"What is it?"

"Why haven't the others come out?"

"I don't know. Do you blame them?"

"Yes. If everyone's fighting, then everyone should be a part of this."

"I don't blame them. They probably each have their own reasons. Not everyone thinks the way we do."

"But we have a purpose and are ready to sacrifice everything for it."

"Yes, but if someone doesn't shout or raise his weapon, it doesn't mean he isn't on our side. They are all with us, you can sure about that. Didn't you see how quickly the doctor agreed to help?"

"Look, there's someone coming. Run up to him; we have to ask him."

"Wait, wait, we have something to ask you."

"What is it?"

"Have you seen our friend? He's wounded; we'd left him here. Maybe you met him along the way?"

"He's tall, wounded in one leg, and had a yellow cap on his head. No, I think he had dropped the cap."

"If he's wounded, how was I supposed to have seen him? He's probably dead. Nobody lives a long life these days."

"He couldn't have died."

"Why not?"

"He had to live longer; he had to start a family. He couldn't have died."

"Don't talk about death in such a cold-hearted way. People have to live for their dreams and desires. He dreamed of starting a family, about having a home and children. Who are you to speak so indifferently about his death?"

"Calm down. I'm sorry, it didn't come out right. That's not what I wanted to say. It's just that there is no value put on a single life today; that's why I said that."

"Why aren't you going to fight?"

"Says who? I'm going."

"Well, good luck."

"What should I do if I see your wounded friend?"

"What should you do? What do you think you should do? Dig a hole and call us."

"Don't be so cruel. He could still be alive."

"Where is he, then? If he's alive, why can't we find him anywhere? We shouldn't have left him alone."

"Poor Nozipa, he's probably bled himself dry under a tree somewhere. He was probably calling out to us when he died."

"He'd be with us now if we hadn't gone to get that doctor."

"But now that we have a doctor in our group, he'll help the remaining wounded."

"At the cost of Nozipa's life?"

"Don't lose hope; we can find him yet."

"Where? Tell me! Do you believe what you're saying?"

"Yes. We were looking for a doctor and we found one, didn't we? We'll find him, too."

"I want to find my friend, not his dead body."

"Me too. Don't shout, I feel you. We have to keep looking for him at all costs."

"I'm going back."

"Why?"

"I'm going; that's that. I have to fight. I'm going back."

"So you've come to terms with Nozipa's death? Don't look at me that way. Fine. Let's go. I don't want…"

"What?"

"We need to win."

ೞ೫

"You said that the boys had come home early from school, right?"

"Yes. But how many times do I have to tell you that only one of my boys goes to school?"

"Why?"

"The other one's still too small."

"Anyway, they've come home early."

"Yes. So what?"

"If they've come home early, how come you haven't seen them? Because it's not that they've come home early, it's that class ended and they went out to roam about instead of coming home."

"I don't know. Why are you asking me? It's like an interrogation."

"It should be; I'm beginning to suspect that one of your boys has stolen some chocolate from me. And not just one piece—a few."

"Says who?"

"Says me."

"What makes you say that?"

"Open their mouths and you'll see—they're covered in black."

"So what? They have bad teeth, that's why they're black. My teeth are black too—have I stolen any of your chocolate?"

"Nozipa, you're a good man. But don't force me to use another tone when I speak with you. Give me the money for the chocolate and I'll forget about it."

"I don't have any money. You know very well that we're barely managing to get by. How can I give you money? And you haven't managed to convince me, anyway. I don't believe that my children would do something like that. It's slander on your part, no doubt. They're good boys; they wouldn't steal."

"You don't know your boys well. They can do anything. Especially that one—Hobo, is it?"

"Your son's the Hobo; don't make fun of my kid again."

"How is it my fault that you've named him Hobo?"

"I've named him Alexander."

"Okay, forget about that. Give me the money for the chocolate tonight. Or else…"

"Or else what?"

"I don't know. Give it to me tonight."

"I'll check. If they've stolen it, I'll give you the money."

"Okay. Wait, don't go, someone's coming to the kiosk. It looks like a foreigner. He'll buy something for sure."

"Hello," I said.

"Hello," the vendor at the kiosk said, sticking her head through the little window as far as possible in the hope that I would buy something.

"Do you have water?" I asked.

"No," said the other person standing next to the vendor. He was around fifty years old. He was looking at me with discontent.

"Would you like some chocolate?" asked the vendor.

"No, I've had some," I said. "I was treated to some."

"By whom?"

"A little boy."

"You see?" the vendor said to the person standing next to her. "I told you so!"

"I'll go find them," the man said, and he left the kiosk. He had a disability and could barely put one of his feet on the ground. He rocked from side to side with every step.

"Don't get angry at them. They're just children. You hear me?" the vendor said.

"Why did he go?" I asked.

"His boys stole some chocolate from my kiosk today. I asked him for the money."

"So it was your kiosk they stole it from?"

"You knew about this?"

"Sort of. I know them. They're great kids."

"Really? Then why steal? Is stealing a good thing?"

"No, of course it isn't. But they—or rather, Hobo—didn't do it on purpose."

"He just happened to steal it, huh? He didn't want to, it just happened," she said with sarcasm.

"I saw how good they were; they're very nice kids. They have lovely dreams. One of them has made up a game, while the other one wants to go to the moon."

"To live there?"

"Yes."

"The way you're talking, it's like you're from the moon, too. Where do you live?"

"I'm staying at a hotel on Union Street. It's close by."

"And?" She said this like she wanted to express an important idea.

"And, I've come here to write a book. I was walking along the streets of Harare and I happened to meet a boy, or rather, a stone fell on my head. It was their stone. The little boy apologized and told me about his brother. I wanted to meet him. He's a very serious kid."

"Come inside," the vendor said matter-of-factly and opened the kiosk door. "Then what happened?"

"I went to their yard; his brother was lying on a cot and had closed his eyes. He looked happy. He was dreaming of beautiful things."

"Like what, for example?"

"I don't know. All I know is that he was dreaming. They argued a little, but I could feel how pure their hearts were and how bright they are."

"Yes, they're Nozipa's boys. He's a good man," she said. Her mood changed instantly and the angry look on her face vanished, replaced by a smile. "I really respect Nozipa, he's a good man. Naturally, his boys would be good kids, too."

"Are you a local?" I asked.

"I'm a Shona. We have our own language, but we speak English, too. Nozipa is a Matabele; have you heard of them?"

"Yes."

"They speak Ndebele, but we can understand each other."

"I see. You said you don't have any water?"

"No, no water. But I can offer you some chocolate."

"What does it cost?"

"My treat."

Zimbabweans are people with big hearts; they welcomed me warmly. But it was time for me to continue my journey. My trip was slowly coming to an end. Before saying goodbye, the vendor said, "Write about Nozipa. He's a good man; he's been in the war. He was wounded, but he has his family now."

"What war?"

Her face was covered in doubt and she withdrew from me. She looked me in the eyes and said nothing.

"Okay," I responded, and I said goodbye to her, Harare, and Zimbabwe. I felt like life would continue on in the same way in Harare without me.

"Sorry to bother you, my father has asked me to return this money to you."

"What money?"

"For the chocolate that I stole."

"No need. Forget about it."[54]

---

54. In 1966 in Salisbury (now Harare), a resistance movement began against the English colonizers who had declared a racist independent state and were organizing acts of violence against the Black population. In those times, several political movements united and dealt a severe blow to the colonizers. Small groups of civilians participated in the fighting as well. On May 18, 1980, Zimbabwe was declared an independent republic.

DAY 51. THE SOUTH AFRICAN REPUBLIC (SAR) PEOPLE

This country is considered one of the most developed in the whole of Africa, if not *the* most developed. And in contrast to the previous countries, I didn't have to search for anything here. Life here was incomparably different. I didn't see any poor or backward neighborhoods or streets. Life was considerably different. I kept asking myself, "Am I still in Africa?" On the one hand, I really wanted the whole continent to be like South Africa, with its high standard of living. On the other hand, I felt like a stranger because it no longer felt like the Africa to which I had grown accustomed.

I was worried by the fact that this country has twelve official languages. I thought that I would have problems communicating with people, but it was a baseless concern that vanished into thin air from the moment that the South African Airways plane landed in Johannesburg. When I heard the pilot's warm announcement, I realized that I was "home." The flight attendant asked us not to leave our seats until the plane came to a complete stop, and she opened an overhead compartment. There was a man sitting next to me, around fifty years old, with a long beard. He hadn't said a word during the whole flight and I had thought that he was a foreigner but, after the landing, he smiled, drew in a deep breath and looked at me happily, reminding me for a minute of the Arab archeologist I had met in Kenya.

"We made it. We finally made it. Our flight was very brief; now I'll put my feet on the ground and feel its warmth. I love you very much," he said, and he kissed my cheek. "It's good, isn't it?"

I looked at him in surprise.

"We'll go and you'll meet my daughter. You'll see our house."

"Are you talking to me?" I asked.

"Yes," he said, looking around. "Is there anyone else here?"

"Yes, there is, actually. In front of you, behind you, on your right. We're in a plane full of people."

"I know that," he said, slightly rudely. "Do I look like an idiot? If it's you I'm looking at, then it's you I'm talking to, isn't it? What's so surprising about that?"

"I thought you were a foreigner, but now you're inviting me to your house. You're talking to me like we've been acquainted for a long time, or we're close friends."

"I'm happy; I've returned home. I've been missed, and now I'm back—isn't that the happiest thing ever? I'm happy to invite the pilot with the raspy voice over to my place as well. I'm happy to treat all the passengers to a meal. Do you understand? Imagine the sun having stayed in the east for a long time, and now it's finally given the chance to go to the west. It would shine down on the west with particular warmth, wouldn't it? But you're trying to dampen my excitement by pretending to be a serious man, by not understanding that people are the same everywhere and you shouldn't treat them differently. You've disappointed me; I won't introduce you to my daughter."

"I'm sorry. It's just that your excited speech came as a surprise to me after your long silence. I hadn't expected it. I even thought that you were confusing me with someone else."

"But you understand now, right?"

"Yes."

"Good. You understand, right, that a new life is beginning for me?"

"Yes."

"That I'm happy and ready for anything?"

"Yes."

The man looked out the window and closed his eyes. Tears flowed down his face. He smiled.

"I'm home. I'm in my home, and I'm not a foreigner here. Is there anything better in the whole world? I've dreamed of two things in life most of all, especially the first one—to come home and live in freedom, to see my daughter."

"And the second thing?"

"The second? Oh, that's nothing. To go up the Nevado Tres Cruces."

"Why?"

"I don't know. I just want to."

"And have you ever been up there?"

"No, it's very far away, in Chile. This isn't a very serious dream."

"When you say home, do you mean South Africa?"

"Why?" he asked, looking at me. "What difference does it make? When I say 'home' I mean all of this—this land, my family."

The plane had long since emptied. I was surprised that we hadn't been asked to leave. I wanted to ask him to continue this conversation outside, but he was so excited that I couldn't bring myself to interrupt him.

"You've probably seen flying monkeys," he said.

"No, you mean with wings?"

"Yes."

"No."

"How about swimming lions?"

"No."

"Walking dolphins?"

"No."

"Well, I've seen them. But for a long time, I haven't seen people, regular people—smiling, happy people, living people. I can see them now," he said, and he wept again.

He was breathing with difficulty and kept running short of breath. I don't know how it happened but, about two minutes later, the stranger closed his eyes and leaned against one of the seats. I only heard the flight attendant say "air." They were saying that he needed air, and a little later they urged me to get off the plane via a mobile staircase that had been deployed. I came down the steps and saw an ambulance below and a few people in uniform. It all happened so fast that I didn't even manage to say a word to the stranger. I was standing slightly off the runway in a prohibited area, and everyone's attention was focused on the inside of the plane while I was looking at the bright sky. A little while later, they carried him down from the plane, supine all the way, and they put him in the ambulance.

"What happened?" I asked one of the doctors, who was an old man and seemed to have a surprising amount of energy for his age.

"Go, and tell the others to leave as well. There's no need to crowd around here," he said.

"What makes you think you can stand here?" a young man, who was probably a police officer, said to me.

"Me? Nothing. What happened to him? We were talking in the plane together a moment ago," I said.

"He's dead."

"How?"

The police officer looked at me indifferently.

"There's only one way to die. You're here one minute, gone the next. Go inside the airport. Walk to that building there."

"Where will they take him?"

"I don't know."

I was in Johannesburg, a big, noisy city. The SAR has three capitals—Bloemfontein is the judicial capital, Pretoria is where the executive branch sits, and Cape Town is the legislative capital.

I don't know why I hadn't chosen any of the capital cities, but I can only say that, as fate would have it, the man I met at the airport changed all my plans. Despite myself, I felt obliged to find the man's daughter and tell her about her father. And I was more than certain that nobody else would be able to better describe what had happened in the plane. But the main problem was that I hadn't been able to find out the daughter's name or their address; I had found out nothing about the man, except for the facts that he was happy and he had returned home.

Hillbrow Tower was visible in the distance, but I never found out the purpose which that structure served. It was huge, immediately distinguishable in a crowd of several other skyscrapers because it was at least two or three times as tall. On the streets of Johannesburg, it was difficult to find someone willing to speak to me. But there was also nobody who looked at me with suspicion or surprise. Naturally, one of the main reasons for this is that around fifteen percent of the population of Johannesburg is white. It was good on the one hand, but it also presented an obstacle to my quest: there was nothing I could do to be seen as a "foreigner."

I was looking at a white business center that stretched up to the sky; it looked quite old-fashioned and majestic.

"Beautiful, isn't it?" someone asked in English.

I turned around; it was a white man around forty years of age with long, curly hair. He wore glasses. For some reason I didn't understand, I assumed he was hungry.

"Yes," I said. "There are many pretty buildings here."

"I am," he said, running out of breath, "I am the architect."

"Really? It's very nice. You're a very talented person."

"I know. But I'm not allowed inside. I can only look at it from a distance."

"Why?"

"I don't know; they feel that I'm not deserving. Or perhaps… I don't know. I have no right to go in."

"But what's the reason?"

"They deny that I was the one who designed this building. I've been an architect for twenty years, but they deny it."

"Are you hungry?'

"Yes."

We were sitting in a pretty café near the business center.

"I'm here every day, waiting for people like you so I can tell you. You can't imagine how relieved I feel after talking to somebody. People are so unfair; I don't know how to fight against them."

"What's the problem?" I asked.

"There's no problem. I don't consider it a problem; it's a tragedy when one person can hate and hold contempt for another. Can I tell you my story?"

"Of course."

"It's a parable. A woman gives birth to a child, but the baby is switched in the maternity ward. They give her someone else's child, who dies several months later. The real baby finds out about his mother only when he's an adult. He comes to his mother and looks at her for a long time, not knowing what to do. His mother smiles and tries to embrace her son, but he rejects his mother and blames her for denying him. Do you know why I told you this story?'

"Why?"

"This is about me. When I look at this building, it looks at me and denies me, blaming me for leaving it and going away. It doesn't know that I am not to blame that my architectural design was confused and I was mixed up with someone else."

"But why don't you go inside? Is there someone who stops you from entering?"

"Yes. Everyone, starting from the windows and ending with the doors. Even the red hat that the doorman wears blocks my path. Look! It's giving me such a stare that I don't know what to do."

"So, there are no people to blame?"

"Of course the people are to blame! I must have given you the impression of being a crazy person, but don't be afraid. It's actually because I'm an artist. If they hadn't distorted my design, I wouldn't be this sad. And the most tragic thing is that, after all this, they decided that I wasn't the architect of this building and they told the doormen that if I come closer than ten meters, they should call the police. They fired me. I lost my house after that and ended up on the street."

"Why? Why would they want to hurt you like that? What was the reason? What had you done to them?"

"Nothing. Nothing at all. I had created my work, that's all. They thought they could trick me out of it and that was exactly what they did. They made some changes so that they could then prove that it wasn't my work. And that was that."

"So what are you going to do now? Are you going to fight?"

"Fight for what? I only fight when I know that I'm going to win. But it's too late this time. My only dream now is to be the architect of a hot air balloon."

"What do you mean?"

"I don't know, either. For some reason, I've decided that a hot air balloon can take to the skies with a different structural design. I really want to build such a balloon one day."

"But hot air balloons aren't built."

"Mine will be."

I had several questions that I wanted to ask him, but the architect apologized and said that he would return in a couple of minutes, then he ran out. A loud noise was heard a little while later. I stepped outside and saw that he had been hit by a car, which had driven away. Nobody had seen the car that had hit him. I walked up to him, but moments later the police and doctors had closed off the area and asked bystanders to keep their distance.

"What happened to him?" I asked one of the police.

"Who let you in here? Get out."

"I was talking to him moments ago," I said.

"Go away; he's dead. Don't block the road."

I didn't know whether this was a coincidence, but I couldn't come to my senses for a long time. I was afraid to talk to anyone else. A desire burned inside me to go to the business center and tell the management there about the architect. I decided to go in. One of the doormen was an old man. He took off his red cap and said in a very warm tone of voice, "What can I do for you?"

"I have to go inside. Did you see that man who died a little while ago?"

"Yes."

"Do you know who he was?"

"The architect of this building."

"You knew that?"

"Of course."

"Does everyone know?"

"Yes. Well, not everyone. Most people."

"But he told me he was tricked."

"He's right. I knew him; he was a good man, a humble man. He didn't like making too much noise. He only had one desire—to look at his building and not see the building looking back in contempt. Everyone knows that he was tricked—he was made to work and was given nothing in return. It's a cruel story."

"But why? If everyone knew, why didn't they help him? That's unfair, after all."

"You're right, it *is* unfair. It's the easiest thing in life, to hold everyone in contempt and not care about what they think. It's very common these days, unfortunately. And what does everyone want? They want freedom. They want their home; they want to live in peace and in the company of their family. They don't want to feel alien. But when your own ideas are alienated, then that can drive you to suicide."

"You're right. Can I come in?"

"Where are you going? Up in the building?"

"Yes."

"No. If it were my decision, there wouldn't be a problem. But this could get me fired. I can't let you in."

"I'll be back quickly. I'll just tell them what I'm thinking, and then come back."

"Keep it inside you. It would be too much of an honor for them. Pokrog's people shouldn't be told what others think of them."

The doorman managed to convince me. After I said goodbye, I saw that he wanted to cross the street, so I came back up to him.

"Where are you going?" I asked.

"I'm going to get lunch."

"Can I come with you?"

"Yes, of course. Come along."

We didn't go to the café where I had sat with the architect. We walked for about five minutes. Then the doorman said, "I'm unhappy, too. But my story is a different one."

I didn't know whether I should hear him out, or shut my ears and run away. I was afraid that something would happen to him, too.

"Don't be afraid," he said. "I see fear in your eyes. If it were up to me, I wouldn't be working here. I'd go to my village—I have some land there; I would rear animals and I would forget about life. That's the most amazing thing—to forget that you are alive. I'd have a farm—cows, horses, and a cat. I've always dreamed of doing that, you know?"

"Doing what?"

"Having a talking cat."

"Why?"

"So I can talk to it," he laughed. "If my daughter wasn't ill, I'd go there and I would enjoy life. But what is there to enjoy now? I need to work hard now and make money, and never stop thinking for a minute."

"What is she ill with?"

He didn't say. He looked around and his eyes welled up, but he did not respond. Then he continued, "Love is a bad thing. You always want to have it and enjoy it, but it tends to come to an end. Like an apple—when you bite into it, the more you bite, the less there is left for you to enjoy."

"Are you talking about your daughter?"

"Yes," he said, straining his voice. "But not just her. You're still too young to understand me. The younger a person is, the more things he believes, the more desires he has; but the older he becomes, the more he realizes that all of that is only for a single purpose—to feel secure, to not feel a stranger to oneself. I don't mean like a foreigner; I mean being alienated from yourself. Perhaps you've read Camus' *The Stranger*? That is more or less what I mean, although the protagonist in that book is much more cold-blooded than I am."

We parted ways. I thought that I would hear a noise at any moment—a blow, an explosion… I didn't want to look back; I was afraid of seeing the doorman die. But I heard nothing. Because of that, I was calm. The doorman had spoken about some very serious things, changing my mood with his words.

"Careful, careful!"

A man appeared in front of me.

"Don't block my way; let me cross," he said.

He carried a huge plastic container on his head and was approaching me slowly. There was some liquid in the container, at least thirty liters. I hadn't done anything wrong, so I was very surprised to hear him shouting at me. It was as if he used that tone to shout at everyone on the street.

"Do you need help?" I asked.

"No," he said, lowering the container from his head. "It's more than thirty kilos, can you imagine? This is the third time I've carried it today. I spilled it the first two times."

"What's in it?"

"Magic potion," he laughed. "Want to drink some?"

"No."

"It's water."

"Regular?"

My question must have seemed strange to him.

"What's regular water?" he asked.

"The one we drink."

"And how is this water different from what you call regular?"

"I don't know. You said it was magical, which is why I asked."

"Yes, it's magical; water itself is magic, it's very expensive today. It's also magic because I've already spilled two containers like this one today. What are you doing here?"

"Walking around. Thinking."

"If you've got nothing else to do, help me move this container."

"Where?"

"To our office; it's close by."

"I have to find a man's daughter."

"Why?" He was already holding on to one of the container's handles.

"I have to tell her about her father."

"Who is this girl?"

"I don't know."

"Who's the father, then?"

"I don't know that, either."

"What do you have to tell her?"

"About life. About how happy her father was, how much joy he felt at having finally made it back home. But unfortunately, he died at the airport."

"Why tell her? If she doesn't know this, then perhaps she shouldn't find out, especially if you're going to say in the end that he died."

"I don't want her to find out from someone else. Someone will call her and say, 'Is this so-and-so?' and she'll say, 'Yes,' and they'll say, 'You know, your father has died.' They'll say he suffocated on the plane and that was that. She'll never find out how happy her father was."

"Let her not know; that would be better. She'll imagine it. What's the point?" He grew silent at that moment, then put the container back on his head, held on to it from both sides, and hurried off. I don't know why he acted that way, but he left as if we had never spoken to each other. I heard a crashing noise a little later. The container had fallen for a third time.

I was walking along the streets of Johannesburg and I was trying to find some sort of an explanation for my journey here. I was finding myself unable to stick to a single story. There were many people with many problems; I didn't know which of them to think about and which to follow. I really wished that I could replay my arrival in South Africa and have everything start over again. I would have taken a seat on the plane in the row ahead, and everything would have been different.

耓考

I was on the plane. We were going to arrive in Johannesburg soon. I had already heard the wheels descend and the pilot's announcement about the landing. A little while later, the flight attendant opened one of the overhead compartments and requested that all passengers stay in place until the plane came to a complete stop. There were many people on the plane. There was a man sitting behind me, around fifty years of age, with a long beard. I had thought that he was a foreigner but, after the landing, he smiled, drew in a deep breath and looked at the person sitting next to him, who I could not see from my seat.

"We made it," I heard the man's voice behind me. "We finally made it. Now I'll put my feet on the ground and feel its warmth. I love you very much. It's good, isn't it? We'll go and you'll meet my daughter. You'll see our house."

"With great pleasure. Let's go. I haven't been home for a long time, either," the passenger next to him replied.

The mobile staircase approached the plane, the door opened, and the passengers began to disembark. I continued to hear their dialogue behind me, but I didn't turn around. I was asked to leave the plane. Once I was inside the terminal, I kept wondering when the ambulance would rush to the runway and when his body would be taken off the plane. I waited a long time, but no ambulance arrived as the man had not suffocated. When I left the airport, a young lady walked up to me and asked in an emotional voice, "Excuse me, were you on the flight from Harare?"

"Yes," I said.

"South African Airways?"

"Yes."

"Have all the passengers gotten off?"

"Yes."

"Has the luggage arrived?"

"I don't have any luggage, so I don't know."

"I'm waiting for my father; he was supposed to finally return home today."

"Why finally? What do you mean?"

"He had been exiled. He had lived in exile for a long time; he'd escaped from jail and gone to Zimbabwe. He was unable to return for a long time. Today, he was finally coming back. He hasn't been home for more than twenty years. But he knew that we were always expecting him to return."

"Does your father have a beard?" I asked.

"I don't know. Maybe. Why?"

"Is he bald?"

"I don't know, I haven't seen him in twenty years. My mother has told me about him, but I don't know him well. I was eight when they exiled him."

"Did he dream of going up the Nevado Tres Cruces, located in Chile?"

The girl looked at me with suspicion.

"How do you know that?"

"He told me."

"So he was on board? Were you sitting next to him?"

The girl was touched. Then she saw her father in the distance, and they looked at each other for a long time before embracing. I headed for the city, where many people were "waiting" for me, but I was sure that, this time, no architect would be hit by a car, no doorman would have to care for his ill daughter and he could raise animals in his village instead, and that another man would not spill the container of water from off his head yet again.

I don't know why I had chosen Johannesburg. Perhaps its people were different...

"Careful," I heard someone say behind me, and then there was a lot of noise and large crowd of people gathered...

DAY 52. SWAZILAND[55]
SWAZI AND

The colorful writing in the distance said "Swaziland," and because it was nighttime, the light inside the letters was shining brightly and illuminating the street. I was standing in front of a shop and there were several antique cars at the curb. There were also two homeless people who had laid down beside a wall and were engaged in conversation. The shop sold household items. One of the homeless people was white, the other Black. I suddenly realized that I understood what they were saying.

I walked toward them behind the cars, so that they wouldn't notice me, then leaned against a wheel and looked in their direction.

"How would you know?" asked the Black man.

"Why do you think that only you can be right?" asked the white man.

"I know what I'm talking about, but you're just imagining things."

"No, you're the one imagining things; you don't know anything about things like politics."

"I didn't understand anything about it several centuries ago, either, did I, when some other white-assed people like you came to Africa and enslaved the locals."

---

55. Swaziland was officially renamed Eswatini in 2018; this story takes place in Swaziland.

"Well, you shouldn't have let them. You should've resisted. That's life. If you don't attack, the other guy will swallow you up," the white man said.

"We resisted, but while we were dunking our arrows in poison and taking aim, you attacked us with your guns and cannons. Who would be able to put up any resistance against that?"

"We were more advanced; we have always been more advanced. Is it my fault that you were backward? You should have thought of something else instead of poison."

"Who would have thought that we would need it?"

"Why not? If you had bows and arrows, then you needed them to defend yourself against someone, didn't you? So, I'm right. What's the difference between sharpening an arrow before an attack or loading a gun? They're both the same aggressions; they're both looking to make a conquest."

"How many European colonies do you know?" asked the Black man.

"What does that have to do with anything? Are you suggesting that you guys are saints, that none of you has ever killed, or robbed, or enslaved anyone?"

"The Africans were sitting peacefully in their homes when the colonizers 'knocked' on our door. As for aggression, what would you do now if you saw a strange person, especially if they were trying to attack and rob you?"

"When the white people first set foot on this land, they came in peace. They were holding a white flag and hadn't come to conquer; they were simply explorers, they didn't want to harm anyone. But when you saw them and attacked them with fear and hostility, they were forced to defend themselves."

"Who were your explorers? The ones who'd brought sacks full of gunpowder, ropes, and guns? The ones who'd heard about gold and diamonds? Or the ones who'd come in small groups to see what was going on, and then returned with large armies?"

"Who are you talking about?"

"White people like you."

"Where did this story come from? How do you know what it was really like? People describe it any way they want to."

"I know it; I know it very well. You blame me, but you also blame yourself because you know that you're wrong. But I only blame you," said the Black man.

"But they gave people like you asylum later, didn't they? They taught you what a life of dignity was like, they gave you a home. The West keeps getting 'blacker' these days, and here you are complaining. Doesn't this mean that you are now doing the same thing?"

"You call that doing a favor? You think that, after being subjected to all kinds of deprivation, after losing one or both parents, after losing your home and family, a person can just switch to living a happy life? You can take that person to Paradise, if you wish.

He will still be miserable. Who needs political asylum if you're a foreigner, if you will be insulted at every turn?"

"But they are going, aren't they? Why don't they stay in Africa then, why do they leave? Why do they want to be better off?"

"They're doing the right thing by leaving; they're going to claim what's rightfully theirs, what has been theirs for ages. You and I wouldn't be in this condition today if everything had been peaceful back in the day."

"Perhaps, but you are far from civilized anyway," said the white man.

"Of course I am; if I don't have a white ass, how could I be civilized?" the Black man asked.

The car whose wheel I was hiding behind moved away. I didn't notice it at first. Then I jumped up. The driver shouted something in Swazi and left. Then the homeless people noticed me. They were startled, and the Black man stood up.

"Hello, how are you?" I said automatically, afraid that they would accuse me of spying on them.

"Hello," said the Black man, "Who brought you here? Have you come to see us?"

"No, I'm just exploring."

The white man looked at his companion and said with sarcasm, "He's an explorer; get your poison arrow ready."

"And you get your gun," the Black man replied.

"Don't be afraid, I come in peace," I said.

They both laughed.

"What do you want? You think we don't know that you were spying on us?" asked the Black man, whose name I never found out, though the white man called him Mpho.

"I didn't want to bother you. I saw that you were quarreling, so I stood aside," I said.

"We weren't quarreling," said the white man, whose name I never found out either, though the Black man called him Leon.

"Who brought you here?" asked Mpho.

"What do you mean?"

"Was it the wind, the lightning, the clouds? Did you come here seated on a leaf?"

"He came on a plane," Leon said.

"A bus," I replied.

"Did you get some sleep on the way?"

"Yes."

"Did you sleep well?"

"No."

"Why are you interrogating him?" Leon asked.

"Because he's white like you."

"Not like me. He's closer to your color than mine. Let him be."

"I have a question," I said.

"Go ahead." They weren't very warm in their reply.

"Why were you quarreling?" I asked.

"We weren't quarreling. It might seem strange to you, but we were having a heartfelt conversation," said Leon.

"See this shop?" asked Mpho.

"Yes."

"If we ask you for a few things, will you buy them for us?"

"What?"

"We don't have any money; the people here aren't rich."

"Tell me what you need."

"Two rolls of toilet paper, toothpaste, two toothbrushes, and…"

"And that's it," Leon interrupted.

"They sell all that here?" I asked.

"Yes. We'll wait here. You go in and quickly get the things. If we're asleep when you get back, wake us up."

"Okay, I'll get the things."

Swaziland. The letters were lit up in the distance, all except for the letter "L". I looked for a few seconds in that direction, then heard Mpho's voice behind me.

"Aren't you going?"

"I'm going," I said.

The inside of the shop seemed badly organized. They were probably getting ready to close. It was late. There were two salespeople—one was an old woman who was seated in a chair and had nodded off, and the other was a young man around twenty years old. I looked around for a while but found none of the requested items, so I was forced to ask him for help.

"What do you need?" he asked.

"There's so much here that I can't see it."

"What do you need?"

"Two toothbrushes, two rolls of toilet paper, and toothpaste."

"We don't sell any of those items here."

"Doesn't this shop sell household items?"

"So what if it does?"

"Well, you should have them then."

"We don't. We don't sell that."

"Where could I find them?"

"I don't know. Is it urgent?"

"Yes."

"If you can wait a bit…" He approached the sleeping woman and said something, then turned back to me. "No, she's asleep. If you wait a couple of hours, then she might wake up. She knows where everything is in the shop."

"So, you do have those things?"

"Maybe we do, but this is my first day here and I don't know where everything is. Our shop is like a warehouse; we get and sell everything in bulk, which is why we don't take things out of their boxes."

"Maybe there's another shop somewhere close by?"

"No, I don't think they'd have the things you need."

"Can't you wake her up?"

"No. When she's asleep, it's not a good idea to wake her. Is it that urgent?"

"It's not for me. It's for the two homeless people on the street."

"Mpho and Leon?"

"Yes."

"Why would they need those things?"

"I don't know; they asked for them. Why would they need them? Personal hygiene."

"Hygiene," he laughed. "You can pick up their stink from the other side of the street; they probably haven't bathed in years. Hygiene isn't likely." Then he changed the subject abruptly. "There are lots of ill people here, you know?"

"I assumed so."

"Aren't you afraid of catching an infection?"

"I am afraid."

"Swaziland has the highest prevalence of AIDS—around 30% of the population. So do Botswana and Zimbabwe. It's very dangerous here," he said in a threatening voice. "Are you sure you're not afraid?"

"I said that I *am* afraid, but what does that have to do with anything? If you're careful, nothing will happen, and you won't get infected."

"If you don't catch the disease then you'll be struck by lightning, and if you're not struck by lightning, you'll be swallowed by a hippo," he laughed. "I'm just kidding, it's just that we have so many hippos here that it's dangerous to go close to the rivers. Have you ever seen a hippo open its mouth?"

"No."

"I have; it has huge teeth, like the horns of a zebu. When it's hungry or during its mating season, it attacks people right away; running away is useless. Even if it's not angry, you don't have much of a chance of staying alive."

"The woman just moved; perhaps she's woken up?" I asked.

"No, she talks in her sleep but doesn't wake up; even if you prick her with a needle, she'll go on sleeping. There aren't too many people of her age here; we live short lives, so she's become a symbol of sorts for us. Let her sleep. Someone had woken her up once, and she'd gotten up and killed that man."

"Then what happened?"

"Then she went back to sleep."

"Why did she kill him?"

"He'd interrupted a dream she was having. She was having a beautiful dream. Our dreams are often more pleasant than our lives."

"Why?"

"In the dream, we can be truly alive."

He left the shop. I followed him. It was true that there weren't too many vehicles or people on the street, but noise immediately cut through the silence. The young man started to smoke. He looked at the letters illuminated in the distance and smiled.

"Pretty letters, aren't they?" he said.

"Yes."

"It's a place like a night club."

"What do you mean?"

"I don't know. I don't go there; I haven't been inside."

"But the letters are huge. I thought at first that they were placed on a hillside or something," I said.

"No, that's the effect of the light. One the letters is missing. It's in English; I don't know it well, but one of the letters is missing."

"Yes, I noticed that, too. The letter 'L' is missing," I said.

"So it says Swazi, end. So that's us, and… the end? The end of the Swazi?" he said.

"No, it's you—the Swazi—*and* someone else."

"What do you mean 'someone else'?" He dropped his cigarette in anger. He looked at the illuminated letters with discontent and went back in. I followed him.

"Go and tell them that we're sold out," he said. "Tell them that we've run out of paper, paste, and toothbrushes."

"Why?"

"I'd be curious to hear what they say."

"Nothing. They'll just ask me to get them from a different shop," I said.

"I'd have found them by then. You go; I'll look for those things."

"Nobody came into your shop during this time?" I asked.

"Who was supposed to come if there's nobody here? Everyone's asleep at home. Why would they come here?"

"So why don't you close the shop then?"

"It was closed; didn't you see the sign? We'd just kept the door open to air the place out."

"What if thieves come in?"

"They won't. There aren't any thieves, either. And even if there are—that's what I'm here for."

I left the shop. I walked towards Mpho and Leon. There were no cars parked near them this time, so I couldn't hide anywhere and listen in on their conversation.

"Did you get the things?" Mpho asked.

"They didn't have them, or rather, it was closed."

"It's not closed; they always leave the door open. You could have gone in."

"I did go in. But they didn't have them."

"Hear that, Leon? He says they didn't have the things."

"I heard," Leon said. "Wasn't the salesman there?"

"There was a woman who was sleeping. And the other guy said that he can't find the things. I have to wait for the woman to wake up."

"I see, so what took you so long?"

"The guy was talking about stuff."

"About what?"

"He told me about the woman's dream, about how she'd killed someone who had woken her up, then he spoke about lightning and hippos."

"Yes," said Mpho. "The hippos here are very dangerous."

"The lightning, too," Leon said. "There isn't a single family who hasn't suffered because of the lightning, one way or the other. It has struck everyone. It's very strong here."

"Have you suffered?" Mpho asked.

"Yes, can't you see that I have?" Leon replied.

"No, I can't."

"That's because you only think about yourself."

"And you think about others?"

"Yes, I'm a civilized person, not like you, who closes his eyes and dreams."

"I don't dream, I sleep. Those are different things."

"Excuse me," I said, "but why did you need those items that you asked me to get?"

"Because he thinks that he's from the cradle of civilization, but he's just a pig like me. He was quarreling with me and thinks that I don't know how to use those things. I decided to ask you to buy them, so that I can show this idiot that I'm more civilized than he is," Mpho said.

"You're good at climbing trees, perhaps you might also be good at running long distances, but all of that is far from being civilized," Leon said.

"I saw you outside the shop, too," Mpho said to me, changing the subject. "You were standing with the salesman and talking. What was he saying? He was talking about us, wasn't he?"

"No. We were talking about those letters that light up in the distance. I was asking why one of the letters wasn't lit."

"What did he say?"

"He didn't know. But he asked what the text means without the 'L'."

"Of course it isn't lit. It was struck by lightning. It rained all of yesterday night."

"So what does it mean?" Leon asked.

I suddenly remembered that I had to return to the hotel. I was afraid of appearing impolite, so I was forced to say, "I have to go. If I see an open shop on my way, I'll buy what you need. If not, I'll come back to this shop in the morning."

"Okay, okay, go," Mpho said matter-of-factly, and then he asked Leon, "So tell me, did you shoot at the letter 'L'?"

"Me? Why? What makes you say that?"

"Those letters are very big. Lightning couldn't damage their glass layer. It was you, wasn't it, with your gun?"

"I don't have a gun."

"Says who, you don't have a gun?"

"No, I don't. Am I supposed to have a gun?"

"There was a time when white-assed people like you all had guns. So now you don't?"

"Well, there was a time when you were much more obedient, as if it gave you pleasure to fulfil our commands."

"Slavery has never given us pleasure. But I know what you mean. That is only natural. Imagine being born and growing up in a cage. Suddenly, one of the bars of the cage is bent and if you apply force, if you make the effort, you can escape. Would you leave the cage? Naturally, you would not. Moreover, you'd straighten that bent iron and close the gap, so that you could stay at home. You changed our lives and, for many of us, this became the new normal because we weren't accustomed to living any other way. But everything was different before you got here."

"No, you're wrong. You've always been slaves because you were born with a mindset of submission. Your role has been to serve. To serve the sun, the wind, nature, and, eventually, people," said Leon.

"But there are different colors in life. You can't just divide us based on Black and white. Can you tell me which is better: night or day?"

"I prefer daytime—the light. Naturally, you would prefer the night, because everyone is asleep and you can roam the streets like a beggar."

"What about you? Aren't you right there with me?" Mpho asked.

"So what if I am? I like the light better," replied Leon.

"But you can't say, can you, that the day is better than the night?"

"I don't know."

"Ha, you see? You don't know because you're no longer racist. You know I'm right. Everyone can be good or evil, except for your kind of people."

"Why?"

"Because you like to rule, to seize; you like it when everyone obeys you."

"I don't like any of that," Leon protested.

"Why did you fire at that letter?"

"I don't have a gun; I didn't fire."

There was silence; only a short distance remained before I would reach my hotel. The street was dark, but I could see that a man was approaching from the distance. He was pushing a cart, which reminded me of the pousse-pousse drivers that I had met in Madagascar. I could hear the squeaking of his cart wheels from a hundred meters way. I walked towards him, and he smiled at me.

"What are you doing at this late hour?" I asked. For some reason, I was scared. If I'd met him at another time of day, I probably wouldn't have even looked at him. He spoke in Swazi, saying something, and then left. I heard a loud sound a little later, like lightning. I ran quickly and entered the hotel, which was on that street. It was a small building with a single floor.

∞∞

Another day went by and my trip to Swaziland, one of three African kingdoms and one of only seven absolute monarchies in the world, was slowly coming to an end.

My entire journey would soon be drawing to a close. Only one country remained, and I felt that Africa kept growing sadder and crueler in my eyes. I had grown used to seeing all that but, on the other hand, I had been unable to see the Africa of my dreams. I wanted to see happy people, healthy people. The start of my journey had been considerably different from the end. I can't say in exactly which country this change started, but at some point, in some place, I had sunk into Africa and had begun to really see the Africans, irrespective of the ethnic group to which they belonged. At some point, I had begun to love Africa in the same way that one could love a woman or a child.

∞∞

The sound that the bottle collectors made on the street was so loud that it forced me to leave my room, especially after a few bottles were dropped and shattered. The bottle collectors said hello to me. They each carried several sacks on their backs and walked slowly. For some reason, the moment I saw them, I remember Mpho and Leon. It was morning; the sun's light brightened the whole street and a bend in the road further ahead shone in such a way that it looked like a shimmering river. Despite myself, I began to walk along the curb with caution, afraid that a hippo might jump out.

I was walking towards the street where that shop was located, remembering that I hadn't delivered the wanted items to Mpho and Leon the previous night. But when I got there, they were nowhere to be seen. A few buckets of water stood in their place. I ran into the shop. The young man wasn't there; it was just the old lady seated in her chair, but she was awake this time. I said hello and asked for two toothbrushes, toilet paper, and toothpaste. The woman looked around for a few minutes, then asked in a lazy voice, "Why do you need all that?"

"You don't have it?" I asked.

"I don't remember where they are. My grandson will come and find them for you; wait a few minutes. But you didn't tell me why you needed all those things."

It was a strange question, but I replied, "It's not for me. There are two homeless people at the end of this street; it's for them."

"Mpho and Leon?" she smirked.

"Yes."

"They don't need it anymore, they died last night."

"What?"

"Yes, they were struck by lightning and died. They didn't get to enjoy life. But don't be too sad for them; they were ill. They were going to die sooner or later," she said indifferently. "Ah, here's my grandson." She turned to him and said, "Give this man two rolls of toilet paper, two toothpastes, and brushes."

"But I don't know where all that is located. Don't you remember that this is only my second day on the job? You have to fiind them for him."

They looked at each other, after which the woman said, "Swazi Mpho and White Leon are dead. Why buy toilet paper or toothpaste? You're free to go."

I left the shop and headed for Lesotho.

In the daylight, all the letters were clearly visible in the distance. But when night fell, they would once again go from "Swaziland" to "Swazi and"…

DAY 53. LESOTHO
THE KINGDOM OF HEAVEN

I was in my last country, a country that was different from all the others. The former Basutoland was located within the South African Republic, and its geographic position makes it unique in the world. This was the only country which I was able to visit only after returning to Johannesburg. The small plane landed in Maseru, or rather, a suburb of that city, which was about twenty kilometers away. With great difficulty, I managed to find a taxi and head into town.

"Moshoeshoe Airport is twenty kilometers away"—these were the first words I heard the driver say.

"From what?" I asked.

"From the city. You said twenty kilometers, but in fact it's eighteen," the driver laughed. "This is Lesotho," he said proudly. "You are in the coldest country in the world and you should be happy about that."

"I'm happy, I'm truly happy. This is the last country."

"The last country of what?"

"Of my travels."

"You're a traveler?"

"I am now."

"Are you going to stay for a long time?"

"I don't know. I'll stay for a day, and then decide."

"Stay for a while. You'll like Lesotho. Where should I take you?"

"To town."

"We're in town already; where should we go?"

"I don't know. I want to see the city."

"I can guide you. I'll take you to interesting places; we can go to my village."

I remembered the truck driver I had met in Burundi.

"Yes, I'll come," I said.

"Before we go to Mokhotlong, there's something I want to show you in Maseru."

"Your village is called Mokhotlong?"

"It's close by."

The car entered a small street, which looked like it was in China. There was a strange building unlike any I'd ever seen before, next to some small, single-story structures. The building looked like a tall pyramid or hat, with something that resembled a cup on top of it. It also looked like a cross. There was also a patio in the middle of the building.

"It's the Basotho Hat," the driver said in a happy voice.

"Who's Basotho?"

"I'm Basotho, everyone's Basotho, or at least most of the population of Lesotho are. It's the name of our nation. Like the Swazi or Malagasy. What nation do you belong to?"

"I'm an Armenian."

"So you must have an Armenian Hat in your country."

"What is this place?"

"It's sacred," he said mysteriously, and he pressed his foot on the gas pedal.

It was humid and rainy; the roads and pavement were wet. Everything around us was green; I had a hard time remembering when I had last seen so many trees. We were going slowly, but the cold wind blew in my face and forced me to squint. The driver's name was Moroesi, and he was very pleasant. I had already heard that the locals were very generous and hospitable, added to which I had promised him 380 rand, the currency of South Africa which was also accepted in Lesotho. Moroesi turned on the radio and began to search for stations. Then he switched it off and took a thick disc from behind his seat and stuffed it into his player.

"Let's listen to some music, so we can get to our destination more easily," he said.

"Do we have a long way to go?"

"No, but it'll take a few hours. I have some good discs; this one has local instruments—the setolo-tolo and lekolulo. Shepherds use the second one. It's like a flute, and the other one's a wind instrument. That's what you call it, right?"

"I suppose so."

The music was wonderful and I would have gladly included it in my book but, alas, books cannot hold music within their pages; otherwise it would have replaced my afterword.

"It's good, isn't it?" he asked.

"Very good."

"So why have you come here?" he asked, growing less formal.

"I'm writing a book."

"That's good. There's lots here you can write about. What are you writing?"

"I don't know yet. I haven't written it. I'd first decided to write during the trip, but then I changed my mind."

"This is the Kingdom of Heaven, that is what we call it."

"Why?"

"Two reasons. First Lesotho is the country with the highest minimum altitude in all of Africa. That is to say, the whole country is more than 1000 meters above sea level. Also, it's one of the rare spots in African where we have snow."

"What's the second reason?"

"The second reason is a fairy tale I've made up about this. Do you want to hear it? One day, a young shepherd comes out of a rondavel, a local hut, and takes his sheep to pasture. After being out in the mountains for a few hours, the shepherd is lost. They search for him for several days, but in vain. Everyone is amazed that the sheep are still alive, but the boy has vanished.

"Then what happened?"

Moroesi was quiet and looked at the clouds. The sky was overcast. It was going to rain. Moroesi braked and stopped the car. He got out. He opened the trunk, took out a plastic bottle full of water, poured the water somewhere, and closed the bottle. He got back in the car.

"Then what happened?" I asked.

"Let's wait a bit, the engine has overheated. The road is going to get worse along the way; it would be good to take a break."

"But what happened? You were telling a story."

"I already told it."

"You didn't complete it."

"That's okay. That story is incomplete."

"Where was the shepherd?"

"He was in the clouds, the wind had blown him away. The sky had grown dark and a storm had started. The sheep came down from the hills, but the boy had vanished."

"So, what does that have to do with the Kingdom of Heaven?"

"Whatever happens here, happens up there—in the air or in the sky. That's why when someone is lost, it means that he or she was taken from the sky. They descend from the Kingdom of Heaven. But that shepherd hasn't descended yet."

"Why? If he's lost, then he must have descended."

"No, he's remained there. I don't want to believe that the shepherd has descended from the Kingdom."

"And why is it a kingdom?"

Moroesi smiled seriously and said very laconically, "Lesotho is a kingdom."

I don't know why, but he seemed very upset. He put his hand on my shoulder and began to sing.

"The story you told was a very beautiful one," I said.

"Really?"

"Really. It was touching and interesting."

"I know that it was touching."

He sang a song about a small boy whose name was Matsepo. I didn't understand all the lyrics, but it had the following meaning, more or less:

> Little boy, come home soon, your lekolulo is on the table waiting for you to play it. Come home quickly so that the sheep don't die of hunger, so that sun can set, run home so the rain can pour down quickly, fly home, so you don't trample the fields, come quickly…

"The car is ready, we can go," he said. "Look, look, it's flown!"

"Who, the boy?"

"No, the eagle," he laughed.

I knew that a moment would come when Moroesi would say goodbye to me and wish me well, embracing me tightly, and I would feel abandoned. I would feel sad and not wish to return home. It was a strange feeling that was difficult to describe. The amazing things I had seen and felt were things I thought I would never come across again. I felt like I was leaving a lover that I had just found. I knew that a moment would come when the world would stop turning for me and I would embrace that part of it which I had always associated with the broadly spread wing of an eagle, and I would hold on to that wing and fly. Unfortunately, Africa is only one wing. It's like a one-winged eagle that is coming in for a landing. A time would come when I would be forced to forget this unforgettable journey that I had been on for fifty-three days.

"Look, look!" I could hear the driver's voice, but it had faded into the background for a moment as I listened to the local music with the lekolulo and the setolo-tolo. "Look!" he shouted.

"What is it?" I asked.

"Look at that tractor; you'll never see anything like it back home."

A tractor was approaching us. We were already on a dirt road at this point. The back of the tractor was round like a circus tent and yellow in color. When it got closer, we could see that it was carrying grass. The driver had wrapped up the grass in such a way that a pile more than a meter and a half high had formed. From a distance, it looked like it was rolling and pushing the vehicle along. The tractor driver approached us. He said a few things in Sotho and left. I tried to listen, but I couldn't understand any of it.

"What did the tractor driver say?" I asked. "He spoke very beautifully."

"Yes, our language is very beautiful. He said that it would rain soon and wash the trees away."

"Why?"

"The wind blows everything away," he said, looking at me in surprise.

"It's overcast. Is the wind here that strong?"

"Yes. If it has blown that young shepherd away, it can take away anything."

"But the boy was light."

"Weight doesn't matter. The wind here doesn't care about weight."

"What did you say to him?" I asked.

"I said that I know, and I wished his animals the best of health."

"Why not to him as well?"

"If his animals stay alive, then he will be healthy."

"Don't most locals speak English?"

"They do. Many people speak English. This land is good. The people here know everything."

"You were a British colony for many years, isn't that so?"

"Yes, we really respect them. All of us respect them."

"But you were their colony."

"I know. Let me give you some advice, or rather, this is an opinion. Imagine that you're falling from a height, you keep gathering speed and someone comes up to you at that point and asks when was the last time that you were at Maletsunyane Falls. What would you do?"

"I don't know. What is one supposed to do?"

"You wouldn't have the time to answer because that person would not be from above. He would be from somewhere else. And he isn't related to you in any way. Suppose he opens fire behind you or starts to torment you. What would you do?"

"I don't know."

"You wouldn't do anything; he wouldn't have the time to fire. He's from somewhere else. That is why we respect everyone, because each person is falling from a different height. But who knows? Some people might not agree with me on this."

We had left the main road a long time ago and our tires had turned red. More clay-like mud lay ahead, squeezing like a sponge when the wheels drove over it, then rising back up after we had passed. The road was narrow and we were making slow progress.

"We'll be there soon. Tired?" he asked.

"No. Where are we going?"

"I haven't told you?" he laughed. "I thought I'd told you. Our village, my house."

"You'd said that. I mean, what kind of a place is it?"

"That is where the world starts. I'm not fooling you, it's really a magical place."

I was extremely happy that I had chosen Lesotho as the final country of my journey.

"We'll get there. We'll go up the hill and see the world. Yes, it's not the highest place in the world, but you can see the whole world from there. The whole continent and the whole sky. You can see the point where the Atlantic and Indian Oceans part ways. When you look out from there, you can see a ship in the distance that seems like the border between the two oceans. Even the southernmost point of Africa, Cape Agulhas, can be seen from there. We're not going to the Himalayas; don't be surprised, we're simply going to the Kingdom of Heaven. Please, when you write about this, use capital letters."

"There's a hill ahead, will the car be able to take it?" I asked.

"Don't worry. If it doesn't, we'll go on foot; it isn't far."

"What about the storm? It was going to rain."

"There's no need to be afraid of the rain. Haven't you heard our motto? It's *Khotso, Pula, Nala.*"

Even if I had read it, that wouldn't have meant anything to me.

"No," I said.

"It's in Sotho: 'peace, rain, prosperity.' So, rain is a peaceful thing."

"What about the trees? You said that they would be washed away."

"The rain knows what to wash away; it won't harm us," he said confidently.

Fortunately, we were able to drive up that hill in the car.

"That's it. We have to go the rest of the way on foot. I have to introduce you to my fellow villagers; they're wonderful people, each of them has a story of their own. Each of them is waiting for a family member to come down from the sky, they are all good people."

We got out of the car. Moroesi did not lock the doors, but he kicked off some of the mud stuck to the tires and walked up the road.

"The door's still open," I said.

"That's okay, you can leave it open. Nobody will come here. Even if they do, they probably won't know how to drive. Even if they do, they probably won't sit at the wheel and take the car. But if they do, let them take it."

The road was difficult. We were slowly going up a mountain and the weather kept getting colder, the wind stronger, and layers of snow were visible in the grass.

"You mentioned a ship," I said.

"That you can see from above?"

"Yes. What ship is it?"

"It was used to take slaves to the south," he said. In reality, he should have said to the north and west.

"Really?"

"No," he laughed. "I'm joking again. I don't know what boat it is, but you can see it well from the top. It's red, the front of it is completely metallic, and there are a few wooden benches in the middle section. It probably has an engine. We like to look at it, but not to get closer to it. In general, we like to keep our distance. Why do you ask?"

"Well, it's strange for there to be a ship in a place that's completely cut off, and for nobody to know what it's for."

"Everyone knows, but no one will tell. Everyone knows how to dream, but no one will share his dream with others."

"Like the story of the young shepherd?"

"Yes."

Naturally, I understood that this altitude would not be high enough to see the Indian Ocean, or the Atlantic Ocean, and particularly not a small boat that was red in color.

"When does night come in your country?" Moroesi suddenly asked.

"When it gets dark, when the sun sets," I replied.

"Do people know that it is the night?"

"Yes."

"Not everyone does over here. Many people here believe that the night is invisible, and it comes only when you are asleep. They think that they cannot see the night. But don't think we're crazy, it's just that people are different."

I began to feel cold and my whole body started to shiver. I had felt this way in Morocco. Moroesi was taking me to a place that had me wondering whether I would be able to return the same day.

Eventually, we arrived. The little huts in the distance, which seemed familiar to me, looked frozen in place. Eight locals stood around twenty meters from us. They were in a shadow, looking at us like stone statues. They were wrapped in various sheets and blankets. The sheets were gray. Some of them had strange instruments in their hands, similar to sickles and plows. Some of them were short. All of them had covered heads and it was difficult to tell their sex. Everything was cold. I was scared. It was like eight ghosts were standing in front of me in those high mountains.

"I told them about you," Moroesi said.

"And?"

"And what?"

"Will they accept me?"

"Why do you think that Africans are savages or cannibals? Are we that frightening?"

"Yes."

"Don't be afraid of those coarse gray blankets. They're cold. That's why they've wrapped themselves up like that."

I came closer. A woman stood in the front. She smiled. The woman was the only one who had a straw hat on her head, and a green necklace hung from her neck. The next person was young, around twenty years old. He held a long metal staff and bent one leg, with the other held back; the impression I got was that he was lame. The young man's eyes were closed; he didn't see me. The next one was a short man, a dwarf, who wore a headpiece and held a stick in his right hand, with his left hand concealed within his sheet. He was the only one who had a relatively colorful sheet. He smiled, too, but said nothing. The next person was behind him. When I walked forward, he retreated slightly, striking the person next to him with his hand, pulling the sheet over his head, and saying something in their language. The fifth person only smiled. His hat covered his head in such a way that only his cheeks and eyes were visible. He smiled with a sincere look on his face and was the only one in the group who wore a bright blue piece of underwear. The sixth, seventh, and eighth people stood further away. The sixth one was the tallest, and he held a guitar-like self-made instrument in his hand. He was the only one who wore white boots. The person standing next to him was different because he had hay tied to his back and he wore a brown hat. I said hello to him as well. I approached the last person, who was either a woman or a man. I couldn't decide; he or she had a very delicate face, but no breasts, although his or her body was completely covered by the sheet. This person didn't look at me, although he or she noticed that I was saying hello. It was only at that moment that I noticed another person behind the first woman. I don't know if he had concealed himself or not, but this was the only person who moved. The others stood still. He approached and looked at me. He was wrapped in a sheet like the others, but his eyes lit up; they were not cold. There was a dark red winter cap on his head.

"*Dumella N'datay,*" he said.

I could clearly make out the words this time.

"He says hello," Moroesi said.

"*Ooo pella jvong?*"

"He's asking 'how are you?'"

I said hello and thanked him.

"*Ke ahlayboha.*"

"He says, 'thank you,'" Moroesi translated.

"*Ooo aah ki?*"

"He's asking where you're going."

"Where? Tell him that I'm going towards the red boat."

Moroesi translated for me. Everyone looked at each other, even the second one, who had closed his eyes. Then the stranger came closer, stood right in front of me, and said, "*Sella hantlai.*"

"What did he say?" I asked Moroesi.

"He said, 'Farewell.'"

"That's it?"

"Yes."

"Who are they?"

"My relatives."

"Don't they speak English?"

"They do. They all speak English. I told them that you wanted to hear Sotho. That is why they spoke that way."

"I thought they were ghosts."

The strangers stood at a distance from us and couldn't hear us talking. Moroesi grew serious for a moment and brought up the 380 rand that I had promised him. I was taken by surprise, but I paid him. He said he would be back soon and went into the forest. I stood there in front of those people. I don't know whether I was shivering with cold or fear, but my skin had never felt this frozen before. Like a scared mouse, I took a first step and approached them.

"It's cold," I said. "Lesotho is a beautiful country. The people, too. Moroesi and I drove a long way. It was supposed to rain; it's quite strange that it hasn't. Moroesi told me that you are relatives of his. He also said that you can understand me. The natural landscape here is amazing. It's like I'm in heaven."

I would probably have continued talking absurdly for another few minutes and smiling at them like an idiot, and my words would have remained without response, if the rain had not come pouring down at that moment. I covered my head with my shirt and ran. They didn't move from their spots. I didn't know where Moroesi had gone but the only thing on my mind at that moment was his worn-out car and its unlocked door. I wanted to get back there as quickly as possible.

I don't know whether I was confused about the location, or if the car had been stolen. I saw the tractor driver on the other side of the street. The tractor was moving so slowly that I caught up with it.

"Have you seen Moroesi's car?" I asked.

He didn't speak English well, but he understood my question.

"He left."

"What do you mean, left?"

"He looked very sad. He's a sad man."

"Do you remember me? You spoke to him a little while ago, and you said that the rain would come and wash away the trees."

I could barely hear my own voice.

"Yes," the tractor driver said indifferently.

"Was he going to the city?"

"What would I do in the city?" Then he looked at me. "Get in, I'll take you there," he said and he cleared a place for me to sit among the grass. I sat down. We were moving very slowly and the journey seemed like it would take forever. I could only see mountains and infinity. I didn't understand why Moroesi had left.

"He was upset with you," he tractor driver said.

"Why?"

"You offended his relatives; you called them ghosts."

"They looked like ghosts," I said.

"They really were ghosts. But you shouldn't say that to a man who believes in immortality. He doesn't accept the fact that people die. In the mountains, very high up, he has a place where he gathers his relatives and meets with them. His son, whom he lost recently, comes there, too; he was a shepherd. The wind had blown that small boy away. Moroesi calls that spot the Kingdom of Heaven."

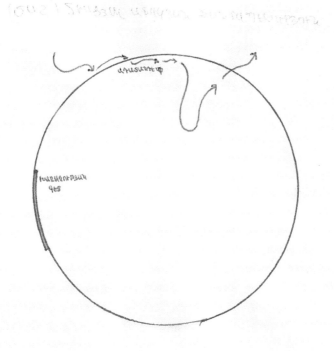

DAY 54. UAR
(UNITED AFRICAN REPUBLIC)[56]
THE CAVEMEN

The red boat gradually approached the shore. We—Someone and I—were in the boat. I didn't know whether we were in the Atlantic Ocean or in the Indian, but we were going to set foot on land in a few minutes, on a land where everything was unknown, a land I was hearing about for the first time. The boat immediately sank into the sand along on the shore. It was normal sand and, at first glance, there was nothing strange about it. All that remained was understanding where we were. I, and Someone who had arrived with me, got off the boat and walked along the length of the beach. There were a few houses in the distance, a volleyball net, and a few children. Their voices came to us and blew past. It was a hot day, like a searing African summer, although a cool breeze would blow from time to time. I thought that we were on Prince Edward Island, because the boat had gone towards the south. That island was not supposed to be a part of my itinerary and, in general, I didn't really know anything about it. But that initial thought vanished quite quickly when I saw the mountains in the distance and the boundless

---

56. "United African Republic" was proposed as a name change for Nigeria in 2021. The term is used more broadly here.

forests. Prince Edward Island could not be that large. It wasn't even marked on many maps, but what lay before us was a huge piece of land, at least several hundred square kilometers. Besides that, out trip had lasted around five hours, and this small boat could not have sped across thousands of kilometers in that span of time. We were in some sort of unknown place. Despite myself, I began to recall the fifty-three countries I had visited, afraid that I had left one of them out. But that didn't help; I had indeed visited all the countries on the itinerary.

"We're lost," Someone who had arrived with me said after a long silence.

"What makes you say that?" I asked.

"Where are we? The boat probably deviated from its course; it's gone north instead of south, and we're somewhere near Madagascar or the northern part of the SAR. Perhaps these are the shores of Mozambique."

"We were going south."

"Fine, then. In that case, where are we? On the moon?"

"I don't know. There are many people over there. We can ask them."

"Ask them where we are? What would they take us for?"

"We'll tell them that we're sailors and that a storm has blown us here," I said.

"Think they'll believe us?"

"At least we'll find out where we are."

"In that case, one of us should stay with the boat, and the other should go check. Otherwise, we might lose the boat."

I went towards the children. They were playing ball. When I was still several meters away, the color of their skin caught my attention. The children were all different in color. They were around five or six years old.

"Hello," I shouted in a confident voice.

They turned around and looked at me in surprise.

"How are you?" I asked. "Doing good?"

They looked at me quietly. One of the children threw the ball at my feet. I kicked it. Then another boy kicked it, then another. The ball beat the net with each blow from feet, head, and knee, and kept coming back.

"Look at that idiot. He was supposed to go find out where we are, but he's out there playing ball with four-year-olds," Someone thought.

I had a lot of fun for about two minutes. The children said almost nothing for that whole time, and I couldn't make out whether or not they understood me.

"Where are your parents?" I asked.

"We have no parents," said one of them, slightly taller than the others and with curly hair.

"You understand me?"

"Yes," he said. "Wasn't I supposed to?"

"Where are your parents?"

"I have no parents."

"Flowers gave birth to him," two other kids shouted from behind him.

"What about your parents? Where are they?"

"They were found by brown bears," the curly-haired one said, his mouth wide open, and he laughed. "Are you coming to play?"

"Where are you from?" I asked.

"Here," he laughed in reply.

"You live here?"

"Yes."

"With whom?"

"With everyone," he laughed. "Come play."

"What is this place?"

"I don't know. What place is it?" he asked in surprise.

"Where are we? Doesn't this place have a name?" I asked.

"It does."

"What is it?"

"The sea," he laughed again. "Come play."

"Is there anyone else here besides you?"

"Yes."

"Where are they?"

"They've gone to the mountains to collect grass. They'll be back soon."

"Who's gone there?"

"Other people. Come play!"

"Who lives in these huts?"

"We do."

"Can I go in?"

"No. The doors are locked."

"When will they be opened?"

"When the people return from the mountains." The child ran towards the ball, and all of us started to play. The flow of conversation was interrupted.

"He's coming back; he's probably found out nothing," Someone thought.

"Well, did you find something out?" he asked.

"No," I said. "They're kids, they don't know anything. They said they don't have any parents, that flowers and brown bears had borne them. They said that there were other people here, too, but that they were in the mountains, to collect grass."

"And you believed them?"

"They know English, so that's good; we're not completely lost. Those huts are theirs, too; they live there. But they said that the doors were closed and locked. I guess their parents had locked them."

"Are you saying that we aren't lost?"

"We have to wait. This could be a resort of some kind."

"Where do you think we are?" Someone asked.

"I don't know. In Africa."

"Is this what your Africa looks like?"

"What do you mean?" I asked.

"Is this your Africa?"

"What do you mean by that?" I asked.

"Fifty-three wasn't enough for you, you wanted one more."

"I don't understand."

"You understand perfectly," he said, offended, then went to the boat and pushed it into the ocean with all his strength.

"What are you doing?"

"Leaving."

"Where?"

"Wherever I can."

"Wait, what about me? You're just leaving me?"

"Yes. You've made all of this up; I'm sure you'll figure a way out."

At that moment, I noticed a few adults near the huts.

"Wait, look! There are people there. Come back! We'll ask them again."

It was very difficult to persuade Someone, but he eventually gave in. We went towards the huts.

The people had sacks in their hands. I noticed two of them going into a hut and leaving the door open behind them. We ran up to them.

"Hello," I said.

The inside of the hut was not big. There were two beds, two chairs, one table, and a few small shelves. A man and a woman were inside. The woman was white, around forty years old with blond hair, while the man was Black and the same age, with watery eyes and cropped hair. They were startled for a moment.

"Hello," said the man. "Have a seat." And he got up from his chair.

The woman nodded hello. She got up as well. They both sat on the bed.

"What do you need?" the man asked.

"We're travelers," I said. "We have a small boat. We've left it at the shore now. When we were at sea, a strong storm began. We barely managed to keep the boat above water. We were afraid of drowning. We didn't know where we were going but we ended up on this beach."

"Way to stretch the story," Someone thought to himself.

"Then what happened?" asked the man.

"Well, we don't know where we are now. We're lost."

"This is an orphanage, the happiest of places," the woman jumped in. "You've probably already seen the kids. There are children of all nationalities here; they are very good and well-behaved." The woman came up to me and I noticed a huge gold ornament hanging from her neck. "So this is a sacred place. Who are you? I see that you are twin brothers. What are you doing in these parts?"

"We're writers. We're writing a book about Africa. We were supposed to return home already, but we suddenly ended up here," Someone said.

"A book is also a sacred thing," said the man, "so you've come to the right place. There's lots to write about here."

"But we've been to all fifty-three countries and it was time for us to return, but then the red boat brought us here."

"You think that by writing about fifty-three countries, you've seen Africa and written about it? What if their number exceeds sixty in one or two years? What will you do then? Will you come back to Africa? A 'country' is a territorial concept today. Africa in reality consists of thousands of nations and ethnic groups, and each of them has the right to their own country. However, I think it would have been good for Africa to be a single country—the Republic of Africa. The United African Republic. That way, it would've been the biggest and most powerful country in the world."

I had actually thought of that earlier. And the man was right, of course. I had travelled to fifty-three countries on this occasion, but perhaps one would need to visit another fifty in the future. So, I had come to the conclusion that Africa was a single entity, and the countries were simply conventional units.

"Where are we?" I asked.

"We already told you—at the orphanage," the man said.

"More specifically?'

"How can I reply to that? You know, life is really interesting; it keeps surprising us. We look into the distance every day and try to see something new. But everything is the same, in reality, and that similarity is what causes us surprise. It is thanks to this that we are alive. If not for these wonderful little ones, we would have considered our lives to have ended. We wouldn't have had the right to continue living. But as long as they are still there, as long as we can keep seeing their smiles, everything makes sense. Life has not yet ended and there is a reason to keep on living."

"We want to know what this place is called," I said.

"This is a marvelous place; we give it various names. Specifically, if you've noticed, the sand in the territory of our orphanage is a bit different. We've imported it from Seychelles, which is why we call this part the White Coast or Diamond Coast. Whichever you like."

"But where are we? What is this land? Is it on the map?"

"I don't know what to say. It's a wonderful place, where people live and enjoy life. We think this is a place where nothing bad exists. You don't believe me, do you? Bernara, call one of the children," the man told his wife. "But this is truly a pure place. Otherwise, we wouldn't have come here and we wouldn't have founded an orphanage here. We wouldn't have gathered so many children to take care of them."

"How many children does the orphanage have?"

"Around fifty."

"They're of different nationalities?"

"Yes. They're all different. Although we have some brothers and sisters—even twin brothers, like you—and they are all good and kind people. Our orphanage is small, though, otherwise we would've taken in a larger number of children. I've already said that there are thousands of nationalities in Africa."

At that moment, the woman walked in, bringing with her the curly-haired boy with whom I had spoken a short while earlier.

"Look at him," the man said. "Look at his eyes. What a good boy he is! Can you find anything bad in him, anything inhuman? If a person is bad, you can already tell by this age. But they are as pure as this beach and as good as the sun."

"They are all separate people," the woman said, "but they are united by this beach, this orphanage."

"Don't they have parents?" I asked.

"No, we only bring children without any parents to the orphanage, those who *need* parents. They were mostly all homeless at one time. By helping one in thousands, we hope that, one day, children like them will return and tell others about this place, tell them that everyone can live together in harmony, health, and, finally, with love for one another."

"Yes," the man continued. "They're still small, and our orphanage is small too, but we hope that a time will come when there won't be a need for the orphanage anymore. There will come a time when these wonderful children will return to their homelands and be able to spread the idea of a united Africa."

"Do you allow them to be adopted?" I asked.

"No, they have no need for adoption."

"Will you ever tell us directly what you mean to say?" Someone asked.

"I mean this beautiful natural landscape and mountains, this wonderful sea and shining sun."

"Are there any other people here?" I asked.

"Of course. You've come to the territory of our orphanage. If you're looking for other people, you have to go to the city. Otherwise, it's just us here, our assistants, and the children. Go in that direction, along the beach—a few kilometers towards the east. You'll see a large sign on the way; take a right there, and continue walking. You'll see the city after you walk a few meters."

"What's in the sacks? The children said you were gathering grass."

"Yes. We make medicinal drinks with it, as well as tea. Our natural resources are wonderful; you can find everything here."

"Thank you," I said. "How can we get back?"

"Where?"

"Towards Lesotho."

"Is that where you're from?"

"Lesotho was the last country we visited."

"It's a wonderful country. Wait, we have a Basotho with us, let me call him."

The man and woman, as well as the curly-haired boy, left the hut. I don't know why, but we left the hut, too, and ran towards the city. I don't know why we didn't want to see the little Basotho, perhaps we were scared of him. I felt embarrassed for the first time, while Someone thought to himself, "Perhaps he thought that, a few seconds later, a little boy named Matsepo would come into the hut, blowing his little flute to call his flock of sheep. Perhaps he was afraid to see that. He was afraid that this lovely story would vanish into thin air, which is why he scrambled out of the hut and started running toward the city."

We were walking along the beach and had already covered one or two kilometers. There was no sign in sight yet. I had forgotten to ask what was supposed to be on the sign. After a long silence, Someone said, "I didn't like the fact that they called us twin brothers."

"Neither did I."

"They never did say where we were."

"They didn't want to."

"Why not?"

"I don't know."

"Perhaps that was what you wanted," Someone said.

"No. I wanted to know where we are."

"So you don't know?"

"No."

He looked offended again and walked off a few steps by himself.

"Now he'll say that the desert and cactuses lay before us, that the sand was as yellow as gold, reminding him of Egypt or Niger, then he'll say that the wind was blowing in our direction and bringing grains of sand with it, and the sign was nowhere to be seen in the distance, although we had already walked for several kilometers," Someone thought.

There was a desert in the distance, but the sand was not the same color as on the beach. It was gray. We had probably slightly changed the direction in which we were walking; there was a paved road to our right. The weather was hot, and there was no wind. I constantly kept thinking about the land on which we had set foot, and it seemed like I was gradually beginning to understand. The city was nowhere to be seen; there was nobody else around. But the paved road was proof that there had been people here, and perhaps there still were.

"Where are we going?" Someone asked.

"We're searching."

"I want to return home. What are we searching for?"

"The city. People. Don't you want to know where we are?"

"You know, you're just torturing me. I'm going back."

"Why?'

"I just am. That's it. I don't want to be with you anymore."

"I've given them the boat as a gift."

"Whom?"

"The orphanage."

"When did you do that? I was with you all along."

"I didn't mention it in the book, which is why you don't know about it. There are many things I haven't mentioned. You can't write it all down. So many things happened over this time that I even began to wish that Africa had a hundred countries, and that my trip would never end."

"Is that why you made this up?"

A huge truck went past us at that moment, and Someone was cut off mid-sentence. Although the truck was moving very quickly, the driver managed to notice us when we raised our hands to the sky, and he stopped the vehicle about fifty meters away from us.

We ran towards the truck. It was the first thing that had suggested that we were still on our planet and in our time.

Unfortunately, there were only two seats in the cab, so one of us had to sit in the back of the truck. I sat down next to the driver. An upset Someone went into the back and covered it over with a huge piece of cloth that was hanging there. Then he looked at a metal chair that was placed there and thought, "He didn't even ask where we were going. He just walked up and sat down next to the driver. What is it he wants?"

The driver was a man around fifty years old. He was large in size and had a protruding belly, a large round nose, and a round white cap on his head; his eyes were round, too. His skin was dark.

"Where are you going?" he asked with a smile. He had a big mouth.

"I don't know; we're returning home," I said. "Back to where we came from."

"Home. That's the best thing. Where everyone misses you and loves you. There are so many people who don't have a home," he said, pulling on his pipe. "Is that your brother?"

"Who?" I asked.

"The guy in the back."

"Yes. Or rather, no."

"Yes or no? He's like a carbon copy."

"Yes and no."

"I don't understand."

"I'm a traveler. Or rather, I'm a writer; I'm writing a book. I started my journey fifty-four days ago, to travel across the whole of Africa, to see people and speak with them. My trip was supposed to have come to an end today. I was in the last country yesterday—Lesotho."

"So what happened?"

"I think the guy in the back is also me."

He braked suddenly.

"I hadn't expected there to be one more country in Africa," I said. "That's probably the reason why I'm not alone here, that there's someone else with me. He was supposed to have gone home."

"That's a good joke," he said, smiling. "I like jokes."

"I'm serious."

"A very good joke," he laughed.

"I'm not joking. Something simply changed here. It was as if I found something I had been searching for."

The driver kept laughing and smoking his pipe.

"Are you going to the city?" I asked.

"Yes. Although, we're in town already. This is a military truck. We transport soldiers in it."

"There are soldiers here?"

"Why does that surprise you? Of course there are. Why wouldn't there be?"

The vehicle moved along the straight road, but I noticed that the shore was curved and it was like we were constantly moving in a circle.

"Why do you need an army? Who are you defending yourself from?"

"Nobody. There are no wars here, so we don't need to defend ourselves. This is the only military vehicle and twenty soldiers can fit in it. The soldiers are on duty at the moment; they're guarding the coast. It's a formality. I take them to their posts in the morning, and then take them back home in the evening. Perhaps you've seen them. They have yellow armbands and yellow metal helmets."

"Why is that?"

"The color yellow protects them from the sun, and their helmets are metallic because seagulls often gather at the beach and, mistaking their shiny helmets for shimmering fish scales, they dive down at them."

"Our boat was blown about by the wind and it brought us to this shore. We don't know where we are," I said.

"You came from Lesotho?"

"Yes."

"I know that country. It's within the South African Republic. You can see the whole world from its mountains. It's no coincidence that you ended up here. This is the UAR. The United African Republic. There is the CAR, the SAR, and the UAR," he laughed. "Isn't that funny?"

I understood for the first time that I had discovered a new country, one that nobody knew or had ever heard about.

"Look," the driver said. "See that building?"

"Yes."

"That is the Ministry of Corruption, Miseducation, and Human Rights Violations."

"Is there anyone there?"

"No."

"So why was that two-story structure built?"

"Specifically so that nobody would ever go there. This is a wonderful country where we have everything that is worth living for."

Perhaps at that moment Someone sitting in the back of the truck was thinking, "The driver is lying, or perhaps joking." But Someone didn't know that we had discovered a new country a few hours ago. He didn't know that everyone was alive here, everyone enjoyed life. He didn't know that we had finally found what he had been searching for all this time.

"Is the population here large?" I asked.

"A million."

"There aren't many cars on the streets."

"Yes, it's the morning now, perhaps that is the reason. Are you hungry? Perhaps we should stop at a café."

"Thank you. Is there an airport here?"

"Of course. Why do you seem so unsure? You don't believe me? It's not my fault that you've never heard of us. We're here, aren't we?"

"Where can I fly to from the airport here?"

"Home," he said, raising his hands upwards.

"What language do you speak?"

"All languages," he laughed. "You shouldn't ask questions like that here. Man has not been created to ask questions and get replies. Only children ask questions to learn about the world. We know the world well. I understand that you are the writer among us, but can I give you a piece of advice?"

"Yes," I said.

"When you write your book, don't ask unnecessary questions." The driver smiled and accelerated.

From far away, somewhere around the sun, the paved road could be seen with a truck speeding along its middle, the driver and I seated in front, with Someone in the back thinking, "You're lying. You've never been to Africa. You've imagined the whole thing." At the other end of the highway, a beautiful city came into view.[57]

---

57. "Africa" is the name of the tribes that lived in the north of Africa, in Carthage. In 1981, the following version of the origin of the continent's name was confirmed—the word "Afri" came from the Berber "ifri" which means "cave."

The Roman suffix "-ca" means country or land. This is the origin of the word Africa.

There are other versions as well—the Greek "aprikie" means hot, without cold, and the Latin "aprika" means bright, happy…

ABOUT THE AUTHOR

Areg Azatyan is an Armenian writer and filmmaker based in the USA. He is the author of six fiction books published by leading publishing houses in Armenia: *Life Beyond the Sun*, *The Trial of the Human*, *Grasping at the Ladybug's Leg*, *The Flying African*, *The Romanticists*, and *During the Lull*. He has also published short fiction in Armenian and international magazines and newspapers.

He was the recipient of one the highest governmental literary awards in Armenia, the Presidential Youth Prize for Literature (2004), as well as Best Writer of the Year (2010) Mesrop Mashtots trophy, and several other international and national literary awards. As a filmmaker, his work has been recognized with several awards and prizes, and he has participated in more than forty international film festivals, including Berlinale, Rotterdam, Sao Paulo, and Gothenburg.

He was selected as a panelist for two AWP sessions: Crossing Languages: From First Draft to Publication (2022) and My Feet, Whose Shoes? Writing and Translating "The Other" (2024).

ABOUT THE TRANSLATOR

Nazareth Seferian was born in Canada, grew up in India and moved to his homeland of Armenia in 1998, where he has been living ever since. His university education was not specific to translation studies, but his love for languages led him to this work in 2001. He began literary translations in 2011 and his published works include the English version of *Yenok's Eye* by Gurgen Khanjyan, *The Clouds of Mount Maruta* by Mushegh Galshoyan, *Ravens Before Noah* by Susanna Harutyunyan, *Jesus' Cat* by Grig, *The Door Was Open* by Karine Khodikyan, and *Robinson* by Aram Pachyan. He has also translated several short stories by other Armenian authors including Artavazd Yeghiazaryan, Levon Shahnur, Armen of Armenia (Ohanyan), Areg Azatyan, Avetik Mejlumyan, and Anna Davtyan. Nazareth produces several pages of translation each day, driven by his desire to promote greater availability and recognition of Armenian culture for English speakers worldwide.

ACCA

PAPER F2

MANAGEMENT
ACCOUNTING

FOR EXAMS IN DECEMBER 2008 AND JUNE 2009

First edition 2007

Second edition June 2008

ISBN 9780 7517 4721 8
(Previous ISBN 9780 7517 3287 0)

British Library Cataloguing-in-Publication Data
A catalogue record for this book
is available from the British Library

Published by

BPP Learning Media Ltd
BPP House, Aldine Place
London W12 8AA

www.bpp.com/learningmedia

Printed in the United Kindgom

We are grateful to the Association of Chartered Certified
Accountants for permission to reproduce past
examination questions. The suggested solutions in the
exam answer bank have been prepared by BPP Learning
Media Ltd, except where otherwise stated.

Your learning materials, published by BPP
Learning Media Ltd, are printed on paper
sourced from sustainable, managed forests.

ii

Contents

How the BPP ACCA-approved Study Text can help you pass

Tackling studying

Studying can be a daunting prospect, particularly when you have lots of other commitments. The **different features** of the text, the **purposes** of which are explained fully on the **Chapter features** page, will help you whilst studying and improve your chances of **exam success**.

Developing exam awareness

Our Texts are completely **focused** on helping you pass your exam.

Our advice on **Studying F2** outlines the **content** of the paper, the **necessary skills** the examiner expects you to demonstrate and any **brought forward knowledge** you are expected to have.

Exam focus points are included within the chapters to highlight when and how specific topics were examined, or how they might be examined in the future.

Using the Syllabus and Study Guide

You can find the syllabus, Study Guide and other useful resources for F2 on the ACCA web site:

www.accaglobal.com/students/study_exams/qualifications/acca_choose/acca/fundamentals/ma

The Study Text covers **all aspects** of the syllabus to ensure you are as fully prepared for the exam as possible.

Testing what you can do

Testing yourself helps you develop the skills you need to pass the exam and also confirms that you can recall what you have learnt.

We include **Questions** – lots of them - both within chapters and in the **Exam Question Bank**, as well as **Quick Quizzes** at the end of each chapter to test your knowledge of the chapter content.

Chapter features

Each chapter contains a number of helpful features to guide you through each topic.

Topic list

Topic list	Syllabus reference

Tells you what you will be studying in this chapter and the relevant section numbers, together the ACCA syllabus references.

Introduction

Puts the chapter content in the context of the syllabus as a whole.

Study Guide

Links the chapter content with ACCA guidance.

Exam Guide

Highlights how examinable the chapter content is likely to be and the ways in which it could be examined.

Knowledge brought forward from earlier studies

What you are assumed to know from previous studies/exams.

FAST FORWARD

Summarises the content of main chapter headings, allowing you to preview and review each section easily.

Examples

Demonstrate how to apply key knowledge and techniques.

Key terms

Definitions of important concepts that can often earn you easy marks in exams.

Exam focus points

Tell you when and how specific topics were examined, or how they may be examined in the future.

Formula to learn

Formulae that are not given in the exam but which have to be learnt.

 Question

Give you essential practice of techniques covered in the chapter.

 Case Study

Provide real world examples of theories and techniques.

Chapter Roundup

A full list of the Fast Forwards included in the chapter, providing an easy source of review.

Quick Quiz

A quick test of your knowledge of the main topics in the chapter.

Exam Question Bank

Found at the back of the Study Text with more comprehensive chapter questions. Cross referenced for easy navigation.

Studying F2

This paper introduces you to costing and management accounting techniques, including those techniques that are used to make and support decisions. It provides a basis for Paper F5 – *Performance Management*.

The examiner for this paper is **David Forster** who was previously the examiner for Paper 1.2. His aims are to test your knowledge of basic costing and management accounting techniques and also to test basic application of knowledge.

1 What F2 is about

F2 is one of the three papers that form the **Knowledge** base for your ACCA studies. Whilst Paper F1 – *The Accountant in Business* gives you a broad overview of the role and function of the accountant, Papers F2 – *Management Accounting* and F3 – *Financial Accounting* give you technical knowledge at a fundamental level of the two major areas of accounting. Paper F2 will give you a good grounding in all the basic techniques you need to know in order to progress through the ACCA qualification and will help you with Papers F5 – *Performance Management* and P5 – *Advanced Performance Management* in particular.

2 What skills are required?

The paper is examined by computer-based exam or a written exam consisting of objective test questions (mainly multiple-choice questions). You are not required, at this level, to demonstrate any written skills. However you will be required to demonstrate the following.

- Core knowledge – classification and treatment of costs, accounting for overheads, budgeting and standard costing, decision-making.

- Numerical and mathematical skills – regression analysis, linear programming.

- Spreadsheet skills – the paper will test your understanding of what can be done with spreadsheets. This section will be particularly useful to you in the workplace.

3 How to improve your chances of passing

You should bear the following points in mind.

- All questions in the paper are compulsory. This means that you cannot avoid studying any part of the syllabus. The examiner can examine any part of the syllabus and you must be prepared for him to do so.

- The best preparation for any exam is to practise lots of questions. Work your way through the **Quick Quizzes** at the end of each chapter in this Study Text and then attempt the questions in the **Exam Question Bank**. You should also make full use of the **BPP Practice and Revision Kit**.

- In the exam, **read the questions carefully**. Beware any question that looks like one you have seen before – it is probably different in some way that you haven't spotted.

- If you really cannot answer something, move on. You can always come back to it.

- If at the end of the exam you find you have not answered all of the questions, have a guess. You are not penalised for getting a question wrong and there is a chance you may have guessed correctly. If you fail to choose an answer, you have no chance of getting any marks.

The exam paper

Format of the paper

Guidance

The exam is a two hour paper that can be taken either as a paper-based or computer-based exam.

There are 50 questions in the paper – 40 questions will be worth two marks each whilst the remaining 10 questions are worth one mark each. There are therefore 90 marks available.

The two mark questions will have a choice of four possible answers (A/B/C/D) whilst the one mark questions will have a choice of two (A/B or True/False) or three possible answers (A/B/C). The one and two mark questions will be interspersed and questions will appear in random order (that is, not in Study Guide order). Questions on the same topic will not necessarily be grouped together.

Questions will be a mix of calculation and non-calculation questions in a similar mix to the pilot paper. The pilot paper can be found on the ACCA web site:
www.accaglobal.com/students/study_exams/qualifications/acca_choose/acca/fundamentals/ma/past_pape
rs.

Before you begin … Are you confident with basic maths?

1 Using this introductory chapter

The Paper F2 – *Management Accounting* syllabus assumes that you have some knowledge of basic mathematics and statistics. The purpose of this introductory chapter is to provide the knowledge required in this area if you haven't studied it before, or to provide a means of reminding you of basic maths and statistics if you are feeling a little rusty in one or two areas!

Accordingly, this introductory chapter sets out from first principles a good deal of the knowledge that you are assumed to possess in the main chapters of the Study Text. You may wish to work right through it now. You may prefer to dip into it as and when you need to. You may just like to try a few questions to sharpen up your knowledge. Don't feel obliged to learn everything in the following pages: they are intended as an extra resource to be used in whatever way best suits you.

2 Integers, fractions and decimals

2.1 Integers, fractions and decimals

An **integer** is a whole number and can be either positive or negative. The integers are therefore as follows.

.....,-5, –4, –3, –2, –1, 0, 1, 2, 3, 4, 5..... .

Fractions (such as $\frac{1}{2}$, $\frac{1}{4}$, $\frac{19}{35}$, $\frac{101}{377}$, ...) and **decimals** (0.1, 0.25, 0.3135 .....) are both ways of showing parts of a whole. Fractions can be turned into decimals by dividing the numerator by the denominator (in other words, the top line by the bottom line). To turn decimals into fractions, all you have to do is remember that places after the decimal point stand for tenths, hundredths, thousandths and so on.

2.2 Significant digits

Sometimes a decimal number has too many digits in it for practical use. This problem can be overcome by rounding the decimal number to a specific number of **significant digits** by discarding digits using the following rule.

If the first digit to be discarded is greater than or equal to five then add one to the previous digit. Otherwise the previous digit is unchanged.

2.3 Example: Significant digits

(a)   187.392 correct to five significant digits is 187.39

Discarding a 2 causes nothing to be added to the 9.

(b)   187.392 correct to four significant digits is 187.4

Discarding the 9 causes one to be added to the 3.

(c)   187.392 correct to three significant digits is 187

Discarding a 3 causes nothing to be added to the 7.

Question

Significant digits

What is 17.385 correct to four significant digits?

Answer

17.39

3 Mathematical notation

3.1 Brackets

Brackets are commonly used to indicate which parts of a mathematical expression should be grouped together, and calculated before other parts. In other words, brackets can indicate a priority, or an order in which calculations should be made. The rule is as follows.

(a)   Do things in brackets before doing things outside them.

(b)   Subject to rule (a), do things in this order.

    (i)   Powers and roots

    (ii)   Multiplications and divisions, working from left to right

    (iii)   Additions and subtractions, working from left to right

Thus brackets are used for the sake of **clarity**. Here are some examples.

(a) $3 + 6 \times 8 = 51$. This is the same as writing $3 + (6 \times 8) = 51$.

(b) $(3 + 6) \times 8 = 72$. The brackets indicate that we wish to multiply the sum of 3 and 6 by 8.

(c) $12 - 4 \div 2 = 10$. This is the same as writing $12 - (4 \div 2) = 10$ or $12 - (4/2) = 10$.

(d) $(12 - 4) \div 2 = 4$. The brackets tell us to do the subtraction first.

A figure outside a bracket may be multiplied by two or more figures inside a bracket, linked by addition or subtraction signs. Here is an example.

$$5(6 + 8) = 5 \times (6 + 8) = 5 \times 6 + 5 \times 8 = 70$$

This is the same as $5(14) = 5 \times 14 = 70$

The multiplication sign after the 5 can be omitted, as shown here $(5(6 + 8))$, but there is no harm in putting it in $(5 \times (6 + 8))$ if you want to.

Similarly:

$$5(8 - 6) = 5(2) = 10; \text{ or}$$
$$5 \times 8 - 5 \times 6 = 10$$

When two sets of figures linked by addition or subtraction signs within brackets are multiplied together, each figure in one bracket is multiplied in turn by every figure in the second bracket. Thus:

$$(8 + 4)(7 + 2) = (12)(9) = 108 \text{ or}$$
$$8 \times 7 + 8 \times 2 + 4 \times 7 + 4 \times 2 =$$
$$56 + 16 + 28 + 8 = 108$$

3.2 Negative numbers

When a negative number (–p) is added to another number (q), the net effect is to subtract p from q.

(a) $10 + (-6) = 10 - 6 = 4$

(b) $-10 + (-6) = -10 - 6 = -16$

When a negative number (-p) is subtracted from another number (q), the net effect is to add p to q.

(a) $12 - (-8) = 12 + 8 = 20$

(b) $-12 - (-8) = -12 + 8 = -4$

When a negative number is multiplied or divided by another negative number, the result is a positive number.

$$-8 \times (-4) = +32$$
$$-18/(-3) = +6$$

If there is only one negative number in a multiplication or division, the result is negative.

$$-8 \times 4 \quad = -32$$
$$3 \times (-2) \quad = -6$$
$$12/(-4) \quad = -3$$
$$-20/5 \quad = -4$$

Work out the following.

(a) $(72 - 8) - (-3 + 1)$

(b) $\dfrac{88 + 8}{12} + \dfrac{(29 - 11)}{-2}$

(c) $8(2 - 5) - (4 - (-8))$

(d) $\dfrac{-36}{9 - 3} - \dfrac{84}{3 - 10} - \dfrac{-81}{3}$

Answer

(a) $64 - (-2) = 64 + 2 = 66$

(b) $8 + (-9) = -1$

(c) $-24 - (12) = -36$

(d) $-6 - (-12) - (-27) = -6 + 12 + 27 = 33$

3.3 Reciprocals

The **reciprocal** of a number is just 1 divided by that number. For example, the reciprocal of 2 is 1 divided by 2, ie ½.

3.4 Extra symbols

You will come across several mathematical signs in this book and there are six which you should learn right away.

(a) $>$ means 'greater than'. So $46 > 29$ is true, but $40 > 86$ is false.
(b) $\geq$ means 'is greater than or equal to'. So $4 \geq 3$ and $4 \geq 4$.
(c) $<$ means ' is less than'. So $29 < 46$ is true, but $86 < 40$ is false.
(d) $\leq$ means ' is less than or equal to'. So $7 \leq 8$ and $7 \leq 7$.
(e) $\neq$ means 'is not equal to'. So we could write $100.004 \neq 100$.
(f) Σ means 'the sum of'.

4 Percentages and ratios

4.1 Percentages and ratios

Percentages are used to indicate the **relative size** or **proportion** of items, rather than their absolute size. For example, if one office employs ten accountants, six secretaries and four supervisors, the **absolute** values of staff numbers and the *percentage* of the total work force in each type would be as follows.

	Accountants	Secretaries	Supervisors	Total
Absolute numbers	10	6	4	20
Percentages	50%	30%	20%	100%

The idea of percentages is that the whole of something can be thought of as 100%. The whole of a cake, for example, is 100%. If you share it out equally with a friend, you will get half each, or $^{100\%}/_2 = 50\%$ each.

To turn a percentage into a fraction or decimal you divide by 100. To turn a fraction or decimal back into a percentage you multiply by 100%. Consider the following.

(a) $0.16 = 0.16 \times 100\% = 16\%$
(b) $^4/_5 = {}^4/_5 \times 100\% = {}^{400}/_5\% = 80\%$
(c) $40\% = {}^{40}/_{100} = {}^2/_5 = 0.4$

There are two main types of situations involving percentages.

(a)   You may be required to calculate a percentage of a figure, having been given the percentage.

   Question: What is 40% of $64?
   Answer: 40% of $64 = $0.4 \times \$64 = \$25.60$.

(b)   You may be required to state what percentage one figure is of another, so that you have to work out the percentage yourself.

   Question: What is $16 as a percentage of $64?

   Answer: $16 as a percentage of $64 $= \dfrac{16}{64} \times 100\% = \dfrac{1}{4} \times 100\% = 25\%$

   In other words, put the $16 as a fraction of the $64, and then multiply by 100%.

4.2 Proportions

A **proportion** means writing a percentage as a proportion of 1 (that is, as a decimal).

100% can be thought of as the whole, or 1. 50% is half of that, or 0.5. Consider the following.

   Question: There are 14 women in an audience of 70. What proportion of the audience are men?

   Answer: Number of men $= 70 - 14 = 56$

   Proportion of men $= \dfrac{56}{70} = \dfrac{8}{10} = 80\% = 0.8$

(a) $^8/_{10}$ or $^4/_5$ is the **fraction** of the audience made up by men.
(b)   80% is the **percentage** of the audience made up by men.
(c)   0.8 is the **proportion** of the audience made up by men.

4.3 Ratios

Suppose Tom has $12 and Dick has $8. The **ratio** of Tom's cash to Dick's cash is 12:8. This can be cancelled down, just like a fraction, to 3:2.

Usually an examination question will pose the problem the other way around: Tom and Dick wish to share $20 out in the ratio 3:2. How much will each receive?

Because 3 + 2 = 5, we must divide the whole up into five equal parts, then give Tom three parts and Dick two parts.

(a) $20 ÷ 5 = $4 (so each part is $4)
(b)   Tom's share = 3 × $4 = $12
(c)   Dick's share = 2 × $4 = $8
(d)   **Check:** $12 + $8 = $20 (adding up the two shares in the answer gets us back to the $20 in the question).

This method of calculating ratios as amounts works no matter how many ratios are involved. Here is another example.

   Question: A, B, C and D wish to share $600 in the ratio 6:1:2:3. How much will each receive?

Answer: (a)   Number of parts   =   6 + 1 + 2 + 3 = 12.

             (b)   Value of each part   = $600 ÷ 12 = $50

             (c)   A: 6 × $50   = $300
                     B: 1 × $50   = $50
                     C: 2 × $50   = $100
                     D   3 × $50   = $150

             (d)   *Check:* $300 + $50 + $100 + $150 = $600.

Question

Ratios

(a)   Peter and Paul wish to share $60 in the ratio 7 : 5. How much will each receive?

(b)   Bill and Ben own 300 and 180 flower pots respectively. What is the ratio of Ben's pots: Bill's pots?

(c)   Tom, Dick and Harry wish to share out $800. Calculate how much each would receive if the ratio used was:

     (i)   3 : 2 : 5;

     (ii)   5 : 3 : 2;

     (iii)   3 : 1 : 1.

(d)   Lynn and Laura share out a certain sum of money in the ratio 4 : 5, and Laura ends up with $6.

     (i)   How much was shared out in the first place?

     (ii)   How much would have been shared out if Laura had got $6 and the ratio had been 5 : 4 instead of 4 : 5?

Answer

(a)   There are 7 + 5 = 12 parts
Each part is worth $60 ÷ 12 = $5
Peter receives 7 × $5 = $35
Paul receives 5 × $5 = $25

(b)   Ben's pots: Bill's pots = 180 : 300 = 3 : 5

(c)   (i)   Total parts = 10
           Each part is worth $800 ÷ 10 = $80
           Tom gets   3 × $80 = $240
           Dick gets   2 × $80 = $160
           Harry gets   5 × $80 = $400

       (ii)   Same parts as (i) but in a different order.
           Tom gets $400
           Dick gets $240
           Harry gets $160

       (iii)   Total parts = 5
           Each part is worth $800 ÷ 5 = $160
           Therefore Tom gets $480
           Dick and Harry each get $160

(d)   (i)   Laura's share = $6 = 5 parts
           Therefore one part is worth $6 ÷ 5 = $1.20
           Total of 9 parts shared out originally
           Therefore total was 9 × $1.20 = = $10.80

       (ii)   Laura's share = $6 = 4 parts
           Therefore one part is worth $6 ÷ 4 = $1.50
           Therefore original total was 9 × $1.50 = $13.50

5 Roots and powers

5.1 Square roots

The square root of a number is a value which, when multiplied by itself, equals the original number.

$$\sqrt{9} = 3, \text{ since } 3 \times 3 = 9$$

Similarly, the cube root of a number is the value which, when multiplied by itself twice, equals the original number.

$$\sqrt[3]{64} = 4, \text{ since } 4 \times 4 \times 4 = 64$$

The nth root of a number is a value which, when multiplied by itself (n – 1) times, equals the original number.

5.2 Powers

Powers work the other way round.
Thus the 6th power of $2 = 2^6 = 2 \times 2 \times 2 \times 2 \times 2 \times 2 = 64$.

Similarly, $3^4 = 3 \times 3 \times 3 \times 3 = 81$.

Since $\sqrt{9} = 3$, it also follows that $3^2 = 9$, and since $\sqrt[3]{64} = 4$, $4^3 = 64$.

When a number with an index (a 'to the power of' value) is multiplied by the *same* number with the same or a different index, the result is that number to the power of the sum of the indices.

(a) $5^2 \times 5 = 5^2 \times 5^1 = 5^{(2+1)} = 5^3 = 125$
(b) $4^3 \times 4^3 = 4^{(3+3)} = 4^6 = 4{,}096$

Similarly, when a number with an index is divided by the *same* number with the same or a different index, the result is that number to the power of the first index minus the second index.

(a) $6^4 \div 6^3 = 6^{(4-3)} = 6^1 = 6$
(b) $7^8 \div 7^6 = 7^{(8-6)} = 7^2 = 49$

Any figure to the power of zero equals one. $1^0 = 1$, $2^0 = 1$, $3^0 = 1$, $4^0 = 1$ and so on.

Similarly, $8^2 \div 8^2 = 8^{(2-2)} = 8^0 = 1$

An index can be a fraction, as in $16^{\frac{1}{2}}$. What $16^{\frac{1}{2}}$ means is the square root of $16 (\sqrt{16}$ or 4). If we multiply $16^{\frac{1}{2}}$ by $16^{\frac{1}{2}}$ we get $16^{(\frac{1}{2}+\frac{1}{2})}$ which equals 16^1 and thus 16.

Similarly, $216^{\frac{1}{3}}$ is the cube root of 216 (which is 6) because $216^{\frac{1}{3}} \times 216^{\frac{1}{3}} \times 216^{\frac{1}{3}} = 216^{(\frac{1}{3}+\frac{1}{3}+\frac{1}{3})}$ $= 216^1 = 216$.

An index can be a negative value. The negative sign represents a reciprocal. Thus 2^{-1} is the reciprocal of, or one over, 2^1

$$= \frac{1}{2^1} = \frac{1}{2}$$

5.3 Example: Roots and powers

(a) $2^{-2} = \dfrac{1}{2^2} = \dfrac{1}{4}$ and $2^{-3} = \dfrac{1}{2^3} = \dfrac{1}{8}$

(b) $5^{-6} = \dfrac{1}{5^6} = \dfrac{1}{15{,}625}$

(c) $4^5 \times 4^{-2} = 4^5 \times \dfrac{1}{4^2} = 4^{5-2} = 4^3 = 64$

When we multiply or divide by a number with a negative index, the rules previously stated still apply.

(a) $9^2 \times 9^{-2} = 9^{(2+(-2))} = 9^0 = 1$ (That is, $9^2 \times \dfrac{1}{9^2} = 1$)

(b) $4^5 \div 4^{-2} = 4^{(5-(-2))} = 4^7 = 16{,}384$

(c) $3^8 \times 3^{-5} = 3^{(8-5)} = 3^3 = 27$

(d) $3^{-5} \div 3^{-2} = 3^{-5-(-2)} = 3^{-3} = \dfrac{1}{3^3} = \dfrac{1}{27}$. (This could be re-expressed as $\dfrac{1}{3^5} \div \dfrac{1}{3^2} = \dfrac{1}{3^5} \times 3^2 = \dfrac{1}{3^3}$.)

Question
Calculations

Work out the following, using your calculator as necessary.

(a) $(18.6)^{2.6}$

(b) $(18.6)^{-2.6}$

(c) $\sqrt[2.6]{18.6}$

(d) $(14.2)^4 \times (14.2)^{\frac{1}{4}}$

(e) $(14.2)^4 + (14.2)^{\frac{1}{4}}$

Answer

(a) $(18.6)^{2.6} = 1{,}998.64$

(b) $(18.6)^{-2.6} = (\dfrac{1}{18.6})^{2.6} = 0.0005$

(c) $\sqrt[2.6]{18.6} = 3.078$

(d) $(14.2)^4 \times (14.2)^{\frac{1}{4}} = (14.2)^{4.25} = 78{,}926.98$

(e) $(14.2)^4 + (14.2)^{\frac{1}{4}} = 40{,}658.69 + 1.9412 = 40{,}660.6312$

6 Equations

6.1 Introduction

So far all our problems have been formulated entirely in terms of specific numbers. However, think back to when you were calculating powers with your calculator earlier in this chapter. You probably used the x^y key on your calculator. x and y stood for whichever numbers we happened to have in our problem, for example, 3 and 4 if we wanted to work out 3^4. When we use letters like this to stand for any numbers we call them **variables**. Today when we work out 3^4, x stands for 3. Tomorrow, when we work out 7^2, x will stand for 7: its value can vary.

The use of variables enables us to state general truths about mathematics.

For example:

$$x = x$$
$$x^2 = x \times x$$

If $y = 0.5 \times x$, then $x = 2 \times y$

These will be true **whatever** values x and y have. For example, let y = 0.5 × x

> If y = 3, x = 2 × y = 6
> If y = 7, x = 2 × y = 14
> If y = 1, x = 2 × y = 2, and so on for any other choice of a value for y.

We can use variables to build up useful **formulae**. We can then put in values for the variables, and get out a value for something we are interested in.

Let us consider an example. For a business, profit = revenue − costs. Since revenue = selling price × units sold, we can say that

> profit = selling price × units sold − costs.

'Selling price × units sold − costs' is a **formula** for profit.

We can then use single letters to make the formula quicker to write.

> Let x = profit
> p = selling price
> u = units sold
> c = cost

Then x = p × u − c.

If we are then told that in a particular month, p = $5, u = 30 and c = $118, we can find out the month's profit.

> Profit = x = p × u − c = $5 × 30 − $118
> = $150 − $118 = $32.

It is usual when writing formulae to leave out multiplication signs between letters. Thus p × u − c can be written as pu − c. We will also write (for example) 2x instead of 2 × x.

6.2 Equations

In the above example, pu − c was a formula for profit. If we write x = pu − c, we have written an equation. It says that one thing (profit, x) is equal to another (pu − c).

Sometimes, we are given an equation with numbers filled in for all but one of the variables. The problem is then to find the number which should be filled in for the last variable. This is called **solving** the equation.

(a)   Returning to x = pu − c, we could be told that for a particular month p = $4, u = 60 and c = $208. We would then have the **equation** x = $4 × 60 − $208. We can solve this easily by working out $4 × 60 − $208 = $240 − $208 = $32. Thus x = $32.

(b)   On the other hand, we might have been told that in a month when profits were $172, 50 units were sold and the selling price was $7. The thing we have not been told is the month's costs, c. We can work out c by writing out the equation.

> $172 = $7 × 50 − c
> $172 = $350 − c

We need c to be such that when it is taken away from $350 we have $172 left. With a bit of trial and error, we can get to c = $178.

Trial and error takes far too long in more complicated cases, however, and we will now go on to look at a rule for solving equations, which will take us directly to the answers we want.

6.3 The rule for solving equations

To solve an equation, we need to get it into the form:

Unknown variable = something with just numbers in it, which we can work out.

We therefore want to get the unknown variable on one side of the = sign, and everything else on the other side.

The rule is that you can do what you like to one side of an equation, so long as you do the same thing to the other side straightaway. The two sides are equal, and they will stay equal so long as you treat them in the same way.

For example, you can do any of the following.

> Add 37 to both sides.
> Subtract 3x from both sides.
> Multiply both sides by −4.329.
> Divide both sides by (x + 2).
> Take the reciprocal of both sides.
> Square both sides.
> Take the cube root of both sides.

We can do any of these things to an equation either before or after filling in numbers for the variables for which we have values.

(a)   In Paragraph 6.2, we had

$$\$172 = \$350 - c.$$

We can then get

$172 + c = $350	(add c to each side)
c = $350 − $172	(subtract $172 from each side)
c = $178	(work out the right hand side).

(b)   450 = 3x + 72   (initial equation: x unknown)
        450 − 72 = 3x   (subtract 72 from each side)

$$\frac{450 - 72}{3} = x$$ (divide each side by 3)

        126 = x   (work out the left hand side).

(c)   3y + 2 = 5y − 7   (initial equation: y unknown)
        3y + 9 = 5y   (add 7 to each side)
            9   = 2y   (subtract 3y from each side)
          4.5   = y   (divide each side by 2).

(d) $$\frac{\sqrt{3x^2 + x}}{2\sqrt{x}} = 7$$ (initial equation: x unknown)

        $$\frac{3x^2 + x}{4x} = 49$$ (square each side)

        $(3x + 1)/4 = 49$ (cancel x in the numerator and the denominator of the left hand side: this does not affect the value of the left hand side, so we do not need to change the right hand side)

        3x + 1 = 196   (multiply each side by 4)
          3x   = 195   (subtract 1 from each side)
           x   = 65   (divide each side by 3).

(e)   Our example in Paragraph 6.1 was x = pu − c. We could change this, so as to give a formula for p.

        x = pu − c

        x + c = pu   (add c to each side)

        $$\frac{x + c}{u} = p$$ (divide each side by u)

        $$p = \frac{x + c}{u}$$ (swap the sides for ease of reading).

        Given values for x, c and u we can now find p. We have *re-arranged* the equation to give p *in terms of* x, c and u.

(f)   Given that $y = \sqrt{3x+7}$, we can get an equation giving x in terms of y.

$$y = \sqrt{3x+7}$$

$$y^2 = 3x + 7 \quad \text{(square each side)}$$

$$y^2 - 7 = 3x \quad \text{(subtract 7 from each side)}$$

$$x = \frac{y^2 - 7}{3} \quad \text{(divide each side by 3, and swap the sides for ease of reading).}$$

(g)   Given that $7 + g = \dfrac{5}{3\sqrt{h}}$, we can get an equation giving h in terms of g.

$$7 + g = \frac{5}{3\sqrt{h}}$$

$$\frac{1}{7+g} = \frac{3\sqrt{h}}{5} \quad \text{(take the reciprocal of each side)}$$

$$\frac{5}{7+g} = 3\sqrt{h} \quad \text{(multiply each side by 5)}$$

$$\frac{5}{3(7+g)} = \sqrt{h} \quad \text{(divide each side by 3)}$$

$$h = \frac{25}{9(7+g)^2} \quad \text{(square each side, and swap the sides for ease of reading).}$$

In equations, you may come across expressions like $3(x + 4y - 2)$ (that is, $3 \times (x + 4y - 2)$). These can be re-written in separate bits without the brackets, simply by multiplying the number outside the brackets by each item inside them. Thus $3(x + 4y - 2) = 3x + 12y - 6$.

Question   Equations

Find the value of x in each of the following equations.

(a) $47x + 256 = 52x$

(b) $4\sqrt{x} + 32 = 40.6718$

(c) $\dfrac{1}{3x + 4} = \dfrac{5}{2.7x - 2}$

(d) $x^3 = 4.913$

(e) $34x - 7.6 = (17x - 3.8) \times (x + 12.5)$

Answer

(a)
$$47x + 256 = 52x$$
$$256 = 5x \quad \text{(subtract 47x from each side)}$$
$$51.2 = x \quad \text{(divide each side by 5).}$$

(b)
$$4\sqrt{x} + 32 = 40.6718$$
$$4\sqrt{x} = 8.6718 \quad \text{(subtract 32 from each side)}$$
$$\sqrt{x} = 2.16795 \quad \text{(divide each side by 4)}$$
$$x = 4.7 \quad \text{(square each side).}$$

(c)
$$\frac{1}{3x + 4} = \frac{5}{2.7x - 2}$$
$$3x + 4 = \frac{2.7x - 2}{5} \quad \text{(take the reciprocal of each side)}$$
$$15x + 20 = 2.7x - 2 \quad \text{(multiply each side by 5)}$$
$$12.3x = -22 \quad \text{(subtract 20 and subtract 2.7x from each side)}$$
$$x = -1.789 \quad \text{(divide each side by 12.3).}$$

(d) x^3 = 4.913

             x = 1.7   (take the cube root of each side).

(e) $34x - 7.6 = (17x - 3.8) \times (x + 12.5)$

This one is easy if you realise that $17 \times 2 = 34$ and $3.8 \times 2 = 7.6$, so

$2 \times (17x - 3.8) = 34x - 7.6$.

We can then divide each side by $17x - 3.8$ to get

      2 = x + 12.5

  −10.5 = x (subtract 12.5 from each side).

Question   Re-arrange

(a)   Re-arrange $x = (3y - 20)^2$ to get an expression for y in terms of x.

(b)   Re-arrange $2(y - 4) - 4(x^2 + 3) = 0$ to get an expression for x in terms of y.

Answer

(a) $x = (3y - 20)^2$

      $\sqrt{x} = 3y - 20$ (take the square root of each side)

      $20 + \sqrt{x} = 3y$ (add 20 to each side)

      $y = \dfrac{20 + \sqrt{x}}{3}$ (divide each side by 3, and swap the sides for ease of reading).

(b) $2(y - 4) - 4(x^2 + 3) = 0$

      $2(y - 4) = 4(x^2 + 3)$ (add $4(x^2 + 3)$ to each side)

      $0.5(y - 4) = x^2 + 3$ (divide each side by 4)

      $0.5(y - 4) - 3 = x^2$ (subtract 3 from each side)

      $x = \sqrt{0.5(y - 4) - 3}$ (take the square root of each side, and swap the sides for ease of reading)

      $x = \sqrt{0.5y - 5}$ (simplify $0.5(y-4) - 3$: this is an optional last step).

7 Linear equations

7.1 Introduction

A linear equation has the general form $y = a + bx$

where   y   is the dependent variable whose value depends upon the value of x;

          x   is the independent variable whose value helps to determine the corresponding value of y;

          a   is a constant, that is, a fixed amount;

          b   is also a constant, being the coefficient of x (that is, the number by which the value of x should be multiplied to derive the value of y).

Let us establish some basic linear equations. Suppose that it takes Joe Bloggs 15 minutes to walk one mile. How long does it take Joe to walk two miles? Obviously it takes him 30 minutes. How did you calculate the time? You probably thought that if the distance is doubled then the time must be doubled. How do you explain (in words) the relationships between the distance walked and the time taken? One explanation would be that every mile walked takes 15 minutes.

That is an explanation in words. Can you explain the relationship with an equation?

First you must decide which is the dependent variable and which is the independent variable. In other words, does the time taken depend on the number of miles walked or does the number of miles walked depend on the time it takes to walk a mile? Obviously the time depends on the distance. We can therefore let y be the dependent variable (time taken in minutes) and x be the independent variable (distance walked in miles).

We now need to determine the constants a and b. There is no fixed amount so a = 0. To ascertain b, we need to establish the number of times by which the value of x should be multiplied to derive the value of y. Obviously y = 15x where y is in minutes. If y were in hours then y = $^x/_4$.

7.2 Example: Deriving a linear equation

A salesman's weekly wage is made up of a basic weekly wage of $100 and commission of $5 for every item he sells. Derive an equation which describes this scenario.

Solution

x = number of items sold
y = weekly wage
a = $100
b = $5
∴ y = 5x + 100

Note that the letters used in an equation do not have to be x and y. It may be sensible to use other letters, for example we could use p and q if we are describing the relationship between the price of an item and the quantity demanded.

8 Linear equations and graphs

8.1 The rules for drawing graphs

One of the clearest ways of presenting the relationship between two variables is by plotting a linear equation as a straight line on a graph.

A graph has a horizontal axis, the x axis and a vertical axis, the y axis. The x axis is used to represent the independent variable and the y axis is used to represent the dependent variable.

If calendar time is one variable, it is always treated as the independent variable. When time is represented on the x axis of a graph, we have a time series.

(a)   If the data to be plotted are derived from calculations, rather than given in the question, make sure that there is a neat table in your working papers.

(b)   The scales on each axis should be selected so as to use as much of the graph paper as possible. Do not cramp a graph into one corner.

(c)   In some cases it is best not to start a scale at zero so as to avoid having a large area of wasted paper. This is perfectly acceptable as long as the scale adopted is clearly shown on the axis. One way of avoiding confusion is to break the axis concerned, as follows.

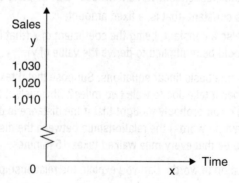

(d)   The scales on the x axis and the y axis should be marked. For example, if the y axis relates to amounts of money, the axis should be marked at every \$1, or \$100 or \$1,000 interval or at whatever other interval is appropriate. The axes must be marked with values to give the reader an idea of how big the values on the graph are.

(e)   A graph should not be overcrowded with too many lines. Graphs should always give a clear, neat impression.

(f)   A graph must always be given a title, and where appropriate, a reference should be made to the source of data.

8.2 Example: Drawing graphs

Plot the graphs for the following relationships.

(a) $y = 4x + 5$
(b) $y = 10 - x$

In each case consider the range of values from $x = 0$ to $x = 10$

Solution

The first step is to draw up a table for each equation. Although the problem mentions $x = 0$ to $x = 10$, it is not necessary to calculate values of y for $x = 1, 2, 3$ etc. A graph of a linear equation can actually be drawn from just two (x, y) values but it is always best to calculate a number of values in case you make an arithmetical error. We have calculated six values. You could settle for three or four.

(a)		(b)	
x	y	x	y
0	5	0	10
2	13	2	8
4	21	4	6
6	29	6	4
8	37	8	2
10	45	10	0

(a)

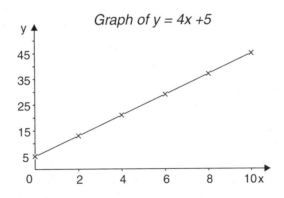

Graph of y = 4x +5

(b)

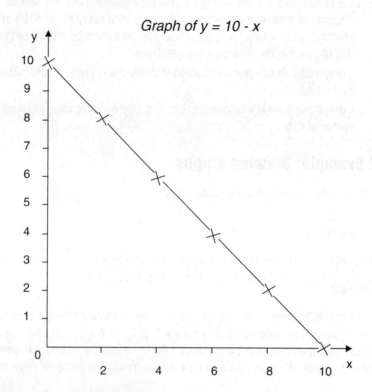

Graph of y = 10 - x

8.3 The intercept and the slope

The graph of a linear equation is determined by two things, the gradient (or slope) of the straight line and the point at which the straight line crosses the y axis.

The point at which the straight line crosses the y axis is known as the intercept. Look back at Paragraph 8.2(a). The intercept of $y = 4x + 5$ is (0, 5) and the intercept of $y = 10 - x$ is (0, 10). It is no coincidence that the intercept is the same as the constant represented by a in the general form of the equation $y = a + bx$. a is the value y takes when x = 0, in other words a constant, and so is represented on a graph by the point (0, a).

The gradient of the graph of a linear equation is $(y_2 - y_1)/(x_2 - x_1)$ where (x_1, y_1) and (x_1, x_2) are two points on the straight line.

The slope of $y = 4x + 5 = (21 - 13)/(4-2) = 8/2 = 4$ where $(x_1, y_1) = (2, 13)$ and $(x_2, y_2) = (4, 21)$

The slope of $y = 10 - x = (6 - 8)/(4 - 2) = -2/2 = -1$.

Note that the gradient of $y = 4x + 5$ is positive whereas the gradient of $y = 10 - x$ is negative. A positive gradient slopes upwards from left to right whereas a negative gradient slopes downwards from right to left. The greater the value of the gradient, the steeper the slope.

Just as the intercept can be found by inspection of the linear equation, so can the gradient. It is represented by the coefficient of x (b in the general form of the equation). The slope of the graph $y = 7x - 3$ in therefore 7 and the slope of the graph $y = 3,597 - 263 x$ is –263.

8.4 Example: intercept and slope

Find the intercept and slope of the graphs of the following linear equations.

(a) $y = \dfrac{x}{10} - \dfrac{1}{3}$

(b) $4y = 16x - 12$

Solution

(a)   Intercept = a = $-\dfrac{1}{3}$ ie $(0, -\dfrac{1}{3})$

Slope = b = $\dfrac{1}{10}$

(b)   4y = 16x − 12

Equation must be form y = a + bx

$y = -\dfrac{12}{4} + \dfrac{16}{4}\, x = -3 + 4x$

Intercept = a = −3 ie (0, − 3)

Slope = 4

9 Simultaneous linear equations

9.1 Introduction

Simultaneous equations are two or more equations which are satisfied by the same variable values. For example, we might have the following two linear equations.

y = 3x + 16
2y = x + 72

There are two unknown values, x and y, and there are two different equations which both involve x and y. There are as many equations as there are unknowns and so we can find the values of x and y.

9.2 Graphical solution

One way of finding a solution is by a graph. If both equations are satisfied together, the values of x and y must be those where the straight line graphs of the two equations intersect.

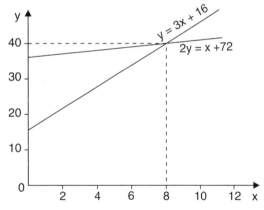

Since both equations are satisfied, the values of x and y must lie on both the lines. Since this happens only once, at the intersection of the lines, the value of x must be 8, and of y 40.

9.3 Algebraic solution

A more common method of solving simultaneous equations is by algebra.

(a)   Returning to the original equations, we have:

y = 3x + 16   (1)
2y = x + 72   (2)

(b) Rearranging these, we have:

$$y - 3x = 16 \qquad (3)$$
$$2y - x = 72 \qquad (4)$$

(c) If we now multiply equation (4) by 3, so that the coefficient for x becomes the same as in equation (3) we get:

$$6y - 3x = 216 \qquad (5)$$
$$y - 3x = 16 \qquad (3)$$

(d) Subtracting (3) from (5) means that we lose x and we get:

$$5y = 200$$
$$y = 40$$

(e) Substituting 40 for y in any equation, we can derive a value for x. Thus substituting in equation (4) we get:

$$2(40) - x = 72$$
$$80 - 72 = x$$
$$8 = x$$

(f) The solution is y = 40, x = 8.

9.4 Example: Simultaneous equations

Solve the following simultaneous equations using algebra.

$$5x + 2y = 34$$
$$x + 3y = 25$$

Solution

$5x + 2y$	$= 34$	(1)	
$x + 3y$	$= 25$	(2)	
$5x + 15y$	$= 125$	(3)	$5 \times (2)$
$13y$	$= 91$	(4)	$(3) - (1)$
y	$= 7$		
$x + 21$	$= 25$		Substitute into (2)
x	$= 25 - 21$		
x	$= 4$		

The solution is x = 4, y = 7.

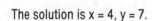

Simultaneous equations

Solve the following simultaneous equations to derive values for x and y.

$$4x + 3y = 23 \qquad (1)$$
$$5x - 4y = -10 \qquad (2)$$

Answer

(a) If we multiply equation (1) by 4 and equation (2) by 3, we will obtain coefficients of +12 and -12 for y in our two products.

$$16x + 12y = 92 \qquad (3)$$
$$15x - 12y = -30 \qquad (4)$$

(b)   Add (3) and (4).

       $31x = 62$
       $x = 2$

(c)   Substitute x = 2 into (1)

       $4(2) + 3y = 23$
       $3y = 23 - 8 = 15$
       $y = 5$

(d)   The solution is x = 2, y = 5.

10 Summary of chapter

Now that you have completed this introductory chapter, you should hopefully feel more confident about dealing with various mathematical techniques. Continue to refer to this chapter throughout your studies, as the techniques are used frequently for solving management accounting problems.

The nature and purpose of cost and management accounting

Information for management

Topic list	Syllabus reference
1 Information	A1 (a)
2 Planning, control and decision making	A1 (b)
3 Financial accounting and cost and management accounting	A2 (a)
4 Presentation of information to management	A1 (a)

Introduction

This and the following two chapters provide an introduction to **Management Accounting**. This chapter looks at **information** and introduces **cost accounting**. Chapters 2 and 3 provide basic information on how costs are classified and how they behave.

Study guide

		Intellectual level
A1	**Accounting for management**	
(a)	Distinguish between 'data' and 'information'	1
(b)	Identify and explain the attributes of good information	1
	Outline the managerial processes of planning, decision making and control	1
	Explain the difference between strategic, tactical and operational planning	1
A2	**Cost and management accounting and financial accounting**	
(a)	Describe the purpose and role of cost and management accounting within an organisation's management information system	1
	Compare and contrast financial accounting with cost and management accounting	1

Exam guide

Exam focus point

Although this chapter is an introductory chapter it is still highly examinable. Candidates should expect questions on every study session including this one.

1 Information

1.1 Data and information

FAST FORWARD

Data is the raw material for data processing. Data relate to facts, events and transactions and so forth.

Information is data that has been processed in such a way as to be **meaningful** to the person who receives it. **Information** is anything that is communicated.

Information is sometimes referred to as **processed data**. The terms 'information' and 'data' are often used interchangeably. It is important to understand the difference between these two terms.

Researchers who conduct market research surveys might ask members of the public to complete questionnaires about a product or a service. These completed questionnaires are **data**; they are processed and analysed in order to prepare a report on the survey. This resulting report is **information** and may be used by management for decision-making purposes.

1.2 Qualities of good information

FAST FORWARD

Good information should be **relevant**, **complete**, **accurate**, **clear**, it should **inspire confidence**, it should be **appropriately communicated**, its **volume** should be manageable, it should be **timely** and its **cost** should be less than the benefits it provides.

Let us look at those qualities in more detail.

(a) **Relevance**. Information must be relevant to the purpose for which a manager wants to use it. In practice, far too many reports fail to 'keep to the point' and contain irrelevant paragraphs which only annoy the managers reading them.

(b) **Completeness**. An information user should have all the information he needs to do his job properly. If he does not have a complete picture of the situation, he might well make bad decisions.

(c) **Accuracy**. Information should obviously be accurate because using incorrect information could have serious and damaging consequences. However, information should only be accurate enough for its purpose and there is no need to go into unnecessary detail for pointless accuracy.

(d) **Clarity**. Information must be clear to the user. If the user does not understand it properly he cannot use it properly. Lack of clarity is one of the causes of a breakdown in communication. It is therefore important to choose the most appropriate presentation medium or channel of communication.

(e) **Confidence**. Information must be trusted by the managers who are expected to use it. However not all information is certain. Some information has to be certain, especially operating information, for example, related to a production process. Strategic information, especially relating to the environment, is uncertain. However, if the assumptions underlying it are clearly stated, this might enhance the confidence with which the information is perceived.

(f) **Communication**. Within any organisation, individuals are given the authority to do certain tasks, and they must be given the information they need to do them. An office manager might be made responsible for controlling expenditures in his office, and given a budget expenditure limit for the year. As the year progresses, he might try to keep expenditure in check but unless he is told throughout the year what is his current total expenditure to date, he will find it difficult to judge whether he is keeping within budget or not.

(g) **Volume**. There are physical and mental limitations to what a person can read, absorb and understand properly before taking action. An enormous mountain of information, even if it is all relevant, cannot be handled. Reports to management must therefore be **clear** and **concise** and in many systems, control action works basically on the 'exception' principle.

(h) **Timing**. Information which is not available until after a decision is made will be useful only for comparisons and longer-term control, and may serve no purpose even then. Information prepared too frequently can be a serious disadvantage. If, for example, a decision is taken at a monthly meeting about a certain aspect of a company's operations, information to make the decision is only required once a month, and weekly reports would be a time-consuming waste of effort.

(i) **Channel of communication**. There are occasions when using one particular method of communication will be better than others. For example, job vacancies should be announced in a medium where they will be brought to the attention of the people most likely to be interested. The channel of communication might be the company's in-house journal, a national or local newspaper, a professional magazine, a job centre or school careers office. Some internal memoranda may be better sent by 'electronic mail'. Some information is best communicated informally by telephone or word-of-mouth, whereas other information ought to be formally communicated in writing or figures.

(j) **Cost**. Information should have some value, otherwise it would not be worth the cost of collecting and filing it. The benefits obtainable from the information must also exceed the costs of acquiring it, and whenever management is trying to decide whether or not to produce information for a particular purpose (for example whether to computerise an operation or to build a financial planning model) a cost/benefit study ought to be made.

Question   Value of information

The value of information lies in the action taken as a result of receiving it. What questions might you ask in order to make an assessment of the value of information?

Answer

(a) What information is provided?
(b) What is it used for?
(c) Who uses it?
(d) How often is it used?
(e) Does the frequency with which it is used coincide with the frequency with which it is provided?

(f)   What is achieved by using it?

(g)   What other relevant information is available which could be used instead?

An assessment of the value of information can be derived in this way, and the cost of obtaining it should then be compared against this value. On the basis of this comparison, it can be decided whether certain items of information are worth having. It should be remembered that there may also be intangible benefits which may be harder to quantify.

1.3 Why is information important?

Consider the following problems and what management needs to solve these problems.

(a)   A company wishes to launch a new product. The company's pricing policy is to charge cost plus 20%. What should the price of the product be?

(b)   An organisation's widget-making machine has a fault. The organisation has to decide whether to repair the machine, buy a new machine or hire a machine. What does the organisation do if its aim is to control costs?

(c)   A firm is considering offering a discount of 2% to those customers who pay an invoice within seven days of the invoice date and a discount of 1% to those customers who pay an invoice within eight to fourteen days of the invoice date. How much will this discount offer cost the firm?

In solving these and a wide variety of other problems, **management need information**.

(a)   In problem (a) above, management would need information about the **cost of the new product**.

(b)   Faced with problem (b), management would need information on the **cost of repairing, buying and hiring the machine**.

(c)   To calculate the cost of the discount offer described in (c), information would be required about **current sales settlement patterns** and **expected changes to the pattern** if discounts were offered.

The successful management of *any* organisation depends on information: non-profit making organisations such as charities, clubs and local authorities need information for decision making and for reporting the results of their activities just as multi-nationals do. For example a tennis club needs to know the cost of undertaking its various activities so that it can determine the amount of annual subscription it should charge its members.

1.4 What type of information is needed?

Most organisations require the following types of information.

- Financial
- Non-financial
- A combination of financial and non-financial information

1.4.1 Example: Financial and non-financial information

Suppose that the management of ABC Co have decided to provide a canteen for their employees.

(a)   The **financial information** required by management might include canteen staff costs, costs of subsidising meals, capital costs, costs of heat and light and so on.

(b)   The **non-financial information** might include management comment on the effect on employee morale of the provision of canteen facilities, details of the number of meals served each day, meter readings for gas and electricity and attendance records for canteen employees.

ABC Co could now **combine financial and non-financial information** to calculate the **average cost** to the company of each meal served, thereby enabling them to predict total costs depending on the number of employees in the work force.

1.4.2 Non-financial information

Most people probably consider that management accounting is only concerned with financial information and that people do not matter. This is, nowadays, a long way from the truth. For example, managers of business organisations need to know whether employee morale has increased due to introducing a canteen, whether the bread from particular suppliers is fresh and the reason why the canteen staff are demanding a new dishwasher. This type of non-financial information will play its part in **planning, controlling** and **decision making** and is therefore just as important to management as financial information is.

Non-financial information must therefore be **monitored** as carefully, **recorded** as accurately and **taken into account** as fully as financial information. There is little point in a careful and accurate recording of total canteen costs if the recording of the information on the number of meals eaten in the canteen is uncontrolled and therefore produces inaccurate information.

While management accounting is mainly concerned with the provision of **financial information** to aid planning, control and decision making, the management accountant cannot ignore **non-financial influences** and should qualify the information he provides with non-financial matters as appropriate.

2 Planning, control and decision making

2.1 Planning

FAST FORWARD

Information for management is likely to be used for **planning**, **control**, and **decision making**.

An organisation should never be surprised by developments which occur gradually over an extended period of time because the organisation should have **implemented a planning process**. Planning involves the following.

- Establishing objectives
- Selecting appropriate strategies to achieve those objectives

Planning therefore forces management to think ahead systematically in both the **short term** and the **long term**.

2.2 Objectives of organisations

FAST FORWARD

An **objective** is the aim or **goal** of an organisation (or an individual). Note that in practice, the terms objective, goal and aim are often used interchangeably. A **strategy** is a possible course of action that might enable an organisation (or an individual) to achieve its objectives.

The two main types of organisation that you are likely to come across in practice are as follows.

- Profit making
- Non-profit making

The main objective of profit making organisations is to **maximise profits**. A secondary objective of profit making organisations might be to increase output of its goods/services.

The main objective of non-profit making organisations is usually to **provide goods and services**. A secondary objective of non-profit making organisations might be to minimise the costs involved in providing the goods/services.

In conclusion, the objectives of an organisation might include one or more of the following.

- Maximise profits
- Maximise shareholder value
- Minimise costs
- Maximise revenue
- Increase market share

Remember that the type of organisation concerned will have an impact on its objectives.

2.3 Strategy and organisational structure

There are two schools of thought on the link between strategy and organisational structure.

- Structure follows strategy
- Strategy follows structure

Let's consider the first idea that **structure follows strategy**. What this means is that organisations develop strategies in order that they can cope with changes in the structure of an organisation. Or do they?

The second school of thought suggests that **strategy follows structure**. This side of the argument suggests that the strategy of an organisation is determined or influenced by the structure of the organisation. The structure of the organisation therefore limits the number of strategies available.

We could explore these ideas in much more detail, but for the purposes of your **Management Accounting** studies, you really just need to be aware that there is a link between **strategy** and the **structure** of an organisation.

2.4 Long-term strategic planning

Key term

> **Long-term planning**, also known as **corporate planning**, involves selecting appropriate strategies so as to prepare a long-term plan to attain the objectives.

The time span covered by a long-term plan depends on the **organisation**, the **industry** in which it operates and the particular **environment** involved. Typical periods are 2, 5, 7 or 10 years although longer periods are frequently encountered.

Long-term strategic planning is a **detailed, lengthy process**, essentially incorporating three stages and ending with a **corporate plan**. The diagram on the next page provides an overview of the process and shows the link between short-term and long-term planning.

2.5 Short-term tactical planning

The **long-term corporate plan** serves as the **long-term framework** for the organisation as a whole but for operational purposes it is necessary to convert the corporate plan into a series of **short-term plans**, usually covering **one year**, which relate to **sections**, **functions** or **departments**. The annual process of short-term planning should be seen as stages in the progressive fulfilment of the corporate plan as each short-term plan steers the organisation towards its long-term objectives. It is therefore vital that, to obtain the maximum advantage from short-term planning, some sort of long-term plan exists.

THE ASSESSMENT STAGE	Assess the external environment	Assess the organisation	Assess the future	Assess expectations

```
                    ↓        ↓           ↓
```

THE OBJECTIVE STAGE → **Evaluate corporate objectives**

LONG-TERM STRATEGY PLANNING

THE EVALUATION STAGE → **Consider alternative ways of achieving objectives**

THE CORPORATE PLAN → **Agree a corporate plan**

Production planning	Resource planning	Product planning	Research and development planning

SHORT-TERM PLANNING

Detailed operational plans which implement the corporate plan on a monthly, quarterly or annual basis. Operational plans include short-term budgets, standards and objectives.

2.6 Control

There are two stages in the **control process**.

(a) The **performance of the organisation** as set out in the detailed operational plans is compared with the actual performance of the organisation on a regular and continuous basis. Any deviations from the plans can then be identified and corrective action taken.

(b) **The corporate plan** is reviewed in the light of the comparisons made and any changes in the parameters on which the plan was based (such as new competitors, government instructions and so on) to assess whether the objectives of the plan can be achieved. The plan is modified as necessary before any serious damage to the organisation's future success occurs.

Effective control is therefore not practical without planning, and planning without control is pointless.

An established organisation should have a system of management reporting that produces control information in a specified format at regular intervals.

Smaller organisations may rely on informal information flows or ad hoc reports produced as required.

2.7 Decision making

Management is decision taking. Managers of all levels within an organisation take decisions. Decision making always involves a **choice between alternatives** and it is the role of the management accountant to provide information so that management can reach an informed decision. It is therefore vital that the management accountant understands the decision making process so that he can supply the appropriate type of information.

2.7.1 Decision making process

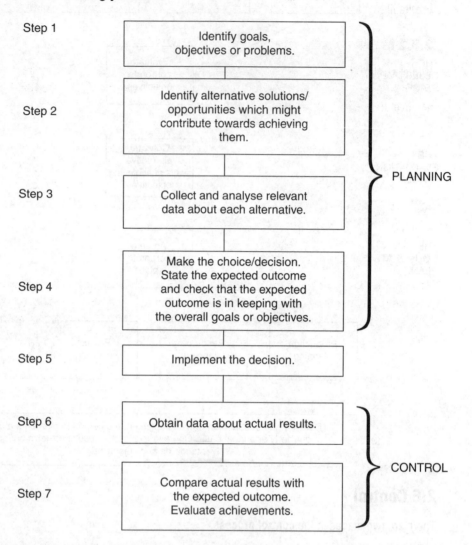

Step 1 — Identify goals, objectives or problems.

Step 2 — Identify alternative solutions/ opportunities which might contribute towards achieving them.

Step 3 — Collect and analyse relevant data about each alternative.

Step 4 — Make the choice/decision. State the expected outcome and check that the expected outcome is in keeping with the overall goals or objectives.

PLANNING

Step 5 — Implement the decision.

Step 6 — Obtain data about actual results.

Step 7 — Compare actual results with the expected outcome. Evaluate achievements.

CONTROL

2.8 Anthony's view of management activity

FAST FORWARD

Anthony divides management activities into **strategic planning**, **management control** and **operational control**.

R N Anthony, a leading writer on organisational control, has suggested that the activities of **planning, control and decision making should not be separated** since all managers make planning and control decisions. He has identified three types of management activity.

(a) **Strategic planning:** 'the process of deciding on objectives of the organisation, on changes in these objectives, on the resources used to attain these objectives, and on the policies that are to govern the acquisition, use and disposition of these resources'.

(b) **Management control:** 'the process by which managers assure that resources are obtained and used effectively and efficiently in the accomplishment of the organisation's objectives'.

(c) **Operational control:** 'the process of assuring that specific tasks are carried out effectively and efficiently'.

2.8.1 Strategic planning

Strategic plans are those which **set or change the objectives**, or **strategic targets** of an organisation. They would include such matters as the selection of products and markets, the required levels of company profitability, the purchase and disposal of subsidiary companies or major fixed assets and so on.

2.8.2 Management control

Whilst strategic planning is concerned with setting objectives and strategic targets, **management control** is concerned with **decisions about the efficient and effective use of an organisation's resources** to achieve these objectives or targets.

(a) **Resources**, often referred to as the **'4 Ms'** (men, materials, machines and money).

(b) **Efficiency** in the use of resources means that optimum **output** is achieved from the **input** resources used. It relates to the combinations of men, land and capital (for example how much production work should be automated) and to the productivity of labour, or material usage.

(c) **Effectiveness** in the use of resources means that the **outputs** obtained are in line with the intended **objectives** or targets.

2.8.3 Operational control

The third, and lowest tier, in Anthony's hierarchy of decision making, consists of **operational control decisions**. As we have seen, operational control is the task of ensuring that **specific tasks** are carried out effectively and efficiently. Just as 'management control' plans are set within the guidelines of strategic plans, so too are 'operational control' plans set within the guidelines of both strategic planning and management control. Consider the following.

(a) Senior management may decide that the company should increase sales by 5% per annum for at least five years – **a strategic plan**.

(b) The sales director and senior sales managers will make plans to increase sales by 5% in the next year, with some provisional planning for future years. This involves planning direct sales resources, advertising, sales promotion and so on. Sales quotas are assigned to each sales territory – **a tactical plan** (management control).

(c) The manager of a sales territory specifies the weekly sales targets for each sales representative. This is **operational planning**: individuals are given tasks which they are expected to achieve.

Although we have used an example of selling tasks to describe operational control, it is important to remember that this level of planning occurs in all aspects of an organisation's activities, even when the activities cannot be scheduled nor properly estimated because they are non-standard activities (such as repair work, answering customer complaints).

The scheduling of unexpected or 'ad hoc' work must be done at short notice, which is a feature of much **operational planning**. In the repairs department, for example, routine preventive maintenance can be scheduled, but breakdowns occur unexpectedly and repair work must be scheduled and controlled 'on the spot' by a repairs department supervisor.

2.9 Management control systems

FAST FORWARD

A **management control system** is a system which measures and corrects the performance of activities of subordinates in order to make sure that the objectives of an organisation are being met and the plans devised to attain them are being carried out.

The management function of control is the measurement and correction of the activities of subordinates in order to make sure that the goals of the organisation, or planning targets are achieved.

The basic elements of a management control system are as follows.

* **Planning:** deciding what to do and identifying the desired results
* **Recording** the plan which should incorporate standards of efficiency or targets

- **Carrying out** the plan and measuring actual results achieved
- **Comparing** actual results against the plans
- **Evaluating** the comparison, and deciding whether further action is necessary
- Where **corrective action** is necessary, this should be implemented

2.10 Types of information

FAST FORWARD

Information within an organisation can be analysed into the three levels assumed in Anthony's hierarchy: **strategic**; **tactical**; and **operational**.

2.10.1 Strategic information

Strategic information is used by senior managers to plan the objectives of their organisation, and to assess whether the objectives are being met in practice. Such information includes **overall** profitability, the profitability of different segments of the business, capital equipment needs and so on.

Strategic information therefore has the following features.

- It is derived from both **internal** and **external** sources.
- It is summarised at a **high level**.
- It is relevant to the **long term**.
- It deals with the **whole organisation** (although it might go into some detail).
- It is often prepared on an **'ad hoc'** basis.
- It is both **quantitative** and **qualitative** (see below).
- It cannot provide complete certainty, given that the future cannot be predicted.

2.10.2 Tactical information

Tactical information is used by middle management to decide how the resources of the business should be employed, and to monitor how they are being and have been employed. Such information includes **productivity measurements** (output per man hour or per machine hour), **budgetary control** or **variance analysis reports**, and **cash flow forecasts** and so on.

Tactical information therefore has the following features.

- It is primarily generated internally.
- It is summarised at a lower level.
- It is relevant to the short and medium term.
- It describes or analyses activities or departments.
- It is prepared routinely and regularly.
- It is based on quantitative measures.

2.10.3 Operational information

Operational information is used by 'front-line' managers such as foremen or head clerks to ensure that specific tasks are planned and carried out properly within a factory or office and so on. In the payroll office, for example, information at this level will relate to day-rate labour and will include the hours worked each week by each employee, his rate of pay per hour, details of his deductions, and for the purpose of wages analysis, details of the time each man spent on individual jobs during the week. In this example, the information is required weekly, but more urgent operational information, such as the amount of raw materials being input to a production process, may be required daily, hourly, or in the case of automated production, second by second.

Operational information has the following features.

- It is derived almost entirely from internal sources.
- It is highly detailed, being the processing of raw data.
- It relates to the immediate term, and is prepared constantly, or very frequently.
- It is task-specific and largely quantitative.

3 Financial accounting and cost and management accounting

3.1 Financial accounts and management accounts

FAST FORWARD

> **Financial accounting systems** ensure that the assets and liabilities of a business are properly accounted for, and provide information about profits and so on to shareholders and to other interested parties. **Management accounting systems** provide information specifically for the use of managers within an organisation.

Management information provides a common source from which is drawn information for two groups of people.

(a) **Financial accounts** are prepared for individuals **external** to an organisation: shareholders, customers, suppliers, tax authorities, employees.

(b) **Management accounts** are prepared for **internal** managers of an organisation.

The data used to prepare financial accounts and management accounts are the same. The differences between the financial accounts and the management accounts arise because the data is analysed differently.

3.2 Financial accounts versus management accounts

Financial accounts	Management accounts
Financial accounts detail the performance of an organisation over a defined period and the state of affairs at the end of that period.	Management accounts are used to aid management record, plan and control the organisation's activities and to help the decision-making process.
Limited liability companies must, by law, prepare financial accounts.	There is no legal requirement to prepare management accounts.
The format of published financial accounts is determined by local law, by International Accounting Standards and International Financial Reporting Standards. In principle the accounts of different organisations can therefore be easily compared.	The format of management accounts is entirely at management discretion: no strict rules govern the way they are prepared or presented. Each organisation can devise its own management accounting system and format of reports.
Financial accounts concentrate on the business as a whole, aggregating revenues and costs from different operations, and are an end in themselves.	Management accounts can focus on specific areas of an organisation's activities. Information may be produced to aid a decision rather than to be an end product of a decision.
Most financial accounting information is of a monetary nature.	Management accounts incorporate non-monetary measures. Management may need to know, for example, tons of aluminium produced, monthly machine hours, or miles travelled by salesmen.
Financial accounts present an essentially historic picture of past operations.	Management accounts are both an historical record and a future planning tool.

Which of the following statements about management accounts is/are true?

(i)   There is a legal requirement to prepare management accounts.

(ii)   The format of management accounts is largely determined by law.

(iii) They serve as a future planning tool and are not used as a historical record.

A   (i) and (ii)

B   (ii) and (iii)

C   (iii) only

D   None of the statements are correct.

Answer

D

Statement (i) is incorrect. Limited liability companies must, by law, prepare **financial** accounts.

The format of published financial accounts is determined by law. Statement (ii) is therefore incorrect.

Management accounts do serve as a future planning tool but they are also useful as a historical record of performance. Therefore all three statements are incorrect and D is the correct answer.

3.3 Cost accounts

FAST FORWARD

Cost accounting and management accounting are terms which are often used interchangeably. It is *not* correct to do so. **Cost accounting is part of management accounting. Cost accounting provides a bank of data for the management accountant to use.**

Cost accounting is concerned with the following.

- Preparing statements (eg budgets, costing)
- Cost data collection
- Applying costs to inventory, products and services

Management accounting is concerned with the following.

- Using financial data and communicating it as information to users

3.3.1 Aims of cost accounts

(a)   The **cost** of goods produced or services provided.

(b)   The **cost** of a department or work section.

(c)   What **revenues** have been.

(d)   The **profitability** of a product, a service, a department, or the organisation in total.

(e)   **Selling prices** with some regard for the costs of sale.

(f)   The **value of inventories of goods** (raw materials, work in progress, finished goods) that are still held in store at the end of a period, thereby aiding the preparation of a balance sheet of the company's assets and liabilities.

(g)   **Future costs** of goods and services (costing is an integral part of budgeting (planning) for the future).

(h)   **How actual costs compare with budgeted costs.** (If an organisation plans for its revenues and costs to be a certain amount, but they actually turn out differently, the differences can be measured and reported. Management can use these reports as a guide to whether corrective action (or 'control' action) is needed to sort out a problem revealed by these differences between budgeted and actual results. This system of control is often referred to as budgetary control.

(i)   **What information management needs** in order to make sensible decisions about profits and costs.

It would be wrong to suppose that cost accounting systems are restricted to manufacturing operations, although they are probably more fully developed in this area of work. **Service industries**, **government departments** and **welfare activities** can all make use of cost accounting information. Within a manufacturing organisation, the cost accounting system should be applied not only to **manufacturing** but also to **administration**, **selling and distribution**, **research and development** and all other departments.

4 Presentation of information to management

4.1 Reports

Data and information are usually presented to management in the form of a **report**. The main features of a report are: TITLE; TO; FROM; DATE; and SUBJECT.

In small organisations it is possible, however, that information will be communicated in a less formal manner than writing a report (orally or using informal reports/memos).

Throughout this Study Text, you will come across a number of techniques which allow financial information to be collected. Once it has been collected it is usually analysed and reported back to management in the form of a **report**.

4.2 Main features of a report

- **TITLE**
  Most reports are usually given a heading to show that it is a report.

- **WHO IS THE REPORT INTENDED FOR?**
  It is vital that the intended recipients of a report are clearly identified. For example, if you are writing a report for Joe Bloggs, it should be clearly stated at the head of the report.

- **WHO IS THE REPORT FROM?**
  If the recipients of the report have any comments or queries, it is important that they know who to contact.

- **DATE**
  We have already mentioned that information should be communicated at the most appropriate time. It is also important to show this timeliness by giving your report a date.

- **SUBJECT**
  What is the report about? Managers are likely to receive a great number of reports that they need to review. It is useful to know what a report is about before you read it!

- **APPENDIX**
  In general, information is summarised in a report and the more detailed calculations and data are included in an appendix at the end of the report.

Chapter roundup

- **Data** is the raw material for data processing. Data relate to facts, events and transactions and so forth.

  Information is data that has been processed in such a way as to be **meaningful** to the person who receives it. **Information** is anything that is communicated.

- Good information should be **relevant, complete, accurate, clear**, it should **inspire confidence**, it should be **appropriately communicated**, its **volume** should be manageable, it should be **timely** and its **cost** should be less than the benefits it provides.

- Information for management accounting is likely to be used for **planning, control** and **decision making**.

- An **objective** is the aim or **goal** of an organisation (or an individual). Note that in practice, the terms objective, goal and aim are often used interchangeably. A **strategy** is a possible course of action that might enable an organisation (or an individual) to achieve its objectives.

- Anthony divides management activities into **strategic planning, management control** and **operational control**.

- A **management control system** is a system which measures and corrects the performance of activities of subordinates in order to make sure that the objectives of an organisation are being met and the plans devised to attain them are being carried out.

- Information within an organisation can be analysed into the three levels assumed in Anthony's hierarchy: **strategic; tactical;** and **operational**.

- **Financial accounting systems** ensure that the assets and liabilities of a business are properly accounted for, and provide information about profits and so on to shareholders and to other interested parties. **Management accounting systems** provide information specifically for the use of managers within the organisation.

- Cost accounting and management accounting are terms which are often used interchangeably. It is not correct to do so. **Cost accounting is part of management accounting. Cost accounting provides a bank of data for the management accountant to use.**

- Data and information are usually presented to management in the form of a report. The main features of a report are: TITLE; TO; FROM; DATE; and SUBJECT.

Quick quiz

1   Define the terms **data** and **information**.

2   The four main qualities of good information are:

    • ....   • ....

    • ....   • ....

3   In terms of management accounting, information is most likely to be used for (1) ....,
   (2) .... or (3) ....

4   A strategy is the aim or goal of an organisation.

   True   ☐   False   ☐

5   **Organisation**   **Objective**

   Profit making
   Non-profit making

6   What are the three types of management activity identified by R N Anthony?

   (1) ....   (3) ....

   (2) ....

7   A management control system is

   A   a possible course of action that might enable an organisation to achieve its objectives ✗

   B   a collective term for the hardware and software used to drive a database system ✗

   C   a set up that measures and corrects the performance of activities of subordinates in order to make
        sure that the objectives of an organisation are being met and their associated plans are being ✓
        carried out

   D   a system that controls and maximises the profits of an organisation ✗

8   List six differences between financial accounts and management accounts.

9   When preparing reports, what are the five key points to remember?

   (1) ....   (4) ....

   (2) ....   (5) ....

   (3) ....

Answers to quick quiz

1   **Data** is the raw material for data processing. **Information** is data that has been processed in such a way as to be meaningful to the person who receives it. **Information** is anything that is communicated.

2   • Relevance   • Accuracy
    • Completeness   • Clarity

3   (1) Planning   (3) Decision making
    (2) Control

4   False. This is the definition of an **objective**. A strategy is a possible course of action that might enable an organisation to **achieve** its objectives.

5   Profit making = maximise profits
    Non-profit making = provide goods and services

6   (1) Strategic planning   (3) Operational control
    (2) Management control

7   C

8   See Paragraph 3.2

9   • Title   • Date
    • Who is the report to   • Subject
    • Who is the report from

    Now try the question below from the Exam Question Bank

Now try the questions below from the Exam Question Bank

Number	Level	Marks	Time
Q1	MCQ	n/a	n/a

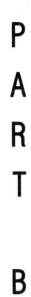

P
A
R
T

B

Cost classification, behaviour and purpose

Cost classification

Topic list	Syllabus reference
1 Total product/service costs	B1 (a)
2 Direct costs and indirect costs	B2 (a)
3 Functional costs	B1 (a)
4 Fixed costs and variable costs	B1 (d)
5 Production and non-production costs	B1 (a)
6 Other cost classifications	B1 (c)
7 Cost units, cost objects and responsibility centres	A1 (a)

Introduction

The **classification of costs** as either **direct** or **indirect**, for example, is essential in the costing method used by an organisation to determine the cost of a unit of product or service.

The **fixed** and **variable cost classifications**, on the other hand, are important in **absorption** and **marginal costing**, **cost behaviour** and **cost-volume-profit analysis**. You will meet all of these topics as we progress through the Study Text.

This chapter therefore acts as a foundation stone for a number of other chapters in the text and hence an understanding of the concepts covered in it is vital before you move on.

Study guide

Exam guide

Cost classification is one of the key areas of the syllabus and you can therefore expect to see it in the exam that you will be facing.

1 Total product/service costs

The total cost of making a product or providing a service consists of the following.

(a) Cost of **materials**

(b) Cost of the **wages** and **salaries** (labour costs)

(c) Cost of **other expenses**

- Rent and rates
- Electricity and gas bills
- Depreciation

2 Direct costs and indirect costs

2.1 Materials, labour and expenses

FAST FORWARD

A **direct cost** is a cost that can be traced in full to the product, service, or department that is being costed. An **indirect cost** (or **overhead**) is a cost that is incurred in the course of making a product, providing a service or running a department, but which cannot be traced directly and in full to the product, service or department.

Materials, labour costs and other expenses can be classified as either **direct costs** or **indirect costs**.

(a) **Direct material costs** are the costs of materials that are known to have been used in making and selling a product (or even providing a service).

(b) **Direct labour costs** are the specific costs of the workforce used to make a product or provide a service. Direct labour costs are established by measuring the time taken for a job, or the time taken in 'direct production work'.

(c) **Other direct expenses** are those expenses that have been incurred in full as a direct consequence of making a product, or providing a service, or running a department.

Examples of indirect costs include supervisors' wages, cleaning materials and buildings insurance.

2.2 Analysis of total cost

Materials	=	Direct materials	+	Indirect materials
+		+		+
Labour	=	Direct labour	+	Indirect labour
+		+		+
Expenses	=	Direct expenses	+	Indirect expenses
Total cost	=	Direct cost	+	Overhead

2.3 Direct material

Key term

> **Direct material** is all material becoming part of the product (unless used in negligible amounts and/or having negligible cost).

Direct material costs are charged to the product as part of the **prime cost**. Examples of direct material are as follows.

(a) **Component parts**, specially purchased for a particular job, order or process.

(b) **Part-finished work** which is transferred from department 1 to department 2 becomes finished work of department 1 and a direct material cost in department 2.

(c) **Primary packing materials** like cartons and boxes.

2.4 Direct labour

Key term

> **Direct wages** are all wages paid for labour (either as basic hours or as overtime) expended on work on the product itself.

Direct wages costs are charged to the product as part of the **prime cost**.

Examples of groups of labour receiving payment as direct wages are as follows.

(a) Workers engaged in **altering** the condition or composition of the product.

(b) Inspectors, analysts and testers **specifically required** for such production.

(c) Foremen, shop clerks and anyone else whose wages are **specifically identified.**

Two **trends** may be identified in **direct labour costs.**

- The ratio of direct labour costs to total product cost is falling as the use of machinery increases, and hence depreciation charges increase.

- Skilled labour costs and sub-contractors' costs are increasing as direct labour costs decrease.

Question | Labour costs

Classify the following labour costs as either direct or indirect.

(a) The basic pay of direct workers (cash paid, tax and other deductions)   *direct*
(b) The basic pay of indirect workers   *indirect*
(c) Overtime premium   *direct & indir*

(d) Bonus payments *ind*

(e) Social insurance contributions *Indir*

(f) Idle time of direct workers *Indir*

(g) Work on installation of equipment *direct*

Answer

Answer

(a) The basic pay of direct workers is a direct cost to the unit, job or process.

(b) The basic pay of indirect workers is an indirect cost, unless a customer asks for an order to be carried out which involves the dedicated use of indirect workers' time, when the cost of this time would be a direct labour cost of the order.

(c) Overtime premium paid to both direct and indirect workers is an indirect cost, except in two particular circumstances.

  (i) If overtime is worked at the specific request of a customer to get his order completed, the overtime premium paid is a direct cost of the order.

  (ii) If overtime is worked regularly by a production department in the normal course of operations, the overtime premium paid to direct workers could be incorporated into the (average) direct labour hourly rate.

(d) Bonus payments are generally an indirect cost.

(e) Employer's National Insurance contributions (which are added to employees' total pay as a wages cost) are normally treated as an indirect labour cost.

(f) Idle time is an overhead cost, that is an indirect labour cost.

(g) The cost of work on capital equipment is incorporated into the capital cost of the equipment.

2.5 Direct expenses

Key term

> **Direct expenses** are any expenses which are incurred on a specific product other than direct material cost and direct wages

Direct expenses are charged to the product as part of the **prime** cost. Examples of direct expenses are as follows.

- The **hire of tools** or equipment for a particular job
- **Maintenance costs** of tools, fixtures and so on

Direct expenses are also referred to as **chargeable expenses.**

2.6 Production overhead

Key term

> **Production (or factory) overhead** includes all indirect material costs, indirect wages and indirect expenses incurred in the factory from receipt of the order until its completion.

Production overhead includes the following.

(a) **Indirect materials** which cannot be traced in the finished product.

- Consumable stores, eg material used in negligible amounts

(b) **Indirect wages**, meaning all wages not charged directly to a product.

- Wages of non-productive personnel in the production department, eg foremen

(c) **Indirect expenses** (other than material and labour) not charged directly to production.

- Rent, rates and insurance of a factory
- Depreciation, fuel, power, maintenance of plant, machinery and buildings

2.7 Administration overhead

Administration overhead is all indirect material costs, wages and expenses incurred in the direction, control and administration of an undertaking.

Examples of administration overhead are as follows.

- **Depreciation** of office buildings and equipment.
- **Office salaries**, including salaries of directors, secretaries and accountants.
- Rent, rates, insurance, lighting, cleaning, telephone charges and so on.

2.8 Selling overhead

Selling overhead is all indirect materials costs, wages and expenses incurred in promoting sales and retaining customers.

Examples of selling overhead are as follows.

- **Printing** and **stationery**, such as catalogues and price lists.
- **Salaries** and **commission** of salesmen, representatives and sales department staff.
- **Advertising** and **sales promotion**, market research.
- Rent, rates and insurance of sales offices and showrooms, bad debts and so on.

2.9 Distribution overhead

Distribution overhead is all indirect material costs, wages and expenses incurred in making the packed product ready for despatch and delivering it to the customer.

Examples of distribution overhead are as follows.

- Cost of packing cases.
- Wages of packers, drivers and despatch clerks.
- Insurance charges, rent, rates, depreciation of warehouses and so on.

Question   Direct labour cost

A direct labour employee's wage in week 5 consists of the following.

		$
(a)	Basic pay for normal hours worked, 36 hours at $4 per hour =	144
(b)	Pay at the basic rate for overtime, 6 hours at $4 per hour =	24
(c)	Overtime shift premium, with overtime paid at time-and-a-quarter ¼ × 6 hours × $4 per hour =	6
(d)	A bonus payment under a group bonus (or 'incentive') scheme – bonus for the month =	30
	Total gross wages in week 5 for 42 hours of work	204

What is the direct labour cost for this employee in week 5?

A $144   B $168   C $198   D $204

Answer

Let's start by considering a general approach to answering multiple choice questions (MCQs). In a numerical question like this, the best way to begin is to ignore the available options and work out your own answer from the available data. If your solution corresponds to one of the four options then mark this as your chosen answer and move on. Don't waste time working out whether any of the other options might be correct. If your answer does not appear among the available options then check your workings. If it still does not correspond to any of the options then you need to take a calculated guess.

Do not make the common error of simply selecting the answer which is closest to yours. The best thing to do is to first eliminate any answers which you know or suspect are incorrect. For example you could eliminate C and D because you know that group bonus schemes are usually indirect costs. You are then left with a choice between A and B, and at least you have now improved your chances if you really are guessing.

The correct answer is B because the basic rate for overtime is a part of direct wages cost. It is only the overtime premium that is usually regarded as an overhead or indirect cost.

3 Functional costs

3.1 Classification by function

Classification by function involves classifying costs as production/manufacturing costs, administration costs or marketing/selling and distribution costs.

In a 'traditional' costing system for a manufacturing organisation, costs are classified as follows.

(a) **Production** or **manufacturing costs.** These are costs associated with the factory.

(b) **Administration costs.** These are costs associated with general office departments.

(c) **Marketing**, or **selling** and **distribution costs.** These are costs associated with sales, marketing, warehousing and transport departments.

Classification in this way is known as **classification by function**. Expenses that do not fall fully into one of these classifications might be categorised as **general overheads** or even listed as a classification on their own (for example research and development costs).

3.2 Full cost of sales

In costing a small product made by a manufacturing organisation, direct costs are usually restricted to some of the production costs. A commonly found build-up of costs is therefore as follows.

	$
Production costs	
Direct materials	A
Direct wages	B
Direct expenses	C
Prime cost	A+B+C
Production overheads	D
Full factory cost	A+B+C+D
Administration costs	E
Selling and distribution costs	F
Full cost of sales	A+B+C+D+E+F

3.3 Functional costs

(a) **Production costs** are the costs which are incurred by the sequence of operations beginning with the supply of raw materials, and ending with the completion of the product ready for warehousing as a finished goods item. Packaging costs are production costs where they relate to 'primary' packing (boxes, wrappers and so on).

(b) **Administration costs** are the costs of managing an organisation, that is, planning and controlling its operations, but only insofar as such administration costs are not related to the production, sales, distribution or research and development functions.

(c) **Selling costs**, sometimes known as marketing costs, are the costs of creating demand for products and securing firm orders from customers.

(d) **Distribution costs** are the costs of the sequence of operations with the receipt of finished goods from the production department and making them ready for despatch and ending with the reconditioning for reuse of empty containers.

(e) **Research costs** are the costs of searching for new or improved products, whereas **development costs** are the costs incurred between the decision to produce a new or improved product and the commencement of full manufacture of the product.

(f) **Financing costs** are costs incurred to finance the business such as loan interest.

Question
Cost classification

Within the costing system of a manufacturing company the following types of expense are incurred.

Reference number

1 (a)	Cost of oils used to lubricate production machinery (a)
2 (c)(d)	Motor vehicle licences for lorries (d)
3 (a)	Depreciation of factory plant and equipment (a)
4 (e)	Cost of chemicals used in the laboratory (a)
5 (	Commission paid to sales representatives (c)
6	Salary of the secretary to the finance director (b)
7	Trade discount given to customers (c)
8	Holiday pay of machine operatives (b)
9	Salary of security guard in raw material warehouse (b)
10	Fees to advertising agency (e)
11	Rent of finished goods warehouse (b)
12	Salary of scientist in laboratory (b)
13	Insurance of the company's premises (
14	Salary of supervisor working in the factory
15	Cost of typewriter ribbons in the general office
16	Protective clothing for machine operatives

Required

Complete the following table by placing each expense in the correct cost classification.

Cost classification	Reference number					
Production costs	1	3	8	9	14	16
Selling and distribution costs	2	5	7	10	11	
Administration costs	6	13	15			
Research and development costs	4	12				

Each type of expense should appear only once in your answer. You may use the reference numbers in your answer.

Answer

Cost classification	Reference number					
Production costs	1	3	8	9	14	16
Selling and distribution costs	2	5	7	10	11	
Administration costs	6	13	15			
Research and development costs	4	12				

4 Fixed costs and variable costs

4.1 Introduction

FAST FORWARD

A different way of analysing and classifying costs is into **fixed costs** and **variable costs**. Many items of expenditure are part-fixed and part-variable and hence are termed **semi-fixed** or **semi-variable costs.**

Key terms

> A **fixed cost** is a cost which is incurred for a particular period of time and which, within certain activity levels, is unaffected by changes in the level of activity.
>
> A **variable cost** is a cost which tends to vary with the level of activity.

4.2 Examples of fixed and variable costs

(a) Direct material costs are **variable costs** because they rise as more units of a product are manufactured.

(b) Sales commission is often a fixed percentage of sales turnover, and so is a **variable cost** that varies with the level of sales.

(c) Telephone call charges are likely to increase if the volume of business expands, but there is also a fixed element of line rental, and so they are a **semi-fixed** or **semi-variable overhead cost.**

(d) The rental cost of business premises is a constant amount, at least within a stated time period, and so it is a **fixed cost.**

5 Production and non-production costs

FAST FORWARD

For the preparation of financial statements, costs are often classified as **production costs** and **non-production costs**. Production costs are costs identified with goods produced for resale. Non-production costs are cost deducted as expenses during the current period.

Production costs are all the costs involved in the manufacture of goods. In the case of manufactured goods, these costs consist of direct material, direct labour and manufacturing overhead.

Non-production costs are taken directly to the profit and loss account as expenses in the period in which they are incurred; such costs consist of selling and administrative expenses.

5.1 Production and non-production costs

The distinction between production and non-production costs is the basis of valuing inventory.

5.2 Example

A business has the following costs for a period:

	$
Materials	600
Labour	1,000
Production overheads	500
Administration overheads	700
	2,800

During the period 100 units are produced. If all of these costs were allocated to production units, each unit would be valued at $28.

This would be incorrect. Only **production** costs are allocated to units of inventory. Administrative overheads are **non-production** costs.

So each unit of inventory should be valued at $21((600 + 1,000 + 500)/100)

This affects both gross profit and the valuation of closing inventory. If during the period 80 units are sold at $40 each, the gross profit will be:

	$
Sales (80 × 40)	3,200
Cost of sales (80 × 21)	(1,680)
Gross profit	1,520

The value of closing (unsold) inventory will be $420 (20 × 21).

6 Other cost classifications

Key terms

> **Avoidable costs** are specific costs of an activity or business which would be avoided if the activity or business did not exist.
>
> **Unavoidable costs** are costs which would be incurred whether or not an activity or sector existed.
>
> A **controllable cost** is a cost which can be influenced by management decisions and actions.
>
> An **uncontrollable cost** is any cost that cannot be affected by management within a given time span.
>
> **Discretionary costs** are costs which are likely to arise from decisions made during the budgeting process. They are likely to be fixed amounts of money over fixed periods of time.

Examples of discretionary costs are as follows.

- Advertising
- Research and Development
- Training

7 Cost units, cost objects and responsibility centres

7.1 Cost centres

FAST FORWARD

> **Cost centres** are collecting places for costs before they are further analysed. Costs are further analysed into cost units once they have been traced to cost centres.

Costs consist of the costs of the following.

- Direct materials
- Direct labour
- Direct expenses
- Production overheads
- Administration overheads
- General overheads

When costs are incurred, they are generally allocated to a **cost centre**. Cost centres may include the following.

- A department
- A machine, or group of machines
- A project (eg the installation of a new computer system)
- Overhead costs eg rent, rates, electricity (which may then be allocated to departments or projects)

Cost centres are an essential 'building block' of a costing system. They are the starting point for the following.

(a) The classification of actual costs incurred.
(b) The preparation of budgets of planned costs.
(c) The comparison of actual costs and budgeted costs (management control).

7.2 Cost units

A **cost unit** is a unit of product or service to which costs can be related. The cost unit is the basic control unit for costing purposes.

Once costs have been traced to cost centres, they can be further analysed in order to establish a **cost per cost unit**. Alternatively, some items of cost may be charged directly to a cost unit, for example direct materials and direct labour costs.

Examples of cost units include the following.

- Patient episode (in a hospital)   • Room (in a hotel)
- Barrel (in the brewing industry)

Question
Cost units

Suggest suitable cost units which could be used to aid control within the following organisations.

(a) A hotel with 50 double rooms and 10 single rooms
(b) A hospital
(c) A road haulage business

Answer

(a) Guest/night   (b) Patient/night   (c) Tonne/mile
     Bed occupied/night   Operation   Mile
     Meal supplied   Outpatient visit

7.3 Cost objects

A **cost object** is any activity for which a separate measurement of costs is desired.

If the users of management information wish to know the cost of something, this something is called a **cost object**. Examples include the following.

- The cost of a product   – The cost of operating a department
- The cost of a service

7.4 Profit centres

Profit centres are similar to cost centres but are accountable for **costs** *and* **revenues**.

We have seen that a cost centre is where costs are collected. Some organisations, however, work on a profit centre basis.

Profit centre managers should normally have control over how revenue is raised and how costs are incurred. Often, several cost centres will comprise one profit centre. The profit centre manager will be able to make decisions about both purchasing and selling and will be expected to do both as profitably as possible.

A profit centre manager will want information regarding both revenues and costs. He will be judged on the profit margin achieved by his division. In practice, it may be that there are fixed costs which he cannot control, so he should be judged on contribution, which is revenue less variable costs. In this case he will want information about which products yield the highest contribution.

7.5 Revenue centres

FAST FORWARD **Revenue centres** are similar to cost centres and profit centres but are accountable for **revenues only**. Revenue centre managers should normally have control over how revenues are raised

A revenue centre manager is not accountable for costs. He will be aiming purely to maximise sales revenue. He will want information on markets and new products and he will look closely at pricing and the sales performance of competitors – in addition to monitoring revenue figures.

7.6 Investment centres

FAST FORWARD An **investment centre** is a profit centre with additional responsibilities for capital investment and possibly for financing, and whose performance is measured by its return on investment.

An investment centre manager will take the same decisions as a profit centre manager but he also has additional responsibility for investment. So he will be judged additionally on his handling of cash surpluses and he will seek to make only those investments which yield a higher percentage than the company's notional cost of capital. So the investment centre manager will want the same information as the profit centre manager and in addition he will require quite detailed appraisals of possible investments and information regarding the results of investments already undertaken. He will have to make decisions regarding the purchase or lease of non-current assets and the investment of cash surpluses. Most of these decisions involve large sums of money.

7.7 Responsibility centres

FAST FORWARD A **responsibility centre** is a department or organisational function whose performance is the direct responsibility of a specific manager.

Cost centres, revenue centres, profit centres and investment centres are also known as **responsibility centres**.

Question
Investment centre

Which of the following is a characteristic of an investment centre?

A   Managers have control over marketing.
B   Management have a sales team.
C   Management have a sales team and are given a credit control function.
D   Managers can purchase capital assets.

Answer

The correct answer is D.

Exam focus point

This chapter has introduced a number of new terms and definitions. The topics covered in this chapter are key areas of the syllabus and are likely to be tested in the F2 – *Management Accounting* examination.

Chapter roundup

- A **direct cost** is a cost that can be traced in full to the product, service or department being costed. An **indirect cost** (or overhead) is a cost that is incurred in the course of making a product, providing a service or running a department, but which cannot be traced directly and in full to the product, service or department.

- **Classification by function** involves classifying costs as production/manufacturing costs, administration costs or marketing/selling and distribution costs.

- A different way of analysing and classifying costs is into **fixed costs** and **variable costs**. Many items of expenditure are part-fixed and part-variable and hence are termed **semi-fixed** or **semi-variable** costs.

- For the preparation of financial statements, costs are often classified as **production costs** and **non-production costs**. Production costs are costs identified with goods produced or purchased for resale. Non-production costs are costs deducted as expenses during the current period.

- **Cost centres** are collecting places for costs before they are further analysed. Costs are further analysed into cost units once they have been traced to cost centres.

- A **cost unit** is a unit of product or service to which costs can be related. The cost unit is the basic control unit for costing purposes.

- A **cost object** is any activity for which a separate measurement of costs is desired.

- **Profit centres** are similar to cost centres but are accountable for both **costs** *and* **revenues**.

- **Revenue centres** are similar to cost centres and profit centres but are accountable for **revenues only**.

- An **investment centre** is a profit centre with additional responsibilities for capital investment and possibly financing, and whose performance is measured by its return on investment.

- A **responsibility centre** is a department or organisational function whose performance is the direct responsibility of a specific manager.

Quick quiz

1   Give two examples of direct expenses.
2   Give an example of an administration overhead, a selling overhead and a distribution overhead.
3   What are functional costs?
4   What is the distinction between fixed and variable costs?
5   What are production costs and non-production costs?
6   What is a cost centre?
7   What is a cost unit?
8   What is a profit centre?
9   What is an investment centre?

Answers to quick quiz

1. - The hire of tools or equipment for a particular job
   - Maintenance costs of tools, fixtures and so on

2. - **Administration overhead** = Depreciation of office buildings and equipment
   - **Selling overhead** = Printing and stationery (catalogues, price lists)
   - **Distribution overhead** = Wages of packers, drivers and despatch clerks

3. Functional costs are classified as follows.

   - **Production** or **manufacturing costs**
   - **Administration costs**
   - **Marketing** or **selling and distribution costs**

4. A **fixed cost** is a cost which is incurred for a particular period of time and which, within certain activity levels, is unaffected by changes in the level of activity.

   A **variable cost** is a cost which tends to vary with the level of activity.

5. **Production costs** are costs identified with a finished product. Such costs are initially identified as part of the value of inventory. They become expenses only when the inventory is sold.

   Non-production costs are costs that are deducted as expenses during the current period without ever being included in the value of inventory held.

6. A **cost centre** acts as a collecting place for certain costs before they are analysed further.

7. A **cost unit** is a unit of product or service to which costs can be related. The cost unit is the basic control unit for costing purposes.

8. A **profit centre** is similar to a cost centre but is accountable for **costs** and **revenues**.

9. An **investment centre** is a profit centre with additional responsibilities for capital investment and possibly financing.

Now try the questions below from the Exam Question Bank

Number	Level	Marks	Time
Q2	MCQ/OTQ	n/a	n/a

Cost behaviour

Topic list	Syllabus reference
1 Introduction to cost behaviour	B3 (b)
2 Cost behaviour patterns	B3 (a)
3 Determining the fixed and variable elements of semi-variable costs	B3 (c)

Introduction

So far in this text we have introduced you to the subject of management information and explained in general terms what it is and what it does. In Chapter 2 we considered the principal methods of classifying costs. In particular, we introduced the concept of the division of costs into those that vary directly with changes in activity levels (**variable costs**) and those that do not (**fixed costs**). This chapter examines further this two-way split of **cost behaviour** and explains one method of splitting semi-variable costs into these two elements, the **high-low** method.

Study guide

		Intellectual level
B3	**Fixed and variable cost**	
(a)	Describe and illustrate graphically different types of cost behaviour	1
(b)	Explain and provide examples of costs that fall into categories of fixed, stepped fixed and variable costs	1
(c)	Use high-low analysis to separate the fixed and variable elements of total costs including situations involving stepped fixed costs and changes in the variable cost per unit	2

Exam guide

Cost behaviour is a key area of the **Management Accounting** syllabus and you need to understand fixed and variable elements and the use of high-low analysis.

1 Introduction to cost behaviour

1.1 Cost behaviour and decision making

FAST FORWARD

Cost behaviour is the way in which costs are affected by changes in the volume of output.

Management decisions will often be based on how costs and revenues vary at different activity levels. Examples of such decisions are as follows.

- What should the **planned activity level** be for the next period?
- Should the **selling price** be reduced in order to sell more units?
- Should a particular component be **manufactured internally** or **bought in**?
- Should a **contract** be undertaken?

1.2 Cost behaviour and cost control

If the accountant does not know the level of costs which should have been incurred as a result of an organisation's activities, how can he or she hope to control costs?

1.3 Cost behaviour and budgeting

Knowledge of cost behaviour is obviously essential for the tasks of **budgeting**, **decision making** and **control accounting**.

Exam focus point

Remember that the behavioural analysis of costs is important for planning, control and decision-making.

1.4 Cost behaviour and levels of activity

There are many factors which may influence costs. The major influence is **volume of output**, or the **level of activity**. The level of activity may refer to one of the following.

- Number of units produced
- Value of items sold
- Number of items sold
- Number of invoices issued
- Number of units of electricity consumed

1.5 Cost behaviour principles

The basic principle of cost behaviour is that **as the level of activity rises, costs will usually rise**. It will cost more to produce 2,000 units of output than it will cost to produce 1,000 units.

This principle is common sense. The problem for the accountant, however, is to determine, for each item of cost, the way in which costs rise and by how much as the level of activity increases. For our purposes here, the level of activity for measuring cost will generally be taken to be the **volume of production**.

1.6 Example: cost behaviour and activity level

Hans Bratch has a fleet of company cars for sales representatives. Running costs have been estimated as follows.

(a) Cars cost $12,000 when new, and have a guaranteed trade-in value of $6,000 at the end of two years. Depreciation is charged on a straight-line basis.

(b) Petrol and oil cost 15 cents per mile.

(c) Tyres cost $300 per set to replace; replacement occurs after 30,000 miles.

(d) Routine maintenance costs $200 per car (on average) in the first year and $450 in the second year.

(e) Repairs average $400 per car over two years and are thought to vary with mileage. The average car travels 25,000 miles per annum.

(f) Tax, insurance, membership of motoring organisations and so on cost $400 per annum per car.

Required

Calculate the average cost per annum of cars which travel 15,000 miles per annum and 30,000 miles per annum.

Solution

Costs may be analysed into fixed, variable and stepped cost items, a stepped cost being a cost which is fixed in nature but only within certain levels of activity.

(a) **Fixed costs**

	$ per annum
Depreciation $(12,000 − 6,000) ÷ 2	3,000
Routine maintenance $(200 + 450) ÷ 2	325
Tax, insurance etc	400
	3,725

(b) **Variable costs**

	Cents per mile
Petrol and oil	15.0
Repairs ($400 ÷ 50,000 miles)*	0.8
	15.8

* If the average car travels 25,000 miles per annum, it will be expected to travel 50,000 miles over two years (this will correspond with the repair bill of $400 over two years).

(c) Step costs are tyre replacement costs, which are $300 at the end of every 30,000 miles.

(i) If the car travels less than or exactly 30,000 miles in two years, the tyres will not be changed. Average cost of tyres per annum = $0.

(ii) If a car travels more than 30,000 miles and up to (and including) 60,000 miles in two years, there will be one change of tyres in the period. Average cost of tyres per annum = $150 ($300 ÷ 2).

(iii) If a car exceeds 60,000 miles in two years (up to 90,000 miles) there will be two tyre changes. Average cost of tyres per annum = $300 ($600 ÷ 2).

The estimated costs per annum of cars travelling 15,000 miles per annum and 30,000 miles per annum would therefore be as follows.

	15,000 miles per annum $	30,000 miles per annum $
Fixed costs	3,725	3,725
Variable costs (15.8c per mile)	2,370	4,740
Tyres	–	150
Cost per annum	6,095	8,615

2 Cost behaviour patterns

2.1 Fixed costs

A **fixed cost** is a cost which tends to be unaffected by increases or decreases in the volume of output.

Fixed costs are a **period charge**, in that they relate to a span of time; as the time span increases, so too will the fixed costs (which are sometimes referred to as period costs for this reason). It is important to understand that **fixed costs always have a variable element**, since an increase or decrease in production may also bring about an increase or decrease in fixed costs.

A sketch graph of fixed cost would look like this.

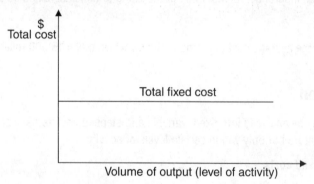

Examples of a fixed cost would be as follows.

- The salary of the managing director (per month or per annum)
- The rent of a single factory building (per month or per annum)
- Straight line depreciation of a single machine (per month or per annum)

2.2 Step costs

A **step cost** is a cost which is fixed in nature but only within certain levels of activity.

Consider the depreciation of a machine which may be fixed if production remains below 1,000 units per month. If production exceeds 1,000 units, a second machine may be required, and the cost of depreciation (on two machines) would go up a step. A sketch graph of a step cost could look like this.

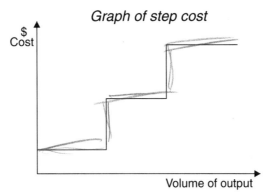

Graph of step cost

Other examples of step costs are as follows.

(a) Rent is a step cost in situations where accommodation requirements increase as output levels get higher.

(b) Basic pay of employees is nowadays usually fixed, but as output rises, more employees (direct workers, supervisors, managers and so on) are required.

(c) Royalties.

2.3 Variable costs

FAST FORWARD

A **variable cost** is a cost which tends to vary directly with the volume of output. The variable cost per unit is the same amount for each unit produced.

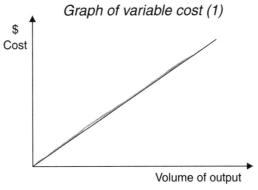

Graph of variable cost (1)

A constant variable cost per unit implies that the price per unit of say, material purchased is constant, and that the rate of material usage is also constant.

(a) The most important variable cost is the **cost of raw materials** (where there is no discount for bulk purchasing since bulk purchase discounts reduce the cost of purchases).

(b) **Direct labour costs** are, for very important reasons, classed as a variable cost even though basic wages are usually fixed.

(c) **Sales commission** is variable in relation to the volume or value of sales.

(d) **Bonus payments** for productivity to employees might be variable once a certain level of output is achieved, as the following diagram illustrates.

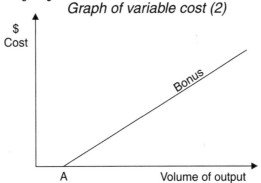

Graph of variable cost (2)

Up to output A, no bonus is earned.

2.4 Non-linear or curvilinear variable costs

If the relationship between total variable cost and volume of output can be shown as a curved line on a graph, the relationship is said to be **curvilinear**.

Two typical relationships are as follows.

(a)   (b)

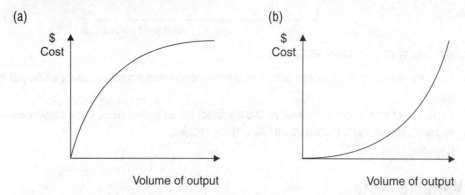

Each extra unit of output in graph (a) causes a **less than proportionate** increase in cost whereas in graph (b), each extra unit of output causes **a more than proportionate** increase in cost.

The cost of a piecework scheme for individual workers with differential rates could behave in a **curvilinear** fashion if the rates increase by small amounts at progressively higher output levels.

2.5 Semi-variable costs (or semi-fixed costs or mixed costs)

A **semi-variable/semi-fixed/mixed cost** is a cost which contains both fixed and variable components and so is partly affected by changes in the level of activity.

Examples of these costs include the following.

(a)   **Electricity and gas bills**

   - Fixed cost = standing charge
   - Variable cost = charge per unit of electricity used

(b)   **Salesman's salary**

   - Fixed cost = basic salary
   - Variable cost = commission on sales made

(c)   **Costs of running a car**

   - Fixed cost = road tax, insurance
   - Variable costs = petrol, oil, repairs (which vary with miles travelled)

2.6 Other cost behaviour patterns

Other cost behaviour patterns may be appropriate to certain cost items. Examples of two other cost behaviour patterns are shown below.

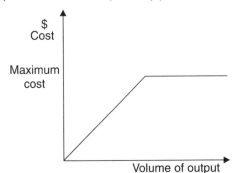

(a) *Cost behaviour pattern (1)*

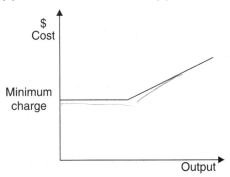

(b) *Cost behaviour pattern (2)*

- Graph (a) represents an item of cost which is variable with output up to a certain maximum level of cost.
- Graph (b) represents a cost which is variable with output, subject to a minimum (fixed) charge.

2.7 Cost behaviour and total and unit costs

The following table relates to different levels of production of the zed. The variable cost of producing a zed is $5. Fixed costs are $5,000.

	1 zed $	10 zeds $	50 zeds $
Total variable cost	5	50	250
Variable cost per unit	5	5	5
Total fixed cost	5,000	5,000	5,000
Fixed cost per unit	5,000	500	100
Total cost (fixed and variable)	5,005	5,050	5,250
Total cost per unit	5,005	505	105

What happens when activity levels rise can be summarised as follows.

- The variable cost per unit remains constant
- The fixed cost per unit falls
- The total cost per unit falls

This may be illustrated graphically as follows.

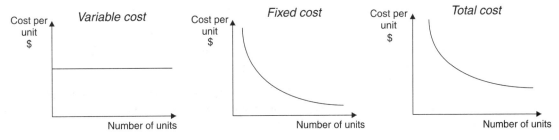

Question   **Fixed, variable, mixed costs**

Are the following likely to be fixed, variable or mixed costs?

(a) Telephone bill
(b) Annual salary of the chief accountant
(c) The management accountant's annual membership fee to CIMA (paid by the company)
(d) Cost of materials used to pack 20 units of product X into a box
(e) Wages of warehousemen

(a) Mixed
(b) Fixed
(c) Fixed
(d) Variable
(e) Variable

An exam question may give you a graph and require you to extract information from it.

2.8 Assumptions about cost behaviour

Assumptions about cost behaviour include the following.

(a) Within the normal or **relevant range** of output, costs are often assumed to be either **fixed**, **variable** or **semi-variable** (mixed).

(b) Departmental costs within an organisation are assumed to be **mixed costs**, with a **fixed** and a **variable** element.

(c) Departmental costs are assumed to rise in a straight line as the volume of activity increases. In other words, these costs are said to be **linear**.

The **high-low method** of determining fixed and variable elements of mixed costs relies on the assumption that mixed costs are linear. We shall now go on to look at this method of cost determination.

3 Determining the fixed and variable elements of semi-variable costs

3.1 Analysing costs

FAST FORWARD

The fixed and variable elements of semi-variable costs can be determined by the **high-low method**.

It is generally assumed that costs are one of the following.

- Variable
- Fixed
- Semi-variable

Cost accountants tend to separate semi-variable costs into their variable and fixed elements. They therefore generally tend to treat costs as either **fixed** or **variable**.

There are several methods for identifying the fixed and variable elements of semi-variable costs. Each method is only an estimate, and each will produce different results. One of the principal methods is the **high-low method**.

3.2 High-low method

Follow the steps below to estimate the fixed and variable elements of semi-variable costs.

Step 1 Review records of costs in previous periods.

- Select the period with the **highest** activity level.
- Select the period with the **lowest** activity level.

Step 2 Determine the following.

- Total cost at high activity level
- Total costs at low activity level
- Total units at high activity level
- Total units at low activity level

Step 3 Calculate the following.

$$\frac{\text{Total cost at high activity level} - \text{total cost at low activity level}}{\text{Total units at high activity level} - \text{total units at low activity level}} = \text{variable cost per unit (v)}$$

Step 4 The fixed costs can be determined as follows. (Total cost at high activity level) –(total units at high activity level × variable cost per unit)

The following graph demonstrates the high-low method.

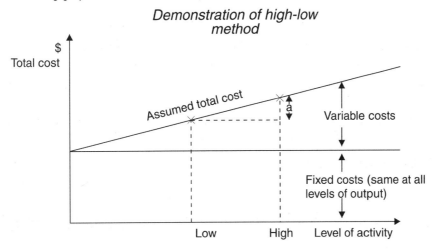

3.3 Example: The high-low method

DG Co has recorded the following total costs during the last five years.

Year	Output volume Units	Total cost $
20X0	65,000	145,000
20X1	80,000	162,000
20X2	90,000	170,000
20X3	60,000	140,000
20X4	75,000	160,000

Required

Calculate the total cost that should be expected in 20X5 if output is 85,000 units.

Solution

Step 1
- Period with highest activity = 20X2
- Period with lowest activity = 20X3

Step 2
- Total cost at high activity level = 170,000
- Total cost at low activity level = 140,000
- Total units at high activity level = 90,000
- Total units at low activity level = 60,000

Step 3 Variable cost per unit

$$= \frac{\text{total cost at high activity level} - \text{total cost at low activity level}}{\text{total units at high activity level} - \text{total units at low activity level}}$$

$$= \frac{170,000 - 140,000}{90,000 - 60,000} = \frac{30,000}{30,000} = \$1 \text{ per unit}$$

LEARNING MEDIA

Step 4   Fixed costs = (total cost at high activity level) – (total units at high activity level × variable
cost per unit)

= 170,000 – (90,000 × 1) = 170,000 – 90,000 = $80,000

Therefore the costs in 20X5 for output of 85,000 units are as follows.

			$
Variable costs =	85,000 × $1 =		85,000
Fixed costs =			80,000
			165,000

3.4 Example: The high-low method with stepped fixed costs

The following data relate to the overhead expenditure of contract cleaners (for industrial cleaning) at two
activity levels.

Square metres cleaned	12,750	15,100
Overheads	$73,950	$83,585

When more than 14,000 square metres are industrially cleaned, it is necessary to have another supervisor
and so the fixed costs rise to $43,350.

Required

Calculate the estimated overhead expenditure if 14,500 square metres are to be industrially cleaned.

Solution

	Units			$
High output	15,100	Total cost		83,585
Low output	12,750	Total cost		73,950
	2,350			9,635

$$\text{Variable cost} = \frac{\$9,635}{2,350}$$

= $4.10 per square metre

Estimated overhead expenditure if 14,500 square metres are to be industrially cleaned:

	$
Fixed costs	43,350
Variable costs (14,500 × $4.10)	59,450
	102,800

3.5 Example: The high-low method with a change in the variable cost per unit

Same data as the previous question.

Additionally, a round of wage negotiations have just taken place which will cost an additional $1 per
square metre.

Solution

Estimated overheads to clean 14,500 square metres.

Variable cost = $\frac{\$9,635}{2,350}$ =		$4.10	per square metre
Additional variable cost		£1.00	per square metre
Total variable cost		$5.10	per square metre

Cost for 14,500 square metres:

	$
Fixed	43,350
Variable costs (14,500 × $5.10)	73,950
	117,300

Question

The Valuation Department of a large firm of surveyors wishes to develop a method of predicting its total costs in a period. The following past costs have been recorded at two activity levels.

	Number of valuations (V)	Total cost (TC)
Period 1	420	82,200
Period 2	515	90,275

The total cost model for a period could be represented as follows.

A	TC = $46,500 + 85V	C	TC = $46,500 – 85V
B	TC = $42,000 + 95V	D	TC = $51,500 – 95V

Answer

Although we only have two activity levels in this question we can still apply the high-low method.

	Valuations V	Total cost $
Period 2	515	90,275
Period 1	420	82,200
Change due to variable cost	95	8,075

∴ Variable cost per valuation = $8,075/95 = $85.

Period 2: fixed cost = $90,275 – (515 × $85)
= $46,500

Using good MCQ technique, you should have managed to eliminate C and D as incorrect options straightaway. The variable cost must be added to the fixed cost, rather than subtracted from it. Once you had calculated the variable cost as $85 per valuation (as shown above), you should have been able to select option A without going on to calculate the fixed cost (we have shown this calculation above for completeness).

Chapter roundup

- **Cost behaviour** is the way in which costs are affected by changes in the volume of output.

- The basic principle of cost behaviour is that **as the level of activity rises, costs will usually rise**. It will cost more to produce 2,000 units of output than it will to produce 1,000 units.

- A **fixed cost** is a cost which tends to be unaffected by increases or decreases in the volume of output.

- A **step cost** is a cost which is fixed in nature but only within certain levels of activity.

- A **variable cost** is a cost which tends to vary directly with the volume of output. The variable cost per unit is the same amount for each unit produced.

- If the relationship between total variable cost and volume of output can be shown as a curved line on a graph, the relationship is said to be **curvilinear**.

- A **semi-variable/semi-fixed/mixed cost** is a cost which contains both fixed and variable components and so is partly affected by changes in the level of activity.

- The fixed and variable elements of semi-variable costs can be determined by the **high-low method**.

Quick quiz

1   Cost behaviour is ....

2   The basic principle of cost behaviour is that as the level of activity rises, costs will usually rise/fall.

3   Fill in the gaps for each of the graph titles below.

(a)

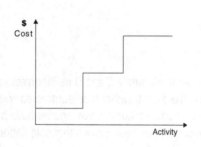

Graph of a ....cost

Example:

(b)

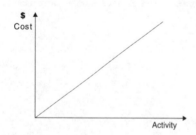

Graph of a ....cost

Example:

(c)

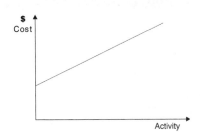

Graph of a ……………………….…..cost

Example:

(d)

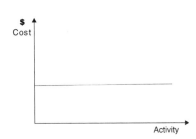

Graph of a ……………………….…..cost

Example:

4   Costs are assumed to be either fixed, variable or semi-variable within the normal or relevant range of output.

True   False

5   The costs of operating the canteen at 'Eat a lot Company' for the past three months is as follows.

Month	Cost	Employees
	$	
1	72,500	1,250
2	75,000	1,300
3	68,750	1,175

Calculate

(a)   Variable cost (per employee per month)
(b)   Fixed cost per month

Answers to quick quiz

1   The variability of input costs with activity undertaken.

2   Rise

3   (a)   Step cost. Example: rent, supervisors' salaries
     (b)   Variable cost. Example: raw materials, direct labour
     (c)   Semi-variable cost. Example: electricity and telephone
     (d)   Fixed. Example: rent, depreciation (straight-line)

4   True

5   (a)   Variable cost = $50 per employee per month
     (b)   Fixed costs = $10,000 per month

	Activity	Cost
		$
High	1,300	75,000
Low	1,175	68,750
	125	6,250

Variable cost per employee = $6,250/125 = $50

For 1,175 employees, total cost = $68,750

Total cost	= variable cost + fixed cost
$68,750	= (1,175 × $50) + fixed cost
∴ Fixed cost	= $68,750 − $58,750
	= $10,000

Now try the questions below from the Exam Question Bank

Number	Level	Marks	Time
Q3	MCQ/OTQ	n/a	n/a

P
A
R
T

C

Business mathematics and computer spreadsheets

Correlation and regression; expected values

4

Introduction

In chapter 3, we looked at how costs behave and how total costs can be split into fixed and variable costs using the **high-low method**. In this chapter, we shall be looking at another method which is used to split total costs. This method is used to determine whether there is a linear relationship between two variables. If a **linear function** is considered to be appropriate, **regression analysis** is used to establish the equation (this equation can then be used to make forecasts or predictions).

Study guide

		Intellectual level
B3	**Fixed and variable costs**	
(a)	Explain the structure of linear functions and equations	1
C1	**Dealing with uncertainty**	
(a)	Explain and calculate an expected value	1
(b)	Demonstrate the use of expected values in simple decision making situations	1
(c)	Explain the limitations of the expected value technique	1
C2	**Statistics for business**	
(a)	Calculate a correlation coefficient and a coefficient of determination	1
(b)	Explain and interpret coefficients calculated	1
(c)	Establish a linear function using regression analysis and interpret the results	2

Exam guide

This is a very important topic and it is vital that you are able to establish linear equations using regression analysis. Remember to continue to refer to the introductory chapter on basic maths if you are struggling with linear equations.

1 Correlation

1.1 Introduction

FAST FORWARD

Two variables are said to be correlated if a change in the value of one variable is accompanied by a change in the value of another variable. This is what is meant by **correlation**.

Examples of variables which might be correlated are as follows.

- A person's height and weight
- The distance of a journey and the time it takes to make it

1.2 Scattergraphs

One way of showing the correlation between two related variables is on a **scattergraph** or **scatter diagram**, plotting a number of pairs of data on the graph. For example, a scattergraph showing monthly selling costs against the volume of sales for a 12-month period might be as follows.

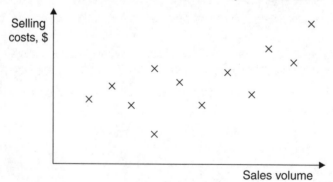

This scattergraph suggests that there is some correlation between selling costs and sales volume, so that as sales volume rises, selling costs tend to rise as well.

1.3 Degrees of correlation

FAST FORWARD

Two variables might be **perfectly correlated**, **partly correlated** or **uncorrelated**. Correlation can be **positive** or **negative**.

The differing degrees of correlation can be illustrated by scatter diagrams.

1.3.1 Perfect correlation

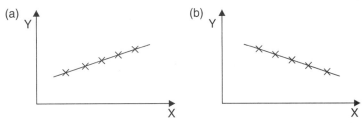

All the pairs of values lie on a straight line. An exact **linear relationship** exists between the two variables.

1.3.2 Partial correlation

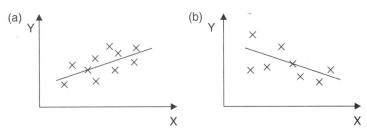

In (a), although there is no exact relationship, low values of X tend to be associated with low values of Y, and high values of X with high values of Y.

In (b) again, there is no exact relationship, but low values of X tend to be associated with high values of Y and vice versa.

1.3.3 No correlation

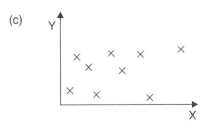

The values of these two variables are not correlated with each other.

1.3.4 Positive and negative correlation

Correlation, whether perfect or partial, can be **positive** or **negative**.

Key terms

Positive correlation means that low values of one variable are associated with low values of the other, and high values of one variable are associated with high values of the other.

Negative correlation means that low values of one variable are associated with high values of the other, and high values of one variable with low values of the other.

2 The correlation coefficient and the coefficient of determination

2.1 The correlation coefficient

FAST FORWARD

The degree of correlation between two variables is measured by the **Pearsonian** (product moment) **correlation coefficient, r**. The nearer r is to +1 or –1, the stronger the relationship.

When we have measured the **degree of correlation** between two variables we can decide, using actual results in the form of pairs of data, whether two variables are perfectly or partially correlated, and if they are partially correlated, whether there is a **high** or **low degree of partial correlation.**

Exam formula

Correlation coefficient, $r = \dfrac{n\sum XY - \sum X \sum Y}{\sqrt{[n\sum X^2 - (\sum X)^2][n\sum Y^2 - (\sum Y)^2]}}$

where X and Y represent pairs of data for two variables X and Y

n = the number of pairs of data used in the analysis

Exam focus point

The formula for the correlation coefficient is given in the exam.

The correlation coefficient, r must always fall between –1 and +1. If you get a value outside this range you have made a mistake.

- r = +1 means that the variables are perfectly positively correlated
- r = –1 means that the variables are perfectly negatively correlated
- r = 0 means that the variables are uncorrelated

2.2 Example: the correlation coefficient

The cost of output at a factory is thought to depend on the number of units produced. Data have been collected for the number of units produced each month in the last six months, and the associated costs, as follows.

Month	Output '000s of units X	Cost $'000 Y
1	2	9
2	3	11
3	1	7
4	4	13
5	3	11
6	5	15

Required

Assess whether there is there any correlation between output and cost.

Solution

$r = \dfrac{n\sum XY - \sum X \sum Y}{\sqrt{[n\sum X^2 - (\sum X)^2][n\sum Y^2 - (\sum Y)^2]}}$

We need to find the values for the following.

(a) $\sum XY$ Multiply each value of X by its corresponding Y value, so that there are six values for XY. Add up the six values to get the total.

(b) ΣX Add up the six values of X to get a total. $(\Sigma X)^2$ will be the square of this total.

(c) ΣY Add up the six values of Y to get a total. $(\Sigma Y)^2$ will be the square of this total.

(d) ΣX^2 Find the square of each value of X, so that there are six values for X^2. Add up these values to get a total.

(e) ΣY^2 Find the square of each value of Y, so that there are six values for Y^2. Add up these values to get a total.

Workings

X	Y	XY	X^2	Y^2
2	9	18	4	81
3	11	33	9	121
1	7	7	1	49
4	13	52	16	169
3	11	33	9	121
5	15	75	25	225
$\Sigma X = 18$	$\Sigma Y = 66$	$\Sigma XY = 218$	$\Sigma X^2 = 64$	$\Sigma Y^2 = 766$

$(\Sigma X)^2 = 18^2 = 324$ $(\Sigma Y)^2 = 66^2 = 4{,}356$

$n = 6$

$$r = \frac{(6 \times 218) - (18 \times 66)}{\sqrt{(6 \times 64 - 324) \times (6 \times 766 - 4{,}356)}}$$

$$= \frac{1{,}308 - 1{,}188}{\sqrt{(384 - 324) \times (4{,}596 - 4{,}356)}}$$

$$= \frac{120}{\sqrt{60 \times 240}} = \frac{120}{\sqrt{14{,}400}} = \frac{120}{120} = 1$$

There is **perfect positive correlation** between the volume of output at the factory and costs which means that there is a perfect linear relationship between output and costs.

2.3 Correlation in a time series

Correlation exists in a time series if there is a relationship between the period of time and the recorded value for that period of time. The correlation coefficient is calculated with time as the X variable although it is convenient to use simplified values for X instead of year numbers.

For example, instead of having a series of years 20X1 to 20X5, we could have values for X from 0 (20X1) to 4 (20X5).

Note that whatever starting value you use for X (be it 0, 1, 2 ... 721, ... 953), the value of r will always be the same.

Question	Correlation

Sales of product A between 20X7 and 20Y1 were as follows.

Year	Units sold ('000s)
20X7	20
20X8	18
20X9	15
20Y0	14
20Y1	11

Required

Determine whether there is a trend in sales. In other words, decide whether there is any correlation between the year and the number of units sold.

Workings

Let 20X7 to 20Y1 be years 0 to 4.

X	Y	XY	X^2	Y^2
0	20	0	0	400
1	18	18	1	324
2	15	30	4	225
3	14	42	9	196
4	11	44	16	121
$\sum X = 10$	$\sum Y = 78$	$\sum XY = 134$	$\sum X^2 = 30$	$\sum Y^2 = 1{,}266$

$(\sum X)^2 = 100 \qquad (\sum Y)^2 = 6{,}084$

$n = 5$

$$r = \frac{(5 \times 134) - (10 \times 78)}{\sqrt{(5 \times 30 - 100) \times (5 \times 1{,}266 - 6{,}084)}}$$

$$= \frac{670 - 780}{\sqrt{(150 - 100) \times (6{,}330 - 6{,}084)}} = \frac{-110}{\sqrt{50 \times 246}}$$

$$= \frac{-110}{\sqrt{12{,}300}} = \frac{-110}{110.90537} = -0.992$$

There is **partial negative correlation** between the year of sale and units sold. The value of r is close to –1, therefore a **high degree of correlation exists**, although it is not quite perfect correlation. This means that there is a **clear downward trend** in sales.

2.4 The coefficient of determination, r^2

FAST FORWARD

The **coefficient of determination**, r^2 (alternatively R^2) measures the proportion of the total variation in the value of one variable that can be explained by variations in the value of the other variable.

Unless the correlation coefficient r is exactly or very nearly +1, –1 or 0, its meaning or significance is a little unclear. For example, if the correlation coefficient for two variables is +0.8, this would tell us that the variables are positively correlated, but the correlation is not perfect. It would not really tell us much else. A more meaningful analysis is available from **the square of the correlation coefficient, r**, which is called the **coefficient of determination**, r^2

The question above entitled 'Correlation' shows that r = –0.992, therefore r^2 = 0.984. This means that over 98% of variations in sales can be explained by the passage of time, leaving 0.016 (less than 2%) of variations to be explained by other factors.

Similarly, if the correlation coefficient between a company's output volume and maintenance costs was 0.9, r^2 would be 0.81, meaning that 81% of variations in maintenance costs could be explained by variations in output volume, leaving only 19% of variations to be explained by other factors (such as the age of the equipment).

Note, however, that if r^2 = 0.81, we would say that 81% of **the variations in y can be explained by variations in x**. We do not necessarily conclude that 81% of variations in y are *caused* by the variations in x. We must beware of reading too much significance into our statistical analysis.

2.5 Correlation and causation

If two variables are well correlated, either positively or negatively, this may be due to **pure chance** or there may be a **reason** for it. The larger the number of pairs of data collected, the less likely it is that the correlation is due to chance, though that possibility should never be ignored entirely.

If there is a reason, it may not be causal. For example, monthly net income is well correlated with monthly credit to a person's bank account, for the logical (rather than causal) reason that for most people the one equals the other.

Even if there is a causal explanation for a correlation, it does not follow that variations in the value of one variable cause variations in the value of the other. For example, sales of ice cream and of sunglasses are well correlated, not because of a direct causal link but because the weather influences both variables.

3 Lines of best fit

3.1 Linear relationships

Correlation enables us to determine the strength of any relationship between two variables but it does not offer us any method of forecasting values for one variable, Y, given values of another variable, X.

If we assume that there is a **linear relationship** between the two variables, however, and we determine the **equation of a straight line (Y = a + bX)** which is a good fit for the available data plotted on a scattergraph, we can use the equation for forecasting: we can substitute values for X into the equation and derive values for Y. If you need reminding about linear equations and graphs, refer to your Basic Maths appendix.

3.2 Estimating the equation of the line of best fit

There are a number of techniques for estimating the equation of a line of best fit. We will be looking at **simple linear regression analysis**. This provides a technique for estimating values for a and b in the equation

$$Y = a + bX$$

where X and Y are the related variables and
a and b are estimated using pairs of data for X and Y.

4 Least squares method of linear regression analysis

4.1 Introduction

Linear regression analysis (the **least squares method**) is one technique for estimating a line of best fit. Once an equation for a line of best fit has been determined, forecasts can be made.

Exam formulae

The **least squares method of linear regression analysis** involves using the following formulae for a and b in Y = a + bX.

$$b = \frac{n\sum XY - \sum X \sum Y}{n\sum X^2 - (\sum X)^2}$$

$$a = \frac{\sum Y}{n} - b\frac{\sum X}{n}$$

where n is the number of pairs of data

Exam focus point

The formulae will be given in the exam.

The line of best fit that is derived represents the **regression of Y upon X**.

A different line of best fit could be obtained by interchanging X and Y in the formulae. This would then represent the regression of X upon Y (X = a + bY) and it would have a slightly different slope. For examination purposes, always use the regression of Y upon X, where X is the independent variable, and Y is the dependent variable whose value we wish to forecast for given values of X. In a time series, X will represent time.

4.2 Example: the least squares method

(a) Given that there is a fairly high degree of correlation between the output and the costs detailed in the example in Paragraph 4.1 (so that a linear relationship can be assumed), calculate an equation to determine the expected level of costs, for any given volume of output, using the least squares method.

(b) Prepare a budget for total costs if output is 22,000 units.

(c) Confirm that the degree of correlation between output and costs is high by calculating the correlation coefficient.

Solution

(a) *Workings*

X	Y	XY	X^2	Y^2
20	82	1,640	400	6,724
16	70	1,120	256	4,900
24	90	2,160	576	8,100
22	85	1,870	484	7,225
18	73	1,314	324	5,329
$\Sigma X = 100$	$\Sigma Y = 400$	$\Sigma XY = 8,104$	$\Sigma X^2 = 2,040$	$\Sigma Y^2 = 32,278$

n = 5 (There are five pairs of data for x and y values)

$$b = \frac{n\Sigma XY - \Sigma X\Sigma Y}{n\Sigma X^2 - (\Sigma X)^2} = \frac{(5 \times 8,104) - (100 \times 400)}{(5 \times 2,040) - 100^2}$$

$$= \frac{40,520 - 40,000}{10,200 - 10,000} = \frac{520}{200} = 2.6$$

$$a = \frac{\Sigma Y}{n} - b\frac{\Sigma X}{n} = \frac{400}{5} - 2.6 \times \left(\frac{100}{5}\right) = 28$$

Y = 28 + 2.6X

where Y = total cost, in thousands of pounds
       X = output, in thousands of units.

Note that the fixed costs are $28,000 (when X = 0 costs are $28,000) and the variable cost per unit is $2.60.

(b) If the output is 22,000 units, we would expect costs to be

28 + 2.6 × 22 = 85.2 = $85,200.

(c) $$r = \frac{520}{\sqrt{200 \times (5 \times 32,278 - 400^2)}} = \frac{520}{\sqrt{200 \times 1,390}} = \frac{520}{527.3} = +0.99$$

4.3 Regression lines and time series

The same technique can be applied to calculate a **regression line** (a **trend line**) for a time series. This is particularly useful for purposes of forecasting. As with correlation, years can be numbered from 0 upwards.

Using the data in the question entitled 'Correlation', calculate the trend line of sales and forecast sales in 20Y2 and 20Y3.

Answer

Using workings from the question entitled 'Correlation':

$$b = \frac{(5 \times 134) - (10 \times 78)}{(5 \times 30) - (10)^2} = \frac{670 - 780}{150 - 100} = -2.2$$

$$a = \frac{\sum Y}{n} - b\frac{\sum X}{n} = \frac{78}{5} - \frac{(-2.2 \times 10)}{5} = 20$$

$\therefore$ Y = 20 – 2.2X where X = 0 in 20X7, X = 1 in 20X8 and so on.

Using the trend line, predicted sales in 20Y2 (year 5) would be:

20 – (2.2 × 5) = 9 ie 9,000 units

and predicated sales in 20Y3 (year 6) would be:

20 – (2.2 × 6) = 6.8 ie 6,800 units.

Regression analysis was used to find the equation Y = 300 – 4.7X, where X is time (in quarters) and Y is sales level in thousands of units. Given that X = 0 represents 20X0 quarter 1 what are the forecast sales levels for 20X5 quarter 4?

Answer

X = 0 corresponds to 20X0 quarter 1

Therefore X = 23 corresponds to 20X5 quarter 4

Forecast sales   = 300 – (4.7 × 23)
                   = 191.9 = 191,900 units

Over a 36 month period sales have been found to have an underlying regression line of Y = 14.224 + 7.898X where Y is the number of items sold and X represents the month.

What are the forecast number of items to be sold in month 37?

Answer

Y   = 14.224 + 7.898X
      = 14.224 + (7.898 × 37)
      = 306.45 = 306 units

5 The reliability of regression analysis forecasts

FAST FORWARD

As with all forecasting techniques, the results from regression analysis will not be wholly reliable. There are a number of factors which affect the reliability of forecasts made using regression analysis.

(a)   **It assumes a linear relationship exists between the two variables** (since linear regression analysis produces an equation in the linear format) whereas a non-linear relationship might exist.

(b)   It assumes that the value of one variable, Y, can be predicted or estimated from the value of one other variable, X. In reality the value of Y might depend on several other variables, not just X.

(c)   When it is used for forecasting, it assumes that what has happened in the past will provide a reliable guide to the future.

(d)   When calculating a line of best fit, there will be a range of values for X. In the example in Paragraph 4.2, the line Y = 28 + 2.6X was predicted from data with output values ranging from X = 16 to X = 24. Depending on the degree of correlation between X and Y, we might safely use the estimated line of best fit to predict values for Y in the future, provided that the value of X remains within the range 16 to 24. We would be on less safe ground if we used the formula to predict a value for Y when X = 10, or 30, or any other value outside the range 16 to 24, because we would have to assume that the trend line applies outside the range of X values used to establish the line in the first place.

  (i)   **Interpolation** means using a line of best fit to predict a value within the two extreme points of the observed range.

  (ii)   **Extrapolation** means using a line of best fit to predict a value outside the two extreme points.

  When linear regression analysis is used for forecasting a time series (when the X values represent time) it **assumes that the trend line can be extrapolated into the future**. This might not necessarily be a good assumption to make.

(e)   As with any forecasting process, **the amount of data available is very important**. Even if correlation is high, if we have fewer than about ten pairs of values, we must regard any forecast as being somewhat unreliable. (It is likely to provide more reliable forecasts than the scattergraph method, however, since it uses all of the available data.)

(f)   **The reliability of a forecast will depend on the reliability of the data collected to determine the regression analysis equation**. If the data is not collected accurately or if data used is false, forecasts are unlikely to be acceptable.

A check on the reliability of the estimated line Y= 28 + 2.6X can be made, however, by calculating the coefficient of correlation. From the answer to the example in Paragraph 4.2, we know that r = 0.99. This is a high positive correlation, and r^2 = 0.9801, indicating that 98.01% of the variation in cost can be explained by the variation in volume. This would suggest that a **fairly large degree of reliance** can probably be placed on estimates .

If there is a **perfect linear relationship** between X and Y (r = ±1) then we can predict Y from any given value of X with **great confidence**.

If correlation is high (for example r = 0.9) the actual values will all lie quite close to the regression line and so predictions should not be far out. If correlation is below about 0.7, predictions will only give a very rough guide as to the likely value of Y.

6 Expected values

An **expected value** (or **EV**) is a weighted average value, based on probabilities. The expected value for a single event can offer a helpful guide for management decisions.

6.1 How to calculate expected values

If the probability of an outcome of an event is p, then the expected number of times that this outcome will occur in n events (the expected value) is equal to n × p.

For example, suppose that the probability that a transistor is defective is 0.02. How many defectives would we expect to find in a batch of 4,000 transistors?

EV = 4,000 × 0.02
      = 80 defectives

6.2 Example: Expected values

The daily sales of Product T may be as follows.

Units	Probability
1,000	0.2
2,000	0.3
3,000	0.4
4,000	0.1
	1.0

Required

Calculate the expected daily sales.

Solution

The EV of daily sales may be calculated by multiplying each possible outcome (volume of daily sales) by the probability that this outcome will occur.

Units	Probability	Expected value Units
1,000	0.2	200
2,000	0.3	600
3,000	0.4	1,200
4,000	0.1	400
		EV of daily sales 2,400

In the long run the expected value should be approximately the actual average, if the event occurs many times over. In the example above, we do not expect sales on any one day to equal 2,400 units, but in the long run, over a large number of days, average sales should equal 2,400 units a day.

6.3 Expected values and single events

The point made in the preceding paragraph is an important one. An **expected value** can be calculated when the **event will only occur once or twice**, but it will not be a true long-run average of what will actually happen, because there is no long run.

6.4 Example: Expected values and single events

Suppose, for example, that a businessman is trying to decide whether to invest in a project. He estimates that there are three possible outcomes.

Outcome	Profit/(loss) $	Probability
Success	10,000	0.2
Moderate success	2,000	0.7
Failure	(4,000)	0.1

The expected value of profit may be calculated as follows.

Profit/(loss)	Probability	Expected value
$		$
10,000	0.2	2,000
2,000	0.7	1,400
(4,000)	0.1	(400)
		Expected value of profit 3,000

In this example, the project is a one-off event, and as far as we are aware, it will not be repeated. The actual profit or loss will be $10,000, $2,000 or $(4,000), and the average value of $3,000 will not actually happen. There is no long-run average of a single event.

Nevertheless, the expected value can be used to help the manager decide whether or not to invest in the project.

Question

Expected values 1

A company manufactures and sells product D. The selling price of the product is $6 per unit, and estimates of demand and variable costs of sales are as follows.

Probability	Demand	Probability	Variable cost per unit
	Units		$
0.3	5,000	0.1	3.00
0.6	6,000	0.3	3.50
0.1	8,000	0.5	4.00
		0.1	4.50

The unit variable costs do not depend on the volume of sales.

Fixed costs will be $10,000.

Required

Calculate the expected profit.

Answer

The EV of demand is as follows.

Demand	Probability	Expected value
Units		Units
5,000	0.3	1,500
6,000	0.6	3,600
8,000	0.1	800
		EV of demand 5,900

The EV of the variable cost per unit is as follows.

Variable costs	Probability	Expected value
$		$
3.00	0.1	0.30
3.50	0.3	1.05
4.00	0.5	2.00
4.50	0.1	0.45
		EV of unit variable costs 3.80

		$
Sales	5,900 units × $6.00	35,400
Less: variable costs	5,900 units × $3.80	22,420
Contribution		12,980
Less: fixed costs		10,000
Expected profit		2,980

Question
Expected values 2

The probability of an organisation making a profit of $180,000 next month is half the probability of it making a profit of $75,000.

What is the expected profit for next month?

A	$110,000	C	$145,000
B	$127,000	D	$165,000

Answer

The correct answer is A.

$$\frac{\left[(180,000 \times 1) + (75,000 \times 2)\right]}{(1+2)} = \$110,000$$

Exam focus point

This is a question from the December 2007 paper and less than 30% of students answered this correctly. Many students answered B, which weights the two profits equally rather than in the ratio given in the question.

6.5 The expected value equation

The expected value is summarised in equation form as follows.

$E(x) = \sum xP(x)$

This is read as 'the expected value of a particular outcome "x" is equal to the sum of the products of each value of x and the corresponding probability of that value of x occurring'.

7 Expectation and decision making

7.1 Decision making

Probability and **expectation** should be seen as an aid to decision making.

The concepts of probability and expected value are vital in **business decision making**. The expected values for single events can offer a helpful guide for management decisions.

- A project with a positive EV should be accepted
- A project with a negative EV should be rejected

Another decision rule involving expected values that you are likely to come across is the choice of an option or alternative which has the **highest EV of profit** (or the **lowest EV of cost**).

Choosing the option with the highest EV of profit is a decision rule that has both merits and drawbacks, as the following simple example will show.

7.2 Example: The expected value criterion

Suppose that there are two mutually exclusive projects with the following possible profits.

Project A		Project B	
Probability	Profit	Probability	Profit/(loss)
	$		$
0.8	5,000	0.1	(2,000)
0.2	6,000	0.2	5,000
		0.6	7,000
		0.1	8,000

Required

Determine which project should be chosen.

Solution

The EV of profit for each project is as follows.

			$
(a)	Project A $(0.8 \times 5,000) + (0.2 \times 6,000)$	=	5,200
(b)	Project B $(0.1 \times (2,000)) + (0.2 \times 5,000) + (0.6 \times 7,000) + (0.1 \times 8,000)$	=	5,800

Project B has a higher EV of profit. This means that on the balance of probabilities, it could offer a better return than A, and so is arguably a better choice.

On the other hand, the minimum return from project A would be $5,000 whereas with B there is a 0.1 chance of a loss of $2,000. So project A might be a safer choice.

Question	Expected values

A company is deciding whether to invest in a project. There are three possible outcomes of the investment:

Outcome	Profit/(Loss)
	$'000
Optimistic	19.2
Most likely	12.5
Pessimistic	(6.7)

There is a 30% chance of the optimistic outcome, and a 60% chance of the most likely outcome arising. The expected value of profit from the project is

A	$7,500	C	$13,930
B	$12,590	D	$25,000

Answer	

B Since the probabilities must total 100%, the probability of the pessimistic outcome = 100% – 60% – 30% = 10%.

Outcome	Profit/(Loss)	Probability	Expected value
	$		$
Optimistic	19,200	0.3	5,760
Most likely	12,500	0.6	7,500
Pessimistic	(6,700)	0.1	(670)
		1.0	12,590

If you selected option A, you calculated the expected value of the most likely outcome instead of the entire project.

If you selected option C, you forgot to treat the 6,700 as a loss, ie as a negative value.

If you selected option D, you forgot to take into account the probabilities of the various outcomes arising.

7.3 Payoff tables

Decisions have to be taken about a wide variety of matters (capital investment, controls on production, project scheduling and so on) and under a wide variety of conditions from **virtual certainty** to **complete uncertainty**.

There are, however, certain common factors in many business decisions.

(a) When a decision has to be made, there will be a range of possible **actions**.

(b) Each action will have certain **consequences**, or **payoffs** (for example, profits, costs, time).

(c) The payoff from any given action will depend on the **circumstances** (for example, high demand or low demand), which may or may not be known when the decision is taken. Frequently each circumstance will be assigned a probability of occurrence. The circumstances are *not* dependent on the action taken.

For a decision with these elements, a **payoff table** can be prepared.

FAST FORWARD A payoff table is simply a table with **rows for circumstances** and **columns for actions** (or vice versa), and the payoffs in the cells of the table.

For example, a decision on the level of advertising expenditure to be undertaken given different states of the economy, would have payoffs in $'000 of profit after advertising expenditure as follows.

		Actions: expenditure		
		High	Medium	Low
Circumstances:	Boom	+50	+30	+15
the state of the	Stable	+20	+25	+5
economy	Recession	0	−10	−35

 Question   **Pay off tables**

In a restaurant there is a 30% chance of five apple pies being ordered a day and a 70% chance of ten being ordered. Each apple pie sells for $2. It costs $1 to make an apple pie. Using a payoff table, decide how many apple pies the restaurant should prepare each day, bearing in mind that unsold apple pies must be thrown away at the end of each day.

Answer

		Prepared	
		Five	Ten
Demand	Five (P = 0.3)	5	0
	Ten (P = 0.7)	5	10

Prepare five, profit = ($5 × 0.3) + ($5 × 0.7) = $5
Prepare ten, profit = ($0 × 0.3) + ($10 × 0.7) = $7

Ten pies should be prepared.

7.4 Limitations of expected values

Evaluating decisions by using expected values have a number of limitations.

(a) The **probabilities** used when calculating expected values are likely to be estimates. They may therefore be **unreliable** or **inaccurate**.

(b) Expected values are **long-term averages** and may not be suitable for use in situations involving **one-off decisions**. They may therefore be useful as a **guide** to decision making.

(c) Expected values do not consider the **attitudes to risk of** the people involved in the decision-making process. They do not, therefore, take into account all of the factors involved in the decision.

(d) The time value of money may not be taken into account: $100 now is worth more than $100 in ten years' time.

Chapter roundup

- Two variables are said to be correlated if a change in the value of one variable is accompanied by a change in the value of another variable. This is what is meant by **correlation**.

- Two variables might be **perfectly correlated**, **partly correlated** or **uncorrelated**. Correlation can be **positive** or **negative**.

- The **degree of correlation** between two variables is measured by the **Pearsonian** (product moment) **correlation coefficient, r**. The nearer r is to +1 or −1, the stronger the relationship.

- The **coefficient of determination, r^2** (alternatively **R^2**) measures the proportion of the total variation in the value of one variable that can be explained by variations in the value of the other variable.

- **Linear regression analysis** (the **least squares method**) is one technique for estimating a line of best fit. Once an equation for a line of best fit has been determined, forecasts can be made.

- As with all forecasting techniques, the results from regression analysis will not be wholly reliable. There are a number of factors which affect the reliability of forecasts made using regression analysis.

- An **expected value** (or EV) is a weighted average value, based on probabilities. The expected value for a single event can offer a helpful guide for management decisions.

- **Probability** and **expectation** should be seen as an aid to decision making.

- A **payoff table** is simply a table with rows for circumstances and columns for actions (or vice versa) and the payoffs in the cells of the table.

Quick quiz

1   .... means that low values of one variable are associated with low values of the other, and high values of one variable are associated with high values of the other.

2   .... means that low values of one variable are associated with high values of the other, and high values of one variable with low values of the other.

3   (i)   Perfect positive correlation,   r = ...
    (ii)   Perfect negative correlation,   r = ...
    (iii) No correlation,   r = ...

The correlation coefficient, r, must always fall within the range .... to ....

4   If the correlation coefficient of a set of data is 0.9, what is the coefficient of determination and how is it interpreted?

5   (a)   The equation of a straight line is given as Y = a + bX. Give two methods used for estimating the above equation.

    (b)   If Y = a + bX, it is best to use the regression of Y upon X where X is the dependent variable and Y is the independent variable.

        True ☐   False ☐

6   List five factors affecting the reliability of regression analysis forecasts.

7   What is an expected value?

Answers to quick quiz

1   Positive correlation

2   Negative correlation

3   (i)   r = +1
     (ii)   r = –1
     (iii) r = 0

     The correlation coefficient, r, must always fall within the range –1 to +1.

4   Correlation coefficient = r = 0.9

     Coefficient of determination = r^2 = 0.9^2 = 0.81 or 81%

     This tells us that over 80% of the variations in the dependent variable (Y) can be explained by variations in the independent variable, X.

5   (a)   • Scattergraph method (line of best fit)
            • Simple linear regression analysis

     (b)   False. When using the regression of Y upon X, X is the independent variable and Y is the dependent variable (the value of Y will depend upon the value of X).

6   (a)   It assumes a linear relationship exists between the two variables.
     (b)   It assumes that the value of one variable, Y, can be predicted or estimated from the value of another variable, X.
     (c)   It assumes that what happened in the past will provide a reliable guide to the future.
     (d)   It assumes that the trend line can be extrapolated into the future.
     (e)   The amount of data available.

7   A weighted average value based on probabilities.

Now try the questions below from the Exam Question Bank

Number	Level	Marks	Time
Q4	MCQ	n/a	n/a

Spreadsheets

Topic list	Syllabus reference
1 Features and functions of spreadsheets	C3 (a)
2 Examples of spreadsheet formula	C3 (a)
3 Basic skills	C3 (b)
4 Spreadsheet construction	C3 (b)
5 Formulae with conditions	C3 (b)
6 Charts and graphs	C3 (b)
7 Spreadsheet format and appearance	C3 (b)
8 Other issues	C3 (b)
9 Three dimensional (multi-sheet) spreadsheets	C3 (b)
10 Macros	C3 (a)
11 Advantage and disadvantages of spreadsheet software	C3 (c)
12 Uses of spreadsheet software	C3 (c)

Introduction

Spreadsheet skills are essential for people working in a management accounting environment as much of the information produces is analysed or presented using spreadsheet software.

This chapter will look at features and functions of commonly used spreadsheet software, its advantages and its disadvantages and how it is used in the day-to-day work of an accountant.

Study guide

		Intellectual level
C3	**Use of spreadsheet models**	
(a)	Explain the role and features of a spreadsheet system	1
(b)	Demonstrate a basic understanding of the use of spreadsheets	1
(c)	Identify applications for spreadsheets in cost and management accounting	1

Exam guide

This topic will account for no more than about 4 marks in the examination and if you are familiar with spreadsheets you may want to skip a lot of this chapter. We have covered this topic in some depth as an aid to those students who do not normally use spreadsheets.

1 Features and functions of spreadsheets

> **FAST FORWARD**
>
> Use of spreadsheets is an essential part of the day-to-day work of an accountant.

1.1 What is a spreadsheet?

> **FAST FORWARD**
>
> A spreadsheet is an electronic piece of paper divided into **rows** and **columns**. The intersection of a row and a column is known as a **cell**.

A spreadsheet is divided into **rows** (horizontal) and **columns** (vertical). The rows are numbered 1, 2, 3 . . . etc and the columns lettered A, B C . . . etc. Each individual area representing the intersection of a row and a column is called a 'cell'. A cell address consists of its row and column reference. For example, in the spreadsheet below the word '*Jan*' is in cell B2. The cell that the cursor is currently in or over is known as the 'active cell'.

The main examples of spreadsheet packages are Lotus 1 2 3 and Microsoft Excel. We will be referring to **Microsoft Excel**, as this is the most widely-used spreadsheet. A simple Microsoft Excel spreadsheet, containing budgeted sales figures for three geographical areas for the first quarter of the year, is shown below.

	A	B	C	D	E	F
1	**BUDGETED SALES FIGURES**					
2		Jan	Feb	Mar	Total	
3		$'000	$'000	$'000	$'000	
4	North	2,431	3,001	2,189	7,621	
5	South	6,532	5,826	6,124	18,482	
6	West	895	432	596	1,923	
7	Total	9,858	9,259	8,909	28,026	
8						

1.2 Why use spreadsheets?

Spreadsheets provide a tool for calculating, analysing and manipulating numerical data. Spreadsheets make the calculation and manipulation of data easier and quicker. For example, the spreadsheet above has been set up to calculate the totals **automatically.** If you changed your estimate of sales in February for the North region to $3,296, when you input this figure in cell C4 the totals (in E4 and C7) would change accordingly.

1.2.1 Uses of spreadsheets

Spreadsheets can be used for a wide range of tasks. Some common applications of spreadsheets are:

- Management accounts
- Cash flow analysis and forecasting
- Reconciliations

- Revenue analysis and comparison
- Cost analysis and comparison
- Budgets and forecasts

1.2.2 Cell contents

The contents of any cell can be one of the following.

(a) **Text**. A text cell usually contains **words**. Numbers that do not represent numeric values for calculation purposes (eg a Part Number) may be entered in a way that tells Excel to treat the cell contents as text. To do this, enter an apostrophe before the number eg '451.

(b) **Values**. A value is a **number** that can be used in a calculation.

(c) **Formulae**. A formula **refers to other cells** in the spreadsheet, and performs some sort of computation with them. For example, if cell C1 contains the formula =A1-B1, cell C1 will display the result of the calculation subtracting the contents of cell B1 from the contents of cell A1. In Excel, a formula always begins with an equals sign: = . There are a wide range of formulae and functions available.

1.2.3 Formula bar

The following illustration shows the formula bar. (If the formula bar is not visible, choose **View**, **Formula bar** from Excel's main menu.)

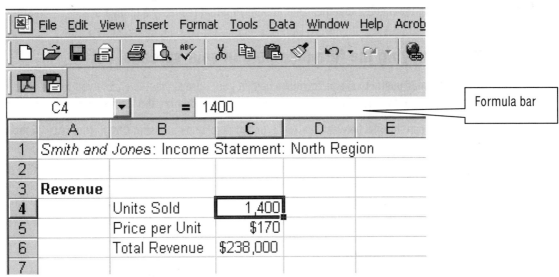

The formula bar allows you to see and edit the contents of the active cell. The bar also shows the cell address of the active cell (C4 in the example above).

Exam focus point

Questions on spreadsheets are likely to focus on the main features of spreadsheets and their issues.

2 Examples of spreadsheet formulae

Formulas in Microsoft Excel follow a specific syntax.

All Excel formulae start with the equals sign =, followed by the elements to be calculated (the operands) and the calculation operators. Each operand can be a value that does not change (a constant value), a cell or range reference, a label, a name, or a worksheet function.

Formulae can be used to perform a variety of calculations. Here are some examples.

(a) =C4*5. This formula **multiplies** the value in C4 by 5. The result will appear in the cell holding the formula.

(b) =C4*B10. This **multiplies** the value in C4 by the value in B10.

(c) =C4/E5. This **divides** the value in C4 by the value in E5. (* means multiply and / means divide by.)

(d) =C4*B10-D1. This **multiplies** the value in C4 by that in B10 and then subtracts the value in D1 from the result. Note that generally Excel will perform multiplication and division before addition or subtraction. If in any doubt, use brackets (parentheses): =(C4*B10)–D1.

(e) =C4*117.5%. This **adds** 17.5% to the value in C4. It could be used to calculate a price including 17.5% sales tax.

(f) =(C4+C5+C6)/3. Note that the **brackets** mean Excel would perform the addition first. Without the brackets, Excel would first divide the value in C6 by 3 and then add the result to the total of the values in C4 and C5.

(g) = 2^2 gives you 2 **to the power** of 2, in other words 2^2. Likewise = 2^3 gives you 2 cubed and so on.

(h) = 4^ (1/2) gives you the **square root** of 4. Likewise 27^(1/3) gives you the cube root of 27 and so on.

Without brackets, Excel calculates a formula from left to right. You can control how calculation is performed by changing the syntax of the formula. For example, the formula =5+2*3 gives a result of 11 because Excel calculates multiplication before addition. Excel would multiply 2 by 3 (resulting in 6) and would then add 5.

You may use parentheses to change the order of operations. For example =(5+2)*3 would result in Excel firstly adding the 5 and 2 together, then multiplying that result by 3 to give 21.

2.1 Displaying the formulae held in your spreadsheet

It is sometimes useful to see all formulae held in your spreadsheet to enable you to see how the spreadsheet works. There are two ways of making Excel **display the formulae** held in a spreadsheet.

(a) You can 'toggle' between the two types of display by pressing **Ctrl** + ` (the latter is the key above the Tab key). Press Ctrl + ` again to get the previous display back.

(b) You can also click on Tools, then on Options, then on View and tick the box next to 'Formulas'.

In the following paragraphs we provide examples of how spreadsheets and formulae may be used in an accounting context.

2.1.1 Example: formulae

	A	B	C	D	E	F
1	BUDGETED SALES FIGURES					
2		Jan	Feb	Mar	Total	
3		$'000	$'000	$'000	$'000	
4	North	2,431	3,001	2,189	7,621	
5	South	6,532	5,826	6,124	18,482	
6	West	895	432	596	1,923	
7	Total	9,858	9,259	8,909	28,026	
8						

(a) In the spreadsheet shown above, which of the cells have had a number typed in, and which cells display the result of calculations (ie which cells contain a formula)?

(b) What formula would you put in each of the following cells?

  (i) Cell B7

  (ii) Cell E6

  (iii) Cell E7

(c) If the February sales figure for the South changed from $5,826 to $5,731, what other figures would change as a result? Give cell references.

Solution

(a) Cells into which you would need to enter a value are: B4, B5, B6, C4, C5, C6, D4, D5 and D6. Cells which would perform calculations are B7, C7, D7, E4, E5, E6 and E7.

(b) (i)   =B4+B5+B6 *or better* =SUM(B4:B6)

    (ii)   =B6+C6+D6 *or better* =SUM(B6:D6)

    (iii) =E4+E5+E6 *or better* =SUM(E4:E6) Alternatively, the three monthly totals could be added across the spreadsheet: = SUM (B7: D7)

(c) The figures which would change, besides the amount in cell C5, would be those in cells C7, E5 and E7. (The contents of E7 would change if any of the sales figures changed.)

Question   **Sum formulae**

The following spreadsheet shows sales of two products, the Ego and the Id, for the period July to September.

	A	B	C	D	E
1	**Sigmund Co**				
2	*Sales analysis - Q3 20X7*				
3		M7	M8	M9	Total
4		$	$	$	$
5	Ego	3,000	4,000	2,000	9,000
6	Id	2,000	1,500	4,000	7,500
7	Total	5,000	5,500	6,000	16,500
8					

Devise a suitable formula for each of the following cells.

(a) Cell B7   (c) Cell E7

(b) Cell E6

Answer

(a) =SUM(B5:B6)   (c) =SUM (E5:E6) *or* =SUM(B7:D7)

(b) =SUM(B6:D6)

or (best of all) =IF(SUM(E5:E6) =SUM(B7:D7),SUM(B7:D7),"ERROR") Don't worry if you don't understand this formula when first attempting this question – we cover IF statements later in this chapter.

Question   **Formulae**

The following spreadsheet shows sales, exclusive of sales tax, in row 6.

	A	B	C	D	E	F	G	H
1	**Taxable supplies Co**							
2	*Sales analysis - Branch C*							
3	*Six months ended 30 June 200X*							
4		Jan	Feb	Mar	Apr	May	Jun	Total
5		$	$	$	$	$	$	$
6	Net sales	2,491.54	5,876.75	3,485.01	5,927.7	6,744.52	3,021.28	27,546.80
7	Sales tax							
8	Total							
9								

Your manager has asked you to insert formulae to calculate sales tax at 17½% in row 7 and also to produce totals.

(a)   Devise a suitable formula for cell B7 and cell E8.

(b)   How could the spreadsheet be better designed?

Answer

(a)   For cell B7   =B6*0.175   For cell E8   =SUM(E6:E7)

(b)   By using a separate 'variables' holding the sales tax rate and possibly the Sales figures. The formulae could then refer to these cells as shown below.

	A	B	C	D	E	F	G	H
1	Taxable Supplies Co							
2	Sales analysis - Branch C							
3	Six months ended 30 June 200X							
4		Jan	Feb	Mar	Apr	May	Jun	Total
5		$	$	$	$	$	$	$
6	Net sales	=B12	=C12	=D12	=E12	=F12	=G12	=SUM(B6:G6)
7	Sales tax	=B6*$B$13	=C6*$B$13	=D6*$B$13	=E6*$B$13	=F6*$B$13	=G6*$B$13	=SUM(B7:G7)
8	Total	=SUM(B6:B7)	=SUM(C6:C7)	=SUM(D6:D7)	=SUM(E6:E7)	=SUM(F6:F7)	=SUM(G6:G7)	=SUM(H6:H7)
9								
10								
11	Variables							
12	Sales	2491.54	5876.75	3485.01	5927.7	6744.52	3021.28	
13	Sales tax rate	0.175						

3 Basic skills

Essential basic skills include how to **move around** within a spreadsheet, how to **enter** and **edit** data, how to **fill** cells, how to **insert** and **delete** columns and rows and how to improve the basic **layout** and **appearance** of a spreadsheet.

In this section we explain some **basic spreadsheeting skills**. We give instructions for Microsoft Excel, the most widely used package. Our examples should be valid with all versions of Excel released since 1997.

You should read this section while sitting at a computer and trying out the skills we describe '**hands-on**'.

3.1 Moving about

The F5 key is useful for moving around within large spreadsheets. If you press the function key **F5**, a **Go To** dialogue box will allow you to specify the cell address you would like to move to. Try this out.

Also experiment by holding down Ctrl and pressing each of the direction arrow keys in turn to see where you end up. Try using the **Page Up** and **Page Down** keys and also try **Home** and **End** and Ctrl + these keys. Try **Tab** and **Shift + Tab**, too. These are all useful shortcuts for moving quickly from one place to another in a large spreadsheet.

3.2 Editing cell contents

Suppose cell A2 currently contains the value 456. If you wish to **change the entry** in cell A2 from 456 to 123456 there are four options – as shown below.

(a)   Activate cell A2, **type** 123456 and press **Enter**.

To undo this and try the next option press **Ctrl + Z**: this will always undo what you have just done.

(b)   **Double-click** in cell A2. The cell will keep its thick outline but you will now be able to see a vertical line flashing in the cell. You can move this line by using the direction arrow keys or the Home and the End keys. Move it to before the 4 and type 123. Then press Enter.

When you have tried this press Ctrl + Z to undo it.

(c)   **Click once** before the number 456 in the formula bar. Again you will get the vertical line and you can type in 123 before the 4. Then press Enter. Undo this before moving onto (d).

(d)   Press the **function key F2**. The vertical line cursor will be flashing in cell A2 at the *end* of the figures entered there (after the 6). Press Home to get to a position before the 4 and then type in 123 and press Enter, as before.

3.3 Deleting cell contents

You may delete the contents of a cell simply by making the cell the active cell and then pressing **Delete**. The contents of the cell will disappear. You may also highlight a range of cells to delete and then delete the contents of all cells within the range.

For example, enter any value in cell A1 and any value in cell A2. Move the cursor to cell A2. Now hold down the **Shift** key (the one above the Ctrl key) and keeping it held down press the ↑ arrow. Cell A2 will stay white but cell A1 will go black. What you have done here is **selected** the range A1 and A2. Now press the Delete key. The contents of cells A1 and A2 will be deleted.

3.4 Filling a range of cells

Start with a blank spreadsheet. Type the number 1 in cell A1 and the number 2 in cell A2. Now select cells A1: A2, this time by positioning the mouse pointer over cell A1, holding down the left mouse button and moving the pointer down to cell A2. When cell A2 is highlighted release the mouse button.

Now position the mouse pointer at the **bottom right hand corner** of cell A2. When you have the mouse pointer in the right place it will turn into a **black cross**.

Then, hold down the left mouse button again and move the pointer down to cell A10. You will see an outline surrounding the cells you are trying to 'fill'.

Release the mouse button when you have the pointer over cell A10. You will find that the software **automatically** fills in the numbers 3 to 10 below 1 and 2.

Try the following variations of this technique.

(a)   Delete what you have just done and type in **Jan** in cell A1. See what happens if you select cell A1 and fill down to cell A12: you get the months **Feb, Mar, Apr** and so on.

(b)   Type the number 2 in cell A1. Select A1 and fill down to cell A10. What happens? The cells should fill up with 2's.

(c)   Type the number 2 in cell A1 and 4 in cell A2. Then select A1: A2 and fill down to cell A10. What happens? You should get 2, 4, 6, 8, and so on.

(d)   Try **filling across** as well as down.

(e)   If you click on the bottom right hand corner of the cell using the **right mouse button**, drag down to a lower cell and then release the button you should see a menu providing a variety of options for filling the cells.

3.5 The SUM button Σ

We will explain how to use the SUM button by way of a simple example. Start with a blank spreadsheet, then enter the following figures in cells A1:B5.

	A	B
1	400	582
2	250	478
3	359	264
4	476	16
5	97	125

Make cell B6 the active cell and click once on the SUM button (the button with a Σ symbol on the Excel toolbar - the Σ symbol is the mathematical sign for 'the sum of'). A formula will appear in the cell saying =SUM(B1:B5). Above cell B6 you will see a flashing dotted line encircling cells B1:B5. Accept the suggested formula by hitting the Enter key.

The formula =SUM(B1:B5) will be entered, and the number 1465 will appear in cell B6.

Next, make cell A6 the active cell and **double-click** on the SUM button. The number 1582 should appear in cell A6.

3.6 Multiplication

Continuing on with our example, next select cell C1. Type in an = sign then click on cell A1. Now type in an **asterisk *** (which serves as a **multiplication sign**) and click on cell B1. Watch how the formula in cell C1 changes as you do this. (Alternatively you can enter the cell references by moving the direction arrow keys.) Finally press Enter. Cell C1 will show the result (232,800) of multiplying the figure in Cell A1 by the one in cell B1.

Your next task is to select cell C1 and **fill in** cells C2 to C5 automatically using the **dragging technique** described above. If you then click on each cell in column C and look above at the line showing what the cell contains you will find that the software has automatically filled in the correct cell references for you: A2*B2 in cell C2, A3*B3 in cell C3 and so on.

(**Note**: The forward slash / is used to represent division in spreadsheet formulae.)

3.7 Inserting columns and rows

Suppose we also want to add each row, for example cells A1 and B1. The logical place to do this would be cell C1, but column C already contains data. We have three options that would enable us to place this total in column C.

(a)   Highlight cells C1 to C5 and position the mouse pointer on one of the **edges**. (It will change to an arrow shape.) Hold down the **left** mouse button and drag cells C1 to C5 into column D. There is now space in column C for our next set of sums. Any **formulae** that need to be changed as a result of moving cells using this method should be changed **automatically** – but always check them.

(b)   The second option is to highlight cells C1 to C5 as before, position the mouse pointer anywhere **within** column C and click on the **right** mouse button. A menu will appear offering you an option **Insert...** . If you click on this you will be asked where you want to shift the cells that are being moved. In this case you want to move them to the right so choose this option and click on OK.

(c)   The third option is to **insert a whole new column**. You do this by clicking on the letter at the top of the column (here C) to highlight the whole of it then proceeding as in (b). The new column will always be inserted to the **left** of the one you highlight.

You can now display the sum of each of the rows in column C.

You can also insert a new row in a similar way (or stretch rows).

(a)   To **insert** one row, perhaps for headings, click on the row number to highlight it, click with the right mouse button and choose insert. One row will be inserted **above** the one you highlighted. Try putting some headings above the figures in columns A to C.

(b)   To insert **several** rows click on the row number immediately **below** the point where you want the new rows to appear and, holding down the left mouse button highlight the number of rows you wish to insert. Click on the highlighted area with the right mouse button and choose Insert (or if you prefer, choose **Insert**, **Rows** from the main menu).

3.8 Changing column width

You may occasionally find that a cell is not wide enough to display its contents. When this occurs, the cell displays a series of hashes #####. There are two options available to solve this problem.

(a)   One is to **decide for yourself** how wide you want the columns to be. Position the mouse pointer at the head of column A directly over the little line dividing the letter A from the letter B. The mouse **pointer** will change to a sort of **cross**. Hold down the left mouse button and, by moving your mouse, stretch Column A to the right, to about the middle of column D, until the words you typed fit. You can do the same for column B. Then make your columns too narrow again so you can try option (b).

(b)   Often it is easier to **let the software decide for you.** Position the mouse pointer over the little dividing line as before and get the cross symbol. Then double-click with the left mouse button. The column automatically adjusts to an appropriate width to fit the widest cell in that column.

You can either adjust the width of each column individually or you can do them all in one go. To do the latter click on the button in the top left hand corner to **select the whole sheet** and then **double-click** on just one of the dividing lines: all the columns will adjust to the **'best fit'** width.

3.9 Keyboard shortcuts and toolbar buttons

Here are a few tips to improve the **appearance** of your spreadsheets and speed up your work. To do any of the following to a cell or range of cells, first **select** the cell or cells and then:

(a)   Press Ctrl + B to make the cell contents **bold.**

(b)   Press Ctrl + I to make the cell contents *italic.*

(c)   Press **Ctrl + C** to **copy** the contents of the cells.

(d)   Move the cursor and press **Ctrl + V** to **paste** the cell you just copied into the new active cell or cells.

There are also **buttons** in the Excel toolbar (shown below) that may be used to carry out these and other functions. The best way to learn about these features is to use them - enter some numbers and text into a spreadsheet and experiment with keyboard shortcuts and toolbar buttons.

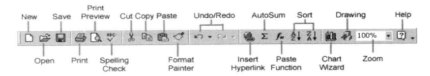

4 Spreadsheet construction

FAST FORWARD

A wide range of **formulae** and functions are available within Excel.

Spreadsheet models that will be used mainly as a calculation tool for various scenarios should ideally be constructed in **three sections**, as follows.

1   An inputs section containing the variables (eg the amount of a loan and the interest rate).

2   A calculations section containing formulae (eg the loan term and interest rate).

Example: spreadsheet construction

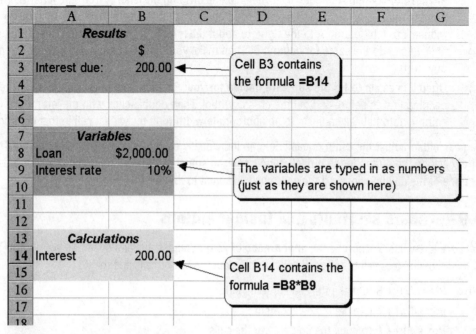

	A	B	C	D	E	F	G
1	*Results*						
2		$					
3	Interest due:	200.00		Cell B3 contains the formula =B14			
4							
5							
6							
7	*Variables*						
8	Loan	$2,000.00					
9	Interest rate	10%		The variables are typed in as numbers (just as they are shown here)			
10							
11							
12							
13	*Calculations*						
14	Interest	200.00		Cell B14 contains the formula =B8*B9			
15							
16							
17							
18							

In practice, in many situations it is often **more convenient** to combine the results and calculations areas as follows.

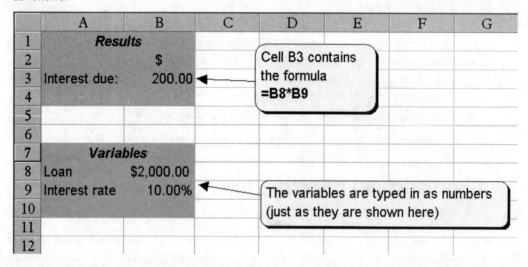

	A	B	C	D	E	F	G
1	*Results*						
2		$					
3	Interest due:	200.00		Cell B3 contains the formula =B8*B9			
4							
5							
6							
7	*Variables*						
8	Loan	$2,000.00					
9	Interest rate	10.00%		The variables are typed in as numbers (just as they are shown here)			
10							
11							
12							

If we took out another loan of $4,789 at an interest rate of 7.25% we would simply need to **overwrite the figures in the variable section** of the spreadsheet with the new figures to calculate the interest.

Question

Answer questions (a) and (b) below, which relate to the following spreadsheet.

	A	B	C	D
1	**Boilermakers Ltd**			
2	*Department B*			
3				
4	*Production data*	Machine A	Machine B	Machine C
5	Shift 1	245.84	237.49	231.79
6	Shift 2	241.14	237.62	261.31
7	Shift 3	244.77	201.64	242.71
8	Shift 4	240.96	238.18	234.50
9				
10	*Usage data*	Machine A	Machine B	Machine C
11	Maintenance	35	71	6
12	Operational	8.47	7.98	9.31
13	Idle	1.42	2.40	0.87
14	Recovery	0	15	4
15				

(a) Cell B9 needs to contain an average of all the preceding numbers in column B. Suggest a formula which would achieve this.

(b) Cell C15 contains the formula

=C11+C12/C13-C14

What would the result be, displayed in cell C15?

Answer

This question tests whether you can evaluate formulae in the correct order. In part (a) you must remember to put brackets around the numbers required to be added, otherwise the formula will automatically divide cell B8 by 4 first and add the result to the other numbers. Similarly, in part (b), the formula performs the multiplication before the addition and subtraction.

(a) =SUM(B5:B8)/4   An alternative is = AVERAGE(B5:B8).

(b) 59.325

4.1 Example: Constructing a cash flow projection

Suppose you wanted to set up a simple six-month cash flow projection, in such a way that you could use it to estimate how the **projected cash balance** figures will **change** in total when any **individual item** in the projection is **altered**. You have the following information.

(a) Sales were $45,000 per month in 20X5, falling to $42,000 in January 20X6. Thereafter they are expected to increase by 3% per month (ie February will be 3% higher than January, and so on).

(b) Debts are collected as follows.

(i) 60% in month following sale. (iii) 7% in third month after sale.
(ii) 30% in second month after sale. (iv) 3% remains uncollected.

(c) Purchases are equal to cost of sales, set at 65% of sales.

(d) Overheads were $6,000 per month in 20X5, rising by 5% in 20X6.

(e) Opening cash is an overdraft of $7,500.

(f) Dividends: $10,000 final dividend on 20X5 profits payable in May.

(g) Capital purchases: plant costing $18,000 will be ordered in January. 20% is payable with order, 70% on delivery in February and the final 10% in May.

4.1.1 Headings and layout

The first step is to put in the various **headings** required for the cash flow projection. At this stage, your spreadsheet might look as follows.

	A	B	C	D	E	F	G
1	**EXCELLENT PLC**						
2	*Cash flow projection - six months ending 30 June 20X6*						
3		*Jan*	*Feb*	*Mar*	*Apr*	*May*	*Jun*
4		$	$	$	$	$	$
5	Sales						
6	*Cash receipts*						
7	1 month in arrears						
8	2 months in arrears						
9	3 months in arrears						
10	Total operating receipts						
11							
12	Cash payments						
13	Purchases						
14	Overheads						
15	Total operating payments						
16							
17	Dividends						
18	Capital purchases						
19	Total other payments						
20							
21	Net cash flow						
22	Cash balance b/f						
23	Cash balance c/f						
24							

Note the following points.

(a) We have **increased the width** of column A to allow longer pieces of text to be inserted. Had we not done so, only the first part of each caption would have been displayed (and printed).

(b) We have developed a **simple style for headings**. Headings are essential, so that users can identify what a spreadsheet does. We have **emboldened** the company name and *italicised* other headings.

(c) When **text** is entered into a cell it is usually **left-aligned** (as for example in column A). We have **centred** the headings above each column by highlighting the cells and using the relevant buttons at the top of the screen.

(d) **Numbers** should be **right-aligned** in cells.

(e) We have left **spaces** in certain rows (after blocks of related items) to make the spreadsheet **easier to use and read**.

4.1.2 Inserting formulae

The next step is to enter the **formulae** required. For example, in cell B10 you want total operating receipts, =SUM(B7:B9).

Look for a moment at cell C7. We are told that sales in January were $42,000 and that 60% of customers settle their accounts one month in arrears. We could insert the formula =B5*0.6 in the cell and fill in the other cells along the row so that it is replicated in each month. However, consider the effect of a change in payment patterns to a situation where, say, 55% of customer debts are settled after one month. This would necessitate a **change to each and every cell** in which the 0.6 ratio appears.

An alternative approach, which makes **future changes much simpler** to execute, is to put the relevant ratio (here, 60% or 0.6) in a cell **outside** the main table and cross-refer each cell in the main table to that cell. This means that, if the percentage changes, the change need only be reflected in **one cell**, following which all cells which are dependent on that cell will **automatically use the new percentage**. We will therefore input such values in separate parts of the spreadsheet, as follows. Look at the other assumptions which we have inserted into this part of the spreadsheet.

	A	B	C	D	E	F
25						
26	*This table contains the key variables for the 20X6 cash flow projections*					
27						
28	Sales growth factor per month		1.03			
29	Purchases as % of sales		-0.65			
30						
31	Debts paid within 1 month		0.6			
32	Debts paid within 2 months		0.3			
33	Debts paid within 3 months		0.07			
34	Irrecoverable debts		0.03			
35						
36	Increase in overheads		1.05			
37						
38	Dividends (May)		-10000			
39						
40	Capital purchases		-18000			
41	January		0.2			
42	February		0.7			
43	May		0.1			
44						
45						
46	*This table contains relevant opening balance data as at Jan 20X6*					
47						
48	Monthly sales 20X5		45000			
49	January 20X6 sales		42000			
50	Monthly overheads 20X5		-6000			
51	Opening cash		-7500			
52						

Now we can go back to cell C7 and input =B5*C31 and then fill this in across the '1 month in arrears' row. (Note that, as we have no December sales figure, we will have to deal with cell B7 separately.) If we assume for the moment that we are copying to cells D7 through to G7 and follow this procedure, the contents of cell D7 would be shown as =C5*D31, and so on, as shown below.

	A	B	C	D	E	F	G
3		*Jan*	*Feb*	*Mar*	*Apr*	*May*	*Jun*
4		$	$	$	$	$	$
5	Sales						
6	*Cash receipts*						
7	1 month in arrears		=B5*C31	=C5*D31	=D5*E31	=E5*F31	=F5*G31
8	2 months in arrears						
9	3 months in arrears						
10	Total operating receipts						
11							

You may have noticed a problem. While the formula in cell C7 is fine - it multiplies January sales by 0.6 (the 1 month ratio stored in cell C31) - the remaining formulae are useless, as they **refer to empty cells** in row 31. This is what the spreadsheet would look like (assuming, for now, constant sales of $42,000 per month).

	A	B	C	D	E	F	G
3		*Jan*	*Feb*	*Mar*	*Apr*	*May*	*Jun*
4		$	$	$	$	$	$
5	Sales	42000	42000	42000	42000	42000	42000
6	*Cash receipts*						
7	1 month in arrears		25200	0	0	0	0
8	2 months in arrears						
9	3 months in arrears						
10	Total operating receipts						
11							

This problem highlights the important distinction between **relative** cell references and **absolute** cell references. Usually, cell references are **relative**. A formula of =SUM(B7:B9) in cell B10 is relative. It does not really mean 'add up the numbers in cells B7 to B9'; it actually means '**add up the numbers in the three cells above this one**'. If this formula was copied to cell C10 (as we will do later), it would become =SUM(C7:C9).

This is what is causing the problem encountered above. The spreadsheet thinks we are asking it to 'multiply the number two up and one to the left by the number twenty-four cells down', and that is indeed the effect of the instruction we have given. But we are actually intending to ask it to 'multiply the number two up and one to the left by the number in cell C31'. This means that we need to create an **absolute** (unchanging) **reference** to cell C31.

Absolute cell references use **dollar signs** ($). A dollar sign before the column letter makes the column reference absolute, and one before the row number makes the row number absolute. You do not need to type the dollar signs - add them as follows.

(a)   Make cell C7 the active cell and press F2 to edit it.

(b)   Note where the cursor is flashing: it should be after the 1. If it is not move it with the direction arrow keys so that it is positioned somewhere next to or within the cell reference C31.

(c)   Press F4.

The **function key F4** adds dollar signs to the cell reference: it becomes $C$31. Press F4 again: the reference becomes C$31. Press it again: the reference becomes $C31. Press it once more, and the simple relative reference is restored: C31.

(a)   A dollar sign **before a letter** means that the **column** reference stays the same when you copy the formula to another cell.

(b)   A dollar sign **before a number** means that the **row** reference stays the same when you copy the formula to another cell.

In our example we have now altered the reference in cell C7 and filled in across to cell G7, overwriting what was there previously. This is the result.

(a)   Formulae

	A	B	C	D	E	F	G
3		Jan	Feb	Mar	Apr	May	Jun
4		$	$	$	$	$	$
5	Sales	42000	42000	42000	42000	42000	42000
6	Cash receipts						
7	1 month in arrears		=B5*$C$31	=C5*$C$31	=D5*$C$31	=E5*$C$31	=F5*$C$31
8	2 months in arrears						
9	3 months in arrears						
10	Total operating receipts						
11							

(b)   Numbers

	A	B	C	D	E	F	G
1		Jan	Feb	Mar	Apr	May	Jun
2		$	$	$	$	$	$
3	Sales	42000	42000	42000	42000	42000	42000
4	Cash receipts						
5	1 month in arrears		25200	25200	25200	25200	25200
6	2 months in arrears						
7	3 months in arrears						
8	Total operating receipts						
9							

Other formulae required for this projection are as follows.

(a)   **Cell B5** refers directly to the information we are given - **sales of $42,000** in January. We have input this variable in cell C49. The other formulae in row 5 (sales) reflect the predicted sales growth of 3% per month, as entered in cell C28.

(b)   Similar formulae to the one already described for row 7 are required in rows 8 and 9.

(c)   **Row 10** (total operating receipts) will display simple **subtotals**, in the form =SUM(B7:B9).

(d)   **Row 13 (purchases)** requires a formula based on the data in row 5 **(sales)** and the value in cell C29 **(purchases** as a % of sales). This model assumes no changes in stock levels from month to month, and that stocks are sufficiently high to enable this. The formula is B5 * $C$29. Note that C29 is negative.

(e)   **Row 15** (total operating payments), like row 10, requires **formulae** to create **subtotals**.

(f)   **Rows 17 and 18** refer to the **dividends and capital purchase data** input in cells C38 and C40 to 43.

(g)   **Row 21** (net cash flow) requires a **total** in the form =B10 + B15 + B21.

(h)   **Row 22** (balance b/f) requires the contents of the **previous month's closing cash** figure.

(i)   **Row 23** (balance b/f) requires the **total** of the **opening cash** figure and the **net cash flow** for the month.

The following image shows the formulae that should now be present in the spreadsheet.

	A	B	C	D	E	F	G
1	EXCELLENT CO						
2	Cash flow projection - six month						
3		Jan	Feb	Mar	Apr	May	Jun
4		$	$	$	$	$	$
5	Sales	=C49	=B5*$C$28	=C5*$C$28	=D5*$C$28	=E5*$C$28	=F5*$C$28
6	Cash receipts						
7	1 month in arrears	=$C$48*$C$31	=B5*$C$31	=C5*$C$31	=D5*$C$31	=E5*$C$31	=F5*$C$31
8	2 months in arrears	=$C$48*$C$32	=$C$48*$C$32	=B5*$C$32	=C5*$C$32	=D5*$C$32	=E5*$C$32
9	3 months in arrears	=$C$48*$C$33	=$C$48*$C$33	=$C$48*$C$33	=B5*$C$33	=C5*$C$33	=D5*$C$33
10	Total operating receipts	=SUM(B7:B9)	=SUM(C7:C9)	=SUM(D7:D9)	=SUM(E7:E9)	=SUM(F7:F9)	=SUM(G7:G9)
11							
12	Cash payments						
13	Purchases	=B5*$C$29	=C5*$C$29	=D5*$C$29	=E5*$C$29	=F5*$C$29	=G5*$C$29
14	Overheads	=$C$50*$C$36	=$C$50*$C$36	=$C$50*$C$36	=$C$50*$C$36	=$C$50*$C$36	=$C$50*$C$36
15	Total operating payments	=SUM(B13:B14)	=SUM(C13:C14)	=SUM(D13:D14)	=SUM(E13:E14)	=SUM(F13:F14)	=SUM(G13:G14)
16							
17	Dividends	0	0	0	0	=C38	0
18	Capital purchases	=C40*C41	=C40*C42	0	0	=C40*C43	0
19	Total other payments	=SUM(B17:B18)	=SUM(C17:C18)	=SUM(D17:D18)	=SUM(E17:E18)	=SUM(F17:F18)	=SUM(G17:G18)
20							
21	Net cash flow	=B10+B15+B19	=C10+C15+C19	=D10+D15+D19	=E10+E15+E19	=F10+F15+F19	=G10+G15+G19
22	Cash balance b/f	=C51	=B23	=C23	=D23	=E23	=F23
23	Cash balance c/f	=SUM(B21:B22)	=SUM(C21:C22)	=SUM(D21:D22)	=SUM(E21:E22)	=SUM(F21:F22)	=SUM(G21:G22)
24							

Be careful to ensure you use the correct sign (negative or positive) when manipulating numbers. For example, if total operating payments in row 15 are shown as **positive**, you would need to **subtract** them from total operating receipts in the formulae in row 23. However if you have chosen to make them **negative**, to represent outflows, then you will need to **add** them to total operating receipts.

Here is the spreadsheet in its normal 'numbers' form.

	A	B	C	D	E	F	G
1	EXCELLENT CO						
2	*Cash flow projection - six months ending 30 June 20X6*						
3		Jan	Feb	Mar	Apr	May	Jun
4		$	$	$	$	$	$
5	Sales	42,000	43,260	44,558	45,895	47,271	48,690
6	*Cash receipts*						
7	1 month in arrears	27,000	25,200	25,956	26,735	27,537	28,363
8	2 months in arrears	13,500	13,500	12,600	12,978	13,367	13,768
9	3 months in arrears	3,150	3,150	3,150	2,940	3,028	3,119
10	Total operating receipts	43,650	41,850	41,706	42,653	43,932	45,250
11							
12	*Cash payments*						
13	Purchases	-27,300	-28,119	-28,963	-29,831	-30,726	-31,648
14	Overheads	-6,000	-6,300	-6,300	-6,300	-6,300	-6,300
15	Total operating payments	-33,300	-34,419	-35,263	-36,131	-37,026	-37,948
16							
17	Dividends	0	0	0	0	-10,000	0
18	Capital purchases	-3,600	-12,600	0	0	-1,800	0
19	Total other payments	-3,600	-12,600	0	0	-11,800	0
20							
21	Net cash flow	6,450	-5,169	6,443	6,521	-4,894	7,302
22	Cash balance b/f	-7,500	-1,050	-6,219	224	6,746	1,852
23	Cash balance c/f	-1,050	-6,219	224	6,746	1,852	9,154
24							

4.1.3 Tidy the spreadsheet up

Our spreadsheet needs a little **tidying up**. We will do the following.

(a) Add in **commas** to denote thousands of dollars.

(b) Put **zeros** in the cells with no entry in them.

(c) Change **negative numbers** from being displayed with a **minus sign** to being displayed in **brackets**.

	A	B	C	D	E	F	G
1	EXCELLENT CO						
2	*Cash flow projection - six months ending 30 June 20X6*						
3		Jan	Feb	Mar	Apr	May	Jun
4		$	$	$	$	$	£
5	Sales	42,000	43,260	44,558	45,895	47,271	48,690
6	*Cash receipts*						
7	1 month in arrears	27,000	25,200	25,956	26,735	27,537	28,363
8	2 months in arrears	13,500	13,500	12,600	12,978	13,367	13,768
9	3 months in arrears	3,150	3,150	3,150	2,940	3,028	3,119
10	Total operating receipts	43,650	41,850	41,706	42,653	43,932	45,250
11							
12	*Cash payments*						
13	Purchases	(27,300)	(28,119)	(28,963)	(29,831)	(30,726)	(31,648)
14	Overheads	(6,300)	(6,300)	(6,300)	(6,300)	(6,300)	(6,300)
15	Total operating payments	(33,600)	(34,419)	(35,263)	(36,131)	(37,026)	(37,948)
16							
17	Dividends	0	0	0	0	(10,000)	0
18	Capital purchases	(3,600)	(12,600)	0	0	(1,800)	0
19	Total other payments	(3,600)	(12,600)	0	0	(11,800)	0
20							
21	Net cash flow	6,450	(5,169)	6,443	6,521	(4,894)	7,302
22	Cash balance b/f	(7,500)	(1,050)	(6,219)	224	6,746	1,852
23	Cash balance c/f	(1,050)	(6,219)	224	6,746	1,852	9,154
24							

4.1.4 Changes in assumptions (what if? analysis)

We referred to earlier to the need to design a spreadsheet so that **changes in assumptions** do **not** require **major changes** to the spreadsheet. This is why we set up two separate areas of the spreadsheet, one for 20X6 assumptions and one for opening balances. Consider each of the following.

(a)   Negotiations with suppliers and gains in productivity have resulted in cost of sales being reduced to 62% of sales.

(b)   The effects of a recession have changed the cash collection profile so that receipts in any month are 50% of prior month sales, 35% of the previous month and 10% of the month before that, with bad debt experience rising to 5%.

(c)   An insurance claim made in 20X5 and successfully settled in December has resulted in the opening cash balance being an overdraft of $3,500.

(d)   Sales growth will only be 2% per month.

All of these changes can be made quickly and easily. The two tables are revised as follows.

	A	B	C	D	E	F
25						
26	This table contains the key variables for the 20X6 cash flow projections					
27						
28	Sales growth factor per month		1.02			
29	Purchases as % of sales		-0.62			
30						
31	Debts paid within 1 month		0.5			
32	Debts paid within 2 months		0.35			
33	Debts paid within 3 months		0.1			
34	Irrecoverable debts		0.05			
35						
36	Increase in overheads		1.05			
37						
38	Dividends (May)		-10000			
39						
40	Capital purchases		-18000			
41	January		0.2			
42	February		0.7			
43	May		0.1			
44						
45						
46	This table contains relevant opening balance data as at Jan 20X6					
47						
48	Monthly sales 19X5		45000			
49	January 1996 sales		42000			
50	Monthly overheads 19X5		-6000			
51	Opening cash		-3500			
52						

The resulting (recalculated) spreadsheet would look like this.

	A	B	C	D	E	F	G
1	**EXCELLENT PLC**						
2	*Cash flow projection - six months ending 30 June 20X6*						
3		Jan	Feb	Mar	Apr	May	Jun
4		$	$	$	$	$	$
5	Sales	42,000	42,840	43,697	44,571	45,462	46,371
6	*Cash receipts*						
7	1 month in arrears	22,500	21,000	21,420	21,848	22,285	22,731
8	2 months in arrears	15,750	15,750	14,700	14,994	15,294	15,600
9	3 months in arrears	4,500	4,500	4,500	4,200	4,284	4,370
10	Total operating receipts	42,750	41,250	40,620	41,042	41,863	42,701
11							
12	*Cash payments*						
13	Purchases	-26,040	-26,561	-27,092	-27,634	-28,187	-28,750
14	Overheads	-6,300	-6,300	-6,300	-6,300	-6,300	-6,300
15	Total operating payments	-32,340	-32,861	-33,392	-33,934	-34,487	-35,050
16							
17	Dividends	0	0	0	0	-10,000	0
18	Capital purchases	-3,600	-12,600	0	0	-1,800	0
19	Total other payments	-3,600	-12,600	0	0	-11,800	0
20							
21	Net cash flow	6,810	-4,211	7,228	7,109	-4,423	7,650
22	Cash balance b/f	-3,500	3,310	-901	6,327	13,436	9,012
23	Cash balance c/f	3,310	-901	6,327	13,436	9,012	16,663
24							

Question

Commission calculations

The following four insurance salesmen each earn a basic salary of $14,000 pa. They also earn a commission of 2% of sales. The following spreadsheet has been created to process their commission and total earnings. Give an appropriate formula for each of the following cells.

(a)   Cell D4   (c)   Cell D9
(b)   Cell E6   (d)   Cell E9

	A	B	C	D	E
1	*Sales team salaries and commissions - 200X*				
2	Name	Sales	Salary	Commission	Total earnings
3		$	$	$	$
4	Northington	284,000	14,000	5,680	19,680
5	Souther	193,000	14,000	3,860	17,860
6	Weston	12,000	14,000	240	14,240
7	Easterman	152,000	14,000	3,040	17,040
8					
9	Total	641,000	56,000	12,820	68,820
10					
11					
12	*Variables*				
13	Basic Salary	14,000			
14	Commission rate	0.02			
15					

Answer

Possible formulae are as follows.

(a)   =B4*$B$14

(b)   =C6+D6

(c)   =SUM(D4:D7)

(d)   There are a number of possibilities here, depending on whether you set the cell as the total of the earnings of each salesman (cells E4 to E7) or as the total of the different elements of remuneration (cells C9 and D9). Even better, would be a formula that checked that both calculations gave the same answer. A suitable formula for this purpose would be:

=IF(SUM(E4:E7)=SUM(C9:D9),SUM(E4:E7),"ERROR")

We will explain this formula in more detail in the next section.

5 Formulae with conditions

FAST FORWARD

If statements are used in conditional formulae.

Suppose the company employing the salesmen in the above question awards a bonus to those salesmen who exceed their target by more than $1,000. The spreadsheet could work out who is entitled to the bonus.

To do this we would enter the appropriate formula in cells F4 to F7. For salesperson Easterman, we would enter the following in cell F7:

=IF(D4>1000,"BONUS"," ")

We will now explain this formula.

IF statements follow the following structure (or syntax).

=IF(logical_test,value_if_true,value_if_false)

The logical_test is any value or expression that can be evaluated to Yes or No. For example, D4>1000 is a logical expression; if the value in cell D4 is over 1000, the expression evaluates to Yes. Otherwise, the expression evaluates to No.

Value_if_true is the value that is returned if the answer to the logical_test is Yes. For example, if the answer to D4>1000 is Yes, and the value_if_true is the text string "BONUS", then the cell containing the IF function will display the text "BONUS".

Value_if_false   is the value that is returned if the answer to the logical_test is No. For example, if the value_if_false is two sets of quote marks "" this means display a blank cell if the answer to the logical test is No. So in our example, if D4 is not over 1000, then the cell containing the IF function will display a blank cell.

Note the following symbols which can be used in formulae with conditions:

<	less than (like L (for 'less') on its side)	>=	greater than or equal to
<=	less than or equal to	>	greater than
=	equal to	<>	not equal to

Care is required to ensure **brackets** and **commas** are entered in the right places. If, when you try out this kind of formula, you get an error message, it may well be a simple mistake, such as leaving a comma out.

5.1 Examples of formulae with conditions

A company offers a discount of 5% to customers who order more than $1,000 worth of goods. A spreadsheet showing what customers will pay might look like this.

	A	B	C	D
1	**Discount Traders Co**			
2	*Sales analysis - April 200X*			
3	Customer	Sales	5% discount	Sales (net)
4		$	$	$
5	Arthur	956.00	0.00	956.00
6	Dent	1423.00	71.15	1351.85
7	Ford	2894.00	144.70	2749.30
8	Prefect	842.00	0.00	842.00
9				

The formula in cell C5 is: =IF(B5>1,000,(0.05*B5),0). This means, if the value in B5 is greater than $1,000 multiply it by 0.05, otherwise the discount will be zero. Cell D5 will calculate the amount net of discount, using the formula: =B5-C5. The same conditional formula with the cell references changed will be found in cells C6, C7 and C8. **Strictly**, the variables $1,000 and 5% should be entered in a **different part** of the spreadsheet.

Here is another example. Suppose the pass mark for an examination is 50%. You have a spreadsheet containing candidate's scores in column B. If a score is held in cell B10, an appropriate formula for cell C10 would be:

=IF(B10<50,"FAILED","PASSED").

6 Charts and graphs

FAST FORWARD

Excel includes the facility to produce a range of charts and graphs. The **chart wizard** provides a tool to simplify the process of chart construction.

Using Microsoft Excel, It is possible to display data held in a range of spreadsheet cells in a variety of charts or graphs. We will use the Discount Traders Co spreadsheet shown below to generate a chart.

	A	B	C	D
1	**Discount Traders Co**			
2	*Sales analysis - April 200X*			
3	Customer	Sales	5% discount	Sales (net)
4		$	$	$
5	Arthur	956.00	0.00	956.00
6	Dent	1423.00	71.15	1351.85
7	Ford	2894.00	144.70	2749.30
8	Prefect	842.00	0.00	842.00
9				

The data in the spreadsheet could be used to generate a chart, such as those shown below. We explain how later in this section.

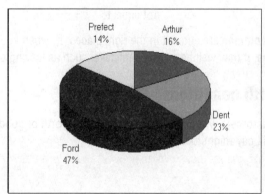
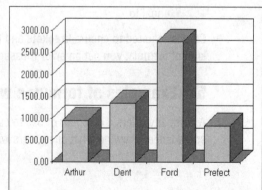

The Chart Wizard, which we explain in a moment, may also be used to generate a line graph. A line graph would normally be used to track a trend over time. For example, the chart below graphs the Total Revenue figures shown in Row 7 of the following spreadsheet.

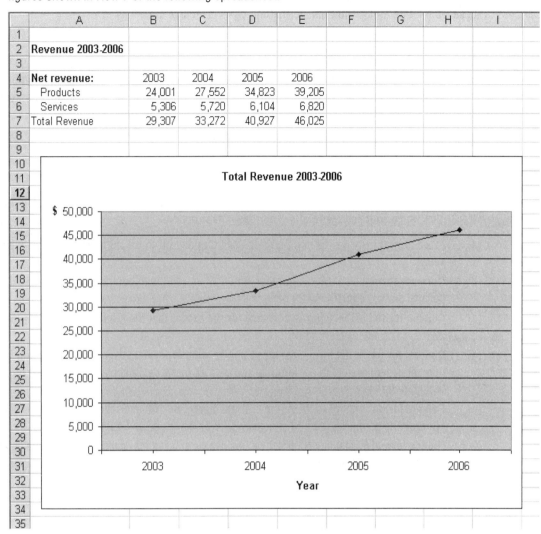

	A	B	C	D	E	F	G	H	I
1									
2	Revenue 2003-2006								
3									
4	Net revenue:	2003	2004	2005	2006				
5	Products	24,001	27,552	34,823	39,205				
6	Services	5,306	5,720	6,104	6,820				
7	Total Revenue	29,307	33,272	40,927	46,025				

7 Spreadsheet format and appearance

FAST FORWARD Good presentation can help people understand the contents of a spreadsheet.

7.1 Titles and labels

A spreadsheet should be headed up with a title which **clearly defines its purpose**. Examples of titles are follows.

(a)   Income statement for the year ended 30 June 200X.

(b)   (i)   Area A: Sales forecast for the three months to 31 March 200X.
         (ii)   Area B: Sales forecast for the three months to 31 March 200X.
         (iii)   Combined sales forecast for the three months to 31 March 200X.

(c)   Salesmen: Analysis of earnings and commission for the six months ended 30 June 200X.

Row and **column** headings (or labels) should clearly identify the contents of the row/column. Any assumptions made that have influenced the spreadsheet contents should be clearly stated.

7.2 Formatting

There are a wide range of options available under the **Format** menu. Some of these functions may also be accessed through toolbar **buttons**. Formatting options include the ability to:

(a) Add **shading** or **borders** to cells.

(b) Use **different sizes of text** and different **fonts**.

(c) Choose from a range of options for presenting values, for example to present a number as a **percentage** (eg 0.05 as 5%), or with commas every third digit, or to a specified number of **decimal places** etc.

Experiment with the various formatting options yourself.

7.2.1 Formatting numbers

Most spreadsheet programs contain facilities for presenting numbers in a particular way. In Excel you simply click on **Format** and then **Cells ...**to reach these options.

(a) **Fixed format** displays the number in the cell rounded off to the number of decimal places you select.

(b) **Currency format** displays the number with a '$' in front, with commas and not more than two decimal places, eg $10,540.23.

(c) **Comma format** is the same as currency format except that the numbers are displayed without the '$'.

(d) **General format** is the format assumed unless another format is specified. In general format the number is displayed with no commas and with as many decimal places as entered or calculated that fit in the cell.

(e) **Percent format** multiplies the number in the display by 100 and follows it with a percentage sign. For example the number 0.548 in a cell would be displayed as 54.8%.

(f) **Hidden format** is a facility by which values can be entered into cells and used in calculations but are not actually displayed on the spreadsheet. The format is useful for hiding sensitive information.

7.3 Gridlines

One of the options available under the **Tools**, **Options** menu, on the **View** tab, is an option to remove the gridlines from your spreadsheet.

Compare the following two versions of the same spreadsheet. Note how the formatting applied to the second version has improved the spreadsheet presentation.

	A	B	C	D	E
1	Sales team salaries and commissions - 200X				
2	Name	Sales	Salary	Commis	Total earnings
3		$	$	$	$
4	Northington	284,000	14,000	5,680	19,680
5	Souther	193,000	14,000	3,860	17,860
6	Weston	12,000	14,000	240	14,240
7	Easterman	152,000	14,000	3,040	17,040
8					
9	Total	641,000	56,000	12,820	68,820
10					

	A	B	C	D	E	
1	Sales team salaries and commissions - 200X					
2	*Name*	*Sales*	*Salary*	*Commission*	*Total earnings*	
3		$	$	$	$	
4	Northington	284,000	14,000	5,680	19,680	
5	Souther	193,000	14,000	3,860	17,860	
6	Weston	12,000	14,000	240	14,240	
7	Easterman	152,000	14,000	3,040	17,040	
8						
9	Total	641,000	56,000	12,820	68,820	
10						

8 Other issues: printing; controls; using spreadsheets with word processing software

Backing up is a key security measure. **Cell protection** and **passwords** can also be used to prevent unauthorised access.

8.1 Printing spreadsheets

The print options for your spreadsheet may be accessed by selecting **File** and then **Page Setup**. The various Tabs contain a range of options. You specify the area of the spreadsheet to be printed in the Print area box on the Sheet tab. Other options include the ability to repeat headings on all pages and the option to print gridlines if required (normally they wouldn't be!)

Experiment with these options including the options available under Header/Footer.

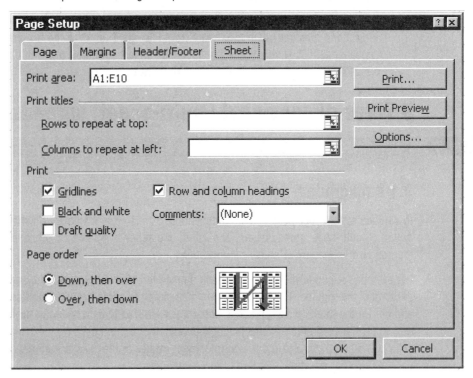

8.2 Controls

There are facilities available in spreadsheet packages which can be used as controls – to prevent unauthorised or accidental amendment or deletion of all or part of a spreadsheet.

(a)   **Saving** and **back-up**. When working on a spreadsheet, save your file regularly, as often as every ten minutes. This will prevent too much work being lost in the advent of a system crash. Spreadsheet files should be included in standard back-up procedures.

(b)   **Cell protection**. This prevents the user from inadvertently changing or erasing cells that should not be changed. Look up how to protect cells using Excel's Help facility. (Select Help from the main menu within Excel, then select Contents and Index, click on the Find tab and enter the words 'cell protection'.)

(c)   **Passwords.** You can set a password for any spreadsheet that you create. In Excel, simply click on **Tools,** then on **Protection,** then on **Protect Sheet** or **Protect Workbook**, as appropriate.

8.3 Using spreadsheets with word processing software

There may be a situation where you wish to incorporate the contents of all or part of a spreadsheet into a **word processed report**. There are a number of options available to achieve this.

(a)   The simplest, but least professional option, is to **print out** the spreadsheet and interleave the page or pages at the appropriate point in your word processed document.

(b)   A neater option if you are just including a small table is to select and **copy** the relevant cells from the spreadsheet to the computer's clipboard by selecting the cells and choosing Edit, Copy. Then switch to the word processing document, and **paste** them in at the appropriate point.

(c)   Office packages, such as Microsoft Office allow you to easily use spreadsheets and word processing files together.

For example, a new, blank spreadsheet can be '**embedded**' in a document by selecting Insert, Object then, from within the Create New tab, selecting Microsoft Excel worksheet. The spreadsheet is then available to be worked upon, allowing the easy manipulation of numbers using all the facilities of the spreadsheet package. Clicking outside the spreadsheet will result in the spreadsheet being inserted in the document.

The contents of an existing spreadsheet may be inserted into a Word document by choosing Insert, Object and then activating the Create from File tab. Then click the Browse button and locate the spreadsheet file. Highlight the file, then click Insert, and then OK. You may then need to move and resize the object, by dragging its borders, to fit your document.

9 Three dimensional (multi-sheet) spreadsheets

FAST FORWARD   Spreadsheet packages permit the user to work with **multiple sheets** that refer to each other.

9.1 Background

In early spreadsheet packages, a spreadsheet file consisted of a single worksheet. Excel provides the option of multi-sheet spreadsheets, consisting of a series of related sheets. Excel files which contain more than one worksheet are often called **workbooks**.

For example, suppose you were producing a profit forecast for two regions, and a combined forecast for the total of the regions. This situation would be suited to using separate worksheets for each region and another for the total. This approach is sometimes referred to as working in **three dimensions**, as you are able to flip between different sheets stacked in front or behind each other. Cells in one sheet may **refer** to cells in another sheet. So, in our example, the formulae in the cells in the total sheet would refer to the cells in the other sheets.

Excel has a series of 'tabs', one for each worksheet at the foot of the spreadsheet.

9.2 How many sheets?

Excel can be set up so that it always opens a fresh file with a certain number of worksheets ready and waiting for you. Click on **Tools ... Options ...** and then the **General** tab and set the number *Sheets in new* *workbook* option to the number you would like each new spreadsheet file to contain (sheets may be added or deleted later).

If you subsequently want to insert more sheets you just **right click** on the index tab after which you want the new sheet to be inserted and choose **Insert** … and then **Worksheet**. By default sheets are called **Sheet 1, Sheet 2** etc. However, these may be changed. To **rename** a sheet in **Excel, right click** on its index tab and choose the rename option.

9.3 Pasting from one sheet to another

When building a spreadsheet that will contain a number of worksheets with identical structure, users often set up one sheet, then copy that sheet and amend the sheet contents. [To copy a worksheet in Excel, from within the worksheet you wish to copy, select Edit, Move or Copy sheet, and tick the Create a copy box.] A 'Total' sheet would use the same structure, but would contain formulae totalling the individual sheets.

9.4 Linking sheets with formulae

Formulae on one sheet may refer to data held on another sheet. The links within such a formula may be established using the following steps.

Step 1   In the cell that you want to refer to a cell from another sheet, type =.

Step 2   Click on the index tab for the sheet containing the cell you want to refer to and select the cell in question.

Step 3   Press Enter or Return.

9.5 Uses for multi-sheet spreadsheets

There are a wide range of situations suited to the multi-sheet approach. A variety of possible uses follow.

(a)   A model could use one sheet for variables, a second for calculations, and a third for outputs.

(b)   To enable quick and easy **consolidation** of similar sets of data, for example the financial results of two subsidiaries or the budgets of two departments.

(c)   To provide **different views** of the same data. For instance you could have one sheet of data sorted in product code order and another sorted in product name order.

10 Macros

FAST FORWARD ▶▶ A **macro** is an automated process that may be written by recording key-strokes and mouse clicks.

If you perform a task repeatedly within a spreadsheet, you may want to make your life easier by automating the task. This is what **macros** are used for.

A macro is a series of commands or functions that are stored in your spreadsheet and can be run each time you want to perform the task.

One example would be the frequent use of long strings of text in formulae. By creating a macro, you can format the cells to which the formula will apply, rather than having to type in the formula each time.

When you record a macro, your spreadsheet package should store information about each step you take as you perform a series of commands. You can then run the macro to repeat the commands. This allows you to check for any errors.

10.1 Working with macros

Always start a macro by **returning the cursor to cell A1** (by pressing Ctrl + Home), even if it is already there. You may well not want to make your first entry in cell A1, but if you select your first real cell (B4 say) **before** you start recording, the macro will always begin at the currently active cell, whether it is B4 or Z256.

Always finish a macro by **selecting the cell** where the **next entry** is required.

If you close down and then re-open the file in which you created the macro, your macro will work again, because it is actually **stored** in that file. If you want your macro to be **available to you whenever** you want it you have the following choices.

(a) Keep this file, with no contents other than your 'name' macro (and any others you may write) and always use it as the basis for any new spreadsheets you create, which will subsequently be saved with new file names.

(b) You can add the macro to your **Personal Macro Workbook.** You do this at the point when you are naming your workbook and choosing a shortcut key, by changing the option in the **Store macro in:** box from This Workbook to Personal Macro Workbook. The macro will then be loaded into memory whenever you start up Excel and be available in any spreadsheet you create.

If you forget to assign a keyboard shortcut to a macro (or do not want to do so), you can still run your macros by clicking on Tools …Macro … Macros. This gives you a list of all the macros currently available. Select the one you want then click on Run.

Do not accept the default names offered by Excel of Macro1, Macro2 etc. You will soon forget what these macros do, unless you give them a meaningful name.

11 Advantages and disadvantages of spreadsheet software

11.1 Advantages of spreadsheets

- Excel is easy to learn and to use
- Spreadsheets make the calculation and manipulation of data easier and quicker
- They enable the analysis, reporting and sharing of financial information
- They enable 'what-if' analysis to be performed very quickly

11.2 Disadvantages of spreadsheets

- A spreadsheet is only as good as its original design, garbage in = garbage out!
- Formulae are hidden from sight so the underlying logic of a set of calculations may not be obvious
- A spreadsheet presentation may make reports appear infallible
- Research shows that a high proportion of large models contain critical errors
- A database may be more suitable to use with large volumes of data

Question   Spreadsheet advantages

An advantage of a spreadsheet program is that it

A   Can answer 'what if?' questions   C   Automatically writes formulae
B   Checks for incorrect entries   D   Can answer 'when is?' questions

Answer

The correct answer is A.

12 Uses of spreadsheet software

Spreadsheets can be used in a variety of accounting contexts. You should practise using spreadsheets, **hands-on experience** is the key to spreadsheet proficiency.

Management accountants will use spreadsheet software in activities such as budgeting, forecasting, reporting performance and variance analysis.

12.1 Budgeting

Spreadsheet packages for budgeting have a number of advantages.

(a) Spreadsheet packages have a facility to perform **'what if' calculations** at great speed. For example, the consequences throughout the organisation of sales growth per month of nil, $\frac{1}{2}$%, 1%, $1\frac{1}{2}$% and so on can be calculated very quickly.

(b) Preparing budgets may be complex; budgets may need to go through several drafts. If one or two figures are changed, the **computer will automatically make all the computational changes to the other figures**.

(c) A spreadsheet model will **ensure that the preparation of the individual budgets is co-ordinated**. Data and information from the production budget, for example, will be automatically fed through to the material usage budget (as material usage will depend on production levels).

These advantages of spreadsheets make them ideal for taking over the **manipulation of numbers**, leaving staff to get involved in the real planning process.

Chapter Roundup

- Use of spreadsheets is an essential part of the day-to-day work of the Management Accountant.

- A spreadsheet is an electronic piece of paper divided into **rows** and **columns**. The intersection of a row and a column is known as a **cell**.

- Formulas in Microsoft Excel follow a specific syntax.

- Essential basic skills include how to **move around** within a spreadsheet, how to **enter** and **edit** data, how to **fill** cells, how to **insert** and **delete** columns and rows and how to improve the basic **layout** and **appearance** of a spreadsheet.

- A wide range of **formulae** and functions are available within Excel.

- **If statements** are used in conditional formulae.

- Excel includes the facility to produce a range of charts and graphs. The **chart wizard** provides a tool to simplify the process of chart construction.

- Good presentation can help people understand the contents of a spreadsheet.

- **Backing up** is a key security measure. **Cell protection** and **passwords** can also be used to prevent unauthorised access.

- Spreadsheet packages permit the user to work with **multiple sheets** that refer to each other.

- A **macro** is an automated process that may be written by recording key-strokes and mouse clicks.

- Spreadsheets can be used in a variety of accounting contexts. You should practise using spreadsheets, **hands-on experience** is the key to spreadsheet proficiency.

Quick quiz

1 List three types of cell contents.
2 What do the F5 and F2 keys do in Excel?
3 What technique can you use to insert a logical series of data such as 1, 2 …. 10, or Jan, Feb, March etc?
4 How do you display formulae instead of the results of formulae in a spreadsheet?
5 Which function key may be used to change cell references within a selected formula from absolute to relative – and vice-versa?
6 List five possible changes that may improve the appearance of a spreadsheet.
7 List three possible uses for a multi-sheet (3D) spreadsheet.
8 You are about to key an exam mark into cell B4 of a spreadsheet. Write an IF statement, to be placed in cell C4, that will display PASS in C4 if the student mark is 50 or above - and or will display FAIL if the mark is below 50 (all student marks are whole numbers).
9 Give two ways of starting Excel's function wizard.

Answers to quick quiz

1 Text, values or formulae.
2 F5 opens a GoTo dialogue box which is useful for navigating around large spreadsheets. F2 puts the active cell into edit mode.
3 You can use the technique of 'filling' - selecting the first few items of a series and dragging the lower right corner of the selection in the appropriate direction.
4 Select Tools, Options, ensure the View tab is active then tick the Formulas box within the window options area.
5 The F4 key.
6 Removing gridlines, adding shading, adding borders, using different fonts and font sizes, presenting numbers as percentages or currency or to a certain number of decimal places.
7 The construction of a spreadsheet model with separate Input, Calculation and Output sheets. They can help consolidate data from different sources. They can offer different views of the same data.
8 =IF(A4>49,"PASS","FAIL ")
9 You could click on the *fx* symbol in the toolbar, or use the menu item Insert, Function, to start the function wizard.

Now try the questions below from the Exam Question Bank

Number	Level	Marks	Time
5	MCQ/OTQ	n/a	n/a

Cost accounting techniques

Material costs

Topic list	Syllabus reference
1 What is inventory control?	D1 (b)
2 The ordering, receipt and issue of raw materials	D1 (a)
3 The storage of raw materials	D1 (c), (d)
4 Inventory control levels	D1 (e)-(h)

Introduction

The investment in inventory is a very important one for most businesses, both in terms of monetary value and relationships with customers (no inventory, no sale, loss of customer goodwill). It is therefore vital that management establish and maintain an **effective inventory control system**.

This chapter will concentrate on a **inventory control system** for materials, but similar problems and considerations apply to all forms of inventory.

Study guide

		Intellectual level
D1	**Accounting for materials**	
(a)	Describe the different procedures and documents necessary for ordering, receiving and issuing materials from inventory	1
(b)	Describe the control procedures used to monitor physical and 'book' inventory and to minimise discrepancies and losses	1
(c)	Interpret the entries and balances in the material inventory account	1
(d)	Identify and explain the costs of ordering and holding inventory	1
(e)	Calculate and interpret optimal recorder quantities	2
(f)	Calculate and interpret optimal reorder quantities when discounts apply	2
(g)	Produce calculations to minimise inventory costs when inventory is gradually replenished	2
(h)	Describe and apply appropriate methods for establishing reorder levels where demand in the lead time is constant	2

Exam guide

Material costs is another key area of the syllabus so expect questions on this topic. Make sure you understand and can use the EOQ formula. It will be given to you in the exam.

1 What is inventory control?

1.1 Introduction

FAST FORWARD

Inventory control includes the functions of inventory ordering and purchasing, receiving goods into store, storing and issuing inventory and controlling levels of inventory.

Classifications of inventories

- Raw materials
- Work in progress
- Spare parts/consumables
- Finished goods

This chapter will concentrate on an **inventory control system** for materials, but similar problems and considerations apply to all forms of inventory. Controls should cover the following functions.

- The **ordering** of inventory
- The **purchase** of inventory
- The **receipt** of goods into store
- **Storage**
- The **issue** of inventory and maintenance of inventory at the most appropriate level

1.2 Qualitative aspects of inventory control

We may wish to **control inventory** for the following reasons.

- Holding costs of inventory may be expensive.
- Production will be disrupted if we run out of raw materials.
- Unused inventory with a short shelf life may incur unnecessary expenses.

If manufactured goods are made out of low quality materials, the end product will be of low quality also. It may therefore be necessary to control the quality of inventory, in order to maintain a good reputation with consumers.

2 The ordering, receipt and issue of raw materials

2.1 Ordering and receiving materials

Every movement of a material in a business should be documented using the following as appropriate: purchase requisition; purchase order; GRN; materials requisition note; materials transfer note and materials returned note.

Proper records must be kept of the physical procedures for ordering and receiving a consignment of materials to ensure the following.

- That enough inventory is held
- That there is no duplication of ordering
- That quality is maintained
- That there is adequate record keeping for accounts purposes

2.2 Purchase requisition

Current inventories run down to the level where a reorder is required. The stores department issues a **purchase requisition** which is sent to the purchasing department, authorising the department to order further inventory. An example of a purchase requisition is shown below.

PURCHASE REQUISITION Req. No.				
Department/job number: Suggested Supplier:			Date	
			Requested by: Latest date required:	
Quantity	Code number	Description	Estimated Cost	
			Unit	$
Authorised signature:				

2.3 Purchase order

The purchasing department draws up a **purchase order** which is sent to the supplier. (The supplier may be asked to return an acknowledgement copy as confirmation of his acceptance of the order.) Copies of the purchase order must be sent to the accounts department and the storekeeper (or receiving department).

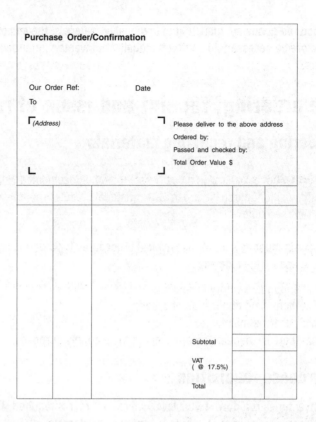

2.4 Quotations

The purchasing department may have to obtain a number of quotations if either a new inventory line is required, the existing supplier's costs are too high or the existing supplier no longer stocks the goods needed. Trade discounts (reduction in the price per unit given to some customers) should be negotiated where possible.

2.5 Delivery note

The supplier delivers the consignment of materials, and the storekeeper signs a **delivery note** for the carrier. The packages must then be checked against the copy of the purchase order, to ensure that the supplier has delivered the types and quantities of materials which were ordered. (Discrepancies would be referred to the purchasing department.)

2.6 Goods received note

If the delivery is acceptable, the storekeeper prepares a **goods received note (GRN)**, an example of which is shown below.

GOODS RECEIVED NOTE	WAREHOUSE COPY

NO 5565

DATE: .... TIME: ....

OUR ORDER NO: .... WAREHOUSE A

SUPPLIER AND SUPPLIER'S ADVICE NOTE NO: ....

QUANTITY	CAT NO	DESCRIPTION

RECEIVED IN GOOD CONDITION: (INITIALS)

A copy of the **GRN** is sent to the accounts department, where it is matched with the copy of the purchase order. The supplier's invoice is checked against the purchase order and GRN, and the necessary steps are taken to pay the supplier. The invoice may contain details relating to discounts such as trade discounts, quantity discounts (order in excess of a specified amount) and settlement discounts (payment received within a specified number of days).

Question   Ordering materials

What are the possible consequences of a failure of control over ordering and receipt of materials?

Answer

(a)   Incorrect materials being delivered, disrupting operations
(b)   Incorrect prices being paid
(c)   Deliveries other than at the specified time (causing disruption)
(d)   Insufficient control over quality
(e)   Invoiced amounts differing from quantities of goods actually received or prices agreed

You may, of course, have thought of equally valid consequences.

2.7 Materials requisition note

Materials can only be issued against a **materials/stores requisition**. This document must record not only the quantity of goods issued, but also the cost centre or the job number for which the requisition is being made. The materials requisition note may also have a column, to be filled in by the cost department, for recording the cost or value of the materials issued to the cost centre or job.

Materials requisition note			
Date required _ _ _ _ _ _ _ _.		Cost centre No/ Job No _ _ _ _ _ _ _ _ _ _ _.	
Quantity	Item code	Description	$
Signature of requisitioning Manager/ Foreman _			Date _ _ _ _ _ _

2.8 Materials transfers and returns

Where materials, having been issued to one job or cost centre, are later transferred to a different job or cost centre, without first being returned to stores, a **materials transfer note** should be raised. Such a note must show not only the job receiving the transfer, but also the job from which it is transferred. This enables the appropriate charges to be made to jobs or cost centres.

Material returns must also be documented on a **materials returned note**. This document is the 'reverse' of a requisition note, and must contain similar information. In fact it will often be almost identical to a requisition note. It will simply have a different title and perhaps be a distinctive colour, such as red, to highlight the fact that materials are being returned.

2.9 Computerised inventory control systems

Many inventory control systems these days are computerised. Computerised inventory control systems vary greatly, but most will have the features outlined below.

(a) **Data must be input into the system**. For example, details of goods received may simply be written on to a GRN for later entry into the computer system. Alternatively, this information may be keyed in directly to the computer: a GRN will be printed and then signed as evidence of the transaction, so that both the warehouse and the supplier can have a hard copy record in case of dispute. Some systems may incorporate the use of devices such as bar code readers.

Other types of transaction which will need to be recorded include the following.

   (i)   **Transfers** between different categories of inventory (for example from work in progress to finished goods)

   (ii) **Despatch**, resulting from a sale, of items of finished goods to customers

   (iii) **Adjustments** to inventory records if the amount of inventory revealed in a physical inventory count differs from the amount appearing on the inventory records

(b) **An inventory master file is maintained**. This file will contain details for every category of inventory and will be updated for new inventory lines. A database file may be maintained.

Question   Inventory master file

What type of information do you think should be held on an inventory master file?

Answer

Here are some examples.

(a) Inventory code number, for reference   (e) Cost per unit
(b) Brief description of inventory item   (f) Selling price per unit (if finished goods)
(c) Reorder level   (g) Amount in inventory
(d) Reorder quantity   (h) Frequency of usage

The file may also hold details of inventory movements over a period, but this will depend on the type of system in operation. In a **batch system**, transactions will be grouped and input in one operation and details of the movements may be held in a separate transactions file, the master file updated in total only. In an **on-line system**, transactions may be input directly to the master file, where the record of movements is thus likely to be found. Such a system will mean that the inventory records are constantly up to date, which will help in monitoring and controlling inventory.

The system may generate orders automatically once the amount in inventory has fallen to the reorder level.

(c) **The system will generate outputs**. These may include, depending on the type of system, any of the following.

   (i)   **Hard copy** records, for example a printed GRN, of transactions entered into the system.

   (ii) Output on a **VDU** screen in response to an enquiry (for example the current level of a particular line of inventory, or details of a particular transaction).

   (iii) Various **printed reports**, devised to fit in with the needs of the organisation. These may include inventory movement reports, detailing over a period the movements on all inventory lines, listings of GRNs, despatch notes and so forth.

A computerised inventory control system is usually able to give more up to date information and more flexible reporting than a manual system but remember that both manual and computer based inventory control systems need the same types of data to function properly.

3 The storage of raw materials

3.1 Objectives of storing materials

- Speedy **issue** and **receipt** of materials
- Full **identification** of all materials at all times
- Correct **location** of all materials at all times
- **Protection** of materials from damage and deterioration
- Provision of **secure stores** to avoid pilferage, theft and fire
- **Efficient** use of storage space
- **Maintenance** of correct inventory levels
- Keeping correct and up-to-date **records** of receipts, issues and inventory levels

3.2 Recording inventory levels

One of the objectives of storekeeping is to maintain accurate records of current inventory levels. This involves the accurate recording of inventory movements (issues from and receipts into stores). The most frequently encountered system for recording inventory movements is the use of bin cards and stores ledger accounts.

3.2.1 Bin cards

A **bin card** shows the level of inventory of an item at a particular stores location. It is kept with the actual inventory and is updated by the storekeeper as inventories are received and issued. A typical bin card is shown below.

Bin card

Part code no _ _ _ _ _ _ _ _ _ _ _			Location _ _ _ _ _ _ _ _ _ _ _ _ _ _ _			
Bin number _ _ _ _ _ _ _ _ _ _ _			Stores ledger no _ _ _ _ _ _ _ _ _ _ _ _			
Receipts			*Issues*			Inventory
Date	Quantity	G.R.N. No.	Date	Quantity	Req. No.	balance

The use of bin cards is decreasing, partly due to the difficulty in keeping them updated and partly due to the merging of inventory recording and control procedures, frequently using computers.

3.2.2 Stores ledger accounts

A typical stores ledger account is shown below. Note that it shows the value of inventory.

Stores ledger account

Material - - - - - - - - - - - - - - - - - - - .				Maximum Quantity _ _ _ _ _ _ _ _ _ _ _ _ _ _ _						
Code - - - - - - - - - - - - - - - - - - -				Minimum Quantity _ _ _ _ _ _ _ _ _ _ _ _ _ _						
Date	Receipts				Issues				Inventory		
	G.R.N No.	Quantity	Unit price $	Amount $	Stores Req. No	Quantity	Unit price $	Amount $	Quantity	Unit price $	Amount $

The above illustration shows a card for a manual system, but even when the inventory records are computerised, the same type of information is normally included in the computer file. The running balance on the stores ledger account allows inventory levels and valuation to be monitored.

3.2.3 Free inventory

Managers need to know the **free inventory balance** in order to obtain a full picture of the current inventory position of an item. Free inventory represents what is really **available for future use** and is calculated as follows.

	Materials in inventory	X
+	Materials on order from suppliers	X
−	Materials requisitioned, not yet issued	(X)
	Free inventory balance	X

Knowledge of the level of physical inventory assists inventory issuing, inventory counting and controlling maximum and minimum inventory levels: knowledge of the level of free inventory assists ordering.

Question   Units on order

A wholesaler has 8,450 units outstanding for Part X100 on existing customers' orders; there are 3,925 units in inventory and the calculated free inventory is 5,525 units.

How many units does the wholesaler have on order with his supplier?

A 9,450   B 10,050   C 13,975   D 17,900

Answer

Free inventory balance	=	units in inventory + units on order − units ordered, but not yet issued
5,525	=	3,925 + units on order − 8,450
Units on order	=	10,050

The correct answer is B.

3.3 Identification of materials: inventory codes (materials codes)

Materials held in stores are **coded** and **classified**. Advantages of using code numbers to identify materials are as follows.

(a)   Ambiguity is avoided.

(b)   Time is saved. Descriptions can be lengthy and time-consuming.

(c)   Production efficiency is improved. The correct material can be accurately identified from a code number.

(d)   Computerised processing is made easier.

(e)   Numbered code systems can be designed to be flexible, and can be expanded to include more inventory items as necessary.

The digits in a code can stand for the type of inventory, supplier, department and so forth.

3.4 The inventory count (stocktake)

FAST FORWARD

The **inventory count (stocktake)** involves counting the physical inventory on hand at a certain date, and then checking this against the balance shown in the inventory records. The count can be carried out on a **continuous** or **periodic** basis.

Periodic stocktaking is a process whereby all inventory items are physically counted and valued at a set point in time, usually at the end of an accounting period.

Continuous stocktaking is counting and valuing selected items at different times on a rotating basis. This involves a specialist team counting and checking a number of inventory items each day, so that each item is checked at least once a year. Valuable items or items with a high turnover could be checked more frequently.

3.4.1 Advantages of continuous stocktaking compared to periodic stocktaking

(a) The annual stocktaking is unnecessary and the disruption it causes is avoided.

(b) Regular skilled stocktakers can be employed, reducing likely errors.

(c) More time is available, reducing errors and allowing investigation.

(d) Deficiencies and losses are revealed sooner than they would be if stocktaking were limited to an annual check.

(e) Production hold-ups are eliminated because the stores staff are at no time so busy as to be unable to deal with material issues to production departments.

(f) Staff morale is improved and standards raised.

(g) Control over inventory levels is improved, and there is less likelihood of overstocking or running out of inventory.

3.4.2 Inventory discrepancies

There will be occasions when inventory checks disclose discrepancies between the physical amount of an item in inventory and the amount shown in the inventory records. When this occurs, the cause of the discrepancy should be investigated, and appropriate action taken to ensure that it does not happen again.

3.4.3 Perpetual inventory

Perpetual inventory refers to a inventory recording system whereby the records (bin cards and stores ledger accounts) are updated for each receipt and issue of inventory as it occurs.

This means that there is a continuous record of the balance of each item of inventory. The balance on the stores ledger account therefore represents the inventory on hand and this balance is used in the calculation of closing inventory in monthly and annual accounts. In practice, physical inventories may not agree with recorded inventories and therefore continuous stocktaking is necessary to ensure that the perpetual inventory system is functioning correctly and that minor inventory discrepancies are corrected.

3.4.4 Obsolete, deteriorating and slow-moving inventories and wastage

Obsolete inventories are those items which have become out-of-date and are no longer required. Obsolete items are written off and disposed of.

Inventory items may be wasted because, for example, they get broken. All **wastage** should be noted on the inventory records immediately so that physical inventory equals the inventory balance on records and the cost of the wastage written off.

Slow-moving inventories are inventory items which are likely to take a long time to be used up. For example, 5,000 units are in inventory, and only 20 are being used each year. This is often caused by overstocking. Managers should investigate such inventory items and, if it is felt that the usage rate is unlikely to increase, excess inventory should be written off as for obsolete inventory, leaving perhaps four or five years' supply in inventory.

4 Inventory control levels

4.1 Inventory costs

Inventory costs include purchase costs, holding costs, ordering costs and costs of running out inventory.

The costs of purchasing inventory are usually one of the largest costs faced by an organisation and, once obtained, inventory has to be carefully controlled and checked.

4.1.1 Reasons for holding inventories

- To ensure sufficient goods are available to meet expected demand
- To provide a buffer between processes
- To meet any future shortages
- To take advantage of bulk purchasing discounts
- To absorb seasonal fluctuations and any variations in usage and demand
- To allow production processes to flow smoothly and efficiently
- As a necessary part of the production process (such as when maturing cheese)
- As a deliberate investment policy, especially in times of inflation or possible shortages

4.1.2 Holding costs

If inventories are too high, **holding costs** will be incurred unnecessarily. Such costs occur for a number of reasons.

(a) **Costs of storage and stores operations.** Larger inventories require more storage space and possibly extra staff and equipment to control and handle them.

(b) **Interest charges**. Holding inventories involves the tying up of capital (cash) on which interest must be paid.

(c) **Insurance costs**. The larger the value of inventories held, the greater insurance premiums are likely to be.

(d) **Risk of obsolescence**. The longer a inventory item is held, the greater is the risk of obsolescence.

(e) **Deterioration**. When materials in store deteriorate to the extent that they are unusable, they must be thrown away with the likelihood that disposal costs would be incurred.

4.1.3 Costs of obtaining inventory

On the other hand, if inventories are kept low, small quantities of inventory will have to be ordered more frequently, thereby increasing the following **ordering or procurement costs**.

(a) **Clerical and administrative costs** associated with purchasing, accounting for and receiving goods

(b) **Transport costs**

(c) **Production run costs**, for inventory which is manufactured internally rather than purchased from external sources

4.1.4 Stockout costs (running out of inventory)

An additional type of cost which may arise if inventory are kept too low is the type associated with running out of inventory. There are a number of causes of **stockout costs**.

- Lost contribution from lost sales
- Loss of future sales due to disgruntled customers
- Loss of customer goodwill
- Cost of production stoppages
- Labour frustration over stoppages
- Extra costs of urgent, small quantity, replenishment orders

4.1.5 Objective of inventory control

The overall objective of inventory control is, therefore, to maintain inventory levels so that the total of the following costs is minimised.

- Holding costs
- Ordering costs

- Stockout costs

4.2 Inventory control levels

FAST FORWARD

> **Inventory control levels** can be calculated in order to maintain inventories at the optimum level. The three critical control levels are reorder level, minimum level and maximum level.

Based on an analysis of past inventory usage and delivery times, inventory control levels can be calculated and used to maintain inventory at their optimum level (in other words, a level which minimises costs). These levels will determine 'when to order' and 'how many to order'.

4.2.1 Reorder level

When inventories reach this level, an order should be placed to replenish inventories. The reorder level is determined by consideration of the following.

- The maximum rate of consumption
- The maximum lead time

The maximum lead time is the time between placing an order with a supplier, and the inventory becoming available for use

Formula to learn

> **Reorder level** = maximum usage × maximum lead time

4.2.2 Minimum level

This is a warning level to draw management attention to the fact that inventories are approaching a dangerously low level and that stockouts are possible.

Formula to learn

> **Minimum level** = reorder level − (average usage × average lead time)

4.2.3 Maximum level

This also acts as a warning level to signal to management that inventories are reaching a potentially wasteful level.

Formula to learn

> **Maximum level** = reorder level + reorder quantity − (minimum usage × minimum lead time)

Question

Maximum inventory level

A large retailer with multiple outlets maintains a central warehouse from which the outlets are supplied. The following information is available for Part Number SF525.

Average usage	350 per day
Minimum usage	180 per day
Maximum usage	420 per day
Lead time for replenishment	11-15 days
Re-order quantity	6,500 units
Re-order level	6,300 units

(a)   Based on the data above, what is the maximum level of inventory?

A 5,250   B 6,500   C 10,820   D 12,800

(b) Based on the data above, what is the approximate number of Part Number SF525 carried as buffer inventory?

A 200   B 720   C 1,680   D 1,750

Answer

(a) Maximum inventory level= reorder level + reorder quantity – (min usage × min lead time)

$$= 6,300 + 6,500 - (180 \times 11)$$
$$= 10,820$$

The correct answer is C.

Using good MCQ technique, if you were resorting to a guess you should have eliminated option A. The maximum inventory level cannot be less than the reorder quantity.

(b) Buffer inventory   = minimum level

Minimum level   = reorder level – (average usage × average lead time)

$$= 6,300 - (350 \times 13) = 1,750.$$

The correct answer is D.

Option A could again be easily eliminated. With minimum usage of 180 per day, a buffer inventory of only 200 would not be much of a buffer!

4.2.4 Reorder quantity

This is the quantity of inventory which is to be ordered when inventory reaches the reorder level. If it is set so as to minimise the total costs associated with holding and ordering inventory, then it is known as the economic order quantity.

4.2.5 Average inventory

The formula for the average inventory level assumes that inventory levels fluctuate evenly between the minimum (or safety) inventory level and the highest possible inventory level (the amount of inventory immediately after an order is received, ie safety inventory + reorder quantity).

Formula to learn

> **Average inventory** = safety inventory + ½ reorder quantity

Question

Average inventory

A component has a safety inventory of 500, a re-order quantity of 3,000 and a rate of demand which varies between 200 and 700 per week. The average inventory is approximately

A 2,000   B 2,300   C 2,500   D 3,500

Answer

Average inventory   = safety inventory + ½ reorder quantity

$$= 500 + (0.5 \times 3,000)$$
$$= 2,000$$

The correct answer is A.

BPP
LEARNING MEDIA

4.3 Economic order quantity (EOQ)

The **economic order quantity (EOQ)** is the order quantity which minimises inventory costs. The EOQ can be calculated using a table, graph or formula.

Economic order theory assumes that the average inventory held is equal to one half of the reorder quantity (although as we saw in the last section, if an organisation maintains some sort of buffer or safety inventory then average inventory = buffer inventory + half of the reorder quantity). We have seen that there are certain costs associated with holding inventory. These costs tend to increase with the level of inventories, and so could be reduced by ordering smaller amounts from suppliers each time.

On the other hand, as we have seen, there are costs associated with ordering from suppliers: documentation, telephone calls, payment of invoices, receiving goods into stores and so on. These costs tend to increase if small orders are placed, because a larger number of orders would then be needed for a given annual demand.

4.3.1 Example: Economic order quantity

Suppose a company purchases raw material at a cost of $16 per unit. The annual demand for the raw material is 25,000 units. The holding cost per unit is $6.40 and the cost of placing an order is $32.

We can tabulate the annual relevant costs for various order quantities as follows.

Order quantity (units)		100	200	300	400	500	600	800	1,000
Average inventory (units)	(a)	50	100	150	200	250	300	400	500
Number of orders	(b)	250	125	83	63	50	42	31	25
		$	$	$	$	$	$	$	$
Annual holding cost	(c)	320	640	960	1,280	1,600	1,920	2,560	3,200
Annual order cost	(d)	8,000	4,000	2,656	2,016	1,600	1,344	992	800
Total relevant cost		8,320	4,640	3,616	3,296	3,200	3,264	3,552	4,000

Notes

(a) Average inventory = Order quantity ÷ 2 (ie assuming no safety inventory)
(b) Number of orders = annual demand ÷ order quantity
(c) Annual holding cost = Average inventory × $6.40
(d) Annual order cost = Number of orders × $32

You will see that the economic order quantity is 500 units. At this point the total annual relevant costs are at a minimum.

4.3.2 Example: Economic order quantity graph

We can present the information tabulated in Paragraph 4.3.1 in graphical form. The vertical axis represents the relevant annual costs for the investment in inventories, and the horizontal axis can be used to represent either the various order quantities or the average inventory levels; two scales are actually shown on the horizontal axis so that both items can be incorporated. The graph shows that, as the average inventory level and order quantity increase, the holding cost increases. On the other hand, the ordering costs decline as inventory levels and order quantities increase. The total cost line represents the sum of both the holding and the ordering costs.

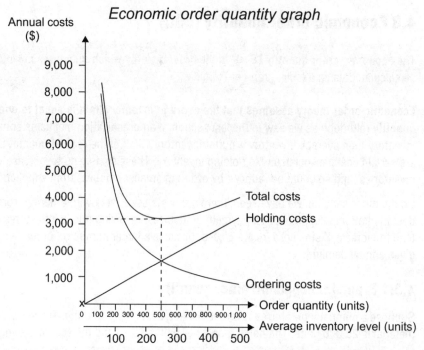

Economic order quantity graph

Note that the total cost line is at a minimum for an order quantity of 500 units and occurs at the point where the ordering cost curve and holding cost curve intersect. **The EOQ is therefore found at the point where holding costs equal ordering costs.**

4.3.3 EOQ formula

The formula for the EOQ will be provided in your examination.

Exam formula

$$EOQ = \sqrt{\frac{2C_0D}{C_H}} \quad \text{(given in exam)}$$

where C_H = cost of holding one unit of inventory for one time period
C_0 = cost of ordering a consignment from a supplier
D = demand during the time period

Question

EOQ

Calculate the EOQ using the formula and the information in Paragraph 4.3.1.

Answer

$$EOQ = \sqrt{\frac{2 \times \$32 \times 25,000}{\$6.40}}$$

$$= \sqrt{250,000}$$

$$= 500 \text{ units}$$

4.4 Economic batch quantity (EBQ)

The **economic batch quantity** (EBQ) is a modification of the EOQ and is used when resupply is gradual instead of instantaneous.

$$EBQ = \sqrt{\frac{2C_0 D}{C_H(1 - D/R)}}$$

Typically, a manufacturing company might hold inventories of a finished item, which is produced in batches. Once the order for a new batch has been placed, and the production run has started, finished output might be used before the batch run has been completed.

4.4.1 Example: Economic batch quantity

If the daily demand for an item of inventory is ten units, and the storekeeper orders 100 units in a batch. The rate of production is 50 units a day.

(a)   On the first day of the batch production run, the stores will run out of its previous inventories, and re-supply will begin. 50 units will be produced during the day, and ten units will be consumed. The closing inventory at the end of day 1 will be 50 – 10 = 40 units.

(b)   On day 2, the final 50 units will be produced and a further ten units will be consumed. Closing inventory at the end of day 2 will be (40 + 50 –10) = 80 units.

(c)   In eight more days, inventories will fall to zero.

The minimum inventory in this example is zero, and the maximum inventory is 80 units. The maximum inventory is the quantity ordered (Q = 100) minus demand during the period of the batch production run which is Q × D/R, where

D   is the rate of demand   R   is the rate of production
Q   is the quantity ordered.

In our example, the maximum inventory is $(100 - \frac{10}{50} \times 100) = 100 - 20 = 80$ units.

The maximum inventory level, given gradual re-supply, is thus $Q - \frac{QD}{R} = Q(1 - D/R)$.

4.4.2 Example: Economic batch quantity graph

The position in Paragraph 4.4.1 can be represented graphically as follows.

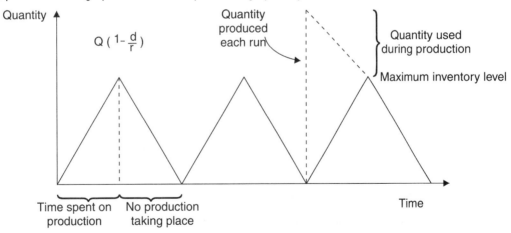

An amended EOQ (economic batch quantity, or EBQ) formula is required because average inventories are not Q/2 but Q(1 – D/R)/2.

4.4.3 EBQ Formula

The **EBQ** is $\sqrt{\dfrac{2C_oD}{C_H(1-DR)}}$ (given in exam)

where
- R = the production rate per time period (which must exceed the inventory usage)
- Q = the amount produced in each batch
- D = the usage per time period
- C_o = the set up cost per batch
- C_H = the holding cost per unit of inventory per time period

Question

Economic production run

A company is able to manufacture its own components for inventory at the rate of 4,000 units a week. Demand for the component is at the rate of 2,000 units a week. Set up costs for each production run are $50. The cost of holding one unit of inventory is $0.001 a week.

Required

Calculate the economic production run.

Answer

$$Q = \sqrt{\frac{2 \times 50 \times 2,000}{0.001(1-2,000/4,000)}} = 20,000 \text{ units (giving an inventory cycle of 10 weeks)}$$

4.5 Bulk discounts

The solution obtained from using the simple EOQ formula may need to be modified if bulk discounts (also called quantity discounts) are available. The following graph shows the effect that discounts granted for orders of certain sizes may have on total costs.

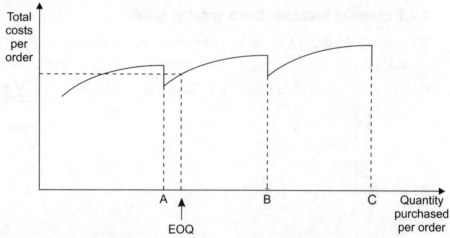

The graph above shows the following.

- Differing bulk discounts are given when the order quantity exceeds A, B and C
- The minimum total cost (ie when quantity B is ordered rather than the EOQ)

To decide mathematically whether it would be worthwhile taking a discount and ordering larger quantities, it is necessary to **minimise** the total of the following.

- Total material costs
- Ordering costs

- Inventory holding costs

The **total cost** will be **minimised** at one of the following.

- At the **pre-discount EOQ level**, so that a discount is not worthwhile
- At the **minimum order size** necessary to earn the discount

4.5.1 Example: Bulk discounts

The annual demand for an item of inventory is 45 units. The item costs $200 a unit to purchase, the holding cost for one unit for one year is 15% of the unit cost and ordering costs are $300 an order.

The supplier offers a 3% discount for orders of 60 units or more, and a discount of 5% for orders of 90 units or more.

Required

Calculate the cost-minimising order size.

Solution

(a) The EOQ ignoring discounts is $\sqrt{\dfrac{2 \times 300 \times 45}{15\% \text{ of } 200}} = 30$

	$
Purchases (no discount) 45 × $200	9,000
Holding costs (W1)	450
Ordering costs (W2)	450
Total annual costs	9,900

Workings

1 **Holding costs**

Holding costs = Average stock × holding cost for one unit of inventory per annum

Average inventory = Order quantity ÷ 2
= 30 ÷ 2 = 15 units

Holding cost for one unit of inventory per annum = 15% × $200
= $30

∴ Holding costs = 15 units × $30
= $450

2 **Ordering costs**

Ordering costs = Number of orders × ordering costs per order ($300)

Number of orders = Annual demand ÷ order quantity
= 45 ÷ 30
= 1.5 orders

∴ ordering costs = 1.5 orders × $300
= $450

(b) With a discount of 3% and an order quantity of 60, units costs are as follows.

	$
Purchases $9,000 × 97%	8,730
Holding costs (W3)	873
Ordering costs (W4)	225
Total annual costs	9,828

Workings

3   Holding costs

Holding costs   = Average inventory × holding cost for one unit of inventory per annum

Average inventory   = Order quantity ÷ 2
= 60 ÷ 2 = 30 units

Holding cost for one unit of inventory per annum = 15% × 97% × $200 = $29.10

Note. 97% = 100% – 3% discount

∴ Holding costs   = 30 units × $29.10
= $873

4   Ordering costs

Ordering costs   = Number of orders × ordering costs per order ($300)

Number of orders   = Annual demand ÷ order quantity
= 45 ÷ 60
= 0.75 orders

∴ Ordering costs   = 0.75 orders × $300
= $225

(c)   With a discount of 5% and an order quantity of 90, units costs are as follows.

	$
Purchases $9,000 × 95%	8,550.0
Holding costs (W5)	1,282.5
Ordering costs (W6)	150.0
Total annual costs	9,982.5

Workings

5   Holding costs

Holding costs   = Average inventory × holding cost for one unit of inventory per annum

Average inventory   = order quantity ÷ 2
= 90 ÷ 2
= 45 units

Holding cost for one unit of inventory per annum   = 15% × 95% × $200
= $28.50

Note. 95% = 100% – 5% discount

∴ Holding costs   = 45 units × $28.50
= $1,282.50

6   Ordering costs

Ordering costs   = Number of orders × ordering costs per order ($300)

Number of orders   = Annual demand ÷ order quantity
= 45 ÷ 90
= 0.5 orders

∴ ordering costs   = 0.5 orders × $300
= $150

The cheapest option is to order 60 units at a time.

Note that the value of C_H varied according to the size of the discount, because C_H was a percentage of the purchase cost. This means that **total holding costs are reduced because of a discount**. This could easily happen if, for example, most of C_H was the cost of insurance, based on the cost of inventory held.

A company uses an item of inventory as follows.

Purchase price: $96 per unit
Annual demand: 4,000 units
Ordering cost: $300
Annual holding cost: 10% of purchase price
Economic order quantity: 500 units

Required

Ascertain whether the company should order 1,000 units at a time in order to secure an 8% discount.

Answer

The total annual cost at the economic order quantity of 500 units is as follows.

	$
Purchases 4,000 × $96	384,000
Ordering costs $300 × (4,000/500)	2,400
Holding costs $96 × 10% × (500/2)	2,400
	388,800

The total annual cost at an order quantity of 1,000 units would be as follows.

	$
Purchases $384,000 × 92%	353,280
Ordering costs $300 × (4,000/1,000)	1,200
Holding costs $96 × 92% × 10% × (1,000/2)	4,416
	358,896

The company should order the item 1,000 units at a time, saving $(388,800 – 358,896) = $29,904 a year.

4.6 Other systems of stores control and reordering

4.6.1 Order cycling method

Under the order cycling method, quantities on hand of each stores item are reviewed periodically (every 1, 2 or 3 months). For low-cost items, a technique called the 90-60-30 day technique can be used, so that when inventories fall to 60 days' supply, a fresh order is placed for a 30 days' supply so as to boost inventories to 90 days' supply. For high-cost items, a more stringent stores control procedure is advisable so as to keep down the costs of inventory holding.

4.6.2 Two-bin system

The two-bin system of stores control (or visual method of control) is one whereby each stores item is kept in two storage bins. When the first bin is emptied, an order must be placed for re-supply; the second bin will contain sufficient quantities to last until the fresh delivery is received. This is a simple system which is not costly to operate but it is not based on any formal analysis of inventory usage and may result in the holding of too much or too little inventory.

4.6.3 Classification of materials

Materials items may be classified as expensive, inexpensive or in a middle-cost range. Because of the practical advantages of simplifying stores control procedures without incurring unnecessary high costs, it may be possible to segregate materials for selective stores control.

(a) Expensive and medium-cost materials are subject to careful stores control procedures to minimise cost.

(b) Inexpensive materials can be stored in large quantities because the cost savings from careful stores control do not justify the administrative effort required to implement the control.

This selective approach to stores control is sometimes called the **ABC method** whereby materials are classified A, B or C according to their expense-group A being the expensive, group B the medium-cost and group C the inexpensive materials.

4.6.4 Pareto (80/20) distribution

A similar selective approach to stores control is the **Pareto (80/20) distribution** which is based on the finding that in many stores, 80% of the value of stores is accounted for by only 20% of the stores items, and inventories of these more expensive items should be controlled more closely.

Chapter roundup

- **Inventory control** includes the functions of inventory ordering and purchasing, receiving goods into store, storing and issuing inventory and controlling the level of inventories.

- Every movement of material in a business should be documented using the following as appropriate: purchase requisition, purchase order, GRN, materials requisition note, materials transfer note and materials returned note.

- The inventory count (stock take) involves counting the physical inventory on hand at a certain date, and then checking this against the balance shown in the inventory records. The inventory count can be carried out on a **continuous** or **periodic** basis.

- **Perpetual inventory** refers to a inventory recording system whereby the records (bin cards and stores ledger accounts) are updated for each receipt and issue of inventory as it occurs.

- **Obsolete inventories** are those items which have become out of date and are no longer required. Obsolete items are written off and disposed of.

- **Inventory costs** include purchase costs, holding costs, ordering costs and costs of running out of inventory.

- **Inventory control levels** can be calculated in order to maintain inventories at the optimum level. The three critical control levels are reorder level, minimum level and maximum level.

- The **economic order quantity** (EOQ) is the order quantity which minimises inventory costs. The EOQ can be calculated using a table, graph or formula.

$$EOQ = \sqrt{\frac{2C_oD}{C_H}}$$

- The **economic batch quantity (EBQ)** is a modification of the EOQ and is used when resupply is gradual instead of instantaneous.

$$EBQ = \sqrt{\frac{2C_oD}{C_H(1-D/R)}}$$

1   List six objectives of storekeeping.

- ....   - ....
- ....   - ....
- ....   - ....

2   Free inventory represents...

3   Free inventory is calculated as follows. (Delete as appropriate)

(a)	+	−	Materials in inventory	X
(b)	+	−	Materials in order	X
(c)	+	−	Materials requisitioned (not yet issued)	X
			Free inventory balance	X

4   How does periodic inventory counting differ from continuous inventory counting?

5   Match up the following.

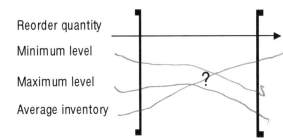

Reorder quantity   Maximum usage × maximum lead time

Minimum level   Safety inventory + ½ reorder level

Maximum level   Reorder level − (average usage × average lead time)

Average inventory   Reorder level + reorder quantity − (minimum usage × minimum lead time)

6    $$EOQ = \sqrt{\frac{2C_oD}{C_H}}$$

Where

(a) C_H = ...

(b) C_o = ...

(c)   D = ...

7   When is the economic batch quantity used?

1
- Speedy **issue** and **receipt** of materials
- Full **identification** of all materials at all times
- Correct **location** of all materials at all times
- **Protection** of materials from damage and deterioration
- Provision of **secure stores** to avoid pilferage, theft and fire
- **Efficient** use of storage space
- **Maintenance** of correct inventory levels
- Keeping correct and up-to-date **records** of receipts, issues and inventory levels

2   Inventory that is readily available for future use.

3   (a)   +
    (b)   +
    (c)   –

4   **Periodic inventory counting.** All inventory items physically counted and valued, usually annually.

   Continuous inventory counting. Counting and valuing selected items at different times of the year (at least once a year).

5

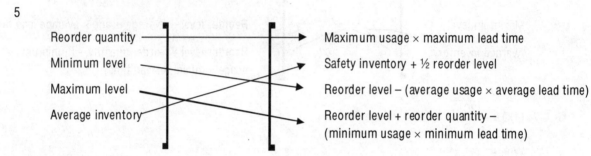

Reorder quantity — Maximum usage × maximum lead time

Minimum level — Safety inventory + ½ reorder level

Maximum level — Reorder level – (average usage × average lead time)

Average inventory — Reorder level + reorder quantity – (minimum usage × minimum lead time)

6   (a)   Cost of holding one unit of inventory for one time period
    (b)   Cost of ordering a consignment from a supplier
    (c)   Demand during the time period

7   When resupply of a product is gradual instead of instantaneous.

Now try the questions below from the Exam Question Bank

Number	Level	Marks	Time
Q6	MCQ	n/a	n/a

7

Labour costs

Topic list	Syllabus reference
1 Measuring labour activity	D2 (a) (f)
2 Remuneration methods	D2 (d)
3 Recording labour costs	D2 (b)
4 Labour turnover	D2 (e)
5 Accounting for labour costs	D2 (c) (g)

Introduction

Just as management need to control inventories and operate an appropriate valuation policy in an attempt to control material costs, so too must they be aware of the most suitable **remuneration policy** for their organisation. We will be looking at a number of methods of remuneration and will consider the various types of **incentive scheme** that exist. We will also examine the procedures and documents required for the accurate **recording of labour costs**. **Labour turnover** will be studied too.

Study guide

		Intellectual level
D2	**Accounting for labour**	
(a)	Calculate direct and indirect labour costs	1
(b)	Explain the methods used to relate input labour costs to work done	1
(c)	Prepare journal and ledger entries to record labour cost inputs and outputs	1
(d)	Describe different remuneration methods, time-based systems, piecework systems and individual and group incentive schemes	1
(e)	Calculate the level, and analyse the costs and causes of, labour turnover	1
(f)	Explain and calculate labour efficiency, capacity and production volume ratios	1
(g)	Interpret the entries in the labour account	1

Exam guide

You may get a question just on labour costs or on working out an employee's pay or you may have to deal with labour as a component of variable cost or overhead.

1 Measuring labour activity

Production and productivity are common methods of measuring labour activity.

1.1 Production and productivity

FAST FORWARD

Production is the quantity or volume of output produced. **Productivity** is a measure of the efficiency with which output has been produced. An increase in production without an increase in productivity will not reduce unit costs

1.2 Example: Production and productivity

Suppose that an employee is expected to produce three units in every hour that he works. The standard rate of productivity is three units per hour, and one unit is valued at $\frac{1}{3}$ of a standard hour of output. If, during one week, the employee makes 126 units in 40 hours of work the following comments can be made.

(a) **Production** in the week is 126 units.

(b) **Productivity** is a relative measure of the hours actually taken and the hours that should have been taken to make the output.

	(i)	**Either**, 126 units should take	42 hours
		But did take	40 hours
		Productivity ratio = 42/40 × 100% =	105%
	(ii)	**Or alternatively**, in 40 hours, he should make (× 3)	120 units
		But did make	126 units
		Productivity ratio = 126/120 × 100% =	105%

A productivity ratio greater than 100% indicates that actual efficiency is better than the expected or 'standard' level of efficiency.

Standard hour of production is a concept used in standard costing, and means the number of units that can be produced by one worker working in the standard way at the standard rate for one hour.

1.3 Planning and controlling production and productivity

Management will wish to **plan** and **control** both production levels and labour productivity.

(a) **Production levels can be raised** as follows.

- Working overtime
- Hiring extra staff
- Sub-contracting some work to an outside firm
- Managing the work force so as to achieve more output.

(b) **Production levels can be reduced** as follows.

- Cancelling overtime
- Laying off staff

(c) **Productivity**, if improved, will enable a company to achieve its production targets in fewer hours of work, and therefore at a lower cost.

1.4 Productivity and its effect on cost

Improved productivity is an important means of reducing total unit costs. In order to make this point clear, a simple example will be used.

1.4.1 Example: Productivity and its effect on cost

Clooney Co has a production department in its factory consisting of a work team of just two men, Doug and George. Doug and George each work a 40 hour week and refuse to do any overtime. They are each paid $100 per week and production overheads of $400 per week are charged to their work.

(a) In week one, they produce 160 units of output between them. Productivity is measured in units of output per man hour.

Production	160 units
Productivity (80 man hours)	2 units per man hour
Total cost	$600 (labour plus overhead)
Cost per man hour	$7.50
Cost per unit	$3.75

(b) In week two, management pressure is exerted on Doug and George to increase output and they produce 200 units in normal time.

Production	200 units (up by 25%)
Productivity	2.5 units per man hour (up by 25%)
Total cost	$600
Cost per man hour	$7.50 (no change)
Cost per unit	$3.00 (a saving of 20% on the previous cost; 25% on the new cost)

(c) In week three, Doug and George agree to work a total of 20 hours of overtime for an additional $50 wages. Output is again 200 units and overhead charges are increased by $100.

Production	200 units (up 25% on week one)
Productivity (100 man hours)	2 units per hour (no change on week one)
Total cost ($600 + $50 + $100)	$750
Cost per unit	$3.75

(d) Conclusions

(i) An increase in production without an increase in productivity will not reduce unit costs (week one compared with week three).

(ii) An **increase in productivity will reduce unit costs** (week one compared with week two).

1.4.2 Automation

Labour cost control is largely concerned with **productivity**. Rising wage rates have increased automation, which in turn has improved productivity and reduced costs.

Where **automation** is introduced, productivity is often, but misleadingly, measured in terms of **output per man-hour**.

1.4.3 Example: Automation

Suppose, for example, that a work-team of six men (240 hours per week) is replaced by one machine (40 hours per week) and a team of four men (160 hours per week), and as a result output is increased from 1,200 units per week to 1,600 units.

	Production	Man hours	Productivity
Before the machine	1,200 units	240	5 units per man hour
After the machine	1,600 units	160	10 units per man hour

Labour productivity has doubled because of the machine, and employees would probably expect extra pay for this success. For control purposes, however, it is likely that a new measure of productivity is required, **output per machine hour**, which may then be measured against a standard output for performance reporting.

1.5 Efficiency, capacity and production volume ratios

Other measures of labour activity include the following.

- Production volume ratio, or activity ratio
- Efficiency ratio (or productivity ratio)
- Capacity ratio

Efficiency ratio	**× Capacity ratio**	**= Production volume ratio**
$\dfrac{\text{Expected hours to make output}}{\text{Actual hours taken}}$	$\times \dfrac{\text{Actual hours worked}}{\text{Hours budgeted}}$	$= \dfrac{\text{Output measured in expected or standard hours}}{\text{Hours budgeted}}$

These ratios are usually expressed as percentages.

1.5.1 Example: Labour activity ratios

Rush and Fluster Co budgets to make 25,000 standard units of output (in four hours each) during a budget period of 100,000 hours.

Actual output during the period was 27,000 units which took 120,000 hours to make.

Required

Calculate the efficiency, capacity and production volume ratios.

Solution

(a) Efficiency ratio $\dfrac{(27,000 \times 4) \text{ hours}}{120,000} \times 100\% = 90\%$

(b) Capacity ratio $\dfrac{120,000 \text{ hours}}{100,000 \text{ hours}} \times 100\% = 120\%$

(c)   Production volume ratio $\dfrac{(27{,}000 \times 4)\ \text{hours}}{100{,}000} \times 100\% = 108\%$

(d)   The production volume ratio of 108% (more output than budgeted) is explained by the 120% capacity working, offset to a certain extent by the poor efficiency (90% × 120% = 108%).

Where efficiency standards are associated with remuneration schemes they generally allow 'normal time' (that is, time required by the average person to do the work under normal conditions) plus an allowance for rest periods and possible delays. There should therefore be a readily achievable standard of efficiency (otherwise any remuneration scheme will fail to motivate employees), but without being so lax that it makes no difference to the rate at which work is done.

2 Remuneration methods

> There are three basic groups of **remuneration** method: **time work**; **piecework schemes**; **bonus/incentive schemes**.

Labour remuneration methods have an effect on the following.

- The cost of finished products and services.
- The morale and efficiency of employees.

2.1 Time work

Formula to learn

> The most common form of **time work** is a **day-rate system** in which wages are calculated by the following formula.
>
> Wages = Hours worked × rate of pay per hour

2.1.1 Overtime premiums

If an employee works for more hours than the basic daily requirement he may be entitled to an **overtime payment**. Hours of overtime are usually paid at a **premium rate**. For instance, if the basic day-rate is $4 per hour and overtime is paid at time-and-a-quarter, eight hours of overtime would be paid the following amount.

	$
Basic pay (8 × $4)	32
Overtime premium (8 × $1)	8
Total (8 × $5)	40

The **overtime premium** is the extra rate per hour which is paid, not the whole of the payment for the overtime hours.

If employees work unsocial hours, for instance overnight, they may be entitled to a **shift premium**. The extra amount paid per hour, above the basic hourly rate, is the **shift premium**.

2.1.2 Summary of day-rate systems

(a)   They are easy to understand.

(b)   They do not lead to very complex negotiations when they are being revised.

(c)   They are most appropriate when the quality of output is more important than the quantity, or where there is no basis for payment by performance.

(d)   There is no incentive for employees who are paid on a day-rate basis to improve their performance.

2.2 Piecework schemes

Formula to learn

In a **piecework scheme**, wages are calculated by the following formula.
Wages = Units produced × Rate of pay per unit

Suppose for example, an employee is paid $1 for each unit produced and works a 40 hour week. Production overhead is added at the rate of $2 per direct labour hour.

Weekly production	Pay (40 hours)	Overhead	Conversion cost	Conversion cost per unit
Units	$	$	$	$
40	40	80	120	3.00
50	50	80	130	2.60
60	60	80	140	2.33
70	70	80	150	2.14

As his output increases, his wage increases and at the same time unit costs of output are reduced.

It is normal for pieceworkers to be offered a **guaranteed minimum wage**, so that they do not suffer loss of earnings when production is low through no fault of their own.

If an employee makes several different types of product, it may not be possible to add up the units for payment purposes. Instead, a **standard time allowance** is given for each unit to arrive at a total of piecework hours for payment.

Question
Weekly pay

Penny Pincher is paid 50c for each towel she weaves, but she is guaranteed a minimum wage of $60 for a 40 hour week. In a series of four weeks, she makes 100, 120, 140 and 160 towels.

Required

Calculate her pay each week, and the conversion cost per towel if production overhead is added at the rate of $2.50 per direct labour hour.

Answer

Week	Output		Pay	Production overhead	Conversion cost	Unit conversion cost
	Units		$	$	$	$
1	100	(minimum)	60	100	160	1.60
2	120		60	100	160	1.33
3	140		70	100	170	1.21
4	160		80	100	180	1.13

There is no incentive to Penny Pincher to produce more output unless she can exceed 120 units in a week. The guaranteed minimum wage in this case is too high to provide an incentive.

2.2.1 Example: Piecework

An employee is paid $5 per piecework hour produced. In a 35 hour week he produces the following output.

	Piecework time allowed per unit
3 units of product A	2.5 hours
5 units of product B	8.0 hours

Required

Calculate the employee's pay for the week.

Solution

Piecework hours produced are as follows.

Product A	3 × 2.5 hours	7.5 hours
Product B	5 × 8 hours	40.0 hours
Total piecework hours		47.5 hours

Therefore employee's pay = 47.5 × $5 = $237.50 for the week.

2.2.2 Differential piecework scheme

Differential piecework schemes offer an incentive to employees to increase their output by paying higher rates for increased levels of production. For example:

up to 80 units per week, rate of pay per unit	=	$1.00
80 to 90 units per week, rate of pay per unit	=	$1.20
above 90 units per week, rate of pay per unit	=	$1.30

Employers should obviously be careful to make it clear whether they intend to pay the increased rate on all units produced, or on the extra output only.

2.2.3 Summary of piecework schemes

- They enjoy fluctuating popularity.
- They are occasionally used by employers as a means of increasing pay levels.
- They are often seen to drive employees to work too hard to earn a satisfactory wage.

Careful inspection of output is necessary to ensure that quality doesn't fall as production increases.

2.3 Bonus/incentive schemes

2.3.1 Introduction

In general, **bonus schemes** were introduced to compensate workers paid under a time-based system for their inability to increase earnings by working more efficiently. Various types of incentive and bonus schemes have been devised which encourage greater productivity. The characteristics of such schemes are as follows.

(a) Employees are paid more for their efficiency.
(b) The profits arising from productivity improvements are shared between employer and employee.
(c) Morale of employees is likely to improve since they are seen to receive extra reward for extra effort.

A bonus scheme must satisfy certain conditions to operate successfully.

(a) Its **objectives** should be **clearly stated** and **attainable** by the employees.
(b) The **rules** and conditions of the scheme should be **easy to understand**.
(c) It must **win** the full **acceptance** of everyone concerned.
(d) It should be seen to be **fair to employees and employers**..
(e) The bonus should ideally be **paid soon after the extra effort has been made** by the employees.
(f) **Allowances** should be made for external factors outside the employees' control which reduce their productivity (machine breakdowns, material shortages).
(g) Only those employees who make the extra effort should be rewarded.
(h) The scheme must be **properly communicated** to employees.

We shall be looking at the following types of incentive schemes in detail.

- High day rate system
- Individual bonus schemes
- Group bonus schemes

- Profit sharing schemes
- Incentive schemes involving shares
- Value added incentive schemes

Some organisations employ a variety of incentive schemes. A scheme for a production labour force may not necessarily be appropriate for white-collar workers. An organisation's incentive schemes may be regularly reviewed, and altered as circumstances dictate.

2.4 High day-rate system

A **high day-rate system** is a system where employees are paid a high hourly wage rate in the expectation that they will work more efficiently than similar employees on a lower hourly rate in a different company.

2.4.1 Example: High day-rate system

For example if an employee would make 100 units in a 40 hour week if he were paid $2 per hour, but 120 units if he were paid $2.50 per hour, and if production overhead is added to cost at the rate of $2 per direct labour hour, costs per unit of output would be as follows.

(a)   Costs per unit of output on the low day-rate scheme would be:

$$\frac{(40 \times \$4)}{100} = \$1.60 \text{ per unit}$$

(b)   Costs per unit of output on the high day-rate scheme would be:

$$\frac{(40 \times \$4.50)}{120} = \$1.50 \text{ per unit}$$

(c)   Note that in this example the labour cost per unit is lower in the first scheme (80c) than in the second (83.3c), but the unit conversion cost (labour plus production overhead) is higher because overhead costs per unit are higher at 80c than with the high day-rate scheme (66.7c).

(d)   In this example, the high day-rate scheme would reward both employer (a lower unit cost by 10c) and employee (an extra 50c earned per hour).

2.4.2 Advantages and disadvantages of high day rate schemes

There are two **advantages** of a high day-rate scheme over other incentive schemes.

(a)   It is **simple** to calculate and **easy** to understand.
(b)   It **guarantees** the employee a consistently **high wage**.

The **disadvantages** of such schemes are as follows.

(a)   **Employees cannot earn more than the fixed hourly rate for their extra effort**. In the previous example, if the employee makes 180 units instead of 120 units in a 40 hour week on a high day-rate pay scheme, the cost per unit would fall to $1 but his wage would be the same – 40 hours at $4.50. All the savings would go to benefit the company and none would go to the employee.

(b)   **There is no guarantee that the scheme will work consistently**. The high wages may become the accepted level of pay for normal working, and supervision may be necessary to ensure that a high level of productivity is maintained. Unit costs would rise.

(c)   **Employees may prefer to work at a normal rate of output**, even if this entails accepting the lower wage paid by comparable employers.

2.5 Individual bonus schemes

An **individual bonus scheme** is a remuneration scheme whereby **individual** employees qualify for a bonus on top of their basic wage, with each person's bonus being calculated separately.

(a) The bonus is **unique** to the individual. It is not a share of a group bonus.

(b) The individual can earn a bonus by working at an **above-target** standard of efficiency.

(c) The individual earns a **bigger bonus the greater his efficiency**, although the bonus scheme might incorporate quality safeguards, to prevent individuals from sacrificing quality standards for the sake of speed and more pay.

To be successful, however, an **individual bonus scheme** must take account of the following factors.

(a) Each individual should be rewarded for the **work done by that individual**. This means that each person's output and time must be measured separately. Each person must therefore work without the assistance of anyone else.

(b) Work should be **fairly routine**, so that standard times can be set for jobs.

(c) The bonus should be **paid soon after the work is done**, to provide the individual with the incentive to try harder.

2.6 Group bonus schemes

A **group bonus scheme** is an incentive plan which is related to the output performance of an entire group of workers, a department, or even the whole factory.

Where individual effort cannot be measured, and employees work as a team, an individual incentive scheme is impracticable but a **group bonus scheme** would be feasible.

The other **advantages** of group bonus schemes are as follows.

(a) They are **easier to administer** because they reduce the clerical effort required to measure output and calculate individual bonuses.

(b) They **increase co-operation** between fellow workers.

(c) They have been found to **reduce** accidents, spoilage, waste and absenteeism.

Serious **disadvantages** would occur in the following circumstances.

(a) The employee groups demand **low efficiency standards** as a condition of accepting the scheme.

(b) Individual employees are browbeaten by their fellow workers for working too slowly.

2.7 Profit-sharing schemes

A **profit sharing scheme** is a scheme in which employees receive a certain proportion of their company's year-end profits (the size of their bonus being related to their position in the company and the length of their employment to date).

The advantage of these schemes is that the company will only pay what it can afford out of actual profits and the bonus can be paid also to non-production personnel.

The disadvantages of profit sharing are as follows.

(a) Employees must **wait until the year end** for a bonus. The company is therefore expecting a long-term commitment to greater efforts and productivity from its workers without the incentive of immediate reward.

(b) **Factors** affecting profit may be **outside the control** of employees, in spite of their greater efforts.

(c) **Too many employees** are involved in a single scheme for the scheme to have a great motivating effect on individuals.

2.7.1 Incentive schemes involving shares

It is becoming increasingly common for companies to use their shares, or the right to acquire them, as a form of incentive.

Key terms

A **share option scheme** is a scheme which gives its members the right to buy shares in the company for which they work at a set date in the future and at a price usually determined when the scheme is set up.

An **employee share ownership plan** is a scheme which acquires shares on behalf of a number of employees, and it must distribute these shares within a certain number of years of acquisition.

Some governments have encouraged companies to set up schemes of this nature in the hope that workers will feel they have a stake in the company which employs them. The **disadvantages** of these schemes are as follows.

(a) The benefits are not certain, as the market value of shares at a future date cannot realistically be predicted in advance.

(b) The benefits are not immediate, as a scheme must be in existence for a number of years before members can exercise their rights.

2.7.2 Value added incentive schemes

Value added is an alternative to profit as a business performance measure and it can be used as the basis of an incentive scheme. It is calculated as follows.

Key term

Value added = sales − cost of bought-in materials and services

The advantage of value added over profit as the basis for an incentive scheme is that it excludes any bought-in costs, and is affected only by costs incurred internally, such as labour.

A basic value added figure would be agreed as the target for a business, and some of any excess value added earned would be paid out as a bonus. For example, it could be agreed that value added should be, say, treble the payroll costs and a proportion of any excess earned, say one third, would be paid as bonus.

Payroll costs for month	$40,000
Therefore, value added target ($\times$ 3)	$120,000
Value added achieved	$150,000
Therefore, excess value added	$30,000
Employee share to be paid as bonus	$10,000

2.7.3 Example: incentive schemes

Swetton Tyres Co manufactures a single product. Its work force consists of 10 employees, who work a 36-hour week exclusive of lunch and tea breaks. The standard time required to make one unit of the product is two hours, but the current efficiency (or productivity) ratio being achieved is 80%. No overtime is worked, and the work force is paid $4 per attendance hour.

Because of agreements with the work force about work procedures, there is some unavoidable idle time due to bottlenecks in production, and about four hours per week per person are lost in this way.

The company can sell all the output it manufactures, and makes a 'cash profit' of $20 per unit sold, deducting currently achievable costs of production but *before* deducting labour costs.

An incentive scheme is proposed whereby the work force would be paid $5 per hour in exchange for agreeing to new work procedures that would reduce idle time per employee per week to two hours and also raise the efficiency ratio to 90%.

Required

Evaluate the incentive scheme from the point of view of profitability.

Solution

The current situation

Hours in attendance	10 × 36	=	360 hours
Hours spent working	10 × 32	=	320 hours
Units produced, at 80% efficiency	$\dfrac{320}{2} \times \dfrac{80}{100}$	=	128 units

	$
Cash profits before deducting labour costs (128 × $20)	2,560
Less labour costs ($4 × 360 hours)	1,440
Net profit	1,120

The incentive scheme

Hours spent working	10 × 34	=	340 hours
Units produced, at 90% efficiency	$\dfrac{340}{2} \times \dfrac{90}{100}$	=	153 units

	$
Cash profits before deducting labour costs (153 × $20)	3,060
Less labour costs ($5 × 360)	1,800
Net profit	1,260

In spite of a 25% increase in labour costs, profits would rise by $140 per week. The company and the workforce would both benefit provided, of course, that management can hold the work force to their promise of work reorganisation and improved productivity.

Question

Labour cost

The following data relate to work at a certain factory.

Normal working day	8 hours
Basic rate of pay per hour	$6
Standard time allowed to produce 1 unit	2 minutes
Premium bonus	75% of time saved at basic rate

What will be the labour cost in a day when 340 units are made?

A $48   B $51   C $63   D $68

Answer

Standard time for 340 units (× 2 minutes)	680 minutes
Actual time (8 hours per day)	480 minutes
Time saved	200 minutes

	$
Bonus = 75% × 200 minutes × $6 per hour	15
Basic pay = 8 hours × $6	48
Total labour cost	63

Therefore the correct answer is C.

Using basic MCQ technique you can eliminate option A because this is simply the basic pay without consideration of any bonus. You can also eliminate option D, which is based on the standard time allowance without considering the basic pay for the eight-hour day. Hopefully your were not forced to guess, but had you been you would have had a 50% chance of selecting the correct answer (B or C) instead of a 25% chance because you were able to eliminate two of the options straightaway.

3 Recording labour costs

Labour attendance time is recorded on, for example, an attendance record or clock card. Job time may be recorded on daily time sheets, weekly time sheets or job cards depending on the circumstances. The manual recording of times on time sheets or job cards is, however, liable to error or even deliberate deception and may be unreliable. The labour cost of pieceworkers is recorded on a piecework ticket/operation card.

3.1 Organisation for controlling and measuring labour costs

Several departments and management groups are involved in the collection, recording and costing of labour. These include the following.

- Personnel
- Production planning
- Timekeeping
- Wages
- Cost accounting

3.2 Personnel department

The **personnel department** is responsible for the following:

- Engagement, transfer and discharge of employees.
- Classification and method of remuneration.

The department is headed by a **professional personnel officer** trained in personnel management, labour laws, company personnel policy and industry conditions who should have an understanding of the needs and problems of the employees.

When a person is engaged a **personnel record card** should be prepared showing full personal particulars, previous employment, medical category and wage rate. Other details to be included are social security number, address, telephone number, transfers, promotions, changes in wage rates, sickness and accidents and, when an employee leaves, the reason for leaving.

Personnel departments sometimes **maintain records of overtime and shift working**. Overtime has to be sanctioned by the works manager or personnel office who advise the time-keepers who control the time booked.

The personnel department is responsible for issuing **reports to management** on normal and overtime hours worked, absenteeism and sickness, lateness, labour turnover and disciplinary action.

3.3 Production planning department

This department is responsible for the following.

- Scheduling work
- Issuing job orders to production departments
- Chasing up jobs when they run late

3.4 Timekeeping department

The **timekeeping department** is responsible for recording the attendance time and job time of the following.

- The time spent in the factory by each worker
- The time spent by each worker on each job

Such timekeeping provides basic data for statutory records, payroll preparation, labour costs of an operation or overhead distribution (where based on wages or labour hours) and statistical analysis of labour records for determining productivity and control of labour costs.

3.5 Attendance time

The bare minimum record of employees' time is a simple **attendance record** showing days absent because of holiday, sickness or other reason. A typical record of attendance is shown as follows.

NAME: A.N. OTHER			DEPT:	072				NI REF: WD 4847 41C									LEAVE ENTITLEMENT: 20										
	1	2	3	4	5	6	7	8	9	10	11	12	**13**	14	15	16	17	18	19	20	21	**22**	23	24	25	26	27	28	29	30	31
JAN																															
FEB																															
MAR																															
APR																															
MAY																															
JUNE																															
JULY																															
AUG																															
SEPT																															
OCT																															
NOV																															
DEC																															

Illness: I	Leave: L	Training: T	Note overleaf: (1) The reasons for special leave (eg bereavement).
Industrial Accident: IA	Unpaid Leave: UL	Jury Service: J	
Maternity: M	Special Leave: SL		(2) Ensure training is noted on personnel card.

RECORD OF ATTENDANCE

It is also necessary to have a record of the following.

- Time of arrival
- Time of breaks
- Time of departure

These may be recorded as follows.

- In a signing-in book
- By using a time recording clock which stamps the time on a clock card
- By using swipe cards (which make a computer record)

An example of a clock card is shown as follows.

No Name			Ending	
HOURS	RATE	AMOUNT	DEDUCTIONS	
Basic O/T Others			Tax Insurance Other	
			Total deduction	
Total Less deductions Net due				

Time	Day	Basic time	Overtime
1230 T			
0803 T			
1700 M			
1305 M			
1234 M			
0750 M			

Signature _ _ _ _ _ _ _ _ _ _

3.6 Job time

Continuous production. Where **routine, repetitive** work is carried out it might not be practical to record the precise details. For example if a worker stands at a conveyor belt for seven hours his work can be measured by keeping a note of the number of units that pass through his part of the process during that time.

Job costing. When the work is not of a repetitive nature the records required might be one or several of the following.

(a) **Daily time sheets**. A time sheet is filled in by the employee as a record of how their time has been spent. The total time on the time sheet should correspond with time shown on the attendance record.

(b) **Weekly time sheets**. These are similar to daily time sheets but are passed to the cost office at the end of the week. An example of a weekly timesheet is shown below.

Time Sheet No. _ _ _ _ _ _ _ _ _ _ _ _ _ _ _ _							
Employee Name _ _ _ _ _ _ _ _ _ Clock Code _ _ _ _ _ _ _ _ _ Dept _ _ _ _ _ _ _							
Date _ _ _ _ _ _ _ _ _ _ _ _ _ _ _ _ _ _ _ Week No. _ _ _ _ _ _ _ _ _ _ _ _ _ _							
Job No.	Start Time	Finish Time	Qty	Checker	Hrs	Rate	Extension

(c) **Job cards**. Cards are prepared for each job or batch. When an employee works on a job he or she records on the job card the time spent on that job. Job cards are therefore likely to contain entries relating to numerous employees. On completion of the job it will contain a full record of the times and quantities involved in the job or batch. A typical job card is shown as follows.

JOB CARD			
Department _ _ _ _ _ _ _ _ _ _ _ _ _ _ _ _ _	Job no _.		
Date _.	Operation no _ _ _ _ _ _ _ _ _ _ _ _ _ _ _ _ _ _		
Time allowance _ _ _ _ _ _ _ _ _ _ _ _ _ _ _ _ _	Time started _ _ _ _ _ _ _ _ _ _ _ _ _ _ _ _ _ _ _		
	Time finished _ _ _ _ _ _ _ _ _ _ _ _ _ _ _ _ _ _		
	Hours on the job _ _ _ _ _ _ _ _ _ _ _ _ _ _ _ _ _.		
Description of job	Hours	Rate	Cost
Employee no_ _ _ _ _ _ _ _ _ _ _ _ _ _ _ _ _ _ _ _	Certified by _		
Signature _ _ _ _ _ _ _ _ _ _ _ _ _ _ _ _ _ _ _			

A job card will be given to the employee, showing the work to be done and the expected time it should take. The employee will record the time started and time finished for each job. Breaks for tea and lunch may be noted on the card, as standard times, by the production planning department. The hours actually taken and the cost of those hours will be calculated by the accounting department.

Piecework. The wages of pieceworkers and the labour cost of work done by them is determined from what is known as a **piecework ticket** or an **operation card**. The card records the total number of items (or 'pieces') produced and the number of rejects. Payment is only made for 'good' production.

OPERATION CARD				
Operator's Name _		Total Batch Quantity _ _ _ _ _ _ _ _ _ _ _ _ _		
Clock No _		Start Time _ _ _ _ _ _ _ _ _ _ _ _ _ _ _ _ _ _		
Pay week No _ _ _ _ _ _ _ _ _ Date _ _ _ _ _ _ _ _		Stop Time _ _ _ _ _ _ _ _ _ _ _ _ _ _ _ _ _ _		
Part No _		Works Order No _ _ _ _ _ _ _ _ _ _ _ _ _ _ _		
Operation _		Special Instructions _ _ _ _ _ _ _ _ _ _ _ _		
Quantity Produced	No Rejected	Good Production	Rate	$
Inspector _		Operative _		
Foreman _		Date _		
PRODUCTION CANNOT BE CLAIMED WITHOUT A PROPERLY SIGNED CARD				

Note that the attendance record of a pieceworker is required for calculations of holidays, sick pay and so on.

Other types of work. Casual workers are paid from job cards or time sheets. Time sheets are also used where outworkers are concerned.

Office work can be measured in a similar way, provided that the work can be divided into distinct jobs. Firms of accountants and advertising agencies, for example, book their staff time to individual clients and so make use of time sheets for salaried staff.

3.7 Salaried labour

Even though salaried staff are paid a flat rate monthly, they may be required to prepare timesheets. The reasons are as follows.

(a)   Timesheets provide management with information (eg product costs).
(b)   Timesheet information may provide a basis for billing for services provided (eg service firms where clients are billed based on the number of hours work done).
(c)   Timesheets are used to record hours spent and so support claims for overtime payments by salaried staff.

An example of a timesheet (as used in the service sector) is shown as follows.

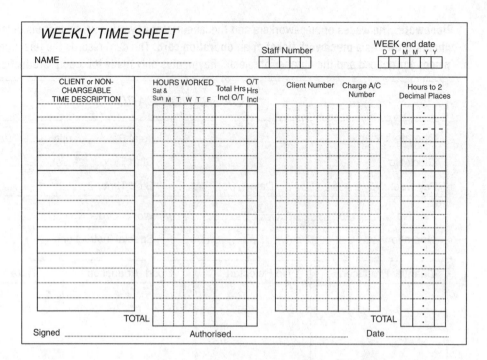

3.8 Idle time

Idle time has a cost because employees will still be paid their basic wage or salary for these unproductive hours and so there should be a record of idle time.

Idle time occurs when employees cannot get on with their work, through no fault of their own. Examples are as follows.

- Machine breakdowns
- Shortage of work

A record of idle time may simply comprise an entry on time sheets coded to 'idle time' generally, or separate idle time cards may be prepared. A supervisor might enter the time of a stoppage, its cause, its duration and the employees made idle on an idle time record card. Each stoppage should have a reference number which can be entered on time sheets or job cards.

3.9 Wages department

Responsibilities of the payroll department include the following.

- Preparation of the payroll and payment of wages.
- Maintenance of employee records.
- Summarising wages cost for each cost centre.
- Summarising the hours worked for each cost centre.
- Summarising other payroll information eg bonus payment, pensions etc.
- Providing an internal check for the preparation and payout of wages.

Attendance cards are the basis for payroll preparation. For **time workers**, the gross wage is the product of time attended and rate of pay. To this is added any overtime premium or bonus. For **piece workers**, gross wages are normally obtained by the product of the number of good units produced and the unit rate, with any premiums, bonuses and allowances for incomplete jobs added.

After calculation of net pay, a pay slip is prepared showing all details of earnings and deductions. The wage envelope or the attendance card may be used for this purpose.

When the payroll is complete, a coin and note analysis is made and a cheque drawn to cover the total amount. On receipt of the cash, the pay envelopes are made up and sealed. A receipt is usually obtained on payout (the attendance card can be used). Wages of absentees are retained until claimed by an authorised person.

Internal checks are necessary to prevent fraud. One method is to distribute the payroll work so that no person deals completely with any transaction. All calculations should be checked on an adding machine where possible. Makeup of envelopes should not be done by persons who prepare the payroll. The cashier should reconcile his analysis with the payroll summary.

3.10 Cost accounting department

The cost accounting department has the following responsibilities.

- The accumulation and classification of all cost data (which includes labour costs).
- Preparation of cost data reports for management.
- Analysing labour information on time cards and payroll.

In order to establish the labour cost involved in products, operations, jobs and cost centres, the following documents are used.

- Clock cards
- Job cards
- Idle time cards
- Payroll

Analyses of labour costs are used for the following.

(a) Charging wages directly attributable to production to the appropriate job or operation.

(b) Charging wages which are not directly attributable to production as follows.

  (i) Idle time of production workers is charged to indirect costs as part of the overheads.

  (ii) Wages costs of supervisors, or store assistants are charged to the overhead costs of the relevant department.

(c) Producing idle time reports which show a summary of the hours lost through idle time, and the cause of the idle time. Idle time may be analysed as follows.

  - Controllable eg lack of materials.
  - Uncontrollable eg power failure.

3.11 Idle time ratio

Formula to learn

$$\text{Idle time ratio} = \frac{\text{Idle hours}}{\text{Total hours}} \times 100\%$$

The idle time ratio is useful because it shows the proportion of available hours which were lost as a result of idle time.

Exam focus point

Make sure you understand the distinction between direct and indirect labour costs and the classification of overtime premium.

4 Labour turnover

FAST FORWARD

Labour turnover is the rate at which employees leave a company and this rate should be kept as low as possible. The cost of labour turnover can be divided into **preventative** and **replacement costs**.

4.1 The reasons for labour turnover

Some employees will leave their job and go to work for another company or organisation. Sometimes the reasons are unavoidable.

- Illness or accidents
- A family move away from the locality
- Marriage, pregnancy or difficulties with child care provision
- Retirement or death

Other causes of labour turnover are to some extent controllable.

- Paying a lower wage rate than is available elsewhere.
- Requiring employees to work in unsafe or highly stressful conditions.
- Requiring employees to work uncongenial hours.
- Poor relationships between management and staff.
- Lack of opportunity for career enhancement.
- Requiring employees to work in inaccessible places (eg no public transport).
- Discharging employees for misconduct, bad timekeeping or unsuitability.

4.2 Measuring labour turnover

Key term

Labour turnover is a measure of the number of employees leaving/being recruited in a period of time expressed as a percentage of the total labour force.

Formula to learn

$$\text{Labour turnover rate} = \frac{\text{Replacements}}{\text{Average number of employees in period}} \times 100\%$$

4.3 Example : Labour turnover rate

Revolving Doors Inc had a staff of 2,000 at the beginning of 20X1 and, owing to a series of redundancies caused by the recession, 1,000 at the end of the year. Voluntary redundancy was taken by 1,500 staff at the end of June, 500 more than the company had anticipated, and these excess redundancies were immediately replaced by new joiners.

The labour turnover rate is calculated as follows.

$$\text{Rate} = \frac{500}{(2,000 + 1,000) \div 2} \times 100\% = 33\%$$

4.4 The costs of labour turnover

The costs of labour turnover can be large and management should attempt to keep labour turnover as low as possible so as to minimise these costs. The **cost of labour turnover** may be divided into the following.

- Preventative costs
- Replacement costs

4.4.1 Replacement costs

These are the costs incurred as a result of hiring new employees. and they include the following.

- Cost of selection and placement
- Inefficiency of new labour; productivity will be lower
- Costs of training
- Loss of output due to delay in new labour becoming available
- Increased wastage and spoilage due to lack of expertise among new staff
- The possibility of more frequent accidents at work
- Cost of tool and machine breakages

4.4.2 Preventative costs

These are costs incurred in order to prevent employees leaving and they include the following.

- Cost of personnel administration incurred in maintaining good relationships
- Cost of medical services including check-ups, nursing staff and so on
- Cost of welfare services, including sports facilities and canteen meals
- Pension schemes providing security to employees

4.5 The prevention of high labour turnover

Labour turnover will be reduced by the following actions.

- Paying satisfactory wages
- Offering satisfactory hours and conditions of work
- Creating a good informal relationship between members of the workforce
- Offering good training schemes and a well-understood career or promotion ladder
- Improving the content of jobs to create job satisfaction
- Proper planning so as to avoid redundancies
- Investigating the cause of an apparently high labour turnover

5 Accounting for labour costs

We will use an example to briefly review the principal bookkeeping entries for wages.

5.1 Example: The wages control account

The following details were extracted from a weekly payroll for 750 employees at a factory.

Analysis of gross pay

	Direct workers $	Indirect workers $	Total $
Ordinary time	36,000	22,000	58,000
Overtime: basic wage	8,700	5,430	14,130
premium	4,350	2,715	7,065
Shift allowance	3,465	1,830	5,295
Sick pay	950	500	1,450
Idle time	3,200	–	3,200
	56,665	32,475	89,140
Net wages paid to employees	$45,605	$24,220	$69,825

Required

Prepare the wages control account for the week.

Solution

(a) **The wages control account** acts as a sort of 'collecting place' for net wages paid and deductions made from gross pay. The gross pay is then analysed between direct and indirect wages.

(b) The first step is to determine which wage costs are **direct** and which are **indirect**. The direct wages will be debited to the work in progress account and the indirect wages will be debited to the production overhead account.

(c) There are in fact only two items of direct wages cost in this example, the ordinary time ($36,000) and the basic overtime wage ($8,700) paid to direct workers. All other payments (including the overtime premium) are indirect wages.

(d) The net wages paid are debited to the control account, and the balance then represents the deductions which have been made for tax, social insurance, and so on.

WAGES CONTROL ACCOUNT

	$		$
Bank: net wages paid	69,825	Work in progress – direct labour	44,700
Deductions control accounts*		Production overhead control:	
($89,140 – $69,825)	19,315	Indirect labour	27,430
		Overtime premium	7,065
		Shift allowance	5,295
		Sick pay	1,450
		Idle time	3,200
	89,140		89,140

* In practice there would be a separate deductions control account for each type of deduction made (for example, tax and social insurance).

5.2 Direct and indirect labour costs

We had a brief look at direct and indirect labour costs in Chapter 3. Have a go at the following questions to remind yourself about the classification of labour costs.

Question   **Direct and indirect costs**

A direct labour employee's wage in week 5 consists of the following.

		$
(a)	Basic pay for normal hours worked, 36 hours at $4 per hour =	144
(b)	Pay at the basic rate for overtime, 6 hours at $4 per hour =	24
(c)	Overtime shift premium, with overtime paid at time-and-a-quarter ¼ × 6 hours × $4 per hour =	6
(d)	A bonus payment under a group bonus (or 'incentive') scheme – bonus for the month =	30
	Total gross wages in week 5 for 42 hours of work	204

Required

Establish which costs are direct costs and which are indirect costs.

Answer

Items (a) and (b) are direct labour costs of the items produced in the 42 hours worked in week 5.

Overtime premium, item (c), is usually regarded as an overhead expense, because it is 'unfair' to charge the items produced in overtime hours with the premium. Why should an item made in overtime be more costly just because, by chance, it was made after the employee normally clocks off for the day?

Group bonus scheme payments, item (d), are usually overhead costs, because they cannot normally be traced directly to individual products or jobs.

In this example, the direct labour employee costs were $168 in direct costs and $36 in indirect costs.

Question   **Overtime**

Jaffa Inc employs two types of labour: skilled workers, considered to be direct workers, and semi-skilled workers considered to be indirect workers. Skilled workers are paid $10 per hour and semi-skilled $5 per hour.

The skilled workers have worked 20 hours overtime this week, 12 hours on specific orders and 8 hours on general overtime. Overtime is paid at a rate of time and a quarter.

The semi-skilled workers have worked 30 hours overtime, 20 hours for a specific order at a customer's request and the rest for general purposes. Overtime again is paid at time and a quarter.

What would be the total overtime pay considered to be a direct cost for this week?

A	$275		C	$375
B	$355		D	$437.50

Answer

		Direct cost $	Indirect cost $
Skilled workers			
Specific overtime	(12 hours × $10 × 1.25)	150	
General overtime	(8 hours × $10 × 1)	80	
	(8 hours × $10 × 0.25)		20
Semi-skilled workers			
Specific overtime	(20 hours × $5 × 1.25)	125	
General overtime	(10 hours × $5 × 1.25)		62.50
		355	82.50

The correct answer is therefore B.

If you selected option A, you forgot to include the direct cost of the general overtime of $80 for the skilled workers.

If you selected option C, you included the overtime premium for skilled workers' general overtime of $20.

If you selected option D, you calculated the total of direct cost + indirect cost instead of the direct cost.

Exam focus point	The study guide for this paper states that candidates should be able to explain the difference between and calculate direct and indirect labour costs.

Chapter roundup

- **Production** is the quantity or volume of output produced. **Productivity** is a measure of the efficiency with which output has been produced. An increase in production without an increase in productivity will not reduce unit costs.

- There are three basic groups of **remuneration** method: **time work**; **piecework schemes**; and **bonus/incentive** schemes.

- Labour attendance time is recorded on, for example, an attendance record or clock card. Job time may be recorded on daily time sheets, weekly time sheets or job cards depending on the circumstances. The manual recording of times on time sheets or job cards, is however, liable to error or even deliberate deception and may be unreliable. The labour cost of pieceworkers is recorded on a piecework ticket/operation card.

- **Idle time** has a cost because employees will still be paid their basic wage or salary for these unproductive hours and so there should be a record of idle time.

- **Labour turnover** is the rate at which employees leave a company and this rate should be kept as low as possible. The cost of labour turnover can be divided into **preventative** and **replacement** costs.

Quick quiz

1 Distinguish between the terms production and productivity.
2 List five types of incentive scheme.
3 What are the requirements for a successful individual bonus scheme?
4 What is a value added incentive scheme?
5 When does idle time occur?
6 What are the responsibilities of a typical wages department?
7 Define the idle time ratio.
8 List six methods of reducing labour turnover.

Answers to quick quiz

1 • **Production** is the quantity or volume of output produced
  • **Productivity** is a measure of the efficiency with which output has been produced

2 Any five from:
  • High day rate system
  • Individual bonus schemes
  • Group bonus schemes
  • Profit sharing schemes
  • Incentive schemes involving shares
  • Value added incentive schemes

3 • Each individual should be rewarded for the work done by that individual
  • Work should be fairly routine, so that standard times can be set for jobs
  • The bonus should be paid soon after the work is done

4 **Value added** is an alternative to profit as a business performance measure and it can be used as the basis of an incentive scheme

  Value added = Sales – cost of bought-in materials and services

5 **Idle time** occurs when employees cannot get on with their work, through no fault of their own, for example when machines break down or there is a shortage of work.

6 • Preparation of the payroll and payment of wages
  • Maintenance of employee records
  • Summarising wages cost for each cost centre
  • Summarising the hours worked for each cost centre
  • Summarising other payroll information, eg bonus payment, pensions etc
  • Providing an internal check for the preparation and payout of wages

7 Idle time ratio = $\dfrac{\text{Idle hours}}{\text{Total hours}} \times 100\%$

8 Any six from:
  • Paying satisfactory wages
  • Offering satisfactory hours and conditions of work
  • Creating a good informal relationship between members of the workforce
  • Offering good training schemes and a well-understood career or promotion ladder
  • Improving the content of jobs to create job satisfaction
  • Proper planning so as to avoid redundancies
  • Investigating the cause of an apparently high labour turnover

Now try the questions below from the Exam Question Bank

Number	Level	Marks	Time
Q7	MCQ	n/a	n/a

Overheads and absorption costing

Topic list	Syllabus reference
1 Overheads	D3 (a)
2 Absorption costing: an introduction	D3 (b)
3 Overhead allocation	D3 (c)
4 Overhead apportionment	D3 (d)
5 Overhead absorption	D3 (e)
6 Blanket absorption rates and departmental absorption rates	D3 (e)
7 Over and under absorption of overheads	D3 (g)
8 Ledger entries relating to overheads	D3 (f)
9 Non-manufacturing overheads	D3 (h)

Introduction

Absorption costing is a method of accounting for overheads. It is basically a method of sharing out overheads incurred amongst units produced.

This chapter begins by explaining why absorption costing might be necessary and then provides an overview of how the cost of a unit of product is built up under a system of absorption costing. A detailed analysis of this costing method is then provided, covering the three stages of absorption costing: **allocation**, **apportionment** and **absorption**.

Study guide

		Intellectual level
D3	**Accounting for overheads 1**	
(a)	Explain the different treatment of direct and indirect expenses	1
(b)	Describe the procedures involved in determining production overhead absorption rates	1
(c)	Allocate and apportion production overheads to cost centres using an appropriate basis	1
(d)	Reapportion service centre costs including the use of the reciprocal method	2
(e)	Select, apply and discuss appropriate bases for absorption rates	2
(f)	Prepare journal and ledger entries for manufacturing overheads incurred and absorbed	1
(g)	Calculate and explain under– and over-absorbed overheads	1
(h)	Apply methods of relating non-production overheads to cost units	1

Exam guide

Overhead apportionment and absorption is one of the most important topics in your Management Accounting studies and is almost certain to appear in the exam. Make sure that you study the contents of this chapter and work through the calculations very carefully.

1 Overheads

FAST FORWARD

Overhead is the cost incurred in the course of making a product, providing a service or running a department, but which cannot be traced directly and in full to the product, service or department.

Overhead is actually the total of the following.

- Indirect materials
- Indirect labour
- Indirect expenses

The total of these indirect costs is usually split into the following categories.

- **Production**
- **Administration**
- **Selling and distribution**

In cost accounting there are two schools of thought as to the correct method of dealing with overheads.

- Absorption costing
- Marginal costing

2 Absorption costing: an introduction

FAST FORWARD

The objective of absorption costing is to include in the total cost of a product an appropriate share of the organisation's total overhead. An appropriate share is generally taken to mean an amount which reflects the amount of time and effort that has gone into producing a unit or completing a job.

An organisation with one production department that produces identical units will divide the total overheads among the total units produced. **Absorption costing is a method for sharing overheads between different products on a fair basis.**

2.1 Is absorption costing necessary?

Suppose that a company makes and sells 100 units of a product each week. The prime cost per unit is $6 and the unit sales price is $10. Production overhead costs $200 per week and administration, selling and distribution overhead costs $150 per week. The weekly profit could be calculated as follows.

	$	$
Sales (100 units × $10)		1,000
Prime costs (100 × $6)	600	
Production overheads	200	
Administration, selling and distribution costs	150	
		950
Profit		50

In absorption costing, overhead costs will be added to each unit of product manufactured and sold.

	$ per unit
Prime cost per unit	6
Production overhead ($200 per week for 100 units)	2
Full factory cost	8

The weekly profit would be calculated as follows.

	$
Sales	1,000
Less factory cost of sales	800
Gross profit	200
Less administration, selling and distribution costs	150
Net profit	50

Sometimes, but not always, the overhead costs of administration, selling and distribution are also added to unit costs, to obtain a full cost of sales.

	$ per unit
Prime cost per unit	6.00
Factory overhead cost per unit	2.00
Administration etc costs per unit	1.50 ✓
Full cost of sales	9.50 ✓

The weekly profit would be calculated as follows.

	$
Sales	1,000 ✓
Less full cost of sales	950
Profit	50

It may already be apparent that the weekly profit is $50 no matter how the figures have been presented. So, how does absorption costing serve any useful purpose in accounting?

The **theoretical justification** for using absorption costing is that all production overheads are incurred in the production of the organisation's output and so each unit of the product receives some benefit from these costs. Each unit of output should therefore be charged with some of the overhead costs.

2.2 Practical reasons for using absorption costing

FAST FORWARD

The main reasons for using absorption costing are for **inventory valuations**, **pricing decisions**, and **establishing the profitability of different products**.

(a) **Inventory valuations**. Inventory in hand must be valued for two reasons.

    (i)   For the closing inventory figure in the statement of financial position

    (ii)   For the cost of sales figure in the statement of comprehensive income

        The valuation of inventory will affect profitability during a period because of the way in which the cost of sales is calculated.

The cost of goods produced
+   the value of opening inventories
−   the value of closing inventories
=   the cost of goods sold.

In our example, closing inventories might be valued at prime cost ($6), but in absorption costing, they would be valued at a fully absorbed factory cost, $8 per unit. (They would not be valued at $9.50, the full cost of sales, because the only costs incurred in producing goods for finished inventory are factory costs.)

(b)   **Pricing decisions**. Many companies attempt to fix selling prices by calculating the full cost of production or sales of each product, and then adding a margin for profit. In our example, the company might have fixed a gross profit margin at 25% on factory cost, or 20% of the sales price, in order to establish the unit sales price of $10. 'Full cost plus pricing' can be particularly useful for companies which do jobbing or contract work, where each job or contract is different, so that a standard unit sales price cannot be fixed. Without using absorption costing, a full cost is difficult to ascertain.

(c)   **Establishing the profitability of different products**. This argument in favour of absorption costing is more contentious, but is worthy of mention here. If a company sells more than one product, it will be difficult to judge how profitable each individual product is, unless overhead costs are shared on a fair basis and charged to the cost of sales of each product.

2.3 International Accounting Standard 2 (IAS 2)

Absorption costing is recommended in financial accounting by IAS 2 *Inventories*. IAS 2 deals with **financial accounting systems**. The cost accountant is (in theory) free to value inventories by whatever method seems best, but where companies integrate their financial accounting and cost accounting systems into a single system of accounting records, the valuation of closing inventories will be determined by IAS 2.

IAS 2 states that costs of all inventories should comprise those costs which have been incurred in the normal course of business in **bringing the inventories to their 'present location and condition'**. These costs incurred will include all related production overheads, even though these overheads may accrue on a time basis. In other words, in financial accounting, closing inventories should be valued at full factory cost, and it may therefore be convenient and appropriate to value inventories by the same method in the cost accounting system.

2.4 Absorption costing stages

FAST FORWARD

The three stages of absorption costing are:

- Allocation
- Apportionment
- Absorption

We shall now begin our study of absorption costing by looking at the process of **overhead allocation**.

3 Overhead allocation

3.1 Introduction

FAST FORWARD

Allocation is the process by which whole cost items are charged direct to a cost unit or cost centre.

Cost centres may be one of the following types.

(a)   A **production department**, to which production overheads are charged

(b)   A **production area service department**, to which production overheads are charged

(c)   An **administrative department**, to which administration overheads are charged (d)　A **selling** or a **distribution department**, to which sales and distribution overheads are charged

(e)　An **overhead cost centre**, to which items of expense which are shared by a number of departments, such as rent and rates, heat and light and the canteen, are charged

The following costs would therefore be charged to the following cost centres via the process of allocation.

- Direct labour will be charged to a production cost centre.
- The cost of a warehouse security guard will be charged to the warehouse cost centre.
- Paper (recording computer output) will be charged to the computer department.
- Costs such as the canteen are charged direct to various overhead cost centres.

3.2 Example: Overhead allocation

Consider the following costs of a company.

Wages of the foreman of department A	$200
Wages of the foreman of department B	$150
Indirect materials consumed in department A	$50
Rent of the premises shared by departments A and B	$300

The cost accounting system might include three overhead cost centres.

Cost centre:　101　Department A
　　　　　　　102　Department B
　　　　　　　201　Rent

Overhead costs would be allocated directly to each cost centre, ie $200 + $50 to cost centre 101, $150 to cost centre 102 and $300 to cost centre 201. The rent of the factory will be subsequently shared between the two production departments, but for the purpose of day to day cost recording, the rent will first of all be charged in full to a separate cost centre.

4 Overhead apportionment

> **Apportionment** is a procedure whereby indirect costs are spread fairly between cost centres. Service cost centre costs may be apportioned to production cost centres by using the reciprocal method.

The following question will be used to illustrate the overhead apportionment process.

4.1 Example: Overhead apportionment - Swotathon

Swotathon Inc has two production departments (A and B) and two service departments (maintenance and stores). Details of next year's budgeted overheads are shown below.

	Total ($)
Heat and light	19,200
Repair costs	9,600
Machinery Depreciation	54,000
Rent and rates	38,400
Canteen	9,000
Machinery insurance	25,000

Details of each department are as follows.

	A	B	Maintenance	Stores	Total
Floor area (m²)	6,000	4,000	3,000	2,000	15,000
Machinery book value ($000)	48	20	8	4	80
Number of employees	50	40	20	10	120
Allocated overheads ($000)	15	20	12	5	50

Service departments' services were used as follows.

	A	B	Maintenance	Stores	Total
Maintenance hours worked	5,000	4,000	----	1,000	10,000
Number of stores requisitions	3,000	1,000	----	----	4,000

4.2 Stage 1: Apportioning general overheads

Overhead apportionment follows on from overhead allocation. The first stage of overhead apportionment is to identify all overhead costs as production department, production service department, administration or selling and distribution overhead. The costs for heat and light, rent and rates, the canteen and so on (ie costs allocated to general overhead cost centres) must therefore be shared out between the other cost centres.

4.2.1 Bases of apportionment

It is considered important that overhead costs should be shared out on a **fair basis**. You will appreciate that because of the complexity of items of cost it is rarely possible to use only one method of apportioning costs to the various departments of an organisation. The bases of apportionment for the most usual cases are given below.

Overhead to which the basis applies	Basis
Rent, rates, heating and light, repairs and depreciation of buildings	Floor area occupied by each cost centre
Depreciation, insurance of equipment	Cost or book value of equipment
Personnel office, canteen, welfare, wages and cost offices, first aid	Number of employees, or labour hours worked in each cost centre

Note that heating and lighting may also be apportioned using volume of space occupied by each cost centre.

4.2.2 Example: Swotathon

Using the Swotathon question above, show how overheads should be apportioned between the four departments.

Solution

Item of cost	Basis of apportionment	Department			
		A	B	Mainten- ance	Stores
		$	$	$	$
Heat and light	Floor area	7,680	5,120	3,840	2,560
Repair costs	Floor area	3,840	2,560	1,920	1,280
Machine dep^n	Machinery value	32,400	13,500	5,400	2,700
Rent and rates	Floor area	15,360	10,240	7,680	5,120
Canteen	No of employees	3,750	3,000	1,500	750
Machine insurance	Machinery value	15,000	6,250	2,500	1,250
Total		78,030	40,670	22,840	13,660

Workings

Overhead apportioned by floor area

$$\text{Overhead apportioned to department} = \frac{\text{Floor area occupied by department}}{\text{Total floor area}} \times \text{total overhead}$$

For example:

$$\text{Heat and light apportioned to Dept A} = \frac{6,000}{15,000} \times 19,200 = \$7,680$$

Overheads apportioned by machinery value

$$\text{Overheads apportioned to department} = \frac{\text{Value of department's machinery}}{\text{Total value of machinery}} \times \text{total overhead}$$

Overheads apportioned by number of employees

$$\text{Overheads apportioned to department} = \frac{\text{No of employees in department}}{\text{Total no of employees}} \times \text{total overhead}$$

4.3 Stage 2 – Apportion service department costs

Only production departments produce goods that will ultimately be sold. In order to calculate a correct price for these goods, we must determine the **total cost** of producing each unit – that is, not just the cost of the labour and materials that are directly used in production, but also the **indirect** costs of services provided by such departments as maintenance, stores and canteen.

Our aim is to apportion all the **service** department costs to the **production** departments, in one of three ways.

(a)   The **direct** method, where the service centre costs are apportioned to production departments only.

(b)   The **step-down** method, where each service centre's costs are not only apportioned to production departments but to some (but not all) of the other service centres that make use of the services provided.

(c)   The **repeated distribution** (or **reciprocal**) method, where service centre costs are apportioned to both the production departments and service departments that use the services. The service centre costs are then gradually apportioned to the production departments. This method is used only when service departments work for each other – that is, **service departments use each other's services** (for example, the maintenance department will use the canteen, whilst the canteen may rely on the maintenance department to ensure its equipment is functioning properly or to replace bulbs, plugs, etc).

The **direct** and **step-down** methods are **not examinable**.

Exam focus point

> Remember that **all** service department costs must be allocated – that is, both **general overheads** that were apportioned and those overheads that are **specific** to the individual departments.

4.3.1 Basis of apportionment

Whichever method is used to apportion service cost centre costs, **the basis of apportionment must be fair**. A different apportionment basis may be applied for each service cost centre. This is demonstrated in the following table.

Service cost centre	Possible basis of apportionment
Stores	Number or cost value of material requisitions
Maintenance	Hours of maintenance work done for each cost centre
Production planning	Direct labour hours worked in each production cost centre

Although both the **direct** and **step-down** methods are **not in your syllabus**, the following illustration will give you an idea of how to carry out simple apportionments before we move onto the more complex reciprocal method.

4.3.2 Example: Swotathon with simple apportionment

Using the information contained in the Swotathon question and the results of the calculations in Section 4.2.2 above, apportion the Maintenance and Stores departments' overheads to production departments A and B and calculate the total overheads for each of these production departments.

Solution

(1) Decide how the **service departments'** overheads will be apportioned. The table above tells us that maintenance overheads can be apportioned according to the **hours of maintenance work done**, whilst we can use the number or cost value of stores/material requisitions for apportioning stores.

The question gives us information about maintenance hours worked and the number of stores requisitions.

(2) **Apportion the overheads** of the **service** department whose services are also used by another service department (in this case, maintenance). This allows us to obtain a total overhead cost for stores.

Total overheads for maintenance department

	$	
General overheads	22,840	(see Section 4.2.2 above)
Allocated overheads	12,000	(from question in Section 4.1)
	34,840	

Apportioned as follows:

$$\frac{\text{Maintenance hours worked in department}}{\text{Total maintenance hours worked}} \times \$34,840$$

Production department A = $\dfrac{5,000}{10,000} \times \$34,840 = \$17,420$

Production department B = $\dfrac{4,000}{10,000} \times \$34,840 = \$13,936$

Stores department = $\dfrac{1,000}{10,000} \times \$34,840 = \$3,484$

(3) Apportion **Stores department's** overheads.

Total overheads for stores

	$	
General overheads	13,660	(see Section 4.2.2 above)
Allocated overheads	5,000	(from question in Section 4.1)
Apportioned from maintenance	3,484	(see above)
	22,144	

Apportioned as follows:

$$\frac{\text{Number of stores requisitions for department}}{\text{Total number of stores requisitions}} \times \$22,144$$

Production department A = $\dfrac{3,000}{4,000} \times \$22,144 = \$16,608$

Production department B = $\dfrac{1,000}{4,000} \times \$22,144 = \$5,536$

(4) **Total overheads** for each production department

	A $	B $	
General overheads	78,030	40,670	(see Section 4.2.2)
Allocated overheads	15,000	20,000	(from question in Section 4.1)
Maintenance	17,420	13,936	
Stores	16,608	5,536	
	127,058	80,142	

4.4 The reciprocal (repeated distribution) method of apportionment

Now that we have looked at the 'simple' scenario of only one service department making use of the other service department's services, we can move onto the more complicated situation of **'reciprocal' servicing**. This is where each service department makes use of the other service department (in the Swotathon example, stores would use maintenance and maintenance would use stores).

4.4.1 Example: Swotathon using repeated distribution method

Suppose the usage of Swotathon's service departments' services were amended to be as follows:

	A	B	Maintenance	Stores	Total
Maintenance hours used	5,000	4,000	-	1,000	10,000
Number of stores requisitions	3,000	1,000	1,000	-	5,000

Show how the Maintenance and Stores departments' overheads would be apportioned to the two production departments and calculate total overheads for each of the production departments.

Solution

Remember to apportion both the general and allocated overheads (see section 4.2.2). The bases of apportionment for Maintenance and Stores are the same as for the example in section 4.2.2 (that is, maintenance hours worked and number of stores requisitions).

	A	B	Maintenance	Stores
	$	$	$	$
Total overheads (general and allocated)	93,030	60,670	34,840	18,660
Apportion maintenance (note (a))	17,420	13,936	(34,840)	3,484
			Nil	22,144
Apportion stores (note (b))	13,286	4,429	4,429	(22,144)
			4,429	Nil
Apportion maintenance	2,215	1,772	(4,429)	442
			Nil	442
Apportion stores (note (c))	332	110	Nil	(442)
Total overheads	126,283	80,917	Nil	Nil

Notes

(a) It does not matter which department you choose to apportion first. Maintenance overheads were apportioned using the calculations illustrated in section 4.3.2.

(b) Stores overheads are apportioned using the same formula as used in section 4.3.2 but with the amended number of stores requisitions given above.

(c) The problem with the repeated distribution method is that you can keep performing the same calculations many times. When you are dealing with a small number (such as $442 above) you can take the decision to apportion the figure between the production departments only. In this case, we ignore the stores requisitions for Maintenance and base the apportionment on the total stores requisitions for the production departments (that is, 4,000). The amount apportioned to production department A was calculated as follows.

$$\frac{\text{Stores requisitions for A}}{\text{Total stores requisitions (A+B)}} \times \text{Stores overheads}$$

$$= \frac{3,000}{4,000} \times \$442 = £332$$

4.5 The reciprocal (algebraic) method of apportionment

FAST FORWARD

> The results of the reciprocal method of apportionment may also be obtained using **algebra** and **simultaneous equations**.

If you are unsure about how to solve simultaneous equations, look at section 9 of the basic maths chapter at the beginning of this text.

4.5.1 Example: Swotathon using the algebraic method of apportionment

Whenever you are using equations you must define each variable.

Let M = total overheads for the Maintenance department
S = total overheads for the Stores department

Remember that total overheads for the Maintenance department consist of general overheads apportioned, allocated overheads and the share of Stores overheads (20%).

Similarly, total overheads for Stores will be the total of general overheads apportioned, allocated overheads and the 10% share of Maintenance overheads.

$M = 0.2S + \$34,840$	(1)		($34,840 was calculated in section 4.3.2)
$S = 0.1M + \$18,660$	(2)		($18,660 was calculated in section 4.3.2)

We now solve the equations.

Multiply equation (1) by 5 to give us

$5M = S + 174,200$	(3), which can be rearranged as
$S = 5M - 174,200$	(4)

Subtract equation (2) from equation (4)

$S = 5M - 174,200$	(4)
$S = 0.1M + 18,660$	(2)

$0 = 4.9M - 192,860$

$4.9M = 192,860$

$$M = \frac{192,860}{4.9} = \$39,359$$

Substitute M = 39,359 into equation (2)

$S = 0.1 \times 39,359 + 18,660$
$S = 3,936 + 18,660 = 22,596$

These overheads can now be apportioned to the production departments using the proportions in section 4.3.1 above.

	A $	B $	Maintenance $	Stores $
Overhead costs	93,030	60,670	34,840	18,660
Apportion maintenance	19,680	15,743	(39,359)	3,936
Apportion stores	13,558	4,519	4,519	(22,596)
Total	126,268	80,932	Nil	Nil

You will notice that the total overheads for production departments A and B are the same regardless of the method used (difference is due to rounding).

Exam focus point

> You must never ignore the existence of reciprocal services unless a question specifically instructs you to do so.

4.6 A full example for you to try

Now that we have worked through the various stages of overhead apportionment, you should try this question to ensure you understand the techniques.

Question   **Reapportionment**

Sandstorm is a jobbing engineering concern which has three production departments (forming, machines and assembly) and two service departments (maintenance and general).

The following analysis of overhead costs has been made for the year just ended.

	$	$
Rent and rates		8,000
Power		750
Light, heat		5,000
Repairs, maintenance:		
Forming	800	
Machines	1,800	
Assembly	300	
Maintenance	200	
General	100	
		3,200
Departmental expenses:		
Forming	1,500	
Machines	2,300	
Assembly	1,100	
Maintenance	900	
General	1,500	
		7,300
Depreciation:		
Plant		10,000
Fixtures and fittings		250
Insurance:		
Plant		2,000
Buildings		500
Indirect labour:		
Forming	3,000	
Machines	5,000	
Assembly	1,500	
Maintenance	4,000	
General	2,000	
		15,500
		52,500

Other available data are as follows.

	Floor area sq. ft	Plant value $	Fixtures & fittings $	Effective horse-power	Direct cost for year $	Labour hours worked	Machine hours worked
Forming	2,000	25,000	1,000	40	20,500	14,400	12,000
Machines	4,000	60,000	500	90	30,300	20,500	21,600
Assembly	3,000	7,500	2,000	15	24,200	20,200	2,000
Maintenance	500	7,500	1,000	5			
General	500	–	500	–	–	–	–
	10,000	100,000	5,000	150	75,000	55,100	35,600

Service department costs are apportioned as follows.

	Maintenance %	General %
Forming	20	20
Machines	50	60
Assembly	20	10
General	10	–
Maintenance	–	10
	100	100

Required

Using the data provided prepare an analysis showing the distribution of overhead costs to departments. Reapportion service cost centre costs using the reciprocal method.

Answer

Analysis of distribution of actual overhead costs

	Basis	Forming $	Machines $	Assembly $	Maint. $	General $	Total $
Directly allocated overheads:							
Repairs, maintenance		800	1,800	300	200	100	3,200
Departmental expenses		1,500	2,300	1,100	900	1,500	7,300
Indirect labour		3,000	5,000	1,500	4,000	2,000	15,500
Apportionment of other overheads:							
Rent, rates	1	1,600	3,200	2,400	400	400	8,000
Power	2	200	450	75	25	0	750
Light, heat	1	1,000	2,000	1,500	250	250	5,000
Depreciation of plant	3	2,500	6,000	750	750	0	10,000
Depreciation of F and F	4	50	25	100	50	25	250
Insurance of plant	3	500	1,200	150	150	0	2,000
Insurance of buildings	1	100	200	150	25	25	500
		11,250	22,175	8,025	6,750	4,300	52,500

Basis of apportionment:

1	floor area	3	plant value
2	effective horsepower	4	fixtures and fittings value

Apportionment of service department overheads to production departments, using the reciprocal method.

	Forming $	Machines $	Assembly $	Maintenance $	General $	Total $
Overheads	11,250	22,175	8,025	6,750	4,300	52,500
	1,350	3,375	1,350	(6,750)	675	
					4,975	
	995	2,985	498	497	(4,975)	
	99	249	99	(497)	50	
	10	30	5	5	(50)	
	1	3	1	(5)		
	13,705	28,817	9,978	0	0	52,500

Exam focus point

Remember that you will never be asked a question of this length in the real exam. However, exam questions may, for example, give you the total general and allocated overheads, and ask you to apportion service department overheads to production departments.

Question

Spaced Out Inc has two production departments (F and G) and two service departments (Canteen and Maintenance). Total allocated and apportioned general overheads for each department are as follows.

F	G	Canteen	Maintenance
$125,000	$80,000	$20,000	$40,000

Canteen and Maintenance perform services for both production departments and Canteen also provides services for Maintenance in the following proportions.

	F	G	Canteen	Maintenance
% of Canteen to	60	25	-	15
% of Maintenance to	65	35	-	-

What would be the total overheads for production department G once the service department costs have been apportioned?

A $90,763   B $100,500   C $99,000   D $100,050

Answer

The correct answer is D.

Total Maintenance overheads	= $40,000 + 15% of Canteen overheads
	= $40,000 + 15% of $20,000
	= $43,000

Of which 35% are apportioned to G = $15,050

Canteen costs apportioned to G = 25% of $20,000 = $5,000

Total overheads for G = $80,000 + 15,050 + 5,000 = $100,050

5 Overhead absorption

5.1 Introduction

FAST FORWARD

Overhead absorption is the process whereby overhead costs allocated and apportioned to production cost centres are added to unit, job or batch costs. Overhead absorption is sometimes called **overhead recovery.**

Having allocated and/or apportioned all overheads, the next stage in the costing treatment of overheads is to add them to, or **absorb them into, cost units.**

Overheads are usually added to cost units using a **predetermined overhead absorption rate**, which is calculated using figures from the budget.

5.2 Calculation of overhead absorption rates

Step 1   Estimate the overhead likely to be incurred during the coming period.

Step 2   Estimate the activity level for the period. This could be total hours, units, or direct costs or whatever it is upon which the overhead absorption rates are to be based.

Step 3   Divide the estimated overhead by the budgeted activity level. This produces the overhead absorption rate.

Step 4   Absorb the overhead into the cost unit by applying the calculated absorption rate.

5.3 Example: The basics of absorption costing

Athena Co makes two products, the Greek and the Roman. Greeks take 2 labour hours each to make and Romans take 5 labour hours. What is the overhead cost per unit for Greeks and Romans respectively if overheads are absorbed on the basis of labour hours?

Solution

Step 1   Estimate the overhead likely to be incurred during the coming period

Athena Co estimates that the total overhead will be $50,000

Step 2   Estimate the activity level for the period

Athena Co estimates that a total of 100,000 direct labour hours will be worked

Step 3   Divide the estimated overhead by the budgeted activity level

$$\text{Absorption rate} = \frac{\$50,000}{100,000 \text{ hrs}} = \$0.50 \text{ per direct labour hour}$$

Step 4   Absorb the overhead into the cost unit by applying the calculated absorption rate

	Greek	Roman
Labour hours per unit	2	5
Absorption rate per labour hour	$0.50	$0.50
Overhead absorbed per unit	$1	$2.50

It should be obvious to you that, even if a company is trying to be 'fair', there is a great lack of precision about the way an absorption base is chosen.

This arbitrariness is one of the main criticisms of absorption costing, and if absorption costing is to be used (because of its other virtues) then it is important that **the methods used are kept under regular review.** Changes in working conditions should, if necessary, lead to changes in the way in which work is accounted for.

For example, a labour intensive department may become mechanised. If a direct labour hour rate of absorption had been used previous to the mechanisation, it would probably now be more appropriate to change to the use of a machine hour rate.

5.4 Choosing the appropriate absorption base

The different **bases of absorption** (or 'overhead recovery rates') are as follows.

*   A percentage of direct materials cost
*   A percentage of direct labour cost
*   A percentage of prime cost
*   A rate per machine hour
*   A rate per direct labour hour
*   A rate per unit
*   A percentage of factory cost (for administration overhead)
*   A percentage of sales or factory cost (for selling and distribution overhead)

The choice of an absorption basis is a matter of judgement and common sense, what is required is an **absorption basis** which realistically reflects the characteristics of a given cost centre and which avoids undue anomalies.

Many factories use a **direct labour hour rate** or **machine hour rate** in preference to a rate based on a percentage of direct materials cost, wages or prime cost.

(a)   A **direct labour** hour basis is most appropriate in a **labour intensive** environment.

(b)   A **machine hour** rate would be used in departments where production is controlled or dictated by machines.

(c)   A **rate per unit** would be effective only if all units were identical.

5.5 Example: Overhead absorption

The budgeted production overheads and other budget data of Bridge Cottage Co are as follows.

Budget	Production dept A	Production dept B
Overhead cost	$36,000	$5,000
Direct materials cost	$32,000	
Direct labour cost	$40,000	
Machine hours	10,000	
Direct labour hours	18,000	
Units of production		1,000

Required

Calculate the absorption rate using the various bases of apportionment.

Solution

Department A

(i) Percentage of direct materials cost

$$\frac{\$36,000}{\$32,000} \times 100\% = 112.5\%$$

(ii) Percentage of direct labour cost

$$\frac{\$36,000}{\$40,000} \times 100\% = 90\%$$

(iii) Percentage of prime cost

$$\frac{\$36,000}{\$72,000} \times 100\% = 50\%$$

(iv) Rate per machine hour

$$\frac{\$36,000}{10,000\,hrs} = \$3.60 \text{ per machine hour}$$

(v) Rate per direct labour hour

$$\frac{\$36,000}{18,000\,hrs} = \$2 \text{ per direct labour hour}$$

The department B absorption rate will be based on units of output.

$$\frac{\$5,000}{1,000\,units} = \$5 \text{ per unit produced}$$

Mat $80
Lab 85   = 165
Labhr 36 hr
Mach 23

5.6 Bases of absorption

The choice of the basis of absorption is significant in determining the cost of individual units, or jobs, produced. Using the previous example, suppose that an individual product has a material cost of $80, a labour cost of $85, and requires 36 labour hours and 23 machine hours to complete. The overhead cost of the product would vary, depending on the basis of absorption used by the company for overhead recovery.

(a) As a percentage of direct material cost, the overhead cost would be

112.5% × $80   = $90.00

(b) As a percentage of direct labour cost, the overhead cost would be

90% × $85   = $76.50

(c) As a percentage of prime cost, the overhead cost would be 50% × $165   = $82.50

(d) Using a machine hour basis of absorption, the overhead cost would be

23 hrs × $3.60   = $82.80

(e) Using a labour hour basis, the overhead cost would be 36 hrs × $2   = $72.00

In theory, each basis of absorption would be possible, but the company should choose a basis for its own costs which seems to be **'fairest'**.

6 Blanket absorption rates and departmental absorption rates

6.1 Introduction

> A **blanket overhead absorption rate** is an absorption rate used throughout a factory and for all jobs and units of output irrespective of the department in which they were produced.

For example, if total overheads were $500,000 and there were 250,000 direct machine hours during the period, the **blanket overhead rate** would be $2 per direct machine hour and all jobs passing through the factory would be charged at that rate.

Blanket overhead rates are not appropriate in the following circumstances.

- There is more than one department.
- Jobs do not spend an equal amount of time in each department.

If a single factory overhead absorption rate is used, some products will receive a higher overhead charge than they ought 'fairly' to bear, whereas other products will be under-charged.

If **a separate absorption rate** is used for each department, charging of overheads will be fair and the full cost of production of items will represent the amount of the effort and resources put into making them.

6.2 Example: Separate absorption rates

The Old Grammar School has two production departments, for which the following budgeted information is available.

	Department A	Department B	Total
Budgeted overheads	$360,000	$200,000	$560,000
Budgeted direct labour hours	200,000 hrs	40,000 hrs	240,000 hrs

If a single factory overhead absorption rate is applied, the rate of overhead recovery would be:

$$\frac{\$560,000}{240,000 \text{ hours}} = \$2.33 \text{ per direct labour hour}$$

If separate departmental rates are applied, these would be:

$$Department\ A = \frac{\$360,000}{200,000 \text{ hours}} = \$1.80 \text{ per direct labour hour}$$

$$Department\ B = \frac{\$200,000}{40,000 \text{ hours}} = \$5 \text{ per direct labour hour}$$

Department B has a higher overhead rate of cost per hour worked than department A.

Now let us consider two separate jobs.

Job X has a prime cost of $100, takes 30 hours in department B and does not involve any work in department A.

Job Y has a prime cost of $100, takes 28 hours in department A and 2 hours in department B.

What would be the factory cost of each job, using the following rates of overhead recovery?

(a) A single factory rate of overhead recovery
(b) Separate departmental rates of overhead recovery

Solution

		Job X		Job Y	
(a)	**Single factory rate**	$		$	
	Prime cost	100		100	
	Factory overhead (30 × $2.33)	70		70	
	Factory cost	170		170	
(b)	**Separate departmental rates**	$		$	
	Prime cost	100		100.00	
	Factory overhead: department A	0	(28 × $1.80)	50.40	
	department B	150	(2 × $5)	10.00	(30 × $5) for Job X
	Factory cost	250		160.40	

Note: (30 × $5) appears beside Job X department B figure.

Using a single factory overhead absorption rate, both jobs would cost the same. However, since job X is done entirely within department B where overhead costs are relatively higher, whereas job Y is done mostly within department A, where overhead costs are relatively lower, it is arguable that job X should cost more than job Y. This will occur if separate departmental overhead recovery rates are used to reflect the work done on each job in each department separately.

If all jobs do not spend approximately the same time in each department then, to ensure that all jobs are charged with their fair share of overheads, it is necessary to establish **separate overhead rates for each department**.

Question

Machine hour absorption rate

The following data relate to one year in department A.

Budgeted machine hours	25,000
Actual machine hours	21,875
Budgeted overheads	$350,000
Actual overheads	$350,000

Based on the data above, what is the machine hour absorption rate as conventionally calculated?

A $12   B $14   C $16   D $18

Answer

Don't forget, if your calculations produce a solution which does not correspond with any of the options available, then eliminate the unlikely options and make a guess from the remainder. Never leave out a multiple choice question.

A common pitfall is to think 'we haven't had answer A for a while, so I'll guess that'. The examiner is *not* required to produce an even spread of A, B, C and D answers in the examination. There is no reason why the answer to *every* question cannot be D!

The correct answer in this case is B.

$$\text{Overhead absorption rate} = \frac{\text{Budgeted overheads}}{\text{Budgeted machine hours}} = \frac{\$350,000}{25,000} = \$14 \text{ per machine hour}$$

7 Over and under absorption of overheads

7.1 Introduction

FAST FORWARD

Over and **under absorption** of overheads occurs because the predetermined overhead absorption rates are based on estimates.

The rate of overhead absorption is based on estimates (of both numerator and denominator) and it is quite likely that either one or both of the estimates will not agree with what actually occurs.

(a)   **Over absorption** means that the overheads charged to the cost of sales are greater then the overheads actually incurred.

(b)   **Under absorption** means that insufficient overheads have been included in the cost of sales.

It is almost inevitable that at the end of the accounting year there will have been an over absorption or under absorption of the overhead actually incurred.

7.2 Example: Over and under absorption

Suppose that the budgeted overhead in a production department is $80,000 and the budgeted activity is 40,000 direct labour hours. The overhead recovery rate (using a direct labour hour basis) would be $2 per direct labour hour.

Actual overheads in the period are, say $84,000 and 45,000 direct labour hours are worked.

	$
Overhead incurred (actual)	84,000
Overhead absorbed (45,000 × $2)	90,000
Over absorption of overhead	6,000

In this example, the cost of produced units or jobs has been charged with $6,000 more than was actually spent. An adjustment to reconcile the overheads charged to the actual overhead is necessary and the over-absorbed overhead will be credited to the profit and loss account at the end of the accounting period.

7.3 The reasons for under-/over-absorbed overhead

The overhead absorption rate is predetermined from budget estimates of overhead cost and the expected volume of activity. Under– or over-recovery of overhead will occur in the following circumstances.

- Actual overhead costs are different from budgeted overheads
- The actual activity level is different from the budgeted activity level
- Actual overhead costs *and* actual activity level differ from the budgeted costs and level

7.4 Example: Reasons for under-/over-absorbed overhead

Pembridge Co has a budgeted production overhead of $50,000 and a budgeted activity of 25,000 direct labour hours and therefore a recovery rate of $2 per direct labour hour.

Required

Calculate the under-/over-absorbed overhead, and the reasons for the under-/over-absorption, in the following circumstances.

(a)   Actual overheads cost $47,000 and 25,000 direct labour hours are worked.
(b)   Actual overheads cost $50,000 and 21,500 direct labour hours are worked.
(c)   Actual overheads cost $47,000 and 21,500 direct labour hours are worked.

Solution

(a)

	$
Actual overhead	47,000
Absorbed overhead (25,000 × $2)	50,000
Over-absorbed overhead	3,000

The reason for the over absorption is that although the actual and budgeted direct labour hours are the same, actual overheads cost less than expected.

(b)

	$
Actual overhead	50,000
Absorbed overhead (21,500 × $2)	43,000
Under-absorbed overhead	7,000

The reason for the under absorption is that although budgeted and actual overhead costs were the same, fewer direct labour hours were worked than expected.

(c)

	$
Actual overhead	47,000
Absorbed overhead (21,500 × $2)	43,000
Under-absorbed overhead	4,000

The reason for the under absorption is a combination of the reasons in (a) and (b).

The distinction between **overheads incurred** (actual overheads) and **overheads absorbed** is an important one which you must learn and understand. The difference between them is known as under– or over-absorbed overheads.

Question	Under-/over-absorbed overhead

The budgeted and actual data for River Arrow Products Co for the year to 31 March 20X5 are as follows.

	Budgeted	Actual
Direct labour hours	9,000	9,900
Direct wages	$34,000	$35,500
Machine hours	10,100	9,750
Direct materials	$55,000	$53,900
Units produced	120,000	122,970
Overheads	$63,000	$61,500

The cost accountant of River Arrow Products Co has decided that overheads should be absorbed on the basis of labour hours.

Required

Calculate the amount of under– or over-absorbed overheads for River Arrow Products Co for the year to 31 March 20X5.

Answer

$$\text{Overhead absorption rate} = \frac{\$63,000}{9,000} = \$7 \text{ per hour}$$

Overheads absorbed by production = 9,900 × $7 = $69,300

	$
Actual overheads	61,500
Overheads absorbed	69,300
Over-absorbed overheads	7,800

You can always work out whether overheads are under– or over-absorbed by using the following rule.

- If Actual overhead incurred – Absorbed overhead = NEGATIVE (N), then overheads are over-absorbed (O) (NO)
- If Actual overhead incurred – Absorbed overhead = POSITIVE (P), then overheads are under-absorbed (U) (PU)

So, remember the NOPU rule when you go into your examination and you won't have any trouble in deciding whether overheads are under– or over-absorbed!

Question
Budgeted overhead absorption rate

A management consultancy recovers overheads on chargeable consulting hours. Budgeted overheads were $615,000 and actual consulting hours were 32,150. Overheads were under-recovered by $35,000.

If actual overheads were $694,075 what was the budgeted overhead absorption rate per hour?

A $19.13   B $20.50   C $21.59   D $22.68

Answer

	$
Actual overheads	694,075
Under-recoverable overheads	35,000
Overheads recovered for 32,150 hours at budgeted overhead absorption rate (x)	659,075

32,150 x = 659,075

$$x = \frac{659,075}{32,150} = \$20.50$$

The correct option is B.

8 Ledger entries relating to overheads

8.1 Introduction

The bookkeeping entries for overheads are not as straightforward as those for materials and labour. We shall now consider the way in which overheads are dealt with in a cost accounting system.

When an absorption costing system is in use we now know that the amount of overhead included in the cost of an item is absorbed at a predetermined rate. The entries made in the cash book and the nominal ledger, however, are the actual amounts.

You will remember that it is highly unlikely that the actual amount and the predetermined amount will be the same. The difference is called **under– or over-absorbed overhead**. To deal with this in the cost accounting books, therefore, we need to have an account to collect under– or over-absorbed amounts for each type of overhead.

8.2 Example: The under-/over-absorbed overhead account

Mariott's Motorcycles absorbs production overheads at the rate of $0.50 per operating hour and administration overheads at 20% of the production cost of sales. Actual data for one month was as follows.

Administration overheads	$32,000
Production overheads	$46,500
Operating hours	90,000
Production cost of sales	$180,000

What entries need to be made for overheads in the ledgers?

Solution

PRODUCTION OVERHEADS

	DR		CR
	$		$
Cash	46,500	Absorbed into WIP (90,000 × $0.50)	45,000
		Under absorbed overhead	1,500
	46,500		46,500

ADMINISTRATION OVERHEADS

	DR		CR
	$		$
Cash	32,000	To cost of sales (180,000 × 0.2)	36,000
Over-absorbed overhead	4,000		
	36,000		36,000

UNDER-/OVER-ABSORBED OVERHEADS

	DR		CR
	$		$
Production overhead	1,500	Administration overhead	4,000
Balance to profit and loss account	2,500		
	4,000		4,000

Less production overhead has been absorbed than has been spent so there is **under-absorbed overhead** of $1,500. More administration overhead has been absorbed (into cost of sales, note, not into WIP) and so there is **over-absorbed overhead** of $4,000. The net over-absorbed overhead of $2,500 is a credit in the income statement.

9 Non-manufacturing overheads

9.1 Introduction

Non-manufacturing overheads may be allocated by choosing a basis for the overhead absorption rate which most closely matches the non-production overhead, or on the basis of a product's ability to bear the costs.

For **external reporting** (eg statutory accounts) it is not necessary to allocate non-manufacturing overheads to products. This is because many of the overheads are non-manufacturing, and are regarded as **period costs**.

For **internal reporting** purposes and for a number of industries which base the selling price of their product on estimates of **total** cost or even actual cost, a **total cost per unit of output** may be required.

Builders, law firms and garages often charge for their services by adding a **percentage profit margin** to actual cost. For product pricing purposes and for internal management reports it may therefore be appropriate to allocate non-manufacturing overheads to units of output.

9.2 Bases for apportioning non-manufacturing overheads

A number of non-manufacturing overheads such as delivery costs or salespersons' salaries are clearly identified with particular products and can therefore be classified as direct costs. The majority of non-manufacturing overheads, however cannot be directly allocated to particular units of output. Two possible methods of allocating such non-manufacturing overheads are as follows.

Method 1: Choose a basis for the overhead absorption rate which most closely matches the non-manufacturing overhead such as direct labour hours, direct machine hours and so on. The problem with such a method is that most non-manufacturing overheads are unaffected in the short term by changes in the level of output and tend to be fixed costs.

Method 2 : Allocate non-manufacturing overheads on the ability of the products to bear such costs. One possible approach is to use the manufacturing cost as the basis for allocating non-manufacturing costs to products.

Formula to learn

The **overhead absorption rate** is calculated as follows.

$$\text{Overhead absorption rate} = \frac{\text{Estimated non-manufacturing overheads}}{\text{Estimated manufacturing costs}}$$

If, for example, budgeted distribution overheads are $200,000 and budgeted manufacturing costs are $800,000, the predetermined distribution overhead absorption rate will be 25% of manufacturing cost. Other bases for absorbing overheads are as follows.

Type of overhead	Possible absorption base
Selling and marketing	Sales value
Research and development	Consumer cost (= production cost minus cost of direct materials) or added value (= sales value of product minus cost of bought in materials and services)
Distribution	Sales values
Administration	Consumer cost or added value

9.3 Administration overheads

The administration overhead usually consists of the following.

- Executive salaries
- Office rent and rates
- Lighting
- Heating and cleaning the offices

In cost accounting, administration overheads are regarded as periodic charges which are charged against the gross costing profit for the year (as in financial accounting).

9.4 Selling and distribution overheads

Selling and distribution overheads are often considered collectively as one type of overhead but they are actually quite different forms of expense.

(a) **Selling costs** are incurred in order to obtain sales

(b) **Distribution costs** begin as soon as the finished goods are put into the warehouse and continue until the goods are despatched or delivered to the customer

Selling overhead is therefore often absorbed on the basis of sales value so that the more profitable product lines take a large proportion of overhead. The normal cost accounting entry for selling overhead is as follows.

DR   Cost of goods sold
CR   Selling overhead control account

Distribution overhead is more closely linked to production than sales and from one point of view could be regarded as an extra cost of production. It is, however, more usual to regard production cost as ending on the factory floor and to deal with distribution overhead separately. It is generally absorbed on a percentage of production cost but special circumstances, such as size and weight of products affecting the delivery charges, may cause a different basis of absorption to be used. The cost accounting entry is as follows.

DR   Cost of goods sold
CR   Distribution overhead control account

184   **8: Overheads and absorption costing** │ Part D Cost accounting techniques

Chapter roundup

- **Overhead** is the cost incurred in the course of making a product, providing a service or running a department, but which cannot be traced directly and in full to the product, service or department.

- The **objective of absorption costing** is to include in the total cost of a product an appropriate share of the organisation's total overhead. An appropriate share is generally taken to mean an amount which reflects the amount of time and effort that has gone into producing a unit or completing a job.

- The main reasons for using absorption costing are for **stock valuations, pricing decisions** and **establishing the profitability of different products.**

- The three stages of absorption costing are:
  - Allocation
  - Apportionment
  - Absorption

- **Allocation** is the process by which whole cost items are charged direct to a cost unit or cost centre.

- **Apportionment** is a procedure whereby indirect costs are spread fairly between cost centres. Service cost centre costs may be apportioned to production cost centres by using the reciprocal method.

- The results of the reciprocal method of apportionment may also be obtained by using **algebra** and **simultaneous equations**.

- **Overhead absorption** is the process whereby overhead costs allocated and apportioned to production cost centres are added to unit, job or batch costs. Overhead absorption is sometimes called **overhead recovery**.

- A **blanket overhead absorption rate** is an absorption rate used throughout a factory and for all jobs and units of output irrespective of the department in which they were produced.

- **Over** and **under absorption of overheads** occurs because the predetermined overhead absorption rates are based on estimates.

- **Non-manufacturing overheads** may be allocated by choosing a basis for the overhead absorption rate which most closely matches the non-production overhead, or on the basis of a product's ability to bear the costs.

Quick quiz

1   What is allocation?

2   Name the three stages in charging overheads to units of output.

3   Match the following overheads with the most appropriate basis of apportionment.

Overhead		Basis of apportionment	
(a)	Depreciation of equipment	(1)	Direct machine hours
(b)	Heat and light costs	(2)	Number of employees
(c)	Canteen	(3)	Book value of equipment
(d)	Insurance of equipment	(4)	Floor area

4   A direct labour hour basis is most appropriate in which of the following environments?

A   Machine-intensive   C   When all units produced are identical
B   Labour-intensive   D   None of the above

5   What is the problem with using a single factory overhead absorption rate?

6   How is under-/over-absorbed overhead accounted for?

7   Why does under– or over-absorbed overhead occur?

Answers to quick quiz

1   The process whereby whole cost items are charged direct to a cost unit or cost centre.

2
- Allocation
- Apportionment
- Absorption

3

(a)	(3)	(c)	(2)
(b)	(4)	(d)	(3)

4   B

5   Because some products will receive a higher overhead charge than they ought 'fairly' to bear and other products will be undercharged.

6   Under-/over-absorbed overhead is written as an adjustment to the income statement at the end of an accounting period.

- Over-absorbed overhead → credit in income statement
- Under-absorbed overhead → debit in income statement

7
- Actual overhead costs are different from budgeted overheads
- The actual activity level is different from the budgeted activity level
- Actual overhead costs *and* actual activity level differ from the budgeted costs and level

Now try the questions below from the Exam Question Bank

Number	Level	Marks	Time
Q8	MCQ/OTQ	n/a	n/a

Marginal and absorption costing

Topic list	Syllabus reference
1 Marginal cost and marginal costing	D4 (a)
2 The principles of marginal costing	D4 (a)
3 Marginal costing and absorption costing and the calculation of profit	D4 (b), (c)
4 Reconciling profits	D4 (d)
5 Marginal costing versus absorption costing	D4 (e)

Introduction

This chapter defines **marginal costing** and compares it with absorption costing. Whereas absorption costing recognises fixed costs (usually fixed production costs) as part of the cost of a unit of output and hence as product costs, marginal costing treats all fixed costs as period costs. Two such different costing methods obviously each have their supporters and so we will be looking at the arguments both in favour of and against each method. Each costing method, because of the different inventory valuation used, produces a different profit figure and we will be looking at this particular point in detail.

Study guide

		Intellectual level
D4	**Marginal and absorption costing**	
(a)	Explain the importance and apply the concept of contribution	1
(b)	Demonstrate and discuss the effect of absorption and marginal costing on inventory valuation and profit determination	2
(c)	Calculate profit or loss under absorption and marginal costing	2
(d)	Reconcile the profits or losses calculated under absorption and marginal costing	2
(e)	Describe the advantages and disadvantages of absorption and marginal costing	1

Exam guide

Look out for questions in your examination which require you to calculate profit or losses using absorption and marginal costing.

1 Marginal cost and marginal costing

1.1 Introduction

FAST FORWARD

Marginal cost is the variable cost of one unit of product or service.

Key term

Marginal costing is an alternative method of costing to absorption costing. In marginal costing, only variable costs are charged as a cost of sale and a contribution is calculated (sales revenue minus variable cost of sales). Closing inventories of work in progress or finished goods are valued at marginal (variable) production cost. Fixed costs are treated as a period cost, and are charged in full to the profit and loss account of the accounting period in which they are incurred.

The **marginal production cost** per unit of an item usually consists of the following.

- Direct materials
- Direct labour
- Variable production overheads

Direct labour costs might be excluded from marginal costs when the work force is a given number of employees on a fixed wage or salary. Even so, it is not uncommon for direct labour to be treated as a variable cost, even when employees are paid a basic wage for a fixed working week. If in doubt, you should treat direct labour as a variable cost unless given clear indications to the contrary. Direct labour is often a step cost, with sufficiently short steps to make labour costs act in a variable fashion.

The **marginal cost of sales** usually consists of the marginal cost of production adjusted for inventory movements plus the variable selling costs, which would include items such as sales commission, and possibly some variable distribution costs.

1.2 Contribution

FAST FORWARD

Contribution is an important measure in marginal costing, and it is calculated as the difference between sales value and marginal or variable cost of sales.

Contribution is of fundamental importance in marginal costing, and the term 'contribution' is really short for 'contribution towards covering fixed overheads and making a profit'.

2 The principles of marginal costing

The principles of marginal costing are as follows.

(a) **Period fixed costs are the same, for any volume of sales and production** (provided that the level of activity is within the 'relevant range'). Therefore, by selling an extra item of product or service the following will happen.

- Revenue will increase by the sales value of the item sold.
- Costs will increase by the variable cost per unit.
- Profit will increase by the amount of contribution earned from the extra item.

(b) Similarly, if the volume of sales falls by one item, the profit will fall by the amount of contribution earned from the item.

(c) **Profit measurement should therefore be based on an analysis of total contribution**. Since fixed costs relate to a period of time, and do not change with increases or decreases in sales volume, it is misleading to charge units of sale with a share of fixed costs. Absorption costing is therefore misleading, and it is more appropriate to deduct fixed costs from total contribution for the period to derive a profit figure.

(d) When a unit of product is made, the extra costs incurred in its manufacture are the **variable production costs**. Fixed costs are unaffected, and no extra fixed costs are incurred when output is increased. It is therefore argued that **the valuation of closing inventories should be at variable production cost** (direct materials, direct labour, direct expenses (if any) and variable production overhead) because these are the only costs properly attributable to the product.

2.1 Example: Marginal costing principles

Rain Until September Co makes a product, the Splash, which has a variable production cost of $6 per unit and a sales price of $10 per unit. At the beginning of September 20X0, there were no opening inventories and production during the month was 20,000 units. Fixed costs for the month were $45,000 (production, administration, sales and distribution). There were no variable marketing costs.

Required

Calculate the contribution and profit for September 20X0, using marginal costing principles, if sales were as follows.

(a) 10,000 Splashes   (c)   20,000 Splashes
(b) 15,000 Splashes

Solution

The stages in the profit calculation are as follows.

- To **identify the variable cost of sales, and then the contribution**.
- Deduct fixed costs from the total contribution to derive the profit.
- Value all closing inventories at marginal production cost ($6 per unit).

	10,000 Splashes		15,000 Splashes		20,000 Splashes	
	$	$	$	$	$	$
Sales (at $10)		100,000		150,000		200,000
Opening inventory	0		0		0	
Variable production cost	120,000		120,000		120,000	
	120,000		120,000		120,000	
Less value of closing inventory (at marginal cost)	60,000		30,000		–	
Variable cost of sales		60,000		90,000		120,000
Contribution		40,000		60,000		80,000
Less fixed costs		45,000		45,000		45,000
Profit/(loss)		(5,000)		15,000		35,000

	10,000 Splashes		15,000 Splashes		20,000 Splashes	
	$	$	$	$	$	$
Profit (loss) per unit		$(0.50)		$1		$1.75
Contribution per unit		$4		$4		$4

The conclusions which may be drawn from this example are as follows.

(a) The **profit per unit varies** at differing levels of sales, because the average fixed overhead cost per unit changes with the volume of output and sales.

(b) The **contribution per unit is constant** at all levels of output and sales. Total contribution, which is the contribution per unit multiplied by the number of units sold, increases in direct proportion to the volume of sales.

(c) Since the **contribution per unit does not change**, the most effective way of calculating the expected profit at any level of output and sales would be as follows.

- First calculate the total contribution.
- Then deduct fixed costs as a period charge in order to find the profit.

(d) In our example the expected profit from the sale of 17,000 Splashes would be as follows.

	$
Total contribution (17,000 × $4)	68,000
Less fixed costs	45,000
Profit	23,000

- If total contribution **exceeds fixed costs**, a profit is made
- If total contribution **exactly equals fixed costs**, no profit or loss is made
- If total contribution is **less than fixed costs**, there will be a loss

Question

Marginal costing principles

Mill Stream makes two products, the Mill and the Stream. Information relating to each of these products for April 20X1 is as follows.

	Mill	Stream
Opening inventory	nil	nil
Production (units)	15,000	6,000
Sales (units)	10,000	5,000
Sales price per unit	$20	$30
Unit costs	$	$
Direct materials	8	14
Direct labour	4	2
Variable production overhead	2	1
Variable sales overhead	2	3
Fixed costs for the month	$	
Production costs	40,000	
Administration costs	15,000	
Sales and distribution costs	25,000	

Required

(a) Using marginal costing principles and the method in 2.1(d) above, calculate the profit in April 20X1.

(b) Calculate the profit if sales had been 15,000 units of Mill and 6,000 units of Stream.

(a)

	$
Contribution from Mills (unit contribution = $20 – $16 = $4 × 10,000)	40,000
Contribution from Streams (unit contribution = $30 – $20 = $10 × 5,000)	50,000
Total contribution	90,000
Fixed costs for the period	80,000
Profit	10,000

(b)   At a higher volume of sales, profit would be as follows.

	$
Contribution from sales of 15,000 Mills (× $4)	60,000
Contribution from sales of 6,000 Streams (× $10)	60,000
Total contribution	120,000
Less fixed costs	80,000
Profit	40,000

2.2 Profit or contribution information

The main advantage of **contribution information** (rather than profit information) is that it allows an easy calculation of profit if sales increase or decrease from a certain level. By comparing total contribution with fixed overheads, it is possible to determine whether profits or losses will be made at certain sales levels. **Profit information**, on the other hand, does not lend itself to easy manipulation but note how easy it was to calculate profits using contribution information in the question entitled *Marginal costing principles*. **Contribution information** is more useful for **decision making** than profit information, as we shall see when we go on to study decision making in Section F of this Study Text.

3 Marginal costing and absorption costing and the calculation of profit

3.1 Introduction

In **marginal costing**, fixed production costs are treated as **period costs** and are written off as they are incurred. In **absorption costing**, fixed production costs are absorbed into the cost of units and are carried forward in inventory to be charged against sales for the next period. Inventory values using absorption costing are therefore greater than those calculated using marginal costing.

Marginal costing as a cost accounting system is significantly different from absorption costing. It is an **alternative method** of accounting for costs and profit, which rejects the principles of absorbing fixed overheads into unit costs.

Marginal costing	Absorption costing
Closing inventories are valued at marginal production cost.	Closing inventories are valued at full production cost.
Fixed costs are period costs.	Fixed costs are absorbed into unit costs.
Cost of sales does not include a share of fixed overheads.	Cost of sales does include a share of fixed overheads (see note below).

Note. The share of fixed overheads included in cost of sales are from the previous period (in opening inventory values). Some of the fixed overheads from the current period will be excluded by being carried forward in closing inventory values.

In **marginal costing**, it is necessary to identify the following.

- Variable costs
- Contribution
- Fixed costs

In **absorption costing** (sometimes known as **full costing**), it is not necessary to distinguish variable costs from fixed costs.

3.2 Example: Marginal and absorption costing compared

The following example will be used to lead you through the various steps in calculating marginal and absorption costing profits, and will highlight the differences between the two techniques.

Big Woof Inc manufactures a single product, the Bark, details of which are as follows.

Per unit	$
Selling price	180.00
Direct materials	40.00
Direct labour	16.00
Variable overheads	10.00

Annual fixed production overheads are budgeted to be $1.6 million and Big Woof expects to produce 1,280,000 units of the Bark each year. Overheads are absorbed on a per unit basis. Actual overheads are $1.6 million for the year.

Budgeted fixed selling costs are $320,000.

Actual sales and production units for the first quarter of 20X8 are given below.

	January – March
Sales	240,000
Production	280,000

There is no opening inventory at the beginning of January.

Prepare income statements for the quarter, using

    (i)   marginal costing   (ii)   absorption costing

Solution

Step 1 Calculate the overhead absorption rate per unit

Remember that overhead absorption rate is based only on budgeted figures.

Overhead absorption rate = $\dfrac{\text{Budgeted fixed overheads}}{\text{Budgeted units}}$

Also be careful with your calculations. You are dealing with a three month period but the figures in the question are for a whole year. You will have to convert these to quarterly figures.

Budgeted overheads (quarterly) = $1.6 million / 4 = $400,000
Budgeted production (quarterly) = 1,280,000 / 4 = 320,000 units

Overhead absorption rate per unit = $400,000 / 320,000 = $1.25 per unit

Step 2 Calculate total cost per unit

Total cost per unit (absorption costing) = Variable cost + fixed production cost
                                      = (40 + 16 + 10) + 1.25
                                        = $67.25

Total cost per unit (marginal costing) = Variable cost per unit = $66

Step 3 Calculate closing inventory in units

Closing inventory = Opening inventory + production – sales
Closing inventory = 0 + 280,000 – 240,000 = 40,000 units

Step 4 Calculate under/over absorption of overheads

This is based on the difference between actual production and budgeted production.

Actual production = 280,000 units
Budgeted production = 320,000 units (see step 1 above)
Under-production = 40,000 units

As Big Woof produced 40,000 fewer units than expected, there will be an **under-absorption** of overheads of 40,000 x $1.25 (see step 1 above) = $50,000. This will be added to production costs in the income statement.

Step 5 Produce income statements

	Marginal costing		Absorption costing	
	$000	$000	$000	$000
Sales (240,000 x $180)		43,200		43,200
Less Cost of Sales				
Opening inventory	0		0	
Add Production cost				
280,000 x $66	18,480			
280,000 x $67.25			18,830	
Less Closing inventory				
40,000 x $66	(2,640)			
40,000 x $67.25			(2,690)	
		(15,840)	16,140	
Add Under absorbed O/H			50	
				(16,190)
Contribution		27,360		
Gross profit				27,010
Less				
Fixed production O/H	400		Nil	
Fixed selling O/H	320		320	
		(720)		(320)
Net profit		26,640		26,690

3.3 No changes in inventory

You will notice from the above calculations that there are **differences** between marginal and absorption costing profits. Before we go on to reconcile the profits, how would the profits for the two different techniques differ if there were **no changes** between opening and closing inventory (that is, if production = sales)?

For the first quarter we will now assume that sales were 280,000 units.

	Marginal costing		Absorption costing	
	$000	$000	$000	$000
Sales (240,000 x $180)		50,400		50,400
Less Cost of Sales				
Opening inventory	0			
Add Production cost				
280,000 x $66	18,480			
280,000 x $67.25			18,830	
Less Closing inventory	Nil		Nil	
		(18,480)	18,830	
Add Under absorbed O/H			50	
				(18,880)
Contribution		31,920		
Gross profit				31,520
Less				
Fixed production O/H	400			
Fixed selling O/H	320		320	
		(720)		(320)
Net profit		31,200		31,200

You will notice that there are now no differences between the two profits. The difference in profits is due to changes in inventory levels during the period.

Question

The overhead absorption rate for product X is $10 per machine hour. Each unit of product X requires five machine hours. Inventory of product X on 1.1.X1 was 150 units and on 31.12.X1 it was 100 units. What is the difference in profit between results reported using absorption costing and results reported using marginal costing?

A   The absorption costing profit would be $2,500 less
B   The absorption costing profit would be $2,500 greater
C   The absorption costing profit would be $5,000 less
D   The absorption costing profit would be $5,000 greater

Answer

Difference in profit = **change** in inventory levels × fixed overhead absorption per unit = (150 – 100) × $10 × 5 = $2,500 **lower** profit, because inventory levels **decreased**. The correct answer is therefore option A.

The key is the change in the volume of inventory. Inventory levels have **decreased** therefore absorption costing will report a **lower** profit. This eliminates options B and D.

Option C is incorrect because it is based on the closing inventory only (100 units × $10 × 5 hours).

4 Reconciling profits

4.1 Introduction

Reported profit figures using marginal costing or absorption costing will differ if there is any change in the level of inventories in the period. If production is equal to sales, there will be no difference in calculated profits using the costing methods.

The difference in profits reported under the two costing systems is due to the different inventory valuation methods used.

If inventory levels increase between the beginning and end of a period, absorption costing will report the higher profit. This is because some of the fixed production overhead incurred during the period will be carried forward in closing inventory (which reduces cost of sales) to be set against sales revenue in the following period instead of being written off in full against profit in the period concerned.

If inventory levels decrease, absorption costing will report the lower profit because as well as the fixed overhead incurred, fixed production overhead which had been carried forward in opening inventory is released and is also included in cost of sales.

4.2 Example: Reconciling profits

The profits reported under absorption costing and marginal costing for January – March in the Big Woof question above can be reconciled as follows.

	$
Marginal costing profit	26,640
Adjust for fixed overhead included in inventory:	
Inventory increase of 40,000 units × $1.25	50,000
Absorption costing profit	76,640

4.3 Reconciling profits – a shortcut

A quick way to establish the difference in profits without going through the whole process of drawing up the income statements is as follows.

Difference in profits = change in inventory level x overhead absorption rate per unit

If inventory levels have **gone up** (that is, closing inventory > opening inventory) then **absorption costing** profit will be **greater** than **marginal costing** profit.

If inventory levels have **gone down** (that is, closing inventory < opening inventory) then **absorption costing** profit will be **less** than **marginal costing** profit.

In the Big Woof example above

Change in inventory = 40,000 units (an increase)

Overhead absorption rate = $1.25 per unit

We would expect absorption costing profit to be **greater** than marginal costing profit by 40,000 x $1.25 = **$50,000**. If you check back to the answer, you will find that this is the case.

Question	Absorption costing profit

When opening inventories were 8,500 litres and closing inventories 6,750 litres, a firm had a profit of $62,100 using marginal costing.

Assuming that the fixed overhead absorption rate was $3 per litre, what would be the profit using absorption costing?

A $41,850	B $56,850	C $67,350	D $82,350

Difference in profit = (8,500 – 6,750) × $3 = $5,250

Absorption costing profit = $62,100 – $5,250 = $56,850

The correct answer is B.

Since inventory levels reduced, the absorption costing profit will be lower than the marginal costing profit. You can therefore eliminate options C and D.

Exam focus point

The effect on profit of using the two different costing methods can be confusing. You *must* get it straight in your mind before the examination. Remember that if opening inventory values are greater than closing inventory values, marginal costing shows the greater profit.

5 Marginal costing versus absorption costing

FAST FORWARD

Absorption costing is most often used for routine profit reporting and must be used for financial accounting purposes. **Marginal costing** provides better management information for planning and decision making. There are a number of arguments both for and against each of the costing systems.

Exam focus point

In your examination you may be asked to calculate the profit for an accounting period using either of the two methods of costing.

The following diagram summarises the arguments in favour of both marginal and absorption costing.

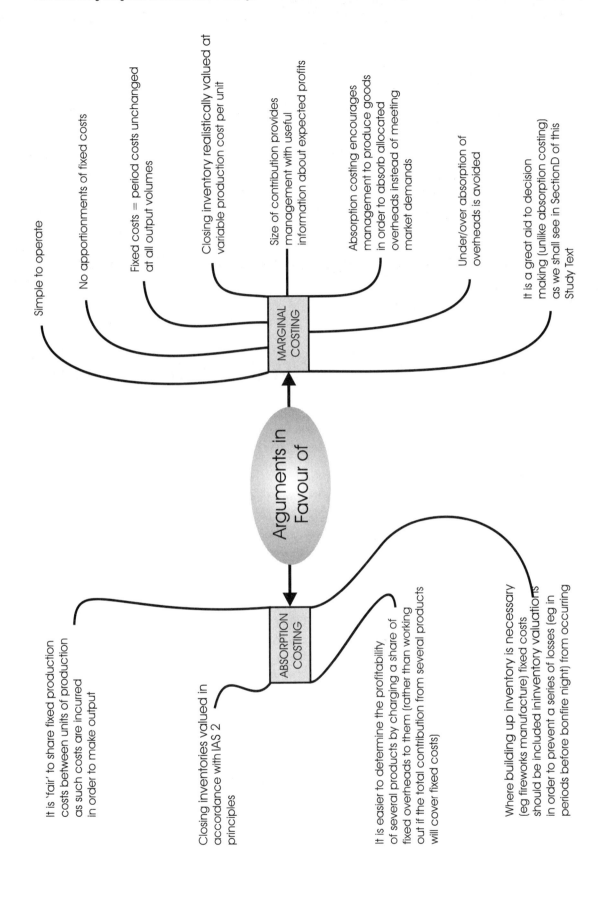

Marginal costing:

- Simple to operate
- No apportionments of fixed costs
- Fixed costs = period costs unchanged at all output volumes
- Closing inventory realistically valued at variable production cost per unit
- Size of contribution provides management with useful information about expected profits
- Absorption costing encourages management to produce goods in order to absorb allocated overheads instead of meeting market demands
- Under/over absorption of overheads is avoided
- It is a great aid to decision making (unlike absorption costing) as we shall see in SectionD of this Study Text

Absorption costing:

- It is 'fair' to share fixed production costs between units of production as such costs are incured in order to make output
- Closing inventories valued in accordance with IAS 2 principles
- It is easier to determine the profitability of several products by charging a share of fixed overheads to them (rather than working out if the total contribution from several products will cover fixed costs)
- Where building up inventory is necessary (eg fireworks manufacture) fixed costs should be included ininventory valuations in order to prevent a series of losses (eg in periods before bonfire night) from occurring

Chapter roundup

- **Marginal cost** is the variable cost of one unit of product or service.

- **Contribution** is an important measure in marginal costing, and it is calculated as the difference between sales value and marginal or variable cost of sales.

- In **marginal costing**, fixed production costs are treated as **period costs** and are written off as they are incurred. In **absorption costing**, fixed production costs are absorbed into the cost of units and are carried forward in inventory to be charged against sales for the next period. Inventory values using absorption costing are therefore greater than those calculated using marginal costing.

- **Reported profit figures using marginal costing or absorption costing will differ if there is any change in the level of inventories in the period**. If production is equal to sales, there will be no difference in calculated profits using these costing methods.

- In your examination you may be asked to calculate the profit for an accounting period using either of the two methods of accounting. **Absorption costing** is most often used for routine profit reporting and must be used for financial accounting purposes. **Marginal costing** provides better management information for planning and decision making. There are a number of arguments both for and against each of the costing systems.

Quick quiz

1   What is marginal costing?

2   What is a period cost in marginal costing?

3   Sales value – marginal cost of sales = ...

4   What is a breakeven point?

5   Marginal costing and absorption costing are different techniques for assessing profit in a period. If there are changes in inventory during a period, marginal costing and absorption costing give different results for profit obtained.

   Which of the following statements are true?

   I   If inventory levels increase, marginal costing will report the higher profit.
   II   If inventory levels decrease, marginal costing will report the lower profit.
   III   If inventory levels decrease, marginal costing will report the higher profit.
   IV   If the opening and closing inventory volumes are the same, marginal costing and absorption costing will give the same profit figure.

   A   All of the above   C   I and IV
   B   I, II and IV   D   III and IV

6   Which of the following are arguments in favour of marginal costing?

   (a)   Closing stock (inventory) is valued in accordance with IAS 2.
   (b)   It is simple to operate.
   (c)   There is no under or over absorption of overheads.
   (d)   Fixed costs are the same regardless of activity levels.
   (e)   The information from this costing method may be used for decision making.

Answers to quick quiz

1   Marginal costing is an alternative method of costing to absorption costing. In marginal costing, only variable costs are charged as a cost of sale and a contribution is calculated (sales revenue – variable cost of sales).

2   A fixed cost

3   Contribution

4   The point at which total contribution exactly equals fixed costs (no profit or loss is made)

5   D

6   (b), (c), (d), (e)

Now try the questions below from the Exam Question Bank

Number	Level	Marks	Time
Q9	MCQ/OTQ	n/a	n/a

Process costing

Topic list	Syllabus reference
1 The basics of process costing	D6 (a), (b), (c)
2 Losses in process costing	D6 (d), (e)
3 Losses with scrap value	D6 (e)
4 Losses with a disposal cost	D6 (i)
5 Valuing closing work in progress	D6 (f), (h)
6 Valuing opening work in progress: FIFO method	D6 (g)
7 Valuing opening work in progress: weighted average cost method	D6 (g)

Introduction

In this chapter we will consider **process costing**. The chapter will consider the topic from basics, looking at how to account for the most simple of processes. We then move on to how to account for any **losses** which might occur, as well as what to do with any **scrapped units** which are sold. We also consider how to deal with any **closing work in progress** and then look at two methods of valuing **opening work in progress**. Valuation of both opening and closing work in progress hinges on the concept of **equivalent units**, which will be explained in detail.

Study guide

		Intellectual level
D6	**Process costing**	
(a)	Describe the characteristics of process costing	1
(b)	Describe situations where the use of process costing would be appropriate	1
(c)	Calculate the cost per unit of process outputs	1
(d)	Explain the concepts of 'normal and abnormal' losses and 'abnormal' gains	1
(e)	Prepare process accounts, involving normal and abnormal losses and abnormal gains	1
(f)	Calculate and explain the concept of equivalent units	1
(g)	Apportion process costs between work remaining in process and transfers out of a process using the weighted average and FIFO methods	2
(h)	Prepare process accounts in situations where work remains incomplete	2
(i)	Prepare process accounts where losses and gains are identified at different stages of the process	1

Note. Situations involving work in process **and** losses in the same process are excluded.

Exam guide

Expect several questions on process costing. The pilot paper has four questions on this topic, and the examiner has stated that this is a good guide to the weighting of exam question topics in the exams for 2008-2009. The questions are shorter than the examples and questions in this chapter, but if you have worked through some long questions you will have covered whatever can come up in a short question.

1 The basics of process costing

1.1 Introduction to process costing

FAST FORWARD

> **Process costing** is a costing method used where it is not possible to identify separate units of production, or jobs, usually because of the continuous nature of the production processes involved.

It is common to identify process costing with **continuous production** such as the following.

- Oil refining
- Paper
- Foods and drinks
- Chemicals

Process costing may also be associated with the continuous production of large volumes of low-cost items, such as **cans** or **tins**.

1.2 Features of process costing

(a) The **output** of one process becomes the **input** to the next until the finished product is made in the final process.

(b) The continuous nature of production in many processes means that there will usually be **closing work in progress which must be valued**. In process costing it is not possible to build up cost records of the cost per unit of output or the cost per unit of closing inventory because production in progress is an **indistinguishable homogeneous mass**.

(c) There is often a **loss in process** due to spoilage, wastage, evaporation and so on.

(d) Output from production may be a single product, but there may also be a **by-product** (or by-products) and/or **joint products**.

The aim of this chapter is to describe how cost accountants keep a set of accounts to record the costs of production in a processing industry. The aim of the set of accounts is to derive a cost, or valuation, for output and closing inventory.

1.3 Process accounts

Where a series of separate processes is required to manufacture the finished product, the output of one process becomes the input to the next until the final output is made in the final process. If two processes are required the accounts would look like this.

PROCESS 1 ACCOUNT

	Units	$		Units	$
Direct materials	1,000	50,000	Output to process 2	1,000	90,000
Direct labour		20,000			
Production overhead		20,000			
	1,000	90,000		1,000	90,000

PROCESS 2 ACCOUNT

	Units	$		Units	$
Materials from process 1	1,000	90,000	Output to finished goods	1,000	150,000
Added materials		30,000			
Direct labour		15,000			
Production overhead		15,000			
	1,000	150,000		1,000	150,000

Note that direct labour and production overhead may be treated together in an examination question as **conversion cost**.

Added materials, labour and overhead in process 2 are added gradually throughout the process. Materials from process 1, in contrast, will often be introduced in full at the start of process 2.

The 'units' columns in the process accounts are for **memorandum purposes** only and help you to ensure that you do not miss out any entries.

1.4 Framework for dealing with process costing

FAST FORWARD

Process costing is centred around **four key steps**. The exact work done at each step will depend on whether there are normal losses, scrap, opening and closing work in progress and so on.

Step 1   Determine output and losses
Step 2   Calculate cost per unit of output, losses and WIP
Step 3   Calculate total cost of output, losses and WIP
Step 4   Complete accounts

Let's look at these steps in more detail

Step 1   **Determine output and losses.** This step involves the following.
- Determining expected output
- Calculating normal loss and abnormal loss and gain
- Calculating equivalent units if there is closing or opening work in progress

Step 2   **Calculate cost per unit of output, losses and WIP.** This step involves calculating cost per unit or cost per equivalent unit.

Step 3   **Calculate total cost of output, losses and WIP**. In some examples this will be straightforward; however in cases where there is closing and/or opening work-in-progress a **statement of evaluation** will have to be prepared.

Step 4   **Complete accounts**. This step involves the following.
- Completing the process account
- Writing up the other accounts required by the question

Exam focus point

In the exam you will only get 2-mark questions, so you will only have to do the equivalent of Step 1, 2 and/or 3. However, you will feel much more confident if you understand all the steps.

2 Losses in process costing

2.1 Introduction

Losses may occur in process. If a certain level of loss is expected, this is known as **normal loss**. If losses are greater than expected, the extra loss is **abnormal loss**. If losses are less than expected, the difference is known as **abnormal gain**.

Key terms

Normal loss is the loss expected during a process. It is not given a cost.

Abnormal loss is the extra loss resulting when actual loss is greater than normal or expected loss, and it is given a cost.

Abnormal gain is the gain resulting when actual loss is less than the normal or expected loss, and it is given a 'negative cost'.

Since normal loss is not given a cost, the cost of producing these units is borne by the 'good' units of output.

Abnormal loss and gain units are valued at the same unit rate as 'good' units. Abnormal events do not therefore affect the cost of good production. Their costs are **analysed separately** in an **abnormal loss or abnormal gain account**.

2.2 Example: abnormal losses and gains

Suppose that input to a process is 1,000 units at a cost of $4,500. Normal loss is 10% and there are no opening or closing stocks. Determine the accounting entries for the cost of output and the cost of the loss if actual output were as follows.

(a)   860 units (so that actual loss is 140 units)
(b)   920 units (so that actual loss is 80 units)

Solution

Before we demonstrate the use of the 'four-step framework' we will summarise the way that the losses are dealt with.

(a)   Normal loss is given no share of cost.

(b)   The cost of output is therefore based on the **expected** units of output, which in our example amount to 90% of 1,000 = 900 units.

(c)   Abnormal loss is given a cost, which is written off to the profit and loss account via an abnormal loss/gain account.

(d)   Abnormal gain is treated in the same way, except that being a gain rather than a loss, it appears as a **debit** entry in the process account (whereas a loss appears as a **credit** entry in this account).

(a)   **Output is 860 units**

Step 1   Determine output and losses

If actual output is 860 units and the actual loss is 140 units:

	Units
Actual loss	140
Normal loss (10% of 1,000)	100
Abnormal loss	40

Step 2   Calculate cost per unit of output and losses

The cost per unit of output and the cost per unit of abnormal loss are based on expected output.

$$\frac{\text{Costs incurred}}{\text{Expected output}} = \frac{\$4,500}{900 \text{ units}} = \$5 \text{ per unit}$$

Step 3   Calculate total cost of output and losses

Normal loss is not assigned any cost.

	$
Cost of output (860 × $5)	4,300
Normal loss	0
Abnormal loss (40 × $5)	200
	4,500

Step 4   Complete accounts

PROCESS ACCOUNT

	Units	$		Units		$
Cost incurred	1,000	4,500	Normal loss	100		0
			Output (finished			
			goods a/c)	860	(× $5)	4,300
			Abnormal loss	40	(× $5)	200
	1,000	4,500		1,000		4,500

ABNORMAL LOSS ACCOUNT

	Units	$		Units	$
Process a/c	40	200	Income statement	40	200

(b)   **Output is 920 units**

Step 1   Determine output and losses

If actual output is 920 units and the actual loss is 80 units:

	Units
Actual loss	80
Normal loss (10% of 1,000)	100
Abnormal gain	20

Step 2   Calculate cost per unit of output and losses

The cost per unit of output and the cost per unit of abnormal gain are based on **expected** output.

$$\frac{\text{Costs incurred}}{\text{Expected output}} = \frac{\$4,500}{900 \text{ units}} = \$5 \text{ per unit}$$

(Whether there is abnormal loss or gain does not affect the valuation of units of output. The figure of $5 per unit is exactly the same as in the previous paragraph, when there were 40 units of abnormal loss.)

Step 3   Calculate total cost of output and losses

	$
Cost of output (920 × $5)	4,600
Normal loss	0
Abnormal gain (20 × $5)	(100)
	4,500

Step 4 Complete accounts

PROCESS ACCOUNT

	Units	$		Units	$
Cost incurred	1,000	4,500	Normal loss	100	0
Abnormal gain a/c	20 (x $5)	100	Output	920 (x $5)	4,600
			(finished goods a/c)		
	1,020	4,600		1,020	4,600

ABNORMAL GAIN

	Units	$		Units	$
Income statement	20	100	Process a/c	20	100

Question
Abnormal losses and gains

Shiny Inc has two processes, Y and Z. There is an expected loss of 5% of input in process Y and 7% of input in process Z. Activity during a four week period is as follows.

	Y	Z
Material input (kg)	20,000	28,000
Output (kg)	18,500	26,100

Is there an abnormal gain or abnormal loss for each process?

	Y	Z
A	Abnormal loss	Abnormal loss
B	Abnormal gain	Abnormal loss
C	Abnormal loss	Abnormal gain
D	Abnormal gain	Abnormal gain

Answer

The correct answer is C.

	Y	Z
Input (kg)	20,000	28,000
Normal loss (kg)	1,000 (5% of 20,000)	1,960 (7% of 28,000)
Expected output	19,000	26,040
Actual output	18,500	26,100
Abnormal loss/gain	500 (loss)	60 (gain)

2.3 Example: Abnormal losses and gains again

During a four-week period, period 3, costs of input to a process were $29,070. Input was 1,000 units, output was 850 units and normal loss is 10%.

During the next period, period 4, costs of input were again $29,070. Input was again 1,000 units, but output was 950 units.

There were no units of opening or closing inventory.

Required

Prepare the process account and abnormal loss or gain account for each period.

Solution

Step 1   Determine output and losses

Period 3

	Units
Actual output	850
Normal loss (10% × 1,000)	100
Abnormal loss	50
Input	1,000

Period 4

	Units
Actual output	950
Normal loss (10% × 1,000)	100
Abnormal gain	(50)
Input	1,000

Step 2   **Calculate cost per unit of output and losses**

For each period the cost per unit is based on expected output.

$$\frac{\text{Cost of input}}{\text{Expected units of output}} = \frac{\$29{,}070}{900} = \$32.30 \text{ per unit}$$

Step 3   **Calculate total cost of output and losses**

Period 3

	$
Cost of output (850 × $32.30)	27,455
Normal loss	0
Abnormal loss (50 × $32.30)	1,615
	29,070

Period 4

	$
Cost of output (950 × $32.30)	30,685
Normal loss	0
Abnormal gain (50 × $32.30)	1,615
	29,070

Step 4   **Complete accounts**

PROCESS ACCOUNT

	Units	$		Units	$
Period 3					
Cost of input	1,000	29,070	Normal loss	100	0
			Finished goods a/c	850	27,455
			(× $32.30)		
			Abnormal loss a/c	50	1,615
			(× $32.30)		
	1,000	29,070		1,000	29,070
Period 4					
Cost of input	1,000	29,070	Normal loss	100	0
Abnormal gain a/c	50	1,615	Finished goods a/c	950	30,685
(× $32.30)			(× $32.30)		
	1,050	30,685		1,050	30,685

ABNORMAL LOSS OR GAIN ACCOUNT

	$		$
Period 3		Period 4	
Abnormal loss in process a/c	1,615	Abnormal gain in process a/c	1,615

A nil balance on this account will be carried forward into period 5.

If there is a closing balance in the abnormal loss or gain account when the profit for the period is calculated, this balance is taken to the income statement: an abnormal gain will be a credit to the income statement and an abnormal loss will be a debit to the income statement.

Question
Process account

3,000 units of material are input to a process. Process costs are as follows.

Material	$11,700
Conversion costs	$6,300

Output is 2,000 units. Normal loss is 20% of input.

Required

Prepare a process account and the appropriate abnormal loss/gain account.

Answer

Step 1   **Determine output and losses**

We are told that output is 2,000 units.
Normal loss = 20% × 3,000 = 600 units
Abnormal loss = (3,000 − 600) − 2,000 = 400 units

Step 2   **Calculate cost per unit of output and losses**

$$\text{Cost per unit} = \frac{\$(11{,}700 + 6{,}300)}{2{,}400} = \$7.50$$

Step 3   **Calculate total cost of output and losses**

		$
Output	(2,000 × $7.50)	15,000
Normal loss		0
Abnormal loss	(400 × $7.50)	3,000
		18,000

Step 4   **Complete accounts**

PROCESS ACCOUNT

	Units	$		Units	$
Material	3,000	11,700	Output	2,000	15,000
Conversion costs		6,300	Normal loss	600	
			Abnormal loss	400	3,000
	3,000	18,000		3,000	18,000

ABNORMAL LOSS ACCOUNT

	$		$
Process a/c	3,000	Income statement	3,000

Charlton Co manufactures a product in a single process operation. Normal loss is 10% of input. Loss occurs at the end of the process. Data for June are as follows.

Opening and closing inventories of work in progress	Nil
Cost of input materials (3,300 units)	$59,100
Direct labour and production overhead	$30,000
Output to finished goods	2,750 units

The full cost of finished output in June was

A $74,250   B $81,000   C $82,500   D $89,100

Answer

Step 1 **Determine output and losses**

	Units
Actual output	2,750
Normal loss (10% × 3,300)	330
Abnormal loss	220
	3,300

Step 2 **Calculate cost per unit of output and losses**

$$\frac{\text{Cost of input}}{\text{Expected units of output}} = \frac{\$89,100}{3,300 - 330} = \$30 \text{ per unit}$$

Step 3 **Calculate total cost of output and losses**

	$
Cost of output (2,750 × $30)	82,500 **(The correct answer is C)**
Normal loss	0
Abnormal loss (220 × $30)	6,600
	89,100

If you were reduced to making a calculated guess, you could have eliminated option D. This is simply the total input cost, with no attempt to apportion some of the cost to the abnormal loss.

Option A is incorrect because it results from allocating a full unit cost to the normal loss: remember that normal loss does not carry any of the process cost.

Option B is incorrect because it results from calculating a 10% normal loss based on *output* of 2,750 units (275 units normal loss), rather than on *input* of 3,300 units.

3 Losses with scrap value

Key term

> **Scrap** is 'Discarded material having some value.'

Loss or spoilage may have scrap value.

FORWARD

- The **scrap value** of normal loss is usually deducted from the cost of materials.
- The **scrap value** of abnormal loss (or abnormal gain) is usually set off against its cost, in an abnormal loss (abnormal gain) account.

As the questions that follow will show, the three steps to remember are these.

Step 1 Separate the **scrap value** of **normal loss** from the **scrap value** of **abnormal loss** or **gain**.

Step 2 In effect, subtract the scrap value of normal loss from the cost of the process, by crediting it to the process account (as a 'value' for normal loss).

Step 3 *Either* subtract the value of abnormal loss scrap from the cost of abnormal loss, by crediting the abnormal loss account.

or subtract the cost of the abnormal gain scrap from the value of abnormal gain, by debiting the abnormal gain account.

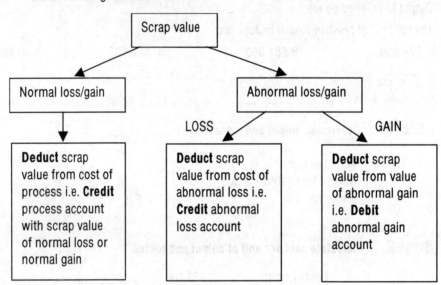

 Question | **Losses and scrap**

3,000 units of material are input to a process. Process costs are as follows.

Material	$11,700
Conversion costs	$6,300

Output is 2,000 units. Normal loss is 20% of input.

The units of loss could be sold for $1 each. Prepare appropriate accounts.

Answer

Step 1 **Determine output and losses**

Input	3,000 units
Normal loss (20% of 3,000)	600 units
Expected output	2,400 units
Actual output	2,000 units
Abnormal loss	400 units

Step 2 **Calculate cost per unit of output and losses**

	$
Scrap value of normal loss	600
Scrap value of abnormal loss	400
Total scrap (1,000 units × $1)	1,000

$$\text{Cost per expected unit} = \frac{\$((11,700 - 600) + 6,300)}{2,400} = \$7.25$$

Step 3   Calculate total cost of output and losses

		$
Output	(2,000 × $7.25)	14,500
Normal loss	(600 × $1.00)	600
Abnormal loss	(400 × $7.25)	2,900
		18,000

Step 4   Complete accounts

PROCESS ACCOUNT

	Units	$		Units	$
Material	3,000	11,700	Output	2,000	14,500
Conversion costs		6,300	Normal loss	600	600
			Abnormal loss	400	2,900
	3,000	18,000		3,000	18,000

ABNORMAL LOSS ACCOUNT

	$		$
Process a/c	2,900	Scrap a/c	400
		P&L a/c	2,500
	2,900		2,900

SCRAP ACCOUNT

	$		$
Normal loss	600	Cash	1,000
Abnormal loss	400		
	1,000		1,000

Question

Two processes, losses and scrap

JJ has a factory which operates two production processes, cutting and pasting. Normal loss in each process is 10%. Scrapped units out of the cutting process sell for $3 per unit whereas scrapped units out of the pasting process sell for $5. Output from the cutting process is transferred to the pasting process: output from the pasting process is finished output ready for sale.

Relevant information about costs for control period 7 are as follows.

	Cutting process		Pasting process	
	Units	$	Units	$
Input materials	18,000	54,000		
Transferred to pasting process	16,000			
Materials from cutting process			16,000	
Added materials			14,000	70,000
Labour and overheads		32,400		135,000
Output to finished goods			28,000	

Required

Prepare accounts for the cutting process, the pasting process, abnormal loss, abnormal gain and scrap.

Answer

(a) Cutting process

Step 1   Determine output and losses

The normal loss is 10% of 18,000 units = 1,800 units, and the actual loss is (18,000 − 16,000) = 2,000 units. This means that there is abnormal loss of 200 units.

Actual output	16,000 units
Abnormal loss	200 units
Expected output (90% of 18,000)	16,200 units

Step 2 **Calculate cost per unit of output and losses**

(i) The total value of scrap is 2,000 units at $3 per unit = $6,000. We must split this between the scrap value of normal loss and the scrap value of abnormal loss.

	$
Normal loss (1,800 × $3)	5,400
Abnormal loss (200 × $3)	600
Total scrap (2,000 units × $3)	6,000

(ii) The scrap value of normal loss is first deducted from the materials cost in the process, in order to calculate the output cost per unit and then credited to the process account as a 'value' for normal loss. The cost per unit in the cutting process is calculated as follows.

	Total cost		Cost per expected unit of output
	$		$
Materials	54,000		
Less normal loss scrap value*	5,400		
	48,600	(÷ 16,200)	3.00
Labour and overhead	32,400	(÷ 16,200)	2.00
Total	81,000	(÷ 16,200)	5.00

* It is usual to set this scrap value of normal loss against the cost of materials.

Step 3 **Calculate total cost of output and losses**

		$
Output	(16,000 units × $5)	80,000
Normal loss	(1,800 units × $3)	5,400
Abnormal loss	(200 units × $5)	1,000
		86,400

Step 4 **Complete accounts**

PROCESS 1 ACCOUNT

	Units	$		Units	$
Materials	18,000	54,000	Output to pasting process *	16,000	80,000
Labour and			Normal loss (scrap a/c) **	1,800	5,400
overhead		32,400	Abnormal loss a/c *	200	1,000
	18,000	86,400		18,000	86,400

* At $5 per unit   ** At $3 per unit

(b) *Pasting process*

Step 1 **Determine output and losses**

The normal loss is 10% of the units processed = 10% of (16,000 + 14,000) = 3,000 units. The actual loss is (30,000 – 28,000) = 2,000 units, so that there is abnormal gain of 1,000 units. These are *deducted* from actual output to determine expected output.

	Units
Actual output	28,000
Abnormal gain	(1,000)
Expected output (90% of 30,000)	27,000

Step 2 **Calculate cost per unit of output and losses**

(i) The total value of scrap is 2,000 units at $5 per unit = $10,000. We must split this between the scrap value of normal loss and the scrap value of abnormal gain. Abnormal gain's scrap value is 'negative'.

			$
Normal loss scrap value	3,000 units × $5		15,000
Abnormal gain scrap value	1,000 units × $5		(5,000)
Scrap value of actual loss	2,000 units × $5		10,000

(ii) The scrap value of normal loss is first deducted from the cost of materials in the process, in order to calculate a cost per unit of output, and then credited to the process account as a 'value' for normal loss. The cost per unit in the pasting process is calculated as follows.

	Total cost		Cost per expected unit of output
	$		$
Materials:			
Transfer from cutting process	80,000		
Added in pasting process	70,000		
	150,000		
Less scrap value of normal loss	15,000		
	135,000	(÷ 27,000)	5
Labour and overhead	135,000	(÷ 27,000)	5
	270,000	(÷ 27,000)	10

Step 3 Calculate total cost of output and losses

		$
Output	(28,000 units × $10)	280,000
Normal loss	(3,000 units × $5)	15,000
		295,000
Abnormal gain	(1,000 units × $10)	(10,000)
		285,000

Step 4 Complete accounts

PASTING PROCESS ACCOUNT

	Units	$		Units	$
From cutting process	16,000	80,000	Finished output *	28,000	280,000
Added materials	14,000	70,000			
Labour and overhead		135,000	Normal loss	3,000	15,000
	30,000	285,000	(scrap a/c)		
Abnormal gain a/c	1,000*	10,000			
	31,000	295,000		31,000	295,000

* At $10 per unit

(c) and (d)

Abnormal loss and abnormal gain accounts

For each process, one or the other of these accounts will record three items.

(i) The cost/value of the abnormal loss/gain (corresponding entry to that in the process account).

(ii) The scrap value of the abnormal loss or gain, to set off against it.

(iii) A balancing figure, which is written to the income statement as an adjustment to the profit figure.

ABNORMAL LOSS ACCOUNT

	Units	$		$
Cutting process	200	1,000	Scrap a/c (scrap value of ab. loss)	600
			Income statement (balance)	400
		1,000		1,000

ABNORMAL GAIN ACCOUNT

	$		Units	$
Scrap a/c (scrap value of abnormal gain units)	5,000	Pasting process	1,000	10,000
Income statement (balance)	5,000			
	10,000			10,000

(e)   **Scrap account**

This is credited with the cash value of actual units scrapped. The other entries in the account should all be identifiable as corresponding entries to those in the process accounts, and abnormal loss and abnormal gain accounts.

SCRAP ACCOUNT

	$		$
Normal loss:		Cash:	
Cutting process (1,800 × $3)	5,400	Sale of cutting process scrap (2,000 × $3)	6,000
Pasting process (3,000 × $5)	15,000	Sale of pasting process scrap (2,000 × $5)	10,000
Abnormal loss a/c	600	Abnormal gain a/c	5,000
	21,000		21,000

FAST FORWARD

Abnormal losses and gains never affect the cost of good units of production. The scrap value of abnormal losses is **not** credited to the process account, and abnormal loss and gain units carry the same **full cost** as a good unit of production.

4 Losses with a disposal cost

4.1 Introduction

You must also be able to deal with losses which have a **disposal cost**.

The basic calculations required in such circumstances are as follows.

(a)   Increase the process costs by the cost of disposing of the units of normal loss and use the resulting cost per unit to value good output and abnormal loss/gain.

(b)   The normal loss is given no value in the process account.

(c)   Include the disposal costs of normal loss on the debit side of the process account.

(d)   Include the disposal costs of abnormal loss in the abnormal loss account and hence in the transfer of the cost of abnormal loss to the income statement.

4.2 Example: Losses with a disposal cost

Suppose that input to a process was 1,000 units at a cost of $4,500. Normal loss is 10% and there are no opening and closing inventories. Actual output was 860 units and loss units had to be disposed of at a cost of $0.90 per unit.

Normal loss = 10% × 1,000 = 100 units. ∴ Abnormal loss = 900 – 860 = 40 units

$$\text{Cost per unit} = \frac{\$4,500 + (100 \times \$0.90)}{900} = \$5.10$$

The relevant accounts would be as follows.

PROCESS ACCOUNT

	Units	$		Units	$
Cost of input	1,000	4,500	Output	860	4,386
Disposal cost of			Normal loss	100	
normal loss		90	Abnormal loss	40	204
	1,000	4,590		1,000	4,590

ABNORMAL LOSS ACCOUNT

	$		$
Process a/c	204	Income statement	240
Disposal cost (40 × $0.90)	36		
	240		240

5 Valuing closing work in progress

5.1 Introduction

FAST FORWARD

When units are partly completed at the end of a period (and hence there is closing work in progress), it is necessary to calculate the **equivalent units of production** in order to determine the cost of a completed unit.

Exam focus point

The Study Guide states that losses and work in progress in the same process will not be examined.

In the examples we have looked at so far we have assumed that opening and closing inventories of work in process have been nil. We must now look at more realistic examples and consider how to allocate the costs incurred in a period between completed output (that is, finished units) and partly completed closing inventory.

Some examples will help to illustrate the problem, and the techniques used to share out (apportion) costs between finished output and closing inventories.

Suppose that we have the following account for Process 2 for period 9.

PROCESS ACCOUNT

	Units	$		Units	$
Materials	1,000	6,200	Finished goods	800	?
Labour and overhead		2,850	Closing WIP	200	?
	1,000	9,050		1,000	9,050

How do we value the finished goods and closing work in process?

With any form of process costing involving closing WIP, we have to apportion costs between output and closing WIP. To apportion costs 'fairly' we make use of the concept of **equivalent units of production**.

5.2 Equivalent units

Key term

Equivalent units are notional whole units which represent incomplete work, and which are used to apportion costs between work in process and completed output.

We will assume that in the example above the degree of completion is as follows.

(a) **Direct materials**. These are added in full at the start of processing, and so any closing WIP will have 100% of their direct material content. (This is not always the case in practice. Materials might be added gradually throughout the process, in which case closing inventory will only be a certain percentage complete as to material content. We will look at this later in the chapter.)

(b) **Direct labour and production overhead.** These are usually assumed to be incurred at an even rate through the production process, so that when we refer to a unit that is 50% complete, we mean that it is half complete for labour and overhead, although it might be 100% complete for materials.

Let us also assume that the closing WIP is 100% complete for materials and 25% complete for labour and overhead.

How would we now put a value to the finished output and the closing WIP?

In **Step 1** of our framework, we have been told what output and losses are. However we also need to calculate **equivalent units**.

STATEMENT OF EQUIVALENT UNITS

		Materials		Labour and overhead	
	Total units	Degree of completion	Equivalent units	Degree of completion	Equivalent units
Finished output	800	100%	800	100%	800
Closing WIP	200	100%	200	25%	50
	1,000		1,000		850

In **Step 2** the important figure is **average cost per equivalent unit**. This can be calculated as follows.

STATEMENT OF COSTS PER EQUIVALENT UNIT

	Materials	Labour and overhead
Costs incurred in the period	$6,200	$2,850
Equivalent units of work done	1,000	850
Cost per equivalent unit (approx)	$6.20	$3.3529

To calculate total costs for **Step 3**, we prepare a statement of evaluation to show how the costs should be apportioned between finished output and closing WIP.

STATEMENT OF EVALUATION

		Materials			Labour and overheads		
Item	Equivalent units	Cost per equivalent units $	Cost $	Equivalent units	Cost per equivalent units $	Cost $	Total cost $
Finished output	800	6.20	4,960	800	3.3529	2,682	7,642
Closing WIP	200	6.20	1,240	50	3.3529	168	1,408
	1,000		6,200	850		2,850	9,050

The process account (work in progress, or work in process account) would be shown as follows.

PROCESS ACCOUNT

	Units	$		Units	$
Materials	1,000	6,200	Finished goods	800	7,642
Labour overhead		2,850	Closing WIP	200	1,408
	1,000	9,050		1,000	9,050

Question

Equivalent units for closing WIP

Ally Inc has the following information available on Process 9.

PROCESS 9 ACCOUNT

		$			$
Input	10,000kg	59,150	Finished goods	8,000kg	52,000
			Closing WIP	2,000kg	7,150
		59,150			59,150

How many equivalent units were there for Closing WIP?

A   1,000   C   2,000
B   1,100

Answer

The correct answer is B.

This question requires you to **work backwards**. You can calculate the cost per unit using the Finished Goods figures.

$$\text{Cost per unit} = \frac{\text{Cost of finished goods}}{\text{Number of kg}} = \frac{52,000}{8,000} = \$6.50$$

If 2,000kg (Closing WIP figure) were fully complete total cost would be

2,000 × $6.50 = $13,000

Actual cost of Closing WIP = $7,150

$$\text{Degree of completion} = \frac{7,150}{13,000} = 55\%$$

Therefore equivalent units = 55% of 2,000 = 1,100kg

Question	Equivalent units

Ashley Inc operates a process costing system. The following details are available for Process 2.

Materials input at beginning of process	12,000 kg, costing $18,000
Labour and overheads added	$28,000

10,000kg were completed and transferred to the Finished Goods account. The remaining units were 60% complete with regard to labour and overheads. There were no losses in the period.

What is the value of Closing WIP in the process account?

A	$4,800	C	$7,667
B	$6,000	D	$8,000

Answer

The correct answer is D.

STATEMENT OF EQUIVALENT UNITS

		Material			Labour	
	Units completion	Degree of units	Equivalent	Units completion	Degree of units	Equivalent
Finished goods	10,000	100%	10,000	10,000	100%	10,000
Closing WIP	2,000	100%	2,000	2,000	60%	1,200
	12,000		12,000	12,000		11,200

COSTS PER EQUIVALENT UNIT

	Material	Labour
Total cost	$18,000	$28,000
Equivalent units	12,000	11,200
Cost per unit	$1.50	$2.50

Total cost per unit = $4.00

Value of Closing WIP = $4 × 2,000 = $8,000

5.3 Different rates of input

In many industries, materials, labour and overhead may be **added at different rates** during the course of production.

(a) Output from a previous process (for example the output from process 1 to process 2) may be introduced into the subsequent process all at once, so that closing inventory is 100% complete in respect of these materials.

(b) Further materials may be added gradually during the process, so that closing inventory is only partially complete in respect of these added materials.

(c) Labour and overhead may be 'added' at yet another different rate. When production overhead is absorbed on a labour hour basis, however, we should expect the degree of completion on overhead to be the same as the degree of completion on labour.

When this situation occurs, **equivalent units**, and a **cost per equivalent unit**, should be calculated separately for each type of material, and also for conversion costs.

5.4 Example: Equivalent units and different degrees of completion

Suppose that Columbine Co is a manufacturer of processed goods, and that results in process 2 for April 20X3 were as follows.

Opening inventory	nil
Material input from process 1	4,000 units

Costs of input:

	$
Material from process 1	6,000
Added materials in process 2	1,080
Conversion costs	1,720

Output is transferred into the next process, process 3.

Closing work in process amounted to 800 units, complete as to:

Process 1 material	100%
Added materials	50%
Conversion costs	30%

Required

Prepare the account for process 2 for April 20X3.

Solution

(a) STATEMENT OF EQUIVALENT UNITS (OF PRODUCTION IN THE PERIOD)

			Process 1 material		Added materials		Labour and overhead	
Input	*Output*	*Total*						
Units		Units	Units	%	Units	%	Units	%
4,000	Completed production	3,200	3,200	100	3,200	100	3,200	100
	Closing inventory	800	800	100	400	50	240	30
4,000		4,000	4,000		3,600		3,440	

Header spanning: *Equivalent units of production*

(b) STATEMENT OF COST (PER EQUIVALENT UNIT)

Input	*Cost*	*Equivalent production in units*	*Cost per unit*
	$		$
Process 1 material	6,000	4,000	1.50
Added materials	1,080	3,600	0.30
Labour and overhead	1,720	3,440	0.50
	8,800		2.30

STATEMENT OF EVALUATION (OF FINISHED WORK AND CLOSING INVENTORIES)

Production	Cost element	Number of equivalent units	Cost per equivalent unit $	Total $	Cost $
Completed production		3,200	2.30		7,360
Closing inventory:	process 1 material	800	1.50	1,200	
	added material	400	0.30	120	
	labour and overhead	240	0.50	120	
					1,440
					8,800

(d) PROCESS ACCOUNT

	Units	$		Units	$
Process 1 material	4,000	6,000	Process 3 a/c	3,200	7,360
Added material		1,080			
Conversion costs		1,720	Closing inventory c/f	800	1,440
	4,000	8,800		4,000	8,800

6 Valuing opening work in progress: FIFO method

6.1 Introduction

FAST FORWARD

Account can be taken of opening work in progress using either the **FIFO** method or the **weighted average cost method**.

Opening work in progress is partly complete at the beginning of a period and is valued at the cost incurred to date. In the example in Paragraph 4.4, closing work in progress of 800 units at the end of April 20X3 would be carried forward as opening inventory, value $1,440, at the beginning of May 20X3.

It therefore follows that the work required to complete units of opening inventory is 100% minus the work in progress done in the previous period. For example, if 100 units of opening inventory are 70% complete at the beginning of June 20X2, the equivalent units of production would be as follows.

Equivalent units in previous period	(May 20X2) (70%)	=	70
Equivalent units to complete work in current period	(June 20X2) (30%)	=	30
Total work done			100

The FIFO method of valuation deals with production on a first in, first out basis. The assumption is that the first units completed in any period are the units of opening inventory that were held at the beginning of the period.

6.2 Example: WIP and FIFO

Suppose that information relating to process 1 of a two-stage production process is as follows, for August 20X2.

Opening inventory 500 units: degree of completion	60%
Cost to date	$2,800

Costs incurred in August 20X2	$
Direct materials (2,500 units introduced)	13,200
Direct labour	6,600
Production overhead	6,600
	26,400

Closing inventory 300 units: degree of completion	80%

There was no loss in the process.

Required

Prepare the process 1 account for August 20X2.

Solution

As the term implies, first in, first out means that in August 20X2 the first units completed were the units of opening inventory.

| Opening inventories: | work done to date = | 60% |
| | plus work done in August 20X2 = | 40% |

The cost of the work done up to 1 August 20X2 is known to be $2,800, so that the cost of the units completed will be $2,800 plus the cost of completing the final 40% of the work on the units in August 20X2.

Once the opening inventory has been completed, all other finished output in August 20X2 will be work started as well as finished in the month.

	Units
Total output in August 20X2 *	2,700
Less opening inventory, completed first	500
Work started and finished in August 20X2	2,200

(* Opening inventory plus units introduced minus closing inventory = 500 + 2,500 – 300)

What we are doing here is taking the total output of 2,700 units, and saying that we must divide it into two parts as follows.

(a)   The opening inventory, which was first in and so must be first out.
(b)   The rest of the units, which were 100% worked in the period.

Dividing finished output into two parts in this way is a necessary feature of the FIFO valuation method.

Continuing the example, closing inventory of 300 units will be started in August 20X2, but not yet completed.

The total cost of output to process 2 during 20X2 will be as follows.

		$
Opening stock	cost brought forward	2,800 (60%)
	plus cost incurred during August 20X2,	
	to complete	x (40%)
		2,800 + x
Fully worked 2,200 units		y
Total cost of output to process 2, FIFO basis		2,800 + x + y

Equivalent units will again be used as the basis for apportioning **costs incurred during August 20X2**. Be sure that you understand the treatment of 'opening inventory units completed', and can relate the calculations to the principles of FIFO valuation.

Step 1   **Determine output and losses**

STATEMENT OF EQUIVALENT UNITS

	Total units		Equivalent units of production in August 20X2
Opening inventory units completed	500	(40%)	200
Fully worked units	2,200	(100%)	2,200
Output to process 2	2,700		2,400
Closing inventory	300	(80%)	240
	3,000		2,640

Step 2   Calculate cost per unit of output and losses

The cost per equivalent unit in August 20X2 can now be calculated.

STATEMENT OF COST PER EQUIVALENT UNIT

$$\frac{\text{Cost incurred}}{\text{Equivalent units}} = \frac{\$26,400}{2,640}$$

Cost per equivalent unit = $10

Step 3   Calculate total costs of output, losses and WIP

STATEMENT OF EVALUATION

	Equivalent units	Valuation $
Opening inventory, work done in August 20X2	200	2,000
Fully worked units	2,200	22,000
Closing inventory	240	2,400
	2,640	26,400

The total value of the completed opening inventory will be $2,800 (brought forward) plus $2,000 added in August before completion = $4,800.

Step 4   Complete accounts

PROCESS 1 ACCOUNT

	Units	$		Units	$
Opening inventory	500	2,800	Output to process 2:		
Direct materials	2,500	13,200	Opening inventory completed	500	4,800
Direct labour		6,600	Fully worked units	2,200	22,000
Production o'hd		6,600		2,700	26,800
			Closing inventory	300	2,400
	3,000	29,200		3,000	29,200

We now know that the value of x is $(4,800 – 2,800) = $2,000 and the value of y is $22,000.

Question   FIFO and equivalent units

Walter Inc uses the FIFO method of process costing. At the end of a four week period, the following information was available for process P.

Opening WIP	2,000 units (60% complete) costing $3,000 to date
Closing WIP	1,500 units (40% complete)
Transferred to next process	7,000 units

How many units were started and completed during the period?

A   5,500 units   C   8,400 units
B   7,000 units   D   9,000 units

Answer

The correct answer is A.

As we are dealing with the FIFO method, Opening WIP must be completed first.

Total output *	7,500 units
Less Opening WIP (completed first)	2,000 units
Units started and completed during the period	5,500 units

* Opening WIP + units introduced – Closing WIP

= 2,000 + 7,000 – 1,500
= 7,500 units

The following information relates to process 3 of a three-stage production process for the month of January 20X4.

Opening inventory

			$
300 units complete as to:			
materials from process 2		100%	4,400
added materials		90%	1,150
labour		80%	540
production overhead		80%	810
			6,900

In January 20X4, a further 1,800 units were transferred from process 2 at a valuation of $27,000. Added materials amounted to $6,600 and direct labour to $3,270. Production overhead is absorbed at the rate of 150% of direct labour cost. Closing inventory at 31 January 20X4 amounted to 450 units, complete as to:

process 2 materials	100%
added materials	60%
labour and overhead	50%

Required

Prepare the process 3 account for January 20X4 using FIFO valuation principles.

Answer

Step 1   Statement of equivalent units

	Total units	Process 2 materials		Added materials		Conversion costs
Opening inventory	300	0	(10%)	30	(20%)	60
Fully worked units *	1,350	1,350		1,350		1,350
Output to finished goods	1,650	1,350		1,380		1,410
Closing inventory	450	450	(60%)	270	(50%)	225
	2,100	1,800		1,650		1,635

* Transfers from process 2, minus closing inventory.

Step 2   Statement of costs per equivalent unit

	Total cost $	Equivalent units	Cost per equivalent unit $
Process 2 materials	27,000	1,800	15.00
Added materials	6,600	1,650	4.00
Direct labour	3,270	1,635	2.00
Production overhead (150% of $3,270)	4,905	1,635	3.00
			24.00

Step 3   Statement of evaluation

	Process 2 materials $		Additional materials $		Labour $		Overhead $	Total $
Opening inventory cost b/f	4,400		1,150		540		810	6,900
Added in Jan 20X4	–	(30x$4)	120	(60x$2)	120	(60x$3)	180	420
	4,400		1,270		660		990	7,320
Fully worked units	20,250		5,400		2,700		4,050	32,400
Output to finished Goods	24,650		6,670		3,360		5,040	39,720
Closing inventory (450x$15)	6,750	(270x$4)	1,080	(225x$2)	450	(225x$3)	675	8,955
	31,400		7,750		3,810		5,715	48,675

Complete accounts

PROCESS 3 ACCOUNT

	Units	$		Units	$
Opening inventory b/f	300	6,900	Finished goods a/c	1,650	39,720
Process 2 a/c	1,800	27,000			
Stores a/c		6,600			
Wages a/c		3,270			
Production o'hd a/c		4,905	Closing inventory c/f	450	8,955
	2,100	48,675		2,100	48,675

Question   **Equivalent units and FIFO**

Cheryl Inc operates a FIFO process costing system. The following information is available for last month.

Opening work in progress	2,000 units valued at	$3,000
Input	60,000 units costing	$30,000
Conversion costs		$20,000
Output	52,000 units	
Closing work in progress	10,000 units	

Opening work in progress was 100% complete with regard to input materials and 70% complete as to conversion. Closing work in progress was complete with regard to input materials and 80% complete as to conversion.

What was the number of equivalent units with regard to conversion costs?

A	44,000		C	51,400
B	50,600		D	52,000

Answer

The correct answer is B.

		Units
Opening work in progress	30% of 2,000 units still to be completed	600
Closing work in progress	80% of 10,000 units completed	8,000
Units started and completed	(Opening WIP + output – closing WIP) – opening WIP	42,000
		50,600

7 Valuing opening work in progress: weighted average cost method

7.1 Introduction

An alternative to FIFO is the **weighted average cost method of inventory valuation** which calculates a weighted average cost of units produced from both opening inventory and units introduced in the current period.

By this method **no distinction is made between units of opening inventory and new units introduced** to the process during the accounting period. The cost of opening inventory is added to costs incurred during the period, and completed units of opening inventory are each given a value of one full equivalent unit of production.

7.2 Example: Weighted average cost method

Magpie produces an item which is manufactured in two consecutive processes. Information relating to process 2 during September 20X3 is as follows.

Opening inventory 800 units

Degree of completion:		$
process 1 materials	100%	4,700
added materials	40%	600
conversion costs	30%	1,000
		6,300

During September 20X3, 3,000 units were transferred from process 1 at a valuation of $18,100. Added materials cost $9,600 and conversion costs were $11,800.

Closing inventory at 30 September 20X3 amounted to 1,000 units which were 100% complete with respect to process 1 materials and 60% complete with respect to added materials. Conversion cost work was 40% complete.

Magpie uses a weighted average cost system for the valuation of output and closing inventory.

Required

Prepare the process 2 account for September 20X3.

Solution

Step 1 Opening inventory units count as a full equivalent unit of production when the weighted average cost system is applied. Closing inventory equivalent units are assessed in the usual way.

STATEMENT OF EQUIVALENT UNITS

	Total units		Process 1 material		Added material		Conversion costs
Opening inventory	800	(100%)	800		800		800
Fully worked units*	2,000	(100%)	2,000		2,000		2,000
Output to finished goods	2,800		2,800		2,800		2,800
Closing inventory	1,000	(100%)	1,000	(60%)	600	(40%)	400
	3,800		3,800		3,400		3,200

(*3,000 units from process 1 minus closing inventory of 1,000 units)

Step 2 The cost of opening inventory is added to costs incurred in September 20X3, and a cost per equivalent unit is then calculated.

STATEMENT OF COSTS PER EQUIVALENT UNIT

	Process 1 material $	Added materials $	Conversion costs $
Opening inventory	4,700	600	1,000
Added in September 20X3	18,100	9,600	11,800
Total cost	22,800	10,200	12,800
Equivalent units	3,800 units	3,400 units	3,200 units
Cost per equivalent unit	$6	$3	$4

Step 3 STATEMENT OF EVALUATION

	Process 1 material $	Added materials $	Conversion costs $	Total cost $
Output to finished goods (2,800 units)	16,800	8,400	11,200	36,400
Closing inventory	6,000	1,800	1,600	9,400
				45,800

Step 4 PROCESS 2 ACCOUNT

	Units	$		Units	$
Opening inventory b/f	800	6,300	Finished goods a/c	2,800	36,400
Process 1 a/c	3,000	18,100			
Added materials		9,600			
Conversion costs		11,800	Closing inventory c/f	1,000	9,400
	3,800	45,800		3,800	45,800

7.3 Which method should be used?

FIFO inventory valuation is more common than the weighted average method, and should be used unless an indication is given to the contrary. You may find that you are presented with limited information about the opening inventory, which forces you to use either the FIFO or the weighted average method. The rules are as follows.

(a) If you are told the degree of completion of each element in opening inventory, but not the value of each cost element, then you must use the **FIFO method**.

(b) If you are not given the degree of completion of each cost element in opening inventory, but you are given the value of each cost element, then you must use the **weighted average method.**

Question	Equivalent units

During August, a factory commenced work on 20,000 units. At the start of the month there were no partly finished units but at the end of the month there were 2,000 units which were only 40% complete. Costs in the month were $3,722,400.

(a) How many equivalent units of closing WIP were there in the month?

A	20,000	C	18,000
B	2,000	D	800

(b) What is the total value of fully completed output which would show in the process account?

A	$3,960,000	C	$3,722,400
B	$3,564,000	D	$3,350,160

Answer	

(a) D   Equivalent units of WIP = 40% × 2,000 = 800

(b) B

Total finished output	18,000	units
Total equivalent units =		
18,000 100%	18,000	
2,000 × 40%	800	
	18,800	
Cost per equivalent unit = 3,722,400/18,800 =	$198	
∴ Value of fully completed output:		
18,000 × 198 =	$3,564,000	

Chapter roundup

- **Process costing** is a costing method used where it is not possible to identify separate units of production or jobs, usually because of the continuous nature of the production processes involved.

- Process costing is centred around **four key steps**. The exact work done at each step will depend on whether there are normal losses, scrap, opening and closing work in progress and so on.

  Step 1. Determine output and losses
  Step 2. Calculate cost per unit of output, losses and WIP
  Step 3. Calculate total cost of output, losses and WIP
  Step 4. Complete accounts

- **Losses** may occur in process. If a certain level of loss is expected, this is known as **normal loss**. If losses are greater than expected, the extra loss is **abnormal loss**. If losses are less than expected, the difference is known as **abnormal gain**.

- The **scrap value** of normal loss is usually deducted from the cost of materials.

- The **scrap value** of abnormal loss (or abnormal gain) is usually set off against its cost, in an abnormal loss (abnormal gain) account

- Abnormal losses and gains never affect the cost of good units of production. The scrap value of abnormal loss is **not** credited to the process account, and abnormal loss and gain units carry the same **full cost** as a good unit of production.

- When units are partly completed at the end of a period (and hence there is closing work in progress), it is necessary to calculate the **equivalent units of production** in order to determine the cost of a completed unit.

- Account can be taken of opening work in progress using either the **FIFO** method or the **weighted average cost method**.

1 Define process costing.

2 Process costing is centred around four key steps.

   Step 1. ....

   Step 2. ....

   Step 3. ....

   Step 4. ....

3 Abnormal gains result when actual loss is less than normal or expected loss.

   True ☐ False ☐

4

   Normal loss (no scrap value)   Same value as good output (positive cost)

   Abnormal loss   **?**   No value

   Abnormal gain   Same value as good output (negative cost)

5 How is revenue from scrap treated?

   A   As an addition to sales revenue   C   As a bonus to employees
   B   As a reduction in costs of processing   D   Any of the above

6 What is an equivalent unit?

7 When there is closing WIP at the end of a process, what is the first step in the four-step approach to process costing questions and why must it be done?

8 What is the weighted average cost method of inventory valuation?

9 Unless given an indication to the contrary, the weighted average cost method of inventory valuation should be used to value opening WIP.

   True ☐ False ☐

Answers to quick quiz

1   **Process costing** is a costing method used where it is not possible to identify separate units of production, or jobs, usually because of the continuous nature of the production processes involved.

2   **Step 1.**   Determine output and losses
    Step 2.   Calculate cost per unit of output, losses and WIP
    Step 3.   Calculate total cost of output, losses and WIP
    Step 4.   Complete accounts

3   True

4

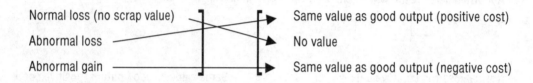

Normal loss (no scrap value)   Same value as good output (positive cost)

Abnormal loss   No value

Abnormal gain   Same value as good output (negative cost)

5   B

6   An **equivalent unit** is a notional whole unit which represents incomplete work, and which is used to apportion costs between work in process and completed output.

7   **Step 1.**   It is necessary to calculate the equivalent units of production (by drawing up a statement of equivalent units). Equivalent units of production are notional whole units which represent incomplete work and which are used to apportion costs between work in progress and completed output.

8   A method where no distinction is made between units of opening inventory and new units introduced to the process during the current period.

9   False. FIFO inventory valuation is more common than the weighted average method and should be used unless an indication is given to the contrary.

Now try the questions below from the Exam Question Bank

Number	Level	Marks	Time
Q10	MCQ/OTQ	n/a	n/a

11

Process costing, joint products and by-products

Introduction

You should now be aware of the most simple and the more complex areas of process costing. In this chapter we are going to turn our attention to the methods of accounting for **joint products** and **by-products** which arise as a result of a **continuous process**.

Study guide

		Intellectual level
D6	**Process costing 2**	
(a)	Distinguish between by-products and joint products	1
(b)	Value by-products and joint products at the point of separation	1
(c)	Prepare process accounts in situations where by-products and/or joint products occur	2

Exam guide

The F2 Pilot paper has four questions on process costing, so make sure you understand all the basics here.

1 Joint products and by-products

1.1 Introduction

FAST FORWARD

Joint products are two or more products separated in a process, each of which has a **significant value** compared to the other. A **by-product** is an incidental product from a process which has an **insignificant value** compared to the main product.

Key terms

Joint products are two or more products which are output from the same processing operation, but which are indistinguishable from each other up to their point of separation.

A **by-product** is a supplementary or secondary product (arising as the result of a process) whose value is small relative to that of the principal product.

(a) Joint products have a **substantial sales value**. Often they require further processing before they are ready for sale. Joint products arise, for example, in the oil refining industry where diesel fuel, petrol, paraffin and lubricants are all produced from the same process.

(b) The distinguishing feature of a by-product is its **relatively low sales value** in comparison to the main product. In the timber industry, for example, by-products include sawdust, small offcuts and bark.

What exactly separates a joint product from a by-product?

(a) A **joint product** is regarded as an important saleable item, and so it should be **separately costed**. The profitability of each joint product should be assessed in the cost accounts.

(b) A **by-product** is not important as a saleable item, and whatever revenue it earns is a 'bonus' for the organisation. Because of their relative insignificance, by-products are **not separately costed**.

Exam focus point

The study guide for Paper F2 states that you must be able to 'distinguish between by-products and joint products'.

1.2 Problems in accounting for joint products

FAST FORWARD

The point at which **joint products** and **by-products** become separately identifiable is known as the **split-off point** or **separation point**. Costs incurred up to this point are called **common costs** or **joint costs**.

Costs incurred prior to this point of separation are **common** or **joint costs**, and these need to be allocated (apportioned) in some manner to each of the joint products. In the following sketched example, there are two different split-off points.

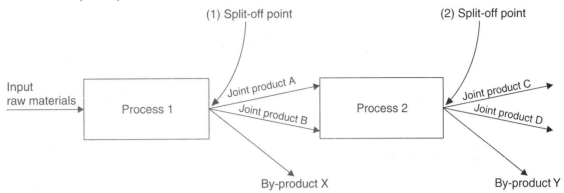

Problems in accounting for joint products are basically of two different sorts.

(a) How common costs should be apportioned between products, in order to put a value to closing inventories and to the cost of sale (and profit) for each product.

(b) Whether it is more profitable to sell a joint product at one stage of processing, or to process the product further and sell it at a later stage.

2 Dealing with common costs

2.1 Introduction

FAST FORWARD

The main methods of apportioning joint costs, each of which can produce significantly different results are as follows.

- Physical measurement
- Relative sales value apportionment method; sales value at split-off point

The problem of costing for joint products concerns **common costs**, that is those common processing costs shared between the units of eventual output up to their 'split-off point'. Some method needs to be devised for sharing the common costs between the individual joint products for the following reasons.

(a) To put a value to closing inventories of each joint product.
(b) To record the costs and therefore the profit from each joint product.
(c) Perhaps to assist in pricing decisions.

Here are some examples of the common costs problem.

(a) How to spread the common costs of oil refining between the joint products made (petrol, naphtha, kerosene and so on).

(b) How to spread the common costs of running the telephone network between telephone calls in peak and cheap rate times, or between local and long distance calls.

Various methods that might be used to establish a basis for apportioning or allocating common costs to each product are as follows.

- Physical measurement
- Relative sales value apportionment method; sales value at split-off point

2.2 Dealing with common costs: physical measurement

With physical measurement, **the common cost is apportioned to the joint products on the basis of the proportion that the output of each product bears by weight or volume to the total output.** An example of this would be the case where two products, product 1 and product 2, incur common costs to the point of separation of $3,000 and the output of each product is 600 tons and 1,200 tons respectively.

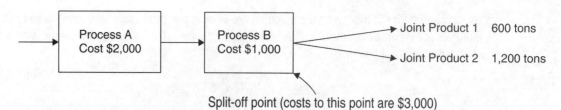

Split-off point (costs to this point are $3,000)

Product 1 sells for $4 per ton and product 2 for $2 per ton.

The division of the common costs ($3,000) between product 1 and product 2 could be based on the tonnage of output.

	Product 1		Product 2	Total
Output	600 tons	+	1,200 tons	1,800 tons
Proportion of common cost	$\dfrac{600}{1,800}$	+	$\dfrac{1,200}{1,800}$	
	$		$	$
Apportioned cost	1,000		2,000	3,000
Sales	2,400		2,400	4,800
Profit	1,400		400	1,800
Profit/sales ratio	58.3%		16.7%	37.5%

Physical measurement has the following limitations.

(a) Where the products separate during the processes into different states, for example where one product is a gas and another is a liquid, this method is unsuitable.

(b) This method does not take into account the relative income-earning potentials of the individual products, with the result that one product might appear very profitable and another appear to be incurring losses.

2.3 Dealing with common costs: sales value at split-off point

The **relative sales value method** is the most widely used method of apportioning joint costs because (ignoring the effect of further processing costs) it assumes that all products achieve the same profit margin.

With relative sales value apportionment of common costs, **the cost is allocated according to the product's ability to produce income**. This method is most widely used because the assumption that some profit margin should be attained for all products under normal marketing conditions is satisfied. The common cost is apportioned to each product in the proportion that the sales (market) value of that product bears to the sales value of the total output from the particular processes concerned. Using the previous example where the sales price per unit is $4 for product 1 and $2 for product 2.

(a) Common costs of processes to split-off point $3,000
(b) Sales value of product 1 at $4 per ton $2,400
(c) Sales value of product 2 at $2 per ton $2,400

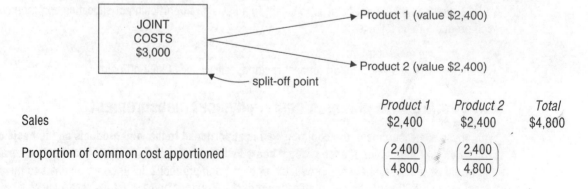

	Product 1	Product 2	Total
Sales	$2,400	$2,400	$4,800
Proportion of common cost apportioned	$\left(\dfrac{2,400}{4,800}\right)$	$\left(\dfrac{2,400}{4,800}\right)$	

	$	$	$
Apportioned cost	1,500	1,500	3,000
Sales	2,400	2,400	4,800
Profit	900	900	1,800
Profit/sales ratio	37.5%	37.5%	37.5%

A comparison of the gross profit margin resulting from the application of the above methods for allocating common costs will illustrate the greater acceptability of the relative sales value apportionment method. Physical measurement gives a higher profit margin to product 1, not necessarily because product 1 is highly profitable, but because it has been given a smaller share of common costs.

Question   Joint products

In process costing, a joint product is

A   A product which is produced simultaneously with other products but which is of lesser value than at least one of the other products

B   A product which is produced simultaneously with other products and is of similar value to at least one of the other products

C   A product which is produced simultaneously with other products but which is of greater value than any of the other products

D   A product produced jointly with another organisation

Answer

The correct answer is B, a product which is of similar value to at least one of the other products.

Question   Sales value method

Two products (W and X) are created from a joint process. Both products can be sold immediately after split-off. There are no opening inventories or work in progress. The following information is available for last period.

Total joint production costs $776,160

Product	Production units	Sales units	Selling price per unit
W	12,000	10,000	$10
X	10,000	8,000	$12

Using the sales value method of apportioning joint production costs, what was the value of the closing inventory of product X for last period?

A $68,992
B $70,560
C $76,032
D $77,616

Answer

The correct answer is D.

Sales value of production:

Product W	(12,000 x $10)	$120,000
Product X	(10,000 x $12)	$120,000

Therefore joint costs are apportioned in the ratio 1:1.

Amount apportioned to product X   (776,160/2) $388,080

20% of X's production is in closing inventory = 20% of $388,080 = $77,616

Exam focus point

The above question is taken from the December 2007 exam. It was highlighted by the examiner as being poorly answered, with less than 30% of students selecting the correct answer. Make sure you split the joint costs according to sales **value** rather than individual selling prices.

3 Joint products in process accounts

This example illustrates how joint products are incorporated into process accounts.

3.1 Example: joint products and process accounts

Three joint products are manufactured in a common process, which consists of two consecutive stages. Output from process 1 is transferred to process 2, and output from process 2 consists of the three joint products, Hans, Nils and Bumpsydaisies. All joint products are sold as soon as they are produced.

Data for period 2 of 20X6 are as follows.

	Process 1	Process 2
Opening and closing inventory	None	None
Direct material		
(30,000 units at $2 per unit)	$60,000	–
Conversion costs	$76,500	$226,200
Normal loss	10% of input	10% of input
Scrap value of normal loss	$0.50 per unit	$2 per unit
Output	26,000 units	10,000 units of Han
		7,000 units of Nil
		6,000 units of Bumpsydaisy

Selling prices are $18 per unit of Han, $20 per unit of Nil and $30 per unit of Bumpsydaisy.

Required

(a)   Prepare the Process 1 account.
(b)   Prepare the Process 2 account using the sales value method of apportionment.
(c)   Prepare a profit statement for the joint products.

Solution

(a)   **Process 1 equivalent units**

	Total units	Equivalent units
Output to process 2	26,000	26,000
Normal loss	3,000	0
Abnormal loss (balance)	1,000	1,000
	30,000	27,000

Costs of process 1

	$
Direct materials	60,000
Conversion costs	76,500
	136,500
Less scrap value of normal loss (3,000 × $0.50)	1,500
	135,000

$$\text{Cost per equivalent unit} = \frac{\$135,000}{27,000} = \$5$$

PROCESS 1 ACCOUNT

	$		$
Direct materials	60,000	Output to process 2 (26,000 × $5)	130,000
Conversion costs	76,500	Normal loss (scrap value)	1,500
		Abnormal loss a/c (1,000 × $5)	5,000
	136,500		136,500

(b) Process 2 equivalent units

	Total units	Equivalent units
Units of Hans produced	10,000	10,000
Units of Nils produced	7,000	7,000
Units of Bumpsydaisies produced	6,000	6,000
Normal loss (10% of 26,000)	2,600	0
Abnormal loss (balance)	400	400
	26,000	23,400

Costs of process 2

	$
Material costs – from process 1	130,000
Conversion costs	226,200
	356,200
Less scrap value of normal loss (2,600 × $2)	5,200
	351,000

Cost per equivalent unit $\dfrac{\$351,000}{23,400}$ = $15

Cost of good output (10,000 + 7,000 + 6,000) = 23,000 units × $15 = $345,000

The sales value of joint products, and the apportionment of the output costs of $345,000, is as follows.

	Sales value $	%	Costs (process 2) $
Hans (10,000 × $18)	180,000	36	124,200
Nils (7,000 × $20)	140,000	28	96,600
Bumpsydaisy (6,000 × $30)	180,000	36	124,200
	500,000	100	345,000

PROCESS 2 ACCOUNT

	$		$
Process 1 materials	130,000	Finished goods accounts	
Conversion costs	226,200	– Hans	124,200
		– Nils	96,600
		– Bumpsydaisies	124,200
		Normal loss (scrap value)	5,200
		Abnormal loss a/c	6,000
	356,200		356,200

(c) PROFIT STATEMENT

	Hans $'000	Nils $'000	Bumpsydaisies $'000
Sales	180.0	140.0	180.0
Costs	124.2	96.6	124.2
Profit	55.8	43.4	55.8
Profit/ sales ratio	31%	31%	31%

Question

Prepare the Process 2 account and a profit statement for the joint products in the above example using the units basis of apportionment.

Answer

PROCESS 2 ACCOUNT

	$		$
Process 1 materials	130,000	Finished goods accounts	
Conversion costs	226,200	– Hans (10,000 × $15)	150,000
		– Nils (7,000 × $15)	105,000
		– Bumpsydaisies (6,000 × $15)	90,000
		Normal loss (scrap value)	5,200
		Abnormal loss a/c	6,000
	356,200		356,200

PROFIT STATEMENT

	Hans $'000	Nils $'000	Bumpsydaisies $'000
Sales	180	140	180
Costs	150	105	90
Profit	30	35	90
Profit/ sales ratio	16.7%	25%	50%

Question

Polly Inc operates a process costing system, the final output from which is three different products: Bolly, Dolly and Folly. Details of the three products for March are as follows.

	Bolly	Dolly	Folly
Selling price per unit	$25	$18	$32
Output for March	6,000 units	10,000 units	4,000 units

22,000 units of material were input to the process, costing $242,000. Conversion costs were $121,000. No losses were expected and there were no opening or closing inventories.

Using the units basis of apportioning joint costs, what was the profit or loss on sales of Dolly for March?

A $(1,500)   C $50,306
B $30,000   D $15,000

Answer

The correct answer is D.

Total output	20,000	units (6,000 + 10,000 + 4,000)
Total input	22,000	units
Abnormal loss	2,000	units

Total cost = $363,000

Cost per unit = $\dfrac{\$363,000}{22,000}$ = $16.50

Cost of 'good' output = 20,000 units × $16.50 = $330,000

$$\text{Amount apportioned to Dolly} \quad = \frac{\text{Units of Dolly}}{\text{Total 'good' units}} \times \$330{,}000$$

$$= (10{,}000/20{,}000) \times \$330{,}000$$

$$= \$165{,}000$$

Profit for Dolly = Sales Revenue – apportioned costs

$$= (10{,}000 \times \$18) - \$165{,}000$$
$$= \$15{,}000$$

4 Accounting for by-products

4.1 Introduction

FAST FORWARD

The most common method of accounting for by-products is to deduct the **net realisable value** of the by-product from the cost of the main products.

A by-product has some commercial value and any income generated from it may be treated as follows.

(a) Income (minus any post-separation further processing or selling costs) from the sale of the by-product may be **added to sales of the main product**, thereby increasing sales turnover for the period.

(b) The sales of the by-product may be **treated as a separate, incidental source of income** against which are set only post-separation costs (if any) of the by-product. The revenue would be recorded in the income statement as 'other income'.

(c) The sales income of the by-product may be **deducted from the cost of production** or cost of sales of the main product.

(d) The **net realisable value of the by-product may be deducted from the cost of production of the main product**. The net realisable value is the final saleable value of the by-product minus any post-separation costs. Any closing inventory valuation of the main product or joint products would therefore be reduced.

The choice of method (a), (b), (c) or (d) will be influenced by the circumstances of production and ease of calculation, as much as by conceptual correctness. The method you are most likely to come across in examinations is method (d). An example will help to clarify the distinction between the different methods.

4.2 Example: Methods of accounting for by-products

During November 20X3, Splatter Co recorded the following results.

Opening inventory   main product P, nil
                           by-product Z, nil
Cost of production $120,000

Sales of the main product amounted to 90% of output during the period, and 10% of production was held as closing inventory at 30 November.

Sales revenue from the main product during November 20X2 was $150,000.

A by-product Z is produced, and output had a net sales value of $1,000. Of this output, $700 was sold during the month, and $300 was still in inventory at 30 November.

Required

Calculate the profit for November using the four methods of accounting for by-products.

Solution

The four methods of accounting for by-products are shown below.

(a)   Income from by-product added to sales of the main product

	$	$
Sales of main product ($150,000 + $700)		150,700
Opening inventory	0	
Cost of production	120,000	
	120,000	
Less closing inventory (10%)	12,000	
Cost of sales		108,000
Profit, main product		42,700

The closing inventory of the by-product has no recorded value in the cost accounts.

(b)   By-product income treated as a separate source of income

	$	$
Sales, main product		150,000
Opening inventory	0	
Cost of production	120,000	
	120,000	
Closing inventory (10%)	12,000	
Cost of sales, main product		108,000
Profit, main product		42,000
Other income		700
Total profit		42,700

The closing inventory of the by-product again has no value in the cost accounts.

(c)   Sales income of the by-product deducted from the cost of production in the period

	$	$
Sales, main product		150,000
Opening inventory	0	
Cost of production (120,000 – 700)	119,300	
	119,300	
Less closing inventory (10%)	11,930	
Cost of sales		107,370
Profit, main product		42,630

Although the profit is different from the figure in (a) and (b), the by-product closing inventory again has no value.

(d)   Net realisable value of the by-product deducted from the cost of production in the period

	$	$
Sales, main product		150,000
Opening inventory	0	
Cost of production (120,000 – 1,000)	119,000	
	119,000	
Less closing inventory (10%)	11,900	
Cost of sales		107,100
Profit, main product		42,900

As with the other three methods, closing inventory of the by-product has no value in the books of accounting, but the value of the closing inventory ($300) has been used to reduce the cost of production, and in this respect it has been allowed for in deriving the cost of sales and the profit for the period.

Randolph manufactures two joint products, J and K, in a common process. A by-product X is also produced. Data for the month of December 20X2 were as follows.

Opening inventories		nil	
Costs of processing	direct materials	$25,500	
	direct labour	$10,000	

Production overheads are absorbed at the rate of 300% of direct labour costs.

		Production Units	Sales Units
Output and sales consisted of:	product J	8,000	7,000
	product K	8,000	6,000
	by-product X	1,000	1,000

The sales value per unit of J, K and X is $4, $6 and $0.50 respectively. The saleable value of the by-product is deducted from process costs before apportioning costs to each joint product. Costs of the common processing are apportioned between product J and product K on the basis of sales value of production.

The individual profits for December 20X2 are:

	Product J	Product K
	$	$
A	5,250	6,750
B	6,750	5,250
C	22,750	29,250
D	29,250	22,750

Answer

The sales value of production was $80,000.

	$	
Product J (8,000 × $4)	32,000	(40%)
Product K (8,000 × $6)	48,000	(60%)
	80,000	

The costs of production were as follows.

	$
Direct materials	25,500
Direct labour	10,000
Overhead (300% of $10,000)	30,000
	65,500
Less sales value of by-product (1,000 × 50c)	500
Net production costs	65,000

The profit statement would appear as follows (nil opening inventories).

		Product J		Product K	Total
		$		$	$
Production costs	(40%)	26,000	(60%)	39,000	65,000
Less closing inventory	(1,000 units)	3,250	(2,000 units)	9,750	13,000
Cost of sales		22,750		29,250	52,000
Sales	(7,000 units)	28,000	(6,000 units)	36,000	64,000
Profit		5,250		6,750	12,000

The correct answer is therefore A.

If you selected option B, you got the profits for each product mixed up.

If you selected option C or D, you calculated the cost of sales instead of the profit.

Chapter roundup

- **Joint products** are two or more products separated in a process, each of which has a **significant value** compared to the other. A **by-product** is an incidental product from a process which has an **insignificant value** compared to the main product.

- The point at which joint and by-products become separately identifiable is known as the **split-off point** or **separation point**. Costs incurred up to this point are called **common costs** or **joint costs**.

- The main methods of apportioning joint costs, each of which can produce significantly different results are as follows: physical measurement; and relative sales value apportionment method; sales value at split-off point

- The **relative sales value method** is the most widely used method of apportioning joint costs because (ignoring the effect of further processing costs) it assumes that all products achieve the same profit margin.

- The most common method of accounting for by-products is to deduct the **net realisable value** of the by-product from the cost of the main products.

Quick quiz

1   What is the difference between a joint product and a by-product?
2   What is meant by the term 'split-off' point?
3   Name two methods of apportioning common costs to joint products.
4   Describe the four methods of accounting for by-products.

Answers to quick quiz

1   A **joint product** is regarded as an important saleable item whereas a **by-product** is not.
2   The **split-off point** (or the **separation point**) is the point at which joint products become separately identifiable in a processing operation.
3   Physical measurement and sales value at split-off point.
4   See paragraph 4.1.

Now try the questions below from the Exam Question Bank			
Number	**Level**	**Marks**	**Time**
Q11	MCQ	n/a	n/a

12

Job, batch and service costing

Topic list	Syllabus reference
1 Costing methods	D5 (a)
2 Job costing	D5 (a), (b), (c), (d)
3 Batch costing	D5 (a), (b), (c), (d)
4 Service costing	D7(a), (b), (c)

Introduction

The first costing method that we shall be looking at is **job costing**. We will see the circumstances in which job costing should be used and how the costs of jobs are calculated. We will look at how the **costing of individual jobs** fits in with the recording of total costs in control accounts and then we will move on to **batch costing**, the procedure for which is similar to job costing.

Service costing deals with **specialist services** supplied to third parties or an **internal service** supplied within an organisation.

Study guide

		Intellectual level
D5	**Job and batch costing**	
(a)	Describe the characteristics of job and batch costing	1
(b)	Describe the situations where the use of job or batch costing would be appropriate	1
(c)	Prepare cost records and accounts in job and batch cost accounting situations	1
(d)	Establish job costs from given information	1
D7	**Service/operation costing**	
(a)	Identify situations where the use of service/operation costing is appropriate	1
(b)	Illustrate suitable unit cost measures that may be used in different service/operation situations	1
(c)	Carry out service cost analysis in simple service industry situations	1

Exam guide

This is a popular topic for MCQs. Make sure that you are able to deal with basic calculations.

1 Costing methods

FAST FORWARD

A **costing method** is designed to suit the way goods are processed or manufactured or the way services are provided.

Each organisation's costing method will therefore have unique features but costing methods of firms in the same line of business will more than likely have common aspects. Organisations involved in completely different activities, such as hospitals and car part manufacturers, will use very different methods.

We will be considering these important costing methods in this chapter.

- Job
- Batch
- Service

2 Job costing

2.1 Introduction

FAST FORWARD

Job costing is a costing method applied where work is undertaken to customers' special requirements and each order is of comparatively short duration.

Key term

A **job** is a cost unit which consists of a single order or contract.

The work relating to a job moves through processes and operations as a **continuously identifiable unit**. Job costing is most commonly applied within a factory or workshop, but may also be applied to property repairs and internal capital expenditure.

2.2 Procedure for the performance of jobs

The normal procedure in jobbing concerns involves:

(a) The prospective customer approaches the supplier and indicates the **requirements** of the job.

(b) A representative sees the prospective customer and agrees with him the **precise details** of the items to be supplied. For example the quantity, quality, size and colour of the goods, the date of delivery and any special requirements.

(c) The estimating department of the organisation then **prepares an estimate for the job**. This will be based on the cost of the materials to be used, the labour expense expected, the cost overheads, the cost of any additional equipment needed specially for the job, and finally the supplier's **profit margin**. The total of these items will represent the **quoted selling price**.

(d) If the estimate is accepted the job can be **scheduled**. All materials, labour and equipment required will be 'booked' for the job. In an efficient organisation, the start of the job will be timed to ensure that while it will be ready for the customer by the promised date of delivery it will not be loaded too early, otherwise storage space will have to be found for the product until the date it is required by (and was promised to) the customer.

2.3 Job cost sheets/cards

> **FAST FORWARD**
>
> Costs for each job are collected on a **job cost sheet** or **job card**.

With other methods of costing, it is usual to produce for inventory; this means that management must decide in advance how many units of each type, size, colour, quality and so on will be produced during the coming year, regardless of the identity of the customers who will eventually buy the product. In job costing, because production is usually carried out in accordance with the **special requirements of each customer**, it is **usual for each job to differ in one or more respects from another job.**

A separate record must therefore be maintained to show the details of individual jobs. Such records are often known as **job cost sheets** or **job cost cards**. An example is shown on the next page.

Either the **detail of relatively small jobs** or a **summary** of direct materials, direct labour and so on **for larger jobs** will be shown on a job cost sheet.

2.4 Job cost information

> **FAST FORWARD**
>
> **Material costs** for each job are determined from **material requisition notes**. **Labour times** on each job are recorded on a **job ticket**, which is then costed and recorded on the job cost sheet. Some labour costs, such as overtime premium or the cost of rectifying sub-standard output, might be charged either directly to a job or else as an overhead cost, depending on the circumstances in which the costs have arisen. **Overhead** is absorbed into the cost of jobs using the predetermined overhead absorption rates.

Information for the direct and indirect costs will be gathered as follows.

2.4.1 Direct material cost

(a) The estimated cost will be calculated by valuing all items on the **bill of materials**. Materials that have to be specially purchased for the job in question will need to be priced by the purchasing department.

(b) The actual cost of materials used will be calculated by valuing materials issues notes for those issues from store for the job and/or from invoices for materials specially purchased. All documentation should indicate the job number to which it relates.

2.4.2 Direct labour cost

(a)   The estimated **labour time requirement** will be calculated from past experience of similar types of work or work study engineers may prepare estimates following detailed specifications. Labour rates will need to take account of any increases, overtime and bonuses.

(b)   The actual labour hours will be available from either time sheets or job tickets/cards, using job numbers where appropriate to indicate the time spent on each job. The actual labour cost will be calculated using the hours information and current labour rates (plus bonuses, overtime payments and so on).

2.4.3 Direct expenses

(a)   The estimated cost of **any expenses likely** to be incurred can be obtained from a supplier.

(b)   The details of actual direct expenses incurred can be taken from invoices.

JOB COST CARD — Job No. B641

Customer	Mr J White	Customer's Order No.		Vehicle make	Peugot 205 GTE
Job Description	Repair damage to offside front door			**Vehicle reg. no.**	G 614 50X
Estimate Ref. 2599		**Invoice No.**			
Quoted price $338.68		**Invoice price** $355.05		**Date to collect**	14.6.00

Material / Labour / Overheads

Date	Req. No.	Qty.	Price	Cost $	Cost c	Date	Emp-loyee	Cost Ctre	Hrs.	Rate	Bonus	Cost $	Cost c	Hrs	OAR	Cost $	Cost c
12.6	36815	1	75.49	75	49	12.6	018	B	1.98	6.50	-	12	87	7.9	2.50	19	75
12.6	36816	1	33.19	33	19	13.6	018	B	5.92	6.50	-	38	48				
12.6	36842	5	6.01	30	05						13.65	13	65				
13.6	36881	5	3.99	19	95												
Total C/F				158	68		**Total C/F**					65	00	**Total C/F**		19	75

Expenses / Job Cost Summary

Date	Ref.	Description	Cost $	Cost c
12.6	-	N. Jolley Panel-beating	50	-
Total C/F			50	-

Job Cost Summary	Actual $	Actual c	Estimate $	Estimate c
Direct Materials B/F	158	68	158	68
Direct Expenses B/F	50	00		
Direct Labour B/F	65	00	180	00
Direct Cost	273	68		
Overheads B/F	19	75		
	293	43		
Admin overhead (add 10%)	29	34		
= Total Cost	322	77	338	68
Invoice Price	355	05		
Job Profit/Loss	32	28		

Comments

Job Cost Card Completed by _

2.4.4 Production overheads

(a) The **estimated production overheads** to be included in the job cost will be calculated from **overhead absorption rates** in operation and the estimate of the basis of the absorption rate (for example, direct labour hours). This assumes the job estimate is to include overheads (in a competitive environment management may feel that if overheads are to be incurred irrespective of whether or not the job is taken on, the minimum estimated quotation price should be based on variable costs only).

(b) The actual production overhead to be included in the job cost will be calculated from the overhead absorption rate and the actual results (such as labour hours coded to the job in question). **Inaccurate overhead absorption rates can seriously harm an organisation**; if jobs are over priced, customers will go elsewhere and if jobs are under priced revenue will fail to cover costs.

2.4.5 Administration, selling and distribution overheads

The organisation may absorb **non-production overheads** using any one of a variety of methods (percentage on full production cost, for example) and estimates of these costs and the actual costs should be included in the estimated and actual job cost.

2.5 Rectification costs

If the finished output is found to be sub-standard, it may be possible to rectify the fault. The sub-standard output will then be returned to the department or cost centre where the fault arose.

Rectification costs can be treated in two ways.

(a) If rectification work is not a frequent occurrence, but arises on occasions with specific jobs to which it can be traced directly, then the rectification costs should be **charged as a direct cost to the jobs concerned.**

(b) If rectification is regarded as a normal part of the work carried out generally in the department, then the rectification costs should be **treated as production overheads**. This means that they would be included in the total of production overheads for the department and absorbed into the cost of all jobs for the period, using the overhead absorption rate.

2.6 Work in progress

At the year end, the **value of work in progress** is simply the **sum of the costs incurred on incomplete jobs** (provided that the costs are lower than the net realisable value of the customer order).

2.7 Pricing the job

FAST FORWARD

The usual method of fixing prices in a jobbing concern is **cost plus pricing**.

Cost plus pricing means that a desired profit margin is added to total costs to arrive at the selling price.

The estimated profit will depend on the particular circumstance of the job and organisation in question. In competitive situations the profit may be small but if the organisation is sure of securing the job the margin may be greater. In general terms, the profit earned on each job should **conform to the requirements of the organisation's overall business plan**.

The final price quoted will, of course, be affected by what competitors charge and what the customer will be willing to pay.

An exam question about job costing may ask you to accumulate costs to arrive at a job cost, and then to determine a job price by adding a certain amount of profit. To do this, you need to remember the following crucial formula.

	%
Cost of job	100
+ profit	25
= selling price	125

Profit may be expressed either as a percentage of job cost (such as 25% (25/100) mark up) or as a percentage of selling price (such as 20% (25/125) margin).

2.8 Job costing and computerisation

Job cost sheets exist in manual systems, but it is **increasingly likely** that in large organisations the **job costing system will be computerised**, using accounting software specifically designed to deal with job costing requirements. A computerised job accounting system is likely to contain the following features.

(a) Every job will be given a **job code number**, which will determine how the data relating to the job is stored.

(b) A separate set of **codes will be given for the type of costs** that any job is likely to incur. Thus, 'direct wages', say, will have the same code whichever job they are allocated to.

(c) In a sophisticated system, **costs can be analysed both by job** (for example all costs related to Job 456), **but also by type** (for example direct wages incurred on all jobs). It is thus easy to perform control analysis and to make comparisons between jobs.

(d) A job costing system might have facilities built into it which incorporate other factors relating to the performance of the job. In complex jobs, sophisticated planning techniques might be employed to ensure that the job is performed in the minimum time possible: time management features may be incorporated into job costing software.

2.9 Example: Job costing

Fateful Morn is a jobbing company. On 1 June 20X2, there was one uncompleted job in the factory. The job card for this work is summarised as follows.

Job Card, Job No 6832

	$
Costs to date	
Direct materials	630
Direct labour (120 hours)	350
Factory overhead ($2 per direct labour hour)	240
Factory cost to date	1,220

During June, three new jobs were started in the factory, and costs of production were as follows.

Direct materials		$
Issued to:	Job 6832	2,390
	Job 6833	1,680
	Job 6834	3,950
	Job 6835	4,420
Damaged inventory written off from stores		2,300

Material transfers	$
Job 6834 to Job 6833	250
Job 6832 to 6834	620

Materials returned to store	$
From Job 6832	870
From Job 6835	170

Direct labour hours recorded

Job 6832	430 hrs
Job 6833	650 hrs
Job 6834	280 hrs
Job 6835	410 hrs

The cost of labour hours during June 20X2 was $3 per hour, and production overhead is absorbed at the rate of $2 per direct labour hour. Production overheads incurred during the month amounted to $3,800. Completed jobs were delivered to customers as soon as they were completed, and the invoiced amounts were as follows.

Job 6832	$5,500
Job 6834	$8,000
Job 6835	$7,500

Administration and marketing overheads are added to the cost of sales at the rate of 20% of factory cost. Actual costs incurred during June 20X2 amounted to $3,200.

Required

(a) Prepare the job accounts for each individual job during June 20X2; (the accounts should only show the cost of production, and not the full cost of sale).

(b) Prepare the summarised job cost cards for each job, and calculate the profit on each completed job.

Solution

(a) **Job accounts**

JOB 6832

	$		$
Balance b/f	1,220	Job 6834 a/c	620
Materials (stores a/c)	2,390	(materials transfer)	
Labour (wages a/c)	1,290	Stores a/c (materials returned)	870
Production overhead (o'hd a/c)	860	Cost of sales a/c (balance)	4,270
	5,760		5,760

JOB 6833

	$		$
Materials (stores a/c)	1,680	Balance c/f	5,180
Labour (wages a/c)	1,950		
Production overhead (o'hd a/c)	1,300		
Job 6834 a/c (materials transfer)	250		
	5,180		5,180

JOB 6834

	$		$
Materials (stores a/c)	3,950	Job 6833 a/c (materials transfer)	250
Labour (wages a/c)	840		
Production overhead (o'hd a/c)	560	Cost of sales a/c (balance)	5,720
Job 6832 a/c (materials transfer)	620		
	5,970		5,970

JOB 6835

	$		$
Materials (stores a/c)	4,420	Stores a/c (materials returned)	170
Labour (wages a/c)	1,230		
Production overhead (o'hd a/c)	820	Cost of sales a/c (balance)	6,300
	6,470		6,470

(b)   **Job cards, summarised**

	Job 6832	Job 6833	Job 6834	Job 6835
	$	$	$	$
Materials	1,530*	1,930	4,320**	4,250
Labour	1,640	1,950	840	1,230
Production overhead	1,100	1,300	560	820
Factory cost	4,270	5,180 (c/f)	5,720	6,300
Admin & marketing o'hd (20%)	854		1,144	1,260
Cost of sale	5,124		6,864	7,560
Invoice value	5,500		8,000	7,500
Profit/(loss) on job	376		1,136	(60)

*$(630 + 2,390 − 620 − 870)
**$(3,950 + 620 − 250)

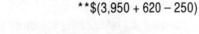

Question   Selling price

The following information relates to job 388886, which is being carried out by Biddy to meet a customer's order.

	Department V	Department Q
Direct materials used	$5,000	$3,000
Direct labour hours	400 hours	200 hours
Direct labour rate per hour	$4	$5
Production overhead per direct labour hour	$4	$4
Administration and other overhead	20% of full production cost	
Profit margin	25% of sales price	

Required

Calculate the selling price of job 388886.

Answer

	Department V	Department Q	Total
	$	$	$
Direct materials	5,000	3,000	8,000
Direct labour	1,600	1,000	2,600
Production overhead	1,600	800	2,400
Full production cost			13,000
Other overheads			2,600
Cost of the job			15,600
Profit (25% of sales=33 $\frac{1}{3}$ % of cost)			5,200
Sales price			20,800

2.10 Job costing for internal services

FAST FORWARD

It is possible to use a job costing system **to control the costs of an internal service department**, such as the maintenance department or the printing department.

If a job costing system is used it is possible to **charge the user departments for the cost of specific jobs carried out, rather than apportioning the total costs of these service departments** to the user departments using an arbitrarily determined apportionment basis.

An internal job costing system for service departments will have the following advantages.

Advantages	Comment
Realistic apportionment	The identification of expenses with jobs and the subsequent charging of these to the department(s) responsible means that costs are borne by those who incurred them.
Increased responsibility and awareness	User departments will be aware that they are charged for the specific services used and may be more careful to use the facility more efficiently. They will also appreciate the true cost of the facilities that they are using and can take decisions accordingly.
Control of service department costs	The service department may be restricted to charging a standard cost to user departments for specific jobs carried out or time spent. It will then be possible to measure the efficiency or inefficiency of the service department by recording the difference between the standard charges and the actual expenditure.
Planning information	This information will ease the planning process, as the purpose and cost of service department expenditure can be separately identified.

Question

Total job cost

A furniture-making business manufactures quality furniture to customers' orders. It has three production departments (A, B and C) which have overhead absorption rates (per direct labour hour) of $12.86, $12.40 and $14.03 respectively.

Two pieces of furniture are to be manufactured for customers. Direct costs are as follows.

	Job XYZ	Job MNO
Direct material	$154	$108
Direct labour	20 hours dept A	16 hours dept A
	12 hours dept B	10 hours dept B
	10 hours dept C	14 hours dept C

Labour rates are as follows: $3.80(A); $3.50 (B); $3.40 (C)

The firm quotes prices to customers that reflect a required profit of 25% on selling price. Calculate the total cost and selling price of each job.

Answer

			Job XYZ		Job MNO
			$		$
Direct material			154.00		108.00
Direct labour:	dept A	(20 × 3.80)	76.00	(16 × 3.80)	60.80
	dept B	(12 × 3.50)	42.00	(10 × 3.50)	35.00
	dept C	(10 × 3.40)	34.00	(14 × 3.40)	47.60
Total direct cost			306.00		251.40
Overhead:	dept A	(20 × 12.86)	257.20	(16 × 12.86)	205.76
	dept B	(12 × 12.40)	148.80	(10 × 12.40)	124.00
	dept C	(10 × 14.03)	140.30	(14 × 14.03)	196.42
Total cost			852.30		777.58
Profit (note)			284.10		259.19
Quoted selling price			1,136.40		1,036.77

(*Note.* If profit is 25% on selling price, this is the same as 33^{1}/$_{3}$% (25/75) on cost.)

Question

A firm uses job costing and recovers overheads on direct labour.

Three jobs were worked on during a period, the details of which are as follows.

	Job 1 $	Job 2 $	Job 3 $
Opening work in progress	8,500	0	46,000
Material in period	17,150	29,025	0
Labour for period	12,500	23,000	4,500

The overheads for the period were exactly as budgeted, $140,000.

Jobs 1 and 2 were the only incomplete jobs.

What was the value of closing work in progress?

A $81,900   B $90,175   C $140,675   D $214,425

Answer

Total labour cost = $12,500 + $23,000 + $4,500 = $40,000

$$\text{Overhead absorption rate} = \frac{\$140,000}{\$40,000} \times 100\% = 350\% \text{ of direct labour cost}$$

Closing work in progress valuation

		Job 1 $		Job 2 $	Total $
Costs given in question		38,150		52,025	90,175
Overhead absorbed	(12,500 × 350%)	43,750	(23,000 × 350%)	80,500	124,250
					214,425

Option D is correct.

We can eliminate option B because $90,175 is simply the total of the costs allocated to Jobs 1 and 2, with no absorption of overheads. Option A is an even lower cost figure, therefore it can also be eliminated.

Option C is wrong because it is a simple total of all allocated costs, including Job 3 which is not incomplete.

3 Batch costing

3.1 Introduction

FAST FORWARD

Batch costing is similar to job costing in that each batch of similar articles is separately identifiable. The **cost per unit** manufactured in a batch is the total batch cost divided by the number of units in the batch.

Key term

A **batch** is a group of similar articles which maintains its identity during one or more stages of production and is treated as a cost unit.

In general, the **procedures for costing batches are very similar to those for costing jobs**.

(a)   The **batch is treated as a job during production** and the costs are collected in the manner already described in this chapter.

(b)   Once the batch has been completed, the **cost per unit can be calculated as the total batch cost divided into the number of units in the batch**.

3.2 Example: Batch costing

Rio manufactures Brazils to order and has the following budgeted overheads for the year, based on normal activity levels.

Production departments	Budgeted Overheads $	Budgeted activity
Welding	12,000	3,000 labour hours
Assembly	20,000	2,000 labour hours

Selling and administrative overheads are 25% of factory cost. An order for 500 Brazils, made as Batch 38, incurred the following costs.

Materials $24,000

Labour   200 hours in the Welding Department at $5 per hour
            400 hours in the Assembly Department at $10 per hour

$1,000 was paid for the hire of x-ray equipment for testing the accuracy of the welds.

Required

Calculate the cost per unit for Batch 38.

Solution

The first step is to calculate the overhead absorption rate for the production departments.

$$\text{Welding} = \frac{\$12,000}{3,000} = \$4 \text{ per labour hour}$$

$$\text{Assembly} = \frac{\$20,000}{2,000} = \$10 \text{ per labour hour}$$

Total cost – Batch 38

		$	$
Direct material			24,000
Direct expense			1,000
Direct labour	200 × $5 =	1,000	
	400 × $10 =	4,000	
			5,000
Prime cost			30,000
Overheads	200 × $4 =	800	
	400 × $10 =	4,000	
			4,800
Factory cost			34,800
Selling and administrative cost (25% of factory cost)			8,700
Total cost			43,500

$$\text{Cost per unit} = \frac{\$43,500}{500} = \$87$$

4 Service costing

4.1 What is service costing?

> Service costing can be used by companies operating in a service industry or by companies wishing to establish the cost of services carried out by some of their departments. Service organisations do not make or sell tangible goods.

Key term

> **Service costing** (or **function costing**) is a costing method concerned with establishing the costs, not of items of production, but of services rendered.

Service costing is used in the following circumstances.

(a) A company operating in a service industry will cost its services, for which sales revenue will be earned; examples are electricians, car hire services, road, rail or air transport services and hotels.

(b) A company may wish to establish the cost of services carried out by some of its departments; for example the costs of the vans or lorries used in distribution, the costs of the computer department, or the staff canteen.

4.2 Service costing versus product costing (such as job or process costing)

(a) With many services, the cost of direct materials consumed will be relatively small compared to the labour, direct expenses and overheads cost. In product costing the direct materials are often a greater proportion of the total cost.

(b) Although many services are revenue-earning, others are not (such as the distribution facility or the staff canteen). This means that the purpose of service costing may not be to establish a profit or loss (nor to value closing inventories for the balance sheet) but may rather be to provide management information about the comparative costs or efficiency of the services, with a view to helping managers to budget for their costs using historical data as a basis for estimating costs in the future and to control the costs in the service departments.

(c) The procedures for recording material costs, labour hours and other expenses will vary according to the nature of the service.

4.3 Specific characteristics of services

> Specific characteristics of services
>
> - Simultaneity
> - Heterogeneity
> - Intangibility
> - Perishability

Consider the service of providing a haircut.

(a) The production and consumption of a haircut are **simultaneous,** and therefore it cannot be inspected for quality in advance, nor can it be returned if it is not what was required.

(b) A haircut is **heterogeneous** and so the exact service received will vary each time: not only will two hairdressers cut hair differently, but a hairdresser will not consistently deliver the same standard of haircut.

(c) A haircut is **intangible** in itself, and the performance of the service comprises many other intangible factors, like the music in the salon, the personality of the hairdresser, the quality of the coffee.

(d) Haircuts are **perishable,** that is, they cannot be stored. You cannot buy them in bulk, and the hairdresser cannot do them in advance and keep them stocked away in case of heavy demand. The incidence of work in progress in service organisations is less frequent than in other types of organisation.

Note the mnemonic **SHIP** for remembering the specific characteristics of services.

4.4 Unit cost measures

The main problem with service costing is the **difficulty in defining a realistic cost unit** that represents a suitable measure of the service provided. Frequently, a composite cost unit may be deemed more appropriate. Hotels, for example, may use the 'occupied bed-night' as an appropriate unit for cost ascertainment and control.

Typical cost units used by companies operating in a service industry are shown below.

Service	Cost unit
Road, rail and air transport services	Passenger/mile or kilometre, ton/mile, tonne/kilometre
Hotels	Occupied bed-night
Education	Full-time student
Hospitals	Patient
Catering establishment	Meal served

Question
Internal services

Can you think of examples of cost units for internal services such as canteens, distribution and maintenance?

Answer

Service	Cost unit
Canteen	Meal served
Vans and lorries used in distribution	Mile or kilometre, ton/mile, tonne/kilometre
Maintenance	Man hour

Each organisation will need to ascertain the **cost unit** most appropriate to its activities. If a number of organisations within an industry use a common cost unit, then valuable comparisons can be made between similar establishments. This is particularly applicable to hospitals, educational establishments and local authorities. Whatever cost unit is decided upon, the calculation of a cost per unit is as follows.

Formula to learn

$$\text{Cost per service unit} = \frac{\text{Total costs for period}}{\text{Number of service units in the period}}$$

4.5 Service cost analysis

Service cost analysis should be performed in a manner which ensures that the following objectives are attained.

(a) Planned costs should be compared with actual costs.

Differences should be investigated and corrective action taken as necessary.

(b) A cost per unit of service should be calculated.

If each service has a number of variations (such as maintenance services provided by plumbers, electricians and carpenters) then the calculation of a cost per unit of each service may be necessary.

(c) The cost per unit of service should be used as part of the control function.

For example, costs per unit of service can be compared, month by month, period by period, year by year and so on and any unusual trends can be investigated.

(d)   Prices should be calculated for services being sold to third parties.

The procedure is similar to job costing. A mark-up is added to the cost per unit of service to arrive at a selling price.

(e)   Costs should be analysed into fixed, variable and semi-variable costs to help assist management with planning, control and decision making.

4.6 Service cost analysis in internal service situations

Service department costing is also used to establish a specific cost for an internal service which is a service provided by one department for another, rather than sold externally to customers eg canteen, maintenance.

4.6.1 Transport costs

'**Transport costs**' is a term used here to refer to the costs of the transport services used by a company, rather than the costs of a transport organisation, such as a rail network.

If a company has a fleet of lorries or vans which it uses to distribute its goods, it is useful to know how much the department is costing for a number of reasons.

(a)   Management should be able to budget for expected costs, and to control actual expenditure on transport by comparing actual costs with budgeted costs.

(b)   The company may charge customers for delivery or 'carriage outwards' costs, and a charge based on the cost of the transport service might be appropriate.

(c)   If management knows how much its own transport is costing, a comparison can be made with alternative forms of transport to decide whether a cheaper or better method of delivery can be found.

(d)   Similarly, if a company uses, say, a fleet of lorries, knowledge of how much transport by lorry costs should help management to decide whether another type of vehicle, say vans, would be cheaper to use.

Transport costs may be analysed to provide the cost of operating one van or lorry each year, but it is more informative to analyse costs as follows.

(a)   The cost per mile or kilometre travelled.

(b)   The cost per ton/mile or tonne/kilometre (the cost of carrying one tonne of goods for one kilometre distance) or the cost per kilogram/metre.

For example, suppose that a company lorry makes five deliveries in a week.

Delivery	Tonnes carried	Distance (one way) Kilometres	Tonne/kilometres carried
1	0.4	180	72
2	0.3	360	108
3	1.2	100	120
4	0.8	250	200
5	1.0	60	60
			560

If the costs of operating the lorry during the week are known to be $840, the cost per tonne/kilometre would be:

$$\frac{\$840}{560 \text{ tonne/kilometre}} = \$1.50 \text{ per tonne/kilometre}$$

Transport costs might be collected under five broad headings.

(a)   **Running costs** such as petrol, oil, drivers' wages

(b)   **Loading costs** (the labour costs of loading the lorries with goods for delivery)

(c) **Servicing, repairs**, spare parts and tyre usage

(d) **Annual direct expenses** such as road tax, insurance and depreciation

(e) **Indirect costs of the distribution department** such as the wages of managers

The role of the cost accountant is to provide a system for **recording and analysing costs**. Just as production costs are recorded by means of material requisition notes, labour time sheets and so on, so too must transport costs be recorded by means of log sheets or time sheets, and material supply notes.

The purpose of a lorry driver's log sheet is to record distance travelled, or the number of tonne/kilometres and the drivers' time.

4.6.2 Canteen costs

Another example of service costing is the cost of a company's **canteen services**. A feature of canteen costing is that some revenue is earned when employees pay for their meals, but the prices paid will be insufficient to cover the costs of the canteen service. The company will subsidise the canteen and a major purpose of canteen costing is to establish the size of the subsidy.

If the costs of the canteen service are recorded by a system of service cost accounting, the likely headings of expense would be as follows.

(a) **Food and drink**: separate canteen stores records may be kept, and the consumption of food and drink recorded by means of 'materials issues' notes.

(b) **Labour costs of the canteen staff**: hourly paid staff will record their time at work on a time card or time sheet. Salaried staff will be a 'fixed' cost each month.

(c) **Consumable stores** such as crockery, cutlery, glassware, table linen and cleaning materials will also be recorded in some form of inventory control system.

(d) **The cost of gas and electricity** may be separately metered; otherwise an apportionment of the total cost of such utilities for the building as a whole will be made to the canteen department.

(e) Asset records will be kept and **depreciation charges** made for major items of equipment like ovens and furniture.

(f) An apportionment of other **overhead costs** of the building (rent and rates, building insurance and maintenance and so on) may be charged against the canteen.

Cash income from canteen sales will also be recorded.

4.6.3 Example: Service cost analysis

Suppose that a canteen recorded the following costs and revenue during the month.

	$
Food and drink	11,250
Labour	11,250
Heating and lighting	1,875
Repairs and consumable stores	1,125
Financing costs	1,000
Depreciation	750
Other apportioned costs	875
Revenue	22,500

The canteen served 37,500 meals in the month.

The size of the subsidy could be easily identified as follows:

	$
The total costs of the canteen	28,125
Revenue	22,500
Loss, to be covered by the company	5,625

The cost per meal averages 75c and the revenue per meal 60c. If the company decided that the canteen should pay its own way, without a subsidy, the average price of a meal would have to be raised by 15 cents.

4.7 The usefulness of costing services that do not earn revenue

4.7.1 Purposes of service costing

The techniques for costing services are similar to the techniques for costing products, but why should we want to establish a cost for 'internal' services, services that are provided by one department for another, rather than sold externally to customers? In other words, what is the purpose of service costing for non-revenue-earning services?

Service costing has two basic purposes.

(a) **To control the costs in the service department**. If we establish a distribution cost per tonne kilometre, a canteen cost per employee, or job costs of repairs, we can establish control measures in the following ways.

    (i)   Comparing actual costs against a target or standard

    (ii)   Comparing current actual costs against actual costs in previous periods

(b) **To control the costs of the user departments**, and prevent the unnecessary use of services. If the costs of services are charged to the user departments in such a way that the charges reflect the use actually made by each department of the service department's services then the following will occur.

    (i)   The overhead costs of user departments will be established more accurately; indeed some service department variable costs might be identified as directly attributable costs of the user department.

    (ii)   If the service department's charges for a user department are high, the user department might be encouraged to consider whether it is making an excessively costly and wasteful use of the service department's service.

    (iii) The user department might decide that it can obtain a similar service at a lower cost from an external service company.

4.7.2 Example: costing internal services

(a) If maintenance costs in a factory are costed as jobs (that is, if each bit of repair work is given a job number and costed accordingly) repair costs can be charged to the departments on the basis of repair jobs actually undertaken, instead of on a more generalised basis, such as apportionment according to machine hour capacity in each department. Departments with high repair costs could then consider their high incidence of repairs, the age and reliability of their machines, or the skills of the machine operatives.

(b) If IT costs are charged to a user department on the basis of a cost per hour, the user department would assess whether it was getting good value from its use of the IT department and whether it might be better to outsource some if its IT work.

4.8 Service cost analysis in service industry situations

4.8.1 Distribution costs

Example: service cost analysis in the service industry

This example shows how a rate per tonne/kilometre can be calculated for a distribution service.

Rick Shaw operates a small fleet of delivery vehicles. Standard costs have been established as follows.

Loading	1 hour per tonne loaded
Loading costs:	
Labour (casual)	$2 per hour
Equipment depreciation	$80 per week
Supervision	$80 per week
Drivers' wages (fixed)	$100 per man per week
Petrol	10c per kilometre

Repairs	5c per kilometre
Depreciation	$80 per week per vehicle
Supervision	$120 per week
Other general expenses (fixed)	$200 per week

There are two drivers and two vehicles in the fleet.

During a slack week, only six journeys were made.

Journey	Tonnes carried (one way)	One-way distance of journey Kilometres
1	5	100
2	8	20
3	2	60
4	4	50
5	6	200
6	5	300

Required

Calculate the expected average full cost per tonne/kilometre for the week.

Solution

Variable costs	Journey	1	2	3	4	5	6
		$	$	$	$	$	$
Loading labour		10	16	4	8	12	10
Petrol (both ways)		20	4	12	10	40	60
Repairs (both ways)		10	2	6	5	20	30
		40	22	22	23	72	100

Total costs

	$
Variable costs (total for journeys 1 to 6)	279
Loading equipment depreciation	80
Loading supervision	80
Drivers' wages	200
Vehicles depreciation	160
Drivers' supervision	120
Other costs	200
	1,119

Journey	Tonnes	One way distance Kilometres	Tonne/kilometres
1	5	100	500
2	8	20	160
3	2	60	120
4	4	50	200
5	6	200	1,200
6	5	300	1,500
			3,680

Cost per tonne/kilometre $\dfrac{\$1,119}{3,680} = \$0.304$

Note that the large element of fixed costs may distort this measure but that a variable cost per tonne/kilometre of $279/3,680 = $0.076 may be useful for budgetary control.

4.8.2 Education

The techniques described in the preceding paragraphs can be applied, in general, to any service industry situation. Attempt the following question about education.

Question

A university with annual running costs of $3 million has the following students.

Classification	Number	Attendance weeks per annum	Hours per week
3 year	2,700	30	28
4 year	1,500	30	25
Sandwich	1,900	35	20

Required

Calculate a cost per suitable cost unit for the university to the nearest cent.

Answer

We need to begin by establishing a cost unit for the university. Since there are three different categories of students we cannot use 'a student' as the cost unit. Attendance hours would seem to be the most appropriate cost unit. The next step is to calculate the number of units.

Number of students	Weeks		Hours		Total hours per annum
2,700	× 30	×	28	=	2,268,000
1,500	× 30	×	25	=	1,125,000
1,900	× 35	×	20	=	1,330,000
					4,723,000

The cost per unit is calculated as follows.

$$\text{Cost per unit} = \frac{\text{Total cost}}{\text{Number of units}} = \$\left(\frac{3,000,000}{4,723,000}\right) = \underline{\underline{\$0.64}}$$

Question

State which of the following are characteristics of service costing.

(i)   High levels of indirect costs as a proportion of total costs
(ii) Use of composite cost units
(iii) Use of equivalent units

A   (i) only
B   (i) and (ii) only

C   (ii) only
D   (ii) and (iii) only

Answer

B   In service costing it is difficult to identify many attributable direct costs. Many costs must be shared over several cost units, therefore characteristic (i) does apply. Composite cost units such as tonne-mile or room-night are often used, therefore characteristic (ii) does apply. Equivalent units are more often used in costing for tangible products, therefore characteristic (iii) does not apply. The correct answer is therefore B.

Chapter roundup

- A **costing method** is designed to suit the way goods are processed or manufactured or the way services are provided.

- **Job costing** is a costing method applied where work is undertaken to customers' special requirements and each order is of comparatively short duration.

- Costs for each job are collected on a **job cost sheet** or **job card.**

- **Material costs** for each job are determined from **material requisition notes**. **Labour times** on each job are recorded on a **job ticket**, which is then costed and recorded on the job cost sheet. Some labour costs, such as overtime premium or the cost of rectifying sub-standard output, might be charged either directly to a job or else as an overhead cost, depending on the circumstances in which the costs have arisen. **Overhead** is absorbed into the cost of jobs using the predetermined overhead absorption rates.

- The usual method of fixing prices within a jobbing concern is **cost plus pricing**.

- It is possible to use a job costing system **to control the costs of an internal service department**, such as the maintenance department or the printing department.

- **Batch costing** is similar to job costing in that each batch of similar articles is separately identifiable. The **cost per unit** manufactured in a batch is the total batch cost divided by the number of units in the batch.

- Service costing can be used by companies operating in a service industry or by companies wishing to establish the cost of services carried out by some of their departments. Service organisations do not make or sell tangible goods.

- Specific characteristics of services

    - Simultaneity
    - Heterogeneity
    - Intangibility
    - Perishability

- The main problem with service costing is the difficulty in **defining a realistic cost unit** that represents a suitable measure of the service provided. Frequently, a composite cost unit may be deemed more appropriate. Hotels, for example, may use the 'occupied bed-night' as an appropriate cost unit for ascertainment and control.

- Service department costing is also used to establish a specific cost for an internal service which is a service provided by one department for another, rather than sold externally to customers eg canteen, maintenance.

1   How are the material costs for each job determined?

2   Which of the following are not characteristics of job costing?

I   Customer driven production
II   Complete production possible within a single accounting period
III   Homogeneous products

A   I and II only   C   II and III only
B   I and III only   D   III only

3   The cost of a job is $100,000

(a)   If profit is 25% of the job cost, the price of the job = $.................
(b)   If there is a 25% margin, the price of the job = $....................

4   What is a batch?

5   How would you calculate the cost per unit of a completed batch?

6   Define service costing

7   Match up the following services with their typical cost units

Service		Cost unit
Hotels		Patient-day
Education	?	Meal served
Hospitals		Full-time student
Catering organisations		Occupied bed-night

8   What is the advantage of organisations within an industry using a common cost unit?

9   Cost per service unit = ...

10   Service department costing is used to establish a specific cost for an 'internal service' which is a service provided by one department for another.

True ☐   False ☐

1 From materials requisition notes, or from suppliers' invoices if materials are purchased specifically for a particular job.

2 D

3 (a) $100,000 + (25\% \times \$100,000) = \$100,000 + \$25,000 = \$125,000$

   (b) Let price of job = x

$$\therefore \text{Profit} = 25\% \times x \text{ (selling price)}$$
$$\text{If profit} = 0.25x$$
$$x - 0.25x = \text{cost of job}$$
$$0.75x = \$100,000$$
$$x = \frac{\$100,000}{0.75}$$
$$= \$133,333$$

4 A group of similar articles which maintains its identity during one or more stages of production and is treated as a cost unit.

5 $\dfrac{\text{Total batch cost}}{\text{Number of units in the batch}}$

6 Cost accounting for services or functions eg canteens, maintenance, personnel (service centres/functions).

7 **Service**   **Cost unit**

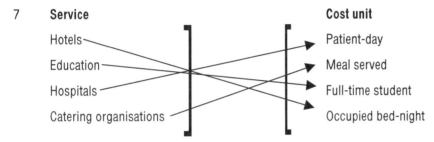

Hotels — Patient-day

Education — Meal served

Hospitals — Full-time student

Catering organisations — Occupied bed-night

8 It is easier to make comparisons.

9 Cost per service unit = $\dfrac{\text{Total costs for period}}{\text{Number of service units in the period}}$

10 True

Now try the questions below from the Exam Question Bank			
Number	**Level**	**Marks**	**Time**
Q12	MCQ/OTQ	n/a	n/a

P

A

R

T

E

Budgeting and standard costing

Budgeting

Topic list	Syllabus reference
1 Budgetary planning and control systems	E1 (a)
2 The preparation of budgets	E1 (b), (c) E2 (a)
3 The sales budget	E2 (b)
4 Production and related budgets	E2 (b)
5 Fixed and flexible budgets	E3 (a)
6 Preparing flexible budgets	E3 (a)
7 Flexible budgets and budgetary control	E3 (a) E5 (a)

Introduction

This chapter covers a new topic, **budgeting**. You will meet the topic at all stages of your future examination studies and so it is vital that you get a firm grasp of it now.

The chapter begins by explaining the **reasons for operating a budgetary planning and control system** (**Section 1**), explains some of the **key terms** associated with budgeting and reminds you of the steps in the preparation of a master budget (**Section 2**).

Study guide

		Intellectual level
E1	**Nature and purpose of budgeting**	
(a)	Explain why organisations use budgeting	1
(b)	Explain the administrative procedures used in the budgeting process	1
(c)	Describe the stages in the budgeting process	1
E2	**Functional budgets**	
(a)	Explain the term 'principal budget factor'	1
(b)	Prepare budgets for sales production, materials (usage and purchase), labour and overheads	1
E3	**Flexible budgets and standard costing**	
(a)	Explain and prepare fixed, flexible and flexed budgets	1
E5	**Reconciliation of budgeted profit and actual profit**	
(a)	Reconcile budgeted profit with actual profit under standard absorption costing	1

Exam guide

This topic was not in the previous syllabus but has been brought into this one – so expect it to be tested.

1 Budgetary planning and control systems

FAST FORWARD

A **budget** is a quantified plan of action for a forthcoming accounting period. A **budget** is a plan of what the organisation is aiming to achieve and what is has set as a target whereas a **forecast** is an estimate of what is likely to occur in the future

Key term

The **budget** is 'a quantitative statement for a defined period of time, which may include planned revenues, expenses, assets, liabilities and cash flows. A budget facilitates planning'.

There is, however, little point in an organisation simply preparing a budget for the sake of preparing a budget. A beautifully laid out budgeted income statement filed in the cost accountant's file and never looked at again is worthless. The organisation should gain from both the actual preparation process and from the budget once it has been prepared.

FAST FORWARD

The **objectives** of a budgetary planning and control system are as follows.

- To ensure the achievement of the organisation's objectives
- To compel planning
- To communicate ideas and plans
- To coordinate activities
- To provide a framework for responsibility accounting
- To establish a system of control
- To motivate employees to improve their performance

Budgets are therefore not prepared in isolation and then filed away but are the fundamental components of what is known as the **budgetary planning and control system**. A budgetary planning and control system is essentially a system for ensuring **communication**, **coordination** and **control** within an organisation. Communication, coordination and control are general objectives: more information is provided by an inspection of the specific objectives of a budgetary planning and control system.

Objective	Comment
Ensure the achievement of the organisation's objectives	Objectives are set for the organisation as a whole, and for individual departments and operations within the organisation. Quantified expressions of these objectives are then drawn up as targets to be achieved within the timescale of the budget plan.
Compel planning	This is probably the most important feature of a budgetary planning and control system. Planning forces management to look ahead, to set out detailed plans for achieving the targets for each department, operation and (ideally) each manager and to anticipate problems. It thus prevents management from relying on ad hoc or uncoordinated planning which may be detrimental to the performance of the organisation. It also helps managers to **foresee potential threats or opportunities**, so that they may **take action now** to avoid or minimise the effect of the threats and to take full advantage of the opportunities.
Communicate ideas and plans	A formal system is necessary to ensure that each person affected by the plans is aware of what he or she is supposed to be doing. Communication might be one-way, with managers giving orders to subordinates, or there might be a two-way dialogue and exchange of ideas.
Coordinate activities	The activities of different departments or sub-units of the organisation need to be coordinated to ensure maximum integration of effort towards common goals. This concept of coordination implies, for example, that the purchasing department should base its budget on production requirements and that the production budget should in turn be based on sales expectations. Although straightforward in concept, coordination is remarkably difficult to achieve, and there is often **'sub-optimality'** and conflict between departmental plans in the budget so that the efforts of each department are not fully integrated into a combined plan to achieve the company's best targets.
Provide a framework for responsibility accounting	Budgetary planning and control systems require that managers of **budget centres** are made responsible for the achievement of budget targets for the operations under their personal control.
Establish a system of control	A budget is a **yardstick** against which actual performance is monitored and assessed. Control over actual performance is provided by the comparisons of actual results against the budget plan. Departures from budget can then be investigated and the reasons for the departures can be divided into **controllable** and **uncontrollable** factors.
Motivate employees to improve their performance	The interest and commitment of employees can be retained via a system of feedback of actual results, which lets them know how well or badly they are performing. The identification of controllable reasons for departures from budget with managers responsible provides an incentive for improving future performance.
Provide a framework for authorisation	Once the budget has been agreed by the directors and senior managers it acts as an authorisation for each budget holder to incur the costs included in the budget centre's budget. **As long as the expenditure is included in the formalised budget** the budget holder can carry out day to day operations without needing to seek separate authorisation for each item of expenditure.

Objective	Comment
Provide a basis for performance evaluation	As well as providing a yardstick for control by comparison, the monitoring of actual results compared with the budget can provide a basis for **evaluating the performance of the budget holder.** As a result of this evaluation the manager might be rewarded, perhaps with a financial bonus or promotion. Alternatively the evaluation process might highlight the need for more investment in staff development and training.

2 The preparation of budgets

Having seen why organisations prepare budgets, we will now turn our attention to the mechanics of budget preparation. We will begin by defining and explaining a number of terms.

2.1 Planning

Key term

> **Planning** is the establishment of objectives, and the formulation of the policies, strategies and tactics required to achieve them. Planning comprises long-term/strategic planning, and short-term operation planning.

2.1.1 The value of long-term planning

A **budgetary planning and control system** operating in **isolation** without any form of long-term planning as a framework is **unlikely to produce maximum potential benefits** for an organisation.

(a)   **Without stated long-term objectives**, managers **do not know what they should be trying to achieve** and so there are **no criteria against which to assess possible courses of action**.

(b)   Without long-term planning, budgets may simply be based on a sales forecast. Performance can therefore only be judged in terms of previous years' results, **no analysis of the organisation's potential** having been carried out.

(c)   Many business **decisions need to be taken on a long-term basis**. For instance, **new products** cannot simply be introduced when sales of existing products begin to decline. Likewise, **capital equipment** cannot necessarily be purchased and installed in the short term if production volumes start to increase.

(d)   With long-term planning, **limiting factors** (other than sales) which might arise can possibly be anticipated, and avoided or overcome.

2.2 The budget period

Except for capital expenditure budgets, the budget period is commonly the accounting year (sub-divided into 12 or 13 control periods).

2.3 The budget manual

Key term

> The **budget manual** is a collection of instructions governing the responsibilities of persons and the procedures, forms and records relating to the preparation and use of budgetary data.

Likely contents of a budget manual	Examples
An explanation of the objectives of the budgetary process	• The purpose of budgetary planning and control • The objectives of the various stages of the budgetary process • The importance of budgets in the long-term planning and administration of the enterprise
Organisational structures	• An organisation chart • A list of individuals holding budget responsibilities
Principal budgets	• An outline of each • The relationship between them
Administrative details of budget preparation	• Membership and terms of reference of the budget committee • The sequence in which budgets are to be prepared • A timetable
Procedural matters	• Specimen forms and instructions for their completion • Specimen reports • Account codes (or a chart of accounts) • The name of the budget officer to whom enquiries must be sent

2.4 The responsibility for preparing budgets

The initial responsibility for preparing the budget will normally be with the managers (and their subordinates) who will be carrying out the budget, selling goods or services and authorising expenditure. However, the budget is normally set as part of a longer process, involving the authorisation of set targets by senior management and the negotiation process with the budget holders. Depending on the size of the organisation there may be a large number of **budget centres** and a separate **budget holder** would be responsible for setting and achieving the budget for the centre.

Examples of the functional budgets that would be prepared and **the managers responsible for their preparation** are as follows.

(a)   The **sales manager** should draft the **sales budget** and **selling overhead** cost centre budgets.

(b)   The **purchasing manager** should draft the **material purchases** budget.

(c)   The **production manager** should draft the **direct production** cost budgets.

(d)   Various **cost centre managers** should prepare the individual production, administration and distribution cost centre budgets for their own cost centre.

(e)   The **cost accountant** will **analyse** the budgeted overheads to determine the overhead absorption rates for the next budget period.

2.5 Budget committee

FAST FORWARD

The **budget committee** is the coordinating body in the preparation and administration of budgets.

The **coordination** and **administration** of budgets is usually the responsibility of a **budget committee** (with the managing director as chairman).

(a)   The budget committee is assisted by a **budget officer** who is usually an accountant. Every part of the organisation should be represented on the committee, so there should be a representative from sales, production, marketing and so on.

(b)   **Functions of the budget committee**

•   **Coordination** of the preparation of budgets, which includes the issue of the budget manual

•   **Issuing of timetables** for the preparation of functional budgets

•   **Allocation of responsibilities** for the preparation of functional budgets

- **Provision of information** to assist in the preparation of budgets
- **Communication of final budgets** to the appropriate managers
- **Comparison** of actual results with budget and the investigation of variances
- **Continuous assessment** of the budgeting and planning process, in order to improve the planning and control function

2.6 Budget preparation

Let us now look at the steps involved in the preparation of a budget. The procedures will differ from organisation to organisation, but the step-by-step approach described in this chapter is indicative of the steps followed by many organisations. The preparation of a budget may take weeks or months, and the budget committee may meet several times before the functional budgets are co-ordinated and the master budget is finally agreed.

2.7 The principal budget factor

FAST FORWARD

The **principal budget factor** should be identified at the beginning of the budgetary process, and the budget for this is prepared before all the others.

The first task in the budgetary process is to identify the **principal budget factor**. This is also known as the **key** budget factor or **limiting** budget factor.

Key term

> The **principal budget factor** is the factor which limits the activities of an organisation.

Likely principal budget factors

(a) The **principal budget factor** is usually **sales demand**: a company is usually restricted from making and selling more of its products because there would be no sales demand for the increased output at a price which would be acceptable/profitable to the company.

(b) Other possible factors

- Machine capacity
- Distribution and selling resources
- The availability of key raw materials
- The availability of cash.

Once this factor is defined then the remainder of the budgets can be prepared. For example, if sales are the principal budget factor then the production manager can only prepare his budget after the sales budget is complete.

Management may not know what the limiting budget factor is until a draft budget has been attempted. The first draft budget will therefore usually begin with the preparation of a draft sales budget.

Question

Budgets

A company that manufactures and sells a range of products, with sales potential limited by market share, is considering introducing a system of budgeting.

Required

(a) List (in order of preparation) the functional budgets that need to be prepared.
(b) State which budgets will comprise the master budget.
(c) Consider how the work outlined in (a) and (b) can be coordinated in order for the budgeting process to be successful.

(a) The **sequence of budget preparation** will be roughly as follows.

- Sales budget. (The market share limits demand and so sales is the principal budget factor. All other activities will depend upon this forecast.)
- Finished goods inventory budget (in units)
- Production budget (in units)
- Production resources budgets (materials, machine hours, labour)
- Overhead budgets for production, administration, selling and distribution, research and development and so on

Other budgets required will be the capital expenditure budget, the working capital budget (receivables and payables) and, very importantly, the cash budget.

(b) The **master budget** is the summary of all the functional budgets. It often includes a summary income statement and balance sheet.

(c) Procedures for preparing budgets can be contained in a **budget manual** which shows which budgets must be prepared when and by whom, what each functional budget should contain and detailed directions on how to prepare budgets including, for example, expected price increases, rates of interest, rates of depreciation and so on.

The formulation of budgets can be coordinated by a **budget committee** comprising the senior executives of the departments responsible for carrying out the budgets: sales, production, purchasing, personnel and so on.

The budgeting process may also be assisted by the use of a **spreadsheet/computer budgeting package**.

3 The sales budget

We have already established that, for many organisations, the principal budget factor is sales volume. The sales budget is therefore **often the primary budget** from which the majority of the other budgets are derived.

Before the sales budget can be prepared a sales forecast has to be made. A **forecast** is an estimate of what is likely to occur in the future. A budget, in contrast, is a plan of what the organisation is aiming to achieve and what it has set as a target.

On the basis of the sales forecast and the production capacity of the organisation, a sales budget will be prepared. This may be subdivided, possible subdivisions being by product, by sales area, by management responsibility and so on.

Once the sales budget has been agreed, related budgets can be prepared.

4 Production and related budgets

If the principal budget factor was production capacity then the production budget would be the first to be prepared. To assess whether production is the principal budget factor, the **production capacity available** must be determined, taking account of a number of factors.

- **Available labour**, including idle time, overtime and standard output rates per hour
- **Availability of raw materials** including allowances for losses during production
- **Maximum machine hours available**, including expected idle time and expected output rates per machine hour

It is, however, normally sales volume that is the constraint and therefore the production budget is usually prepared after the sales budget and the finished goods inventory budget.

The production budget will show the quantities and costs for each product and product group and will tie in with the sales and inventory budgets. This co-ordinating process is likely to show any shortfalls or excesses in capacity at various times over the budget period.

If there is likely to be a **shortfall** then consideration should be given to how this can be avoided. Possible **options** include the following.

- Overtime working
- Subcontracting
- Machine hire
- New sources of raw materials

A significant shortfall means that production capacity is, in fact, the limiting factor.

If **capacity exceeds sales volume** for a length of time then consideration should be given to **product diversification**, a **reduction in selling price** (if demand is price elastic) and so on.

Once the production budget has been finalised, the labour, materials and machine budgets can be drawn up. These budgets will be based on budgeted activity levels, planned inventory positions and projected labour and material costs.

4.1 Example: the production budget and direct labour budget

Landy manufactures two products, A and B, and is preparing its budget for 20X3. Both products are made by the same grade of labour, grade Q. The company currently holds 800 units of A and 1,200 units of B in inventory, but 250 of these units of B have just been discovered to have deteriorated in quality, and must therefore be scrapped. Budgeted sales of A are 3,000 units and of B 4,000 units, provided that the company maintains finished goods inventories at a level equal to three months' sales.

Grade Q labour was originally expected to produce one unit of A in two hours and one unit of B in three hours, at an hourly rate of $2.50 per hour. In discussions with trade union negotiators, however, it has been agreed that the hourly wage rate should be raised by 50c per hour, provided that the times to produce A and B are reduced by 20%.

Required

Prepare the production budget and direct labour budget for 20X3.

Solution

The expected time to produce a unit of A will now be 80% of 2 hours = 1.6 hours, and the time for a unit of B will be 2.4 hours. The hourly wage rate will be $3, so that the direct labour cost will be $4.80 for A and $7.20 for B (thus achieving a saving for the company of 20c per unit of A produced and 30c per unit of B).

(a) **Production budget**

		Product A Units	Product A Units		Product B Units	Product B Units
Budgeted sales			3,000			4,000
Closing inventories	($^3/_{12}$ of 3,000)	750		($^3/_{12}$ of 4,000)	1,000	
Opening inventories (minus inventories scrapped)		800			950	
(Decrease)/increase in inventories						50
			(50)			
Production			2,950			4,050

(b) **Direct labour budget**

	Grade Q Hours	Cost $
2,950 units of product A	4,720	14,160
4,050 units of product B	9,720	29,160
Total	14,440	43,320

It is assumed that there will be no idle time among grade Q labour which, if it existed, would have to be paid for at the rate of $3 per hour.

4.2 The standard hour

Key term

A **standard hour** or standard minute is the amount of work achievable at standard efficiency levels in that time period.

This is a useful concept in budgeting for labour requirements. For example, budgeted **output of different products or jobs** in a period could be converted into standard hours of production, and a labour budget constructed accordingly.

Standard hours are particularly useful when management wants to monitor the production levels of a variety of dissimilar units. For example product A may take five hours to produce and product B, seven hours. If four units of each product are produced, instead of saying that total output is eight units, we could state the production level as $(4 \times 5) + (4 \times 7)$ standard hours = 48 standard hours.

4.3 Example: direct labour budget based on standard hours

Truro manufactures a single product, Q, with a single grade of labour. Its sales budget and finished goods inventory budget for period 3 are as follows.

Sales	700 units
Opening inventories, finished goods	50 units
Closing inventories, finished goods	70 units

The goods are inspected only when production work is completed, and it is budgeted that 10% of finished work will be scrapped.

The standard direct labour hour content of product Q is three hours. The budgeted productivity ratio for direct labour is only 80% (which means that labour is only working at 80% efficiency).

The company employs 18 direct operatives, who are expected to average 144 working hours each in period 3.

Required

(a) Prepare a production budget.
(b) Prepare a direct labour budget.
(c) Comment on the problem that your direct labour budget reveals, and suggest how this problem might be overcome.

Solution

(a) **Production budget**

	Units
Sales	700
Add closing inventory	70
	770
Less opening inventory	50
Production required of 'good' output	720
Wastage rate	10%

Total production required $\quad 720 \times \dfrac{100\,^*}{90} = 800$ units

(* Note that the required adjustment is 100/90, not 110/100, since the waste is assumed to be 10% of total production, not 10% of good production.)

(b) Now we can prepare the **direct labour budget**.

Standard hours per unit	3
Total standard hours required = 800 units × 3 hours	2,400 hours
Productivity ratio	80%

Actual hours required $\quad 2,400 \times \dfrac{100}{80} = 3,000$ hours

(c)   If we look at the **direct labour budget** against the information provided, we can identify the problem.

	Hours
Budgeted hours available (18 operatives × 144 hours)	2,592
Actual hours required	3,000
Shortfall in labour hours	408

The (draft) budget indicates that there will not be enough direct labour hours to meet the production requirements.

(d)   **Overcoming insufficient labour hours**

(i)   **Reduce the closing inventory** requirement below 70 units. This would reduce the number of production units required.

(ii)   Persuade the workforce to do some **overtime** working.

(iii)   Perhaps **recruit** more direct labour if long-term prospects are for higher production volumes.

(iv)   **Improve** the **productivity** ratio, and so reduce the number of hours required to produce the output.

(v)   If possible, **reduce** the **wastage** rate below 10%.

4.4 Example: the material purchases budget

Tremor manufactures two products, S and T, which use the same raw materials, D and E. One unit of S uses 3 litres of D and 4 kilograms of E. One unit of T uses 5 litres of D and 2 kilograms of E. A litre of D is expected to cost $3 and a kilogram of E $7.

Budgeted sales for 20X2 are 8,000 units of S and 6,000 units of T; finished goods in inventory at 1 January 20X2 are 1,500 units of S and 300 units of T, and the company plans to hold inventories of 600 units of each product at 31 December 20X2.

Inventories of raw material are 6,000 litres of D and 2,800 kilograms of E at 1 January, and the company plans to hold 5,000 litres and 3,500 kilograms respectively at 31 December 20X2.

The warehouse and stores managers have suggested that a provision should be made for damages and deterioration of items held in store, as follows.

Product S :	loss of 50 units	Material D :	loss of 500 litres
Product T :	loss of 100 units	Material E :	loss of 200 kilograms

Required

Prepare a material purchases budget for the year 20X2.

Solution

To calculate material purchase requirements, it is first of all necessary to calculate the budgeted production volumes and material usage requirements.

	Product S		Product T	
	Units	Units	Units	Units
Sales		8,000		6,000
Provision for losses		50		100
Closing inventory	600		600	
Opening inventory	1,500		300	
(Decrease)/increase in inventory		(900)		300
Production budget		7,150		6,400

	Material D		Material E	
	Litres	Litres	Kg	Kg
Usage requirements				
To produce 7,150 units of S		21,450		28,600
To produce 6,400 units of T		32,000		12,800
Usage budget		53,450		41,400
Provision for losses		500		200
		53,950		41,600
Closing inventory	5,000		3,500	
Opening inventory	6,000		2,800	
(Decrease)/increase in inventory		(1,000)		700
Material purchases budget		52,950		42,300
	Material D		Material E	
Cost per unit	$3 per litre		$7 per kg	
Cost of material purchases	$158,850		$296,100	
Total purchases cost		$454,950		

Question — Material purchases budget

J purchases a basic commodity and then refines it for resale. Budgeted sales of the refined product are as follows.

	April	May	June
Sales in kg	9,000	8,000	7,000

- The basic raw material costs $3 per kg.
- Material losses are 10% of finished output.
- The target month-end raw material inventory level is 5,000 kg plus 25% of the raw material required for next month's budgeted production.
- The target month-end inventory level for finished goods is 6,000 kg plus 25% of next month's budgeted sales.

What are the budgeted raw material purchases for April?

A   8,500 kg   C   9,447 kg
B   9,350 kg   D   9,722 kg

Answer

The correct answer is C.

	March	April	May
	kg	kg	kg
Required finished inventory:			
Base inventory	6,000	6,000	6,000
+ 25% of next month's sales	2,250	2,000	1,750
= Required inventory	8,250	8,000	7,750
Sales for month		9,000	8,000
		17,000	15,750
Less: opening inventory		8,250	8,000
Required finished production		8,750	7,750
Wastage rate as % of finished output		10%	10%

Raw material required

$$8,750 \times \frac{100}{90} \qquad 7,750 \times \frac{100}{90}$$

$$= 9,722 \text{ kg} \qquad = 8,611 \text{ kg}$$

| | March | April | May |
	kg	kg	kg
Required material inventory:			
Base inventory	5,000.00	5,000.00	
+ 25% of material for next month's production	2,406.25	2,131.25	
= Required closing material inventory	7,406.25	7,131.25	
Production requirements		9,722.00	
		16,853.25	
Less: opening inventory		7,406.25	
Required material purchases		9,447.00	

4.5 Non-production overheads

In the modern business environment, an increasing proportion of overheads are not directly related to the volume of production, such as administration overheads and research and development costs.

4.6 Key decisions in the budgeting process for non-production overheads

Deciding which fixed costs are committed (will be incurred no matter what) and which fixed costs will depend on management decisions.

Deciding what factors will influence the level of variable costs. Administration costs for example may be partly governed by the number of orders received.

5 Fixed and flexible budgets

Fixed budgets remain unchanged regardless of the level of activity; **flexible budgets** are designed to flex with the level of activity.

Flexible budgets are prepared using marginal costing and so mixed costs must be split into their fixed and variable components (possibly using the **high/low method**).

5.1 Fixed budgets

The master budget prepared before the beginning of the budget period is known as the **fixed** budget. By the term 'fixed', we do not mean that the budget is kept unchanged. Revisions to a fixed master budget will be made if the situation so demands. The term 'fixed' means the following.

(a) The budget is prepared on the basis of an estimated volume of production and an estimated volume of sales, but no plans are made for the event that actual volumes of production and sales may differ from budgeted volumes.

(b) When actual volumes of production and sales during a control period (month or four weeks or quarter) are achieved, a fixed budget is not adjusted (in retrospect) to represent a new target for the new levels of activity.

The major purpose of a fixed budget lies in its use at the planning stage, when it seeks to define the broad objectives of the organisation.

Key term

A **fixed budget** is a budget which is normally set prior to the start of an accounting period, and which is not changed in response to changes in activity or costs/revenues.

Fixed budgets (in terms of a **pre-set expenditure limit**) are also useful for **controlling any fixed cost**, and **particularly non-production fixed costs** such as advertising, because such costs should be unaffected by changes in activity level (within a certain range).

5.2 Flexed budgets

Comparison of a fixed budget with the actual results for a different level of activity is of little use for **budgetary control purposes**. Flexible budgets should be used to show what cost and revenues should have been for the actual level of activity. Differences between the flexible budget figures and actual results are **variances**.

Key term

A **flexible budget** is a budget which is designed to change as volume of activity changes.

Two uses of flexible budgets

(a) **At the planning stage**. For example, suppose that a company expects to sell 10,000 units of output during the next year. A master budget (the fixed budget) would be prepared on the basis of these expected volumes. However, if the company thinks that output and sales might be as low as 8,000 units or as high as 12,000 units, it may prepare **contingency** flexible budgets, at volumes of, say 8,000, 9,000, 11,000 and 12,000 units, and then assess the possible outcomes.

(b) **Retrospectively.** At the end of each control period, flexible budgets can be used to compare actual results achieved with what results should have been under the circumstances. Flexible budgets are an essential factor in budgetary control.

    (i) Management needs to know about how good or bad actual performance has been. To provide a measure of performance, there must be a yardstick (budget/ standard) against which actual performance can be measured.

    (ii) Every business is dynamic, and actual volumes of output cannot be expected to conform exactly to the fixed budget. Comparing actual costs directly with the fixed budget costs is meaningless.

    (iii) For useful control information, it is necessary to compare actual results at the actual level of activity achieved against the results that should have been expected at this level of activity, which are shown by the flexible budget.

6 Preparing flexible budgets

6.1 Example: fixed and flexible budgets

Suppose that Gemma expects production and sales during the next year to be 90% of the company's output capacity, that is, 9,000 units of a single product. Cost estimates will be made using the high-low method and the following historical records of cost.

Units of output/sales	Cost of sales
	$
9,800	44,400
7,700	38,100

The company's management is not certain that the estimate of sales is correct, and has asked for flexible budgets to be prepared at output and sales levels of 8,000 and 10,000 units. The sales price per unit has been fixed at $5 .

Required

Prepare appropriate budgets.

Solution

If we assume that within the range 8,000 to 10,000 units of sales, all costs are fixed, variable or mixed (in other words there are no stepped costs, material discounts, overtime premiums, bonus payments and so on) the fixed and flexible budgets would be based on the estimate of fixed and variable cost.

		$
Total cost of 9,800 units	=	44,400
Total cost of 7,700 units	=	38,100
Variable cost of 2,100 units	=	6,300

The variable cost per unit is $3.

		$
Total cost of 9,800 units	=	44,400
Variable cost of 9,800 units (9,800 × $3)	=	29,400
Fixed costs (all levels of output and sales)	=	15,000

The fixed budgets and flexible budgets can now be prepared as follows.

	Flexible budget 8,000 units $	Fixed budget 9,000 units $	Flexible budget 10,000 units $
Sales (× $5)	40,000	45,000	50,000
Variable costs (× $3)	24,000	27,000	30,000
Contribution	16,000	18,000	20,000
Fixed costs	15,000	15,000	15,000
Profit	1,000	3,000	5,000

6.2 The need for flexible budgets

We have seen that flexible budgets may be prepared in order to plan for variations in the level of activity above or below the level set in the fixed budget. It has been suggested, however, that since many cost items in modern industry are fixed costs, the value of flexible budgets in planning is dwindling.

(a) In many manufacturing industries, plant costs (depreciation, rent and so on) are a very large proportion of total costs, and these tend to be fixed costs.

(b) Wage costs also tend to be fixed, because employees are generally guaranteed a basic wage for a working week of an agreed number of hours.

(c) With the growth of service industries, labour (wages or fixed salaries) and overheads will account for most of the costs of a business, and direct materials will be a relatively small proportion of total costs.

Flexible budgets are nevertheless necessary, and even if they are not used at the planning stage, they must be used for budgetary control variance analysis.

7 Flexible budgets and budgetary control

FAST FORWARD

Budgetary control is based around a system of **budget centres**. Each centre has its own budget which is the responsibility of the **budget holder**.

In other words, individual managers are held responsible for investigating differences between budgeted and actual results, and are then expected to take corrective action or amend the plan in the light of actual events.

It is therefore vital to ensure that valid comparisons are being made. Consider the following example.

7.1 Example

Penny manufactures a single product, the Darcy. Budgeted results and actual results for May are as follows.

	Budget	Actual	Variance
Production and sales of the Darcy (units)	7,500	8,200	
	$	$	$
Sales revenue	75,000	81,000	6,000 (F)
Direct materials	22,500	23,500	1,000 (A)
Direct labour	15,000	15,500	500 (A)
Production overhead	22,500	22,800	300 (A)
Administration overhead	10,000	11,000	1,000 (A)
	70,000	72,800	2,800 (A)
Profit	5,000	8,200	3,200 (F)

Note. (F) denotes a favourable variance and (A) an unfavourable or adverse variance.

In this example, the variances are meaningless for the purposes of control. All costs were higher than budgeted but the volume of output was also higher; it is to be expected that actual variable costs would be greater those included in the fixed budget. However, it is not possible to tell how much of the increase is due to **poor cost control** and how much is due to the **increase in activity**.

Similarly it is not possible to tell how much of the increase in sales revenue is due to the increase in activity. Some of the difference may be due to a difference between budgeted and actual selling price but we are unable to tell from the analysis above.

For control purposes we need to know the answers to questions such as the following.

- Were actual costs higher than they should have been to produce and sell 8,200 Darcys?
- Was actual revenue satisfactory from the sale of 8,200 Darcys?

Instead of comparing actual results with a fixed budget which is based on a different level of activity to that actually achieved, the correct approach to budgetary control is to compare actual results with a budget which has been **flexed** to the actual activity level achieved.

Suppose that we have the following estimates of the behaviour of Penny's costs.

(a) Direct materials and direct labour are variable costs.
(b) Production overhead is a semi-variable cost, the budgeted cost for an activity level of 10,000 units being $25,000.
(c) Administration overhead is a fixed cost.
(d) Selling prices are constant at all levels of sales.

Solution

The **budgetary control analysis** should therefore be as follows.

	Fixed budget	Flexible budget	Actual results	Variance
Production and sales (units)	7,500	8,200	8,200	
	$	$	$	$
Sales revenue	75,000	82,000 (W1)	81,000	1,000(A)
Direct materials	22,500	24,600 (W2)	23,500	1,100 (F)
Direct labour	15,000	16,400 (W3)	15,500	900 (F)
Production overhead	22,500	23,200 (W4)	22,800	400 (F)
Administration overhead	10,000	10,000 (W5)	11,000	1,000 (A)
	70,000	74,200	72,800	1,400 (F)
Profit	5,000	7,800	8,200	400 (F)

Workings

1 Selling price per unit = $75,000 ÷ 7,500 = $10 per unit
   Flexible budget sales revenue = $10 × 8,200 = $82,000

2 Direct materials cost per unit = $22,500 ÷ 7,500 = $3
   Budget cost allowance = $3 × 8,200 = $24,600

3   Direct labour cost per unit = $15,000 ÷ 7,500 = $2
     Budget cost allowance = $2 × 8,200 = $16,400

4   Variable production overhead cost per unit = $(25,000 − 22,500)/(10,000 − 7,500)
                                                = $2,500/2,500 = $1 per unit

     ∴ Fixed production overhead cost = $22,500 − (7,500 × $1) = $15,000
     ∴ Budget cost allowance = $15,000 + (8,200 × $1) = $23,200

5   Administration overhead is a fixed cost and hence budget cost allowance = $10,000

Comment

(a) In selling 8,200 units, the expected profit should have been, not the fixed budget profit of $5,000, but the flexible budget profit of $7,800. Instead actual profit was $8,200 ie $400 more than we should have expected.

     One of the reasons for this improvement is that, given output and sales of 8,200 units, the cost of resources (material, labour etc) was $1,400 lower than expected. (A comparison of the fixed budget and the actual costs in Example 7.1 appeared to indicate that costs were not being controlled since all of the variances were adverse).

     Total cost variances can be analysed to reveal how much of the variance is due to lower resource prices and how much is due to efficient resource usage.

(b) The sales revenue was, however, $1,000 less than expected because a lower price was charged than budgeted.

     We know this because flexing the budget has eliminated the effect of changes in the volume sold, which is the only other factor that can affect sales revenue. You have probably already realised that this variance of $1,000 (A) is a **selling price variance**.

     The lower selling price could have been caused by the increase in the volume sold (to sell the additional 700 units the selling price had to fall below $10 per unit). We do not know if this is the case but without flexing the budget we could not know that a different selling price to that budgeted had been charged. Our initial analysis above had appeared to indicate that sales revenue was ahead of budget.

The difference of $400 between the flexible budget profit of $7,800 at a production level of 8,200 units and the actual profit of $8,200 is due to the net effect of cost savings of $1,400 and lower than expected sales revenue (by $1,000).

The difference between the original budgeted profit of $5,000 and the actual profit of $8,200 is the total of the following.

(a) The savings in resource costs/lower than expected sales revenue (a net total of $400 as indicated by the difference between the flexible budget and the actual results).

(b) The effect of producing and selling 8,200 units instead of 7,500 units (a gain of $2,800 as indicated by the difference between the fixed budget and the flexible budget). This is the **sales volume contribution variance**.

A **full variance analysis statement** would be as follows.

	$	$
Fixed budget profit		5,000
Variances		
Sales volume	2,800 (F)	
Selling price	1,000 (A)	
Direct materials cost	1,100 (F)	
Direct labour cost	900 (F)	
Production overhead cost	400 (F)	
Administration overhead cost	1,000 (A)	
		3,200 (F)
Actual profit		8,200

If management believes that any of the variances are large enough to justify it, they will investigate the reasons for their occurrence to see whether any corrective action is necessary.

| Question | Flexible budget |

Flower budgeted to sell 200 units and produced the following budget.

	$	$
Sales		71,400
Variable costs		
Labour	31,600	
Material	12,600	
		44,200
Contribution		27,200
Fixed costs		18,900
Profit		8,300

Actual sales turned out to be 230 units, which were sold for $69,000. Actual expenditure on labour was $27,000 and on material $24,000. Fixed costs totalled $10,000.

Required

Prepare a flexible budget that will be useful for management control purposes.

| Answer |

	Budget 200 units $	Budget per unit $	Flexed budget 230 units $	Actual 230 units $	Variance $
Sales	71,400	357	82,110	69,000	13,110 (A)
Variable costs					
Labour	31,600	158	36,340	27,000	9,340 (F)
Material	12,600	63	14,490	24,000	9,510 (A)
	44,200	221	50,830	51,000	
Contribution	27,200	136	31,280	18,000	13,280 (A)
Fixed costs	18,900		18,900	10,000	8,900 (F)
Profit	8,300		12,380	8,000	4,380 (A)

7.2 Flexible budgets, control and computers

The production of flexible budget control reports is an area in which computers can provide invaluable assistance to the cost accountant, calculating flexed budget figures using fixed budget and actual results data and hence providing detailed variance analysis. For control information to be of any value it must be produced quickly: speed is one of the many advantages of computers.

7.3 The link between standard costing and budget flexing

The calculation of standard cost variances and the use of a flexed budget to control costs and revenues are **very similar in concept**.

For example, a direct material total variance in a standard costing system is calculated by **comparing the material cost that should have been incurred for the output achieved, with the actual cost that was incurred**.

Exactly the same process is undertaken when a budget is flexed to provide a basis for comparison with the actual cost: **the flexible budget cost allowance for material cost is the same as the cost that should**

have been incurred for the activity level achieved. In the same way as for standard costing, this is then compared with the actual cost incurred in order to practice control by comparison.

However, there are differences between the two techniques.

(a) **Standard costing variance analysis is more detailed**. The total material cost variance is analysed further to determine how much of the total variance is caused by a difference in the price paid for materials (the material price variance) and how much is caused by the usage of material being different from the standard (the material usage variance). In flexible budget comparisons only total cost variances are derived.

(b) **For a standard costing system to operate it is necessary to determine a standard unit cost for all items of output**. All that is required to operate a flexible budgeting system is an understanding of the cost behaviour patterns and a measure of activity to use to flex the budget cost allowance for each cost element.

Exam focus point

Make sure you understand the **principal budget factor** and the difference between **fixed** and **flexible** budgets.

Chapter Roundup

- A **budget** is a quantified plan of action for a forthcoming accounting period. A **budget** is a plan of what the organisation is aiming to achieve and what is has set as a target, whereas a **forecast** is an estimate of what is **likely** to occur in the future

- The **objectives** of a budgetary planning and control system are as follows.

    - To ensure the achievement of the organisation's objectives
    - To compel planning
    - To communicate ideas and plans
    - To coordinate activities
    - To provide a framework for responsibility accounting
    - To establish a system of control
    - To motivate employees to improve their performance

- The **budget committee** is the coordinating body in the preparation and administration of budgets.

- The **principal budget factor** should be identified at the beginning of the budgetary process, and the budget for this is prepared before all the others.

- **Fixed budgets** remain unchanged regardless of the level of activity; **flexible budgets** are designed to flex with the level of activity.

- **Flexible budgets** are prepared using marginal costing and so mixed costs must be split into their fixed and variable component.

- Comparison of a fixed budget with the actual results for a different level of activity is of little use for **budgeting control purposes**. Flexible budgets should be used to show what cost and revenues should have been for the actual level of activity. Differences between the flexible budget figures and actual results are **variances.**

- Budgetary control is based around a system of **budget centres**. Each centre has its own budget which is the responsibility of the **budget holder**.

Quick Quiz

1   Which of the following is not an objective of a system of budgetary planning and control?

   A   To establish a system of control
   B   To coordinate activities
   C   To compel planning
   D   To motivate employees to maintain current performance levels

2   Sales is always the principal budget factor and so it is always the first budget to be prepared. *True or false?*

3   *Choose the appropriate words from those highlighted.*

   A **forecast/budget** is an **estimate/guarantee** of what is **likely to occur in the future/has happened in the past**.

   A **forecast/budget** is a **quantified plan/unquantified plan/guess** of what the organisation is aiming to **achieve/spend**.

4   *Fill in the blanks.*

   When preparing a production budget, the quantity to be produced is equal to sales ....
   opening inventory .... closing inventory.

Answers to Quick Quiz

1   D. The objective is to motivate employees to *improve* their performance.

2   False. The budget for the principal budget factor must be prepared first, but sales is not always the principal budget factor.

3   A forecast is an estimate of what is likely to occur in the future.

   A budget is a quantified plan of what the organisation is aiming to achieve.

4   When preparing a production budget, the quantity to be produced is equal to sales minus opening inventory plus closing inventory.

Now try the questions below from the Exam Question Bank

Number	Level	Marks	Time
Q13	MCQ/OTQ	n/a	n/a

14

Standard costing

Topic list	Syllabus reference
1 What is standard costing?	E3 (a)
2 Setting standards	E3 (b)

Introduction

Just as there are **standards** for most things in our daily lives (cleanliness in hamburger restaurants, educational achievement of nine year olds, number of trains running on time), there are standards for the costs of products and services. Moreover, just as the standards in our daily lives are not always met, the standards for the costs of products and services are not always met. We will not, however, be considering the standards of cleanliness of hamburger restaurants in this chapter but we will be looking at standards for **costs**, what they are used for and how they are set.

In the next chapter we will see how **standard costing** forms the basis of a process called **variance analysis**, a vital management control tool.

Study guide

		Intellectual level
E3	**Flexible budgets and standard costing**	
(a)	Explain the purpose and principles of standard costing	1
(b)	Establish the standard cost per unit under absorption and marginal costing	1

Exam guide

Standard costing can be applied under both absorption and marginal costing and is important in calculating variances, which we look at in the next chapter. You may be given the standard cost and required to calculate the variance.

1 What is standard costing?

1.1 Introduction

FAST FORWARD

A **standard cost** is a **predetermined estimated unit cost**, used for inventory valuation and control.

The building blocks of standard costing are standard costs and so before we look at standard costing in any detail you really need to know what a standard cost is.

1.2 Standard cost card

FAST FORWARD

A **standard cost card** shows full details of the standard cost of each product.

The standard cost card of product 1234 is set out below.

STANDARD COST CARD – PRODUCT 1234

	$	$
Direct materials		
Material X – 3 kg at $4 per kg	12	
Material Y – 9 litres at $2 per litre	18	
		30
Direct labour		
Grade A – 6 hours at $1.50 per hour	9	
Grade B – 8 hours at $2 per hour	16	
		25
Standard direct cost		55
Variable production overhead – 14 hours at $0.50 per hour		7
Standard variable cost of production		62
Fixed production overhead – 14 hours at $4.50 per hour		63
Standard full production cost		125
Administration and marketing overhead		15
Standard cost of sale		140
Standard profit		20
Standard sales price		160

Notice how the total standard cost is built up from standards for each cost element: standard quantities of materials at standard prices, standard quantities of labour time at standard rates and so on. It is therefore determined by management's estimates of the following.

- The expected prices of materials, labour and expenses
- Efficiency levels in the use of materials and labour
- Budgeted overhead costs and budgeted volumes of activity

We will see how management arrives at these estimates in Section 2.

But why should management want to prepare standard costs? Obviously to assist with standard costing, but what is the point of standard costing?

1.3 The uses of standard costing

Standard costing has a variety of uses but its two principal ones are as follows.

(a) To **value inventories** and **cost production** for cost accounting purposes.

(b) To act as a **control device** by establishing standards (planned costs), highlighting (via **variance analysis** which we will cover in the next chapter) activities that are not conforming to plan and thus **alerting management** to areas which may be out of control and in need of corrective action.

Question

Standard cost card

Bloggs makes one product, the joe. Two types of labour are involved in the preparation of a joe, skilled and semi-skilled. Skilled labour is paid $10 per hour and semi-skilled $5 per hour. Twice as many skilled labour hours as semi-skilled labour hours are needed to produce a joe, four semi-skilled labour hours being needed.

A joe is made up of three different direct materials. Seven kilograms of direct material A, four litres of direct material B and three metres of direct material C are needed. Direct material A costs $1 per kilogram, direct material B $2 per litre and direct material C $3 per metre.

Variable production overheads are incurred at Bloggs Co at the rate of $2.50 per direct labour (skilled) hour.

A system of absorption costing is in operation at Bloggs Co. The basis of absorption is direct labour (skilled) hours. For the forthcoming accounting period, budgeted fixed production overheads are $250,000 and budgeted production of the joe is 5,000 units.

Administration, selling and distribution overheads are added to products at the rate of $10 per unit.

A mark-up of 25% is made on the joe.

Required

Using the above information draw up a standard cost card for the joe.

Answer

STANDARD COST CARD – PRODUCT JOE

	$	$
Direct materials		
A – 7 kgs × $1	7	
B – 4 litres × $2	8	
C – 3 m × $3	9	
		24
Direct labour		
Skilled – 8 × $10	80	
Semi-skilled – 4 × $5	20	
		100
Standard direct cost		124
Variable production overhead – 8 × $2.50		20
Standard variable cost of production		144
Fixed production overhead – 8 × $6.25 (W)		50
Standard full production cost		194
Administration, selling and distribution overhead		10
Standard cost of sale		204
Standard profit (25% × 204)		51
Standard sales price		255

Working

Overhead absorption rate = $\dfrac{\$250,000}{5,000 \times 8}$ = $6.25 per skilled labour hour

Question

What would a standard cost card for product joe show under a marginal system?

Answer

STANDARD COST CARD – PRODUCT JOE

	$
Direct materials	24
Direct labour	100
Standard direct cost	124
Variable production overhead	20
Standard variable production cost	144
Standard sales price	255
Standard contribution	111

Although the use of standard costs to simplify the keeping of cost accounting records should not be overlooked, we will be concentrating on the **control** and **variance analysis** aspect of standard costing.

Key term

> **Standard costing** is a control technique which compares standard costs and revenues with actual results to obtain variances which are used to improve performance.

Notice that the above definition highlights the control aspects of standard costing.

1.4 Standard costing as a control technique

FAST FORWARD

> Differences between actual and standard costs are called **variances**.

Standard costing therefore involves the following.

- The establishment of predetermined estimates of the costs of products or services
- The collection of actual costs
- The comparison of the actual costs with the predetermined estimates.

The predetermined costs are known as **standard costs** and the difference between standard and actual cost is known as a **variance**. The process by which the total difference between standard and actual results is analysed is known as **variance analysis**.

Although standard costing can be used in a variety of costing situations (batch and mass production, process manufacture, jobbing manufacture (where there is standardisation of parts) and service industries (if a realistic cost unit can be established)), the greatest benefit from its use can be gained if there is a **degree of repetition** in the production process. It is therefore most suited to **mass production** and **repetitive assembly work**.

2 Setting standards

2.1 Introduction

Standard costs may be used in both absorption costing and in marginal costing systems. We shall, however, confine our description to standard costs in absorption costing systems.

As we noted earlier, the standard cost of a product (or service) is made up of a number of different standards, one for each cost element, each of which has to be set by management. We have divided this section into two: the first part looks at setting the monetary part of each standard, whereas the second part looks at setting the resources requirement part of each standard.

2.2 Types of performance standard

Performance standards are used to set efficiency targets. There are four types: ideal, attainable, current and basic.

The setting of standards raises the problem of how demanding the standard should be. Should the standard represent a perfect performance or an easily attainable performance? The type of performance standard used can have behavioural implications. There are four types of standard.

Type of standard	Description
Ideal	These are based on **perfect operating conditions**: no wastage, no spoilage, no inefficiencies, no idle time, no breakdowns. Variances from ideal standards are useful for pinpointing areas where a close examination may result in large savings in order to maximise efficiency and minimise waste. However ideal standards are likely to have an unfavourable motivational impact because reported variances will always be adverse. Employees will often feel that the goals are unattainable and not work so hard.
Attainable	These are based on the hope that a standard amount of work will be carried out efficiently, machines properly operated or materials properly used. **Some allowance is made for wastage and inefficiencies**. If well-set they provide a useful psychological incentive by giving employees a realistic, but challenging target of efficiency. The consent and co-operation of employees involved in improving the standard are required.
Current	These are based on **current working conditions** (current wastage, current inefficiencies). The disadvantage of current standards is that they do not attempt to improve on current levels of efficiency.
Basic	These are **kept unaltered over a long period of time**, and may be out of date. They are used to show changes in efficiency or performance over a long period of time. Basic standards are perhaps the least useful and least common type of standard in use.

Ideal standards, attainable standards and current standards each have their supporters and it is by **no means clear which of them is preferable**.

Question

Performance standards

Which of the following statements is not true?

A   Variances from ideal standards are useful for pinpointing areas where a close examination might result in large cost savings.

B   Basic standards may provide an incentive to greater efficiency even though the standard cannot be achieved.

C   Ideal standards cannot be achieved and so there will always be adverse variances. If the standards are used for budgeting, an allowance will have to be included for these 'inefficiencies'.

D   Current standards or attainable standards are a better basis for budgeting, because they represent the level of productivity which management will wish to plan for.

Answer

The correct answer is B.

Statement B is describing ideal standards, not basic standards.

2.3 Direct material prices

Direct material prices will be estimated by the purchasing department from their knowledge of the following.

- Purchase contracts already agreed
- Pricing discussions with regular suppliers
- The forecast movement of prices in the market
- The availability of bulk purchase discounts

Price inflation can cause difficulties in setting realistic standard prices. Suppose that a material costs $10 per kilogram at the moment and during the course of the next twelve months it is expected to go up in price by 20% to $12 per kilogram. What standard price should be selected?

- The current price of $10 per kilogram
- The average expected price for the year, say $11 per kilogram

Either would be possible, but neither would be entirely satisfactory.

(a)   If the **current price** were used in the standard, the reported price variance will become adverse as soon as prices go up, which might be very early in the year. If prices go up gradually rather than in one big jump, it would be difficult to select an appropriate time for revising the standard.

(b)   If an **estimated mid-year price** were used, price variances should be favourable in the first half of the year and adverse in the second half of the year, again assuming that prices go up gradually throughout the year. Management could only really check that in any month, the price variance did not become excessively adverse (or favourable) and that the price variance switched from being favourable to adverse around month six or seven and not sooner.

2.4 Direct labour rates

Direct labour rates per hour will be set by discussion with the personnel department and by reference to the payroll and to any agreements on pay rises with trade union representatives of the employees.

(a)   A separate hourly rate or weekly wage will be set for each different labour grade/type of employee.

(b)   An average hourly rate will be applied for each grade (even though individual rates of pay may vary according to age and experience).

Similar problems when dealing with inflation to those described for material prices can be met when setting labour standards.

2.5 Overhead absorption rates

When standard costs are fully absorbed costs, the **absorption rate** of fixed production overheads will be **predetermined**, usually each year when the budget is prepared, and based in the usual manner on budgeted fixed production overhead expenditure and budgeted production.

For selling and distribution costs, standard costs might be absorbed as a percentage of the standard selling price.

Standard costs under marginal costing will, of course, not include any element of absorbed overheads.

2.6 Standard resource requirements

To estimate the materials required to make each product (**material usage**) and also the labour hours required (**labour efficiency**), **technical specifications** must be prepared for each product by production experts (either in the production department or the work study department).

(a)   The **'standard product specification'** for materials must list the quantities required per unit of each material in the product. These standard input quantities must be made known to the operators in the production department so that control action by management to deal with **excess material wastage** will be understood by them.

(b)   The **'standard operation sheet'** for labour will specify the expected hours required by each grade of labour in each department to make one unit of product. These standard times must be carefully set (for example by work study) and must be understood by the labour force. Where necessary, **standard procedures** or **operating methods** should be stated.

Exam focus point

An exam question may give you actual costs and variances and require you to calculate the standard cost.

Chapter roundup

- A **standard cost** is a **predetermined estimated unit cost**, used for inventory valuation and control.

- A **standard cost card** shows full details of the standard cost of each product.

- Differences between actual and standard cost are called **variances**.

- **Performance standards** are used to set efficiency targets. There are four types: ideal, attainable, current and basic.

Quick quiz

1   A standard cost is ....

2   What are two main uses of standard costing?

3   A control technique which compares standard costs and revenues with actual results to obtain variances which are used to stimulate improved performance is known as:

    A   Standard costing
    B   Variance analysis
    C   Budgetary control
    D   Budgeting

4   Standard costs may only be used in absorption costing.

    True ☐   False ☐

5   Two types of performance standard are

    (a)   ....   (b)   ....

Answers to quick quiz

1   A planned unit cost.

2   (a)   To value inventories and cost production for cost accounting purposes.

    (b)   To act as a control device by establishing standards and highlighting activities that are not
          conforming to plan and bringing these to the attention of management.

3   A

4   False. They may be used in a marginal costing system as well.

5   (a)   Attainable
    (b)   Ideal

Now try the questions below from the Exam Question Bank

Number	Level	Marks	Time
Q14	MCQ/OTQ	n/a	n/a

Basic variance
analysis

Introduction

The actual results achieved by an organisation during a reporting period (week, month, quarter, year) will, more than likely, be different from the expected results (the expected results being the standard costs and revenues which we looked at in the previous chapter). Such differences may occur between individual items, such as the cost of labour and the volume of sales, and between the total expected profit/contribution and the total actual profit/contribution.

Management will have spent considerable time and trouble setting standards. Actual results have differed from the standards. The wise manager will consider the differences that have occurred and use the results of these considerations to assist in attempts to attain the standards. The wise manager will use **variance analysis** as a method of **control**.

This chapter examines **variance analysis** and sets out the method of calculating the variances stated below in the Study Guide.
We will then go on to look at the reasons for and significance of cost variances.

Chapter 16 of this **Management Accounting** Study Text will build on the basics set down in this chapter by introducing **sales variances** and **operating statements**.

Study guide

		Intellectual level
E4	**Basic variance analysis under absorption and marginal costing**	
(a)	Calculate the following variances (i) Materials total, price and usage (ii) Labour total, rate and efficiency (iii) Variable overhead total, expenditure and efficiency (iv) Fixed overhead total, expenditure and, where appropriate, volume capacity and efficiency	1
(b)	Interpret all the variances above	1
(c)	Explain possible causes of all the variances above	1
(d)	Describe the interrelationships between the variances above	1

Exam guide

Variance calculation is a very important part of your Management Accounting studies and it is vital that you are able to calculate all of the different types of variance included in the syllabus.

1 Variances

FAST FORWARD

A **variance** is the difference between a planned, budgeted, or standard cost and the actual cost incurred. The same comparisons may be made for revenues. The process by which the **total** difference between standard and actual results is analysed is known as **variance analysis**.

When actual results are better than expected results, we have a **favourable variance** (F). If, on the other hand, actual results are worse than expected results, we have an **adverse variance** (A).

Variances can be divided into three main groups.

- Variable cost variances
- Sales variances
- Fixed production overhead variances.

In the remainder of this chapter we will consider, in detail, variable cost variances and fixed production overhead variances.

2 Direct material cost variances

2.1 Introduction

FAST FORWARD

The direct material total variance can be subdivided into the **direct material price** variance and the **direct material usage** variance.

The **direct material total variance** is the difference between what the output actually cost and what it should have cost, in terms of material.

The **direct material price variance.** This is the **difference between the standard cost and the actual cost for the actual quantity of material used or purchased.** In other words, it is the difference between what the material did cost and what it should have cost.

The **direct material usage variance.** This is the **difference between the standard quantity of materials that should have been used for the number of units actually produced, and the actual quantity of materials used, valued at the standard cost per unit of material.** In other words, it is the difference between how much material should have been used and how much material was used, valued at standard cost.

2.2 Example: Direct material variances

Product X has a standard direct material cost as follows.

10 kilograms of material Y at $10 per kilogram = $100 per unit of X.

During period 4, 1,000 units of X were manufactured, using 11,700 kilograms of material Y which cost $98,600.

Required

Calculate the following variances.

(a)   The direct material total variance
(b)   The direct material price variance
(c)   The direct material usage variance

Solution

(a)   **The direct material total variance**

This is the difference between what 1,000 units should have cost and what they did cost.

	$
1,000 units should have cost (× $100)	100,000
but did cost	98,600
Direct material total variance	1,400 (F)

The variance is **favourable** because the units cost less than they should have cost.

Now we can break down the direct material total variance into its two constituent parts: the direct material **price** variance and the direct material **usage** variance.

(b)   **The direct material price variance**

This is the difference between what 11,700 kgs should have cost and what 11,700 kgs did cost.

	$
11,700 kgs of Y should have cost (× $10)	117,000
but did cost	98,600
Material Y price variance	18,400 (F)

The variance is **favourable** because the material cost less than it should have.

(c)   **The direct material usage variance**

This is the difference between how many kilograms of Y should have been used to produce 1,000 units of X and how many kilograms were used, valued at the standard cost per kilogram.

1,000 units should have used (× 10 kgs)	10,000 kgs
but did use	11,700 kgs
Usage variance in kgs	1,700 kgs (A)
× standard cost per kilogram	× $10
Usage variance in $	$17,000 (A)

The variance is **adverse** because more material than should have been used was used.

(d) **Summary**

	$
Price variance	18,400 (F)
Usage variance	17,000 (A)
Total variance	1,400 (F)

2.3 Materials variances and opening and closing inventory

FAST FORWARD Direct material price variances are usually extracted at the time of the **receipt** of the materials rather than at the time of usage.

Suppose that a company uses raw material P in production, and that this raw material has a standard price of $3 per metre. During one month 6,000 metres are bought for $18,600, and 5,000 metres are used in production. At the end of the month, inventory will have been increased by 1,000 metres. In variance analysis, the problem is to decide the **material price variance**. Should it be calculated on the basis of **materials purchased** (6,000 metres) or on the basis of **materials used** (5,000 metres)?

The answer to this problem depends on how **closing inventories** of the raw materials will be valued.

(a) If they are valued at **standard cost**, (1,000 units at $3 per unit) the price variance is calculated on material **purchases** in the period.

(b) If they are valued at **actual cost** (FIFO) (1,000 units at $3.10 per unit) the price variance is calculated on materials **used in production** in the period.

A **full standard costing system** is usually in operation and therefore the price variance is usually calculated on **purchases** in the period. The variance on the full 6,000 metres will be written off to the costing profit and loss account, even though only 5,000 metres are included in the cost of production.

There are two main advantages in extracting the material price variance at the time of **receipt**.

(a) If variances are extracted at the time of receipt they will be **brought to the attention of managers earlier** than if they are extracted as the material is used. If it is necessary to correct any variances then management action can be more timely.

(b) Since variances are extracted at the time of receipt, **all inventories will be valued at standard price**. This is administratively easier and it means that all issues from inventory can be made at standard price. If inventories are held at actual cost it is necessary to calculate a separate price variance on each batch as it is issued. Since issues are usually made in a number of small batches this can be a time-consuming task, especially with a manual system.

The price variance would be calculated as follows.

	$
6,000 metres of material P purchased should cost (× $3)	18,000
but did cost	18,600
Price variance	600 (A)

3 Direct labour cost variances

3.1 Introduction

The direct labour total variance can be subdivided into the **direct labour rate** variance and the **direct labour efficiency** variance.

Key terms

The **direct labour total variance** is the difference between what the output should have cost and what it did cost, in terms of labour.

The direct labour rate variance. This is similar to the direct material price variance. It is the **difference between the standard cost and the actual cost for the actual number of hours paid for.**

In other words, it is the difference between what the labour did cost and what it should have cost.

The direct labour efficiency variance is similar to the direct material usage variance. It is the **difference between the hours that should have been worked for the number of units actually produced, and the actual number of hours worked, valued at the standard rate per hour.**

In other words, it is the difference between how many hours should have been worked and how many hours were worked, valued at the standard rate per hour.

The calculation of **direct labour variances** is very similar to the calculation of direct material variances.

3.2 Example: Direct labour variances

The standard direct labour cost of product X is as follows.

>   2 hours of grade Z labour at $5 per hour = $10 per unit of product X.

During period 4, 1,000 units of product X were made, and the direct labour cost of grade Z labour was $8,900 for 2,300 hours of work.

Required

Calculate the following variances.

(a)   The direct labour total variance
(b)   The direct labour rate variance
(c)   The direct labour efficiency (productivity) variance

Solution

(a)   **The direct labour total variance**

This is the difference between what 1,000 units should have cost and what they did cost.

	$
1,000 units should have cost (× $10)	10,000
but did cost	8,900
Direct labour total variance	1,100 (F)

The variance is **favourable** because the units cost less than they should have done.

Again we can analyse this total variance into its two constituent parts.

(b)   **The direct labour rate variance**

This is the difference between what 2,300 hours should have cost and what 2,300 hours did cost.

	$
2,300 hours of work should have cost (× $5 per hr)	11,500
but did cost	8,900
Direct labour rate variance	2,600 (F)

The variance is **favourable** because the labour cost less than it should have cost.

(c)   **The direct labour efficiency variance**

1,000 units of X should have taken (× 2 hrs)	2,000 hrs
but did take	2,300 hrs
Efficiency variance in hours	300 hrs (A)
× standard rate per hour	× $5
Efficiency variance in $	$1,500 (A)

The variance is **adverse** because more hours were worked than should have been worked.

(d)   **Summary**

	$
Rate variance	2,600 (F)
Efficiency variance	1,500 (A)
Total variance	1,100 (F)

4 Variable production overhead variances

FAST FORWARD

> The variable production overhead total variance can be subdivided into the variable production overhead **expenditure** variance and the variable production overhead **efficiency** variance (**based on actual hours**).

4.1 Example: Variable production overhead variances

Suppose that the variable production overhead cost of product X is as follows.

   2 hours at $1.50 = $3 per unit

During period 6, 400 units of product X were made. The labour force worked 820 hours, of which 60 hours were recorded as idle time. The variable overhead cost was $1,230.

Calculate the following variances.

(a)   The variable overhead total variance
(b)   The variable production overhead expenditure variance
(c)   The variable production overhead efficiency variance

Since this example relates to variable production costs, the total variance is based on actual units of production. (If the overhead had been a variable selling cost, the variance would be based on sales volumes.)

	$
400 units of product X should cost (× $3)	1,200
but did cost	1,230
Variable production overhead total variance	30 (A)

In many variance reporting systems, the variance analysis goes no further, and expenditure and efficiency variances are not calculated. However, the adverse variance of $30 may be explained as the sum of two factors.

(a)   The hourly rate of spending on variable production overheads was higher than it should have been, that is there is an expenditure variance.

(b)   The labour force worked inefficiently, and took longer to make the output than it should have done. This means that spending on variable production overhead was higher than it should have been, in other words there is an efficiency (productivity) variance. The variable production overhead efficiency variance is exactly the same, in hours, as the direct labour efficiency variance, and occurs for the same reasons.

It is usually assumed that **variable overheads are incurred during active working hours**, but are not incurred during idle time (for example the machines are not running, therefore power is not being consumed, and no indirect materials are being used). This means in our example that although the labour force was paid for 820 hours, they were actively working for only 760 of those hours and so variable production overhead spending occurred during 760 hours.

> The **variable production overhead expenditure variance** is the difference between the amount of variable production overhead that should have been incurred in the actual hours actively worked, and the actual amount of variable production overhead incurred.

(a)

	$
760 hours of variable production overhead should cost (× $1.50)	1,140
but did cost	1,230
Variable production overhead expenditure variance	90 (A)

> The **variable production overhead efficiency variance**. If you already know the direct labour efficiency variance, the variable production overhead efficiency variance is exactly the same in hours, but priced at the variable production overhead rate per hour.

(b)   In our example, the efficiency variance would be as follows.

400 units of product X should take (× 2hrs)	800 hrs
but did take (active hours)	760 hrs
Variable production overhead efficiency variance in hours	40 hrs (F)
× standard rate per hour	× $1.50
Variable production overhead efficiency variance in $	$60 (F)

(c)   **Summary**

	$
Variable production overhead expenditure variance	90 (A)
Variable production overhead efficiency variance	60 (F)
Variable production overhead total variance	30 (A)

5 Fixed production overhead variances

5.1 Introduction

> The fixed production overhead total variance can be subdivided into an **expenditure** variance and a **volume** variance. The fixed production overhead volume variance can be further subdivided into an efficiency and capacity variance.

You may have noticed that the method of calculating cost variances for variable cost items is essentially the same for labour, materials and variable overheads. Fixed production overhead variances are very different. In an **absorption costing system**, they are an attempt to explain the **under– or over-absorption of fixed production overheads** in production costs. We looked at under/over absorption of fixed overheads in Chapter 8.

The fixed production overhead total variance (ie the under– or over-absorbed fixed production overhead) may be broken down into two parts as usual.

* An **expenditure** variance

* A **volume** variance. This in turn may be split into two parts

  – **A volume efficiency variance**   – **A volume capacity variance**

You will find it easier to calculate and understand **fixed overhead variances**, if you keep in mind the whole time that you are trying to 'explain' (put a name and value to) any under– or over-absorbed overhead.

You will need to be able to distinguish between marginal and absorption costing. The variances introduced above and discussed below relate to an absorption costing system. Marginal costing is dealt with in Chapter 16. In the marginal costing system the only fixed overhead variance is an expenditure variance.

5.2 Under/over absorption

Remember that the **absorption rate** is calculated as follows.

$$\text{Overhead absorption rate} = \frac{\text{Budgeted fixed overhead}}{\text{Budgeted activity level}}$$

Remember that the budgeted fixed overhead is the **planned** or **expected** fixed overhead and the budgeted activity level is the **planned** or **expected** activity level.

If either of the following are incorrect, then we will have an under– or over-absorption of overhead.

- The numerator (number on top) = Budgeted fixed overhead
- The denominator (number on bottom) = Budgeted activity level

5.3 The fixed overhead expenditure variance

The fixed overhead expenditure variance occurs if the numerator is incorrect. It measures the under– or over-absorbed overhead caused by the **actual total overhead** being different from the budgeted total overhead.

Therefore, fixed overhead expenditure variance = **Budgeted (planned) expenditure – Actual Expenditure**.

5.4 The fixed overhead volume variance

As we have already stated, the fixed overhead volume variance is made up of the following sub-variances.

- Fixed overhead efficiency variance
- Fixed overhead capacity variance

These variances arise if the denominator (ie the budgeted activity level) is incorrect.

The fixed overhead efficiency and capacity variances measure the under– or over-absorbed overhead caused by the **actual activity level** being different from the budgeted activity level used in calculating the absorption rate.

There are two reasons why the **actual activity** level may be different from the **budgeted activity level** used in calculating the absorption rate.

(a) The workforce may have worked more or less efficiently than the standard set. This deviation is measured by the **fixed overhead efficiency variance.**

(b) The hours worked by the workforce could have been different to the budgeted hours (regardless of the level of efficiency of the workforce) because of overtime and strikes etc. This deviation from the standard is measured by the **fixed overhead capacity variance.**

5.5 How to calculate the variances

In order to clarify the overhead variances which we have encountered in this section, consider the following definitions which are expressed in terms of how each overhead variance should be calculated.

Fixed overhead total variance is the difference between fixed overhead incurred and fixed overhead absorbed. In other words, it is the under– or over-absorbed fixed overhead.

Fixed overhead expenditure variance is the difference between the budgeted fixed overhead expenditure and actual fixed overhead expenditure.

Fixed overhead volume variance is the difference between actual and budgeted (planned) volume multiplied by the standard absorption rate per *unit*.

Fixed overhead volume efficiency variance is the difference between the number of hours that actual production should have taken, and the number of hours actually taken (that is, worked) multiplied by the standard absorption rate per *hour*.

Fixed overhead volume capacity variance is the difference between budgeted (planned) hours of work and the actual hours worked, multiplied by the standard absorption rate per *hour*.

You should now be ready to work through an example to demonstrate all of the fixed overhead variances.

5.6 Example: Fixed overhead variances

Suppose that a company plans to produce 1,000 units of product E during August 20X3. The expected time to produce a unit of E is five hours, and the budgeted fixed overhead is $20,000. The standard fixed overhead cost per unit of product E will therefore be as follows.

5 hours at $4 per hour = $20 per unit

Actual fixed overhead expenditure in August 20X3 turns out to be $20,450. The labour force manages to produce 1,100 units of product E in 5,400 hours of work.

Task

Calculate the following variances.

(a)   The fixed overhead total variance
(b)   The fixed overhead expenditure variance
(c)   The fixed overhead volume variance
(d)   The fixed overhead volume efficiency variance
(e)   The fixed overhead volume capacity variance

Solution

All of the variances help to assess the under– or over-absorption of fixed overheads, some in greater detail than others.

(a)   **Fixed overhead total variance**

	$
Fixed overhead incurred	20,450
Fixed overhead absorbed (1,100 units × $20 per unit)	22,000
Fixed overhead total variance	1,550 (F)
(= under-/over-absorbed overhead)	

The variance is favourable because more overheads were absorbed than budgeted.

(b)   **Fixed overhead expenditure variance**

	$
Budgeted fixed overhead expenditure	20,000
Actual fixed overhead expenditure	20,450
Fixed overhead expenditure variance	450 (A)

The variance is adverse because actual expenditure was greater than budgeted expenditure.

(c)   **Fixed overhead volume variance**

The production volume achieved was greater than expected. The fixed overhead volume variance measures the difference at the standard rate.

	$
Actual production at standard rate (1,100 × $20 per unit)	22,000
Budgeted production at standard rate (1,000 × $20 per unit)	20,000
Fixed overhead volume variance	2,000 (F)

The variance is **favourable** because output was greater than expected.

(i)   The labour force may have worked efficiently, and produced output at a faster rate than expected. Since overheads are absorbed at the rate of $20 per unit, more will be absorbed if units are produced more quickly. This **efficiency variance** is exactly the same in hours as the direct labour efficiency variance, but is valued in $ at the standard absorption rate for fixed overhead.

(ii)   The labour force may have worked longer hours than budgeted, and therefore produced more output, so there may be a **capacity variance**.

(d)   **Fixed overhead volume efficiency variance**

The volume efficiency variance is calculated in the same way as the labour efficiency variance.

1,100 units of product E should take (× 5 hrs)	5,500 hrs
but did take	5,400 hrs
Fixed overhead volume efficiency variance in hours	100 hrs (F)
× standard fixed overhead absorption rate per hour	× $4
Fixed overhead volume efficiency variance in $	$400 (F)

The labour force has produced 5,500 standard hours of work in 5,400 actual hours and so output is 100 standard hours (or 20 units of product E) higher than budgeted for this reason and the variance is **favourable**.

(e)   **Fixed overhead volume capacity variance**

The volume capacity variance is the difference between the budgeted hours of work and the actual active hours of work (excluding any idle time).

Budgeted hours of work	5,000 hrs
Actual hours of work	5,400 hrs
Fixed overhead volume capacity variance	400 hrs (F)
× standard fixed overhead absorption rate per hour	× $4
Fixed overhead volume capacity variance in $	$1,600 (F)

Since the labour force worked 400 hours longer than planned, we should expect output to be 400 standard hours (or 80 units of product E) higher than budgeted and hence the variance is **favourable**.

The variances may be summarised as follows.

	$
Expenditure variance	450 (A)
Efficiency variance	400 (F)
Capacity variance	1,600 (F)
Over-absorbed overhead (total variance)	$1,550 (F)

Do not worry if you find fixed production overhead variances more difficult to grasp than the other variances we have covered. Most students do. Read over this section again and then try the following practice questions.

The following information relates to the questions shown below

Barbados has prepared the following standard cost information for one unit of Product Zeta.

Direct materials	4kg @ $10/kg	$40.00
Direct labour	2 hours @ $4/hour	$8.00
Fixed overheads	3 hours @ $2.50	$7.50

The fixed overheads are based on a budgeted expenditure of $75,000 and budgeted activity of 30,000 hours.

Actual results for the period were recorded as follows.

Production	9,000 units
Materials – 33,600 kg	$336,000
Labour – 16,500 hours	$68,500
Fixed overheads	$70,000

 Question   **Material variances**

The direct material price and usage variances are:

	Material price $	Material usage $
A	–	24,000 (F)
B	–	24,000 (A)
C	24,000 (F)	–
D	24,000 (A)	–

Answer

Material price variance

	$
33,600 kg should have cost (× $10/kg)	336,000
and did cost	336,000
	–

Material usage variance

9,000 units should have used (× 4kg)	36,000 kg
but did use	33,600 kg
	2,400 kg (F)
× standard cost per kg	× $10
	24,000 (F)

The correct answer is therefore A.

The direct labour rate and efficiency variances are:

	Labour rate	Labour efficiency
	$	$
A	6,000 (F)	2,500 (A)
B	6,000 (A)	2,500 (F)
C	2,500 (A)	6,000 (F)
D	2,500 (F)	6,000 (A)

Answer

Direct labour rate variance

	$
16,500 hrs should have cost (× $4)	66,000
but did cost	68,500
	2,500 (A)

Direct labour efficiency variance

9,000 units should have taken (× 2 hrs)	18,000 hrs
but did take	16,500 hrs
	1,500 (F)
× standard rate per hour (× $4)	× $4
	6,000 (F)

The correct answer is therefore C.

The total fixed production overhead variance is:

A $5,000 (A)
B $5,000 (F)
C $2,500 (A)
D $2,500 (F)

Answer

	$
Fixed production overhead absorbed ($7.50 × 9,000)	67,500
Fixed production overhead incurred	70,000
	2,500 (A)

The correct answer is therefore C.

6 The reasons for cost variances

There are many possible reasons for cost variances arising, as you will see from the following list of possible causes.

This is not an exhaustive list and in an examination question you should review the information given and use your imagination and common sense in analysing possible reasons for variances.

Variance	Favourable	Adverse
(a) Material price	Unforeseen discounts received More care taken in purchasing Change in material standard	Price increase Careless purchasing Change in material standard
(b) Material usage	Material used of higher quality than standard More effective use made of material Errors in allocating material to jobs	Defective material Excessive waste Theft Stricter quality control Errors in allocating material to jobs
(c) Labour rate	Use of apprentices or other workers at a rate of pay lower than standard	Wage rate increase Use of higher grade labour
(d) Idle time	The idle time variance is always adverse	Machine breakdown Non-availability of material Illness or injury to worker
(e) Labour efficiency	Output produced more quickly than expected because of work motivation, better quality of equipment or materials, or better methods. Errors in allocating time to jobs	Lost time in excess of standard allowed Output lower than standard set because of deliberate restriction, lack of training, or sub-standard material used Errors in allocating time to jobs
(f) Overhead expenditure	Savings in costs incurred More economical use of services	Increase in cost of services used Excessive use of services Change in type of services used
(g) Overhead volume efficiency	Labour force working more efficiently (favourable labour efficiency variance)	Labour force working less efficiently (adverse labour efficiency variance)
(h) Overhead volume capacity	Labour force working overtime	Machine breakdown, strikes, labour shortages

7 The significance of cost variances

7.1 Introduction

Materiality, controllability, the type of standard being used, the interdependence of variances and the cost of an investigation should be taken into account when deciding whether to investigate reported variances.

Once variances have been calculated, management have to decide whether or not to investigate their causes. It would be extremely time consuming and expensive to investigate every variance therefore managers have to decide which variances are worthy of investigation.

There are a number of factors which can be taken into account when deciding whether or not a variance should be investigated.

(a) **Materiality.** A standard cost is really only an **average** expected cost and is not a rigid specification. Small variations either side of this average are therefore bound to occur. The problem is to decide whether a variation from standard should be considered **significant** and worthy of investigation. **Tolerance limits** can be set and only variances which exceed such limits would require investigating.

(b) **Controllability.** Some types of variance may not be controllable even once their cause is discovered. For example, if there is a general worldwide increase in the price of a raw material there is nothing that can be done internally to control the effect of this. If a central decision is made to award all employees a 10% increase in salary, staff costs in division A will increase by this amount and the variance is not controllable by division A's manager. Uncontrollable variances call for a change in the plan, not an investigation into the past.

(c) **The type of standard being used.**

  (i) The efficiency variance reported in any control period, whether for materials or labour, will depend on the **efficiency level** set. If, for example, an **ideal standard** is used, variances will always be **adverse**.

  (ii) A similar problem arises if **average price levels** are used as standards. If inflation exists, favourable price variances are likely to be reported at the beginning of a period, to be offset by adverse price variances later in the period as inflation pushes prices up.

(d) **Interdependence between variances** . Quite possibly, individual variances should not be looked at in isolation. One variance might be inter-related with another, and much of it might have occurred only because the other, inter-related, variance occurred too. We will investigate this issue further in a moment.

(e) **Costs of investigation.** The costs of an investigation should be weighed against the benefits of correcting the cause of a variance.

7.2 Interdependence between variances

When two variances are interdependent (interrelated) one will usually be adverse and the other one favourable.

7.3 Interdependence – materials price and usage variances

It may be decided to purchase cheaper materials for a job in order to obtain a favourable **price variance**. This may lead to higher materials wastage than expected and therefore, **adverse usage variances occur**. If the cheaper materials are more difficult to handle, there might be some **adverse labour efficiency variance** too.

If a decision is made to purchase more expensive materials, which perhaps have a longer service life, the price variance will be adverse but the usage variance might be favourable.

7.4 Interdependence – labour rate and efficiency variances

If employees in a workforce are paid higher rates for experience and skill, using a highly skilled team should incur an **adverse rate variance** at the same time as a **favourable efficiency variance**. In contrast, a **favourable rate variance** might indicate a high proportion of inexperienced workers in the workforce, which could result in an **adverse labour efficiency variance** and possibly an **adverse materials usage variance** (due to high rates of rejects).

Chapter roundup

- A **variance** is the difference between a planned, budgeted, or standard cost and the actual cost incurred. The same comparisons can be made for revenues. The process by which the **total** difference between standard and actual results is analysed is known as the **variance analysis**.

- The direct material total variance can be subdivided into the **direct material price** variance and the **direct material usage** variance.

- Direct material price variances are usually extracted at the time of **receipt** of the materials, rather than at the time of usage.

- The direct labour total variance can be subdivided into the **direct labour rate** variance and the **direct labour efficiency** variance.

- If **idle time** arises, it is usual to calculate a separate idle time variance, and to base the calculation of the efficiency variance on **active hours** (when labour actually worked) only. It is always an **adverse** variance.

- The variable production overhead total variance can be subdivided into the variable production overhead **expenditure** variance and the variable production overhead **efficiency** variance **(based on active hours)**.

- The fixed production overhead total variance can be subdivided into an **expenditure** variance and a **volume** variance. The fixed production overhead volume variance can be further subdivided into an **efficiency** and a **capacity** variance.

- Materiality, controllability, the type of standard being used, the interdependence of variances and the cost of an investigation should be taken into account when deciding whether to investigate reported variances.

Quick quiz

1   Subdivide the following variances.

    (a)   Direct materials cost variance

    (b)   Direct labour cost variance

    (c)   Variable production overhead variance

2   What are the two main advantages in calculating the material price variance at the time of receipt of materials?

3   Idle time variances are always adverse.

    True ☐   False ☐

4   Adverse material usage variances might occur for the following reasons.

I	Defective material	III	Theft
II	Excessive waste	IV	Unforeseen discounts received

A	I	C	I, II and III
B	I and II	D	I, II, III and IV

5   List the factors which should be taken into account when deciding whether or not a variance should be investigated.

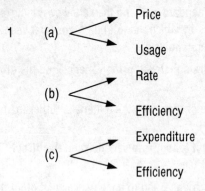

1   (a)   Price

    Usage

    (b)   Rate

    Efficiency

    (c)   Expenditure

    Efficiency

2   (a)   The earlier variances are extracted, the sooner they will be brought to the attention of managers.
    (b)   All inventories will be valued at standard price which requires less administration effort.

3   True

4   C

5   • Materiality   • Interdependence between variances
    • Controllability   • Costs of investigation
    • Type of standard being used

Now try the questions below from the Exam Question Bank

Number	Level	Marks	Time
Q15	MCQ/OTQ	n/a	n/a

Further variance analysis

Introduction

The objective of cost variance analysis, which we looked at in the previous chapter, is to assist management in the **control of costs**. Costs are, however, only one factor which contribute to the achievement of planned profit. **Sales** are another important factor and sales variances can be calculated to aid management's control of their business. We will therefore begin this chapter by examining **sales variances**.

Having discussed the variances you need to know about, we will be looking in Section 2 at the **ways in which variances should be presented to management** to aid their control of the organisation.

We then consider in Section 3 how **marginal cost variances** differ from absorption cost variances and how marginal costing information should be presented.

Finally we will consider **how actual data can be derived from standard cost details and variances**.

Study guide

		Intellectual level
E4	**Basic variance analysis under absorption and marginal costing**	
(a)	Calculate interpret and explain sales price and volume variance	1
(b)	Calculate actual or standard figures where the following variances are given:	1
	(i) Sales price and volume	
	(ii) Materials total, price and usage	
	(iii) Labour total, rate and efficiency	
	(iv) Variable overhead total, expenditure and efficiency	
	(v) Fixed overhead total, expenditure and, where appropriate, volume, capacity and efficiency	
E5	**Reconciliation of budgeted profit and actual profit**	
(a)	Reconcile budgeted profit with actual profit under standard absorption costing	1
(b)	Reconcile budgeted profit or contribution with actual profit or contribution under standard marginal costing	1

Exam guide

Variance analysis is traditionally a very popular exam topic. Make sure that you are able to prepare operating statements and explain why calculated variances have occurred. You will not be expected to prepare a whole operating statement in the exam, but you may be tested on your understanding of these statements.

1 Sales variances

1.1 Selling price variance

FAST FORWARD

> The **selling price variance** is a measure of the effect on expected profit of a different selling price to standard selling price. It is calculated as the difference between what the sales revenue should have been for the actual quantity sold, and what it was.

1.2 Example: Selling price variance

Suppose that the standard selling price of product X is $15. Actual sales in 20X3 were 2,000 units at $15.30 per unit. The selling price variance is calculated as follows.

	$
Sales revenue from 2,000 units should have been (× $15)	30,000
but was (× $15.30)	30,600
Selling price variance	600 (F)

The variance calculated is **favourable** because the price was higher than expected.

1.3 Sales volume profit variance

FAST FORWARD

> The **sales volume profit variance** is the difference between the actual units sold and the budgeted (planned) quantity, valued at the standard profit per unit. In other words, it measures the increase or decrease in standard profit as a result of the sales volume being higher or lower than budgeted (planned).

1.4 Example: Sales volume profit variance

Suppose that a company budgets to sell 8,000 units of product J for $12 per unit. The standard full cost per unit is $7. Actual sales were 7,700 units, at $12.50 per unit.

The **sales volume profit variance** is calculated as follows.

Budgeted sales volume	8,000 units
Actual sales volume	7,700 units
Sales volume variance in units	300 units (A)
× standard profit per unit ($(12–7))	× $5
Sales volume variance	$1,500 (A)

The variance calculated above is **adverse** because actual sales were less than budgeted (planned).

Question	Selling price variance

Jasper Ltd has the following budget and actual figures for 20X4.

	Budget	Actual
Sales units	600	620
Selling price per unit	$30	$29

Standard full cost of production = $28 per unit.

Required

Calculate the selling price variance and the sales volume profit variance.

Answer

Sales revenue for 620 units should have been (× $30)	18,600
but was (× $29)	17,980
Selling price variance	620 (A)

Budgeted sales volume	600 units
Actual sales volume	620 units
Sales volume variance in units	20 units (F)
× standard profit per unit ($(30 − 28))	× $2
Sales volume profit variance	$40 (F)

1.5 The significance of sales variances

The possible **interdependence** between sales price and sales volume variances should be obvious to you. A reduction in the sales price might stimulate bigger sales demand, so that an adverse sales price variance might be counterbalanced by a favourable sales volume variance. Similarly, a price rise would give a favourable price variance, but possibly at the cost of a fall in demand and an adverse sales volume variance.

It is therefore important in analysing an unfavourable sales variance that the overall consequence should be considered, that is, has there been a counterbalancing favourable variance as a direct result of the unfavourable one?

2 Operating statements

2.1 Introduction

FAST FORWARD ➤➤ **Operating statements** show how the combination of variances reconcile budgeted profit and actual profit.

So far, we have considered how variances are calculated without considering how they combine to reconcile the difference between budgeted profit and actual profit during a period. This reconciliation is usually presented as a report to senior management at the end of each control period. The report is called an **operating statement** or **statement of variances**.

Key term

> An **operating statement** is a regular report for management of actual costs and revenues, usually showing variances from budget.

An extensive example will now be introduced, both to revise the variance calculations already described, and also to show how to combine them into an operating statement.

2.2 Example: Variances and operating statements

Sydney manufactures one product, and the entire product is sold as soon as it is produced. There are no opening or closing inventories and work in progress is negligible. The company operates a standard costing system and analysis of variances is made every month. The standard cost card for the product, a boomerang, is as follows.

STANDARD COST CARD – BOOMERANG

		$
Direct materials	0.5 kilos at $4 per kilo	2.00
Direct wages	2 hours at $2.00 per hour	4.00
Variable overheads	2 hours at $0.30 per hour	0.60
Fixed overhead	2 hours at $3.70 per hour	7.40
Standard cost		14.00
Standard profit		6.00
Standing selling price		20.00

Selling and administration expenses are not included in the standard cost, and are deducted from profit as a period charge.

Budgeted (planned) output for the month of June 20X7 was 5,100 units. Actual results for June 20X7 were as follows.

Production of 4,850 units was sold for $95,600.
Materials consumed in production amounted to 2,300 kgs at a total cost of $9,800.
Labour hours paid for amounted to 8,500 hours at a cost of $16,800.
Actual operating hours amounted to 8,000 hours.
Variable overheads amounted to $2,600.
Fixed overheads amounted to $42,300.
Selling and administration expenses amounted to $18,000.

Required

Calculate all variances and prepare an operating statement for the month ended 30 June 20X7.

Solution

(a)

	$
2,300 kg of material should cost (× $4)	9,200
but did cost	9,800
Material price variance	600 (A)

(b)

4,850 boomerangs should use (× 0.5 kgs)	2,425 kg
but did use	2,300 kg
Material usage variance in kgs	125 kg (F)
× standard cost per kg	× $4
Material usage variance in $	$ 500 (F)

(c)

	$
8,500 hours of labour should cost (× $2)	17,000
but did cost	16,800
Labour rate variance	200 (F)

(d)

4,850 boomerangs should take (× 2 hrs)	9,700 hrs
but did take (active hours)	8,000 hrs
Labour efficiency variance in hours	1,700 hrs (F)
× standard cost per hour	× $2
Labour efficiency variance in $	$3,400 (F)

(e) **Idle time variance** 500 hours (A) × $2 $1,000 (A)

(f)

	$
8,000 hours incurring variable o/hd expenditure should cost (× $0.30)	2,400
but did cost	2,600
Variable overhead expenditure variance	200 (A)

(g) **Variable overhead efficiency variance** in hours is the same as the labour efficiency variance:

1,700 hours (F) × $0.30 per hour $ 510 (F)

(h)

	$
Budgeted fixed overhead (5,100 units × 2 hrs × $3.70)	37,740
Actual fixed overhead	42,300
Fixed overhead expenditure variance	4,560 (A)

(i)

	$
4,850 boomerangs should take (× 2 hrs)	9,700 hrs
but did take (active hours)	8,000 hrs
Fixed overhead volume efficiency variance in hrs	1,700 hrs (F)
× standard fixed overhead absorption rate per hour	× $3.70
Fixed overhead volume efficiency variance in $	6,290 (F)

(j)

	$
Budgeted hours of work (5,100 × 2 hrs)	10,200 hrs
Actual hours of work	8,000 hrs
Fixed overhead volume capacity variance in hrs	2,200 hrs (A)
× standard fixed overhead absorption rate per hour	× $3.70
Fixed overhead volume capacity variance in $	8,140 (A)

(k)

		$
Revenue from 4,850 boomerangs should be (× $20)		97,000
but was		95,600
Selling price variance		1,400 (A)

(l)

Budgeted sales volume	5,100 units
Actual sales volume	4,850 units
Sales volume profit variance in units	250 units
× standard profit per unit	× $6 (A)
Sales volume profit variance in $	$1,500 (A)

There are several ways in which an operating statement may be presented. Perhaps the most common format is one which **reconciles budgeted profit to actual profit**. In this example, sales and administration costs will be introduced at the end of the statement, so that we shall begin with 'budgeted profit before sales and administration costs'.

Sales variances are reported first, and the total of the budgeted profit and the two sales variances results in a figure for 'actual sales minus the standard cost of sales'. The cost variances are then reported, and an actual profit (before sales and administration costs) calculated. Sales and administration costs are then deducted to reach the actual profit for June 20X7.

SYDNEY – OPERATING STATEMENT JUNE 20X7

		$	$
Budgeted (planned) profit before sales and administration costs			30,600
Sales variances:	price	1,400 (A)	
	volume	1,500 (A)	
			2,900 (A)
Actual sales minus the standard cost of sales			27,700

	(F)	(A)	
Cost variances	$	$	
Material price		600	
Material usage	500		
Labour rate	200		
Labour efficiency	3,400		
Labour idle time		1,000	
Variable overhead expenditure		200	
Variable overhead efficiency	510		
Fixed overhead expenditure		4,560	
Fixed overhead volume efficiency	6,290		
Fixed overhead volume capacity		8,140	
	10,900	14,500	3,600 (A)

Actual profit before sales and administration costs	24,100
Sales and administration costs	18,000
Actual profit, June 20X7	6,100

Check	$	$
Sales		95,600
Materials	9,800	
Labour	16,800	
Variable overhead	2,600	
Fixed overhead	42,300	
Sales and administration	18,000	
		89,500
Actual profit		6,100

3 Variances in a standard marginal costing system

3.1 Introduction

FAST FORWARD

There are two main differences between the variances calculated in an absorption costing system and the variances calculated in a marginal costing system.

- In the marginal costing system **the only fixed overhead variance is an expenditure variance**.
- The sales volume variance is **valued at standard contribution margin**, not standard profit margin.

In all of the examples we have worked through so far, a system of standard absorption costing has been in operation. If an organisation uses **standard marginal costing** instead of standard absorption costing, there will be two differences in the way the variances are calculated.

(a) In marginal costing, fixed costs are not absorbed into product costs and so there are no fixed cost variances to explain any under or over absorption of overheads. There will, therefore, be **no fixed overhead volume variance**. There will be a fixed overhead expenditure variance which is calculated in exactly the same way as for absorption costing systems.

(b) The **sales volume variance** will be valued at **standard contribution margin** (sales price per unit minus variable costs of sale per unit), **not** standard **profit** margin.

3.2 Preparing a marginal costing operating statement

Returning once again to the example of Sydney, the variances in a system of standard marginal costing would be as follows.

(a) There is **no fixed overhead volume variance** (and therefore no fixed overhead volume efficiency and volume capacity variances).

(b) The standard contribution per unit of boomerang is $(20 − 6.60) = 13.40, therefore the **sales volume contribution variance** of 250 units (A) is valued at ($\times$ $13.40) = $3,350 (A).

The other variances are unchanged. However, this operating statement differs from an absorption costing operating statement in the following ways.

(a) It begins with the budgeted **contribution** ($30,600 + budgeted fixed production costs $37,740 = $68,340).

(b) The subtotal before the analysis of cost variances is actual sales ($95,600) less the standard **variable** cost of sales ($4,850 $\times$ $6.60) = $63,590.

(c) **Actual contribution** is highlighted in the statement.

(d) Budgeted (planned) fixed production overhead is adjusted by the fixed overhead expenditure variance to show the **actual** fixed production overhead expenditure.

Therefore a marginal costing operating statement might look like this.

SYDNEY – OPERATING STATEMENT JUNE 20X7

	$	$	$
Budgeted (planned) contribution			68,340
Sales variances: volume		3,350 (A)	
price		1,400 (A)	
			4,750 (A)
Actual sales minus the standard variable cost of sales			63,590
	(F)	(A)	
Variable cost variances			
Material price		600	
Material usage	500		
Labour rate	200		
Labour efficiency	3,400		
Labour idle time		1,000	
Variable overhead expenditure		200	
Variable overhead efficiency	510		
	4,610	1,800	
			2,810 (F)
Actual contribution			66,400
Budgeted (planned) fixed production overhead		37,740	
Expenditure variance		4,560 (A)	
Actual fixed production overhead			42,300
Actual profit before sales and administration costs			24,100
Sales and administration costs			18,000
Actual profit			6,100

Notice that the actual profit is the same as the profit calculated by standard absorption costing because there were no changes in inventory levels. Absorption costing and marginal costing do not always produce an identical profit figure.

Question   Variances

Piglet, a manufacturing firm, operates a standard marginal costing system. It makes a single product, PIG, using a single raw material LET.

Standard costs relating to PIG have been calculated as follows.

Standard cost schedule – PIG	Per unit
	$
Direct material, LET, 100 kg at $5 per kg	500
Direct labour, 10 hours at $8 per hour	80
Variable production overhead, 10 hours at $2 per hour	20
	600

The standard selling price of a PIG is $900 and Piglet Co produce 1,020 units a month.

During December 20X0, 1,000 units of PIG were produced. Relevant details of this production are as follows.

Direct material LET

90,000 kgs costing $720,000 were bought and used.

Direct labour

8,200 hours were worked during the month and total wages were $63,000.

Variable production overhead

The actual cost for the month was $25,000.

Inventories of the direct material LET are valued at the standard price of $5 per kg.

Each PIG was sold for $975.

Required

Calculate the following for the month of December 20X0.

(a) Variable production cost variance
(b) Direct labour cost variance, analysed into rate and efficiency variances
(c) Direct material cost variance, analysed into price and usage variances
(d) Variable production overhead variance, analysed into expenditure and efficiency variances
(e) Selling price variance
(f) Sales volume contribution variance

Answer

(a) This is simply a 'total' variance.

	$
1,000 units should have cost ($\times$ $600)	600,000
but did cost (see working)	808,000
Variable production cost variance	208,000 (A)

(b) **Direct labour cost variances**

	$
8,200 hours should cost ($\times$ $8)	65,600
but did cost	63,000
Direct labour rate variance	2,600 (F)

1,000 units should take ($\times$ 10 hours)	10,000 hrs
but did take	8,200 hrs
Direct labour efficiency variance in hrs	1,800 hrs (F)
$\times$ standard rate per hour	$\times$ $8
Direct labour efficiency variance in $	$14,400 (F)

Summary	$
Rate	2,600 (F)
Efficiency	14,400 (F)
Total	17,000 (F)

(c) **Direct material cost variances**

	$
90,000 kg should cost ($\times$ $5)	450,000
but did cost	720,000
Direct material price variance	270,000 (A)

1,000 units should use ($\times$ 100 kg)	100,000 kg
but did use	90,000 kg
Direct material usage variance in kgs	10,000 kg (F)
$\times$ standard cost per kg	$\times$ $5
Direct material usage variance in $	$50,000 (F)

Summary	$
Price	270,000 (A)
Usage	50,000 (F)
Total	220,000 (A)

(d) **Variable production overhead variances**

	$
8,200 hours incurring o/hd should cost ($\times$ $2)	16,400
but did cost	25,000
Variable production overhead expenditure variance	8,600 (A)

Efficiency variance in hrs (from (b))		1,800 hrs (F)
× standard rate per hour		× $2
Variable production overhead efficiency variance		$3,600 (F)

Summary

		$
Expenditure		8,600 (A)
Efficiency		3,600 (F)
Total		5,000 (A)

(e) **Selling price variance**

		$
Revenue from 1,000 units should have been (× $900)		900,000
but was (× $975)		975,000
Selling price variance		75,000 (F)

(f) **Sales volume contribution variance**

Budgeted sales		1,020 units
Actual sales		1,000 units
Sales volume variance in units		20 units (A)
× standard contribution margin ($(900 − 600))		× $300
Sales volume contribution variance in $		$6,000 (A)

Workings

		$
Direct material		720,000
Total wages		63,000
Variable production overhead		25,000
		808,000

Exam focus point

> The question above is much longer than what will appear in your exam, but any one of these variances, individually, may be the subject of a 2-mark question.

 Question   **Operating statements**

Diddly Inc earned a profit of $305,000 in the last month. Variances were as follows.

Labour:	rate	15,250 (F)
	efficiency	(10,750)
Material:	usage	(8,675)
	price	9,825 (F)
Variable overheads:	efficiency	(6,275)
	expenditure	2,850 (F)
Fixed overheads:	expenditure	7,000 (F)
Sales:	price	(25,000)
	volume	32,000

What was Diddly Inc's budgeted profit for last month?

A	$321,225		C	$371,925
B	$288,775		D	$254,300

Remember you are working in **reverse** (you have been given actual profit), so all **adverse** variances have to be **added back** to actual profit and **favourable** variances **deducted** to arrive at budgeted profit.

The correct answer is B.

		Fav. $	Adv. $	$
Actual profit				305,000
Variances:				
Labour:	rate	(15,250)		
	efficiency		10,750	
Material:	price	(9,825)		
	usage		8,675	
Variable overheads:	efficiency		6,275	
	expenditure	(2,850)		
Fixed overheads:	expenditure	(7,000)		
Sales:	price		25,000	
	volume	(32,000)		
		(66,925)	50,700	
Net favourable variance				(16,225)
Budgeted profit				288,775

Reconciling contributions

A company uses standard marginal costing. Last month the standard contribution on actual sales was $10,000 and the following variances arose.

	$
Total variable costs variance	2,000 (Adverse)
Sales price variance	500 (Favourable)
Sales volume contribution variance	1,000 (Adverse)

What was the actual contribution for last month?

A	$7,000	C	$8,000
B	$7,500	D	$8,500

The correct answer is D.

	$
Standard contribution on actual sales	10,000
Add: favourable sales price variance	500
Less: adverse total variable costs variance	(2,000)
Actual contribution	8,500

The above question was an actual question from December 2007 which was highlighted by the examiner as one where less than 30% of students selected the correct answer. The most popular choice made by students was B – these students overlooked the fact that 'standard contribution on actual sales' (which is given in the question) would have been obtained by adjusting the budgeted contribution by the sales volume contribution variance. This variance should therefore have been ignored in answering the question.

4 Deriving actual data from standard cost details and variances

FAST FORWARD

Variances can be used to derive actual data from standard cost details.

Rather than being given actual data and asked to calculate the variances, you may be given the variances and required to calculate the actual data on which they were based. See if you can do these two questions.

Question

Rate of pay

XYZ uses standard costing. The following data relates to labour grade II.

Actual hours worked	10,400 hours
Standard allowance for actual production	8,320 hours
Standard rate per hour	$5
Rate variance (adverse)	$416

What was the actual rate of pay per hour?

A	$4.95	C	$5.04
B	$4.96	D	$5.05

Answer

Rate variance per hour worked = $\dfrac{\$416}{10,400}$ = $0.04 (A)

Actual rate per hour = $(5.00 + 0.04) = $5.04.

The correct answer is C.

You should have been able to eliminate options A and B because they are both below the standard rate per hour. If the rate variance is adverse then the actual rate must be above standard.

Option D is incorrect because it results from basing the calculations on standard hours rather than actual hours.

Question

Quantity of material

The standard material content of one unit of product A is 10kg of material X which should cost $10 per kilogram. In June 20X4, 5,750 units of product A were produced and there was an adverse material usage variance of $1,500.

Required

Calculate the quantity of material X used in June 20X4.

Let the quantity of material X used = Y

5,750 units should have used (× 10kg)	57,500 kg
but did use	Y kg
Usage variance in kg	(Y – 57,500) kg
× standard price per kg	× $10
Usage variance in $	$1,500 (A)

∴ $10(Y - 57,500)$ = 1,500

       $Y - 57,500$ = 150

∴   Y   = 57,650 kg

Exam focus point

One way that the examiner can test your understanding of variance analysis is to provide information about variances from which you have to 'work backwards' to determine the actual results.

Make sure that you understand the questions covering this technique that we have provided. This type of question **really** tests your understanding of the subject. If you simply memorise variance formulae you will have difficulty in answering such questions.

Chapter roundup

- The **selling price variance** is a measure of the effect on expected profit of a different selling price to standard selling price. It is calculated as the difference between what the sales revenue should have been for the actual quantity sold.

- The **sales volume profit variance** is the difference between the actual units sold and the budgeted (planned) quantity, valued at the standard profit per unit. In other words, it measures the increase or decrease in standard profit as a result of the sales volume being higher or lower than budgeted (planned).

- **Operating statements** show how the combination of variances reconcile budgeted profit and actual profit.

- There are two main differences between the variances calculated in an absorption costing system and the variances calculated in a marginal costing system.

   - In a marginal costing system **the only fixed overhead variance is an expenditure variance.**
   - The sales volume variance is **valued at standard contribution margin**, not standard profit margin.

- Variances can be used to derive actual data from standard cost details.

Quick quiz

1   What is the sales volume profit variance?

2   A regular report for management of actual cost, and revenue, and usually comparing actual results with budgeted (planned) results (and showing variances) is known as

    A   Bank statement   C   Budget statement
    B   Variance statement   D   Operating statement

3   If an organisation uses standard marginal costing instead of standard absorption costing, which two variances are calculated differently?

Answers to quick quiz

1   It is a measure of the increase or decrease in standard profit as a result of the sales volume being higher or lower than budgeted (planned).

2   D

3   (a)   In marginal costing there is no fixed overhead volume variance (because fixed costs are not absorbed into product costs).

    (b)   In marginal costing, the sales volume variance will be valued at standard contribution margin and not standard profit margin.

Now try the questions below from the Exam Question Bank

Number	Level	Marks	Time
Q16	MCQ	n/a	n/a

P
A
R
T

F

Short-term decision-making techniques

Cost-volume-profit (CVP) analysis

17

Topic list	Syllabus reference
1 CVP analysis and breakeven point	F1 (a)
2 The contribution to sales (C/S) ratio	F1 (b)
3 The margin of safety	F1 (a)
4 Breakeven arithmetic and profit targets	F1 (d)
5 Breakeven charts, contribution charts and profit/volume charts	F1 (c)
6 Limitations of CVP analysis	F1 (d)

Introduction

You should by now realise that the cost accountant needs estimates of **fixed** and **variable costs**, and **revenues**, at various output levels. The cost accountant, must also be fully aware of **cost behaviour** because, to be able to estimate costs, he must know what a particular cost will do given particular conditions.

An understanding of cost behaviour is not all that you may need to know, however. The application of **cost-volume-profit analysis**, which is based on the cost behaviour principles and marginal costing ideas, is sometimes necessary so that the appropriate decision-making information can be provided. As you may have guessed, this chapter is going to look at that very topic, **cost-volume-profit analysis** or **breakeven analysis**.

Study guide

		Intellectual level
F1	**Cost-volume-profit (CVP) analysis**	
(a)	Calculate and interpret a breakeven point and a margin of safety	2
(b)	Understand and use the concepts of a target profit or revenue and a contribution to sales ratio	2
(c)	Identify the elements in traditional and contribution breakeven charts and profit/volume charts	1
(d)	Apply CVP analysis to single product situations	2

Note. Multi-product breakeven charts and profit/volume charts are excluded.

Exam guide

A question on this topic may give you a breakeven chart and ask you to extract data from it.

1 CVP analysis and breakeven point

1.1 Introduction

FAST FORWARD

Cost-volume-profit (CVP)/breakeven analysis is the study of the interrelationships between costs, volume and profit at various levels of activity.

The management of an organisation usually wishes to know the profit likely to be made if the aimed-for production and sales for the year are achieved. Management may also be interested to know the following.

(a) The **breakeven** point which is the activity level at which there is neither profit nor loss.
(b) The **amount** by which actual **sales can fall** below anticipated sales, **without** a **loss** being incurred.

1.2 Breakeven point

FAST FORWARD

$$\text{Breakeven point} = \frac{\text{Total fixed costs}}{\text{Contribution per unit}} = \frac{\text{Contribution required to break even}}{\text{Contribution per unit}}$$

$$= \text{Number of units of sale required to break even.}$$

1.3 Example: breakeven point

Expected sales	10,000 units at $8 = $80,000
Variable cost	$5 per unit
Fixed costs	$21,000

Required

Compute the breakeven point.

Solution

The contribution per unit is $(8–5)	=	$3
Contribution required to break even	=	fixed costs = $21,000
Breakeven point (BEP)	=	21,000 ÷ 3
	=	7,000 units
In revenue, BEP	=	(7,000 × $8) = $56,000

Sales above $56,000 will result in profit of $3 per unit of additional sales and sales below $56,000 will mean a loss of $3 per unit for each unit by which sales fall short of 7,000 units. In other words, profit will improve or worsen by the amount of contribution per unit.

	7,000 units	7,001 units
	$	$
Revenue	56,000	56,008
Less variable costs	35,000	35,005
Contribution	21,000	21,003
Less fixed costs	21,000	21,000
Profit	0 (= breakeven)	3

2 The contribution to sales (C/S) ratio

FAST FORWARD

$$\frac{\text{Contribution required to breakeven}}{\text{C/S ratio}} = \frac{\text{Fixed costs}}{\text{C/S ratio}} = \text{Breakeven point in terms of sales revenue}$$

(The contribution/sales (C/S) ratio is also sometimes called a **profit/volume** or **P/V ratio**).

An alternative way of calculating the breakeven point to give an answer in terms of sales revenue.

In the example in Paragraph 1.3 the C/S ratio is $\dfrac{\$3}{\$8} = 37.5\%$

Breakeven is where sales revenue equals $\dfrac{\$21,000}{37.5\%} = \$56,000$

At a price of $8 per unit, this represents 7,000 units of sales.

FAST FORWARD

The C/S ratio (or P/V ratio) is a measure of how much contribution is earned from each $1 of sales.

The C/S ratio of 37.5% in the above example means that for every $1 of sales, a contribution of 37.5c is earned. Thus, in order to earn a total contribution of $21,000 and if contribution increases by 37.5c per $1 of sales, sales must be:

$$\frac{\$1}{37.5c} \times \$21,000 = \$56,000$$

Question
Breakeven point

The C/S ratio of product W is 20%. IB, the manufacturer of product W, wishes to make a contribution of $50,000 towards fixed costs. How many units of product W must be sold if the selling price is $10 per unit?

Answer

$$\frac{\text{Required contribution}}{\text{C/S ratio}} = \frac{\$50,000}{20\%} = \$250,000$$

∴ Number of units = $250,000 ÷ $10 = 25,000.

Question
C/S ratio

A company manufactures a single product with a variable cost of $44. The contribution to sales ratio is 45%. Monthly fixed costs are $396,000. What is the breakeven point in units?

Answer

Contribution per unit = $44/0.55 × 0.45
= $36

Breakeven point = Fixed costs/contribution per unit
= $396,000/$36
= 11,000 units

3 The margin of safety

The **margin of safety** is the difference in units between the **budgeted sales volume** and the **breakeven sales volume**. It is sometimes expressed as a percentage of the budgeted sales volume. The margin of safety may also be expressed as the difference between the **budgeted sales revenue** and **breakeven sales revenue** expressed as a percentage of the budgeted sales revenue.

3.1 Example: margin of safety

Mal de Mer makes and sells a product which has a variable cost of $30 and which sells for $40. Budgeted fixed costs are $70,000 and budgeted sales are 8,000 units.

Required

Calculate the breakeven point and the margin of safety.

Solution

(a) Breakeven point $= \dfrac{\text{Total fixed costs}}{\text{Contribution per unit}} = \dfrac{\$70,000}{\$(40-30)}$

$= 7,000$ units

(b) Margin of safety $= 8,000 - 7,000$ units $= 1,000$ units

which may be expressed as $\dfrac{1,000 \text{ units}}{8,000 \text{ units}} \times 100\% \times 100\% = 12\frac{1}{2}\%$ of budget

(c) The margin of safety indicates to management that actual sales can fall short of budget by 1,000 units or 12½% before the breakeven point is reached and no profit at all is made.

4 Breakeven arithmetic and profit targets

At the **breakeven point**, sales revenue equals total costs and there is no profit. At the breakeven point **total contribution = fixed costs**.

Formula to learn

> S   = V + F
> where S   = Sales revenue
>   V   = Total variable costs
>   F   = Total fixed costs
> Subtracting V from each side of the equation, we get:
>   S − V = F, that is, **total contribution = fixed costs**

BPP
LEARNING MEDIA

4.1 Example: breakeven arithmetic

Butterfingers makes a product which has a variable cost of $7 per unit.

Required

If fixed costs are $63,000 per annum, calculate the selling price per unit if the company wishes to break even with a sales volume of 12,000 units.

Solution

Contribution required to break even (= Fixed costs)	=	$63,000	
Volume of sales	=	12,000 units	
			$
Required contribution per unit (S – V)	=	$63,000 ÷ 12,000 =	5.25
Variable cost per unit (V)	=		7.00
Required sales price per unit (S)	=		12.25

4.2 Target profits

FAST FORWARD

The **target profit** is achieved when S = V + F + P. Therefore the total contribution required for a target profit = **fixed costs + required profit.**

A similar formula may be applied where a company wishes to achieve a certain profit during a period. To achieve this profit, sales must cover all costs and leave the required profit.

Formula to learn

> The **target profit** is achieved when: S = V + F + P,
>
> where   P = required profit
>
> Subtracting V from each side of the equation, we get:
>
>   S – V   = F + P, so
>
> Total contribution required   = F + P

4.3 Example: target profits

Riding Breeches makes and sells a single product, for which variable costs are as follows.

	$
Direct materials	10
Direct labour	8
Variable production overhead	6
	24

The sales price is $30 per unit, and fixed costs per annum are $68,000. The company wishes to make a profit of $16,000 per annum.

Required

Determine the sales required to achieve this profit.

Solution

Required contribution = fixed costs + profit = $68,000 + $16,000 = $84,000

Required sales can be calculated in one of two ways.

(a) $\dfrac{\text{Required contribution}}{\text{Contribution per unit}}$ = $\dfrac{\$84,000}{\$(30-24)}$ = 14,000 units, or $420,000 in revenue

(b) $\dfrac{\text{Required contribution}}{\text{C/S ratio}}$ $=$ $\dfrac{\$84,000}{20\%\,*}$ = \$420,000 of revenue, or 14,000 units.

* C/S ratio = $\dfrac{\$30 - \$24}{\$30}$ = $\dfrac{\$6}{\$30}$ = 0.2 = 20%.

Question

Seven League Boots wishes to sell 14,000 units of its product, which has a variable cost of $15 to make and sell. Fixed costs are $47,000 and the required profit is $23,000.

Required

Calculate the sales price per unit.

Answer

Required contribution	=	fixed costs plus profit
	=	$47,000 + $23,000
	=	$70,000
Required sales		14,000 units

	$
Required contribution per unit sold	5
Variable cost per unit	15
Required sales price per unit	20

4.4 Decisions to change sales price or costs

You may come across a problem in which you have to work out the effect of altering the selling price, variable cost per unit or fixed cost. Such problems are slight variations on basic breakeven arithmetic.

4.5 Example: Change in selling price

Stomer Cakes bake and sell a single type of cake. The variable cost of production is 15c and the current sales price is 25c. Fixed costs are $2,600 per month, and the annual profit for the company at current sales volume is $36,000. The volume of sales demand is constant throughout the year.

The sales manager, Ian Digestion, wishes to raise the sales price to 29c per cake, but considers that a price rise will result in some loss of sales.

Required

Ascertain the minimum volume of sales required each month to raise the price to 29c.

Solution

The minimum volume of demand which would justify a price of 29c is one which would leave total profit at least the same as before, ie $3,000 per month. Required profit should be converted into required contribution, as follows.

	$
Monthly fixed costs	2,600
Monthly profit, minimum required	3,000
Current monthly contribution	5,600

Contribution per unit (25c – 15c)	10c
Current monthly sales	56,000 cakes

The minimum volume of sales required after the price rise will be an amount which earns a contribution of $5,600 per month, no worse than at the moment. The contribution per cake at a sales price of 29c would be 14c.

$$\text{Required sales} = \frac{\text{required contribution}}{\text{contribution per unit}} = \frac{\$5,600}{14c} = 40,000 \text{ cakes per month.}$$

4.6 Example: Change in production costs

Close Brickett makes a product which has a variable production cost of $8 and a variable sales cost of $2 per unit. Fixed costs are $40,000 per annum, the sales price per unit is $18, and the current volume of output and sales is 6,000 units.

The company is considering whether to have an improved machine for production. Annual hire costs would be $10,000 and it is expected that the variable cost of production would fall to $6 per unit.

Required

(a) Determine the number of units that must be produced and sold to achieve the same profit as is currently earned, if the machine is hired.

(b) Calculate the annual profit with the machine if output and sales remain at 6,000 units per annum.

Solution

The current unit contribution is $(18 − (8+2)) = $8

(a)

	$
Current contribution (6,000 × $8)	48,000
Less current fixed costs	40,000
Current profit	8,000

With the new machine fixed costs will go up by $10,000 to $50,000 per annum. The variable cost per unit will fall to $(6 + 2) = $8, and the contribution per unit will be $10.

	$
Required profit (as currently earned)	8,000
Fixed costs	50,000
Required contribution	58,000
Contribution per unit	$10
Sales required to earn $8,000 profit	5,800 units

(b) **If sales are 6,000 units**

	$	$
Sales (6,000 × $18)		108,000
Variable costs: production (6,000 × $6)	36,000	
sales (6,000 × $2)	12,000	
		48,000
Contribution (6,000 × $10)		60,000
Less fixed costs		50,000
Profit		10,000

Alternative calculation

	$
Profit at 5,800 units of sale (see (a))	8,000
Contribution from sale of extra 200 units (× $10)	2,000
Profit at 6,000 units of sale	10,000

4.7 Sales price and sales volume

It may be clear by now that, given no change in fixed costs, **total profit is maximised when the total contribution is at its maximum**. Total contribution in turn depends on the unit contribution and on the sales volume.

An increase in the sales price will increase unit contribution, but sales volume is likely to fall because fewer customers will be prepared to pay the higher price. A decrease in sales price will reduce the unit contribution, but sales volume may increase because the goods on offer are now cheaper. The **optimum combination** of sales price and sales volume is arguably the one which **maximises total contribution**.

4.8 Example: Profit maximisation

C has developed a new product which is about to be launched on to the market. The variable cost of selling the product is $12 per unit. The marketing department has estimated that at a sales price of $20, annual demand would be 10,000 units.

However, if the sales price is set above $20, sales demand would fall by 500 units for each 50c increase above $20. Similarly, if the price is set below $20, demand would increase by 500 units for each 50c stepped reduction in price below $20.

Required

Determine the price which would maximise C's profit in the next year.

Solution

At a price of $20 per unit, the unit contribution would be $(20 − 12) = $8. Each 50c increase (or decrease) in price would raise (or lower) the unit contribution by 50c. The total contribution is calculated at each sales price by multiplying the unit contribution by the expected sales volume.

		Unit price $	Unit contribution $	Sales volume Units	Total contribution $
		20.00	8.00	10,000	80,000
(a)	**Reduce price**				
		19.50	7.50	10,500	78,750
		19.00	7.00	11,000	77,000
(b)	**Increase price**				
		20.50	8.50	9,500	80,750
		21.00	9.00	9,000	81,000
		21.50	9.50	8,500	80,750
		22.00	10.00	8,000	80,000
		22.50	10.50	7,500	78,750

The total contribution would be maximised, and therefore profit maximised, at a sales price of $21 per unit, and sales demand of 9,000 units.

Question   Breakeven output level

Betty Battle manufactures a product which has a selling price of $20 and a variable cost of $10 per unit. The company incurs annual fixed costs of $29,000. Annual sales demand is 9,000 units.

New production methods are under consideration, which would cause a $1,000 increase in fixed costs and a reduction in variable cost to $9 per unit. The new production methods would result in a superior product and would enable sales to be increased to 9,750 units per annum at a price of $21 each.

If the change in production methods were to take place, the breakeven output level would be:

| | A | 400 units higher | C | 100 units higher |
| | B | 400 units lower | D | 100 units lower |

	Current	Revised	Difference
	$	$	
Selling price	20	21	
Variable costs	10	9	
Contribution per unit	10	12	
Fixed costs	$29,000	$30,000	
Breakeven point (units)	2,900	2,500	**400 lower**

Breakeven point $= \dfrac{\text{Total fixed costs}}{\text{Contribution per unit}}$

Current BEP $= \dfrac{\$29,000}{\$10} = 2,900$ units

Revised BEP $= \dfrac{\$30,000}{\$12} = 2,500$ units

The correct answer is therefore B.

5 Breakeven charts, contribution charts and profit/volume charts

Refer to section 8 of the introductory chapter 'Basic Maths' for further help with how to draw graphs.

5.1 Breakeven charts

FAST FORWARD

The breakeven point can also be determined graphically using a breakeven chart or a contribution breakeven chart. These charts show approximate levels of profit or loss at different sales volume levels within a limited range.

A breakeven chart has the following axes.

- A **horizontal** axis showing the **sales/output** (in value or units)
- A **vertical axis** showing $ for **sales revenues** and **costs**

The following lines are drawn on the breakeven chart.

(a) The **sales line**

- Starts at the origin
- Ends at the point signifying expected sales

(b) The **fixed costs line**

- Runs parallel to the horizontal axis
- Meets the vertical axis at a point which represents total fixed costs

(c)   The **total costs line**

- Starts where the fixed costs line meets the vertical axis
- Ends at the point which represents anticipated sales on the horizontal axis and total costs of anticipated sales on the vertical axis

The **breakeven point** is the **intersection** of the **sales line** and the **total costs line**.

The distance between the **breakeven point** and the **expected (or budgeted) sales**, in units, indicates the **margin of safety**.

5.2 Example: A breakeven chart

The budgeted annual output of a factory is 120,000 units. The fixed overheads amount to $40,000 and the variable costs are 50c per unit. The sales price is $1 per unit.

Required

Construct a breakeven chart showing the current breakeven point and profit earned up to the present maximum capacity.

Solution

We begin by calculating the profit at the budgeted annual output.

	$
Sales (120,000 units)	120,000
Variable costs	60,000
Contribution	60,000
Fixed costs	40,000
Profit	20,000

Breakeven chart (1) is shown on the following page.

The chart is drawn as follows.

(a)   The **vertical axis** represents **money** (costs and revenue) and the **horizontal axis** represents the **level of activity** (production and sales).

(b)   The fixed costs are represented by a **straight line parallel to the horizontal axis** (in our example, at $40,000).

(c)   The **variable costs** are added 'on top of' fixed costs, to give **total costs**. It is assumed that fixed costs are the same in total and variable costs are the same per unit at all levels of output.

The line of costs is therefore a straight line and only two points need to be plotted and joined up. Perhaps the two most convenient points to plot are total costs at zero output, and total costs at the budgeted output and sales.

- At zero output, costs are equal to the amount of fixed costs only, $40,000, since there are no variable costs.

- At the budgeted output of 120,000 units, costs are $100,000.

	$
Fixed costs	40,000
Variable costs 120,000 × 50c	60,000
Total costs	100,000

(d)   The sales line is also drawn by plotting two points and joining them up.

- At zero sales, revenue is nil.
- At the budgeted output and sales of 120,000 units, revenue is $120,000.

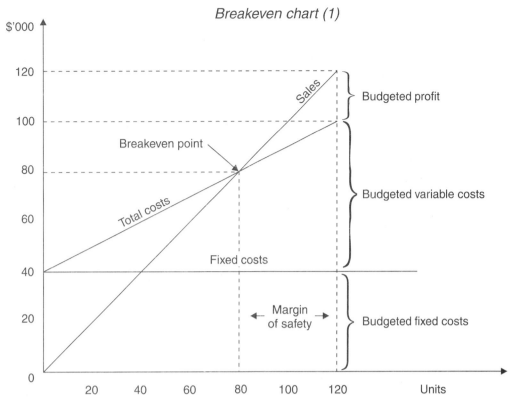

Breakeven chart (1)

The breakeven point is where total costs are matched exactly by total revenue. From the chart, this can be seen to occur at output and sales of 80,000 units, when revenue and costs are both $80,000. This breakeven point can be proved mathematically as:

$$\frac{\text{Required contribution (= fixed costs)}}{\text{Contribution per unit}} = \frac{\$40,000}{50c \text{ per unit}} = 80,000 \text{ units}$$

The margin of safety can be seen on the chart as the difference between the budgeted level of activity and the breakeven level.

5.3 The value of breakeven charts

Breakeven charts are used as follows.

- To **plan** the production of a company's products
- To **market** a company's products
- To give a **visual display** of breakeven arithmetic

5.4 Example: Variations in the use of breakeven charts

Breakeven charts can be used to **show variations** in the possible **sales price**, **variable costs** or **fixed costs**. Suppose that a company sells a product which has a variable cost of $2 per unit. Fixed costs are $15,000. It has been estimated that if the sales price is set at $4.40 per unit, the expected sales volume would be 7,500 units; whereas if the sales price is lower, at $4 per unit, the expected sales volume would be 10,000 units.

Required

Draw a breakeven chart to show the budgeted profit, the breakeven point and the margin of safety at each of the possible sales prices.

Solution

Workings

	Sales price $4.40 per unit $		Sales price $4 per unit $
Fixed costs	15,000		15,000
Variable costs (7,500 × $2.00)	15,000	(10,000 × $2.00)	20,000
Total costs	30,000		35,000
Budgeted revenue (7,500 × $4.40)	33,000	(10,000 × $4.00)	40,000

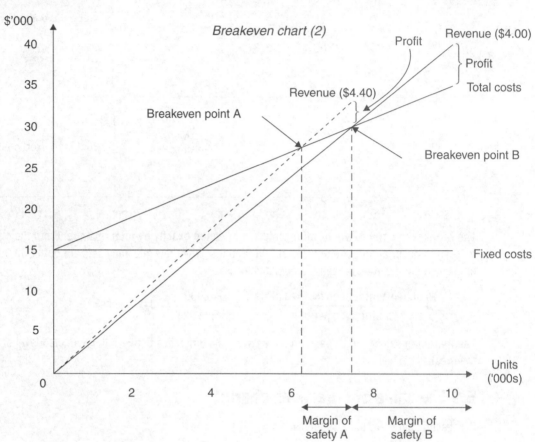

Breakeven chart (2)

(a) **Breakeven point A** is the breakeven point at a sales price of $4.40 per unit, which is 6,250 units or $27,500 in costs and revenues.

$$\text{(check: } \frac{\text{Required contribution to breakeven}}{\text{Contribution per unit}} \quad \frac{\$15,000}{\$2.40 \text{ per unit}} = 6,250 \text{ units)}$$

The margin of safety (A) is 7,500 units – 6,250 units = 1,250 units or 16.7% of expected sales.

(b) **Breakeven point B** is the breakeven point at a sales price of $4 per unit which is 7,500 units or $30,000 in costs and revenues.

$$\text{(check: } \frac{\text{Required contribution to breakeven}}{\text{Contribution per unit}} \quad \frac{\$15,000}{\$2 \text{ per unit}} = 7,500 \text{ units)}$$

The margin of safety (B) = 10,000 units – 7,500 units = 2,500 units or 25% of expected sales.

Since a price of $4 per unit gives a higher expected profit and a wider margin of safety, this price will probably be preferred even though the breakeven point is higher than at a sales price of $4.40 per unit.

Contribution (or contribution breakeven) charts

As an alternative to drawing the fixed cost line first, it is possible to start with that for variable costs. This is known as a **contribution chart**. An example is shown below using the example in Paragraphs 5.2 and 5.4.

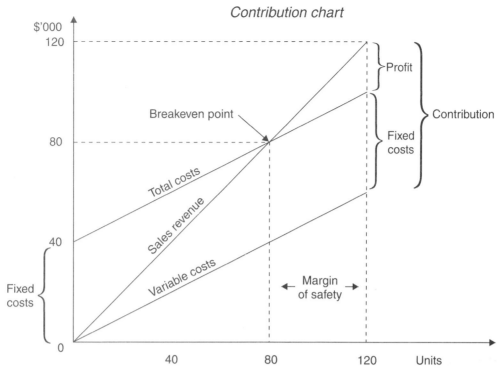

Contribution chart

One of the **advantages** of the contribution chart is that is shows clearly the **contribution** for **different levels of production** (indicated here at 120,000 units, the budgeted level of output) as the 'wedge' shape between the sales revenue line and the variable costs line. At the **breakeven point**, the **contribution equals fixed costs** exactly. At levels of output **above** the **breakeven** point, the **contribution** is **larger**, and not only covers fixed costs, but also leaves a profit. **Below** the **breakeven** point, the **loss** is the amount by which contribution fails to cover fixed costs.

5.5 The Profit/Volume (P/V) chart

FAST FORWARD

> The **profit/volume (P/V) chart** is a variation of the breakeven chart which illustrates the relationship of costs and profits to sales and the margin of safety.

A P/V chart is constructed as follows (look at the chart in the example that follows as you read the explanation).

(a)   'P' is on the y axis and actually comprises not only 'profit' but contribution to profit (in monetary value), extending above and below the x axis with a zero point at the intersection of the two axes, and the negative section below the x axis representing fixed costs. This means that at zero production, the firm is incurring a loss equal to the fixed costs.

(b)   'V' is on the x axis and comprises either volume of sales or value of sales (revenue).

(c)   The profit-volume line is a straight line drawn with its starting point (at zero production) at the intercept on the y axis representing the level of fixed costs, and with a gradient of contribution/unit (or the P/V ratio if sales value is used rather than units). The P/V line will cut the x axis at the breakeven point of sales volume. Any point on the P/V line above the x axis represents the profit to the firm (as measured on the vertical axis) for that particular level of sales.

5.6 Example: P/V chart

Let us draw a P/V chart for our example. At sales of 120,000 units, total contribution will be 120,000 × $(1 − 0.5) = $60,000 and total profit will be $20,000.

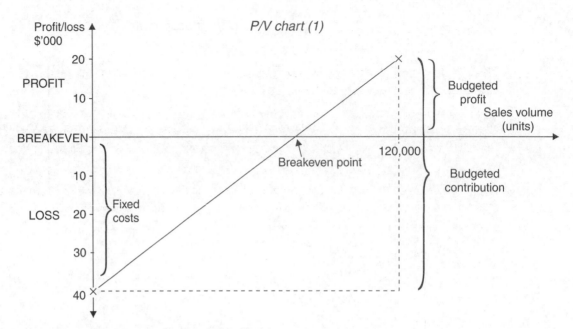

P/V chart (1)

5.7 The advantage of the P/V chart

The P/V chart shows clearly the effect on profit and breakeven point of any changes in selling price, variable cost, fixed cost and/or sales demand.

If the budgeted selling price of the product in our example is increased to $1.20, with the result that demand drops to 105,000 units despite additional fixed costs of $10,000 being spent on advertising, we could add a line representing this situation to our P/V chart.

At sales of 105,000 units, contribution will be 105,000 × $(1.20 – 0.50) = $73,500 and total profit will be $23,500 (fixed costs being $50,000).

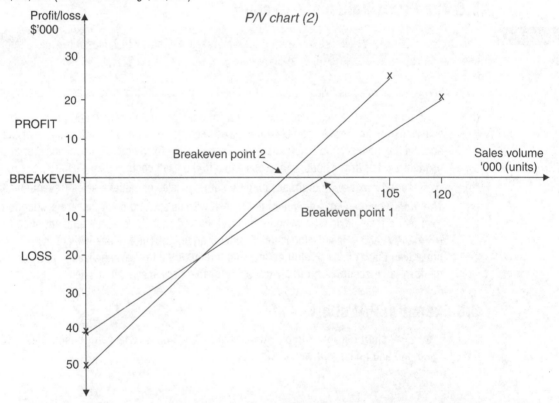

P/V chart (2)

The diagram shows that if the selling price is increased, the breakeven point occurs at a lower level of sales revenue (71,429 units instead of 80,000 units), although this is not a particularly large increase when viewed in the context of the projected sales volume. It is also possible to see that for sales above

50,000 units, the profit achieved will be higher (and the loss achieved lower) if the price is $1.20. For sales volumes below 50,000 units the first option will yield lower losses.

The P/V chart is the clearest way of presenting such information; two conventional breakeven charts on one set of axes would be very confusing.

Changes in the variable cost per unit or in fixed costs at certain activity levels can also be easily incorporated into a P/V chart. The profit or loss at each point where the cost structure changes should be calculated and plotted on the graph so that the profit/volume line becomes a series of straight lines.

For example, suppose that in our example, at sales levels in excess of 120,000 units the variable cost per unit increases to $0.60 (perhaps because of overtime premiums that are incurred when production exceeds a certain level). At sales of 130,000 units, contribution would therefore be 130,000 × $(1 – 0.60) = $52,000 and total profit would be $12,000.

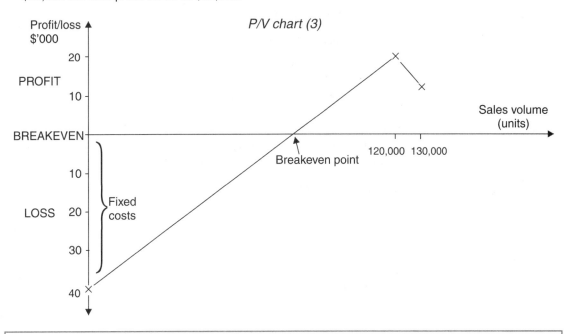

P/V chart (3)

Exam focus point

You may be given a breakeven or PV chart and required to extract the information from it.

6 Limitations of CVP analysis

FAST FORWARD

Breakeven analysis is a useful technique for managers as it can provide **simple** and **quick** estimates. **Breakeven charts** provide a **graphical representation** of breakeven arithmetic. Breakeven analysis does, however, have number of limitations.

- It **can only apply to a single product** or a single mix of a group of products
- A breakeven chart may be **time-consuming** to prepare
- It **assumes** fixed costs are constant at all levels of output.
- It **assumes** that **variable costs** are the **same** per unit at all levels of output
- It **assumes** that **sales prices** are **constant** at all levels of output
- It assumes **production** and **sales** are the **same** (inventory levels are ignored)
- It **ignores** the **uncertainty** in the estimates of fixed costs and variable cost per unit

Chapter roundup

- **Cost-volume– profit (CVP)/breakeven analysis** is the study of the interrelationships between costs, volume and profits at various levels of activity.

- **Breakeven point** = Number of units of sale required to breakeven

$$= \frac{\text{Total fixed costs}}{\text{Contribution per unit}}$$

$$= \frac{\text{Contribution required to break even}}{\text{Contribution per unit}}$$

- **Breakeven point in terms of sales revenue**

$$= \frac{\text{Contribution required to break even}}{\text{C/S ratio}}$$

$$= \frac{\text{Fixed costs}}{\text{C/S ratio}}$$

- The **C/S ratio** (or **P/V ratio**) is a measure of how much contribution is earned from each \$1 of sales.

- The **margin of safety** is the difference in units between the **budgeted sales volume** and the **breakeven sales volume**. It is sometimes expressed as a percentage of the budgeted sales volume. The **margin of safety** may also be expressed as the difference between the **budgeted sales revenue** and the **breakeven sales revenue** expressed as a percentage of the budgeted sales revenue.

- At the **breakeven point**, sales revenue = total costs and there is no profit. At the breakeven point **total contribution = fixed costs.**

- The **target profit** is achieved when S = V + F + P. Therefore the **total contribution required** for a target profit = **fixed costs + required profit.**

- The breakeven point can also be determined graphically using a **breakeven chart** or a **contribution breakeven chart**. These charts show approximate levels of profit or loss at different sales volume levels within a limited range.

- The **profit/volume (PV) chart** is a variation of the breakeven chart which illustrates the relationship of costs and profits to sales and the margin of safety.

- The **P/V chart** shows clearly the effect on profit and breakeven point of any changes in selling price, variable cost, fixed cost and/or sales demand.

- **Breakeven analysis** is a useful technique for managers as it can provide simple and quick estimates. **Breakeven charts** provide a graphical representation of breakeven arithmetic. Breakeven analysis does, however, have a number of **limitations.**

1   What does CVP analysis study?

2   The **breakeven point** is the ....…..............
      or... ....

3   Use the following to make up three formulae which can be used to calculate the breakeven point.

Contribution per unit
Contribution per unit
Fixed costs
Fixed costs
Contribution required to breakeven
Contribution required to breakeven
C/S ratio
C/S ratio

(a)   Breakeven point (sales units)   =   _____

                                           or   _____

(b)   Breakeven point (sales revenue)   =   _____

                                           or   _____

4   The C/S ratio is a measure of how much profit is earned from each $1 of sales.

      True ☐   False ☐

5   The **margin of safety** is the difference in units between the budgeted sales volume and the breakeven sales volume. How is it sometimes expressed?

6   Profits are maximised at the breakeven point.

      True ☐   False ☐

7   At the breakeven point, total contribution = ...

8   The total contribution required for a **target profit** = ...…... .

9   Give three uses of breakeven charts.

10   Breakeven charts show approximate levels of profit or loss at different sales volume levels within a limited range. Which of the following are true?

      I   The sales line starts at the origin
      II   The fixed costs line runs parallel to the vertical axis
      III   Breakeven charts have a horizontal axis showing the sales/output (in value or units)
      IV   Breakeven charts have a vertical axis showing $ for revenues and costs
      V   The breakeven point is the intersection of the sales line and the fixed cost line

      A   I and II   C   I, III and IV
      B   I and III   D   I, III, IV, and V

11   On a breakeven chart, the distance between the breakeven point and the expected (or budgeted) sales, in units, indicates the ....

12   Give seven limitations of CVP analysis.

- ....
- ....
- ....
- ....
- ....
- ....
- ....

Answers to quick quiz

1   The interrelations between **costs, volume** and **profits** of a product at various activity levels.

2   The **breakeven point** is the number of units of sale required to breakeven or the sales revenue required to breakeven.

3   (a)   Breakeven point (sales units)   = $\dfrac{\text{Fixed costs}}{\text{Contribution per unit}}$

or $\dfrac{\text{Contribution required to breakeven}}{\text{Contribution per unit}}$

(b)   Breakeven point (sales revenue)   = $\dfrac{\text{Fixed costs}}{\text{C/S ratio}}$

or $\dfrac{\text{Contribution required to breakeven}}{\text{C/S ratio}}$

4   False. The C/S ratio is a measure of how much **contribution** is earned from each $1 of sales.

5   As a **percentage** of the budgeted sales volume.

6   False. At the breakeven point there is no profit.

7   At the breakeven point, total contribution = fixed costs

8   Fixed costs + required profit

9
- To plan the production of a company's products
- To market a company's products
- To give a visual display of breakeven arithmetic

10   C

11   Margin of safety

12
- It **can only apply to a single product** or a single mix of a group of products.
- A breakeven chart may be **time-consuming** to prepare.
- It **assumes** fixed costs are constant at all levels of output.
- It **assumes** that **variable costs** are the **same** per unit at all levels of output.
- It **assumes** that **sales prices** are **constant** at all levels of output.
- It assumes **production** and **sales** are the **same** (inventory levels are ignored).
- It **ignores** the **uncertainty** in the estimates of fixed costs and variable cost per unit.

Now try the questions below from the Exam Question Bank

Number	Level	Marks	Time
Q17	MCQ	n/a	n/a

Relevant costing and decision making

Topic list	Syllabus reference
1 Relevant costs	F2 (a)-(d)
2 Choice of product (product mix) decisions	F3 (a), (b)

Introduction

Management at all levels within an organisation take decisions. The overriding requirement of the information that should be supplied by the cost accountant to aid decision making is that of **relevance**. This chapter therefore begins by looking at the costing technique required in decision-making situations, that of **relevant costing**, and explains how to decide which costs need taking into account when a decision is being made and which costs do not.

We then go on to see how to apply relevant costing to product mix decisions.

Study guide

		Intellectual level
F2	**Relevant costing**	
(a)	Explain the concept of relevant costing	1
(b)	Calculate the relevant costs for materials, labour and overheads	2
(c)	Calculate the relevant costs associated with non-current assets	1
(d)	Explain and apply the concept of opportunity cost	1
F3	**Limiting factors**	
(a)	Identify a single limiting factor	1
(b)	Determine the optimal production plan where an organisation is restricted by a single limiting factor	2

Exam guide

Relevant costing is one of the key syllabus topics for Paper F2. Make sure that you can calculate relevant costs for materials and labour and the deprival value of an asset. Multiple choice questions are a good way of testing your understanding of this subject.

1 Relevant costs

1.1 Relevant costs

FAST FORWARD

Relevant costs are future cash flows arising as a direct consequence of a decision.

- Relevant costs are **future costs**
- Relevant costs are **cash flows**
- Relevant costs are **incremental costs**

Decision making should be based on relevant costs.

(a) **Relevant costs are future costs**. A decision is about the future and it cannot alter what has been done already. Costs that have been incurred in the past are totally irrelevant to any decision that is being made 'now'. Such costs are **past costs** or **sunk costs**.

Costs that have been incurred include not only costs that have already been paid, but also costs that have been **committed**. A **committed cost** is a future cash flow that will be incurred anyway, regardless of the decision taken now.

(b) **Relevant costs are cash flows**. Only cash flow information is required. This means that costs or charges which do not reflect **additional cash spending** (such as depreciation and notional costs) should be ignored for the purpose of decision making.

(c) **Relevant costs are incremental costs**. For example, if an employee is expected to have no other work to do during the next week, but will be paid his basic wage (of, say, $100 per week) for attending work and doing nothing, his manager might decide to give him a job which earns the organisation $40. The net gain is $40 and the $100 is irrelevant to the decision because although it is a future cash flow, it will be incurred anyway whether the employee is given work or not.

Other terms are sometimes used to describe relevant costs.

1.2 Avoidable costs

Avoidable costs are costs which would not be incurred if the activity to which they relate did not exist.

One of the situations in which it is necessary to identify the avoidable costs is in deciding whether or not to **discontinue a product**. The only costs which would be saved are the **avoidable costs** which are usually the variable costs and sometimes some specific costs. Costs which would be incurred whether or not the product is discontinued are known as **unavoidable costs**.

1.3 Differential costs and opportunity costs

FAST FORWARD

Relevant costs are also **differential costs** and **opportunity costs**.

- **Differential cost** is the difference in total cost between alternatives.
- An **opportunity cost** is the value of the benefit sacrificed when one course of action is chosen in preference to an alternative.

For example, if decision option A costs $300 and decision option B costs $360, the **differential cost** is $60.

1.3.1 Example: Differential costs and opportunity costs

Suppose for example that there are three options, A, B and C, only one of which can be chosen. The net profit from each would be $80, $100 and $70 respectively.

Since only one option can be selected option B would be chosen because it offers the biggest benefit.

	$
Profit from option B	100
Less opportunity cost (ie the benefit from the most profitable alternative, A)	80
Differential benefit of option B	20

The decision to choose option B would not be taken simply because it offers a profit of $100, but because it offers a differential profit of $20 in excess of the next best alternative.

1.4 Controllable and uncontrollable costs

We came across the term **controllable costs** at the beginning of this study text. **Controllable costs** are items of expenditure which can be directly influenced by a given manager within a given time span.

As a general rule, **committed fixed costs** such as those costs arising from the possession of plant, equipment and buildings (giving rise to depreciation and rent) are largely **uncontrollable** in the short term because they have been committed by longer-term decisions.

Discretionary fixed costs, for example, advertising and research and development costs can be thought of as being **controllable** because they are incurred as a result of decisions made by management and can be raised or lowered at fairly short notice.

1.5 Sunk costs

FAST FORWARD

A **sunk cost** is a past cost which is not directly relevant in decision making.

The principle underlying decision accounting is that management decisions can only affect the future. In decision making, managers therefore require information about **future costs and revenues** which would be affected by the decision under review. They must not be misled by events, costs and revenues in the past, about which they can do nothing.

Sunk costs, which have been charged already as a cost of sales in a previous accounting period or will be charged in a future accounting period although the expenditure has already been incurred, are irrelevant to decision making.

1.5.1 Example: Sunk costs

An example of a sunk cost is development costs which have already been incurred. Suppose that a company has spent $250,000 in developing a new service for customers, but the marketing department's most recent findings are that the service might not gain customer acceptance and could be a commercial failure. The decision whether or not to abandon the development of the new service would have to be taken, but the $250,000 spent so far should be ignored by the decision makers because it is a **sunk cost**.

1.6 Fixed and variable costs

FAST FORWARD

In general, variable costs will be relevant costs and fixed costs will be irrelevant to a decision.

Exam focus point

Unless you are given an indication to the contrary, you should assume the following.

- Variable costs will be relevant costs.
- Fixed costs are irrelevant to a decision.

This need not be the case, however, and you should analyse variable and fixed cost data carefully. Do not forget that 'fixed' costs may only be fixed in the short term.

1.6.1 Non-relevant variable costs

There might be occasions when a variable cost is in fact a sunk cost (and therefore a **non-relevant variable cost**). For example, suppose that a company has some units of raw material in inventory. They have been paid for already, and originally cost $2,000. They are now obsolete and are no longer used in regular production, and they have no scrap value. However, they could be used in a special job which the company is trying to decide whether to undertake. The special job is a 'one-off' customer order, and would use up all these materials in inventory.

(a) In deciding whether the job should be undertaken, the relevant cost of the materials to the special job is nil. Their original cost of $2,000 is a **sunk cost**, and should be ignored in the decision.

(b) However, if the materials did have a scrap value of, say, $300, then their relevant cost to the job would be the **opportunity cost** of being unable to sell them for scrap, ie $300.

1.6.2 Attributable fixed costs

There might be occasions when a fixed cost is a relevant cost, and you must be aware of the distinction between **'specific'** or **'directly attributable' fixed costs**, and general fixed overheads.

Directly attributable fixed costs are those costs which, although fixed within a relevant range of activity level are relevant to a decision for either of the following reasons.

(a) They could increase if certain extra activities were undertaken. For example, it may be necessary to employ an extra supervisor if a particular order is accepted. The extra salary would be an **attributable fixed cost**.

(b) They would decrease or be eliminated entirely if a decision were taken either to reduce the scale of operations or shut down entirely.

General fixed overheads are those fixed overheads which will be unaffected by decisions to increase or decrease the scale of operations, perhaps because they are an apportioned share of the fixed costs of items which would be completely unaffected by the decisions. General fixed overheads are not relevant in decision making.

1.6.3 Absorbed overhead

Absorbed overhead is a **notional** accounting cost and hence should be ignored for decision-making purposes. **It is overhead incurred which may be relevant to a decision**.

1.7 The relevant cost of materials

The relevant cost of raw materials is generally their **current replacement cost**, *unless* the materials have already been purchased and would not be replaced once used. In this case the relevant cost of using them is the **higher** of the following.

- Their current resale value
- The value they would obtain if they were put to an alternative use

If the materials have no resale value and no other possible use, then the relevant cost of using them for the opportunity under consideration would be nil.

| Question | | Relevant cost of materials |

O'Reilly has been approached by a customer who would like a special job to be done for him, and who is willing to pay $22,000 for it. The job would require the following materials.

Material	Total units required	Units already in inventory	Book value of units in inventory $/unit	Realisable value $/unit	Replacement cost $/unit
A	1,000	0	-	-	6
B	1,000	600	2	2.50	5
C	1,000	700	3	2.50	4
D	200	200	4	6.00	9

Material B is used regularly by O'Reilly, and if units of B are required for this job, they would need to be replaced to meet other production demand.

Materials C and D are in inventory as the result of previous over-buying, and they have a restricted use. No other use could be found for material C, but the units of material D could be used in another job as substitute for 300 units of material E, which currently costs $5 per unit (of which the company has no units in inventory at the moment).

Required

Calculate the relevant costs of material for deciding whether or not to accept the contract.

| Answer |

(a)   **Material A** is not yet owned. It would have to be bought in full at the replacement cost of $6 per unit.

(b)   **Material B** is used regularly by the company. There are existing inventories (600 units) but if these are used on the contract under review a further 600 units would be bought to replace them. Relevant costs are therefore 1,000 units at the replacement cost of $5 per unit.

(c)   1,000 units of **material C** are needed and 700 are already in inventory. If used for the contract, a further 300 units must be bought at $4 each. The existing inventories of 700 will not be replaced. If they are used for the contract, they could not be sold at $2.50 each. The realisable value of these 700 units is an opportunity cost of sales revenue forgone.

(d)   The required units of **material D** are already in inventory and will not be replaced. There is an opportunity cost of using D in the contract because there are alternative opportunities either to sell the existing inventories for $6 per unit ($1,200 in total) or avoid other purchases (of material E), which would cost 300 × $5 = $1,500. Since substitution for E is more beneficial, $1,500 is the opportunity cost.

(e)   **Summary of relevant costs**

	$
Material A (1,000 × $6)	6,000
Material B (1,000 × $5)	5,000
Material C (300 × $4) plus (700 × $2.50)	2,950
Material D	1,500
Total	15,450

Question

Relevant material costs

A company regularly uses a material. It currently has 100kg in inventory for which it paid $200. If it were sold it could be sold for $3 per kg. The market price is now $4 per kg. A customer has placed an order that will use 200kg of the material. The relevant cost of the 200kg is:

A	$500	C	$700
B	$600	D	$800

Answer

The material is in regular use and so 200kg will be purchased. The relevant cost is therefore 200 × $4 = $800. Answer D.

1.8 The relevant cost of labour

The relevant cost of labour, in different situations, is best explained by means of an example.

1.8.1 Example: Relevant cost of labour

LW is currently deciding whether to undertake a new contract. 15 hours of labour will be required for the contract. LW currently produces product L, the standard cost details of which are shown below.

STANDARD COST CARD
PRODUCT L

	$/unit
Direct materials (10kg @ $2)	20
Direct labour (5 hrs @ $6)	30
	50
Selling price	72
Contribution	22

(a)   What is the relevant cost of labour if the labour must be hired from outside the organisation?
(b)   What is the relevant cost of labour if LW expects to have 5 hours spare capacity?
(c)   What is the relevant cost of labour if labour is in short supply?

Solution

(a)   Where labour must be hired from outside the organisation, the relevant cost of labour will be the variable costs incurred.

       Relevant cost of labour on new contract = 15 hours @ $6 = $90

(b)   It is assumed that the 5 hours spare capacity will be paid anyway, and so if these 5 hours are used on another contract, there is no additional cost to LW.

Relevant cost of labour on new contract

	$
Direct labour (10 hours @ $6)	60
Spare capacity (5 hours @ $0)	0
	60

(c) Contribution earned per unit of Product L produced = $22

If it requires 5 hours of labour to make one unit of product L, the contribution earned per labour hour = $22/5 = $4.40.

Relevant cost of labour on new contract

	$
Direct labour (15 hours @ $6)	90
Contribution lost by not making product L ($4.40 × 15 hours)	66
	156

It is important that you should be able to identify the relevant costs which are appropriate to a decision. In many cases, this is a fairly straightforward problem, but there are cases where great care should be taken. Attempt the following question.

Question   Customer order

A company has been making a machine to order for a customer, but the customer has since gone into liquidation, and there is no prospect that any money will be obtained from the winding up of the company.

Costs incurred to date in manufacturing the machine are $50,000 and progress payments of $15,000 had been received from the customer prior to the liquidation.

The sales department has found another company willing to buy the machine for $34,000 once it has been completed.

To complete the work, the following costs would be incurred.

(a) Materials: these have been bought at a cost of $6,000. They have no other use, and if the machine is not finished, they would be sold for scrap for $2,000. ↩

(b) Further labour costs would be $8,000. Labour is in short supply, and if the machine is not finished, the work force would be switched to another job, which would earn $30,000 in revenue, and incur direct costs of $12,000 and absorbed (fixed) overhead of $8,000.

(c) Consultancy fees $4,000. If the work is not completed, the consultant's contract would be cancelled at a cost of $1,500.

(d) General overheads of $8,000 would be added to the cost of the additional work.

Required

Assess whether the new customer's offer should be accepted.

Answer

(a) Costs incurred in the past, or revenue received in the past are not relevant because they cannot affect a decision about what is best for the future. Costs incurred to date of $50,000 and revenue received of $15,000 are 'water under the bridge' and should be ignored.

(b) Similarly, the price paid in the past for the materials is **irrelevant**. The only relevant cost of materials affecting the decision is the opportunity cost of the revenue from scrap which would be forgone – $2,000.

(c) **Labour costs**

	$
Labour costs required to complete work	8,000
Opportunity costs: contribution forgone by losing	
other work $(30,000 – 12,000)	18,000
Relevant cost of labour	26,000

(d) The **incremental cost** of consultancy from completing the work is $2,500.

	$
Cost of completing work	4,000
Cost of cancelling contract	1,500
Incremental cost of completing work	2,500

(e) **Absorbed overhead is a notional accounting cost** and should be ignored. Actual overhead incurred is the only overhead cost to consider. General overhead costs (and the absorbed overhead of the alternative work for the labour force) should be ignored.

(f) **Relevant costs may be summarised as follows.**

		$	$
Revenue from completing work			34,000
Relevant costs			
Materials:	opportunity cost	2,000	
Labour:	basic pay	8,000	
	opportunity cost	18,000	
Incremental cost of consultant		2,500	
			30,500
Extra profit to be earned by accepting the order			3,500

1.9 The relevant cost of an asset

FAST FORWARD

The **relevant cost** of an asset represents the amount of money that a company would have to receive if it were deprived of an asset in order to be no worse off than it already is. We can call this the **deprival value**.

Exam focus point

The study guide for Paper F2 states that candidates must be able to calculate the relevant costs associated with non-current assets.

The deprival value of an asset is best demonstrated by means of an example.

1.9.1 Example: Deprival value of an asset

A machine cost $14,000 ten years ago. It is expected that the machine will generate future revenues of $10,000. Alternatively, the machine could be scrapped for $8,000. An equivalent machine in the same condition would cost $9,000 to buy now. What is the deprival value of the machine?

Solution

Firstly, let us think about the relevance of the costs given to us in the question.

Cost of machine = $14,000 = past/sunk cost
Future revenues = $10,000 = revenue expected to be generated
Net realisable value = $8,000 = scrap proceeds
Replacement cost = $9,000

When calculating the **deprival value** of an asset, use the following diagram.

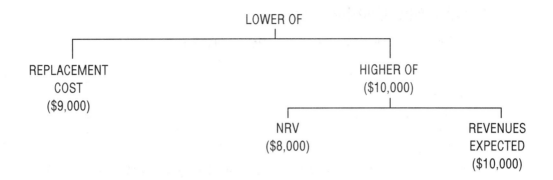

LOWER OF

REPLACEMENT COST ($9,000)

HIGHER OF ($10,000)

NRV ($8,000)

REVENUES EXPECTED ($10,000)

Therefore, the deprival value of the machine is the lower of the replacement cost and $10,000. The deprival value is therefore $9,000.

Exam focus point

Your exam will use the term 'relevant cost' rather than 'deprival value', but you may find that 'deprival value' is a useful concept to bear in mind when considering a non-current asset.

2 Choice of product (product mix) decisions

2.1 The limiting factor

FAST FORWARD

A **limiting factor** is a factor which limits the organisation's activities. In a **limiting factor situation**, contribution will be maximised by earning the biggest possible contribution per unit of limiting factor.

A limiting factor is anything which limits the activity of the entity. This could be the level of demand for its product or it could be one or more scarce resources which limit production to below that level.

Possible limiting factors are:

(a)   **Sales**. There may be a limit to sales demand

(b)   **Labour**. There may be a limit to total quantity of labour available or to labour having particular skills

(c)   **Materials**. There may be insufficient available materials to produce enough units to satisfy sales demand

(d)   **Manufacturing capacity**. There may not be sufficient machine capacity for the production required to meet sales demand

One of the more common decision-making problems is a situation where there are not enough resources to meet the potential sales demand, and so a decision has to be made about what mix of products to produce, using what resources there are as effectively as possible.

A **limiting factor** could be sales if there is a limit to sales demand but any one of the organisation's resources (labour, materials and so on) may be insufficient to meet the level of production demanded.

It is assumed in limiting factor accounting that management wishes to maximise profit and that **profit will be maximised when contribution is maximised** (given no change in fixed cost expenditure incurred). In other words, **marginal costing ideas are applied**.

Contribution will be maximised by earning the biggest possible contribution from each unit of limiting factor. For example if grade A labour is the limiting factor, contribution will be maximised by earning the biggest contribution from each hour of grade A labour worked.

The limiting factor decision therefore involves the determination of the contribution earned by each different product from each unit of the limiting factor.

2.2 Example: Limiting factor

AB makes two products, the Ay and the Be. Unit variable costs are as follows.

	Ay $	Be $
Direct materials	1	3
Direct labour ($3 per hour)	6	3
Variable overhead	1	1
	8	7

The sales price per unit is $14 per Ay and $11 per Be. During July 20X2 the available direct labour is limited to 8,000 hours. Sales demand in July is expected to be 3,000 units for Ays and 5,000 units for Bes.

Required

Determine the profit-maximising production mix, assuming that monthly fixed costs are $20,000, and that opening inventories of finished goods and work in progress are nil.

Solution

Step 1   Confirm that the limiting factor is something other than sales demand.

	Ays	Bes	Total
Labour hours per unit	2 hrs	1 hr	
Sales demand	3,000 units	5,000 units	
Labour hours needed	6,000 hrs	5,000 hrs	11,000 hrs
Labour hours available			8,000 hrs
Shortfall			3,000 hrs

Labour is the limiting factor on production.

Step 2   Identify the contribution earned by each product per unit of limiting factor, that is per labour hour worked.

	Ays $	Bes $
Sales price	14	11
Variable cost	8	7
Unit contribution	6	4
Labour hours per unit	2 hrs	1 hr
Contribution per labour hour (= unit of limiting factor)	$3	$4

Although Ays have a higher unit contribution than Bes, two Bes can be made in the time it takes to make one Ay. Because labour is in short supply it is more profitable to make Bes than Ays.

Step 3   Determine the **optimum production plan**. Sufficient Bes will be made to meet the full sales demand, and the remaining labour hours available will then be used to make Ays.

(a)

Product	Demand	Hours required	Hours available	Priority of manufacture
Bes	5,000	5,000	5,000	1st
Ays	3,000	6,000	3,000 (bal)	2nd
		11,000	8,000	

(b)

Product	Units	Hours needed	Contribution per unit $	Total $
Bes	5,000	5,000	4	20,000
Ays	1,500	3,000	6	9,000
		8,000		29,000
Less fixed costs				20,000
Profit				9,000

In conclusion

(a)   Unit contribution is **not** the correct way to decide priorities.

(b)   Labour hours are the scarce resource, and therefore contribution **per labour hour** is the correct way to decide priorities.

(c)   The Be earns $4 contribution per labour hour, and the Ay earns $3 contribution per labour hour. Bes therefore make more profitable use of the scarce resource, and should be manufactured first.

Question

The following details relate to three products made by DSF Co.

	V	A	L
	$ per unit	$ per unit	$ per unit
Selling price	120	170	176
Direct materials	30	40	60
Direct labour	20	30	20
Variable overhead	10	16	20
Fixed overhead	20	32	40
	80	118	140
Profit	40	52	36

All three products use the same direct labour and direct materials, but in different quantities.

In a period when the labour used on these products is in short supply, the most and least profitable use of the labour is

	Most profitable	Least profitable
A	L	V
B	L	A
C	V	A
D	A	L

Answer

The correct answer is B.

	V	A	L
	$	$	$
Selling price per unit	120	170	176
Variable cost per unit	60	86	100
Contribution per unit	60	84	76
Labour cost per unit	$20	$30	$20
Contribution per $ of labour	$3	$2.80	$3.80
Ranking	2	3	1

Question

Jam Co makes two products, the K and the L. The K sells for $50 per unit, the L for $70 per unit. The variable cost per unit of the K is $35, that of the L $40. Each unit of K uses 2 kg of raw material. Each unit of L uses 3 kg of material.

In the forthcoming period the availability of raw material is limited to 2,000 kg. Jam Co is contracted to supply 500 units of K. Maximum demand for the L is 250 units. Demand for the K is unlimited.

What is the profit-maximising product mix?

	K	L
A	250 units	625 units
B	1,250 units	750 units
C	625 units	250 units
D	750 units	1,250 units

Answer

The correct answer is C.

	K	L
Contribution per unit	$15	$30
Contribution per unit of limiting factor	$15/2 = $7.50	$30/3 = $10
Ranking	2	1

Production plan	Raw material used kg
Contracted supply of K (500 x 2 kg)	1,000
Meet demand for L (250 x 3 kg)	750
Remainder of resource for K (125 x 2 kg)	250
	2,000

Chapter roundup

- **Relevant costs** are future cash flows arising as a direct consequence of a decision.

    - Relevant costs are **future costs**
    - Relevant costs are **cashflows**
    - Relevant costs are **incremental costs**

- Relevant costs are also **differential costs** and **opportunity costs.**

    - **Differential cost** is the difference in total cost between alternatives.

    - An **opportunity cost** is the value of the benefit sacrificed when one course of action is chosen in preference to an alternative.

- A **sunk cost** is a past cost which is not directly relevant in decision making.

- **In general**, variable costs will be relevant costs and fixed costs will be irrelevant to a decision.

- The **relevant cost** of an asset represents the amount of money that a company would have to receive if it were deprived of an asset in order to be no worse off than it already is. We can call this the **deprival value**.

- A **limiting factor** is a factor which limits the organisation's activities. In a **limiting factor situation**, contribution will be maximised by earning the biggest possible contribution per unit of limiting factor.

1   Relevant costs are:

   (a)   (d)
   (b)   (e)
   (c)

2   Sunk costs are directly relevant in decision making.

     True ☐   False ☐

3   The following information relates to machine Z.

     Purchase price = $7,000

     Expected future revenues = $5,000

     Scrap value = $4,000

     Replacement cost = $4,500

     Complete the following diagram in order to calculate the relevant cost of machine Z.

```
                              LOWER OF  [          ]
                                   |
         ┌─────────────────────────┴─────────────────────┐
   REPLACEMENT                                        HIGHER OF
      COST                                         [          ]
   [          ]                            ┌────────────┴────────────┐
                                          NRV                    REVENUES
                                       [          ]            [          ]
```

     The relevant cost of machine Z is ....

4   A limiting factor is a factor which ....

5   A sunk cost is:

     A   a cost committed to be spent in the current period
     B   a cost which is irrelevant for decision making
     C   a cost connected with oil exploration in the North Sea
     D   a cost unaffected by fluctuations in the level of activity

Answers to quick quiz

1　(a)　Future costs　　　　　　　　(d)　Differential costs
　(b)　Cash flows　　　　　　　　　(e)　Opportunity costs
　(c)　Incremental costs

2　False

3

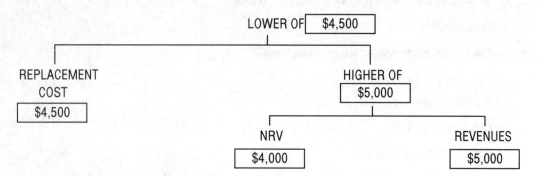

The relevant cost of machine Z is **$4,500**.

4　Limits the organisation's activities.

5　B

Now try the questions below from the Exam Question Bank

Number	Level	Marks	Time
Q18	MCQ/OTQ	n/a	n/a

Linear programming

Topic list	Syllabus reference
1 The problem	F3 (a), (b)
2 Formulating the problem	F3 (c)
3 Graphing the model	F3 (d)
4 Finding the best solution	F3 (c)
5 The graphical method using simultaneous equations	F3 (e)

Introduction

We are now going to look at a decision-making technique which involves **allocating resources in order to achieve the best results**. The name '**linear programming**' sounds rather formidable and the technique *can* get very complicated. Don't worry though: you are only expected to be able to analyse the simplest examples.

Study guide

		Intellectual level
F3	**Limiting factors**	
(a)	Identify a single limiting factor	1
(b)	Determine the optimal production plan where an organisation is restricted by a single limiting factor	2
(c)	Formulate a linear programming problem involving two variables	1
(d)	Determine the optimal solution to a linear programming problem using a graphical approach	1
(e)	Use simultaneous equations where appropriate, in the solution of a linear programming problem	1

Exam guide

The Pilot paper has four questions on this part of the syllabus. Make sure you understand both the graphical approach and the method using simultaneous equations.

Remember to refer to the introductory chapter 'Basic maths' if you are having difficulties with this chapter – sections 6 - 9 will be particularly useful.

1 The problem

FAST FORWARD

A **limiting factor** limits the organisation's production. It could be a limited supply of labour, inventory, machine hours or some other factor. The production plan must aim to maximise the **contribution per unit of limiting factor**.

A typical business problem is to decide how a company should **divide up its production among the various types of product** it manufactures in order to obtain the **maximum possible profit**. A business cannot simply aim to produce as much as possible because there will be **limitations** or **constraints** within which the production must operate. Such constraints could be one or more of the following.

- Limited quantities of raw materials available
- A fixed number of man-hours per week for each type of worker
- Limited machine hours

Moreover, since the profits generated by different products vary, it may be better not to produce any of a less profitable line, but to concentrate all resources on producing the more profitable ones. On the other hand limitations in market demand could mean that some of the products produced may not be sold.

Refer back to Chapter 18 for simple production planning. In this chapter we look at the approach using linear programming.

2 Formulating the problem

Linear programming is a technique for solving problems of profit maximisation or cost minimisation and resource allocation. 'Programming' has nothing to do with computers: the word is simply used to denote a series of events.

Linear programming, at least at this fairly simple level, is a technique that can be carried out in a fairly 'handle turning' manner once you have got the basic ideas sorted out. The steps involved are as follows.

1	Define variables	5	Establish feasible region
2	Establish constraints	6	Add iso-profit/contribution line
3	Construct objective function	7	Determine optimal solution
4	Graph constraints		

Let us imagine that B makes just two models, the Super and the Deluxe, and that the **only constraint** faced by the company is that **monthly machine capacity is restricted to 400 hours**. The Super requires 5 hours of machine time per unit and the Deluxe 1.5 hours. Government restrictions mean that the maximum number of units that can be sold each month is 150, that number being made up of any combination of the Super and the Deluxe.

Let us now work through the steps involved in setting up a linear programming model.

Step 1   Define variables

What are the quantities that the company can vary? Obviously not the number of machine hours or the maximum sales, which are fixed by external circumstances beyond the company's control. The only things which it can determine are the number of each type of unit to manufacture. It is these numbers which have to be determined in such a way as to get the maximum possible profit. Our variables will therefore be as follows.

Let x = the number of units of the Super manufactured.
Let y = the number of units of the Deluxe manufactured.

Step 2   Establish constraints

Having defined these two variables we can now translate the two constraints into inequalities involving the variables.

Let us first consider the machine hours constraint. Each Super requires 5 hours of machine time. Producing five Supers therefore requires $5 \times 5 = 25$ hours of machine time and, more generally, producing x Supers will require $5x$ hours. Likewise producing y Deluxes will require $1.5y$ hours. The total machine hours needed to make x Supers and y Deluxes is $5x + 1.5y$. We know that this cannot be greater than 400 hours so we arrive at the following inequality.

$5x + 1.5y \leq 400$

We can obtain the other inequality more easily. The total number of Supers and Deluxes made each month is $x + y$ but this has to be less than 150 due to government restrictions. The sales order constraint is therefore as follows.

$x + y \leq 150$

Non-negativity

The variables in linear programming models should usually be non-negative in value. In this example, for instance, you cannot make a negative number of units and so we need the following constraints.

$x \geq 0; y \geq 0$

Do not forget these non-negativity constraints when formulating a linear programming model.

Step 3 — Construct objective function

We have yet to introduce the question of profits. Let us assume that the profit on each model is as follows.

	$
Super	100
Deluxe	200

The **objective** of B is to **maximise profit** and so the **function** to be maximised is as follows.

Profit (P) = 100x + 200y

The problem has now been reduced to the following four inequalities and one equation.

$$5x + 1.5y \leq 400$$
$$x + y \leq 150$$
$$x \geq 0$$
$$y \geq 0$$
$$P = 100x + 200y$$

Have you noticed that **the inequalities are all linear expressions**? If plotted on a graph, they would all give **straight lines**. This explains why the technique is called **linear programming** and also gives a hint as to how we should proceed with trying to find the solution to the problem.

Question

Constraints

Patel manufactures two products, X and Y, in quantities x and y units per week respectively. The contribution is $60 per X and $70 per Y. For practical reasons, no more than 100 Xs can be produced per week. If Patel plc uses linear programming to determine a profit-maximising production policy and on the basis of this information, which one of the following constraints is correct?

A $x \leq 60$ C $x \leq 100$

B $y \leq 100$ D $60x + 70y \leq 100$

Answer

The correct answer is C because the question states that the number of Xs produced cannot exceed 100 and so $x \leq 100$.

Option A has no immediate bearing on the number of units of X produced which must be ≤ 100. ($60 represents the contribution per unit of X).

We have no information on the production volume of Product Y and option B is therefore incorrect.

The contribution earned per week is given by 60x + 70y but we have no reason to suppose that this must be less than or equal to 100. Option D is therefore incorrect.

Exam focus point

> Students often have problems with constraints of the style 'the quantity of one type must not exceed twice that of the other'. This can be interpreted as follows: the quantity of one type (say X) must not exceed (must be less than or equal to) twice that of the other (2Y) (ie $X \leq 2Y$).

We have looked at how to **formulate a problem** and in the next section we will look at solving a problem using graphs.

3 Graphing the model

FAST FORWARD

A graphical solution is only possible when there are two variables in the problem. One variable is represented by the x axis and one by the y axis of the graph. Since non-negative values are not usually allowed, the graph shows only zero and positive values of x and y.

A linear equation with one or two variables is shown as a straight line on a graph. Thus y = 6 would be shown as follows.

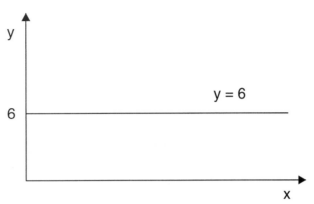

If the problem included a constraint that y could not exceed 6, the **inequality** y ≤ 6 would be represented by the shaded area of the graph below.

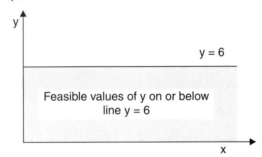

The equation 4x + 3y = 24 is also a straight line on a graph. To draw any straight line, we need only to plot two points and join them up. The easiest points to plot are the following.

(a)   x = 0 (in this example, if x = 0, 3y = 24, y = 8)
(b)   y = 0 (in this example, if y = 0, 4x = 24, x = 6)

By plotting the points, (0, 8) and (6, 0) on a graph, and joining them up, we have the line for 4x + 3y = 24.

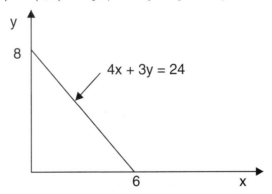

If we had a constraint 4x + 3y ≤ 24, any combined value of x and y within the shaded area below (on or below the line) would satisfy the constraint.

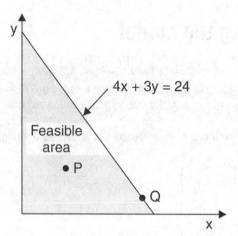

For example, at point P where (x = 2, y = 2) 4x + 3y = 14 which is less than 24; and at point Q where x = 5.5, y = 2/3, 4x + 3y = 24. Both P and Q lie within the **feasible area** (the area where the inequality is satisfied, also called the feasible region). A **feasible area** enclosed on all sides may also be called a **feasible polygon**.

The inequalities $y \geq 6$, $x \geq 6$ and $4x + 3y \geq 24$, would be shown graphically as follows.

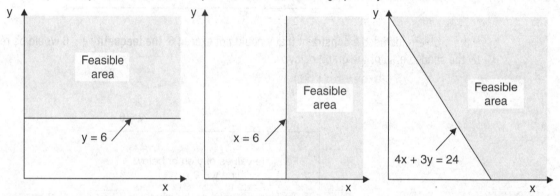

When there are several constraints, the feasible area of combinations of values of x and y must be an area where all the inequalities are satisfied.

Thus, if $y \leq 6$ *and* $4x + 3y \leq 24$ the feasible area would be the shaded area in the graph following.

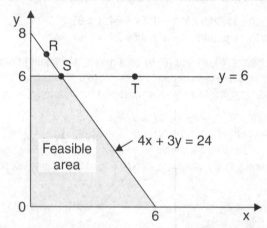

(a)   Point R (x = 0.75, y = 7) is not in the feasible area because although it satisfies the inequality $4x + 3y \leq 24$, it does not satisfy $y \leq 6$.

(b)   Point T (x = 5, y = 6) is not in the feasible area, because although it satisfies the inequality $y \leq 6$, it does not satisfy $4x + 3y \leq 24$.

(c)   Point S (x = 1.5, y = 6) satisfies both inequalities and lies just on the boundary of the feasible area since y = 6 exactly, and $4x + 3y = 24$. Point S is thus at the intersection of the two equation lines.

Similarly, if $y \geq 6$ and $4x + 3y \geq 24$ but $x \leq 6$, the feasible area would be the shaded area in the graph below.

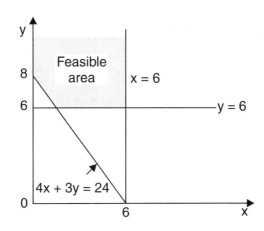

Question

Feasible region

Draw the feasible region which arises from the constraints facing B Co (see Section 2).

Answer

If $5x + 1.5y = 400$, then if $x = 0$, $y = 267$ and if $y = 0$, $x = 80$.
If $x + y = 150$, then if $x = 0$, $y = 150$ and if $y = 0$, $x = 150$

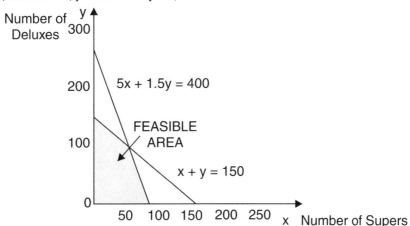

Question

Linear programming problem

In a linear programming problem, one of the constraints is given by $2x \le 3y$. Which of the following statements about the graphical presentation of this constraint is correct?

I   The constraint line passes through the point $x = 2$, $y = 3$.
II   The constraint line passes through the origin.
III The constraint line passes through the point $x = 3$, $y = 2$.
IV   The region below the constraint line is part of the feasible area.

A	I and II only	C	II and III only
B	I and III only	D	II, III and IV only

Answer

When $x = 0$ then y must also equal 0, therefore statement II is correct.

When $x = 3$, $6 = 3y$ and hence $y = 2$, therefore statement III is correct.

Statements II and III are correct and therefore option C is the right answer.

Statement I is incorrect since when $x = 2$, $4 = 3y$ and $y = 1.33$ and y does not equal 3 when $x = 2$.

Statement IV is incorrect since $3y$ is greater than $2x$ above the line, not below it.

4 Finding the best solution

4.1 Introduction

Having found the **feasible region** (which includes all the possible solutions to the problem) we need to find which of these possible solutions is **'best'** in the sense that it yields the **maximum possible profit**. We could do this by finding out what profit each of the possible solutions would give, and then choosing as our 'best' combination the one for which the profit is greatest.

Consider, however, the feasible region of the problem faced by B Co (see the solution to the question entitled Feasible region). Even in such a simple problem as this, there are a great many possible solution points within the feasible area. Even to write them all down would be a time consuming process and also an unnecessary one, as we shall see.

4.2 Example: Finding the best solution

Let us look again at the graph of B's problem.

Consider, for example, the point A at which 40 Supers and 80 Deluxes are being manufactured. This will yield a profit of $((40 \times 100) + (80 \times 200)) = \$20,000$. We would clearly get more profit at point B, where the same number of Deluxes are being manufactured but where the number of Supers being manufactured has increased by five, or from point C where the same number of Supers but 10 more Deluxes are manufactured. This argument suggests that **the 'best' solution is going to be a point on the edge of the feasible area rather than in the middle of it.**

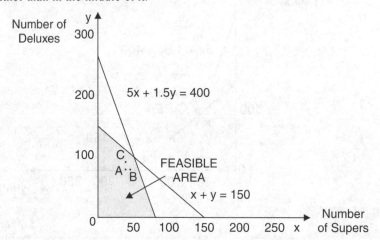

This still leaves us with quite a few points to look at but there is a way we can narrow down the candidates for the best solution still further. Suppose that B Co wish to make a profit of $10,000. The company could sell the following combinations of Supers and Deluxes.

(a)   100 Super, no Deluxe

(b)   No Super, 50 Deluxe

(c)   A proportionate mix of Super and Deluxe, such as 80 Super and 10 Deluxe or 50 Super and 25 Deluxe

The possible combinations of Supers and Deluxes required to earn a profit of $10,000 could be shown by the straight line $100x + 200y = 10,000$.

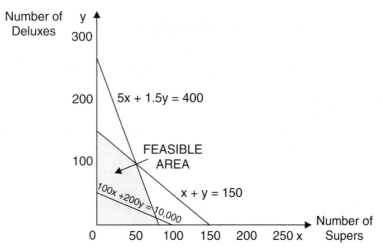

For a total profit of $15,000, a similar line 100x + 200y = 15,000 could be drawn to show the various combinations of Supers and Deluxes which would achieve the total of $15,000.

Similarly a line 100x + 200y = 8,000 would show the various combinations of Supers and Deluxes which would earn a total profit of $8,000.

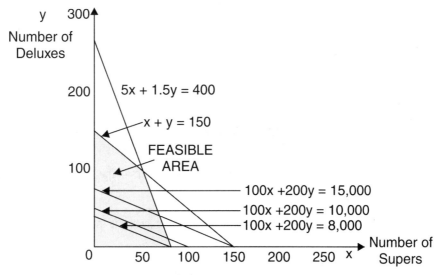

These profit lines are all parallel. (They are called **iso-profit lines**, 'iso' meaning equal.) A similar line drawn for any other total profit would also be parallel to the three lines shown here. This means that if we wish to know the slope or gradient of the profit line, for any value of total profit, we can simply draw one line for any convenient value of profit, and we will know that all the other lines will be parallel to the one drawn: they will have the same slope.

Bigger profits are shown by lines further from the origin (100x + 200y = 15,000), **smaller profits by lines closer to the origin** (100x + 200y = 8,000). As B Co try to **increase possible profit** we need to **slide the profit line outwards from the origin**, while always keeping it **parallel** to the other profit lines.

As we do this there will come a point at which, if we were to move the profit line out any further, it would cease to lie in the feasible region and therefore larger profits could not be achieved in practice because of the constraints. In our example concerning B Co this will happen, as you should test for yourself, where the profit line is just passing through the intersection of x + y = 150 with the y axis (at (0, 150)). The point (0, 150) will therefore give us the best production combination of the Super and the Deluxe, that is, to produce 150 Deluxe models and no Super models.

4.3 Example: A maximisation problem

Brunel manufactures plastic-covered steel fencing in two qualities, standard and heavy gauge. Both products pass through the same processes, involving steel-forming and plastic bonding.

Standard gauge fencing sells at $18 a roll and heavy gauge fencing at $24 a roll. Variable costs per roll are $16 and $21 respectively. There is an unlimited market for the standard gauge, but demand for the heavy gauge is limited to 1,300 rolls a year. Factory operations are limited to 2,400 hours a year in each of the two production processes.

	Processing hours per roll	
Gauge	Steel-forming	Plastic-bonding
Standard	0.6	0.4
Heavy	0.8	1.2

What is the production mix which will maximise total contribution and what would be the total contribution?

Solution

(a) Let S be the number of standard gauge rolls per year.

Let H be the number of heavy gauge rolls per year.

The objective is to maximise 2S + 3H (contribution) subject to the following constraints.

$$0.6S + 0.8H \leq 2,400 \quad \text{(steel-forming hours)}$$
$$0.4S + 1.2H \leq 2,400 \quad \text{(plastic-bonding hours)}$$
$$H \leq 1,300 \quad \text{(sales demand)}$$
$$S, H \geq 0$$

Note that **the constraints are inequalities**, and are not equations. There is no requirement to use up the total hours available in each process, nor to satisfy all the demand for heavy gauge rolls.

(b) If we take the production constraint of 2,400 hours in the steel-forming process

$$0.6S + 0.8H \leq 2,400$$

it means that since there are only 2,400 hours available in the process, output must be limited to a maximum of:

(i) $\dfrac{2,400}{0.6}$ = 4,000 rolls of standard gauge;

(ii) $\dfrac{2,400}{0.8}$ = 3,000 rolls of heavy gauge; or

(iii) a proportionate combination of each.

This maximum output represents the boundary line of the constraint, where the inequality becomes the equation

$$0.6S + 0.8H = 2,400.$$

(c) The line for this equation may be drawn on a graph by joining up two points on the line (such as S = 0, H = 3,000; H = 0, S = 4,000).

(d) The other constraints may be drawn in a similar way with lines for the following equations.

$$0.4S + 1.2H = 2,400 \quad \text{(plastic-bonding)}$$
$$H = 1,300 \quad \text{(sales demand)}$$

(e)

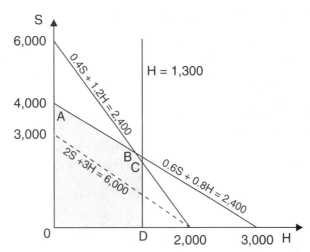

To satisfy all the constraints simultaneously, the values of S and H must lie on or below each constraint line. The outer limits of the **feasible polygon** are the lines, but all combined values of S and H within the shaded area are **feasible solutions**.

(f) The next step is to find the **optimal solution**, which **maximises the objective function**. Since the objective is to **maximise contribution**, the solution to the problem must involve relatively high values (within the feasible polygon) for S, or H or a combination of both.

If, as is likely, there is only one combination of S and H which provides the optimal solution, this combination will be one of the **outer corners of the feasible polygon**. There are four such corners, A, B, C and D. However, it is possible that any combination of values for S and H on the boundary line between two of these corners might provide solutions with the same total contribution.

(g) To solve the problem we establish **the slope of the iso-contribution lines**, by drawing a line for any one level of contribution. In our solution, a line 2S + 3H = 6,000 has been drawn. (6,000 was chosen as a convenient multiple of 2 and 3). **This line has no significance except to indicate the slope, or gradient, of every iso-contribution line for 2S + 3H.**

Using a ruler to judge at which corner of the feasible polygon we can draw an **iso– contribution line** which is as far to the right as possible, (away from the origin) but which still touches the **feasible polygon**.

(h) This occurs at corner B where the constraint line 0.4S + 1.2H = 2,400 crosses with the constraint line 0.6S + 0.8H = 2,400. At this point, there are simultaneous equations, from which the exact values of S and H may be calculated.

0.4S +	1.2H	=	2,400	(1)
0.6S +	0.8H	=	2,400	(2)
1.2S +	3.6H	=	7,200	(3) ((1) × 3)
1.2S +	1.6H	=	4,800	(4) ((2) × 2)
	2H	=	2,400	(5) ((3) − (4))
	H	=	1,200	(6)

Substituting 1,200 for H in either equation, we can calculate that S = 2,400.

The contribution is maximised where H = 1,200, and S = 2,400.

	Units	Contribution per unit $	Total contribution $
Standard gauge	2,400	2	4,800
Heavy gauge	1,200	3	3,600
			8,400

The Dervish Chemical Company operates a small plant. Operating the plant requires two raw materials, A and B, which cost $5 and $8 per litre respectively. The maximum available supply per week is 2,700 litres of A and 2,000 litres of B.

The plant can operate using either of two processes, which have differing contributions and raw materials requirements, as follows.

Process	Raw materials consumed (litres per processing hour)		Contribution per hour
	A	B	$
1	20	10	70
2	30	20	60

The plant can run for 120 hours a week in total, but for safety reasons, process 2 cannot be operated for more than 80 hours a week.

Formulate a linear programming model, and then solve it, to determine how many hours process 1 should be operated each week and how many hours process 2 should be operated each week.

Answer

The decision variables are processing hours in each process. If we let the processing hours per week for process 1 be P_1 and the processing hours per week for process 2 be P_2 we can formulate an objective and constraints as follows.

The objective is to maximise $70P_1 + 60P_2$, subject to the following constraints.

$$
\begin{array}{lll}
20P_1 + 30P_2 & \leq\ 2{,}700 & \text{(material A supply)} \\
10P_1 + 20P_2 & \leq\ 2{,}000 & \text{(material B supply)} \\
P_2 & \leq\ 80 & \text{(maximum time for } P_2) \\
P_1 + P_2 & \leq\ 120 & \text{(total maximum time)} \\
P_1\,,\ P_2 & \geq\ 0 & \text{(non-negativity)}
\end{array}
$$

The feasible area is ABCDO. The optimal solution, found by moving the iso-contribution line outwards, is at point A, where $P_1 = 120$ and $P_2 = 0$. Total contribution would be $120 \times 70 = \$8{,}400$ a week.

4.4 Multiple solutions

It is possible that the optimum position might lie, not at a particular corner, but all along the length of one of the sides of the feasibility polygon. This will occur if the iso-contribution line is exactly parallel to one of the constraint lines.

If this happens then there is no one optimum solution but a **range of optimum solutions**. All of these will maximise the objective function at the same level. However, *any* value of the decision variables that happens to satisfy the constraint between the points where the constraint line forms part of the feasibility region would produce this optimum level of contribution.

4.5 Minimisation problems in linear programming

Although decision problems with limiting factors usually involve the maximisation of contribution, there may be a requirement to **minimise costs**. A graphical solution, involving two variables, is very similar to that for a maximisation problem, with the exception that instead of finding a contribution line touching the feasible area as far away from the origin as possible, we look for a **total cost line touching the feasible area as close to the origin as possible**.

4.5.1 Example: A minimisation problem

Claire Speke Co has undertaken a contract to supply a customer with at least 260 units in total of two products, X and Y, during the next month. At least 50% of the total output must be units of X. The products are each made by two grades of labour, as follows.

	X Hours	Y Hours
Grade A labour	4	6
Grade B labour	4	2
Total	8	8

Although additional labour can be made available at short notice, the company wishes to make use of 1,200 hours of Grade A labour and 800 hours of Grade B labour which has already been assigned to working on the contract next month. The total variable cost per unit is $120 for X and $100 for Y.

Claire Speke Ltd wishes to minimise expenditure on the contract next month. How much of X and Y should be supplied in order to meet the terms of the contract?

Solution

(a)   Let the number of units of X supplied be x, and the number of units of Y supplied be y.

The objective is to minimise 120x + 100y (costs), subject to the following constraints.

$x + y$	$\geq$	260	(supply total)
x	$\geq$	$0.5\,(x + y)$	(proportion of x in total)
$4x + 6y$	$\geq$	1,200	(Grade A labour)
$4x + 2y$	$\geq$	800	(Grade B labour)
x, y	$\geq$	0	

The constraint $x \geq 0.5\,(x + y)$ needs simplifying further.

$$x \geq 0.5\,(x + y)$$
$$2x \geq x + y$$
$$x \geq y$$

In a graphical solution, the line will be x = y. Check this carefully in the following diagram.

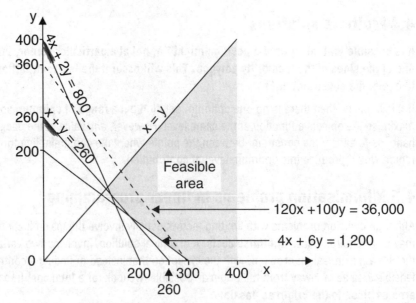

(b) The cost line 120x + 100y = 36,000 has been drawn to show the slope of every cost line 120x + 100 y. **Costs are minimised where a cost line touches the feasible area as close as possible to the origin of the graph**. This occurs where the constraint line 4x + 2y = 800 crosses the constraint line x + y = 260. This point is found as follows.

x + y	=	260	(1)
4x + 2y	=	800	(2)
2x + y	=	400	(3) ((2) ÷ 2)
x	=	140	(4) ((3) – (1))
y	=	120	(5)

(c) Costs will be minimised by supplying the following.

	Unit cost $	Total cost $
140 units of X	120	16,800
120 units of Y	100	12,000
		28,800

The proportion of units of X in the total would exceed 50%, and demand for Grade A labour would exceed the 1,200 hours minimum.

4.6 The use of simultaneous equations

You might think that a lot of time could be saved if we started by solving the simultaneous equations in a linear programming problem and did not bother to draw the graph.

Certainly, this procedure may give the right answer, but in general, it is *not* recommended until you have shown graphically which constraints are effective in determining the optimal solution. To illustrate this point, consider the following graph.

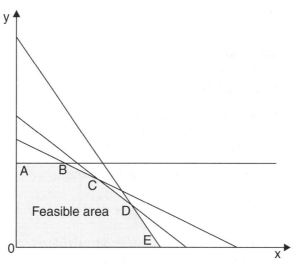

No figures have been given on the graph but the feasible area is OABCDE. When solving this problem, we would know that the optimum solution would be at one of the corners of the feasible area. We need to work out the profit at each of the corners of the feasible area and pick the one where the profit is greatest.

Once the optimum point has been determined graphically, simultaneous equations can be applied to find the exact values of x and y at this point.

5 The graphical method using simultaneous equations

FAST FORWARD

The optimal solution can also be found using **simultaneous equations**.

Simultaneous equations are covered in section 9 of the introductory chapter 'Basic maths'.

5.1 Example: using simultaneous equations

An organisation manufactures plastic-covered steel fencing in two qualities: standard and heavy gauge. Both products pass through the same processes involving steel forming and plastic bonding.

The standard gauge sells at $15 a roll and the heavy gauge at $20 a roll. There is an unlimited market for the standard gauge but outlets for the heavy gauge are limited to 13,000 rolls a year. The factory operations of each process are limited to 2,400 hours a year. Other relevant data is given below.

Variable costs per roll

	Direct material	Direct wages	Direct expense
	$	$	$
Standard	5	7	1
Heavy	7	8	2

Processing hours per 100 rolls

	Steel forming Hours	Plastic bonding Hours
Standard	6	4
Heavy	8	12

Required

Calculate the allocation of resources and hence the production mix which will maximise total contribution.

Solution

Step 1   **Define variables**
Let the number of rolls of standard gauge to be produced be x and the number of rolls of heavy gauge be y.

Step 2   **Establish objective function**
Standard gauge produces a contribution of $2 per roll ($15 – $(5 + 7 + 1)) and heavy gauge a contribution of $3 ($20 – $(7 + 8 + 2)).

Therefore the objective is to maximise contribution (C) = 2x + 3y subject to the constraints below.

Step 3   **Establish constraints**
The constraints are as follows.

$0.06x + 0.08y \leq 2,400$ (steel forming hours)
$0.04x + 0.12y \leq 2,400$ (plastic bonding hours)
$y \leq 13,000$ (demand for heavy gauge)
$x, y \geq 0$ (non-negativity)

Step 4   **Graph problem**
The graph of the problem can now be drawn.

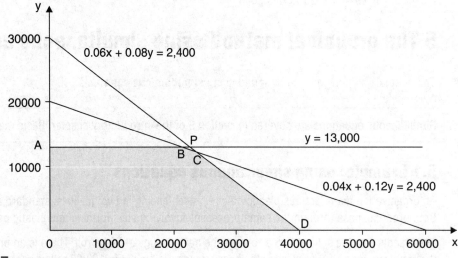

Step 5   **Define feasible area**
The combinations of x and y that satisfy all three constraints are represented by the area OABCD.

Step 6   **Determine optimal solution**
Which combination will maximise contribution? Obviously, the more units of x and y, the bigger the contribution will be, and the optimal solution will be at point B, C or D. It will not be at A, since at A, y = 13,000 and x = 0, whereas at B, y = 13,000 (the same) and x is greater than zero.

Using **simultaneous equations** to calculate the value of x and y at each of points B, C and D, and then working out total contribution at each point from this, we can establish the contribution-maximising product mix.

Point B
$$y = 13,000 \quad (1)$$
$$0.04x + 0.12y = 2,400 \quad (2) \text{ (Plastic forming hours)}$$
$$0.12y = 1,560 \quad (3) ((1) \times 0.12) (13,000 \times 0.12)$$
$$0.04x = 840 \quad (4) ((2) - (3)) (2,400 - 1,560$$
$$x = 21,000 \quad (5) (840 \div 0.04)$$

Total contribution = (21,000 × $2) + (13,000 × $3) = $81,000.

Note. At **Point B** we can see from the graph that y =13,000, so we only need to find x. At **Point C** we have to find x and y.

Point C

$$0.06x + 0.08y = 2,400 \quad (1) \text{ (Steel forming hours)}$$
$$0.04x + 0.12y = 2,400 \quad (2) \text{ (Plastic bonding hours)}$$
$$0.12x + 0.16y = 4,800 \quad (3) \ ((1) \times 2)$$
$$0.12x + 0.36y = 7,200 \quad (4) \ ((2) \times 3)$$
$$0.2y = 2,400 \quad (5) \ ((4) - (3))$$
$$y = 12,000 \quad (6)$$
$$0.06x + 960 = 2,400 \quad (7) \text{ (substitute in (1)) } (960 = 0.08y)$$
$$x = 24,000 \quad (8)$$

Here we produce two equations in which the value of X is the same. This enables us to calculate Y

Total contribution = $(24,000 \times \$2) + (12,000 \times \$3) = \$84,000$.

Point D

Total contribution = $40,000 \times \$2 = \$80,000$.

Comparing B, C and D, we can see that contribution is maximised at C, by making 24,000 rolls of standard gauge and 12,000 rolls of heavy gauge, to earn a contribution of $84,000.

Exam focus point

In exam questions involving the graphical method, you will not be expected to draw a complete graph. However, you may be given an incomplete graph that you may be required to complete to gain the marks available.

Chapter roundup

- A **limiting factor** limits the organisation's production, It could be a limited supply of labour, inventory, machine hours or some other factor. The production plan must aim to maximise the **contribution per unit of limiting factor.**

- **Linear programming** is a technique for solving problems of profit maximisation or cost minimisation and resource allocation. 'Programming' has nothing to do with computers: the word is simply used to denote a series of events.

- **Linear programming**, at least at this fairly simple level, is a technique that can be carried out in a fairly 'handle-turning' manner once you have got the basic ideas sorted out. The steps involved are as follows.

1	Define variables	5	Establish feasible region
2	Establish constraints	6	Add iso-profit/contribution line
3	Construct objective function	7	Determine optimal solution
4	Graph constraints		

- A graphical solution is only possible when there are two variables in the problem. One variable is represented by the x axis and one by the y axis of the graph. Since non-negative values are not usually allowed, the graph only shows zero and positive values of x and y.

- The optimal solution can also be found using **simultaneous** equations.

Quick quiz

1   What are the three main steps involved in setting up a linear programming model?

    Step 1. ....

    Step 2. ....

    Step 3. ....

2   Draw the inequality $4x + 3y \leq 24$ on the graph below.

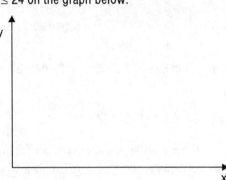

3   A feasible area enclosed on all sides may also be called a ....

4   How does the graphical solution of minimisation problems differ from that of maximisation problems?

5   The graphical method cannot be used when there are more than two decision variables.

    True ☐   False ☐

BPP LEARNING MEDIA

1 **Step 1.** Define variables

    Step 2. Establish constraints

    Step 3. Establish objective function

2

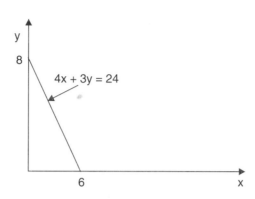

3 Feasible polygon.

4 Instead of finding a contribution line touching the feasible area as far away from the origin as possible, we look for a total cost line touching the feasible area **as close to the origin as possible**.

5 True

Now try the questions below from the Exam Question Bank			
Number	**Level**	**Marks**	**Time**
Q19	MCQ	n/a	N/a

APPENDIX
Exam formulae

Regression analysis

$$a = \frac{\sum y}{n} - \frac{b \sum x}{n}$$

$$b = \frac{n \sum xy - \sum x \sum y}{n \sum x^2 - (\sum x)^2}$$

$$r = \frac{n \sum xy - \sum x \sum y}{\sqrt{[n \sum x^2 - (\sum x)^2][n \sum y^2 - (\sum y)^2]}}$$

Economic order quantity $= \sqrt{\dfrac{2C_0 D}{C_h}}$

Economic batch quantity $= \sqrt{\dfrac{2C_0 D}{C_h \left(1 - \dfrac{D}{R}\right)}}$

Exam question and answer bank

1 Information for management

(a)   Which of the following statements is/are true?

    I   Information is the raw material for data processing
    II   External sources of information include an organisation's financial accounting records
    III   The main objective of a non-profit making organisation is usually to provide goods and services

    A   I and III only   C   II and III only
    B   I, II and III   D   III only   **(2 marks)**

(b)   Which of the following statements is not true?

    A   Management accounts detail the performance of an organisation over a defined period and
         the state of affairs at the end of that period

    B   There is no legal requirement to prepare management accounts

    C   The format of management accounts is entirely at management discretion   **(1 mark)**

(c)   Which of the following could higher level management carry out?

    A   taking long-term decisions
    B   taking short-term decisions
    C   taking long-term and short-term decisions   **(1 mark)**

(d)   Which of the following statements is not correct?

    A   Financial accounting information can be used for internal reporting purposes

    B   Routine information can be used to make decisions regarding both the long term and the
         short term

    C   Management accounting provides information relevant to decision making, planning,
         control and evaluation of performances

    D   Cost accounting can only be used to provide inventory valuations for internal reporting
                                                                      (2 marks)

2 Cost classification

(a)   Which of the following items might be a suitable cost unit within the accounts payable department
       of a company?

    (i)   Postage cost   (iii)   Supplier account
    (ii)   Invoice processed

    A   Item (i) only   C   Item (iii) only
    B   Item (ii) only   D   Items (ii) and (iii) only   **(2 marks)**

(b)   Which of the following are direct expenses?

    (i)   The cost of special designs, drawing or layouts
    (ii)   The hire of tools or equipment for a particular job
    (iii)   Salesman's wages
    (iv)   Rent, rates and insurance of a factory

    A   (i) and (ii)   C   (i) and (iv)
    B   (i) and (iii)   D   (iii) and (iv)   **(2 marks)**

(c)   Which of the following would be appropriate cost units for a passenger coach company?

		Appropriate	Not appropriate
(a)	Vehicle cost per passenger-kilometre	X	
(b)	Fuel cost for each vehicle per kilometre	X	
(c)	Fixed cost per kilometre		X

                                                                      (2 marks)

(d)   A cost which contains both fixed and variable elements, and so is partly affected by changes in the level of activity, is called

      A   A direct cost   C   An unavoidable cost

      (B)   A semi-variable cost   **(1 mark)**

(e)   A cost unit is

      A   A measure of output of work in a standard hour

      (B)   A unit of product or service in relation to which costs are ascertained

      C   The cost per hour of operating a machine   **(1 mark)**

3 Cost behaviour

(a)   Variable costs are conventionally deemed to

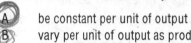

      (A)   be constant per unit of output

      (B)   vary per unit of output as production volume changes

      C   be constant in total when production volume changes   **(1 mark)**

(b)   The following is a graph of total cost against level of activity.

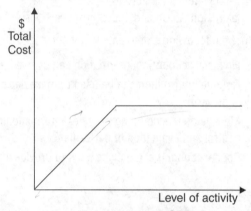

To which one of the following costs does the graph correspond?

A   Photocopier rental costs, where a fixed rental is payable up to a certain number of copies each period. If the number of copies exceeds this amount, a constant charge per copy is made for all subsequent copies during that period.

(B)   Vehicle hire costs, where a constant rate is charged per mile travelled, up to a maximum monthly payment regardless of the miles travelled.

C   Supervisor salary costs, where one supervisor is needed for every five employees added to the staff.

D   The cost of direct materials, where the unit rate per kg purchased reduces when the level of purchases reaches a certain amount.

(c) Identify which type of cost is being described in (a)-(d) below.

VARIABLE COST	FIXED COST	STEPPED FIXED COST	SEMI-VARIABLE COST

(a) This type of cost stays the same, no matter how many products you produce

F I

(b) This type of cost increases as you produce more products. The sum of these costs are also known as the marginal cost of a product

VARI

(c) This type of cost is fixed but only within certain levels of activity

STC P

(d) This type of cost contains both fixed and variable elements

SEM I

(2 marks)

4 Correlation and regression

(a) A company's weekly costs ($C) were plotted against production level (P) for the last 50 weeks and a regression line calculated to be C = 1,000 + 250P. Which statement about the breakdown of weekly costs is true?

A Fixed costs are $1,000. Variable costs per unit are $5.
B Fixed costs are $250. Variable costs per unit are $4.
C Fixed costs are $250. Variable costs per unit are $1,000.
D Fixed costs are $1,000. Variable costs per unit are $250.   **(2 marks)**

(b) The value of the correlation coefficient between x and y is 0.9. Which of the following is correct?

A There is a weak relationship between x and y
B x is 90% of y
C If the values of x and y were plotted on a graph, the line relating them would have a slope of 0.9
D There is a very strong relationship between x and y   **(2 marks)**

5 Spreadsheets

(a) A chart wizard can be used to generate graphs. Which type of chart would be best used to track a trend over time?

A A pie chart   C A multiple bar chart
B A line graph   D A radar chart   **(2 marks)**

(b) A **macro** is used for occasional complicated tasks in spreadsheets.

True ☐   False ☒   **(1 mark)**

(c) The following statements relate to spreadsheet formulae

I Absolute cell references (B3) change when you copy formulae to other locations
II The F4 key is used to change cell references from absolute to relative
III Relative cell references ($B$3) stay the same when you copy formulae to other locations

Which statements are correct?

A I and II only   C II and III only
B I and III only   D II only   **(2 marks)**

Questions (d) to (f) refer to the spreadsheet shown below.

	A	B	C	D
1	Unit selling price	$65	Annual volume	10,000
2				
3	Seasonal variations			
4	Quarter 1	-20%		
5	Quarter 2	-35%		
6	Quarter 3	10%		
7	Quarter 4	45%		
8				
9	**Sales budgets**	Seasonal variations (units)	Quarterly volume	Quarterly turnover
10	Quarter 1			
11	Quarter 2			
12	Quarter 3			
13	Quarter 4			
14				

(d)   The cell B10 shows the seasonal variation in units for quarter 1. Which of the following would be a suitable formula for this cell?

A   =$D$1/4*B4   C   =$D$1/4*B1

B   =(D1/4)*B4   D   =D1/4*$B$4   **(2 marks)**

(e)   The cell C10 shows the sales volume in units for quarter 1. Which of the following would be a suitable formula for this cell?

A   =$D$1/4+B10   C   =D1+B10

B   =D1/4+$B$10   **(1 mark)**

(f)   The cell D10 shows the turnover in Quarter 1 Which of the following would be a suitable formula for this cell?

A   =D1*$B$1   C   =C10*$B$1

B   =C10-B10   D   =(C10+B10)*$B$1   **(2 marks)**

6 Material costs

(a)   The following data relates to an item of raw material

Unit cost of raw material	$20
Usage per week	250 units
Cost of ordering material, per order	$400
Annual cost of holding inventory, as a % of cost	10%
Number of weeks in a year	48

What is the economic order quantity, to the nearest unit?

A   316 units   C   1,549 units

B   693 units   D   2,191 units   **(2 marks)**

(b)   The following data relates to the stores ledger control account of Duckboard, a manufacturing company, for the month of October.

	$
Opening inventory	18,500
Closing inventory	16,100
Deliveries from suppliers	142,000
Returns to suppliers	2,300
Cost of indirect materials issued	25,200

The issue of direct materials would have been recorded in the cost accounts as follows.

			$	$
A	Debit	Stores ledger control account	119,200	
	Credit	Work in progress control account		119,200
B	Debit	Work in progress control account	119,200	
	Credit	Stores ledger control account		119,200
C	Debit	Stores ledger control account	116,900	
	Credit	Work in progress control account		116,900
(D)	Debit	Work in progress control account	116,900	
	Credit	Stores ledger control account		116,900

(2 marks)

(c)   The Economic Order Quantity (EOQ) model is used to minimise

A   Inventory holding costs
B   Costs associated with running out of inventory
(C)   The sum of inventory ordering and inventory holding costs   (1 mark)

7 Labour costs

(a)   Gross wages incurred in department 1 in June were $54,000. The wages analysis shows the following summary breakdown of the gross pay.

		Paid to direct labour	Paid to indirect labour
		$	$
Ordinary time		25,185	11,900
Overtime:	basic pay	5,440	3,500
	premium	1,360	875
Shift allowance		2,700	1,360
Sick pay		1,380	300
		36,065	17,935

What is the direct wages cost for department 1 in June?

A	$25,185	C	$34,685	
(B)	$30,625	D	$36,065	(2 marks)

(b)   The wages control account for A Co for February is shown below.

WAGES CONTROL ACCOUNT

	$		$
Bank	128,400	Work in progress control	79,400
Balance c/d	12,000	Production overhead control	61,000
	140,400		140,400
		Balance b/d	12,000

Which of the following statements about wages for February is *not* correct?

A   Wages paid during February amounted to $128,400
(B)   Wages for February were prepaid by $12,000
C   Direct wages cost incurred during February amounted to $79,400
D   Indirect wages cost incurred during February amounted to $61,000   (2 marks)

8 Overheads and absorption costing

A company absorbs overheads based on labour hours. Data for the latest period are as follows.

Budgeted labour hours	8,500
Budgeted overheads	$148,750
Actual labour hours	7,928
Actual overheads	$146,200

(a) Based on the data given above, what is the labour hour overhead absorption rate?

- A $17.20 per hour
- B $17.50 per hour
- C $18.44 per hour
- D $18.76 per hour   **(2 marks)**

(b) Based on the data given above, what is the amount of under-/over-absorbed overhead?

- A $2,550 under-absorbed overhead
- B $2,550 over-absorbed overhead
- C $7,460 over-absorbed overhead
- D $7,460 under-absorbed overhead   **(2 marks)**

(c) The budgeted production overheads and other budget data of Eiffel Co are as follows.

Budget	Production dept X
Overhead cost	$36,000
Direct materials cost	$32,000
Direct labour cost	$40,000
Machine hours	10,000
Direct labour hours	18,000

What would be the absorption rate for Department X using the various bases of apportionment?

(a) % of direct material cost = ☐

(b) % of direct labour cost = ☐

(c) % of total direct cost = ☐

(d) Rate per machine hour = ☐

(e) Rate per direct labour hour = ☐   **(2 marks)**

9 Marginal and absorption costing

(a) The overhead absorption rate for product Y is $2.50 per direct labour hour. Each unit of Y requires 3 direct labour hours. Stock of product Y at the beginning of the month was 200 units and at the end of the month was 250 units. What is the difference in the profits reported for the month using absorption costing compared with marginal costing?

- A The absorption costing profit would be $375 less
- B The absorption costing profit would be $125 greater
- C The absorption costing profit would be $375 greater
- D The absorption costing profit would be $1,875 greater   **(2 marks)**

(b) B Company makes a product which has a variable production cost of $21 per unit and a sales price of $39 per unit. At the beginning of 20X5, there was no opening inventory and sales during the year were 50,000 units. Fixed costs (production, administration, sales and distribution) totalled $328,000. Production was 70,000 units.

(a) The contribution per unit is $ ☐ .   **(2 marks)**

(b) The profit per unit is $ ☐ .   **(2 marks)**

(c) A company does not hold any opening or closing inventories.

Which of the following statements is true?

- A Profits will be higher if absorption costing is used
- B Profits will be the same if either absorption costing or marginal costing were used
- C Profits will be higher if marginal costing is used   **(1 mark)**

(d) In a marginal costing system, the formula 'Sales – Variable Costs' is used to calculate

- A Net profit
- B Contribution
- C Gross profit   **(1 mark)**

10 Process costing

The following data relates to questions (a) and (b)

A chemical is manufactured in two processes, X and Y. Data for process Y for last month are as follows.

Material transferred from process X	2,000 litres @ $4 per litre
Conversion costs incurred	$12,250
Output transferred to finished goods	1,600 litres
Closing work in progress	100 litres

Normal loss is 10% of input. All losses are fully processed and have a scrap value of $4 per litre.

Closing work in progress is fully complete for material, but is only 50 per cent processed.

(a)   What is the value of the completed output (to the nearest $)?

A	$15,808	C	$17,244	
B	$17,289	D	$17,600	**(2 marks)**

(b)   What is the value of the closing work in progress (to the nearest $)?

A	$674	C	$750	
B	$728	D	$1,100	**(2 marks)**

(c)   20,000 litres of liquid were put into a process at the beginning of the month at a cost of $4,400. The output of finished product was 17,000 litres. The normal level of waste in this process is 20% and the waste which is identified at the end of the process can be sold at $0.50 per litre. Use this information to complete the process account below.

PROCESS ACCOUNT

	Litres	$		Litres	$
Materials			Normal waste		
Abnormal gains	____	____	Finished goods	____	____
	====	====		====	====

(2 marks)

(d)   A food manufacturing process has a normal wastage of 10% of input. In a period, 3,000 kg of material was input and there was an abnormal loss of 75 kg. No inventories are held at the beginning or end of the process.

The quantity of good production achieved was ⬚ kg.   **(2 marks)**

(e)   A company makes a product, which passes through a single process.

Details of the process for the last period are as follows.

Materials	5,000 kg at 50c per kg
Labour	$700
Production overheads	200% of labour

Normal losses are 10% of input in the process, and without further processing any losses can be sold as scrap for 20c per kg.

The output for the period was 4,200 kg from the process.

There was no work in progress at the beginning or end of the period.

The value of the abnormal loss for the period is $ ⬚   **(2 marks)**

(f)   In a process account, abnormal losses are valued

A   At good production cost less scrap value
B   At their scrap value
C   The same as good production   **(1 mark)**

11 Joint products and by-products

(a) SH Ltd manufactures three joint products and one by-product from a single process.

Data for May are as follows.

Opening and closing inventories	Nil
Raw materials input	$90,000
Conversion costs	$70,000

Output

		Units	Sales price $ per unit
Joint product	J	2,500	36
	K	3,500	40
	L	2,000	35
By-product M		4,000	1

By-product sales revenue is credited to the process account. Joint costs are apportioned on a physical units basis.

What were the full production costs of product K in May?

A	$45,500	C	$68,250	
B	$46,667	D	$70,000	**(2 marks)**

(b) Samakand Preparations operates a continuous process producing three products and one by-product. Output from the process for one month was as follows.

	Selling price per unit $	Output Units
Joint product		
A	38	20,000
B	54	40,000
C	40	35,000
By-product		
D	4	20,000

Total output costs were $4,040,000.

The saleable value of the by-product is deducted from process costs before apportioning costs to each joint product. Using the sales revenue basis for allocating joint costs, the unit valuation for joint product B was (to 2 decimal places):

A	$49.50	C	$50.00	
B	$45.00	D	$100.00	**(2 marks)**

12 Job, batch and service costing

(a) Which of the following would be appropriate cost units for a transport business?

(i) Cost per tonne-kilometre
(ii) Fixed cost per kilometre
(iii) Maintenance cost of each vehicle per kilometre

A	(i) only	C	(i) and (iii) only	
B	(i) and (ii) only	D	All of them	**(2 marks)**

(b) JC Co operates a job costing system. The company's standard net profit margin is 20 per cent of sales value.

The estimated costs for job B124 are as follows.

Direct materials	3 kg @ $5 per kg
Direct labour	4 hours @ $9 per hour

Production overheads are budgeted to be $240,000 for the period, to be recovered on the basis of a total of 30,000 labour hours.

Other overheads, related to selling, distribution and administration, are budgeted to be $150,000 for the period. They are to be recovered on the basis of the total budgeted production cost of $750,000 for the period.

The price to be quoted for job B124 is $ [   ]   **(2 marks)**

(c)   In which of the following situation(s) will job costing normally be used?

[   ]   Production is continuous

[V   ]   Production of the product can be completed in a single accounting period

[✓   ]   Production relates to a single special order   **(1 mark)**

(d)   Consider the following features and identify whether they relate to job costing, contract costing, service costing or none of these costing methods.

J =   Job costing
C =   Contract costing
S =   Service costing
N =   None of these costing methods

(i)   Production is carried out in accordance with the wishes of the customer | C | J

(ii)   Work is usually of a relatively long duration | N | C

(iii)   Work is usually undertaken on the contractor's premises | N |

(iv)   Costs are averaged over the units produced in the period | S | S

(v)   It establishes the costs of services rendered | N | S

                                                                                      (2 marks)

(e)   Ali Pali Ltd is a small jobbing company. Budgeted direct labour hours for the current year were 45,000 hours and budgeted direct wages costs were $180,000.

Job number 34679, a rush job for which overtime had to be worked by skilled employees, had the following production costs.

	$	$
Direct materials		2,000
Direct wages		
Normal rate (400 hrs)	2,000	
Overtime premium	500	
		2,500
Production overhead		4,000
		8,500

Production overhead is based on a direct labour hour rate

If production overhead had been based on a percentage of direct wages costs instead, the production cost of job number 34679 would have been:

A $5,500   C $10,250
B $9,000   D $10,750   **(2 marks)**

13 Budgeting

(a) What does the statement 'sales is the principal budget factor' mean?

    A   The level of sales will determine the level of cash at the end of the period

    B   The level of sales will determine the level of profit at the end of the period

    C   The company's activities are limited by the level of sales it can achieve   **(1 mark)**

(b) When preparing a production budget, the quantity to be produced equals

    A   sales quantity + opening inventory of finished goods + closing inventory of finished goods

    B   sales quantity – opening inventory of finished goods + closing inventory of finished goods

    C   sales quantity – opening inventory of finished goods – closing inventory of finished goods

    D   sales quantity + opening inventory of finished goods – closing inventory of finished goods

    (2 marks)

(c) PQ Co plans to sell 24,000 units of product R next year. Opening inventory of R is expected to be 2,000 units and PQ Co plans to increase inventory by 25 per cent by the end of the year. How many units of product R should be produced next year?

    A   23,500 units   C   24,500 units

    B   24,000 units   D   30,000 units   **(2 marks)**

(d) Each unit of product Alpha requires 3 kg of raw material. Next month's production budget for product Alpha is as follows.

Opening inventories:

Raw materials	15,000 kg
Finished units of Alpha	2,000 units
Budgeted sales of Alpha	60,000 units

Planned closing inventories:

Raw materials	7,000 kg
Finished units of Alpha	3,000 units

The number of kilograms of raw materials that should be purchased next month is:

    A   172,000   C   183,000

    B   175,000   D   191,000   **(2 marks)**

(e) Budgeted sales of X for December are 18,000 units. At the end of the production process for X, 10% of production units are scrapped as defective. Opening inventories of X for December are budgeted to be 15,000 units and closing inventories will be 11,400 units. All inventories of finished goods must have successfully passed the quality control check. The production budget for X for December, in units is

    A   12,960   C   15,840

    B   14,400   D   16,000   **(2 marks)**

(f) In a situation where there are no production resource limitations, which of the following must be available for the material usage budget to be completed? Tick all that apply.

(a)	Production volume from the production budget	✔
(b)	Budgeted change in materials inventory	
(c)	Standard material usage per unit	✔ **(2 marks)**

(g) If a company has no production resource limitations, in which order would the following budgets be prepared?

	Order
Material usage budget	2
Sales budget	1
Material purchase budget	6
Finished goods inventory budget	2
Production budget	5
Material inventory budget	4

(2 marks)

(h)

		True	False
(a)	Budgetary control procedures are useful only to maintain control over an organisation's expenditure	✓	✓
(b)	A prerequisite of flexible budgeting is a knowledge of cost behaviour patterns	✓	✓
(c)	Fixed budgets are not useful for control purposes		✓

(2 marks)

14 Standard costing

(a) Which of the following would *not* be used to estimate standard direct material prices?

A   The availability of bulk purchase discounts
B   Purchase contracts already agreed
C   The forecast movement of prices in the market
D   Performance standards in operation   **(2 marks)**

(b) JC Co operates a bottling plant. The liquid content of a filled bottle of product T is 2 litres. During the filling process there is a 30% loss of liquid input due to spillage and evaporation. The standard price of the liquid is $1.20 per litre. The standard cost of the liquid per bottle of product T, to the nearest penny, is

A	$2.40	C	$3.12	
B	$2.86	D	$3.43	**(2 marks)**

(c) Standard costing provides which of the following? Tick all that apply.

(a)	Targets and measures of performance	✓
(b)	Information for budgeting	✓
(c)	Simplification of inventory control systems	
(d)	Actual future costs	✓ **(2 marks)**

(d) Calculate the standard cost of producing 100 wheels for a toy car using the information given below. Fill in the shaded box.

	Bending	Cutting	Assembly
Standard labour rates of pay per hour $	4	6	5
Standard labour rates per 100 wheels (hours)	0.8	0.5	1.2

STANDARD COST CARD			
Toy car wheels	Part number 5917B - 100 wheels		Date:
	Quantity	*Rate/price*	*Total* $
Direct materials			
Tyres	100	10c each	
Steel strip	50	$10.40 per 100	
Wire	1000	2c each	
Direct labour	hours	$	
Bending			
Cutting			
Assembly			
STANDARD COST			

(2 marks)

(e) What is an attainable standard?

A   A standard that can be attained under perfect operating conditions, and which does not include an allowance for wastage, spoilage, machine breakdowns and other inefficiencies

B   A standard that is based on currently attainable working conditions

C   A standard that can be attained if production is carried out efficiently, machines are operated properly and/or materials are used properly, with some allowance being made for waste and inefficiencies **(1 mark)**

15 Basic variance analysis

(a) The standard cost information for SC's single product shows the standard direct material content to be 4 litres at $3 per litre.

Actual results for May were:

Production   1,270 units
Material used   5,000 litres at a cost of $16,000

All of the materials were purchased and used during the period. The direct material price and usage variances for May are:

	Material price	*Material usage*
A	$1,000 (F)	$240 (F)
B	$1,000 (A)	$240 (F)
C	$1,000 (F)	$240 (A)
D	$1,000 (A)	$256 (F)

(2 marks)

The following information relates to questions (b) and (c)

The standard variable production overhead cost of product B is as follows.

4 hours at $1.70 per hour = $6.80 per unit

During period 3 the production of B amounted to 400 units. The labour force worked 1,690 hours, of which 30 hours were recorded as idle time. The variable overhead cost incurred was $2,950.

(b) The variable production overhead expenditure variance for period 3 was

A	$77 adverse	C	$128 favourable
B	$128 adverse	D	$230 adverse

(2 marks)

(c)   The variable production overhead efficiency variance for period 3 was

     A $102 favourable   C $105 adverse

     B $102 adverse   D $153 adverse   **(2 marks)**

(d)   Which of the following would help to explain a favourable direct material price variance?

		Would help to explain variance	Would not help to explain variance
(a)	The standard price per unit of direct material was unrealistically high		
(b)	Output quantity was greater than budgeted and it was possible to obtain bulk purchase discounts		
(c)	The material purchased was of a higher quality than standard		

(2 marks)

16 Further variance analysis

(a)   W uses a standard absorption costing system. The following data relates to one of its products.

	$ per unit	$ per unit
Selling price		27.00
Variable costs	12.00	
Fixed costs	9.00	
		21.00
Profit		6.00

Budgeted sales for control period 7 were 2,400 units, but actual sales were 2,550 units. The revenue earned from these sales was $67,320.

Profit reconciliation statements are drawn up using absorption costing principles. What sales variances would be included in such a statement for period 7?

	Price	Volume
A	$1,530 (F)	$900 (F)
B	$1,530 (A)	$900 (F)
C	$1,530 (F)	$900 (A)
D	$1,530 (A)	$900 (A)

(2 marks)

(b)   A standard marginal costing system:

     (i)   calculates fixed overhead variances using the budgeted absorption rate per unit

     (ii)   calculates sales volume variances using the standard contribution per unit

     (iii)   values finished goods stock at the standard variable cost of production

Which of the above statements is/are correct?

     A   (i), (ii) and (iii)   C   (ii) and (iii) only

     B   (i) and (ii) only   D   (i) and (iii) only   **(2 marks)**

17 Cost-volume profit analysis

(a)   A company manufactures a single product for which cost and selling price data are as follows.

Selling price per unit	$12
Variable cost per unit	$8
Fixed costs per month	$96,000
Budgeted monthly sales	30,000 units

The margin of safety, expressed as a percentage of budgeted monthly sales, is (to the nearest whole number):

A	20%	C	73%	
B	25%	D	125%	**(2 marks)**

(b)

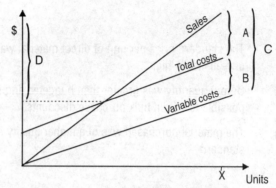

In the above breakeven chart, the contribution at level of activity x can be read as:

A	distance A	C	distance C	
B	distance B	D	distance D	**(2 marks)**

18 Relevant costing and decision making

(a)   Sue is considering starting a new business and she has already spent $5,000 on market research and intends to spend a further $2,000.

In the assessment of the relevant costs of the decision to set up the business, market research costs are:

A   a sunk cost of $7,000
B   a sunk cost of $5,000 and an incremental cost of $2,000
C   a sunk cost of $2,000 and an incremental cost of $5,000
D   an opportunity cost of $7,000   **(2 marks)**

(b)   ABC Ltd is in the process of deciding whether or not to accept a special order. The order will require 100 litres of liquid X. ABC Ltd has 85 litres of liquid X in inventory but no longer produces the product which required liquid X. It could therefore sell the 85 litres for $2 per litre if it rejected the special order. The liquid was purchased three years ago at a price of $8 per litre but its replacement cost is $10 per litre. What is the relevant cost of liquid X to include in the decision-making process?

A	$200	C	$800	
B	$320	D	$1,000	**(2 marks)**

(c)   V Co manufactures three products which have the following selling prices and costs per unit.

	V1	V2	V3
	$	$	$
Selling price	30.00	36.00	34.00
Costs per unit			
Direct materials	8.00	10.00	20.00
Direct labour	4.00	8.00	3.60
Overhead			
Variable	2.00	4.00	1.80
Fixed	9.00	6.00	2.70
	23.00	28.00	28.10
Profit per unit	7.00	8.00	5.90

All three products use the same type of labour.

In a period in which labour is in short supply, the rank order of production is:

V1 ....

V2 ....

V3 ....   **(2 marks)**

(d) S Co manufactures a single product, V. Data for the product are as follows.

	$ per unit
Selling price	40
Direct material cost	8
Direct labour cost	6
Variable production overhead cost	4
Variable selling overhead cost	2
Fixed overhead cost	10
Profit per unit	10

The profit/volume ratio for product V is [   ]   **(2 marks)**

(e) Fast Fandango Co manufactures a single product, the FF, which sells for $10. At 75% capacity, which is the normal level of activity for the factory, sales are $600,000 per period.

The cost of these sales are as follows.

Direct cost per unit	$3
Production overhead	$156,000 (including variable costs of $30,000)
Sales costs	$ 80,000
Distribution costs	$ 60,000 (including variable costs of $15,000)
Administration overhead	$ 40,000 (including variable costs of $9,000)

The sales costs are fixed with the exception of sales commission which is 5% of sales value.

(a) The contribution per unit of product FF is $ [   ]   **(2 marks)**

(b) The fixed cost per period is $ [   ]   **(2 marks)**

(c) The breakeven volume of sales per period is [   ] units   **(2 marks)**

19 Linear programming

(a) A company produces two types of orange juice, ordinary (X cartons per year) and premium (Y cartons per year). Which of the following inequalities represents the fact that the amount of ordinary orange juice produced must be no more than twice the amount of premium orange juice produced.

A $X \geq 2Y$ C $2X \leq Y$

B $2X \geq Y$ D $X \leq 2Y$ **(2 marks)**

(b) In a linear programming problem, the constraints are $X \leq 41$ and $Y \geq 19$. Describe the feasible region, assuming where appropriate that the axes also constitute boundaries.

A   A rectangle to the left of X = 41 and below Y = 19

B   An infinite rectangle to the right of X = 41 and below Y = 19

C   An infinite region above Y = 19 and to the right of X = 41

D   An infinite rectangle to the left of X = 41 and above Y = 19   **(2 marks)**

ANSWERS

1 Information for management

(a)   D   **Data** is the raw material for data processing. **Information** is data that has been processed in such a way as to be meaningful to the person who receives it. Statement I is therefore incorrect.

An organisation's financial accounting records are an example of an **internal** source of information. Statement II is therefore incorrect.

The main objective of a non-profit making organisation is usually to provide goods and services. Statement III is therefore correct.

(b)   A   **Financial accounts** (not management accounts) detail the performance of an organisation over a defined period and the state of affairs at the end of that period. **Management accounts** are used to aid management record, plan and control the organisation's activities and to help the decision-making process.

(c)   C   Higher level management are likely to be involved with taking decisions at all levels within an organisation.

(d)   D   Cost accounting can also be used to provide inventory valuations for external reporting.

2 Cost classification

(a)   D   It would be appropriate to use the cost per invoice processed and the cost per supplier account for control purposes. Therefore items (ii) and (iii) are suitable cost units and the correct answer is D.

Postage cost, item (i), is an expense of the department, therefore option A is not a suitable cost unit.

If you selected option B or option C you were probably rushing ahead and not taking care to read all the options. Items (ii) and (iii) *are* suitable cost units, but neither of them are the *only* suitable suggestions.

(b)   A   Special designs, and the hire of tools etc for a particular job can be traced to a specific cost unit. Therefore they are direct expenses and the correct answer is A.

Item (iii) is a selling and distribution overhead and item (iv) describes production overheads.

(c)

		Appropriate	Not appropriate
(a)	Vehicle cost per passenger - kilometre	√	
(b)	Fuel cost for each vehicle per kilometre	√	
(c)	Fixed cost per kilometre		√

(d)   B   A direct cost is one that can be directly related to a unit of output; an unavoidable cost is one that would be incurred whether or not a certain activity took place.

(e)   B   The cost per hour of operating a machine is an example of the cost of input resource, which might form part of the total cost of a cost unit.

A measure of output of work in a standard hour is an indication of productivity.

3 Cost behaviour

(a) A Variable costs are conventionally deemed to increase or decrease in direct proportion to changes in output. Therefore the correct answer is A. Description B implies a changing unit rate, which does not comply with this convention. Description C relates to a fixed cost.

(b) B The cost depicted begins as a linear variable cost, increasing at a constant rate in line with activity. At a certain point the cost becomes fixed regardless of the level of activity. The vehicle hire costs follow this pattern.

Graphs for the other options would look like this.

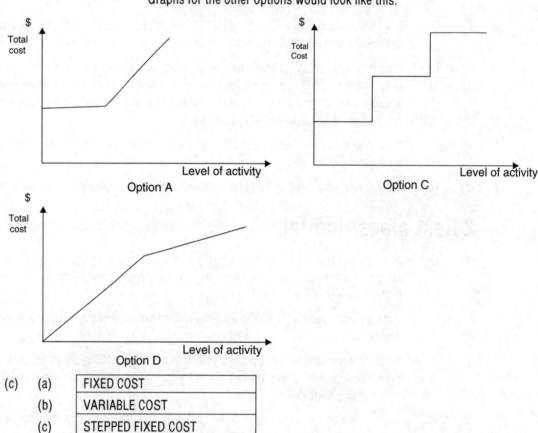

(c) (a) | FIXED COST |
     (b) | VARIABLE COST |
     (c) | STEPPED FIXED COST |
     (d) | SEMI-VARIABLE COST |

4 Correlation and regression

(a) D If C = 1,000 + 250P, then fixed costs are $1,000 and variable costs are $250 per unit.

(b) D The correlation coefficient of 0.9 is very close to 1 and so there is a very strong relationship between x and y.

5 Spreadsheets

(a) B A line graph is the best way of illustrating a trend over time.

(b) False

A macro is used for automating frequently repeated tasks

(c) D II only

Relative cell references (B3) change when you copy formulae to other locations. Absolute cell references ($B$3) stay the same when you copy formulae to other locations.

(d)   A   =$D$1/4*B4

This formula will divide the annual turnover by 4 and multiply the result by the seasonal variation. The $ signs show that the cell reference for D1 is absolute so the reference will stay the same when the formula is copied into the cells below.

(e)   A   =$D$1/4+B10

This formula will divide the annual turnover by 4 and add the result to the seasonal variation found in cell B10. The $ signs show that the cell reference for D1 is absolute so the reference will stay the same when the formula is copied into the cells below.

(f)   C   =C10*$B$1

This formula will multiply the quarterly volume in units from cell C10 by the unit selling price in cell B1. The $ signs show that the cell reference for B1 is absolute so the reference will stay the same when the formula is copied into the cells below

6 Material costs

(a)   D $EOQ = \sqrt{\dfrac{2 \times \$400 \times (250 \times 48)}{\$20 \times 10\%}} = 2{,}191$

Therefore the correct answer is D.

If you selected option A you used **weekly** usage in the calculations instead of the annual usage.

If you selected option B you did not take ten per cent of the material cost as the annual inventory holding cost.

If you selected option C you omitted the 2.

(b)   D   The easiest way to solve this question is to draw up a stores ledger control account.

STORES LEDGER CONTROL ACCOUNT

	$		$
Opening stock b/f	18,500	Payables (returns)	2,300
Payables/cash (deliveries)	142,000	Overhead account (indirect materials)	25,200
		WIP (balancing figure)	116,900
		Closing inventory c/f	16,100
	160,500		160,500

If you selected option C you determined the correct value of the direct materials issued but you **reversed the entries**.

If you selected options A or B you placed the figure for returns on the **wrong side of your account**, and in option A you **reversed the entries** for the issue of direct materials from stores.

(c)   C   There is a trade off between inventory ordering and inventory holding costs. If we assume that the cost of purchasing an item of inventory remains constant, the EOQ formula calculates the order size at which the total of these two costs is minimised.

7 Labour costs

(a)   B   The only direct costs are the wages paid to direct workers for ordinary time, plus the basic pay for overtime.

$25,185 + $5,440 = $30,625.

If you selected option A you forgot to include the basic pay for overtime of direct workers, which is always classified as a direct labour cost.

If you selected option C you have included overtime premium and shift allowances, which are usually treated as indirect costs. However, if overtime and shiftwork are incurred specifically for a particular cost unit, then they are classified as direct costs of that cost unit. There is no mention of such a situation here.

Option D includes sick pay, which is classified as an indirect labour cost.

(b)   B   The credit balance on the wages control account indicates that the amount of wages incurred and analysed between direct wages and indirect wages was **higher** than the wages paid through the bank. Therefore there was a $12,000 balance of **wages owing** at the end of February and statement B is not correct. Therefore the correct option is B.

Statement A is correct. $128,400 of wages was paid from the bank account.

Statement C is correct. $79,400 of direct wages was transferred to the work in progress control account.

Statement D is correct. $61,000 of indirect wages was transferred to the production overhead control account.

8 Overheads and absorption costing

(a)   B $\text{Overhead absorption rate} = \dfrac{\text{budgeted overheads}}{\text{budgeted labour hours}} = \dfrac{\$148,750}{8,500} = \$17.50 \text{ per hr}$

If you selected option A you divided the actual overheads by the budgeted labour hours. Option C is based on the actual overheads and actual labour hours. If you selected option D you divided the budgeted overheads by the actual hours.

(b)   D

	$
Overhead absorbed = $17.50 × 7,928 =	138,740
Overhead incurred =	146,200
Under-absorbed overhead =	7,460

If you selected options A or B you calculated the difference between the budgeted and actual overheads and interpreted it as an under or over absorption. If you selected option C you performed the calculations correctly but misinterpreted the result as an over absorption.

(c)

(a)	% of direct material cost =	112.5%
(b)	% of direct labour cost =	90%
(c)	% of total direct cost =	50%
(d)	Rate per machine hour =	$3.60
(e)	Rate per direct labour hour =	$2

Workings

(a)   % of direct materials cost $\dfrac{\$36,000}{\$32,000} \times 100\% = 112.5\%$

(b)   % of direct labour cost $\dfrac{\$36,000}{\$40,000} \times 100\% = 90\%$

(c)   % of total direct cost $\dfrac{\$36,000}{\$72,000} \times 100\% = 50\%$

(d) Rate per machine hour $\dfrac{\$36,000}{10,000\,hrs}$ = \$3.60 per machine hour

(e) Rate per direct labour hour $\dfrac{\$36,000}{18,000\,hrs}$ = \$2 per direct labour hour

9 Marginal and absorption costing

(a) C Difference in profit = change in inventory level × fixed overhead per unit
                 = (200 − 250) × (\$2.50 × 3)
                 = \$375

The absorption costing profit will be greater because inventories have increased.

If you selected option A you calculated the correct profit difference but the absorption costing profit would be greater because fixed overheads are carried forward in the increasing inventory levels.

If you selected option B you multiplied the inventory difference by the direct labour-hour rate instead of by the total overhead cost per unit, which takes three hours.

If you selected option D you based the profit difference on the closing inventory only (250 units × \$2.50 × 3).

(b) (a) The contribution per unit is \$900,000/50,000 = \$18

(b) The profit per unit is \$572,000/50,000 = \$11.44

	\$'000	\$'000
Sales (at \$39 per unit)		1,950
Opening inventory	–	
Variable production cost (\$21 × 70,000)	1,470	
Less closing inventory (\$21 × 20,000)	420	
Variable cost of sales		1,050
Contribution		900
Less fixed costs		328
Profit		572

(c) B Profits will be the same under both methods, as opening inventory equals closing inventory.

It is changes in inventory levels that cause these two costing systems to give different profit figures.

(d) B Gross profit is used in an absorption costing system; net profit = contribution − fixed costs.

10 Process costing

(a) D **Step 1. Determine output and losses**

			Equivalent units of production			
Input	Output	Total	Process X		Conversion costs	
Units		Units	Units	%	Units	%
2,000	Finished units	1,600	1,600	100	1,600	100
	Normal loss	200				
	Abnormal loss (balance)	100	100	100	100	100
	Closing inventory	100	100	100	50	50
2,000		2,000	1,800		1,750	

Step 2. Calculate cost per unit of output, losses and WIP

Input	Cost $	Equivalent units	Cost per equivalent unit $
Process X material ($8,000 – 800)	7,200	1,800	4
Conversion costs	12,250	1,750	7
			$\overline{11}$

Step 3. Calculate total cost of output

Cost of completed production = $11 × 1,600 litres = $17,600

If you selected option A you included the normal loss in your equivalent units calculation, but these units do not carry any of the process costs. If you selected option B you did not allow for the fact that the work in progress units were incomplete as regards conversion costs. If you selected option C you reduced the process costs by the scrap value of all lost units, instead of the normal loss units only.

(b) C Using the unit rates from answer (a) step 2, we can proceed again to step 3.

Calculate the total cost of work in progress

	Cost element	Number of equivalent units	Cost per equivalent unit $	Total $
Work in progress	Process X material	100	4	400
	Conversion costs	50	7	350
				$\overline{750}$

If you selected option A you included the normal loss in your equivalent units calculation. If you selected option B you reduced the process costs by the scrap value of all lost units, instead of the normal loss units only. Option D does not allow for the fact that the work in progress (WIP) is incomplete when calculating the total cost of WIP.

(c)

PROCESS ACCOUNT

	Litres	$		Litres	$
Materials	20,000	4,400	Normal waste		
			(4,000 × $0.50)	4,000	2,000
			Finished goods	17,000	2,550
Abnormal gain	1,000	150			
	21,000	4,550		21,000	4,550

Workings

Normal loss = 20% × 20,000 litres = 4,000 litres

Expected output = 20,000 – 4,000 = 16,000 litres

$$\text{Cost per unit} = \frac{\text{Process costs - scrap proceeds of normal loss}}{\text{Expected output}}$$

$$= \frac{\$4,400 - (4,000 \times \$0.50)}{16,000\,\text{litres}}$$

$$= \frac{\$4,400 - \$2,000}{16,000\,\text{litres}}$$

$$= \frac{\$2,400}{16,000\,\text{litres}}$$

$$= \$0.15$$

(d) The quantity of good production achieved was [2,625] kg.

   Good production = input – normal loss – abnormal loss
                     = 3,000 – (10% × 3,000) – 75
                     = 3,000 – 300 – 75
                     = 2,635 kg

(e) The value of the abnormal loss for the period is $ [300]

	kg
Input	5,000
Normal loss (10% × 5,000 kg)	(500)
Abnormal loss	(300)
Output	4,200

Cost per kg $= \dfrac{\text{Input costs } - \text{ scrap value of normal loss}}{\text{Expected output}}$

$= \dfrac{\$4,600^* - \$100}{5,000 - 500}$

$= \dfrac{\$4,500}{4,500} = \$1.00$

Value of abnormal loss = 300 × $1.00 = $300

	$
*Materials (5,000 kg × 0.5)	2,500
Labour	700
Production overhead	1,400
	4,600

(f) C Abnormal losses have the same value as good production.

11 Joint products and by-products

(a) C Net process costs

	$
Raw materials	90,000
Conversion costs	70,000
Less by-product revenue	(4,000)
Net process costs	156,000

Apportionment of net process costs

		Units	$	Apportioned costs $
Product	J	2,500	$156,000 × (2,500/8,000)	48,750
	K	3,500	$156,000 × (3,500/8,000)	68,250
	L	2,000	$156,000 × (2,000/8,000)	39,000
		8,000		156,000

If you selected option A or B you apportioned a share of the process costs to the by-product, and with option B or D you did not deduct the by-product revenue from the process costs.

(b)   A   *Workings*

	Sales revenue	
Joint product	$	
A	760,000	($38 × 20,000)
B	2,160,000	($54 × 40,000)
C	1,400,000	($40 × 35,000)
Total sales revenues	4,320,000	

Joint costs to be allocated = Total output costs − sales revenue from by-product D

= $4,040,000 − $80,000 ($4 × 20,000)

= $3,960,000

Costs allocated to joint product B $\quad = \dfrac{\$2,160,000}{\$4,320,000} \times \$3,960,000$

$\qquad\qquad\qquad\qquad\qquad\qquad\quad = \$1,980,000$

Unit valuation (joint product B) $\quad = \dfrac{\$1,980,000}{40,000}$

$\qquad\qquad\qquad\qquad\qquad\qquad\quad = \$49.50$ (to 2 decimal places)

If you selected option B, you forgot to deduct the sales revenue (from by-product D) from the joint costs to be allocated.

If you selected option C, you excluded by-product D from your calculations completely.

If you selected option D, you divided the total sales revenue (instead of the joint costs to be allocated) by the number of units of joint product D.

12 Job, batch and service costing

(a)   C   Cost per tonne – kilometre (i) is appropriate for cost control purposes because it combines the distance travelled and the load carried, **both of which affect cost**.

The fixed cost per kilometre (ii) is not particularly useful for control purposes because it **varies with the number of kilometres travelled**.

The maintenance cost of each vehicle per kilometre (iii) can be useful for control purposes because it **focuses on a particular aspect** of the cost of operating each vehicle. Therefore the correct answer is C.

(b)   The price to be quoted for job B124 is $ 124.50

Production overhead absorption rate = $240,000/30,000 = $8 per labour hour

Other overhead absorption rate = ($150,000/$750,000) × 100% = 20% of total production cost

Job B124	$
Direct materials (3 kg × $5)	15.00
Direct labour (4 hours × $9)	36.00
Production overhead (4 hours × $8)	32.00
Total production cost	83.00
Other overhead (20% × $83)	16.60
Total cost	99.60
Profit margin: 20% of sales (× $^{20}/_{80}$)	24.90
Price to be quoted	124.50

(c)

✓	Production of the product can be completed in a single accounting period
✓	Production relates to a single special order

Job costing is appropriate where each cost unit is **separately identifiable** and is of relatively **short duration**.

(d) (i)   Production is carried out in accordance with the wishes of the customer | J |

(ii) Work is usually of a relatively long duration | C |

(iii) Work is usually undertaken on the contractor's premises | N |

(iv) Costs are averaged over the units produced in the period | S |

(v) It establishes the costs of services rendered | S |

(e) D

Hours for job 34679	= 400 hours
Production overhead cost	$4,000
∴ Overhead absorption rate ($4,000 ÷ 400)	$10 per direct labour hour
Budgeted direct labour hours	45,000
∴ Total budgeted production overheads	$450,000
Budgeted direct wages cost	$180,000
∴ Absorption rate as % of wages cost	= $450,000/$180,000 × 100%
	= 250%

Cost of job 34679

	$
Direct materials	2,000
Direct labour, including overtime premium *	2,500
Overhead (250% × $2,500)	6,250
Total production cost	10,750

* The overtime premium is a direct labour cost because the overtime was worked specifically for this job.

If you selected option A you got your calculation of the overhead absorption rate 'upside down' and derived a percentage rate of 40 per cent in error. If you selected option B you did not include the overtime premium and the corresponding overhead. If you selected option C you did not include the overtime premium in the direct labour costs.

13 Budgeting

(a) C The **principal budget factor** is the factor which limits the activities of an organisation.

Although cash and profit are affected by the level of sales (options A and B), sales is not the only factor which determines the level of cash and profit.

(b) B Any opening inventory available at the beginning of a period will **reduce** the additional quantity required from production in order to satisfy a given sales volume. Any closing inventory required at the end of a period will **increase** the quantity required from production in order to satisfy sales and leave a sufficient volume in inventory. Therefore we need to **deduct** the opening inventory and **add** the required closing inventory.

(c) C

	Units
Required for sales	24,000
Required to increase inventory (2,000 × 0.25)	500
	24,500

If you selected option A you subtracted the change in inventory from the budgeted sales. However, if inventories are to be increased then **extra units must be made for inventory**.

Option B is the budgeted sales volume which would only be equal to budgeted production if there were no planned changes to inventory volume.

If you selected option D you increased the sales volume by 25 per cent, instead of adjusting inventory by this percentage.

(d) B

	Units
Required increase in finished goods inventory	1,000
Budgeted sales of Alpha	60,000
Required production	61,000

	kg
Raw materials usage budget (× 3 kg)	183,000
Budgeted decrease in raw materials inventory	(8,000)
Raw material purchase budget	175,000

If you selected option A you made no allowance for the increase in finished goods inventory. If you selected option C you did not adjust for the budgeted decrease in raw materials inventory and option D adjusts for an increase in raw material inventory, rather than a decrease.

(e) D

	Units
Budgeted sales	18,000
Budgeted reduction in finished goods	(3,600)
Budgeted production of completed units	14,400
Allowance for defective units (10% of output = 1/9 of input)	1,600
Production budget	16,000

If you selected option A you deducted a ten per cent allowance for defective units, instead of adding it, and option B makes no allowance for defective units at all. If you selected option C you added ten per cent to the required completed units to allow for the defective units, but the ten per cent **should be based on the total number of units output**, ie ten per cent of 16,000 = 1,600 units.

(f) (a) Production volume from the production budget ✓

(b) Budgeted change in materials inventory

(c) Standard material usage per unit ✓

Since there are no production resource limitations, the production budget would be prepared before the material usage budget (a). The standard material usage per unit (c) would then indicate the total material usage required to produce the budgeted production volume.

It would not be necessary to know the budgeted change in materials inventory (b) since this would affect the material purchases, rather than the material usage.

(g)

	Order
Material usage budget	4
Sales budget	1
Material purchase budget	6
Finished goods inventory budget	2
Production budget	3
Material inventory budget	5

		True	False
(a)	Budgetary control procedures are useful only to maintain control over an organisation's expenditure		✓
(b)	A prerequisite of flexible budgeting is a knowledge of cost behaviour patterns	✓	
(c)	Fixed budgets are not useful for control purposes		✓

Comments

(a)   Budgetary control procedures can also be useful to maintain control over an organisation's revenue.

(b)   A knowledge of cost behaviour patterns is necessary so that the variable cost allowance can be flexed in line with changes in activity.

(c)   Fixed budgets may be useful for control purposes when:

   (i)   Variable costs are negligible or non-existent
   (ii)   Activity levels are not subject to change

14 Standard costing

(a)   D   Performance standards would be taken into account when estimating **material usage**, they would not have a direct effect on material price. Therefore the correct answer is D.

All of the other factors would be used to estimate standard material prices for a forthcoming period.

(b)   D   Required liquid input = 2 litres $\times \dfrac{100}{70}$ = 2.86 litres

Standard cost of liquid input = 2.86 × $1.20 = $3.43 (to the nearest cent)

If you selected option A you made no allowance for spillage and evaporation. Option B is the figure for the quantity of material input, not its cost. If you selected option C you simply added an extra 30 per cent to the finished volume. However, the wastage is 30 per cent of the liquid **input**, not 30 per cent of output.

(c)

(a)	Targets and measures of performance	✓
(b)	Information for budgeting	✓
(c)	Simplification of inventory control systems	✓
(d)	Actual future costs	

Standard costing provides targets for achievement, and yardsticks against which actual performance can be monitored (**item (a)**). It also provides the unit cost information for evaluating the volume figures contained in a budget (**item (b)**). Inventory control systems are simplified with standard costing. Once the variances have been eliminated, all inventory units are evaluated at standard price (**item (c)**).

Item (d) is incorrect because standard costs are an estimate of what will happen in the future, and a unit cost target that the organisation is aiming to achieve.

(d)

STANDARD COST CARD			
Toy car wheels	Part number 5917B - 100 wheels		Date:
	Quantity	*Rate/price*	*Total* $
Direct materials			
Tyres	100	10c each	10.00
Steel strip	50	$10.40 per 100	5.20
Wire	1000	2c each	20.00
			35.20
Direct labour	hours	$	
Bending	4	0.8	3.20
Cutting	6	0.5	3.00
Assembly	5	1.2	6.00
			12.20
STANDARD COST			47.40

(e)   C   **Attainable standards** may provide an incentive for employees to work harder as they represent a realistic but challenging target of efficiency.

A standard that is based on currently attainable working conditions describes a **current standard**. Current standards do not attempt to improve current levels of efficiency.

A standard that can be attained under perfect operating conditions, and which **does not** include an allowance for wastage, spoilage, machine breakdowns and other inefficiencies describes an **ideal standard**. Ideal standards are not very useful for day-to-day control and they can demotivate employees because they are highly unlikely to be achieved.

15 Basic variance analysis

(a)   B

	$
Material price variance	
5,000 litres did cost	16,000
But should have cost (× $3)	15,000
	1,000 (A)

Material usage variance	
1,270 units did use	5,000 litres
But should have used (× 4 litres)	5,080 litres
Usage variance in litres	80 (F)
× standard cost per litre	$3
	240 (F)

If you selected options A or C you calculated the money values of the variances correctly but misinterpreted their direction.

If you selected option D you valued the usage variance in litres at the actual cost per litre instead of the standard cost per litre.

(b)   B

	$
1,660 hours of variable production overhead should cost (× $1.70)	2,822
But did cost	2,950
	128 (A)

If you selected option A you based your expenditure allowance on all of the labour hours worked. However, it is usually assumed that **variable overheads are incurred during active working hours**, but are not incurred during idle time.

If you selected option C you calculated the correct money value of the variance but you misinterpreted its direction.

Option D is the variable production overhead total variance.

(c)   B

400 units of Product B should take (× 4 hours)	1,600 hours
But did take (active hours)	1,660 hours
Efficiency variance in hours	60 hours (A)
× standard rate per hour	× $1.70
	102 (A)

If you selected option A you calculated the correct money value of the variance but you misinterpreted its direction.

If you selected option C you valued the efficiency variance in hours at the actual variable production overhead rate per hour. Option D bases the calculation on all of the hours worked, instead of only the active hours.

(d)

		Would help to explain variance	Would not help to explain variance
(a)	The standard price per unit of direct material was unrealistically high	✓	
(b)	Output quantity was greater than budgeted and it was possible to obtain bulk purchase discounts	✓	
(c)	The material purchased was of a higher quality than standard		✓

Statement (a) is consistent with a favourable material price variance. If the standard is high then actual prices are likely to be below the standard.

Statement (b) is consistent with a favourable material price variance. Bulk purchase discounts would not have been allowed at the same level in the standard, because purchases were greater than expected.

Statement (c) is not consistent with a favourable material price variance. Higher quality material is likely to cost more than standard, resulting in an adverse material price variance.

16 Further variance analysis

(a)   B

	$
Revenue from 2,550 units should have been (× $27)	68,850
but was	67,320
Sales price variance	1,530 (A)

Actual sales	2,550 units
Budgeted sales	2,400 units
Variance in units	150 units (F)
x standard profit per unit ($(27 − 12))	× $6
Sales volume variance in $	$900 (F)

If you selected option A, C or D, you calculated the monetary values of the variances correctly, but misinterpreted their direction.

(b)   C   Statement (i) is not correct. Fixed overhead is not absorbed into production costs in a marginal costing system.

Statement (ii) is correct. Sales volume variances are calculated using the standard contribution per unit (and not the standard profit per unit which is used in standard absorption costing systems).

Statement (iii) is correct. As stated above, fixed overhead is not absorbed into production costs in a marginal costing system.

17 Cost-volume profit analysis

(a)   A   Breakeven point $= \dfrac{\text{Fixed costs}}{\text{Contribution per unit}} = \dfrac{\$96,000}{\$(12-8)} =$ 24,000 units

Budgeted sales   <u>30,000</u> units
Margin of safety   <u>6,000</u> units

Expressed % of budget $= \dfrac{6,000}{30,000} \times 100\% = 20\%$

If you selected option B you calculated the correct margin of safety in units, but you then expressed this as a percentage of the breakeven point. If you selected option C you divided the fixed cost by the selling price to determine the breakeven point, but the selling price also has to cover the variable cost. You should have been able to eliminate option D; the margin of safety expressed as a percentage must always be less than 100 per cent.

(b)   C   Contribution at level of activity x = sales value less variable costs, which is indicated by distance C. Distance A indicates the profit at activity x, B indicates the fixed costs and D indicates the margin of safety in terms of sales value.

18 Relevant costing and decision making

(a)   B $5,000 has been spent on market research already and is therefore a sunk cost and irrelevant to the decision. The further $2,000 will only be spent if Sue continues with the project, therefore it is an incremental (relevant) cost of the decision to go ahead.

The cost is not an opportunity cost (option D) because Sue has not forgone an alternative use for the resources.

(b)   B   The relevant cost of the material in inventory is the opportunity cost of $2 per litre, because the material would be sold if the order was rejected. The remainder of the required material must be purchased at $10 per litre.

Relevant cost is therefore $(85 \times \$2) + (15 \times \$10) = \$320$.

If you selected option A you valued all of the 100 litres required at $2 per litre, but this opportunity cost only applies to the 85 litres in inventory. Option C values the inventory items at their original cost of $8 per litre, but this is a sunk cost which is not relevant to decisions about the future use of the material. Option D values all the material at replacement cost, but the items in inventory will not be replaced by ABC.

(c)   V1 = 1st
         V2 = 3rd
         V3 = 2nd

	V1	V2	V3
	$	$	$
Selling price per unit	30	36	34.00
Variable costs per unit	<u>14</u>	<u>22</u>	<u>25.40</u>
Contribution per unit	<u>16</u>	<u>14</u>	<u>8.60</u>
Labour cost per unit	$4	$8	$3.60
Contribution per $ of labour cost	$4	$1.75	$2.39
Rank order of production	1	3	2

(d) The profit/volume ratio for product V is $\boxed{50}$ %

The profit/volume ratio (P/V ratio) is another term used to describe the contribution/sales ratio (C/S ratio)

$$P/V\ ratio = \frac{Contribution\ per\ unit}{Selling\ price\ per\ unit}$$

$$= \frac{\$(40-8-6-4-2)}{\$40} \times 100\% = 50\%$$

(e) (a) The contribution per unit of product FF is $5.60.

Workings

Sales are 60,000 units at the normal level of activity. Variable costs at 60,000 units of production/sales are as follows.

	$	$ per unit
Production overhead	30,000	0.50
Sales costs (5% of $600,000)	30,000	0.50
Distribution costs	15,000	0.25
Administration overhead	9,000	0.15
	84,000	1.40
Direct costs	180,000	3.00
Total variable costs	264,000	4.40
Sales revenue	600,000	10.00
Contribution	336,000	5.60

(b) The fixed cost per period is $252,000.

Fixed costs	$
Production overhead	126,000
Sales costs	50,000
Distribution costs	45,000
Administration overhead	31,000
	252,000

(c) The breakeven volume of sales per period is 45,000 units.

Workings

$$Breakeven\ point = \frac{fixed\ costs}{contribution\ per\ unit}$$

$$= \frac{\$252,000}{\$5.60}$$

$$= 45,000\ units$$

19 Linear programming

(a) D   This inequality states that X must be at most 2Y, as required.

The inequality in **option A** states that X must be at least 2Y, whereas 2Y is meant to be the very maximum value of X.

The inequality in **option B** states that Y must be at most 2X, whereas X is meant to be at most 2Y.

The inequality in **option C** states that Y must be at least 2X, whereas X is meant to be at most 2Y.

(b)   D   The region to the left of X = 41 satisfies $X \leq 41$ while that above Y = 19 satisfies $Y \geq 19$.

Option A is incorrect because the region you have described is bounded by $X \leq 41$, but $Y \leq 19$ instead of $Y \geq 19$.

Option B is incorrect because the region you have described is bounded by $X \geq 41$ and $Y \leq 19$ instead of by $X \leq 41$ and $Y \geq 19$.

Option C is incorrect because the region you have described is bounded by $Y \geq 19$ but by $X \geq 41$ instead of $X \leq 41$.

Index

Review Form & Free Prize Draw – Paper F2 Management Accounting (6/08)

All original review forms from the entire BPP range, completed with genuine comments, will be entered into one of two draws on 31 January 2009 and 31 July 2009. The names on the first four forms picked out on each occasion will be sent a cheque for £50.

Name: _____ Address: _____

_____

_____

How have you used this Text?
(Tick one box only)

☐ Home study (book only)

☐ On a course: college _____

☐ With 'correspondence' package

☐ Other _____

Why did you decide to purchase this Text? *(Tick one box only)*

☐ Have used BPP Texts in the past

☐ Recommendation by friend/colleague

☐ Recommendation by a lecturer at college

☐ Saw advertising

☐ Saw information on BPP website

☐ Other _____

During the past six months do you recall seeing/receiving any of the following?
(Tick as many boxes as are relevant)

☐ Our advertisement in *ACCA Student Accountant*

☐ Our advertisement in *Pass*

☐ Our advertisement in *PQ*

☐ Our brochure with a letter through the post

☐ Our website www.bpp.com

Which (if any) aspects of our advertising do you find useful?
(Tick as many boxes as are relevant)

☐ Prices and publication dates of new editions

☐ Information on Text content

☐ Facility to order books off-the-page

☐ None of the above

Which BPP products have you used?

Text	☑	Success CD	☐	Learn Online	☐
Kit	☐	i-Learn	☐	Home Study Package	☐
Passcard	☐	i-Pass	☐	Home Study PLUS	☐

Your ratings, comments and suggestions would be appreciated on the following areas.

	Very useful	Useful	Not useful
Introductory section (Key study steps, personal study)	☐	☐	☐
Chapter introductions	☐	☐	☐
Key terms	☐	☐	☐
Quality of explanations	☐	☐	☐
Case studies and other examples	☐	☐	☐
Exam focus points	☐	☐	☐
Questions and answers in each chapter	☐	☐	☐
Fast forwards and chapter roundups	☐	☐	☐
Quick quizzes	☐	☐	☐
Question Bank	☐	☐	☐
Answer Bank	☐	☐	☐
Index	☐	☐	☐

Overall opinion of this Study Text	Excellent ☐	Good ☐	Adequate ☐	Poor ☐

Do you intend to continue using BPP products?   Yes ☐   No ☐

On the reverse of this page are noted particular areas of the text about which we would welcome your feedback. The BPP author of this edition can be e-mailed at: lesleybuick@bpp.com

Please return this form to: Lesley Buick, ACCA Publishing Manager, BPP Learning Media Ltd, FREEPOST, London, W12 8BR

Review Form & Free Prize Draw (continued)

TELL US WHAT YOU THINK

Please note any further comments and suggestions/errors below

Free Prize Draw Rules

1   Closing date for 31 January 2009 draw is 31 December 2008. Closing date for 31 July 2009 draw is 30 June 2009.

2   Restricted to entries with UK and Eire addresses only. BPP employees, their families and business associates are excluded.

3   No purchase necessary. Entry forms are available upon request from BPP Learning Media. No more than one entry per title, per person. Draw restricted to persons aged 16 and over.

4   Winners will be notified by post and receive their cheques not later than 6 weeks after the relevant draw date.

5   The decision of the promoter in all matters is final and binding. No correspondence will be entered into.